Praise for *The Firs*

'R.R. Virdi's *The First Binding* is engrossing and beautiful, joyous and painful – always entertaining, sometimes profound. This book makes me remember why I love epic fantasy' Kevin J. Anderson, *New York Times* bestselling author

'Crafted with patience, passion and, most importantly, tremendous love. Read R.R. Virdi'

Jim Butcher, *New York Times* bestselling author of the Dresden Files

'R.R. Virdi spins a very personal epic fantasy about the consequences of our actions and the nature of heroism. Rich world-building, plenty of action, and devious twists abound. Very highly recommended'

Jonathan Maberry, *New York Times* bestselling author

'An epic like no other – grand, sweeping, dramatic, a love letter to fantasy burning with the dust and heat and mythos of South Asia. It reads like magic and tastes like saffron'

Yudhanjaya Wijeratne, bestselling author of *The Salvage Crew*

'If you loved *The Name of the Wind* and *The Lies of Locke Lamora*, this is your next reading addiction' Dyrk Ashton, author of the Paternus Trilogy

'*The First Binding* is epic fantasy at its finest – an homage to storytelling and legend, richly told and endlessly engaging. Complex and luxuriant, this is an emotional, multifaceted gem of a book that examines the twists and turns a story takes on its journey from the truth'

Andrea Stewart, *Sunday Times* bestselling author of *The Bone Shard War*

'Lavish in detail, a saga colourfully flavoured with the mythos of India, R.R. Virdi's *The First Binding* is a fantasy debut recommended for the exceptional promise that *The Name of the Wind* enthusiasts have been pining to discover and read' Janny Wurts, author of *The Wars of Light and Shadow*

'A work of extraordinary depth; readers will be unpicking the secrets of Tremaine for years to come'

Richard Swan, *Sunday Times* bestselling author of *The Justice of Kings*

'An ode to storytelling, complete with a rich mythology, turbulent adventures, and a flawed hero you'll root for' Kirkus

'*The First Binding* is a masterpiece of epic fantasy storytelling'
Michael Mammay, author of The Planetside series

'The pattern woven by the recurring elements is beguiling. You'll want to sit down with this Storyteller again' *SFX*

'This is a SPECTACULAR book, deep and rich and intense. It takes my breath away' Faith Hunter, *New York Times* bestselling author

'There is little else out there to rival *The First Binding.* It is an entire mythos and world, epic fantasy and autobiography, a comprehensive retelling of one man's life' *The Wall Street Journal*

'A work of staggering ambition born out of a fathoms-deep love for epic fantasy, *The First Binding* marks the arrival of an author and protagonist who are both trickster heroes on a multi-layered legendary journey'
Samit Basu, author of *The City Inside*

'Lyrical and enchanting. A new star has risen in the firmament of epic fantasy'
D.J. Butler, Dragon Award-winning author of *Witchy Eye*

'Filled with astute nods to South Asian lore, *The First Binding* is a classic in every way: layered, nuanced, and luxurious. A story that forces you to examine reality and truth, and the power of legends themselves'
Kritika H. Rao, author of *The Surviving Sky*

'A mysterious odyssey through the ancient legends and culture of South Asia that weaves an enchanting tale of theatre, thievery and richly fleshed binding-magic. The story within a story unravels like a Matryoshka doll and each discovery pulses with music and wonder and sometimes even deceit. The Old Gods will be pleased with this marathon of lyrical prose. Perfect for history-mythology geeks' Gourav Mohanty, author of *Sons of Darkness*

THE FIRST BINDING

TALES *of* TREMAINE

R.R. Virdi

This edition first published in Great Britain in 2023

First published in Great Britain in 2022 by Gollancz
an imprint of The Orion Publishing Group Ltd
Carmelite House, 50 Victoria Embankment
London EC4Y 0DZ

An Hachette UK Company

The authorised representative in the EEA is Hachette Ireland,
8 Castlecourt Centre, Dublin 15, D15 XTP3 Ireland (email: info@hbgi.ie)

5 7 9 10 8 6 4

A CIP catalogue record for this book is available from the British Library.

ISBN (Mass Market Paperback) 978 1 473 23400 0

Typeset by Input Data Services Ltd, Bridgwater, Somerset

Printed in Great Britain by Clays Ltd, Elcograph S.p.A

www.gollancz.co.uk

To the ones who held the heart, whole in hand and full-fast, then let it fall just as quick and all too short to last.

To Jim Butcher

For saving my life all those years ago on a night that should have been my last. He knows why, what he did, and why it mattered. For telling me that one day I could be where he was: signing books, getting on an award ballot alongside him, maybe an anthology with him, panel alongside him, and many more things. Many of which have happened. A few more secrets to come. And, for telling me to write the book I wanted. This book. And that if I did my job right, it would sell itself. It did. And he was right.

Thank you.

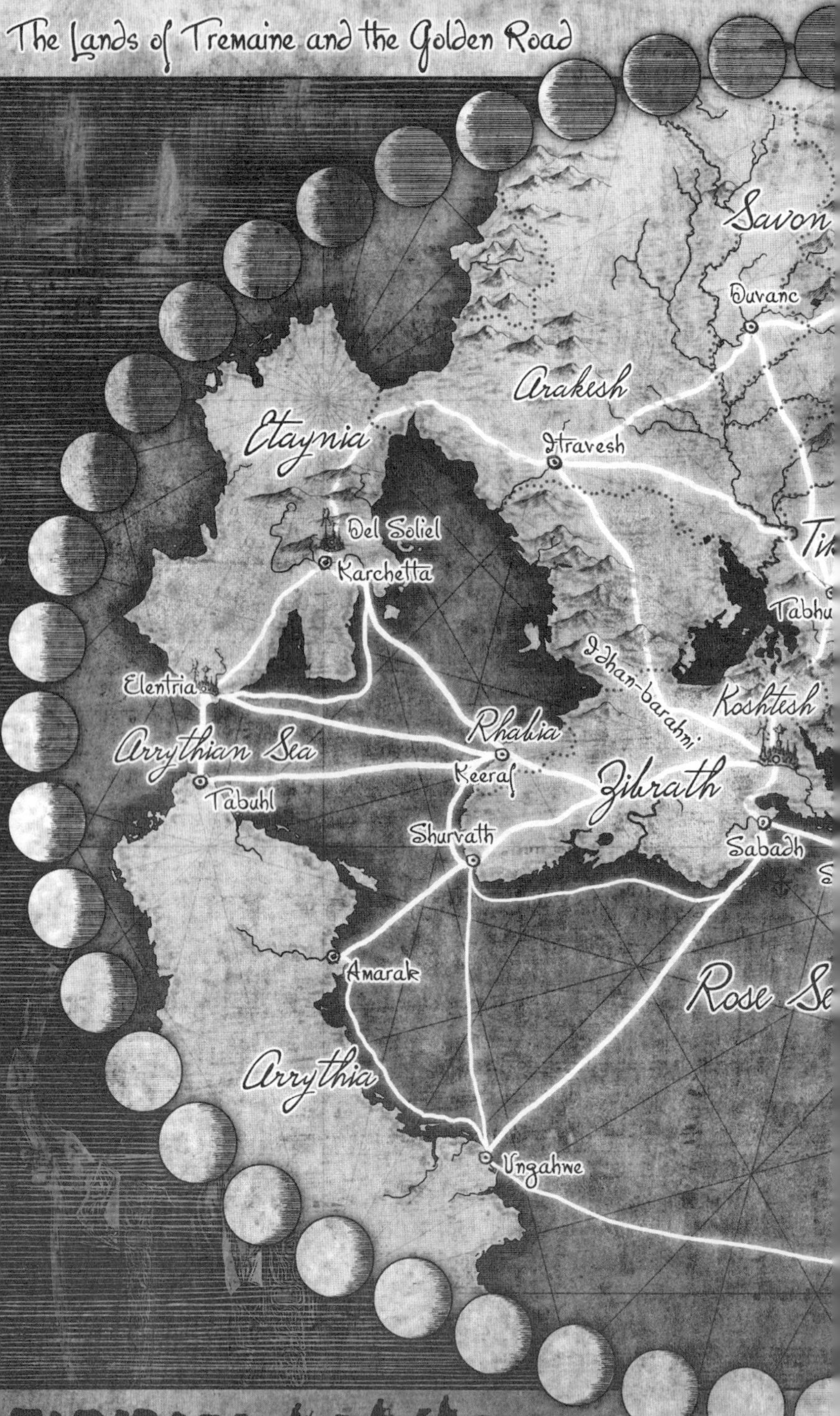

The Lands of Tremaine and the Golden Road
Savon
Duvanc
Arakesh
Etaynia
Itravesh
Del Soliel
Karchetta
Idhan-barahni
Koshtesh
Elentria
Rhakia
Arrythian Sea
Keeras
Zikrath
Tabuhl
Shurvath
Sabadh
Amarak
Arrythia
Ungahwe

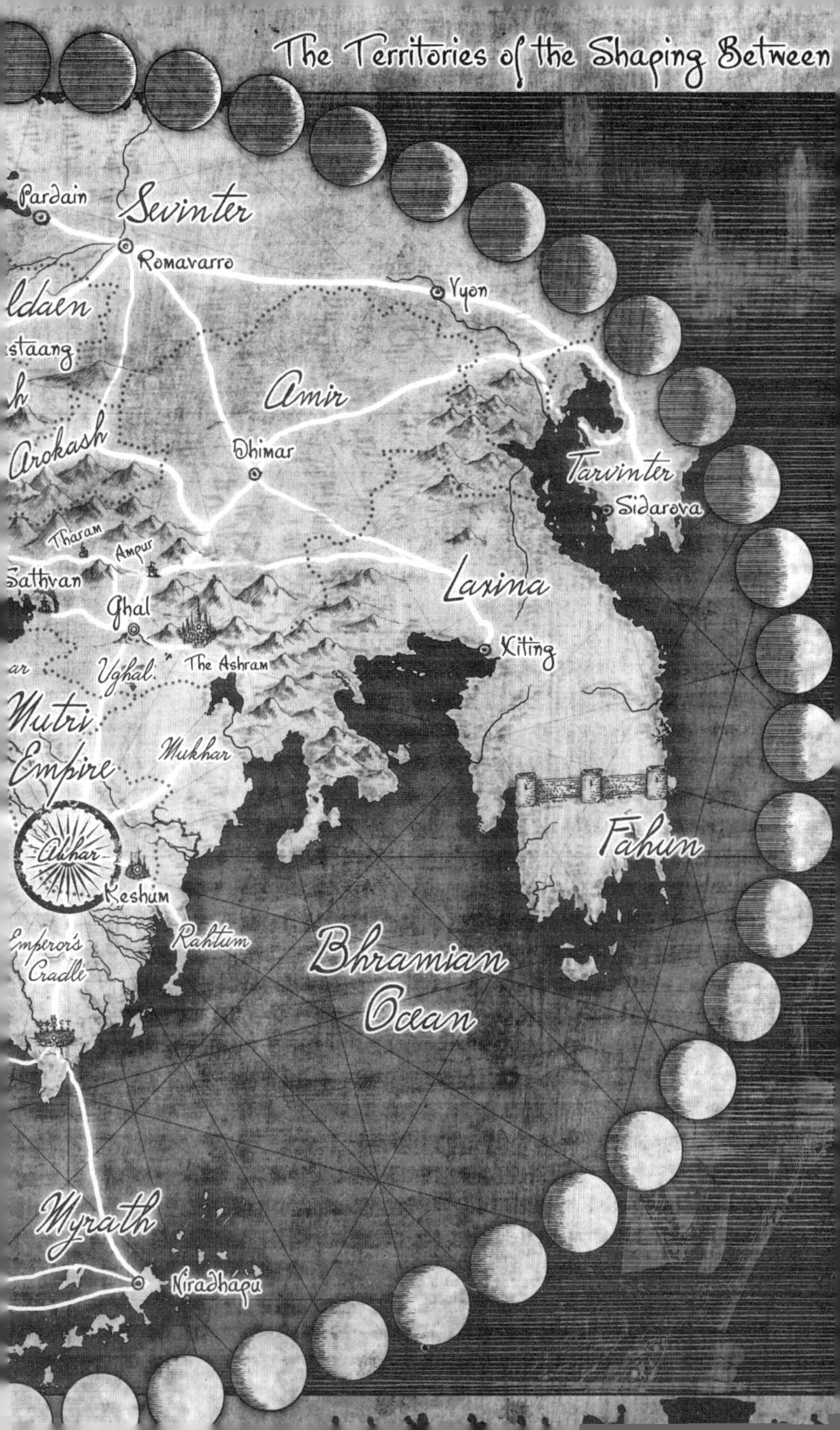

The Territories of the Shaping Between

Pardain
Sevinter
Romavarro
ldaen
Vyon
staang
Amir
Arokash
Dhimar
Tarvinter
Sidarova
Tharam
Ampur
Sathvan
Laxina
Ghal
Xiting
ar
The Ashram
Ughal
Mutri
Empire
Mukhar
Akhar
Fahun
Keshum
Emperor's
Cradle
Rahtum
Bhramian
Ocean
Myrath
Niradhápu

ONE

A Conversation in Stillness

I walked into the tavern in search of the most important thing in the world.

A story.

And I ended up swept into the most dangerous one of all.

The worst sort of prison held the Three Tales Tavern.

An emptiness.

A stillness.

And that is always meant to be broken.

It hung like a cord gone taut, quivering and waiting to snap. It was the quiet of held breaths, wanting for a voice, but ready to bite at any that dare make noise. It was the soundlessness of men too tired to speak and with an ear to hear even less. And all the stillness of an audience waiting for the play to begin.

The perfect stage for me. And I had just the thing to rouse them—ensnare them. But all good performances need one thing, and mine required a drink.

The tavern's lone mirror glinted from behind the counter with the hazy light I'd seen accompany mirages. It pulled my attention past the oiled and polished floors, away from the pitted, but solid wooden beams holding the place up, and to the counter.

I made my way over to it and sat down—alone.

The barkeeper took note of that, staring at me over the rim of a glass he polished with mechanical coldness. He looked to be in his middle years. His hair carried more streaks of chalk and iron than it should have at his age, thinning along the top. He had a soft, slightly protruding belly, not aided in appearance by a brown shirt gone tight around his waist nor his barrel of a chest. His eyes were lined with creases that could have come from both too much time in the sun and frequent smiling.

Though, he wasn't smiling now.

I eyed the barkeeper, adding another layer of stillness to the place. The air thickened into something chewable as I let curiosity flood the elderly men sitting in the far corner. They watched me with the interest only those with too much time on their hands could muster, which is what I wanted.

I know how to work my audience—build anticipation like feeding wood to a fire.

Layers.

I added another film of intrigue when I reached over my shoulder to grab one of the journals bound to my back. I tugged it free, thumbing it open to pull free a sheet of paper. Producing the pen was a simple thing, but I added a flare by rolling my wrist as I retrieved it from the folds of my robes. To those unskilled in sleight of hand, it looked as if the pen had sprung from my palm.

Theatricality and showmanship go a long way in making an impression. And the long case I'd set down to one side would do just the same.

Curiosity. It filled them now.

The slender piece of horn and silver inlay sat as an old comfort in my hand. A hollow thing with a narrow reservoir to hold just enough ink for my needs. I scrawled slowly, smoothly, across the sheet.

The barkeep watched with feigned disinterest, blanketing the place with another form of stillness. He shuffled over a few steps until he stood before me. The man passed off the action as if he needed to place the glass he'd finished cleaning somewhere nearby.

I knew better and made use of his act, pushing the sheet of paper in his direction. I looked up and smiled—waiting.

The barkeeper glanced at the sheet, then blinked and stared past me to the trio of patrons in the back. Another moment of stillness slipped by before he relented and plucked the paper between a thumb and forefinger. His eyes were the color of morning fog over water, a bleak gray masking the faintest hints of washed-out blue. They hardened into cold slate as he read over my note. If he took umbrage at my odd request, he didn't show it.

The man turned to pull a wooden mug from a brass hook hanging overhead. He took a measured step to the side and flicked the tap of a cask, waiting as a liquid the color of wet earth poured into the mug. The barkeep shut the valve and turned with a quarter step to place the drink before me. He stood and loomed like a figure of stone, wanting to know just as much as the men in the back what came next.

I kept them waiting as I pulled the mug toward me. It was one thing to order a drink. It was another matter to ask for one without a word, much less pay. It had the intended effect.

Hollow moans echoed through the tavern as chair legs scraped against the floor.

I looked toward the source of the noise without turning my head. The three men in the corner had all moved to face me now. I returned my attention to the contents of my drink. I'd asked for tea. He'd given me an ale.

I didn't say anything. I know when I'm being pressed—tested. And I know how to play back. Most innkeepers do not want to deal with prickly performers, easily slighted and twice the trouble than they're worth in coin. I shrugged my cowl free, letting it fall along my collar as I tipped the mug back.

Notes of cinnamon, cardamom, and woodruff sparked against my tongue. The faintest touch of anise made itself present through the clearness and crispness of the drink. I took care not to smack my lips or exhale a pleasurable sigh at its taste.

Stillness.

I continued to build it until I could almost hear the men's hearts pumping in agitation, answering their buried questions: Who am I? Who is the stranger in the red cloak and cowl? What rests within the case at my side?

I took another sip and waited for them to break the quiet that lingered before I'd even come in.

The barkeeper hovered before me, staring with the clear intent of wanting recompense for the beverage.

He'd get it and more.

One of the men sputtered. "It moved. His cloak moved on its own."

It did. And the silence broke.

Another of the men, old enough to be someone's grandfather, brushed aside wisps of white hair from over his eyes. "Swore the thing was . . . bleeding for a moment."

It was.

I let them gossip. And when I shifted in my seat, resting my staff in plain view, their whispers grew all the louder.

"Man comes in silence, doesn't spit so much as a word. Staff and cowl. Mess of books on his back," said one of the men.

All true.

"Only heard of one man like that. Hear it that he keeps his words inside him—deep, like a burning fire. When he speaks, everyone listens like magic. Can't no man turn away from his tales. He's that storyteller."

I grabbed my staff, spinning in place and slamming its base against the floorboards. A thunderous *crack* echoed through the tavern and my voice boomed with it. "I am."

And stillness returned in the beat between words.

I seized it. The pauses now belonged to me. And I decided when to break them.

One of the men fidgeted, grinding the tip of a worn boot against the floor. He wore dark breeches and a matching shirt. His coat had seen better days, the seams littered with dangling threads, some frayed. Dust from the road marred its already dull gray color. The man looked to be carved from driftwood left in the rain and cold to crack. His face was old leather, dark and lined. He bounced a leg in anticipation.

"I am *the* Storyteller. I've entertained the duke of Tarvinter with tales of daring and heroism. I've collected the world's secrets, forgotten stories, greatest legends, and tonight . . . I'll share them with you. But, every storyteller needs a willing audience. So find me one if you want an earful you'll never forget." I bowed, rolling my hands in a flourish.

The three men ran for the exit with more energy in their step than someone half their age could have mustered.

I turned back to the barkeeper, smiling in earnest and tipping back more of the ale. The next sip earned me my repressed sigh as I pulled the mug from my lips. "That's good." I hooked a thumb over a shoulder toward the door. "And, that's why you gave it to me for free. How many people do you think they'll rally for tonight?"

The barkeeper placed his hands against the counter. "Folk in Karchetta have been starved for outside news—stories. Place will be packed tonight." A hint of light filled his eyes. "Busy. Customers willing to spend money. Wanting entertainment. I hope you live up to your reputation."

I raised the mug. "I always do."

The bartender snorted. "You're just as bad as the woman."

I arched a brow, waiting for him to explain.

He looked over to the staircase to our side. "You'll run across her, no doubt. Has a mouth—fire in her. Not quite sure why I haven't booted her out myself." The barkeeper grabbed a rag, idly polishing a spot on the counter while regarding me.

Quiet returned, but I'd had my fill of that. "You said people are hungry for word from outside. What of news here? By the look of the people, I'd say it's grim."

The barkeeper pulled the rag away from the spot, frowning as he stared deeply into it. "You don't know?"

It's a rare thing for me not to know stories, the happenings of and in the world, but there are those moments. And I sought something more important than the local gossip.

I shook my head.

He exhaled. "There's a reason the Three Tales is without any stories of late.

Etaynia has enough of her own keeping people's attention. The prince-elect was murdered over a set ago."

I did the mental calculation of days the region used to mark a notable passing of time. It came out to fourteen, and two of those comprised a month here. Sets of days varied through countries along the Golden Road. No standardized monthly cycle existed as of yet, and the political tension between some countries made it nearly impossible to get there. I waved for him to continue.

"His younger brother took his place as an *efante,* but the election will be held again. The other household princes used the death to plead the church for reconsideration. Seven *efantes* are back to fighting, worrying people of what's to come. But it'll be the same. Prince-elect to king. Once that happens, people will breathe easier. There'll be more room for stories, I hope. Never know what the next man on the throne will do, and one prince or two already have their eye on joining the wars sprouting up around the world." The barkeeper resumed polishing the indiscriminate spot on the counter.

"Though, if you ask me—not that anyone does, mind you—I'd say we ought to be staying out of the affairs of other countries. Not the *efantes,* though. Some of them seem too keen to be king just to stick our noses where we'll be stung for it. Mark my words, Storyteller."

Murdered. My thoughts remained on that singular word. So I asked the question I shouldn't have, but being a storyteller is being part gossip. "Who do you think did it?" I tilted the mug, watching him over the rim as I drank.

He held his composure better than I credited him to do. The muscles in his neck went tight, shooting a rod through his collar and shoulders that straightened his posture noticeably. "Don't know. I'm far from a wise man, but I'd echo what they'd say here. It's not healthy for a man to think on that. More so to finger a man for doing so."

I decided to change the subject. If the town of Karchetta was worried over their country's election, talking about it would only sour the locals against me. And I needed them to like me—love me—if I wanted to earn free meals and a place to sleep that didn't involve dangerously close proximities with a horse. Accidentally speaking ill of one of Etaynia's princes would all but guarantee that outcome.

One never knew whom another person favored as a leader.

"Have you heard any other stories? Anything worthwhile pass through here?" I leaned forward, resting on my elbows.

The barkeeper snorted. "You mean any stories *you* deem worthwhile. I've heard you're a picky fellow."

I smiled. "I am. I've heard almost every story the world's had to tell. Witnessed some legends." *And been part of my fair share. Though, I wish I hadn't.* "I'm still seeking that special one, the tale of tales that needs a proper teller to tell it."

The barkeeper's eyes lost their focus as he silently mouthed along with what I had said. "Bit of a mouthful there."

"I do that on occasion. Nature of my profession."

The barkeeper snorted. "I've heard a bit about that too." He paused, frowning at a spot near the corner of the counter. Its wood was the color of sandstone smothered in honey, and a portion of its surface refused to carry the luster of the rest. The barkeeper breathed over the spot, putting more weight behind his polishing. The area still turned away the light. "Ah." He tossed the rag toward me.

I snatched it out of the air, waving it before folding it into a tight square. The cloth was the color found in dried blood, hanging somewhere between a rotten plum and red wine. The fabric's fibers had been worn to the point they'd tear soon. A hint of pressure and my thumbs would punch clean through.

He always used this rag, but a glance past the man revealed several others. Newer, by the looks of them, stacked alongside a pair of bottles.

The question was: Why?

And the answer was equally as simple: It was important. There was a story behind it.

There's a story behind everything and everyone—powerful tales, even if they don't seem it on the surface. There's power in stories. There's magic in them. And each person's life is a story itself, and with that, every person carries magic within them.

And all of us are taught over the years how to forget it—lose it.

My job is to remind you.

I gestured to the spot he'd been trying to clean. "May I?"

The barkeeper pushed off the counter, crossing his arms as he nodded. "Be my guest."

"I intend to." I rose, slipping off the sling of books hanging over my shoulder. The leather thong bound a handful of stories I'd collected over years. And one in particular contained some things that should only have been recorded, but never shared and said aloud.

Some secrets need to be buried.

I set the bundle down on my stool, straightening my staff as I moved by. My thumbs and forefingers kneaded the cloth as I came to the spot. "What's the story behind this?"

"What?"

My fingers brushed over the counter. It felt like river stone, smooth, but hints of a porous surface remained. "The story behind this old piece of cloth. Or is there not a reason you've held on to it for so long when there are several perfectly usable ones behind you." I didn't bother looking up, regarding the lackluster portion of the counter. The wood was old, yet held bands of morning light across its grain, nearly glimmering.

I breathed it in. It smelled of lemon and oils. He'd treated it regularly.

Most innkeepers tended to their establishments with the care you'd expect of a business owner knowing the worth of their investment. This went beyond that. The Three Tales Tavern was special to him. At least, parts of it were.

I took the rag and leaned closer to the counter's surface, breathing lightly over the spot.

"You'll laugh at me." The barkeeper let out a rueful chuckle. "It's a silly thing—a woman was involved."

There always is—always. I motioned for him to go on as I exhaled onto the wood again.

"How old do you think this place is?"

I missed a beat, blinking and forgetting about the blemished wood. There were many answers, many ways to be right. I could tell him it was at least a few decades. I'd be right, yet off the mark. I could say it had been around long enough to become an important place in Karchetta. It was the truth.

But all of it would fall short of the best answer I could give—the needed one.

"I don't know, but I'd like to hear that story as well." *Because I have a feeling they're tied together.*

Everyone has stories they've collected inside them, and one of the most important things you can do is let those be given voice. People need to be able to share their memories with an audience that cares.

And I could be that audience.

He cleared his throat, turning to grab the glass he'd cleaned earlier. He ran a thumb over its lip, and the edge of it sang with a low but audible hum. He filled his glass from the same cask as before with the measured patience of someone who had all the time in the world.

"It's better in glass," he said after taking a long, slow sip. "People don't know that. Not many. And no one tells you. I didn't know myself till I met her."

Her. How so many stories start. My mouth broke into a smile, but it was short-lived. I knew how those sorts of stories often ended.

"I didn't have much in life." The barkeeper shook his head, more to himself, tipping his glass back for another swallow. "Didn't think I'd go anywhere either." A lazy grin spread over his face as he looked around his tavern. "Guess you could say I still haven't. But it was her that changed things."

I placed the folded cloth over the blemish, rubbing it more for appearance's sake than anything else.

"Karchetta isn't much of a place, you know? Everyone goes west eventually to the seas. Fishing, now that's a good life. Bring home food if you don't make bits. But Etaynia is a land for fishing." He spoke matter-of-factly.

"But truth be told, and it's a shameful thing for a man to admit here, I can't swim. Not much use for a fisherman that can't weather the sea. So what's a young man to do?"

I polished harder, giving him my full attention.

"Can't fish, well, you sail. Keep hearing tell there's a whole wide world out there to see." He paused for a long moment, eyeing me sideways. "*See*, sailors. Because of the sea?"

I gave him a thin smile. "Clever. I must be tired is all." I scrubbed harder, losing myself in the repetitive action. My mind slipped into a series of folds. First, in half. I became aware of only two things: the dull spot on the counter, and the now distant words of the barkeeper. Another fold, now into fours. My mind cleared and there was only the mark on the counter. The other three places were without thought or image. My mind folded again. Eight places.

Just the spot on the counter remained. A portion of wood unlike the rest, but needing to be restored. The thought intensified and I strung another image to it. I envisioned the counter as it once was. The wood carried a deeper light, new and warm.

"Was like many men, young and full of ideas. Not a whit of a notion on how to make any of them happen. And, well, could always farm. But, need a herd, or at least enough bits to have the start of one. Where's a man to get that? Wasn't much good with my hands either. Couldn't build, couldn't apprentice to anyone in a craft that made you a decent living, and that's what I wanted. So, I tell myself to just go out and travel. Travel does a man a lot of good, or so I've heard."

It does.

"But that takes money, too. You can see I'm not good at planning. Life's too"—he waved a dismissive hand—"it just happens, you know? Not much a man can do to deal with that. So, what could I do?"

I stayed silent, folding my mind again. There was just the nature of the counter, clean but for one spot. Then there was the truth inside running opposite to the one before me. In my mind, the wood was uniform and perfect. I held to that image. My mind folded again; each square, like parchment, carried the singular vision I'd crafted.

"Well, figured first ought to clear my thoughts. Headed for the only tavern around." He laughed to himself. "And no, wasn't this place. Not yet, anyhow."

The words rang dull and hollow to me. I remained fixed on my task. Every fiber of my being, my mind, believed in that spot matching the rest of the counter's luster.

I breathed over it again. "Start with whent." My mind folded again, becoming a multifaceted lens all mirroring the same image countless times. More faith than I'd called on in a long time welled inside me, and I applied it to the belief that the bar was as bright and flawless as when it was made. "Then go to ern." I wiped the cloth along the spot, pulling it back.

A perfectly polished counter sat before me, reflecting things better left unseen.

I'd grown a few days' worth of coal beard over my face. My hair was dark as night and just as wild. The long locks fell to just below my chin, caught between being waves and curls. My eyes were a shade darker than the counter. A color somewhere between bright amber and cedar.

"Solus and shadow, boy! I thought you were going to try your hand at cleaning a spot, not the whole counter. Didn't even see you move." The barkeeper blinked hard before rubbing a palm against each eye. He downed his glass the next instant. "Must've gotten lost in my own tale." He snorted, putting the drink down. "It's good to see this old thing like this, but it's not like it was. I can see myself in it, hah!" He let out a rolling laugh that faded into a heavy sigh. "Wish you could've seen it, Rita."

I perked up, shaking myself of the reverie and the hint of power I'd called upon. "Who's Rita?"

I had an idea, but some stories are better left in the hands of those that lived them. Some tales just aren't meant for professionals. There are things missing from them: the way your voice changes speaking about someone you love, the hollow knots that fill you and make their way out of your mouth when talking about pain, and the hot metal that comes with rage.

A good storyteller can mimic those, but some stories are best served raw.

"Hm? Oh, Rita was . . . she was behind all this." He waved a hand absently to our surroundings. "Found me young, the best time for a boy to meet that special girl, you know? Though, come to think of it"—he frowned deeply—"suppose there's no wrong time to meet them, so long as you do. There's a change in luck—fortune—in meeting the right one. Anyhow, was lost without wind and sails, if you'll pardon the expression."

I nodded, understanding.

Etaynia was a coastal kingdom, reaping its riches from trade, fishing, exploration, and an immeasurable amount of wealth from salt. Everything revolved around the sun and seas here. The warm climate allowed for vast swaths of land to be dedicated to agriculture, grains in particular. These were well cared for, and by hardworking people. The only thing ever keeping them down was religion and the affairs of their seven *efantes*—princes.

He went on as if I hadn't lost myself in thought. "Rita was a thing."

Was. My heart ached for a moment.

I knew where this story was going.

"She had a mind and the wit to go with it. Caught me at Solus du Novre, festival of the new sun. Season of gray skies and hard seas, little light, all past. We were back to clear and bright mornings. Should've seen her, Storyteller. Dressed like the sun she was. All rippling red and orange. She'd made it herself. Always good with her hands." He smiled, the sort where it reached his eyes and made him look years younger. "Was like watching leaves twirling in the wind, the way she spun and danced. You know what that's like?"

I kept silent, letting him find his own answer.

"But you're young. Suspect you've found a fair few girls to tumble with." He fixed me with a knowing look. "But not *the* one, am I right?"

He wasn't, but I nodded.

"Well, don't know how, but she took to me. Never questioned it much after that. Man shouldn't question good luck and fortune. When Solus gives, he gives bountifully. That's what the sun does, hm? She convinced me that I did have a way to make a life and way in this world. Wasn't much good at a craft, but I was strong and willing. I took whatever work I could find. Carried loads for merchants out by the coast, far from home. Sent money back to Rita, and you know, she waited for me. She did." His smile grew.

"I moved lumber for shipbuilders. Cleaned decks and scraped ships clear of filth. Worked for glassmakers far out where the bigger churches are, helping lift the big pieces they fit up high in the towers.

"Did it for years, visiting back when I could. We grew closer, Rita and I. We talked about things that young people do. Dreams and such. I spoke of wanting roots back here—home. Didn't know how to make it happen. Didn't matter much. See, I'd fallen in love with a terribly clever woman. She'd been putting away every spare bit, septas when I could earn them, all for keeping. And she'd gotten to working with her hands." He tapped the counter.

"Made this first. A piece, a promise. The idea that one day we'd own our own home, a tavern, a place for all those travelers I never got to be like to come through and rest. A home set in my home. Not a bad dream, huh?"

"No." It was all I could say at the moment.

"Well, I set back out. Not for long this time, mind you. Got working till I heard word that the old tavern'd burned down." He frowned, the light leaving his eyes as his face hardened. "Wasn't the best of places, but it was a good one."

He cleared his throat and extended a hand, gesturing with a thrust of chin to the rag.

I passed it to him.

He took it in silence, polishing the counter despite no need for it. "We'd lost a bit of home and that shook me. Was starting to think I should take what money we'd put away and finally go somewhere else. Rita stood firm as any old oak, telling me she wouldn't budge on the dream. Remember that, not much more stubborn in this world than a woman when she knows she's right. Which"—he winked my way—"is almost all of the time. Least, it's healthier if you live that way. Trust me.

"But she didn't move. Told me we'd offer to buy what was left of the place, which wasn't much. But she was as good as her word. Woman spent a day and a night at old Abraham's door—foreign fellow from off far east who'd settled here. She stood just as firm and solid as she did before me, not budging till he gave in. That was that. Place was ours." He sucked in a heavy breath before picking up his glass, draining it in a single go.

"So we took to it. I'd leave for a set or two, taking up most of a month. Come home with money and get to work rebuilding the place. First thing we did was put this"—he rapped his knuckles against the countertop—"in place. Built the rest of the Three Tales around it. Took us seven months all told. Most of the whole year went by just so in our labor. But, we'd done it, Rita and I." He leaned back against the shelf lined with bottles and casks, crossing his arms and letting the day's stress visibly leave his shoulders and neck.

"We'd made a home and we tended to it. And it went as well as you'd imagine for two young ones who'd gotten ahead of themselves with dreams and love. We had our mishaps. Nearly lost the place a couple of times to our own fires, unscrupulous folk, and a tax collector riling Rita the wrong way so as to catch the rough side of her tongue." He shook his head and suppressed a laugh. "Bet the fellow still remembers that lashing. But her bark was always worse than her bite."

I'd met my fair share of folk like that as well.

"But we held on." His voice grew hollow, a tone I recognized. The sound a story makes when it's about to change. When a tale turns on its head and you realize it's not the happily ever after you expected.

This was a tragedy.

And I knew those all too well.

After all, I'd played my part in a fair few.

History would remember those.

"Comes to two years later. We're doing fine for ourselves, but I'm running the place more and more on my own. See, Rita, strong as she was, was getting more tired by the day. She slept in later. Needed help carrying things. Wasn't sure what was wrong at first. Thought she'd caught something ill." He swallowed, taking a long look at the counter. "I was right, but I didn't think things would go as poorly as they did. That's for the stories, you know?"

I did.

"She grew paler. Lost the color of the sun in her skin. Her hair went thin, but used to be like, like . . ." He exhaled and tossed the rag beside the clean ones. "It was a dream. It was something." He picked the rag back up on instinct, folding and kneading it much as I had. "No amount of money, nothing I could do. No prayers to Solus. The church. Nothing could turn away what'd come over her. I did what I could, I swear it."

"I believe you." My words carried more weight than I'd intended, reverberating through the nearly empty place.

That seemed to steady him. He nodded to himself. "I did. But, months came and went, as they do. After the fourth, Rita didn't come back." He turned from me, bringing the glass over to the cask and refilling it. "That was so many years ago, likely before you were born." He took a large swig of ale. "But this"—he shook the rag—"is something to remember her by.

"When we fixed up the place, didn't have much left over for the smaller things, the forgotten ones. Like things to clean. Rita laughed and just tore a patch from her old dress. Then another, and another, sewing them together. Easy, just like that." He waved the cloth. "Then she set to wiping, still laughing all the while." The barkeeper smiled, a thin thing trying to be more, like a gash in stone.

"And, well . . . that's my story."

I inhaled, bowing my head. "Thank you for sharing that . . ." I let the pause hang in the air.

"Dannil." He held out his hand.

I took it, holding firm as I shook it. "And you know me by my reputation."

He snorted. "We'll see that tonight. I gave you a story. Expect some glorious ones back, the kind folk here won't soon forget."

"I promise you that."

His earlier curiosity returned and Dannil looked over the counter. The man's gaze fell on the blackwood-and-leather oiled case I'd set on the floor. "Can I ask?"

I nodded, bringing the case up and setting it on the counter. Its clasps snapped open with a hard metallic sound that I had almost forgotten from years past. An old treasure sat inside.

A thing of well-worked wood and polished to a gloss. The black of rich tar and the sunburst orange of dawn. The mandolin lay in two pieces, broken along the neck clean as hammer and chisel parting stone. Its strings cut by a knife as fine as glass. If you were to try to strum the strings, they would play one final note that would say a single word. A word for which there is no word but which could come to mean many things. *Profound sorrow. Pain. Regret. Please come back. Begging forgiveness.* And most of all, *I'm sorry.*

But the strings could not be strummed, so there was no word.

No more melody. The mandolin was broken.

And it would never play again.

I could mend many broken things, but not this.

I shut the case. Sometimes the price of memories is too great for remembrance, so the best thing we can do is close the door to those parts of our lives.

Dannil let out a heavy sigh at seeing the state of the instrument. "I'd have asked if you play but—"

"I don't." I returned the case to the ground. "But my stories have no need for music. I'll give you one to remember."

"Good. But for now, I'll settle for an explanation." He gestured to the restored counter again.

My voice was softer than a breeze sifting through low-cut grass, nearly inaudible. "There are ten bindings all men must know." I hadn't realized I'd spoken. Old memories and training had risen to the surface, drilled into me over time.

"What's that?"

I shook my head. "Nothing. Would you like a hand setting up for tonight? I expect a good crowd."

He nodded and we set to work.

TWO

A Dark and Wild Woman

Night fell over the village of Karchetta, and with it came another kind of stillness. The sort accompanying anticipation. The kind you knew would be broken, it was just a question of when. There was a reprieve in smashing that stillness with noise and reverie.

But the waiting could kill a man.

I busied myself with arranging the last of the stools, helping form a semicircle before the white-stone fireplace. The setup would allow me to move with ease and address the crowd.

Dannil moved with the efficiency of someone used to catering to large crowds, prepping tin platters with portions of toasted bread no larger than one's palms. He spread small pats of butter over each piece, sprinkling hints of salt and pepper with the care expected of a chef. Next came thin fish, shimmering like slender pieces of silver and the size of my smallest finger.

The traditional snack within Etaynia. People within the region had a deep-held love for the *baquerene* fish, gutted and dried.

Dannil brought up a handful of tomatoes, slicing them into thin rings before dicing cubes smaller than a fingernail. He layered them just as carefully over the fish. A clear container, fashioned from glass, appeared in his hands with almost the same level of skill I'd displayed in producing my pen. It was shaped like an upturned bell, with a flat and narrow base that curved outward to form a wide mouth.

Dannil tilted the container, holding a thumb over the narrow spout. A stream of oil pooled in the crack of space left between, spilling thin bands over the pieces of toast.

I'd seen revered craftsmen who didn't pay half as much care as Dannil did to that food. I watched without a word, fetching my staff and sling of books. My mind slipped into an old and familiar pattern as I flipped open the first of my tomes. Stories blurred by as I tumbled through the pages. I'd memorized all of the tales and information stored within ages ago. But there was something soothing in the process of going over them again.

I wouldn't need to look at any of them in particular for the night's performance. Good storytelling is seldom about the truth. In fact, oftentimes, it's about the lies—the good ones.

I'd know. I'd spent years spreading several about myself. Because of them, I could travel the world without much fear, sitting wherever I chose and only ever being seen as a famed entertainer.

It was easier that way.

The door slammed open with a *thud* reserved for a drum. People spilled into the room, clamoring amongst themselves.

I feigned inattention as I peered at my books, but kept my ears trained on the smattering of conversations. The crowd's mood and gossip would decide what story they needed.

"Terrible business, the things happening with the *efante*," said a man somewhere in his forties. He was built like a rake, and thin and knotted-hard as some roots. His features were dark and as craggy as one of the men I'd seen earlier. They spoke of lots of time spent under the sun without reprieve. He wore thick clothing, weathered and the matching colors of the earth—browns and faded greens. A farmer, likely. "I swear it by Solus' beard, one of them *efantes* will have us marching on our neighbors. Sons dying in fields, daughters left widows. Something's twisted in some of those men—tainted. I'm telling you."

A woman, who could have been his wife, cuffed his shoulder. She hissed sharp enough to cut a groove in stone. "Shouldn't be talking of that. Leave princely concerns to them and the church. It's not for us. Solus knows who'll hear, and what'll happen then, hm?"

"Hoping to hear something grand, y'know? Something heroic. That's the sort of stuff he tells. Least I've heard as such." The speaker was a young man, not even in his twenties. He had a slender build and carried the smooth muscles of someone whose day was spent carrying out strenuous work. He wore a simple spun shirt and the breeches to match. Splotches of gray clay, possibly mortar, had dried along his hands. A few rogue drops peppered his cheeks. I caught sight of the scantest traces of the material along some of the dark strands of his hair. It didn't do much to dull his boyish looks.

The rest of the growing crowd murmured similar sentiments.

"Want to hear something to wash away the ills going around. Too much foul and sad talk these days."

"Wouldn't mind one of the old legends, the things no one talks of but the church. Want it done properly by someone wanting to do more than preach. I'd like that."

They were the same sort of folk and all of a similar mind. You'd find no nobles among this group—none of the *burgesa*. These were common men and women. And as such, they wanted an uncommon tale. Something of daring and heroism. Something to aspire to, dream of. They wanted legends. Proper ones.

The troubles and tribulations of their own princes brought them down. They wanted to hear of the nobles of old. A time when royalty fought for the common man's good. Stories where the low-down—lowborn—rose high and walked taller than those raised in castles with silver spoons.

They wanted a story like Antoine, the farmer soldier become a prince of the sun.

I smiled to myself. It was a good tale to tell, and I'd do it in a manner that'd have them waxing about it for years to come. I stood, lowering the leather thong and books to the floor as I picked up my staff. It would be a crime to start the story early, orating with people still bustling about and making noises of their own.

No.

They needed to want it more. To be willing to hold their breaths in anticipation for my first words. The Three Tales Tavern needed to fall back to the stillness of when I'd first entered.

So I waited, a statue washed in blood. The oddest and brightest figure as the fire's light washed over the crimson of my cloak and cowl.

People found seating to their liking. Some opted for the lengthy tables running along the far side of the tavern, sitting close enough together they'd rub elbows the entire night. Others moved to the farthest corners of the place, almost outside the edges of my vision. A string of folk passed by and made their way up the stairs. They vanished out of sight as the passage wound its way behind the fireplace, leading up to a mezzanine. Tables lined the edges behind wooden railings, offering those seated in place a good view.

Through it all, I caught wandering eyes and whispers. The kind I'd expected to hear and the ones I wanted.

"That him?"

"Looks like."

"Has to."

"Never seen someone like him."

"The cloak . . . Haven't drunk a drop, but something's not right with it. And it can't be me."

"It's you. Looks to be fine . . ." The voice trailed off as if reconsidering.

"What's with the staff? He lame? Maybe he needs a walking cane?"

"Doesn't look like it. See how he's standing. He's young and fit. Though, can't make much of his face out underneath that hood of his."

A young woman slipped past me while the crowd continued muttering.

She wore a dress the mixed colors of autumn leaves. They blended together across her chest and waist so that you couldn't tell where one shade began and another ended. Her skirt fell to just above her ankles. A sash, the color of pressed olives, was bound tight against her waist. The ensemble left her arms and parts of her back bare.

If anyone rivaled me in terms of grandeur this night, it was her.

Her hair was bound in a loose tail, coiled over one shoulder, with strands flitting free at her temples. She had the Etaynian complexion, kissed by the sun and smooth as river stone. Bright eyes. Full lips. The sort that gave young men all sorts of ideas.

She ran over to Dannil, throwing her arms around him with the joy a daughter might greet her father with. He returned the hug and leaned over to whisper in her ear, following with a nod toward a group of patrons. She returned the gesture and went behind the bar to grab a tray.

A pair of girls, dressed similarly, entered moments later. They skipped the greetings and set to the same task, doling out drinks and food.

I waited for them to placate the masses.

The people were hungry and tired. A day's work had gotten to them. The world around them grew tighter with talks of scheming princes and an overbearing church. They needed a few moments amongst themselves, trading simpler stories. Talks of how their days went. Local gossip. Whose daughter fancies who. What trouble sons are up to. Rumors and things that made them feel connected, safe, and away from the larger problems in the world.

Minutes passed, slipping into an hour. I stayed on my feet the entire time. Fading into the backdrop was as much an art as performing.

The talks and hollering quieted to low rumbles after a while. People moved more languidly as the food and drink got to them. A couple of lazy looks passed over the taproom.

And suddenly people remembered the figure in blood red.

Eyes slowly fixed on me, and the old rumor-mongering returned.

I didn't pay attention to it this time. Instead, I turned, brushing my cloak back far and wide as I closed in on the fire. My mind folded in half once again. I saw the division between both its sides, clean—unmarred, like fresh parchment. I folded it again. Segmenting emptiness into larger fields of nothingness. My mind blanked.

Only tendrils of vermilion, lining bands of bright yellow, remained. A sea of carmine embers sifted below it all. The fire's light dominated every square of my mind.

Fire. It was as old as the world itself, coming to life alongside my people, who sprung up around it to tell tales—the first stories of the world.

I knew it. I had an intimate understanding of fire and the story behind it. I knew its inner workings the way a playwright knows their productions.

When you know something's story, you know the truth of it—and the bits meant to be hidden. You know what's lacking and where to find it.

Another fold. All sound fled my ears, leaving me deaf to the goings-on within the Three Tales.

The fire before me had a twin, bound deep in my chest. I pulled on it—tugged. It was the heat that comes with love, or anger. The fire that spurs people on in the face of adversity. The kind that fuels the pursuit of dreams.

I brought the grooved and knotted tip of my staff to my lips. A breath formed deep inside me, more in the pit of my stomach than my lungs. I tethered it to the countless fires burning in my mind. The image of my breath sailed upward, past my chest, where I envisioned binding it to the flame around my heart. I exhaled, releasing warm air over my wooden tool.

My mind folded again, and now I saw a dozen images of air bound to the head of my staff.

"Ahn." My breath coursed over the wood in an unseen current. It flowed, hot as when it'd left my lungs, warming by the second. I tipped the staff toward the hearth, slipping the head into the fire.

"Whent." My voice stayed low, hidden within the edges of my cowl. I held firm to the visions in my head, the belief that fire burned inside. The bands of breath around my staff were its perfect conduit. Of that, I had no doubt.

Unshakable belief that they were all one and the same. I kept to that.

"Ern." I held the staff in the fire. Its fingers licked at the rod's head, surging with serpentine grace to wind over and flow through the whisper of air I'd breathed. The fire held and twined, unfading.

I turned, planting the butt of the staff against the floorboards with a solid *thump*.

Every person in the Three Tales Tavern froze, forgetting their breaths in the process.

I banged the staff again. It resonated like a thunderclap.

Again.

Thunder.

A third time.

A heavenly boom followed.

The audience joined me, stomping fists and feet in unison with my beat.

I held my tempo until no other sounds remained but the drumming.

I stopped.

And the audience followed.

Stillness returned to the Three Tales Tavern.

I took hold of it, kept them waiting, eyeing them all without moving.

Their breaths remained still—distant.

I drew the stillness longer then, took a step forward, careful not to make a sound.

People twitched. Cast sidelong looks to one another. None dared speak, however. And just when it got to be too much for them, I acted.

I stormed toward the row of people sitting on the nearest stools. "So, people of Karchetta!"

The crowd shook and gasped.

A simple thing, but the little stunt roused them true enough. Hearts pounding, eyes wide, they were mine now.

I lunged to my right, throwing my cloak out wide to one side with a flick of my hand. The weaving of fire around my staff flickered as I bent low, placing its tip between my face and the closest patrons.

They yelped, collecting themselves the next instant. A low chorus of chuckles broke through the room.

"You want to hear a story?" I didn't give them time to answer, leaping back toward the fireplace, twirling my cloak with practiced motions. "A tale of daring and bravery. Of men come from nothing who changed a world. Or at least . . . a country. Maybe even a place like here." I pounded the base of my staff against the floor. "A place called . . . Etaynia. Home of the children of the sun—Solus. People whose skin he has kissed. Whose hair and brows are reminders of the nights before he came to this world.

"You want a story that reminds you of your old blood. The potential in you. The deep and boundless courage you know to be stored in all your hearts. You want to know, be reminded, that a little bit of Solus"—I brought the staff close again, breathing into the bands of fire until they blossomed—"lives within you!" The flare drew excited gasps and exclamations from the crowd before the fire resettled itself.

"That is what you want." It wasn't a question. Their hearts and minds were mine now, and I could tell them the stories they needed, and they'd nod and agree as if the idea was their own.

I let another pause take over. The people's thoughts must have run wild as they tried to guess which story I'd pluck from their rich history. On what adventure would I take them?

Something jangled from the shadows, like metal against glass. Clear, crystalline it chimed and jingled.

A sound like a rain of iron beads on panes of frozen glass.

I turned to the source, ripped from my performance to find I'd been wrong about which woman rivaled me in grandeur that night.

I've told many a story in my life, been part of nearly as many, and *she* before me could have walked off the pages of any of them.

Hair, darker than a raven's wing, fell behind her in thick and wild curls. A band the color of rouge ran through her black tresses. The ribbon wound down her head and around her neck, disappearing between her breasts. Golden hoops hung from her ears, hooking my gaze as they caught the firelight, and her skin was a shade lighter than the people of Karchetta's. It was like sugar, cooked low and golden with spices, promising to be as warm and sweet to kiss and touch as it looked.

We traded glances and I nearly lost the folds of my mind, and the binding with it. The fire around my staff snapped and flickered, almost in rebuke.

Her eyes carried an unruly intensity, like a sea in storm. They were deep emeralds washed with sage and flecks of bright pear. The sash tied tightly around her waist mirrored them, enriching them all the more.

The woman's outfit was the antithesis of mine. Her blouse was the white of snow, cut low to reveal her shoulders and tease a view most boys would flush at. Gold bangles hooped her wrists. They chimed every other step. She walked barefoot, ringing twice over due to the anklets at her feet. The metal contrasted the brightness of her violet skirt.

She hummed, low and long, with the clarity of silver and brass.

The sound threatened to rip me from the folds of my mind. My hold over my bindings wavered, the fire sputtering like it'd been doused with water. The unseen and ever-so-fine threads of air quivered as if ready to snap.

I had folded my mind enough times to risk a violent backlash should I abandon the weavings of magic so suddenly. Belief, once formed, must be held with an iron will . . . or it shatters. And adding another fold to solidify my workings could have meant losing my mind in an inescapable vortex of mirror images and twisting thoughts. Instead, I repeated my bindings more to bolster myself.

Her voice had robbed me of the audience's attention. The woman's lips, wide and full, quirked to one side in a smoldering smile that promised many things.

"Story and song tonight?" said someone in the crowd.

"Lucky twice over, seems like. Praise Solus."

"Knew it'd be a good idea to come here. Said so, didn't I?"

"You did."

The patrons slipped into quiet murmuring, dismantling the atmosphere I'd labored to build.

I ground my teeth, glaring at the woman with a heat that dwarfed the fire behind me.

She returned the look with a dazzling and mischievous one I didn't know how to process.

Instead, I cleared my throat in the hopes of recapturing my audience. "Praise Solus indeed! And with that, let us begin the story of his chosen son. The lowest of men, risen to heir of sunlight and first *efante* of Etaynia!" I blew a steady current of air into the burning staff. Fire blossomed to mimic the sun in miniature.

The crowd gasped, some clapping and letting all manner of raucous noises flood the room.

"I'll sing." The woman stepped over to the man nearest her, running a finger from one end of his collar to the other. "After the storyteller works his magic."

She was poking—prodding—testing my composure.

Very well. I resolved to give her a performance she'd remember.

Let me risk another binding. To fold one's mind—envisioning countless reflections of a few select images—was one thing. It took another kind of skill to push that aside without burying it, all to the end of convincing your brain to hold to another set of beliefs.

The workings tasked with imbuing my staff with wind and fire slipped to the side as I imagined half the world within me going blank as fresh parchment. A cord, fine as a lock of my own hair, hung suspended in my mind. It trailed from my lungs to my throat. I breathed out. "Whent." The end of the cord left my mouth, fraying as it spread through the room, binding my voice to the air. "Ern."

The crowd shifted anxiously.

I spoke, and the air bowed and rippled before my words. I gave voice to thunder. "Listen and listen well. For now we go back far—to a time before this was Etaynia. To an era when the lands to the east were at war, which spilled over into this fertile and prosperous country. When brothers to the south, across the Arrythian Sea, failed to answer your ancestors' calls for help. *This* is the story of one man, of common salt and earth—with the sun on his face and in his heart. A man who'd stand up to any that meant harm to those who called these golden lands *home*."

I slipped into the story as the Three Tales Tavern fell into the deepest stillness yet.

THREE

A Prince of Sunlight

To a time once forgotten, and not far from where we now stand, was Carmeaum. The heartland of what became Etaynia. A place untouched by neighboring wars, but that would soon change.

I lunged and worked the folds of my mind to hold more shapes. A weaker thought, but still taxing. The light from my staff ebbed, and a new light cast long shadows across the wall. The shapes of men arced through the tavern in vast armies, drawing the attention of the audience with long-drawn gasps.

Within this place was a man, strong of heart and mind, but not of back and brow. His name was Antoine.

He labored twice as long and hard as the rest of the men, never giving thought to anything other than the day's labor.

And it is that strength of character that made him into something more.

Solus, the sun, took note of this and watched over the young man. Though Solus loved Antoine from afar, God Above never intervened in the farmer's life. Even as the War of Shadows crept closer, great Solus sat idle.

And what a terrible time for him to do so.

For Des Embras—the Ten Shadows, first of creation, first to be forgotten—walked the world again. They took root in the hearts and minds of many men, pushing them to hatred and a war of conquest. Brother turned on brother. Kings looked with newfound greed to lands outside their grasps.

Ten of the shadows I'd cast grew in size, dominating the tavern wall until they held the eyes of every patron. A few huddled closer together. Some . . . averted their eyes.

Swords fell on noble and commoner alike. And people learned an important truth: All blood spills the same. And it colors all things the same sickly shade.

I stepped closer to the front row of the audience—shadows trailing behind me as I did. They swarmed over the crowd, pulling a few cries from the listeners. I worked a hint of my will into the folds, reimagining my firelight to take a darker tone of red, and soon the color of blood bled through the glow.

As the war raged, those fighting men lost themselves under the passing nights of bloodshed. They fell. Their souls twisted and twined, stretching and slipping into something not like men at all—shadow. They grew into hollow hungry things. Nothing satiated the children of the Ten Shadows. Nothing but death and to turn any kingdom touched by sun into one of ash and embers.

So, their sights soon fell on what place but Carmeaum.

The day that changed Antoine's life began like any other—awake before the sun had risen. He dressed himself and went outside of his humble cottage to regard the field upon which he lived. A cool morning's air kissed him, giving him a sweet gift with which to start. He smiled and blew a breath back to the wind in silent thanks.

The weather held clean and warm. It was a field day—a good one.

So Antoine started as he should have. He knelt, plunging his fingers into the rich earth he'd been gifted to steward. "Thank you, salt and soil, earth below, for granting me the boons above you." Antoine looked at the grains sprouting in the near distance. "Thank you for providing me with that I take in, to give me the power to shape that outside me, field and farm." Young Antoine looked to the sky and gave thanks to the sun, which even hidden from sight, still had his love and faith. "Thank you, light and warmth of the world, for giving me life. Let me repay you with another day of hard work and bountiful growth."

And Antoine was as good as his word.

Evening came over Carmeaum, and with it came a young woman to Antoine's field.

I let one of the folds in my mind dwindle, taking the shadows with it. A simple movement of my staff and a repositioning of my hand made the silhouette of a shrouded lady stand tall against the tavern wall.

He had finished his work, moving to rest by the walls of his little cottage. The man waited as the woman, dressed in the loose and flowing garb of a shepherd, approached him.

She lowered her white shepherd's hood, revealing a face kissed to hold all the warmth and bronze of the sun. And just as bright and lovely as a thing could be.

This was Etaynia, destined to become mother and namesake for a country of hardy folk. Men and women born of the sun and sea. Proud folk. Brave ones. And deep within her gentle and kind face burned the sun's own fire to give those traits to generations to come. But first, she would share it with the man she loved.

She brought him a meal, as she always did when his work went on into the nights.

"I'm frightened, Antoine," she said.

He held her hand, not speaking in return.

"My father has traveled far of late, feeding and tending to his flock. The traders at the end of our borders say war is coming here and nothing will stop it."

Antoine remained silent, choosing instead to lose himself in the soft and warm browns of her eyes.

"My father has since gone south, staying to our side of the sea to ask those who cross over if their people will be of any help. They told him that they would not. That the war could come here, but it would never cross the Arrythian Sea. And for that, they had no need of worry or to help." Etaynia held to Antoine's hand hoping he'd have an answer that'd soothe the ache in her heart.

Antoine finished his meal, thinking to himself over what his sweet love had told him. "The war will come here. When it does, Carmeaum's people will have two choices: Leave across the sea to new lands and hope the war never passes over. Or they will have to stand and fight."

Etaynia watched Antoine from within a seat of the same stillness he'd held to before.

"I'm . . . not a strong man. But, when shadow crosses into these lands of sun, I'll put aside the farmer's sickle and take up the sword. I'll stand before the sea of darkness and keep them away from you. I promise." And Antoine cupped Etaynia's face, leaning in to kiss her deeply.

The loving pair parted that night, both nursing worries of what lingered beyond morning's first light. For they knew one day there'd come a darkness where shadows followed. And though they spoke with hope and bravery, they feared that their land's light would be swallowed.

Antoine went to bed and gave thanks to the sun for another day's light with which he could make his livelihood. But this time, he didn't end with a profession of gratitude. Antoine lay there and asked the sun for guidance.

What then will I do when the shadow comes here? I spoke bravely before Etaynia, but I'm no warrior—no swordsman. My arms are better suited to the shovel and hoe than they are the sword and shield. His thoughts, unknown to him, echoed through the dark to reach the ears of the one being that could help.

A knock came at his door, rousing poor Antoine from the sleep he so desperately needed. He answered to find a stranger standing before him.

The shadow of Etaynia I'd shaped fell away—replaced now by a tall and hooded man. The figure hunched and loomed over the front row of the crowd, forcing some of them to shy away from his darkened gaze.

The stranger's features were a near mirror for Antoine's. But for where our hero was slender in face and build, the man in the doorway was broad and strong of jaw. His eyes seemed to burn with candlelights, unwavering and bright even in the dead of night. He had the short-cropped hair of a soldier and a beard just as neat and trim. "Apologies, but I am lost. I saw your cottage and your field. I am in need of help: a night's rest, food, if you have any to spare, and perhaps, a story to lull me to bed."

Antoine, never one to refuse help, stepped aside to welcome the stranger. "My home is open to all who call these lands under the sun home. I can see by your face and clothing you are from here. Forgive me, but I do not recall seeing you." Antoine reached to take his guest's cloak, setting it on a chair beside a table.

"Thank you," said the stranger. "And you have seen me, Antoine. Every day of your life. I've watched over these lands since before you were born. And I'll watch over them still in the ages to come." The stranger sat down on the floor beside the dying fire. A sign of things to come.

I reached into the folds of my mind, willing the firelight to dim. Darkness took more of the Three Tales Tavern, and the audience drew closer together. Closer to my flame.

Antoine swallowed, unsure of what to make of the strange words. But, he had made an offer of kindness to him. And he intended to fulfill it. He fetched what he could to prepare a meal. "I don't have much at the moment. I take what I need from the field when it's ready, and even then, it's only enough to fill my belly."

The stranger nodded in understanding. "And the rest comes from sweet Etaynia, I know."

Antoine bristled. "And what do you know of her?"

The stranger exhaled, accepting the food from Antoine. "Everything."

Antoine recoiled as the man's hands brushed against his. True warmth, the kind radiating from the sun at its zenith, washed over him. It penetrated him, striking his heart and holding him in place. Heat and joy blossomed inside—uncontrollable. He wept without knowing why. As Antoine stood, beside himself with emotion, the stranger rose to his feet beside our hero-to-be.

"I know everything and everyone under my watchful eyes. I know their minds. I know their habits. And I know their hearts, dear Antoine. I am no stranger lost in the night." And the stranger raised his hands above his head.

I banged my staff hard against the tavern floor, muttering another binding beneath the thunderous clap of wood on wood. "Ahn." The image of the rod, fixed in place, sat within my mind. And it came to pass. The staff stood firmly rooted and I returned to the folds holding the firelight. I breathed it into something larger then.

Golden light blossomed from the man. It washed away the dimness within Antoine's home. The aura pulled the aches and pangs from his body, soothed his skin, and sent bands of immeasurable comfort and joy down to his bones.

I fed my stolen firelight, fanning it into something to rival a sun within the tavern. It swelled until no eyes could bear to look upon it, finding refuge behind raised hands.

The light settled, weakening to a steady glow around the man. It thrummed with unseen power—quivering ribbons flitting around the stranger's form. Antoine knew that only the brightness had changed. The full strength of the warmth still sat inside the man, ready to be called if he so desired.

I let some of my will bleed out of the binding of light, letting the ball of fire dim. And the audience breathed in relief as their sight cleared.

Antoine fell to his knees, looking up at the stranger, who no longer bore the appearance of a road-weary traveler.

The stranger's features sharpened. His eyes looked like twin suns, pooling swaths of violent oranges streamed with yellow. Thin lengths of fire, fine as strands of hair, wove themselves into a crown above his head. Ill-fitting robes melted away to reveal a set of armor that shone like morning rays. It was as if someone had fashioned the pieces from the sun's corona.

The lone shadow I'd left of the stranger along the wall now became my focus. I poured my thoughts into the folds, shaping them into something new. I went to the side of the tavern, placing a hand there to take in the darkened figure I'd cast along it. Now his form held the bands of fire coursing around my staff. And I spoke the bindings to make it true.

"Ahl." The flames leapt from my staff as if thrown free. "Ahn." They bound themselves to the wall.

The audience gasped. Dannil let loose a cry of protest. He envisioned his tavern burning, I wagered.

But it would not be so. I muttered another pair of bindings then. "Whent. Ern." And the flames spread through the shadow to give truth to what I'd said. Pools of firelight burned in the shadow's eyes. A crown of flames wove itself into being above the dark shape. A crest of sunlight burned from the man's chest. I returned to the story.

Antoine sat frozen, fighting for words, but none answered his call.

The golden stranger extended a hand. "Rise."

And Antoine did. "Who are you?"

"I am Solus. I am the one who shepherds your mornings and gives fire to your heart. I am the one who eases your burdens when you feel too weak to carry on. I am the morning sun and light. I am the humble stranger you welcomed open and bravely, without fear, with only kindness and servitude. Now I have need of you, Antoine."

"Of me?" said Antoine.

Solus nodded. "As I have served you every morning, bringing life to your fields, strength to your limbs, I need you to serve me. Shadow comes to these lands. I watch over a great many, but this place, your home, is important. This is the seat of my power. This is where my children—*you*—prosper and will continue to do so. And your children one day will follow. *If* you do as I ask.

"You worry your arms do not have the strength to bear shield and sword. I say to you now, they do. You worry your heart isn't full of enough fire to burn brightly back against the dark. I tell you, it does. You worry you will fail Etaynia—that darkness may take her. And I say that it will not. Will you serve me, faithfully, in this quest as you have lived in gratitude to me all your life?"

Antoine did not fear in that moment. A life's worth of dedication flooded him—steeled him before his lord and life-giver. Fire and iron filled his eyes and heart. "Yes."

Solus nodded. No smile broke across the Lord of Sunlight's face, for he knew the answer Antoine would give before he had asked. And he knew the path on which he set his soldier—son.

Solus placed both hands on Antoine's shoulders and spoke with the strength and clarity only a king could. "So be it, then. Antoine of Carmeaum, I name you my arm. My sword. My shield. To venture out and cast back the darkness, the Des Embras, wherever you find it—them. To be a Prince of Sunlight, my chosen. So long as the sun shines above, you will have no equal in strength—growing stronger by the passing hour under my light. You will not know weariness or fear. No foe will be able to cut you down. And when the sun's hour passes, your strength will hold—but grow no stronger—by the moon's glow. For she too carries my light. You will be shepherded by us day and night."

The heat of a forge fire filled Antoine. It screamed through his skin, pushing past muscle and sinew, down into the marrow of his bones. It was the fire that purified iron and turned it to molten pools—what was needed to make something new—something stronger. And Antoine's body and soul were remade from inside to better serve his new lord.

He bore it silently, enduring the pain, knowing it to be a small price to take on the mantle needed to save his country. Where once he stood tall and reedy, now he carried the muscles to shame a smith. Antoine knew his lord had spoken truly. He had arms that would never weaken, able to cleave through anything before him with proper sword in hand. Shoulders that could bear any strain—hold any shield as a bulwark against darkness.

To that end, the Lord of Morning reached up, pulling his golden plate from his chest. He passed it to Antoine. "Let my skin protect yours. Let my light shield your heart." He fastened the piece to Antoine's chest, slowly stripping more of his armor to fix to his champion. Solus worked with the care and tenderness of a father clothing his son. When he was done, the Caster of Light clapped his hands together, sparking a pool of celestial radiance between them.

He pulled his fingers away from each other, heavenly bands of gold streaming between them like thread. Solus squeezed, stretched—singing to the light as he wove it into something glorious. A sword, with all the glow of sunbeams, sat in his grip. Simple in form, yet thrumming with a power that bowed and bent the very air around it. Solus passed it to Antoine. "*Lanzia de Reyl,* the Raycaster. My gift to you, with which you will cast back the encroaching shadow."

Antoine took it, gasping in reverence as its power coursed through him.

I pulled the light from my shadow-cast Solus, reworking the folds of my mind and the bindings. I whispered the words and drew the flames into a single lance I ripped free from the wall. The lance of firelight shone above the crowd—a beam of pure sunlight if ever there was one.

Some of the crowd murmured, some recoiled. And a few brave souls reached out toward it, stopping short of the tendrils of fire.

The Morning Lord wasn't done. Just as he'd given Antoine the sword to cut through evil, he would see fit to gift the man with the means to shield others from darkness. With the same movements as before, he bound air and light to form a great curved shield, shaped in his own visage—the sun. Nameless, the piece still quivered with the same energy as radiated from the sword. "With this, no shadow will be able to take the lives and minds of those behind it. With this, you are a wall of heaven's light, unbreachable. With this, you are ready." And Solus, Light Bringer, cupped Antoine's face as he lowered his head to touch his prince's. "I'm sorry to send you to this fate, but there is no man better suited to the task."

Antoine said nothing, closing his eyes for but a moment. He opened them then to find Solus gone. But he'd left enough of himself behind for our hero to remember him, in the armor—the sword and the shield. And Antoine put them to good use.

For the shadow had come to Carmeaum.

"Tak. Roh." The film of firelight hanging as a lance above the crowd winked out of existence. Its flames streamed to a new point fixed in my mind—the head of my staff. The current of air I'd once bound to it had never left, and now served as a conduit for the returned fire once again. But this time, the flames

did not form a full fireball. Something weaker. Something fragile. A bulb of light that could be blown from existence with a careless breath. The Three Tales Tavern sat in darkness but for the candle flame I held before them.

They came like waves of darkness, crashing hard—mercilessly into the outermost edges of the land. Men and women fell to be consumed by the Des Embras' power. Twisted—turned, they became instruments of the Ten Shadows, wraiths that set out against friend and family.

I mimed more shadows, this time only using my hands and what light I had, casting them into a march toward the audience.

Among the sea of black, one man stood and cried challenge: Antoine.

I undid the binding holding my staff to the tavern floor, wrenching the tool free and running hard through the crowd. They made way for me until I stood far at the other end of the tavern, holding up my light in opposition to the shadows I'd played against the wall.

And true to his lord's word, Antoine did not tire as he cut through the darkness. His blade shone with the promised power of the sun, blinding his foes as he split them one by one. His shield rebuked their shadowy clutches, burning them at a touch. He was a lone vanguard against the nightly tide. Antoine's strength grew by the passing hour from dawn to noon, where it peaked and held until the moon's glow sustained him as best it could.

I swung my staff hard, like a soldier sending his sword through his enemies. Trails of embers and light arced through the air, lingering for a moment before fading from existence.

But no matter what heavenly body filled the sky, no shadow could match Antoine's might. He fought where the thickest of darkness swept over the lands—unflinching, shining ever bright. He turned away the blackness from village to village, never resting, spinning myths that he need not hunger nor sleep.

Bleeding some of my will back into the flame, I fanned it as large as a man's head, better symbolizing Antoine's brightness.

A year passed, but the shadows persisted. Still Antoine held firm and fought on as the Prince of Sunlight.

But everything changed when the greatest of the Des Embras decided to enter the conflict of Carmeaum himself. Umbras, the formless one. A being of true darkness—shadow given form—and all the terror of the night coalesced. He walked over fresh grass, turning all underfoot to salt and ash. Life and color bled from this world at his presence.

I let the light dwindle and returned to the front of the tavern. Now I worked another binding, shaping a larger shadow than any before to form against the tavern wall. It grew, showing no signs of stopping until its head touched the ceiling. It loomed. It hunched, a mantle of black spreading far from its shoulders to enshroud the front rows.

A child cried. Someone protested and began to utter prayers to Solus. And the rest of the audience swallowed their breaths, keeping them tight within their throats and chests.

I kept them there in the stillness. In the quiet. All before the dark frightening shadow. Then I reminded them of what story I was telling.

I leapt, letting the size bleed from the shadow as I fueled the fire of my staff larger still. The brightness washed away more of the darkness—drawing gasps from the crowd. And I resumed the tale.

Antoine stood firm before the darkest of shadows, pointing his sword—bright as sun—at the threat. "Turn back, Umbras. Turn and take the blackness—your death and despair—back to the ends of the world. And once there, throw yourself over it to rid us all of your foulness."

Umbras stood as night itself, cloaked in a wind gone black as ink and charcoal, swallowing any light that dared get too close. But the greatest shadow did not raise a hand to strike at Antoine. No. He extended it much as a friend would. He pleaded—called to the Prince of Sunlight. "You serve a false master. You don't know the truth of things. I offer you my hand, a power greater than that which you now call your own. I offer you truth and freedom from a blinding light of lies. I call you to forsake the liar—charlatan—who plays at being a god. He's bound you light and air. Tethered them to your life, breaking the greatest binding of all in doing so. You do not know what you are doing. But you have the power to change that with a choice. Join me."

Antoine would not be swayed. He raised his sword high, calling on the light as he dedicated the first blow to his lord, Solus. The Prince of Sunlight swung, striking hard against Umbras' mantle of darkness.

I swung my staff as Antoine must have done his sword. Cast after tumble-cast, all toward the shadow of Umbras I'd shaped against the wall.

Alas, to no avail.

His sword of sunlight did not break the curtain of black hanging around the first of shadows. But Antoine carried the very fire of the sun within him and did not relent. He swung, again and again, burning as bright as his lord father.

Light and dark clashed for all in Carmeaum to see. An eclipse, two celestial powers, parted the air itself as they danced with one another. A false night amongst the mid of day.

I let the folds die, holding everything but the firelight of my staff. Once done, I angled its head to the darkest corner of the tavern, casting the orange glow of a sun amidst a blackened world behind it. The shadows formed a ring around the light, promising to come in and swallow it whole.

Shadow flickered harmlessly against Antoine's golden shield. Raycaster lanced out to meet a wall of impenetrable dark, the first thing to turn away the blade's brilliance and unstoppable edge.

They fought for days and nights. Yet the horizons never shifted all the while, caught in what looked like an eternal moment of morning and midnight. Each tried to take the other over in the sky. Darkness bled against light, golden fingers trying to edge back against the black.

I pulled away, lunging to thrust the tip of my burning staff toward the darkened wall. The flames ebbed as I worked the folds of my mind to hold a dwindling fire. Then I fanned and fueled them brighter. Lunge—thrust. Back and forth, I repeated the movements like two men exchanging blows. Flame against shadow.

But neither foe fell.

And neither tired.

"Yield. This serves no purpose to the both of us. Yield, foolish child of light. If you will not walk in the shadows, then leave. Do not throw away your life." Umbras stopped, holding out his hand once more to tempt our hero to take it.

But Antoine refused. "No. For if I cast aside my oaths and arms, you will take more than I can bear to lose. You will not only take my home, but the heart of mine not shielded by this golden plate." And fire filled his eyes before he spoke the next words. "My sweet Etaynia."

Umbras pulled away, fast as ink flung into a stream. "Then I shall reap the greater of your two hearts to show you truth—to take the whole of you." And the greatest of the Des Embras fled.

He took Etaynia, holding her in his grasp at the crest of the hill he'd fought Antoine on days ago. "By the hours of morning, I ask you to cast down your arms and leave. By the coming of twilight, I say again, leave and end your crusade against the shadows. And by the falling of night, I speak thricely; let the sunlight pass—leave, and fade." Umbras grabbed Etaynia by her throat, holding her high for Antoine to see.

Our hero said nothing, throwing his head back to unleash a roar that great Solus himself would hear high in the heavens. He charged, all fear burned away. He plunged his sword toward shadow and threw his shield aside. Both hands drove the blade into Umbras' cloak of midnight.

The being of darkness held firm, chiding Antoine for his recklessness. Umbras swung a hand of talons past the Prince of Sunlight. For he meant to finally strike at the man's true heart—Etaynia. But Antoine had not been foolish, having thrown his shield to his beloved. The boon promised to repel any and all darkness.

And it upheld its oath. Screaming against Umbras' touch to blind the dark lord.

Antoine put all of himself into the next blow, lunging again.

Umbras howled, lashing out to grab the hero's throat, now without shield to repel his blackened touch. His fingers dug in and broke flesh, pouring darkness into him.

But Antoine's light burned deep and powerful in that moment, for he'd learned a truth of this world: To strike at shadow, you must open yourself to it. And by discarding his shield, he'd tempted Umbras into a fatal mistake. For so long as the shadow held him, it was vulnerable.

Antoine's blow struck true and clean, sinking into the very heart of darkness. It pierced Umbras' chest and flooded him with golden light. His cloak peeled away from him like strands of black hair caught in a hurricane.

This time I plunged the staff toward the black wall, holding it in place as if wanting to burn through the mortar of Dannil's home. The fire left no mark, but it washed away most of the shadows along the wall.

But he would not go quietly. "Fool. You've damned it all. All too willing to burn away truth and salvation in your blindness. In love." Umbras used his final breath to scream a curse as he squeezed Antoine's throat. "Then die in blindness. I bind you to it. Blind you from the light. You will die in darkness, twisted and shaped by it. I bind you to the night, now and ever." Umbras passed with those words. And with his passing, so did the rest of the Des Embras, nevermore to plague this world.

I pulled away from the wall and raised my staff high, fueling the fire to burn brighter. Another breath to billow it brighter still. And the flame bloomed into a sun to shield your eyes against.

But Antoine did not fall into blindness as cursed. Though, the battle had taken its toll. Our hero knelt beside his love, breathing weak and weary. The shadow had pierced his throat—taken his voice. The wound was lethal and Etaynia knew what would come.

Antoine did not tarry. He pressed his mouth to hers, kissing her long and deep with all of the fire and warmth a Prince of Sunlight could muster. "I love you. And when I pass, I'll join my father's fire, burning brighter to watch over you—to keep the dark ever far away."

She pulled her lips from his, throwing her arms around his body and holding tight. "I know."

And Antoine of Carmeaum, Prince of Sunlight, husband to Etaynia—for which this land came to be named—passed.

I delved into my mind, sifting through the countless folds and separations. Undoing them was as simple as exhaling. Bit by bit, belief and bindings vanished, leaving my mind as clear and empty as the surface of a pond after spring's thaw.

The weaving of air and fire flickered out of sight, taking with it the flames of the hearth as well.

It all dwindled—dimmed, then died. The Three Tales Tavern returned to stillness. And darkness.

The story ended.

I pulled my cowl low so no one could see my face.

And I wept.

FOUR

Songs and Lies

Silence hung in the aftermath of my story. It came as a thin film you could almost see. Something so delicate that just a breath would tear it and bring sound crashing back.

The audience sat, hands over mouths, some rubbing their eyes.

They knew the story and they knew it'd end in tragedy. But even with having that in mind, knowing I had planned to string them through heartache, they loved me for it. Because Antoine's tale filled them with something they needed—hope, against the dark, confusing things in the world. They wanted to hold to the idea that the troubles over the horizon would fail to harm their home. And should they try, someone, another Antoine, could come and turn back the shadow. They believed those kinds of people could exist. They had to.

We all do.

One of the serving girls worked in the dark to kindle a flame, lighting several candles as quickly as she could.

I smiled and kept my voice low, murmuring another pair of bindings. "Tak. Roh." The folds of my mind fixed on one of the candle flames, drawing it forth and down toward the hearth at my back. The fire rekindled with the snap of cracking twigs, casting its orange light throughout the place once again.

And with that, the final act of my performance concluded.

The sun and its warmth had returned to the audience. The curtain of darkness . . . lifted.

Three Tales Tavern erupted. People sobbed, full and heavily now. Some screamed their cheers. Men raised mugs and bottles, bellowing incoherently. Women clapped. Some pined.

I remained in place—waiting, letting the noise simmer from the raucous cries and applause. Once it had, I headed toward the bar, inclining my head to Dannil. It almost felt wrong, perverse, to speak after such a story. I felt like there wouldn't be any point in using words after what I'd done. So I leaned against the counter, staring.

A few of the nearby patrons held steady gazes on me.

Dannil looked back, unblinking, as he polished an empty glass.

Between the conversation and noise, lingering through clinking drinks and drumming fists on tables, another sliver of quiet entered the place. A strand hanging between me and Dannil.

I took hold of it, letting the edges of my mouth betray the slightest hints of a smile.

Dannil had returned to the stony mask he wore when I'd first seen him.

It had gone on long enough, and the folk wanted none of the little game.

"Speak, dammit. Say something, man!" One of the men clapped my back.

"*That* is what truly pays for my drink, and more." I smiled, full and wide. If I could catch a look at myself in the mirror, I was sure to find a light dancing between my eyes.

Dannil threw his head back and laughed. "You insufferable, dramatic, theatrical ass! Wait here." He pulled away from the bar, still chuckling to himself. Dannil vanished through a door near the stairs. He returned less than a minute later, carrying a small mug—porcelain in make. Steam billowed from it. Dannil set it down with care before me. "That tea you asked for." He winked.

I had the dignity not to snort and accepted the drink with a deeper bow of my head. The beverage was a color somewhere between pinewood and molasses. Dannil must have added milk to it. I brought it to my lips, breathing slow and steady to help cool the first sip.

It should be noted that the Etaynians did not have a great love for tea.

That was no clearer than when the taste of honey and cloves overwhelmed my palate. The drink lacked the flavor—notes of spice I'd come to associate with a place far off in the east I could, when feeling generous, call home. I drank on regardless.

It's a rude guest that doesn't finish an offered drink.

I drained the contents and set the mug down. "It's by no random chance I happen to be here, Dannil. I'm looking for something." I let the words hang in the air like quivering strings, teasing the nearby crowd.

"And what's that?" He pulled a customer's mug without looking, turning in place to fill it with a level of grace that could shame some dancers.

"For me to know." I fought down the smile, knowing people would be irritated at the obvious setup now. "But, I can do with lodgings for a bit. Know of any reputable taverns, some seeking entertainment of the sort only *I* can provide?" I left the extra question unspoken. Any tavern owner worth his name in salt and coin would know what was owed to one of my kind.

Dannil didn't miss a beat, to his credit. He pulled out his purse, pinching two bronze coins as large as a man's eyes. The tavern owner pressed them against the counter and slid them toward me.

I kept my surprise to myself, taking another long sip of the tea. Two septas wasn't a great deal of money for me. But it wasn't an insignificant sum either.

Sometimes the worth of things depends on those around you and what it can do for them.

Each coin held the value of seventy bits. Some of the folks near me wouldn't see that amount of money for a full season. Even then, most of it would have been spent on the means to get by rather than collected in a tidy pair of bronze septas.

I hesitated in accepting them. "And this is for?"

"Tonight's performance"—Dannil pulled the coins back an inch for drama's sake—"and the promise of more." It wasn't a question. "Your room'll be third from left up top. Highest floor. Best room I can give away, mind you." He gave me a knowing look. The implication was clear: I was to perform—well.

"I can meet that obligation," I said, placing a hand over his. "But I'm afraid not for the cost you have in mind." My face slipped into a somber mask that could make stone look lively by comparison.

Everyone stilled.

I drew the moment out before smiling again. "I'll take the septa, provided the other goes to as many drinks it can cover for the fine folk in this wonderful place."

And another chorus of applause broke out, all to the tune of "Storyteller!"

There's an art to making the crowd love you, and it goes past the telling of tales. It's making them feel valued. Something all people want—yearn for. It rarely costs anything, in fact, so give it to them. Value them.

For what's a world, a people, without value?

Once the clamor of clapping died down, the most beautiful face within the Three Tales came to stare at me. Stopping her humming did nothing to make her any less musical. She chimed—rang—every step a bright and vibrant note through the noise around us. Singular. It drew me in.

I flashed the best smile I could from beneath my cowl.

She met it. "Generous." The lone word brimmed with more music than in a trouper's song. "Does that offer extend to me?" She raised a dark brow, lips quirking at the ends in what promised to be a molten smile, but never came.

"Most certainly. Anything she wants, Dannil." I turned on my stool, brushing back my cowl and facing the singer. "But I feel terrible referring to you as only 'she.'"

"Then I imagine you'll be feeling terrible for quite some time. Shame." She frowned. "I'd hoped for more stories. Especially like that one. Though now I worry you don't have any." She flashed a sympathetic look, going so far as to bat her lashes as she rested a hand on my shoulder.

"The only shame is that I didn't catch your name." I took her fingers in mine.

She slipped out of my weak hold, gliding a few steps away. Her hand trailed along the counter as she moved. "I don't remember letting it loose to be caught." A smile—wide and full, carrying all of the heat I had imagined. She hummed again and I found my questions dying. "But maybe"—the smile grew wicked—"there's a chance you can earn it."

Dannil moved over to her, pushing one of the crystal glasses from earlier toward her. A light amber drink sloshed inside. He knew what she liked.

I made note of that.

"Thank you, Dannil." She kept her eyes on me as she took a few sips. None of the drink left a trail of foam and froth across her lips. It was like it refused to adhere.

One of the men by me staggered by, jostling my shoulder. "Song." He looked around for support, raising a hand. "Song-song-song! Come on, then. We've had a tale—true and marvelous. Best I've heard of that telling, in fact. Now give us a song to go with it. Something lively. Something to get us going and forget the tears."

My fingers dug into the wooden counter, and I'm not ashamed to say that it took all my mental fortitude to keep from rounding on the fellow.

The woman's eyes never left me as she slinked farther back. "A bit longer of a wait, then, for that chance of yours." She moved deftly, the sort of way a gentle breeze does over sapling leaves. "They've asked for a song, and like your story, wouldn't it be the worst of shames to deny them *that*?" She'd phrased it as a question, but the bemused look she gave me told me the truth.

We both knew the answer.

I stayed in place, not pursuing, and settled myself for her performance.

"I can get you something heavier than the tea, if you want it? Something that'll set you back a bit. Put the mind on softer thoughts. Trust me, Storyteller, you'll want it for this bird's singing." Dannil shoved me gently.

I waved him off. Nothing to dull my mind. If her singing was every bit as good as her promise showed, I wanted to remember it—clearly.

She stepped lithely to where I'd stood earlier. A faint jingle of the bands along her limbs filled my ears. Then a step—quick, crashing. *Chime, jingle.* Bright and clear. The clinking jewelry set into something of a rhythm.

The faint metallic chords slowly lulled everyone from their conversations and to her. Soon, there was only the sound of her. She hummed again, drawing it out, low and long.

I quivered along with the vibrations of her voice—skin and hair thrumming in anticipation for when she'd break into something more. It strummed a chord in me almost like the touch of magic. Almost.

Then she stopped.

The force of the abrupt ending jarred me, sending an electric shock through my spine that settled in the base of my neck. My eyes ached. *Why would she stop?* A look around the place showed me everyone else nursed similar thoughts.

But she didn't. Her lips quirked again. The same teasing smile from before. She was playing with us. Building us up like a breath too long wanting to be let out.

"A song. Simple and rousing. You want something to set you on your feet. A song to kindle the fires in you and have you dancing and singing. I can do that." She clapped her hands. *Chime. Chime.* Then she broke into the song.

> *"Hi-ho,*
> *off we go,*
> *on a quest to see*
> *all that can be*
> *from here to there,*
> *from sea to endless,*
> *shining sea.*
>
> *"Hi-ho,*
> *off we go,*
> *to dream and dare*
> *without worry*
> *or a care,*
> *to chase treasure o' gold*
> *and be like them,*
> *those heroes brave,*
> *and the bold.*
>
> *"Hi-ho . . ."*

She trailed off, clapping and ushering the crowd to join her. And they did without a second's hesitation.

I'd forgotten about everything else in that moment. She'd turned the simplest song in the world, a low-down tavern tune, into something more. She sang it with the skill and passion I'd seen people give to their masterworks. I'd forgotten how to breathe during the whole of it, chest binding tight.

She went again, dancing all the while. *Chime, clink,* she went between the thundering fists and stomping feet as the crowd sang along. She twirled, a dervish of purple and white. Threads of gold caught in the light, glinting through the dance.

It was like watching the lone flickering of a candle in the darkest of nights. Everything else fell away. Only the flame remained—snapping—ebbing, dipping, and dancing in a way that pulled your eyes. You caught every curving spark until the image burned itself into your mind.

She stopped, extending a leg as she dipped into a deep bow.

The crowd clapped and I joined them.

But her performance hadn't ended. Not yet.

She hummed again, shifting to one side of the tavern. Hand outstretched, fingers dancing before the chins of eager and close men. They followed her with their eyes and hands until they nearly fell from their stools.

"Oh, daughter of moon,
sweet of heart,
lover gone so soon,
weeping of a sun lost,
a prince of light,
who paid the greatest cost.
A daughter strong and steadfast,
in the face of shadowy invasion,
a woman not to cower in desperation.

"She whose love stopped the tide,
oh, daughter of moon,
who stood by her prince's side.
Only when all was said and done,
darkness' hour passed,
the battle won,
she fell to her knees,
and cried."

The men had turned their gazes away, racked with another bout of heartache. Their faces twisted in the conflict of emotions between wanting her and remembering Etaynia's sacrifice, the one little thought of.

The songstress had set them to their feet—roused and cheery. Then she'd spun them around to drop them flat with a song echoing the heaviest pains from my story.

It was well done.

She was playing us again. And she made it look easy.

A part of me throbbed over Etaynia's loss as well, getting a taste of my own medicine, as it were. Another side appreciated her showmanship. She had the crowd wound around the tip of her finger. A simple bend and she'd have them toppling over one another to follow her next move.

Another hum, drawn out loud and undulating like a lute's cord plucked left to thrum. She chimed again and again as she came toward my side of the tavern.

Our eyes met for the flash between a second and she winked at me. It carried more warmth than tea and fire.

"Oh, what to tell,
what to sing?
What song to sell,
what thing?
Tell me, brave men.
Speak to me.
What song do you hear?
Oh, what do you see?
Tell me.
Tell me.

"Oh, my sisters dear,
say to me,
what to sing,
what to hear?
Tell me,
tell me,
sisters sweet,
what song to sing?
What treat?"

She moved like she was music herself. The air felt like it slipped out of her way for fear of disturbing her work.

I watched it all—silent. Still.

She'd sung several complicated songs and made them look easy enough for a child to belt out. Doing that after making a common inn song sound difficult was a feat worth remembering.

But now?

She'd turned a simple question into a song itself and, with it, bought herself a reprieve as quiet returned.

The crowd turned inward, debating what to ask for. And what could they say? There were countless songs for her to call on. All of which gave her peace in the moment.

I smiled to myself. *Clever.* In essence, she was holding the next performance hostage, building the anticipation during the pause. But, she'd given everyone a choice. So now the fault was with them for why soundlessness filled the Three Tales again. But I had a way to break that.

I leaned forward, putting a hand to my mouth to call out a song that would surely stump her. "What about—"

"Sing 'The Binding of Fire'!" came the cry, cutting me off. The source of the request was one of the old men from when I'd entered the tavern earlier in the day.

I gripped my staff tighter, heart pounding as I narrowed my gaze on him.

If the choice of song had bothered the young woman, she didn't show it. She broke back into the same humming as she stepped toward the fire. "You want a song, short and sweet, about *that* man? A legend, a villain to some. A man who's more than that? Some say he's closer to a god. Others say he's nothing more than a myth—a lie. Someone with a lion's heart of courage and could bind fire into something everlasting—eternal."

The man nodded and the audience bobbed in agreement.

I knew the song he wanted. It was short, but nothing close to sweet. At least for those who knew the truth. The temptation to quell all sound within the tavern again overwhelmed me, but I shut my eyes and buried it. I didn't have that right.

"Darkest hair, a wild mane.
A lion of wit and courage,
speaking a secret, a hidden language,
lost powers did he gain.

"What did he find?
What could he bind?

"First flame flitted, flew—flying free.
Angry, sparking, flickering it came.
Kindled, bright, this man made it tame.
Charming lion pulled it,
wove and tethered;
he bound an unseen ring of everlasting flame."

And once again, she'd ensnared the people in the Three Tales Tavern. Rightfully so. She'd sung it in a way that, had I been of another mind, it would have pulled at me, heart and soul.

But she may as well have slapped me.

I turned back to Dannil. "What do you have that's strong enough to tip me back a bit, but nothing so potent that I won't be able to make it up to my room?"

His brows knotted together and his lips pursed. He looked from me to the woman, then back to me. "Having trouble enjoying her?"

I am. "Not at all. But I felt the drink would make for an even better time. Sometimes being tilted lends to an extra appreciation for the finer things." I gave him a knowing wink.

He smiled and nodded as he turned to fetch me a drink. Small kindness he didn't ask for any remuneration.

Something dark sloshed through the drink Dannil returned with and nearly kissed the rim before settling down.

I didn't speak, fixing him with a quizzical look.

"Erella mahd. Rich, malty, sharp bite of earth and spice at the end. Savor it. Good stuff." He raised both brows and gave me a look implying it wasn't cheap. The drink was to be properly considered.

I bowed my head in thanks and pulled it close, raising it to his health.

A hand fell on my wrist, staying me before I could take the sip. The songstress. She smiled, pulling the glass from my fingers and laying it down on the table. "Walk with me?"

I flashed a look to Dannil.

The tavern owner suddenly developed an overwhelming interest in the spot I'd polished earlier.

It's worth noting: Men are utterly useless at aiding one another when it comes to matters involving the fairer sex.

I gave the drink one last look and feigned a long-suffering sigh. "I thought you'd never ask." I gave the woman my best smile, fetching my case and slipping by her side as she led the way. It was a shorter walk than I'd hoped for.

Most men, when in the company of a beautiful woman, harbor the notion that they'll stroll for hours under a midnight canvas threaded with stars.

We stopped after climbing the first five stairs, rounding the bend to lean against the railing. It gave us a decent view of the patrons before us. But as far as lonesome and romantic, it was rather lacking. I lowered my case onto the stairs, keeping it close by my feet.

"Many a woman has brought me to many a place, but none quite . . . like this." I gave her a sideways look.

"Many a woman might have had a great many other things in mind. But none quite like what I do." She matched my look.

"And what's that?" I edged closer to her, and this time, she didn't move away.

"A question." A fire, one that made the hearth's look like the first spark on tinder, burned within her eyes.

"Oh, well ask away. I've told a thousand stories and heard thousands more. I can answer anything about any of them. Of things remembered, and many forgotten. If there's something you wish to know, chances are, I've got a bit of what you're looking for."

She didn't waste a breath, cutting to the heart of the matter, and mine. "Why did you lie?"

I blinked. The question caught me off guard, leaving me to fish for a response. But my mind had turned to dark waters and nothing was in sight. In the end, I came up short for an appropriate reply. "What do you mean?"

She turned to look at the crowd. "The story, 'Etaynia.' You've told it the same way as it's been told as far back as I can remember. . . ." She let the words sit in the air as her stare turned distant, falling onto a place that only she could see.

"What other way is there to tell it?"

My question snapped her back to the moment. She shook her head, still not looking at me. "But you know how it really ends. I saw it in your face. And that's why you were crying." She turned to me, the heat in her eyes simmering to wistful embers. It was a silent plea. "Say it for me, please."

I licked my lips, unsure what to do. It had been a long time since someone had challenged me on one of my stories. Longer still since someone had challenged their truth. And it was a first for one of them to be right.

I bowed my head. "Etaynia was no child of the sun. She came from a people older, of starlight and carrying the moon's subtle glow. That did not make her any less, however. Does the moon not shine with the sun's mighty light when it passes out of sight? And so too did she, daughter of stars and moon, carry her beloved Antoine's light onward against the shadow . . . as he fell not to the sword, but darkness and shadow himself, a Prince of Sunlight—eclipsed.

"And a new servant of lightlessness was born that day. For it is always that way. There will be Des Embras—ten. No less. No more." I swallowed and decided to look for that unseen spot she'd been gazing at earlier.

"Why did you hide that from them, the truth?"

I scoffed. "People don't want the truth. Not always. And most certainly not now. They need the little lies, and the big. They need something to keep going. So I gave them the story they needed. For the truth might surely break them." *And me.*

She pursed her lips, but didn't argue. In fact, the look on her face said she understood. "What happened to her?"

I shook free of my reverie. "Her? Etaynia?"

The woman nodded.

"She did the bravest thing anyone could do: She tried to save him—Antoine. She fought the Des Embras, alone. A woman made of starfire and the cold steel and glow of the moon. All while brandishing the sun's own shield and sword."

"Did she kill him?" The singer moved closer, watching me with intent.

"She did something worse." I paused, letting that sit with her. "She died for him, making sure it was by his hand. And that final deed saved a part of him. But what's left is said to be a broken, twisted thing. Something tormented by the echoes of who he was, and the voice of his beloved. The sight of what he'd become. The vision of what he'd done. Oh, poor Etaynia."

A bead of moisture welled at the corner of the woman's left eye. She brushed it away, acting like it hadn't been there.

I ignored its existence as well. It was politer that way.

She cleared her throat and placed a hand on me, pulling me closer to her. "You almost make them sound like they're real. The Des Embras."

I gave her a thin, brittle smile. "Almost." My right side twinged, and I winced through the pain.

She didn't think anything of the sudden movement. Instead, she leaned close, breathing hot against the side of my neck. Her lips were close enough that, should she want, she could place a gentle kiss against my earlobe. "I've given many names to many people, all of them lies. But to thank you for telling me the truth about something I truly wished to know, you'll hear no lies from me." She pulled back, stopping to press her lips against my cheek.

I smiled, hoping that would pull my thoughts from the heat rising in my face. "And that truthful name would be?"

She grinned like a cat. "I said I would tell no lies, not that I would give you my name." Silence. Fast and like the aftermath of a hammer fall.

I fought for words, replaying what she'd said. *Tricky.* "Then you'll have to forgive me, but the most beautiful woman in any story always has a name. One usually just as striking as her. May I gift you one?"

She arched both brows, turning to look at me over a shoulder in a look of false shock. "Is that what we are? In a story? And, you may."

I could have sworn the edges of her mouth tugged into a pleased smile, though it could have been a trick of the light. "We're all stories. Every one of us. Each important, more than any one could ever know. A story of those who came before us, of where we are, and where we're headed. The lives we've touched, and those we've lost. We are, all of us, the most important things in the world. For what's more important than a story? What's more important than the hero of their own tale?"

She still stayed facing away from me, but her posture shifted, bringing her closer. "My, careful, sweet storyteller. You keep saying things like that and I just might have to fall in love with you."

The words rocked me like a club to the skull. I can't recall just how long passed exactly before I found my wits again. "There are a great deal of stories surrounding love and lovers."

"Some romantic. Endlessly so, no doubt," she added.

And some far more tragic than I've the heart to tell. I kept the thought to myself.

"Ah, you call that singin'?" Someone stumbled forward from their table, slurring through a string of incoherent babble. "Woman's a fine thing to look at. I'll give you that. But if I had tits and an ass like that, I'd own the whole world by now. But since I don't"—a violent hiccup rocked his body—"I'll show you how it's done." He teetered in place.

I hadn't realized I'd gripped the railing hard until the beds of my fingernails ached and nearly changed in color.

The songstress placed a hand on mine, squeezing gently. "Let it go. I've seen that look many times. A man, quick to anger, ready to defend my honor. It usually ends in trouble for everyone involved. And I'd so hate to find another place to sleep tonight." She smiled, and I found the rage melting away. "Let him sing. For people like us, sometimes there's pleasure in the . . . uninitiated trying their hand, or voice, at what we do." She gave me a mischievous wink.

She had a point. Most women always do. But it can be a terrible danger to let them know you know that.

I relaxed, leaning against the railing in hopes of enjoying the bungled show-to-be.

The old man shambled for a bit, doing interesting things to what little hair lined the sides of his head. He wore a poor man's crown of willow-thin strands. He was dressed in simple canvas clothing and looked like someone's old coot of a grandfather.

The special sort parents warn never to listen to.

He cleared his throat again, louder. "Listen up, listen well. I've got a song to tell. Or is it sing?" He squinted at the crowd as if looking to them for the answer. When nothing came, he waved dismissively at them. "I got a song you'll be wanting to hear. A short thing, but true as the warmth of that fire. True as I'm going bald." He tugged on the wisps of hair left, drawing a round of chuckles and titters from the audience. "A story about *him*. Man who tangled with the Shaen. Most beautiful of all folk, not of this world. He fought for love. For one of their own. For their princess.

"I'll tell you—sing to you, of a man not a man. But something more." He hiccupped again. "I'll tell you, I will. Of a man wielding a fire no others can see. A man wrapped in blood, unable to ever wash it off. A man who could whisper and bend the skies themselves to his will and every wish. I'll tell you of a man who could call up a storm and lay low the Shaen!"

The crowd froze. Earthenware jugs stayed mid-pour. Drinks rested a couple inches above the table, people caught between taking a sip or putting them down. Uncomfortable looks were traded.

Some folk saw the man of which the grandpa spoke as a villain. Others, a hero. Regardless of the case, the frightening thing about him was that he was real. Or, at least, had been.

There's nothing more terrible than the idea of a real monster. A real legend. The old man had stolen the stage, their attention, and every one of them partly wished he hadn't. But he went on.

"O'er his heart, a ring of unseen flame.
Around him—a blood-red hame.
With but a whisper,
he called the sky's hidden true name.
For Alune,
on eagle's wings of lightning he came.
Khir Na Edderith he struck,
their foe eternal he became.

"Him that is,
he that was.
A man no more,
made fire his.
Learned the skies' lost laws.
Something more.
Magic for sure.
But a man?

"A war he began.
Bloody and long.
One where,
they'd sing not a single song.

For too horrible a thing,
would it be to sing.

"O'er his heart, a ring of unseen flame.
Around him—a blood-red hame.
With but a whisper,
he called the sky's hidden true name.
For Alune,
on eagle's wings of lightning he came.
Khir Na Edderith he struck,
their foe eternal he became."

The old man stopped to a conflicted crowd, torn between murmuring and reluctant cheering at the piece. And none of them heard me go on to speak the remaining hidden verses.

"O' poor Alune, daughter of stars,
for her passing—he's to blame."

My voice was a whisper of wind through hollow wood. Dry and weak, but echoing nonetheless. I felt the songstress' eyes and ears on me and gave silent thanks hers seemed to be the only attentive pairs in the tavern.

It was a good note on which to end.

I smiled to my nameless singer, brushing by her as I moved up the stairs.

"Wait," she said.

I did, turning to regard her.

"You promised me a name, Storyteller."

I had. It would have been poor of me to leave without fulfilling my word. "Eloine, like those that came here before. Shining, sun-kissed—ever bright. My very own princess of warmth and sunlight." I bowed.

Because I could never love another daughter of the moon. Not today. Most especially this night.

Her face lit up at that, radiant and living up to the name I'd gifted her.

I left her with that minor gift and grabbed my case before leaving to find my room. The trip didn't last nearly long enough. I passed through the door, giving the place no thought but for the bed. My staff clattered to the floor. My books followed. But I took as much care as possible in lowering the case to the ground. I collapsed and tried to clear my mind of the last two lines of the song.

I failed.

I folded my mind a dozen times. And when that wasn't enough, a dozen more.

But Alune flooded every one of them.

I don't remember falling asleep.

Only the tears.

FIVE

QUESTIONS

A procession of tin drums sounded above, rousing me from my sleep. I lay in bed, listening to the rain—losing myself in the staccato. It seemed fitting, mimicking the noise inside my head. I took in the room from where I rested.

Dannil had certainly weighed my skills and talents properly. The place would have run a paying customer enough bits to be out a full bronze septa before long.

All of which meant he intended to get his use out of me.

A washtub, large enough for me to almost lie in, stood a few feet from the end of the bed. The jug beside it had been painted a color of spring skies. It glistened with a soft sheen.

The rest of the room fell out of my mind save for the painted changing screen in one corner. A farmer's field took up most of the view. The sun beat down in full strength. A lone man, reedy and well-tanned, toiled under it.

Antoine. I smiled at the thought, thankful for the reprieve from the images that had haunted me prior to falling asleep. The idea of a bath appealed to me, but the notion of lingering and stewing in silence did not. It would only be more time to think. And that was the last thing I needed to do.

I rose from the bed, taking my staff in hand as I regarded my books and the case on the floor. No one here would tamper with them, much less steal them. Most folk didn't care much for stories save for when the proper person performed them. Past that, they were seen as old scribbles, nothing more. And the case would be but a cumbersome weight for someone to carry—nothing worthwhile.

It's one of the world's greatest shames that the most important things are often overlooked.

I bent over at the waist, taking up the closest of my tomes. Books deserved as much care as a man could offer, and I gave them that, stacking one atop another till I was done. Carefully—reverently almost, I wound the leather thong binding around the set until it went tight. Confident they wouldn't shift or fall out of alignment, I made my way over to the desk.

A brass key sat atop it that I hadn't noticed upon first inspection. I snatched it up, slipping a finger from my other hand through the loop at its end, leaving me free to pull open the largest drawer. It shuddered before groaning to a shaky open as if it protested the action. I gently lowered my books into it, exercising the same care in shutting the compartment.

The key resisted slipping into its place for a moment almost as if it had long since forgotten the well-worn entry. I jiggled it, working it into place and turning it to a satisfying and heavy *click*.

It may have been nothing more than self-indulgence, but I wriggled the bulky key through my fingers, tumbling it back as it arced over the knuckle of my small finger. A quick shake of my robes sent the cuff sliding over the object to obscure it. I tucked it away inside a pocket lining my sleeve.

There's something to be said for practicing old skills, no matter how impractical they might seem. Trials a lifetime ago had taught me nothing ever loses its usefulness. And that being prepared pays well, sometimes in saving one's life.

I moved the key from inside the sleeve, never breaking through the openings in my robe, to another pocket against my chest. Content with my exercise, I made my way out of the room. The door eased shut behind me soundlessly.

Candlelight, each flame flickering no larger than the tip of a man's thumb, illuminated the hall. The only clue to the state of the world outside came from the lone panel of glass at the end. Darkness, streaked with fleeting moments of white as rain spattered the glass, waited for me.

I headed toward the stairs, making my way down with the tentative measure of a cat—silent. One of the boards flexed, yet gave off no sound, as if it had reconsidered the action.

Old training flooded me as I slipped into the familiar way of stepping lightly—oddly—down the stairs. A way to move without making sound. My ankles ached more from the memory of injuries and endless practice than in actuality. I reached the last stair, grimacing at the distant aches. The only relief came from the fact I hadn't banged and clattered my staff along the way.

I grinned at the thought, thinking back to halls of stone and ivy. Water trickling through the mausoleum of earth. And the threats against my life.

The taproom of the Three Tales Tavern was as I'd found it earlier. I aimed to preserve the stillness of the place. I'd made my way to the door when the faint chime of metal sent frozen bands of ice through my chest.

I whirled about, leveling my staff in the direction of the noise.

She stepped out of the shadows hiding most of the far corner in front of me. Her mouth pulled to one corner in a smile of self-satisfaction. "Going somewhere?"

"Eloine." I took a step back and bowed. A flick of my wrist and an extension of will sent my cloak billowing to one side in a flourish. "My, what surprise."

"A lovely one, I hope." Her voice hovered between curiosity and amusement, sounding just as rich in the dead of night as it had in the height of her performance.

"If there's something beyond lovely, it would most certainly be you. So, yes, at the very least, this is quite the lovely surprise. And I'm hoping it can come to be more than that." I chanced a look up to see her smile had widened.

"You might be getting a little ahead of yourself . . ."

I held her gaze, matching her pause.

Her eyes went wide and she gasped. An act, a good one. Eloine went as far as bringing a hand to her mouth to feign outrage. "You've done me a terrible rudeness. Don't deny it, I recall it freshly. You gave me a name, a gift, but you never gave me yours. It's a terrible thing to deny a woman what she wishes to know."

The muscles in my mouth twitched, working to betray me and break into a smile. The lady was serious, in part. It made sense to act in kindness. I inclined my head solemnly. "Forgive me, Eloine. I'd not have wronged you so had I known. But, I'm puzzled." I pursed my lips. "For I already gave you a name. Are you saying you'd like another? Two seems a tad too many for any person to get any use out of. After all, how many names does one really ever need?"

She met me wit for wit. "You tell me. You have the face and act of a man who's gone through many, all said and told. Possibly more than me."

Now that's something.

"And, that's twice you've done me wrong, sir. I asked you a question as to where you're going." A faint light kindled in her eyes. She was enjoying this.

"I believe you asked if I was going somewhere. And as a matter of fact, I am." I grinned, wide and foolish as a young boy a bit too happy with his own cleverness.

Perhaps I shouldn't have been that pleased.

Her brows knitted together and her lips went tight. "Am I to take that as a dismissal, then? I had hoped that you might have wanted some good company. Though, you'll have to settle for mine." She'd taken a tone that spelled danger to any man with functioning ears. It was a thing sharp and brittle, like the first snap of winter's ice over a lake.

I faltered for the briefest of moments, working the scant hint of saliva in my mouth back to back. "I could think of no better company—the best, in fact—than you." I rolled my wrist as I extended my hand to her. "In fact, let me take your warning to heart about me getting too far ahead of myself. Would you do me the courtesy of ensuring I don't stray too far from your side?"

She placed her hand in mine. Her touch pulled a smile out of me then and left me feeling like I'd left my palms open under a summer sun. "Mhm. Reining a man in isn't an easy thing to do, but I suppose I'll have to manage. I've only ever broken in an Altayan." She turned her face from me, eyeing me sideways. "I have the feeling the horse is easier than the man."

I pressed my lips together, blowing a puff of air through them in an imitation of an unruly horse. A part of me filed away what she'd let slip—Altayan. They were a breed of hardy, shaggy horses found in the mountains far to the east.

She sighed, placing a hand on her chest while shaking her head. "I wanted a man to walk with me under rain and a moonless night. Instead, you gave me a boy pretending to be a horse." Eloine's shoulders slumped as she moved toward the door.

I caught her fleeting look out of the corners of her eyes before she averted it. "*Neigh*"—I put as much equine emphasis on it as I could—"you've found a man, full and proper."

She stopped, staring at me deadpan. "You didn't."

"I did."

"I'm not sure if I should leave you here alone for that, or ensure that you come with me so you'll be drenched."

I smiled. "I believe I was already headed that way myself." I held out a hand to her. "Will I be getting wet alone?"

Eloine blew out a breath that let me know she'd caught the meaning behind my words and found it just as amusing as she did wearisome. She took my hand. "I've yet to come across a man who can make that the case for both parties involved. Maybe tonight will be different?" She arched a brow, appraising me, but said nothing further.

I pushed open the door of the Three Tales Tavern and stepped into the rain with the most beautiful woman in the world. Beads of water peppered my cloak. The steady sound helped draw my mind away from the darker thoughts flooding it.

"I've always been fond of the rain."

I faced Eloine. The water plastered her hair to her skull, doing nothing to dull her beauty as it pressed her clothes against the lines of her body. I looked away to the path ahead.

"That's a first."

I said nothing and walked slowly, keeping my fingers twined with hers.

"Most men wouldn't have stopped staring, you know?"

I did. But most men were too used to getting their way. Theirs was the sort of appraising stare used by a child never told "No." They look and they take without consequence. And I'd seen where that look led . . . and the damage caused when it went unchecked.

Sometimes the most beautiful things are killed with a wrong look.

"Did you find it pleasing?"

A loaded question, one that would trap many a man. But I walked into it nonetheless with the only thing one should carry: the truth. "Yes."

"But you wouldn't stare." It wasn't a question.

I returned to her earlier comment, feeling it best to address it and put the subject to rest. "I'm not most men. And for that, you'll either find me wildly entertaining, or odd and irritating. That's been my experience with women, at least." The cobblestone road pushed back hard against my feet as I moved over a section that had been recently restored.

A few shops, single-story buildings with flat roofs, still carried flickering hints of candlelight behind shuttered windows. Another inn came into view down the road. A small building sat nestled next to it, its walls hugging the inn's.

Even at the late hour, I could have used the distraction and change of scene. The Three Tales Tavern would be home for the coming set of days, at the very least. And in the moment, I needed any other place but home.

"I think you're doing yourself a disservice, my teller of tales." A throaty and warm current filled Eloine's voice. "You've managed to be odd and diverting. Entertaining and irritating." We didn't exchange looks but I had the feeling she was smiling deep as she said it.

"Happy to supersede all expectations, m'lady."

"Is that so?" She let out a little laugh. "Now that *is* a first. No one's ever called me a lady before. Not with any real feeling. They're always fawning, dripping with hunger and that noise that comes into men's mouths when they're trying too hard to get something they can't have. You, you meant what you said."

I looked up at her. Even under the rain and a lightless night, the sight of her left me without words. A shadow fell over the curve of her mouth, bringing out the fullness of her lips and filling me with the desire to press mine against them. But I tempered the thought and decided it better to aim elsewhere.

I pulled her hand closer to my mouth, brushed my lips against it. "I did mean what I said. You're a lady to me, in all the measure of the term, from the ones filling stories, to the ones strewn through all the arts in the world. You're a lady, true and proper. Beautiful without compare." I moved beside her before leading the way forward.

"Mhm. You know . . ." She trailed off for a moment. "I wish more men thought along the lines you do." Hollowness hung in the words and that distant echo spoke of something.

Regret. Pain.

I've heard those enough times in the voices of people. The notes change, surely. No two people sound the same. But the way they pull at your tone, weigh it down and push it far off—it's always the same.

I didn't push it. Leaving her to another moment's quiet would do no harm. Instead, I pulled my cloak and cowl tighter around myself. The surface of the cloak settled considerably, no longer resembling a boiling pool of crimson under every droplet of water to come in contact with it.

"I'd hate to keep you in the rain, Eloine—"

"Then don't." She stopped me, pulling me close and pressing herself against me. We traded a look, long and deep. The sort they talk about in stories. But unlike the stories, it didn't last. She broke away after a second, turning her attention down the road. "Take me somewhere—anywhere. I'm not sure it matters. Just . . ." She bit her lip, breathing just loud enough for me to hear over the pattering rain.

"I can do that." I took the lead, guiding her toward the other inn I'd spotted.

She murmured something under her breath that sounded like it was supposed to have gone unheard, but came short of that. "Thank you."

I had half a mind to acknowledge it, but the way she'd said it struck me. The hushed whisper was uncertainty, relief that couldn't be expressed properly, and newness. My thoughts turned to what kind of life could have left her surprised by a simple kindness.

The inn drew near and I led her up the steps, pushing open the door to let her in first. It shut behind me as I slipped in after her.

Unlike the Three Tales, within this inn faint bulbs of orange still burned and danced from scattered candles. They all served to bring out the disarray of glass bottles, their varied colors like gemstones, lining the back wall behind the counter. The tables had gone through a nightly cleaning after a crowd had come and gone. The floor had gotten the same treatment.

A wooden carving stole my attention. It stood well taller than most men. Broad shouldered, carrying the build one expected from the most exaggerated of heroes. The figure was in his middle years, strong jawed and bearded. He looked fatherly, warm though his features were sharp. He wore farmer's clothing, but it was the crown of fire on his head that made clear who he was.

Solus, Lord of Morning Light, without his shining armor. They'd made God and brought him low to the world of the commoners. Made him dress like them. It probably made them feel closer to him.

I couldn't blame them.

For all our bravery and feats, we're frightened things when it comes to many of life's avenues. Uncertainty, loneliness, even a dark and long road leaves us wishing for someone's company. And who better than a god? It's in those quiet and scared moments we turn in hope of a silent watcher.

I met Solus' eyes for a moment that stretched out longer than I could recall.

"What do you want?"

I blinked, returning to the present.

The innkeeper here stood at my height, well weathered by years and stress. The set of face made it obvious he'd gone past his patience hours ago. Nothing remarkable stood out about him to distinguish him from the average Etaynian. He ran a hand through a mess of shaggy dark hair threaded with lines of salt. It matched his trimmed, but just as messy beard.

"A place to sit, a fire to think by, and if it's not too much trouble, drinks and food." I gave him my best smile.

He glowered.

Eloine leaned closer, almost bringing her lips to my earlobe. "I think you should learn to smile better."

I scowled.

"Not like that." She breathed hot against the side of my head. "Like this." Eloine pulled away and flashed the innkeeper a smile that would have had any man tripping over his own feet, and any woman glaring daggers at the back of her when she turned around.

"I'm sure I can find something." The innkeeper scratched at the side of his face. "Anything in particular?" Something hung unsaid in the words. The question of: Can you pay, and if so, how much?

I reached into the folds of my cloak, fingering one of the slender pockets. Rough-worn leather brushed back against my touch. I pinched the mouth of the purse and pulled it free. The familiar clink of metal sounded from within the bag.

The tavern owner bobbed his head in acquiescence and moved behind the counter. "What would you like? Most of my girls have left, not sure if there's one or two still milling about. I'll fetch what I can, but you'll be mostly making do with what I've got ready and easy on hand, *sieta*?"

Eloine and I nodded and spoke in unison. "*Sieta*."

"Something warm would probably do for drinks. Chocolate?" The drink wasn't as common farther north and out toward the west, but Etaynia traded well enough with their neighbors to the south that I could hold out a small hope.

The innkeeper nodded. "Woman looks like she'll need more than one." His voice had stayed carefully neutral, but I could tell his concern rested in selling another drink more than Eloine's health.

"One will be fine," Eloine said. "I rather enjoy the rain against my skin. It doesn't chill quite so much. You wouldn't happen to have any leftover stew, perchance?"

The innkeeper nodded. "Pork, carrots, sugar, and marrow—farrow-grain. Will that do you?"

"Gods yes." Eloine moved to a nearby table.

She'd missed the innkeeper's lip stiffening at her comment. His eyes darkened a shade and a shadow fell over his brow. "There's only *one* god." He nodded brusquely over to the statue of Solus. "Our Sun, our Lord of Light and Harvest. Don't care for what other people preach and pray to outside these borders, but a woman such as yourself, dark and kissed by his light, you should remember that. Should dress proper like one of ours too. . . ." He trailed off, brows furrowing as he shuffled off to get what we'd asked for. I waited till he had passed fully out of earshot before I came by Eloine's side.

She smiled, gesturing for me to take a seat.

I did, holding her look as a question bubbled to mind.

Her lips pursed for the span of a breath. "A gentleman would have refused, giving me his hand first and easing me into my seat." She gave me a knowing look, mouth quirking again to one side. It was a good act, but she'd made it clear my behavior hadn't bothered her.

I raised my hands palms up nonchalantly. "It may come as a shock to you, but I am no gentleman. I can play one, sure—perfectly in fact. I'm nothing of the sort, however."

"Mhm. Good." She moved to me, slipping behind me as one of her hands fell to my shoulder.

I fought to suppress a shiver and willed my cloak into the definition of stillness.

One of her fingers trailed along my collar, gliding to the other side as she passed by. Eloine sat beside me, eyeing my cloak more than me now. "Odd."

"What's that?"

"Your cloak." Her eyes narrowed as her face twisted in puzzlement. "I'm soaking wet, yet there's not a drop on you." She blinked and re-trained her stare like she wasn't sure if she'd seen right the first time. "It was warm to the touch like someone's skin after sitting under the sun. But the way it felt . . . it was like, like . . ." She trailed off, looking away and biting a corner of her lower lip.

I said nothing. Most people came to various conclusions about my cloak, normally settling upon the rational answer—the believable one: It was well-made, expensive, a material that defied what little they knew of the world.

It was easier to accept than the truth.

"Like *blood*." She swallowed, looking more through me than at me now. "What is it?"

I opened my mouth to speak, but she waved me off with her hand, turning her attention to the table now with the same distant stare.

"Around him—a blood-red hame." Recognition filled her eyes and, slowly, she turned to look at me as if just realizing I was there.

And stillness returned, almost like it had been following me all along rather than filling the Three Tales. I would have given anything to know how to break it. But in the moment, I didn't.

The silence stretched out, making me acutely aware of the emptiness of the place. The soundlessness threatened to go on into the stonelike deadness of noise that could drive men mad until, finally, a reprieve.

"I'm going to ask you a question. I know I have no right to it, not with how I've slipped yours, but I'm going to regardless."

All I could do was nod.

"Are you *him*?" She didn't have to add anything else. The question was enough.

But I avoided it all the same. "Him, who?"

Something dark and hot kindled within her eyes. "Don't. Many men have thought many things about me. All of them wrong. The one thing I cannot—will not—abide is thinking that I am stupid."

Silence for the space of a heartbeat.

She broke it again.

"Over a dozen stories—legends—all so similar, yet worlds apart in other details. It's almost as if someone, someone clever, twisted the tales over the years to be accounts of a dozen different men. But do you know what I've long since wondered?" She fixed me with a look that could have burned clean through oak.

I did, in fact, know. She'd all but handed me the answer, but I gave her what she needed to hear, knowing she'd return with the one thing I couldn't bear to hear anyone speak. "No."

"What if they were all one and the same? One man, one legend. One set of stories told over and over, warped the way a song is over time. Purposefully. Masterfully. By a storyteller, perhaps? By you." She didn't end on a question, doubling the intensity of her look. "Are you him that struck Khir Na Ed-derith, setting off a war with the Shaen? The one that broke the Rokashi? He who drowned the Zahinbahari in a storm. A man with a thousand faces. Are they in fact all one and the same? Is it all you?"

I spoke once of how the truth could break some people. I'd been right, and I wished I hadn't been.

"Yes." The word carried more weight and strength behind it than I'd anticipated. Wood creaked through the tavern as if come under a great pressure. Motes of dust, which somehow avoided the late-night cleaning, leapt to the air and scattered through the place. The world dimmed as candles flickered under a gust of wind that was not there.

Then, stillness.

"Ari." She breathed my name like it was something forbidden. "The sword, the eagle, the lion. Fire binder. Lightning rider. Princesskiller." The last one struck like a hammer to my heart, and the blow rang through me, threatening to break me to pieces.

"What do you know? What does anyone?" My words were acid, strong enough to gnaw at iron. Wood shuddered against my fingernails as I raked the surface of the table in a momentary fit.

"Only the bits told tall and loud through taverns across the world. Only the tales you've told, preened and molded, to suit your purpose. Gods can only guess what that is?"

I glared at her. It wasn't a thing of small and fleeting anger. It was hot and hard, like an iron rod pulled from a forge. "My *purpose*? My purpose is whatever I damn well please. My purpose is to, for once, be free to walk this world without a cadre of forgotten beings, the blackened Shaen, hounding me. My purpose is to maybe do some good. Do something as little, silly, and undeniably good as make people laugh and smile. It's the least I can do after living the life I have." *And brought about all of its consequences.*

"My purpose is to be able to move wherever I see fit, when I see fit. If I want the stars for company for a night. I will do so. If I want a nice tavern bed. Then I'll choose so. *That* is my purpose."

Eloine had sat with the stillness to shame the wooden carving of Solus. She licked her lips, still holding my gaze, looking like she was searching for the right words. "I know what that's like." She had spoken so softly that a simple puff of wind could have drowned the words into nothingness.

I didn't know if what she'd said was meant for me, or if it was just an exclamation driven by something deep inside her not meant for the ears of others.

The innkeeper arrived just then to set down a pair of mugs for us. He took a step, half turning to address us. "When I come back with your food, I'm expecting a certain number of things." He held up a finger. "Some coin, and not kept tight in your purse. Some eating and drinking of the quiet and content sort. And that you two will keep your damn lovers' spats to yourselves. Don't much care for your problems. Don't have the ear to hear them. And that goes doubly so for the folk sleeping here tonight. Understand?"

He didn't wait to hear the answer.

I turned the heated look I'd given Eloine on his back. My fingers flexed against my staff until dull pressure radiated through my knuckles.

Eloine's hand fell on one of my shoulders and squeezed hard.

I blinked, slipping out of the folds of my mind and the binding I'd been working toward. Numbers passed by as I counted by odds in an effort to calm myself. It didn't work.

Her hand fell to my cheek, putting a gentle pressure as she slid it down along my jaw.

I turned and followed the moving of her hand. Words fell through my lips before I realized what I was doing. "There are ten bindings all men must know." The simple tenet steeled me, driving home the grueling lessons and philosophy of a life past.

"What was that?"

"Nothing." I took her hand within mine. "Nothing. Just a memory." I picked up my mug with the weak hope of losing myself in it. A hint of almond tickled my nose followed by a tinge of something else as well. I took a sip and clicked my tongue as the faintest bite of cayenne made itself known. *Spiced chocolate.*

I took the next sip with the intent of letting it sit in my mouth, savoring it. The smooth softness of the chocolate rolled through me. It tempered the sharpness of the pepper in the best of ways, sending a sweet heat through my mouth that washed my mind clean of our stroll through the rain.

Eloine had only taken one sip, watching me over the rim of her mug. "If I ask you to tell me, to tell me all of it. Every bit of your story. Will you?"

I don't know what prompted me to answer as I did. A beautiful face? A certain something, indescribable, about her? The weight of my own past and story, clawing at my sternum and the hollow of my throat for a way out. That maybe if she heard it all, she'd understand. She was different, of course.

Any storybook romantic answer would have done. They were all wrong. And they were all right in that moment.

"Yes."

Because there's nothing so horrible as a locked-away story.

SIX

A Dinner Interrupted

Our meal arrived, and I'd never been so relieved for the break in conversation. The innkeeper bent slightly and placed a pair of wooden bowls and tin spoons before us. Two cups of the same metal, holding water, were placed next to them. A great deal can be learned about a place by the crockery used.

Some taverns prided themselves on their cutlery and other utensils. One place would take the painstaking effort of having every bit detailed and of the highest quality. Most fell somewhere in between, trying to balance their budget with what they could carry to entice a better kind of customer.

This place was not such an establishment. There was nothing wrong with it, but another look around spoke volumes. This was a place for the common man, with no idea of ever entertaining anyone beyond that. And the innkeeper liked it that way. The sturdiness of everything within the tavern, including the statue of Solus, inspired familiarity for his clientele.

Nothing was lavish or ornate. Nothing would make someone feel out of place here. And nothing would prompt him to ill behavior all under the watchful eye of his god.

Our meal threw up wisps of steam and pulled at me with the smell of meat and spices. Slivers of shredded carrot floated through it along with nubs of potatoes.

I took a spoonful, blowing a steady breath over it. The first taste filled me with warmth. Marrow and cream made themselves known in the stew's broth. Eloine and I ate with a quiet speed only known to travelers and performers. Silent. Focused on our food.

We'd downed over a third of the contents before revisiting the topic we'd let sit.

Eloine sucked a spoonful of the broth only, chasing it down with a swig of water. Her mouth moved for a second without sound like she was debating what to say next. "Why?" The single word was enough, I suppose.

I rolled my wrist and signaled for her to elaborate as I shoveled a few more spoonfuls of stew into my mouth.

"Why hide it all—hide yourself, your story?" She shook her head, dark hair still wet but springing a hint from the action. Her mouth pulled tight in a way that did nothing to thin the fullness of her lips. "The stories: Ari, Aresh, Ba'shaen, the sword, the Lion of Amir . . ." Eloine exhaled before draining the last dregs of her chocolate, "They're all just you," her voice but a whisper, suggesting she could scarcely believe the truth. "How? Why? Does anyone else know?"

"How else? Because. And a few people, and some things that fall well outside that term." I took another spoonful of stew, deciding to follow her example and drained my chocolate in full. The last note of sweet and spice was a wonderful spark against the backs of my throat and tongue.

Eloine's eyes flashed hot again. "When I asked for a clever man, I'd hoped he'd be clever enough to know when not to be."

I permitted myself the shadow of a smile. Going too far in prodding a woman was never conducive to one's health.

"Why turn the stories the way you have, then? The same tale, depending on who tells it, paints you as hero or villain. They've all been twisted so many ways most people can't even believe they're true, despite—" She waved to our surroundings. "Amir marches on Sevinter. People across the world report raiding parties of Shaen—Shaen! Stories come to life, turning peaceful hamlets and villages into smoldering ruins amidst a winter's freeze . . . all in the middle of a warm spring? What's anyone to believe?"

I pushed my bowl away from me, giving her a calm and level stare. "Whatever they want. That's the point. That's why I let the stories get out of hand, tweaking them when and where I could. Something gets told enough times by the wrong sorts of tongues, well, it goes on to take a life of its own. Several lives in fact. Each as true and false as the ones before it. The fact it exists as a story makes it true to itself. The fact it gets the details wrong just makes it false in accuracy, that's all."

She arched a brow. "Cavalier way to look at something your people hold so dear."

I froze, eyeing her unblinkingly. "My people?"

"It's in the look of you, but more than that." Eloine furrowed her brows and stared at me, taking in every detail. "It was *how* you spoke when you told the story. The air shook and bowed. There was . . . magic in your voice. It was the gift of the Ruma, the second folk to walk this world. A people born of fire and the distant echoes of the first folk. You huddled for warmth around man's light, and with the faint voices of your ancestors, you wove sounds into stories. The first tellers."

The saliva ran dry in my mouth as I tried to swallow my shock. "Where did you hear that? How do you know of the Ruma?"

She waggled a finger in admonishment. "No. It's not your turn for asking. Gods far and wide know that you've raised plenty enough questions for me. It's time for you to answer. You promised, after all."

I wanted to point out that while I had agreed, I'd never promised. But my deliberation in breaking into my story had served me in other ways. I'd learned a bit more about Eloine the longer we spoke.

She had handled a specific breed of horse from far into the east. Her clothing and performances spoke of gifts I've never seen in all my life, which says a great deal by itself. And she knew the truth, even if partly, about me, as well as had an understanding of my people.

The last one was far out of the ordinary. Enough so for me to wager comfortably she wasn't some common traveler, beauty notwithstanding, trading songs and dances for rooms and meals. She was something else—something more.

And every bit of me burned in wanting to know *what*—know more. I wanted to know her from the curls of her dark hair to the arches of her feet. I couldn't say why. It was a yearning, like I was tethered to her like the sun and moon, each following the other in an endless cycle. Yet, they never truly shared sky together.

In those brief instances where one danced too close, eclipsing the other, they brought about moments neither could enjoy.

I pushed the thought away as I realized how we could both get what we wanted. "I'll tell you everything, though I'm not quite sure where to begin."

"You, *the* Storyteller, don't know how to start your own tale?" A chiding grin spread across her face.

"I've spent the years painstakingly crafting enough variations of my story to leave any two men arguing over the true accounting. All that time, all those little lies. I suppose I know where to begin, but . . ." I trailed off and gave her a knowing look.

"*But*"—she rolled the word around her mouth, stressing it like she knew it was coming—"you want something in return." Eloine propped her chin on balled fists, eyeing me and batting her lashes. "What could it be? What would a storyteller ask for? What's burning away at his heart and mind?" She paused, pursing her lips thoughtfully. "Let me guess. My story?" She widened her eyes, parting her mouth in mock surprise.

"I could think of nothing more wondrous than that to trade for." I leaned closer to her. At this distance, even though she'd been washed with rain, I could smell subtle traces of sandalwood and juniper.

She shied away from me. "It would be a sad story—a tragedy. Not the sort of thing to tell in taverns through the world. Not the sort of thing you'd want to hear." Eloine's mouth curved into a forced and brittle smile.

The sight of it banded my chest with hot iron, but I kept the feelings from my face. "I think I'm best suited to decide what stories I do and don't want to hear, hm? Besides"—smoke and stone filled my voice—"what makes you think my story is any different?"

She perked up at that, watching me intently.

The innkeeper returned before she could speak. He stood much like his statue, looming over us. His fingers twitched before he rubbed an index and middle finger against a thumb.

I inhaled slowly, returning to the folds of my mind, but keeping them empty. "How much?"

"Chocolate's pricey." It was a matter-of-fact statement.

I nodded.

He rubbed his chin thoughtfully, eyeing the pair of us. His gaze seemed to linger a bit too long over Eloine before he turned back to me. "Stew was leftovers, but still good meat. Good meat runs a good cost." He was giving me a run, believing he could get away with it. "All in all, twenty pewter bits."

I didn't miss a beat as I raised a hand to stay him. "Water's free, that is if I remember my Etaynian history. Like Solus blessed Antoine to never thirst, so shall all Etaynians never thirst for water. No man or woman crossing these lands will be far from Solus' blessing. All tongues wet. All mouths quenched."

He bristled, but remained silent.

"Going rate for chocolate is about five bits for ten pieces of ten grams, yes?" I didn't wait for his answer. "Don't bother, I've traveled with enough traders of late to know it is. Now you didn't use close to that for two mugs of this. The stew? Good meat, surely. But leftovers are leftovers. You made it regardless and not fresh for us. Ten bits, and I'm being generous."

His eyes turned to slits and heavy creases formed above his brow. The lines of jaw visibly hardened as he held the look. It was impressive, but all puff.

He relented a moment later and held out his hand.

I didn't bother with my purse, producing the bronze septa I'd earned earlier from Dannil. People had odd reactions to being given foreign currencies, and that's all that sat in my purse at the moment.

He took it, eyes lighting up.

I knew the calculations going through his mind. "I know it's clear I'm not from here, but let me warn you that I know more than the worth of chocolate and stew, *sieta*?"

He worked his teeth against each other before giving me a brusque bow of his head. "*Sieta.*" The owner pulled free his own purse, dropping the coin in as he fished out the appropriate change. His mouth tightened as he plucked ten pewter bits to drop on the table unceremoniously. He repeated the action until sixty of the notched triangular coins littered the wooden surface. "*Disfra e comi, basha.*" The innkeeper cinched the pouch and left, making it clear he had no intention of coming back to check on us.

Eloine had stiffened beside me when he'd finished speaking. "You should have whittled him down for more." Her voice could have peeled curls of wood from the table.

"You understood that?" I had only grasped one of the words he'd spoken. Despite my travels, Etaynian was one of the few languages I never bothered to pick up, as they spoke the Trader's Tongue as well as their own speech.

"He told us, 'Enjoy your meal, trash.'"

"You're not Etaynian." I collected my coins, stuffing them into another pocket in my cloak.

She gave me a cool and calculated look. "Oh, am I not?"

"You could pass, of course. But for our dark features, we're not of this land, or any nearby I know of." I hooked a thumb to my chest. "I know of my home, but yours?"

Eloine gave me a smile that made the lingering aftertaste of chocolate seem bitter in comparison.

I exhaled, raising my hands in a gesture of resignation. "Fine. Back to our previous conversation, then. My story for yours."

"You'd hold your story hostage?" She readopted an expression of feigned astonishment, going so far as to place a hand to her breast. The action drew my eyes from hers and down to the hollow of her throat. A few rogue beads of rainwater still sat along the exposed line of her collar, glistening even now in the candlelight.

"I would." I flashed a roguish smile. *It's not the first time I've had to do so. Though I wished the first had been the last.* "And it's the greatest story you'll ever hear. This I know to be truth."

"*That* is a devilish thing to do to a woman."

"Haven't you heard the stories? On account of several of them, I *am* a devilish man." My grin turned wolfish.

Eloine's face went tight, visibly fighting the urge to smile. Her eyes twinkled as she lunged and jabbed my ribs with an elbow. "You know full well I've only heard parts of the stories. Clearly not the good parts, like how you came by this." She reached out, pausing an inch from brushing my cloak, then pinching a bit of the material between a thumb and forefinger. "It's still slick to the touch, but"—she wiped her fingers together—"nothing."

"Is that where you'd like to start?" I gave her a teasing smile. "Would you like to know how I came to possess a blood-red cloak?" I pursed my lips, looking up at the ceiling. "Hm, it's a good ways into the story of my life, and it leaves out a great deal." I stopped there, letting the words sit for a moment, knowing they'd rile her.

"The beginning." She bounced in her seat almost like a child, giddy at the prospect of hearing all about my past.

It warmed a part of me to see that.

Everyone wants their story to matter, and they do. But people forget that. Everyone wants someone, just that right someone, to listen attentively with wonder and happiness to the greater moments of their life. And everyone wants someone who'll sit by and listen without judgment over the moments we fell. Especially when we've gone too far, at least for ourselves.

I think I found that person in Eloine.

"Very well. From the beginning then. You'll give me a moment to compose myself?" I looked ahead, but shifted my gaze to the corner of my eyes to stare slyly at her.

She matched my laugh. "I've heard something similar from men before, but the following performances, *mhm,* lasted too short for my liking." An impish smile spread over her with the light to match the one burning in her eyes. "I hope yours delivers something more fulfilling—longer."

I blinked, cheeks growing hot.

It's not proper for a storyteller of my caliber to lose their poise. I cleared my throat and dove into the folds of my mind, splitting it into two before making it four. Each blank state of my will and imagination mirrored an endless plain of white, much like a painter's canvas. The perfect field with which to bring something to life, whether it be a story, or a firmly held belief to shape my surroundings with.

But I turned it elsewhere now. Another place, and another time. To a place unlike Etaynia in almost every way imaginable. A place that I could have called "home."

The door to the tavern crashed open, and the trio who entered looked used to bulling people around. Two men stood to either side of a woman I marked to be a decade short of midlife. The pair around her were dressed in chain mail, white cloaks hanging from their shoulders, trailing down to their knees front and back. A golden ring, lined with spiked edges, emblazoned the pristine fabric.

A sun. The clergos. I swallowed what little saliva had built in my mouth, turning away from them, though my eyes lingered.

The woman's features were stone and razor. Her face, hard and angular with all the severity of cold metal drawn to a point.

She wore a coat the color of dried plums, leather pants a shade of olive, and a blade on her hip that prompted me to take a longer look. A thin hilt with a curving wire guard.

That's a sword for nobility. Or an officer. I frowned. The clergos were the Etaynian knights of the church. Bound to serve the religious body to the extreme. And they did just that. If a member of the church with any power commanded them so, the clergos would burn man and mortar alike, letting Solus sort out the rest. They were ruthless, fanatical, and the perfect instrument of terror for a theocracy like Etaynia.

I leaned close to Eloine. "I feel my story will have to wait . . . for obvious reasons. Not the sort of people I want knowing who I am." A rueful grin spread across my face, fading just as fast when I saw her expression.

Eloine had frozen. Her lips were parted, eyes wide, moisture beading at her throat. "They've not a care for who you are, past or present." She took a breath that sounded choked off. She turned, bending closer to her bowl of stew while bringing up an arm to shield her face. She passed the gesture off by propping the limb on the table like she was weary and needed the support.

I slid closer, taking the silent cue. My cloak billowed in agitation as my blood pressure rose. I spread an arm wide, casting my garment over Eloine as I held her close. "Hope this isn't terribly presumptuous of me."

"Presume away." Her voice shook, her fire and humor now cold and distant.

"Innkeeper." The woman's voice was ice over iron. Hard. Resolute. Ringing the way only someone accustomed to absolute authority could do.

The man from earlier bustled into view, muttering a string of obscenities and dark curses before drawing up short. He stammered for a second before collecting himself. "Ah, Justice—"

"Yes." She cut through the innkeeper's sputtering with a sharpness that could rival her sword. "It's late. You sent word?"

Word. Sent? What she had said hung in my mind, but it left a question: For what purpose?

"Uh, yes, Justice . . ." The innkeeper wrung his hands together, shying away from meeting her eyes.

"My name is of no consequence, *sieta*? Only my rank."

The innkeeper nodded before tilting his head in my direction.

I stiffened, hand gripping my staff tighter. *Nothing rash.* I considered the thought, stifling a laugh at my advice. It was good. I wouldn't follow it.

I never did.

The justice was atop me in the time it took to exhale. She loomed, giving me a look that carried all the contempt for someone beneath her she could muster.

I did the only thing I could in that situation. The thing to rankle the elite and those who think silver and gold flows through their veins rather than the same red as us all. I gave her a look, staring at her less as the sword of the church, and more like the village sweetheart you'd moon after. "Twice blessed I am, for now I'm surrounded by another face of stunning beauty."

Her nose twitched. "If you want beauty, find a mirror. You're pretty enough to preen after yourself."

I didn't let the comment alter my perfectly staged smile. It only pushed me to raise my performance. "And what would happen if we found a mirror large enough for the both of us. That would certainly paint a picture of unrivaled looks."

The justice said nothing, then raised an index finger with the stiffness of steel. She touched it to a pendant at her breast. It was a circle of solid metal, ribbed with a fan of curved edges like the tips of flames. A ring of fire much like the corona of the sun. An iron one.

"Do you know what this is?" Her eyes narrowed in the faintest of amounts.

"I do."

She gave the briefest of nods. "I carry the iron judgment of the pontifex himself. His iron arm"—she gestured with a thrust of her chin to her sheathed blade—"and sword." The justice touched two fingers to the iron ring. "This means my words ring with the authority of Solus himself. I say. It is truth. I think. It is done. This means you will address me with respect, *sieta*." It wasn't a question. "You will answer me, *sieta*."

I inclined my head, but didn't turn to fully face her. Any further movement would force me to pull my cloak away from obscuring Eloine. Taking the chance to will my garment to cover her in that situation would only reveal the unnaturalness of it.

"You are not from here—not Etaynian."

I shook my head.

She scrutinized me, still looking down her nose at me. "Ah, the storyteller."

"*The* Storyteller." I emphasized my title and the singular fact I was the best of the whole damn lot. I didn't spend all those years building my reputation brick by brick to be lumped alongside any old spinner of tales.

It was in my blood. The gift of my people. And I had earned the right to become the greatest of them.

She sniffed once, a gesture of dismissal. "And she is?" The justice shifted her posture a shade, leaning to the side to try and get a look over my cloak.

"Tired. Hungry. Road-weary and in need of a good meal to enjoy"—molten iron flooded my eyes and voice—"*in peace*."

The justice's mouth parted. The boldness and heat of my comment jarred her, something she wasn't used to in her position.

I'd bet a good septa that her intimidation routine and rank served well enough to get her way without so much as a disgruntled whisper.

The justice drew her sword in a smooth and practiced motion. A length of silver emerged, catching the errant candlelight along its edge. The blade held its form like a strip of grass, narrow and fine and ever so sharp. She leveled it, point first, before my right eye.

I didn't blink, having been threatened at swordpoint many times before.

"If I run you through with this, no one would question it. No one would care. No one would remember you by the time your blood ran cold."

"That's a shame. I would have sworn I'd built a better reputation than that." I pursed my lips in mock thoughtfulness. "We could fix that. Give me ten minutes of your time alone—I'm a fast worker—and I'm sure I can have you remember me."

She went as pale as a girl in the deep of winter before color flushed her face like someone after their first kiss.

The two clergos by her side traded wide-eyed looks between themselves and quickly set to searching the room almost as if wanting a place to hide.

Her icy composure finally shattered. The justice's lips twisted into a snarl, giving way under a rolling scream. She lunged at my cloak and ripped it free from where Eloine sat. "You're doing a poor job blending in, *basha*." The word dripped with venom.

Trash. Her? I thought back to the innkeeper's earlier comment and put it together. It wasn't an errant insult hurled at us for coming in late and being troublesome. He'd directed it at her. Eloine's reaction had made it clear she'd heard it before and that it only stung mildly by now.

Eloine swallowed a lump in her throat as she faced the justice. Her eyes remained on me the whole time, however. "I *hate* that word."

The justice's mouth twisted into something cruel. A razor's slit in a sheet of ice. "We feel the same about your kind."

Something hot and angry took me over, burning to the heart of me.

One of the clergos must have noticed the expression on my face. His hand went to his weapon, a short and stocky club of dark wood. Iron bands were fastened along its head to give it an extra weight and impact.

The justice moved her sword from me to the hollow of Eloine's throat. "Running you through would be like killing a pretty little lamb. People would celebrate if they knew what you were. But"—dark and dangerous light flecked to life in the justice's eyes—"taking you before the church would be better. A public showing, then." Her twisted smile widened. "Take her."

SEVEN

A Devil in Red

My mind tumbled into a fold. Then another. Within the span of a second, I'd folded it a dozen times. Each space within my imagination carried this single mirror thought: my voice bound to the air itself, proud and shaking. A thunderclap over the quietest of days.

Whent. Ern.

I stood to my feet. "Enough!" The sound rocked the wares on the table, sending the clergos a step back on their heels. And the wooden statue of Solus looked to flex under the weight of my bolstered voice.

The justice went rigid.

"Run." I said the word without truly raising my pitch, but the binding I'd worked blew it into a leonine roar.

True fear, the sort overtakes a rabbit's eyes when it's spotted by the hawk, filled Eloine. In that moment, all of her subtle insecurities and panicked minor motions were clear to me. Her chest heaved. Her eyelids fluttered as if she could blink the trouble away. And her bare toes curled anxiously against the wooden flooring.

"Go!" The final bark shook her from the reverie, driving her forward as if shoved by an almighty gust of wind.

She didn't spare me a second glance as she tore toward the doorway.

The clergos closest to her reached out, trying to grab the loose and flowing material of her shift.

I kicked the base of my staff and whirled it about. It thumped hard against the knight's armored wrist, batting it away.

The justice roused herself from the stupor of my deafening voice. She barked an order in Etaynian, jabbing a finger after Eloine, then whipped her blade toward me.

The folds of my mind washed clean to be replaced by another set of images. I stood rooted in place, immovable as the greatest trees in the world. I was the antithesis to the three before me. A being so fundamentally different, the space around me was compelled to repel them.

"Ahn." The command burned in me as the blade closed in. "Ahl!"

The binding over my voice had shattered, now making me a living ward for the immediate space around me.

Her sword struck an unseen wall of air. The impact threw her arm back just as one of the clergos' clubs struck a spot to the side of my head. He tumbled backward from the rejecting force.

The justice's skin blanched. She looked at me as if finally realizing my existence. Now she truly saw me—more than just a performer. More than just a man.

"Magic." The word left her like a curse, but a note of hushed awe quivered beneath it.

"Of the oldest sort. The ten bindings all men must know." The mantra came to me once again on instinct and years of repetition.

"Devil." She jabbed the sword at me in a fit of forgetful rage. Its point met the space before my chest, a hand's breadth from my heart, ending in the same result as before. She reeled back as if someone had driven an open palm hard against her sternum.

"I've been called that, and worse. But in truth, there have been moments in my life where I've warranted that label." The heat from earlier built within me like a great kiln, promising to burn me from my bones outward. "Let me show you." I broke the first half of my binding, returning to my mastery of inner forces. The working to safeguard the area around me had now been channeled along my insides as well. *Start with whent. Then go to ern.*

The lines came to me like the names of old friends. I reached deep inside me, pulling at a band of flame round my heart. A source of endless heat . . . and pain. The folds of my mind now burned bright as sunlight. Then hotter. Hellish carmine, threaded with fiery oranges, flooded me. *Whent*. I linked the fire within to my breath as I exhaled. *Ern*.

Violent flames spurted from my mouth in a flash, fanning wide before me. They licked through the air with thin fingers trying to snap at the faces of the trio. Each tongue of fire fell short, only serving to send the religious soldiers tumbling back.

One of the clergos stammered something incoherent in his native tongue. He clarified a second later. *"Diavello. Diavello!"* He pointed at me, kicking his feet against the floorboards to backpedal.

Devil, devil, went his call. And he was right. In part. If I were truly in that mood and manner, I'd have set fire to the inn atop them all. But I didn't.

I puffed another breath of flame, wide and long. It bathed the place in the sort of light you couldn't bear to look at. Everyone's arms went up to shield themselves from the brightness and I seized my moment.

I slipped free of the bindings, wincing through the momentary ache assailing my forehead. It had been a while since I'd done a proper three-piece working. I turned on a heel, lurching around the table and past the stunned innkeeper.

He pawed blindly after me.

I grasped the center of my staff, lashing out with its head toward the man. It cracked hard against his hand with the force to break small bones.

He yowled, stumbling back and gingerly reaching out to the crippled limb.

Serves him right. I made my way over to the staircase at the far end of the room and grabbed onto the railing as I leaned forward. My momentum carried me to swing around and rush up the first few steps.

The justice and her cadre had recovered, setting their jaws in grim determination as they followed suit.

Good. They'd forgotten about Eloine for the moment.

I hurtled up the staircase, stopping a few steps short of the top. I turned around and planted myself firmly as the first of the clergos ascended after me. My fingers slipped into one of the endless pockets within my cloak, brushing against cool metal. I pulled free one of the triangular bits I'd gotten back from the innkeeper. *Another binding, then.*

My head reeled at the thought, but I gritted through it. I held the image of being fixed to the staircase itself—a part of it. *Ahn.* A pewter bit sat pinched between my thumb and forefinger in front of my chest. I envisioned throwing all of my weight behind it, repelling it from me as if neither of us could be within a breath's space of another. *Ahl.*

The bit shot free from my grip like an arrow, tumbling through the air until it collided with the first of the clergos climbing the stairs. It crashed against his chest with the full force of a man's body thrown against him.

I rocked from the binding's impact, using it to drive me up the final steps.

He'd tumbled back, head over heels, going down the stairs to bowl over the second of the armored men.

The justice had stopped short at the foot of the stairs, stepping out of the way as her men crashed at her feet. She gave them a withering look that lasted a second but promised a set's worth of punishment. Stepping over them, she came after me.

I didn't wait for her to clear the stairs and honor her word of running me through. My feet beat across the wooden floor as I thumped the gnarled head of my staff against every door on my way.

Shouting erupted from inside some of the rooms, patrons flinging their doors open to take out frustration on the would-be disturber. All it served to do was bar the way for my pursuer as the new barriers forced her to weave her way through.

The hall ahead broke to the left, another set of stairs leading to the third story. What interested me was the window in front of me. The single pane of glass, cheap by the looks of it, was slightly larger than me. It looked to flex under each drop of rain pelting it.

I increased my pace, leaping as I neared the window. My will flowed through my cloak and cowl in the same manner of thought in moving one's own fingers. It fluttered to life, blanketing me in a cocoon as I crashed into the glass. The window shattered, not with a sharp screech, but the hollow crunching of thin ice carrying too much weight.

I sailed through it, spotting the flat roof of the building hugging the inn.

Its top was closer to the ground than I remembered.

Rain pattered against me as I fell.

I winced, leaning forward as I braced for the impact. My hand snapped out, sending my staff clattering along the roof.

There's an art to falling and scampering along rooftops. The sudden stop in momentum leads to a singular result: ending up flatter than a strip of bacon. Your forward inertia is your greatest asset.

I tucked properly, coming down at an angle on the balls of my feet. My body somersaulted forward. The brunt of the collision washed over my backside, blossoming into dull flowers of agony through my shoulders and below. I came back to my feet in a spring. The roll had driven me toward my staff, which I snatched up as I hobbled toward the lip of the roof.

The next building stood too far for me to jump.

I scanned the space between the structures, looking for anything that could serve me. A small stretch of canvas sat between poles fixed to the side of a vendor's cart. The items looked to be cleared from it, so the damage would be minimal. The fabric had been set up to likely keep the sun's heat from the owner's face during a long day of hawking wares.

A stream of Etaynian, probably obscenities given the tone, echoed from the frame of the broken window.

I turned, smiling in defiance as I tipped two fingers to my forehead in a salute. Satisfied the justice had spotted me, I pushed off the roof, falling toward the street as far as she was concerned.

My body struck the tarp, its fabric going tight under me. It buoyed me for the time it took to exhale before I heard it failing. Its seams cried out as cloth does under great stress, making it clear it'd tear under my weight. I cursed and rolled off of it. My fingers clung to its edge as I fell, helping to steady my impact.

It may have been a rash decision.

The whole of the cart upended from the sudden shift in weight, coming down before me in a clatter of wood on stone.

I hissed, whipping my head about for any sign of Eloine.

Nothing.

My fiasco had roused enough folks that there'd be constabulary looking for me before long. Their search would lead them to the Three Tales eventually.

My stories. A hand of ice squeezed my heart, refusing to let go until the muscles of my breast ached and my breath came shallow. *Rippling water, let it sit, stills.* The old lesson burned in me.

I took a deep breath and walked between the buildings, heading away from the central road. My mind stayed fixed on Eloine's face when I'd seen her perform. The single image became the occupation of every fold within my mind as it broke it into countless pieces. She stared back at me over a dozen times, looking out of broken panes of glass.

My fear for my collected stories abated and I'd steadied myself. I turned at the end of the street, debating risking any more bindings. The rainfall muted most of the sounds I would have relied on in avoiding any more trouble this night. But the option of another working would tax me further.

Shadow take her, where is that woman? Something she'd told me echoed through my mind. She'd said she liked the rain. My attention turned to the skyline, taking in the highest points nearby.

Eloine wouldn't have gone far. At least, that's what I told myself. She'd taken a room at the Three Tales Tavern. That much was clear if she'd been performing there. My gaze fell on the building.

Like the rest of the buildings in Etaynia, it had a flat roof with small slits set into the stone to allow for drainage during storms. People took advantage of the surfaces during nicer weather to take in the sun. But the top of the Three Tales offered just a place for someone wanting to enjoy either rain or shine.

Let me be right. I hurried in the direction of the tavern. A few rogue drops of rain struck my face like flecks of glass, stinging with the promise of reddening my skin. I found myself back before the Three Tales before I knew it. A look over my shoulder showed me that the justice and her clergos hadn't set down the main street after me.

Small fortune. I pushed my way into the tavern, stopping as my foot slid against the smooth floor. Despite the darkness, I managed to make out a hint of discoloration against the grain of the wood. I knelt and touched my index and middle fingers to the spot. *Wet.*

Eloine had come this way, to fetch her things and flee, or to find solace atop the roof. I prayed for the latter as I made my way toward the stairs.

"*Eyo diavello.*"

I froze, stilling my breath, much to the dismay of my heaving and tight chest.

A figure emerged from a doorway behind the bar. They shambled forward, an arm rubbing against their face from tiredness.

I didn't wait for my vision to properly adjust. It wasn't a stretch to guess their identity. "Dannil—"

"*Maedre de* . . ." He trailed off, coming closer. "You?"

I nodded.

He ground the heels of his palms against his eyes. "Is something wrong?" He stifled a yawn. "Problem with the bed—the room?" His eyes widened at that thought. "No, no. I gave you one of my best." Another yawn. "Couldn't sleep." He nodded more to himself. "I didn't have that problem. Fell out of it in the back after tidying up." Dannil stretched his arms overhead, smacking his lips. "So, what is it?" His voice dropped conspiratorially. "The woman, eh?"

"It's always a woman." I kept my voice level, but gave him a knowing look.

"Tricky things. If my Rita was around, I'd pull her ear to give you some advice."

I had a feeling the ear pulling would have gone the other way, but kept the thought to myself. "Appreciate it, but there's something else I need to tell you."

He frowned.

"How much do you value this place? What's a good series of nights and performances to you? What of the performers?" I didn't know how he'd answer, only hoped.

"You know what this place is built on?" Dannil waved a hand to our surroundings. "Stories. Three of them."

I perked up at that, waiting for him to elaborate.

"One day I might tell them to you. But, Rita once told me that a tavern's only ever as good as the people running it. Only does as well as the people it hires and cares for." His chest swelled with pride. "That's why I own the best in the country. My people mean everything to me."

Time to find out if that's true. To test how far it goes.

"A justice crossed my path during my late-night stroll." I stopped and let the words sit for a moment.

Dannil exhaled, but said nothing.

"She had two clergos with her, and they were intent on taking our songstress friend. I couldn't tell you why for the life of me."

The tavern owner took a deep breath, eyes fluttering. "What happened? Not sure I want to know, but I have to."

I told him most of the truth. Nobody needed to know about my use of bindings. The vast majority of the world still believed the practices to be nothing more than story fodder. What little believed in it, truly so, felt it closer to devilry than a gift.

Dannil winced, placing a hand over his face as if he could shield himself from the trouble to come. "And you came back here? You don't make trouble with that sort, ever. If they come looking and ask folk . . . people will tell them." His eyes hardened. "The truth."

"I figured as much. But I'm more interested in what you will say to them if asked." My hand clenched hard to my staff, but I kept any threat from showing on my face.

Dannil groaned. "Rita would knock me sideways for a set of days for not helping someone in need, but shadow take you, boy. What were you thinking?"

Truthfully, I wasn't. But I've done some of my best work that way. "That wanting to execute someone because you can is wrong. That wanting to take someone before your church to make an example is wrong. Hear me well and clear, damn it all what this place's rules and laws are."

Dannil's eyes narrowed in the dimness, his jaw tightening.

The quickest way to offend a man was to attack his beliefs and customs.

But the truth of the world is this: Some men are worth offending, especially when there is something vastly greater on the line. Something irreplaceable. Invaluable. Like a life.

"What would your Solus think of your church, the people said to represent *his* will, attacking a woman?" I paused for a moment for that to settle in before delivering the punch to his gut. "What would your Rita think?"

His shoulder moved, indicating what was to come. Dannil's fist shot out toward the side of my jaw.

For the space it takes a thought to pass, my mind turned to honed reflexes—not forgotten—wanting me to catch the blow and bring Dannil to the ground. Instead, I did the necessary thing—the hard one.

My cheek cried out as his hand connected, driving me a few steps to the side. Dull pain radiated through the side of my skull, but I'd managed to keep my footing. Dannil may have looked like a slightly portly innkeeper, but he'd tucked away years of muscle from his laborious youth under that fat.

"Not many things will get a man clapped across the head, but bringing up his woman is on that list. You'd do well to remember it." Dannil's tone had hardened to stone.

"And what happens when someone endangers her?" I kept my voice painfully neutral, and his eyes widened, mouth going slack as if I'd been the one to hit him. Realization set in.

"How much do the laws of this land—no, the people making those—weigh over the folk themselves? How high do you place the church over the ones you serve here? That's what's at stake right now. One of your own. A tavern traveler, a performer. Someone who brings you coin and laughter. Someone who's done you no harm and makes no threats to your sovereignty, the way you want to live your life." I glared at him and resisted the urge to call on any more bindings to drive my point home.

Dannil exhaled, shaking his head. "Shadow take us all. And keep your voice down. Don't go waking people who paid good money to be here." He turned his head, mouth moving silently along with a lengthy stream of what I imagined were obscenities. Dannil huffed and rubbed a hand against his face. "*Ai-e Solus.* You're asking me to lie to a justice."

"I am." I inclined my head, reaching out to put a hand on his shoulder. "And I'll make it worth your while."

He stiffened.

Bribing a man was a tricky thing. You had to know them down to their heartstrings and hopes for it to work. Some men jumped at the promise of coin. Others, favors. Some men moved for entirely other reasons. For someone like Dannil, growing up destitute with nothing but dreams and love, he was motivated by the idea of something else.

"I'll perform like no one ever has within the Three Tales. I'd say my story earlier was more than enough, but I'll give you something that makes a king's theater look like a ragged troupe in comparison. I'll make the Three Tales Tavern the talk of the country." I bled every bit of passion and confidence into those final words, tugging on what Dannil truly wanted.

The dream of seeing his tavern prosperous beyond measure. The idea that his humble little inn, built with his love, could have its name reach farther and wider with more renown than he imagined.

He took a step back from me, nodding.

I thanked him wordlessly, moving by until he caught me by the biceps. "What?"

"She's not just some woman, you know?" He gave me a look that said I should have caught on to his meaning.

I didn't.

He waved a hand dismissively. "She'll tell you, if you can whittle it out of her, but there's a reason the justice would be going this far." Dannil offered me nothing else and released his hold.

I slipped past him, making my way up the stairs, not stopping off on the floor where my room lay. The steps ended and I walked toward a lone door that I hoped led to the roof. My hand fell on it with barely any weight before it slowly drifted open.

The rain had turned into a mist of gossamer-thin strands.

I stepped into it, closing my eyes as I took in the solace the rooftop offered. Some believe the rain is without smell. They're wrong. It's a cleanness that only the sky can bring. An absence of other odors, washed away for an air of crispness—softness. It is light and soothing as spring in its fullness.

I took a deep breath, holding it in me with the thought of pushing it down into the pit of my stomach. The folds of my mind bled into view with stark whiteness. They begged for me to flood them with another binding, anything—a trace of more magic. I exhaled slowly, letting the breath filter out of me over the course of several seconds. The urge passed and I rested my back against the door.

"A gentleman," came the voice, "would offer to sit with a woman in the rain so she wasn't cold and alone."

I fought the smile etching its way across my face and turned toward Eloine.

She sat, knees tucked to her chest, a few feet to my side. The young woman hugged her legs, watching me intently with a look that spoke of several things: How did I find her? What happened after she'd left? And would I say anything about her current state?

The whole of her called to me, and I answered in kind, taking her in. Her hair resisted the rain in part, holding on to a hint of the curls I'd seen earlier. A single drop had run down the curved and elegant bridge of her nose to settle on the tip. Her lids had darkened from the water, but I also noticed something else. A slight sheen hung in her eyes, and it hadn't come from the rain.

Tears. I didn't acknowledge them, knowing she wouldn't want me to. Another reason she might have chosen a spot outside during the rain.

I came to her side and kneeled.

She smiled at that. "And I thought you told me that you *weren't* a gentleman."

My back rested against the wall as I slid down to my bottom. I raised an arm, spreading my cloak in a silent offer. She leaned forward and allowed me to slip my limb behind her. A quick pull and I had her snugly against me under the shelter of my red shroud. "I think I'll play one tonight, for you."

"Mhm." She pursed her lips thoughtfully, touching the tip of an index finger to the bow of her upper lip. "And gentlemen usually do as ladies ask." It wasn't a question. She slid nearer to me, rubbing her shoulders against my chest.

"Usually." A hint of uncertainty crept into my voice.

"And if I ask you to make good on your promise?" She looked at me, her eyes seeming all the wider now in her closeness.

I almost lost myself in the depths of the green, which had now gone the color of pine boughs under fog. They'd faded to something softer. Something brittle. A silent plea hung in her request. The sort of thing I'd heard before in people wanting a story for other reasons than entertainment.

An escape. A reprieve from something burdensome, an unshakable weight that threatened to pull them back somewhere deep inside them they'd fought tooth and claw to escape.

I inclined my head in agreement. Offering an avenue of departure from the here and now was within my power. No matter how fleeting the distraction would be, for those moments, Eloine would be spared whatever gnawed at her.

"A part of me is still loath to the idea of sharing my story." I watched her out of the corners of my eyes, letting a teasing smile spread across my face.

Then I exhaled, drawing the air back into me a second later. If I did this thing, shared with her my past, unvarnished with all the follies and misdeeds intact, there was no telling how she'd take it. I chewed over that for another moment, finding myself all the more enamored with Eloine for not pressing me as I deliberated.

"This is a story of many things. A story spanning thousands of miles and different skies. Some truths. Good deeds. Legends. And lies . . . A story of how I came to be known as The Dragon of Rokash, the fire among the frozen steppes and its people. Of how I became the Sword of the Jade Halls in Laxina, far in the east where the earth begins to kiss the lowest of the heavens. I am the Eagle of Edderith, the lion who kindled everlasting flame. He who struck at the Shaen, all for love of a princess. One I failed. And I incurred the eternal wrath of the black riders.

"I have learned the ten bindings all men must know and mastered them all. I have spent one hundred and one nights with Enshae, and kidnapped her from between the grips of warring Morning Lords. And in the end, I walked away bound to return, hamed in blood-red so as to guarantee I keep my word." My collar tightened around my throat before loosening the next instant.

"I have seen the faces of a dozen beings all said to be the one true god, and I've bested them all. I've set fire to the fabled Ashram and buried the village of Ampur under a mountain of ice and snow.

"I have stolen lost magics, best forgotten, and was cursed for it. I've robbed merchant kings and sailed to the ends of the world. And I've lost more money than ten lords could dare to dream of having. I've collected the greatest of tales, and locked one of them away. I've seduced beings of myth, born to sing and twist the minds and hearts of men. I've done these things and a thousand more that could be legends for all time. But among them, I've come to carry the greatest sin imaginable.

"I've set loose that which will swallow this world—consume it all, light and hope." My hand fell over my heart as it ached in agony. I pulled against the fabric of my clothing, squeezing it tight.

"This is not a story of only wonder, but just as much of horror. Of heroism, and the moments I've fallen far short into villainy. It is, in its whole, a tragedy. And it's something that has left me searching for a salvation I'm not so sure exists. A story, first of all kind, the truth of all things within it. Chasing behind this thing to find the roots and follow them to the end. But, it's all unfolding before me still to this day. This is a story of how I've killed the world, and no one but me knows it yet. This is the truth of why most people fear the real me."

Eloine squeezed my shoulder tight, looking at me with burning resolution in her eyes. "I'm not afraid of you."

I took her hand within mine, pulling it away from me. "You should be. Now let me tell you why."

EIGHT
Sounds and Stages

My story begins far to the east. A place of sand-swept streets and high walls of stone. Of homes, tall and fashioned of hard brick and mortar. The country of marble and gold. The land of salt and spice. The center of all trade and wealth.

Though, it would be a lie to say I'd ever seen any of that in my youth.

And in my younger years is the place to start, in the kingdom of Abhar, richest within the Mutri Empire. Notably the poorest as well, especially along the streets I lived under in the city of Keshum. It all depended on who you were.

I bring this up because it's what I wonder drove my parents to be rid of me. It's not for sympathy I tell you this. Just understanding. I have no other reason, still to this day, why I've been alone for as long as I can remember.

I don't remember their faces, their voices. Nothing.

But I remember the first place I called home.

❧

The understage was a thing pulled from a child's dreams . . . or nightmare.

A place as large as mountain caverns with all the cold dark stone to match. Repurposed wood, rock, and metalworks littered the place, casting odd and long shadows if given the slightest bit of light. The kinds of shapes young children would inevitably think of as monsters come for them. It was a place of ropes and pulleys, winding above you to form a tangled web that should never have functioned. Yet, no two lengths of twine rubbed against each other or caught tight.

The hollow tubes along one wall made me think of tall reedy men in the night keeping watch over me. The low burning fire off to one side, nestled in an old rusted iron mouth, could have been a dragon. At least, I often saw it as such when I couldn't fall asleep.

In truth, the understage was a living wonder to me, albeit one of cold dead things that had found a new purpose under my hands. To breathe and move and perform. A motley assembly of contraptions that would bring another set of voices to any theater play.

And one voice led it all.

"Clink, boy. Clink!"

I heeded the rough call, rushing forward to grab a length of rope. The whole of my weight fell against it as I pulled. I didn't carry the strength to yank it down with the force needed, having to throw myself toward the ground.

The crude and worn pulley shivered in its mounting above. It *clinked* like a glass bottle tapping against metal.

A chorus of laughter, tinged with light clapping, echoed from what might as well have been a world away.

I smiled despite my weariness. My arms ached, not accustomed to the laborious days yet.

"Thump!"

I released my hold on the rope, scrambling over a raised wooden platform before me. My knees throbbed with days-old pains that had manifested in the form of palm-sized bruises. I cleared the obstruction, rounding its side and reaching for another rope. The old twine, frayed and tough, bit lightly against the flesh of my palms as I jerked it.

A canted lever above me moved, swinging its broad and cloth-wrapped head into a wide drum. It struck with thunderous resonance and clapped with the full force of a storm.

"Rain." The call had lost much of the bark and bluster driving it.

I answered it, scurrying through the little wooden realm of tools and mechanisms. My haste had driven my shin into a block, used as a step, knocking it aside and driving renewed agony through my leg. The pain settled into my already suffering knee, of course. I winced through it and ignored the light and chiding *tsk* that came from the darkened corner of the room.

A series of bamboo pillars occupied a good portion of the wall to my side. Even though I couldn't see past the rest of their length past the ceiling, I knew they ran up well into the air on the floor above. Small knobs protruded from the tops of them just out of my reach. I cursed myself for forgetting the obvious and rushed back to fetch the step.

The voice didn't call this time, silently observing my mistake with the cool collectedness of usual.

The step clattered to the ground before me with a sound much like the drum. I clambered on top and reached up to pull the first knob. A wooden disc slid back, not fully out of the bamboo, releasing the endless grains of sand and discarded metal shavings held above. They cascaded within the tubing and down what I knew were sets of grooves varying in thickness.

The sound of gentle rain filled my ears and echoed through the shaft into the stage above. I repeated the process, enthusiasm filling my motions and making them slightly erratic. My fingers pinched another knob, and I pulled.

More rain.

I hadn't learned my lesson of patience and leaned on the unsteady step to grasp at the last of the knobs. Its bulbous head hung just at the edge of my fingertips, leaving me only able to brush it in futility. My legs and sides quaked as I bent at an angle only children could manage. My thumb and forefinger found a small bit of purchase against the knob and I pulled.

The disc pulled free to the gentle susurrus of added rain.

It failed to muffle the noise as I toppled from my precarious perch, crashing onto the ground with a *thumpfh*. The step slid back and clattered against the wall with a woody racket.

"Bellows," called the voice without a trace of emotion. It was the gruff and short tone of someone ordering about a performance with no time for anything but action.

I scrabbled to my feet, lurching a few steps as bright spots of pain flared to life through my body. Wincing through them was my only recourse as I hobbled toward a black iron stove.

Its bulbous body had been repurposed, tapering to a thin pipe that led far above to the stage overhead. An opening had been fashioned to one of its sides with a working set of bellows to manipulate the fire as needed.

My hands clasped tight to the handles of the rigid boards and I set to the task. My arms ached, thin cords of muscle flexing while I pumped air into the makeshift furnace. Smoke churned to life as I renewed the intensity of the fire within the iron body. I knew black clouds would billow far above onto the stage, bringing another layer of life to the performance.

I knew from the two years of working below the stage what play went on above simply by the routine I ran in the understage. The muscles along my sides tensed, crying in fatigue as I continued working the bellows.

"Crank."

I huffed out a short breath, not bothering to wipe the sweat from my brow as I pulled away from the hot stove. My hair had plastered itself to my skull. Some of the locks tickled the tops of my ears where they brushed against the soft and sensitive flesh. I reached the two wheels, rings of steel with four spokes running through each. A small lever had been fixed to a point along both of their rims for ease in turning them.

I took each in hand, grunting and putting my weight into pushing against them. Each of them juddered in protest against my sudden effort. They relented the next second and spun lazily despite my best efforts. A light squealing, from metal long in need of oiling, filled the understage as I cranked along.

The curtain call. My motions had to be smooth and strong, ensuring the fabrics above the stage would come to gentle and flowing close to hide the performers. I kept that in mind as I pumped my arms for every bit of strength I could manage out of them. The wheels shook to a sudden halt, refusing to go any farther.

I let go and doubled over now that my job was done. Each labored breath came as a relief, cool and sweet, even though the temperature was anything but. My breeches, if they could be called that—tattered and torn in places—served as a serviceable cloth to wipe my grimy hands on. Better than my face. What little bits of sweat and filth remained ended up on my worn and weathered shirt.

The once-white clothing had faded to an old gray. It was the shade of cobblestones after years of trampling feet and unforgiving rains. No matter how hard I worked, I couldn't wipe clean the few soot stains lining the edges of my wrists.

"Stop that. You'll wear out what little you've got." The source of the voice finally emerged from the dark corner of the room. He stood a few hairs short of six feet with a wiry build that came from both years of tough labor and not quite getting all the meals he required. His cotton shirt and pants hung off his frame, loose and flitting occasionally as errant breezes rolled through.

I closed my eyes, inhaling and pulling the air down deep in my chest, holding on to the refreshing breath.

"*Mazashad*." The man spat. "Someone left the door out to the back open again." He repeated the earlier curse, not bothering to hack up spittle and fling it anywhere in the understage.

"Wasn't me, Khalim. Promise." I raised a hand to my heart, emphasizing my honesty. It would have been convincing had I not been averting my gaze.

Khalim snorted, coming close. He had a fatherly manner about him. It manifested best and clearest in his face. His head was solid and thick, the sort you'd normally attribute to thugs and bandits in plays. But upon a closer look, one could see where he differed from those kinds of people. He had a narrow forehead lacking the broad and sloping appearance of the more brutish elements of society. Even under the dim light in the understage, I could see the patchy stubble running along the side of his skull and some of the top.

He'd started going bald years before I met him, choosing now to keep himself clean shaven, beard and head. It added a softness to the hard angles of his face. Khalim's nose sat crooked in a manner that said one thing: It had been made so courtesy of another man's fist.

I knew the story behind it. He'd once saved another child, long ago, and given them a home here. The act had earned him a thrashing.

Khalim kneeled before me, placing his large hands on my shoulders.

I flinched instinctively.

"Oi, I'm not going to hit you, Ari." Khalim gripped me tightly, giving me a gentle shake. "I'll work you like a dog, but that's the price for this life. But I'm not like those people, huh?" Another shake.

I nodded. He'd lived up to his word, so far. But everyone hit you eventually. It was a matter of time. All it took was a bad day, a poor earning, and you being the closest thing around when they snapped. But I kept the doubts from showing on my face.

I may not have been allowed to perform onstage, but that didn't mean I hadn't learned a hint of the craft.

"You're a clever boy, Ari."

I grinned.

"But sometimes being clever is a bad thing. And do you know what's worse than being clever?" He gave me a long, knowing look.

I shook my head.

"Being a clever little shit." Khalim reached out and tweaked my nose between a thumb and forefinger.

"Ow!" I lashed out, brushing aside his arm and grabbing my face. The sensation only lasted a couple of seconds.

"That's for leaving the door open. It'll get cold down here. Maybe your"—he placed a hand on my chest, giving me a little shove that rocked me back a step—"little body, young and fit, can take that. I cannot." Khalim hooked a thumb to his own sternum, then rubbed it. "Old chest gets cold." He moved his hands down to his knees, massaging them. "These too. They creak and clank just like those." Khalim nodded to the pulleys and wheels.

The man didn't look past his middle years, but a life hovering between abject poverty, and worse, aged him prematurely. He grew tired at times from acts of simple labor that men a decade older could perform with little trouble. On winter nights, when the wind grew dry and biting, he struggled to breathe properly. His words weren't exactly meant to chastise me, but they had the same effect.

I fixed my gaze on the ground, unable to meet his eyes. "Sorry, Khalim. Won't happen again." One of my hands went to my throat, resting over the hollow of it. I pinched the area gently like I was choking off the space my voice came from. "Promise."

He winked once, eyes twinkling. "That's what you said the last time, ah?" Khalim placed a hand on my head, running his fingers through my hair before jostling me. "Now, on to more important things."

I sobered immediately, knowing a test ran through his mind.

"What story were they performing, hm?"

Picking through my routine normally served as the best way to pin the play onstage. The family had been going through a series of news of late, though. Khalim had made a point of intensifying my quizzes in frequency and difficulty during this time. Not something I enjoyed as a child, as you can imagine.

My mind tumbled, recalling the sequence I'd gone through. The pulley had moved a pair of canvas sacks dressed to look like wraiths. At least, that's what they had been fashioned to resemble the last time I'd worked the mechanism. The drums and rain signaled a storm. That only narrowed it down to a handful of possible stories. The key rested in the smoke.

"When come they demons—ash and ember
on clouds of reddest smoke
with cries of rain
and sounds of thunder
two things man must remember:
burn quick and fast
purest white,
and truest oak
to cast Ashura asunder."

The lines had come to me in an instant, surprising me. "*Demons in Dinture*."

Khalim smiled. Not wide and brimming. No obvious, beaming pride there. It was a gentle and content thing.

But to me, it meant as much as a thing could to a child.

"Good man." He gave me another gentle shake. "It's a good man that knows his stories, ah?" Khalim jabbed a pointer finger to my chest lightly. "It's in your blood. You keep to that, master it, and you'll be the greatest teller of tales this world's seen."

My smile came thin and forced this time, like stretching the thin film that forms over boiled milk. I took care to not let it break into something obviously so fake. Khalim's comment had tugged at a part of me I hadn't managed to properly bury. A hollowness aching to be filled with the knowledge of my parents. The question left my mouth before I'd realized it. "What *is* my blood, Khalim?"

He opened his mouth to speak, but I rode over him.

"Who were they?" My voice carried leaden weight on the last word. "You never talk about my parents. But you always bring up the blood."

The skin around Khalim's eyes wrinkled as he gave me a kind and sympathetic look. His mouth moved through a series of expressions as if struggling to find the right one.

After all, what face do you make when trying to answer an orphan boy's request? Especially one that's been long avoided?

"They were ravel and trash." The voice echoed down from a passage on the left. It was smooth and rich like fresh cream, carrying a touch of honeyed sweetness. Though none of that made it into the words themselves. Somehow, through the softness of it all, a hard edge ran through what he'd said.

I turned to face the speaker.

Makham strode toward me, his loose and flowing skirt swishing as he moved. He wore a shirt made of the same soft and slack material. His entire ensemble had been dyed several times to finally reach a rich shade of blue somewhere between morning skies and sapphires. He had a face sharp as a knife, and his eyes were canted slits of the dark brown of freshly turned earth. He may have carried himself tall and proud as a cat, but he came off as a worm to me.

I glared at him, fighting to keep my breath steady as my chest heaved.

Makham ran a thumb and forefinger over the neatly trimmed and slender scrap of hairs he called a beard. His hand moved through the short and greasy curls atop his head. Each dark lock pressed flat to his skull before springing back into shape. "Your parents were gutter crawlers, *ji*? They rooted around for garbage to pilfer and peddle. Then one day, they found the jewel of the lot"—his gaze settled knowingly on me—"you."

Khalim's hands gripped me tight, fingers digging into what little meat I carried in my shoulders. His eyes were undoubtebly boring holes into the side of my head in a look I'd grown to know all too well. A warning to keep calm and not let the performer rankle me.

"So, what else would they do but sell you." A smile, like a slit in cold stone, passed across his face. "And what else would come of it but Khalim taking you in." Makham put a hand over his heart, squeezing the spot in mock agony. "He has a soft spot for collecting broken bits of trash."

I let the comment pass, clenching my jaw hard enough to crack a tooth or two. "We're all Sullied here, Makham."

The performer blinked. He worked his mouth as if chewing over a particularly tough piece of meat. It looked as if I'd bested him and he'd turn to leave, deciding digging into me wasn't worth it this night.

I was wrong.

His lips twitched, pulling to one corner in an expression fit for a snake. "True. We're the lowest of the low of castes here, but what does that make you, ah?" He touched a finger to the tip of his nose. "You're casteless, orphaned. Your blood isn't worth piss and shit. And that's about all you got from your parents, *ji*? They were bloodless curs who—"

I pulled free of Khalim's grip and charged Makham. My scream echoed through the understage, taking on an odd and resonant tone as it warbled through the metal workings.

I reached Makham's side before he could register what was happening. My clenched fist hammered into the space below his navel, causing him to buckle. Another blow landed just above his hip. The hailstorm of punches came without thought. It was the bone-deep anger of a kid full of questions with no answers. Something that needed a place to be directed.

And Makham just so happened to be the perfect fit for it.

One of his hands snapped to the side of my head, cuffing me with enough force to send me off-balance.

I flailed, hands grabbing tight to his skirt. Fabric tore as Makham shoved me away, trying to stop me exposing his genitals. The motion caused me to rock back toward him. A primal scream left my lungs, and I opened my mouth. My teeth found a home in the soft meat of his thigh.

Makham cried out.

"*Kala mahl,* Ari!" A pair of hands clasped my shoulders and wrenched.

Khalim's words finally registered with me. He'd effectively said, "Blackened shit."

I lashed out with frenzied kicks, trying to reach Makham but falling short.

Khalim hauled me farther away and swore under his breath.

The performer's chest heaved, a dangerous light kindling in his eyes. "You bastard. *Gutiya!*"

A flash of white strobed through my vision. Soft red peppered my sight next, muting the scenery of the understage. Makham's slap rang out with a fleshy impact that could have rivaled the drum from earlier.

"*Qutha!*" Another slap.

Khalim didn't stop it, using his strength to keep me from retaliating. But he barked something I couldn't quite make out. His words warbled and sounded distant like he was underwater.

Makham raised another hand, his eyes dark slits and glimmering.

"Enough!" I finally registered Khalim's voice. "You kill him, you'll be working the understage, *ji-ah*?" Khalim held out a hand between myself and Makham.

The performer sucked in a breath, lowering his hand and glowering at me. Makham racked his throat and spat a glob of spittle, the color of dirt, at me.

It struck my left cheek and rolled down to the side of my chin. I flailed harder against Khalim's hold, unable to break it.

"Stop. Stop." He squeezed me tighter until I relented. Satisfied I wasn't going to shake my way free and charge after Makham, he released me.

I pinched a part of my shirt, the only suitable piece of cloth I had to my name, and brought it to my face to wipe away the spit. It stained the fabric over the month's grime, dust, and oil that had accumulated in my work. *Parna.*

The residue came from a leaf that, when mixed with lime paste, served as a cheap chewing tobacco. It also provided a state of mental euphoria and stimulation. The plant managed to addict most people within a few uses.

I had developed an immeasurable abhorrence for it. Mostly because the cruelest person in my life happened to chew it, and its stains ran down through the understage—my home—courtesy of that same abusive person.

I stared at the stain with a level of heat that could have set the clothing aflame.

Khalim pulled me out of my reverie by turning me to face him. "You shaken up here?" He tapped my temple twice. "Ah?" He shook my head. "Oi, speak."

"You heard what he—"

Khalim waved my protests off. "I don't care what he said. He's one of my leads. If he leaves, who's going to take his place, ah?" I opened my mouth to speak but he talked over me. "You? No. You've never spent a day onstage. We're *Sullied,* boy. It's hard enough getting someone to act in this troupe. Most people won't spend a copper round on us if they can avoid it. They want us to beg for tin chips." He thrust his chin up at that, dismissing the notion with a look. "We may be skilled and talented—among the best—but our caste is our caste. Makham is irreplaceable, *ji-ah*?"

I knew better than to argue with him then. "*Ji.*" I conceded, noting that Khalim had said nothing about my worth. If he so desired, he could easily dredge up another urchin or orphan, teaching them what I knew in a matter of weeks. So I moved the subject back to something else he'd said. "I could act. You said yourself, all the things about my blood." I hoped my enthusiasm didn't bleed into my voice.

If he had picked up on desire, he didn't show it. Khalim looked me levelly in the eyes. A soft sigh escaped his lips, an odd sound in the understage, so usually filled with the raucousness of contraptions. "Maybe one day, ah? Maybe. But first get that temper under control. You think I'm hard on you?" He arched a brow. "I work every actor harder than an ass."

I tried not to snicker at that, then worked doubly so when I thought of how well the word fit Makham.

"And you do have the blood. A stock to be proud of. Something any of us Sullied would give all of our own souls for. But that doesn't mean anything right now. Not today." He cupped a hand to the cheek Makham had spit on, giving it a few gentle slaps. "One day though." Khalim rose, turning to leave.

"Wait." I reached out for him unconsciously, catching myself in the act and pulling my hand back. "You were going to tell me about my parents?" I failed to keep the plea out of my voice, hearing it crack at the end like a pane of glass under stone.

Khalim didn't face me, keeping his gaze fixed down the hall. "You struck Makham, one of my performers. Ari, I like you, but that can't pass. Makham will talk. You know how he runs his mouth. I can't have my actors thinking some whip of a boy can get away with that. If any of them leave. *Any.* I am ruined. You're going to bed without food. I'll tell you about your parents another time . . . *if* you behave. *Ji-ah*?"

I didn't answer, looking down to my bare feet and wriggling my toes. No response came to me no matter how hard I tried to find one. He'd denied me something every sinew inside me screamed for. All I had ever gotten was little snippets of my parents, usually the same old bits of how they'd given me up. Worse if Makham or the other actors were around.

Moisture welled along my eyes, forcing me to blink them shut. The tears ran along my face down the same path Makham's spittle had. I sniffed and brought my shirt to my face a second time, wiping with the knowledge I'd end up dirtier for it than if I left my cheeks alone.

I don't know if you're aware of what it's like to be deprived of your past, your parents. The idea that there is nothing connecting you to anyone in this world apart from your work. There is a certain hollowness, singular and all encompassing, that fills you. The notion that you are all that is—nothing more—and when you're not much on your own, it's a rather crushing thing.

I didn't know my family name. I couldn't remember my parents' faces—their voices. No memories of their touch, what they smelled like. It was like I existed for the sole purpose of running the understage. I was born to scurry beneath a world of imagination and storytelling, eternally deprived of the opportunity to ever be part of it. Only to watch, listen.

A knot formed in my stomach, drawing my attention to a different kind of emptiness. I pressed a hand to my abdomen. I'd run myself ragged working the understage, and the adrenaline had finally passed, bringing to light my hunger. All of which would go unassuaged now.

I cleared my throat and stifled my sniffling. A bone-deep weariness took over, urging me to head to bed and end the night. It seemed the practical thing to do. After all, we're all spared the hardness of the world and its pains when we sleep. And our gnawing hungers follow.

My appetite plus the chastisement reminded me just how small I was. And the understage only served to accentuate that as I moved through it.

The ceiling sat far enough out of reach that it would take at least six of me standing on top of each other to brush my fingertips against it. Each piece of stone, unlike the next and mortared irregularly, was larger than my skull.

Every contraption meant to add to a performance stood a beastly thing beside my rail-thin body. It was as if everything inside the place was meant to drive home just how pitifully tiny I was in comparison. How insignificant.

Just like Makham said. Just like Khalim had implied; maybe not by intent, but he'd done so nonetheless.

I shook my head clear of the thoughts, making my way to the farthest wall. None of the contraptions needed for my job littered this space. I'd kept it meticulously clean. Well, as clean as possible.

A series of wooden beams protruded from cracks in the stone flooring, held in place by cement that had been unceremoniously dumped into the holes. Flat planks ran across the tops of the pillars and created a crude scaffolding. No ladder or construction marked out a clear way to climb it.

Countless nails, each thicker than a man's pointer finger, lined one of the wooden beams. I'd collected them—which is to say, stolen—from excess stage materials Khalim had bought. Hammering them into the beams had taken me a considerable bit of effort and time in having to go through bricks. They tended to fail under the repeated stress of driving a nail into thick wood. Scrounging up more had been a sizeable part of the endeavor.

But in the end, I had my place. A part of the understage free from anyone. Somewhere safe and all to my own. Out of reach.

I grabbed hold of one of the nails, wincing as it flexed within the wood. My body told me I was undernourished of late. The shifting piece of metal told another story. I clambered up the makeshift rungs, blotting out the acute spots of pain from where the edges of the flat heads dug into my tender heels. It didn't get easier no matter how many times I'd done it. And my feet had refused to build up the calluses that would have spared me. I slapped my hands to the platform and climbed atop, rolling onto my back.

A low sigh of relief passed through my lips. The bars of tension that had formed through my back and arms slowly softened. The momentary reprieve from the pain and stiffness left me with no delusions. I knew I'd be sore as a pack mule the next morning. But for now, I had peace.

Thin bands of pain across my face, still stinging, reminded me that it was a hard-won peace. I inhaled and let myself nurse dark thoughts of Makham as my eyes turned to the window nestled above. The twin panes of glass sat neatly within the dark wall. A lip, almost a full foot in length, protruded from where the window rested. The temptation took hold of me to get to my feet and grab hold of the edge. A little more effort and I could look out and catch a bit more of the outside.

Of a world I barely knew and, according to some, I would never get to see any more of than a fleeting glimpse.

Fatigue won out over temptation and I rolled to my side in defeat. I grabbed an old pair of grain sacks, each longer than me by a foot. I had found each of them by the far exit to the theater over a month ago. They weren't terribly comfortable, sinking in places as I shifted in the night. And without anything keeping their mouths properly sealed, they were prone to puffing out clouds of soot and sawdust. The odd bits of hair trimmings and fabric scraps would occasionally find their way free as well. I wasn't burdened with an abundance of proper stuffing for the makeshift mattresses.

Satisfied that I'd placed both of them close enough together to prevent me from slipping into their pinched ends, I eased myself onto the sacks. My hand went to the side, brushing against coarse wall as I fumbled blindly for my blanket. The patchwork of discarded clothing caught against my pinky. I snatched it, pulling it over myself. The cloth's hem tickled my ankles, and no amount of shuffling or kicking would ever make it so it would cover the ends of my feet. The next sigh I released came from resignation, not weary relief.

But, I'd returned to my true home now. The home within the understage—my bed. My place of dreams and where I could run errant and free in worlds not bound by my birth, caste, and the crushing weight of the opinions of others who never cared to know me better than what they saw me as.

For some of us, the only true safety we have is in our dreams.

My bed was a place I could escape to any world in. Any legend, myth, or adventure. There were no bars here.

My eyes drifted back to the window, but I shut them. A different promise drowned out the one of the outside. The idea that tomorrow was another day, one where I could possibly impress Khalim. A perfect performance could be all that led me from the understage to the theater itself. I lost myself in the thought, and just before a dream could coalesce around the comforting idea, a sharp sound tore me away from it all.

Another *crack*, like a thin, flat stone against glass.

Something was at my window.

NINE
A Promise of a Story

There's a certain kind of fear that comes to all children in the middle of the night. It's an unseen hand of ice that takes hold of your heart. The kind of cold that spreads through the rest of you until you chill entirely. It's the unknown something that lurks just outside your reach, and with but a step, it can take you. The shapeless fear that a child's mind can all too quickly give monstrous form to.

I lay there, stiff as the boards beneath me and nursing a silent string of curses that my blanket didn't cover the whole of me.

The noise outside had softened from harsh snaps to something gentler. *Tap. Tap. Tap.* They were measured and almost rhythmic.

Realization set in, drawing me out of fear's grip. I scrambled to my feet and clawed against the wall. My fingers found purchase in the crevices I'd chiseled in when I'd built the platform. I made it to the lip before the window, reaching out with my other hand to trip the latch.

The window slid up and revealed a girl close to my own age. Her hair was shorter than mine in places, no longer than my little finger. The strands curled wildly like she'd run her fingers through them with oil. She flashed me a smile as bright as the moon's own glow. "Ari."

I could have counted to ten before I found my voice. "Nisha, you're not supposed to be here tonight." I leaned away from the opening as she squeezed her way through. My fingers ached as I held myself in place.

She grinned, and the firelight from outside brought her features to better clarity. The warm glow did interesting things to her skin. It gave a slightly red tinge to the rich bronze of her face. She had eyes the color of burnished cedar with the slightest hints of muted orange, and the bits of light dancing across her face only brightened those notes. Her mouth parted wide as if something had just struck her. "Wait."

I blinked, gritting my teeth as the small muscles in my hands fell under a heat much like that when I'd been struck earlier. "Hurry, please."

If she heard my complaint, she didn't show any signs. "Here, I brought things." She eased her way back through the window with something filling her arms.

The smell hit me first. A strong wave of spices with an undercurrent that brought back just how hungry I truly was. As if on cue, my stomach grumbled in equal parts discontent and ravenous desire.

Nisha set down a tin bowl no larger than her fist. A faint wisp of steam wafted from it, and she laid a long length of wrinkled parchment beside the metal container. Bits of the paper carried dark splotches like something had seeped into the material.

I eyed her. "What is it?"

"Buttered bread and stew." Her mouth pulled into a thin and uneven frown. "I know you don't always get to eat."

I bristled, knowing she meant well, but the comment pricked me like a barb. My life wasn't glamorous by any means. I held on to no delusions about that. But I'd fought to make the best of it I could, and her words struck at the root of my pride. Some of the heat and acid building in my stomach made its way into my reply. "I eat fine." I eased myself down from the lip to the first set of crevices. My stomach rumbled loud enough to reveal my lie.

Nisha said nothing, leaning forward close enough to bring her nose nearly to the tip of mine. "It's still hot." She sighed, looking away. "But . . . if you don't want it . . ."

I gave voice to the groan that had buried itself in my stomach. "I do." My weakening hold on the wall was all that kept me from lunging for the food. Instead, a moment's reason won out and I lowered myself to my bed.

Nisha reached behind herself, revealing an old cloth. One side of the fabric could have been simply sand and sweat, but the other remained unmarred, the rich color of saffron. She carefully laid it down, almost as if performing a religious act, smoothing out any rumples within the material. Nisha placed the bread in the center before taking as much time and effort to rest the dish of stew atop. She made a few short movements to fold excess cloth out of the way before cinching the food package together at the top.

I bit back my desire to hurry her.

Nisha didn't respond well to pressure. And an instance of anger, even a child's impatience, could send her running away with no knowing when she'd return.

"Here." She grunted, leaning over the sill while maintaining a solid hold on it. Nisha lowered the makeshift sack toward me.

I jumped, grabbing hold of the pack's neck, struggling to keep it steady as I landed on the platform. My crude bed wobbled, forcing me to place an arm against the stone wall for some semblance of support. Relieved I hadn't dropped my meal or toppled from the perch, I placed the food down by my feet and glanced up to Nisha. "Wait, don't try to—"

She had already taken to placing her feet against the nooks and crannies, finding purchase and scrambling down with the grace and skill of an acrobat. Nisha plopped down beside me, flashing me a lopsided smile of self-satisfaction.

"When did you learn to do that?" I had asked the question carefully, keeping my tone to that of someone discussing how someone's day had gone.

I hadn't done a good enough job, it seemed.

Nisha shied away from my look, managing to say more with that than if she had taken a minute to answer me in detail.

I decided to move the conversation to a safer subject. "Thank you for the food. Khalim and Makham came down on me tonight. I can't say I didn't earn it. But Makham—"

Nisha pressed her fingers against my lips, hushing me. "No. Not now." She pulled the sack into her lap, undoing the knot she'd tied. "Just eat. We don't have to talk about them and the bad things. Not tonight"—she chewed on her lip and turned her gaze away again—"please?"

I acquiesced in silence. There isn't much to do when a friend makes a plea like that. And doubly when they're the only real companion you can have.

Nisha placed the tin before me and the bread, watching as I tore into it.

The bread folded in my hands easily. It held form like the dough was more rubber than anything else, letting me shape it into a crude shovel as I plunged it into the stew. The first bite filled my mouth with the subtle taste of mild peppers and garlic. A strong wash of onion followed, chased by hints of coriander. I swallowed it mostly whole, not bothering to chew as I continued fishing through the stew with the bread. My eyes grew owlish as I plucked a piece of red meat. "How did you pay for something with goat in it?"

She smiled. "You like it?" Nisha avoided the question, pressing me again if I was happy with the meal.

I persevered. "Did Koli ask you to steal tonight?"

Nisha went rigid as a cat stroked with a wet hand. She glared at me, shuffling away along the platform.

I reached out for her, stopping when she recoiled. "Sorry, sorry. Nisha, I didn't mean to. I won't ask about Koli—"

"I don't like when he makes me do things." She sniffed once and still refused to meet my eyes. "I don't like being a bad person. And I don't like you thinking about me doing those things, Ari."

Life mandates a great many things, and for one of the casteless, without opportunity and safety, stealing is sometimes one of them. Imagine a child—a friend—worried they're something horrible for their sheer want of survival.

The remnants of the understage, hot and heavy, filled my chest in that moment. I didn't have the right words to soothe Nisha, so I grabbed the first I could find and hoped they'd be enough.

"Thank you for dinner. I wish I had something for you . . ." I trailed off as my words kindled an idea. "And maybe I do." I flashed her a wide smile. "How long has it been since you've heard a story?"

She swiveled to face me, beaming. "I heard one on the streets two mornings ago . . . but he didn't tell it like you do. He was from one of the temples." Nisha sniffed and it had nothing to do with her mood. "You know how they say things. Always shouting and never telling."

I didn't know, which Nisha was aware of on some level, but I didn't press it. My life hadn't allowed me to wander the streets within the Mutri Empire. The whole of my world rested in the understage. So I nodded as she told a little story of her own, and I could see her calm a bit.

Nisha jabbed an accusing finger at my chest. "You have all strayed from the love and wisdom of Brahm. He who . . ." She bit off the next words, shaking her head. "I didn't like how he did it. He stopped the story to yell at the crowds before asking for money."

That sounded more like what I'd heard Khalim grouse about when it came to the "holy" and "wizened" men of religious life.

God and salvation will always be the greatest hook . . . and the greatest grift for a con man. And more often than not, men of the cloth are both, and just as often better than the honest thieves and actors of the world at it.

I kept that bit of Khalim's wisdom to myself, and bowed my head once again to what Nisha said. "Not everyone can tell a proper story the way it needs to be." I puffed up my chest a little, clearing my throat as if I were about to roll into a tale myself.

Nisha sighed, picking at a length of wood with her fingernails. "I know. It's so hard to find someone who's good at those." She eyed me askance before turning her attention to the planks beneath us. "Who do you think is the best in the theater, Ari?"

I huffed and narrowed my eyes at her. "You know it's me. But if you don't want to hear a story from me, I guess I can go ask Khalim or Makham to come down and tell you all the stories you'd ever want to hear." A lopsided smile crossed my face.

She laughed, and the sound warmed me to my heart. "No! You tell me one. Tell me one about Brahm. The start of everything."

Bristling at a request was beneath a proper performer, especially of the kind I aimed to be. So I squirmed instead.

Of all the stories ever told, why Nisha wanted one of the most trod on and spat about of all, I didn't know. But a look in her eyes at that moment told me enough of a reason as to why I should tell it for her. And so I did.

I cleared my throat and began, "Of Brahm and all things."

TEN

Brahm

First, before skies and world, before stream and stone, was black. It was wide and expansive, covering all things.

Except, then there was light. A kindling white flame, ebbing, fighting against the blackness. It refused to wink out.

An egg, a stone, a pearl.

It shone like mirrorglass far out in the dark—stark—and alone. In it rested the first thing in all of creation, the hand that would shape all things. Fateweaver, Threadpuller, the one who bound the first flame and gave us light. The one who gave the moon its pale guiding glow, a beacon for our night.

In it rested Brahm.

But in deep slumber he laid, leaving all to nothingness and all things unmade.

This was before time, the making of the Sithre, and the Fallen's first crime.

Only nothingness and Brahm.

And then, one day, the heavenly pearl split. Streams of orange and red flame screamed through the crack. They broke apart the first egg and all silence and stillness. The fire spread, howling against the empty blackness almost in protest. And through it all . . . came Brahm.

In fire. In brightness and light. Into the darkness came Brahm as the first of all things. It's said no one knows, still to this day, what he truly looked like. Too grand, beyond all words and ways to describe. Just know that there was once black, and then Brahm came to life in it—against it—burning away nothingness.

And like that, the first thing he experienced was hollowness.

There's nothing here. It's all empty but for me. I'm alone. His chest ached, and Brahm first knew pain. *I can't see a thing for as far as I can see, and there are no ends to that. It's just me. Only me.* And the hollow space in him grew larger. Something he wished to fill.

So Brahm wandered, lost and lonely. He carried the broken remnants of his egg wherever he went, stopping to sleep beside it when he felt tired. But what light and flame had been within the egg, given it its warmth, had since gone out. It was now in Brahm. So he slept cold, unsure what to do or where to go.

There's nothing no matter how far I go. Where I search. All I see is blackness. And nothing wants to fill it. I'm cold. Please make it stop.

And when he could not sleep anymore, he picked up the pieces of his pearl and wandered again.

Somewhere along the way, Brahm's solitude overtook him and he began to weep in the dark.

It hurts. The emptiness is too much—so vast. Make it bright. Give me something, anything—a light. Something warm like it was before I was born.

The blackness had gotten to him, overcoming his light, and left Brahm, shaper of all things, hollow and sad. So he shed his tears over this.

I feel heavy and brittle like my egg. I'm breaking now. I want for something. Please.

And the light of his pearl poured out from his eyes. Beads of white fire dropped from his lids, spilling from between his fingers. He felt their warmth and spread his hands, casting the droplets far and wide. They caught among the black and hung like sequins to glimmer in the wideness of night.

Warmth, he thought. *Brightness.* He reached out to grab the first of these and cradled their flames. *It feels alive. Safe. And real. Something to fill the darkness. Something besides just me. It's so warm.* He held it close to him, letting the ball of fire take away the loneliness.

And thus Brahm created the first things, the first flitting flames. He made the stars.

Some flickered, threatening to wink out of existence. And to them, he gave his breath, billowing them into something great. He blew to life all manner of fire to hang across the dark.

No. Don't go—don't die. Please. He gave them another bit of breath. *Dance, breathe, play with me now. Don't leave.* He coaxed them, bled for them, keeping his first friends kindled and alive as best he could. And then they hung as still as anything of fire could and can do, and he gave them names.

"Mahor. The first." The star he'd given life to at the beginning pulsed and orbited him until Brahm forgot the deep of darkness and all the solitude it had brought him. Now he had his own lights and makings to fill the void with.

Some stars remained hot as when he first cried those tears, shimmering motes of white. Others grew into angry things the color of our sun, large enough to swallow our world.

It's said if you look out at night, far, far at the corners of the sky, you can catch sight of some of these stars. The ones that Brahm pushed to the ends of darkness, the ones he had to forsake. So their anger wouldn't spread to the light around them. So their pain wouldn't taint the other things Brahm would come to make. Realizing what he had done, Brahm cried out his final few tears, flicking them free of his fingertips to have the last stars hang in the night.

I'm sorry. Some of you are holding to too much of my hurt, and in that, you can come to break what I do next. It hurts again. He placed a hand on his chest, aching in grief for pushing his first lights away.

Remember me, for I will always care for you. I will give you all the names you deserve and ensure everything knows them until the end of time.

He brushed his face dry, understanding the depth of power and flame inside him. Something that would never falter, never wane. So Brahm stood straight and set to wandering again, his eyes now clear and fixed with purpose. To find a place perfect for his loneliness to end. A spot with which to shape something new—somewhere to his talents spend.

I need to move on. Make more. Create and fill. Lights are only the beginning and the darkness needs more than that to keep the emptiness at bay. To keep all the hollow pains and loneliness away.

He came across where we are now, it's said. Distant, dark, and empty. Somewhere with which to sew creation's next thread. To place the seeds for life's first bounty.

This place is too far dark and away from every star I've made. This place is as good as can be for new ground and makings to be laid. "So cold a place. So empty. This is like from before. Just so hollow and waiting to be filled. Will . . . you let me fill you, empty place in space?"

Brahm waited. He listened. Not wanting to intrude on the quiet stillness of where he was. And when he felt it, the silent agreement that only he could hear, he knew he could begin his making.

He breathed a breath, hot and thin, carrying flame and his own soul within. Through cupped hands he blew, the first winds of creation that would come to shape me and you.

Please let this hold. Let my hope and let my love fill this making and its band. Let my vision and my dream come to take and form this land.

Brahm spun the air into a band and shaped it with gentle care. He pressed it firm like shaping clay and poured more of his fire into our world, knowing a piece of him was the price to pay. Then he breathed a breath so cool, to harden the threads of this freshly made place, creation's first new jewel.

But this world was empty save for stone. Hard of skin and hot in core, it was lacking, and needed something more. Knowing that his tears were flame, Brahm could not shape like before—the same. He brought hand to mouth and bit firmly deep. He drew his blood and birthed the flood that would waters bring to this great world. He poured it free and spread it wide till this place became of stone and tide—his salt and bone.

It hurts again. Each time I make, a precious piece of myself must I forsake. He looked at where he'd torn of himself to give to our world. "It's beautiful. A thing unlike any other—all its own. A place of possibility to fill with new wonders and new sights."

"But what to do, and what to make?" *All I've known is the blackness and what it means to be empty. How do I fill a thing that has so long gone unfilled in me?*

He looked around him and realized what he had to do. All he'd done was create and fill, and he still had more of that ahead of him.

This making of his was wet and firm, but that was all. It had no life. Nothing like him. Little else but shape and form.

"Another pain then to endure, to bring about something more."

So he took his flesh in hand and pulled it hard till skin tore and sinew followed. "Take my flesh, and take my body. I want you to have of me because what you offer in return, world, is something greater." With this fresh piece of himself, Brahm laid down the first part of true land on this world—Ibrahmia, now the Mutri Empire, and our home.

But the world hardly looked changed. "Is this not enough? More then? Please and take." He twisted locks of his hair, twining them tight and seeding them over all he could. Watered with another offering of his blood, Brahm birthed the first green things in our world, letting them flourish and spread of their own. Every bit he plucked free of himself came back as if it had never left, just like his fire.

It hurts less now the more I give. He smiled, caressing the edges of his newest making. "Tell me and I will listen. What else do you need? What else do you want for, world?"

And the world answered him, but no one knows what she said.

With this, Brahm knew he could come to shape something truly magnificent. He set to the task, making all things as carefully as he could from his own core. He rent tooth and bone to form mountain and highest stone. He whispered wind upon the world, bound by breath, set to ever flowing paths unseen, to move full free—unhampered, and with an edge cold and keen.

"More. I'll give you more. And for each thing I give, you've given dozens back in beauty and return. Thank you. Thank you." Brahm had been lying to himself, though. For all his sacrifices still hurt. Yet, the joy of seeing what he made buried that pain so deep even a god could not feel them.

He fanned the first flame at this world's core once more. Bringing renewed warmth to new mounds of land, but it was not enough. This place still lacked something needing, a spark to make it lively, and a world true. It lacked me and you.

"What? What? What else is there to do? Why are you so empty still? What else can I give you? Please, won't you talk to me now?" Brahm reached out, cradling the world, asking—hoping for her to tell him again what she might need.

But she was silent for once.

So Brahm had no idea of what shape for these things to take, of how to another kind of life make. "No. Not now. Please. Speak, and I will listen."

But she didn't.

In his confusion, he tore once again at himself, hoping for something new to spring. A new form of being to bring.

"What then? What? Is this enough? Do I have to give more of myself then? Watch me. See it done. I will. I will!" *Oh, but it hurts so much again. Will this be the last of what's asked of me? The last shaping for me to make?*

In this moment, Brahm pulled at something past his body—his own self and soul. And thus he gave birth to the next of the gods we would come to know—new life, proud and whole.

The next flame to be born. All of pride and fury bound, full-formed from Brahm's loneliness and all suffering freshly torn.

Oh, but how beautiful you are. "Let me look at you, first of my true makings. Let me hear you. Please, say something—anything. Will . . . will you let me know you?"

And this first new flame did cry out, and Brahm knew him then and gave him name. "Oh, Saithaan. My first. My own son."

Saithaan, prince of white fire and starlight. He would come to aid his father in his plight.

"Will you help me? Will you shape with me so that I may not have to do this alone?"

And his son answered. "Yes, Father." Hand in hand, they took pieces of themselves to birth children, brothers and sisters more, crafting one by one to the score.

> *We know them by their names and their deeds:*
> *First comes Rathiya, who sees to love and all hearts' things.*
> *Then came Sivu,*
> *who listens to the green, and this world's buried needs.*
> *Followed by Arnia—the one who sat silent,*
> *she listened,*

she watched,
deciding over which to take and rule,
waiting for things to be shaped even further,
and until man would come to be;
before it was decided, she knew—she could see
that she would come to be the one to tend to the wise
and counsel minds of the lowly to this world's kings.
But her brother born next, would come to be vexed
for so many mantles had been chosen,
from hearts and love to earth and fires bright,
leaving him to take things in his own hands
to become the god of strength and one's own might;
he is Hahn,
who would come to shepherd the strong and champions under his sight,
guiding them take wrongs and make them right.
But the making continued,
and the gods and goddesses came to be
intent to watch over all things for eternity.

And for time uncounted, they did, trading stories and talking of their roles for those who had chosen. The others sat quiet and content at Brahm's side as his other shapings were still to come. This was before the first mortal life had been formed, you see, before man and Shaen came to be.

But even still Brahm's solitude the new gods failed to quell. Something was still missing in creation, but what . . . he could not tell.

Something's still not right. Something lacking—something beyond my grasp and my sight. But what? Maybe it's not for me to think on or to know. Maybe my children will have the answers.

So he convened with his children and asked them for their thoughts. They offered to do what had been done before, to split of him and themselves to make something new again. Brahm thought on this as it had worked before. But what else was left to make? What other paths in creation were there to take?

He told them, "No. This time will not be the same. It is time to end the birthing of gods and flame." *Is there nothing more to make? Must it all be the same, something birthed of my blood and of my everlasting flame? I want something else—something more yet less.* He wanted something not as grand and all powerful. But something different, smaller—and close to mortal.

So this time he didn't sacrifice himself or the other gods. He asked them to offer—to will pieces of their own fire and mantles out into nothingness. "Will you, my children, follow in my stead? Will you give of yourselves, body and soul, be willing to be bled?" Brahm wanted his children to think and hold firmly to faith in something coming to life where there was none. And their efforts were rewarded.

"What are they, Father?" asked Saithaan.

"Listen close, my son, and you tell me. There is a power in that, and if you hone it, they will tell you themselves—their stories and their names. And you'll know them by and for that then."

"Sithre," spoke Brahm's first-made.

The first of the Sithre, the Sirathrae, the holy beings of lesser light and fire. Each with a smaller dominion of creation to oversee. They were not like the gods in many ways that it pleased Brahm. Something fresh had come to being.

"Look at them! So empty and full of possibility. Unsure of how to bind and shape and make. They know nothing. So unlike us. So . . . *new*!" *So ready for me to be with.*

And so Brahm set to task with his children to teach the Sithre. And he taught them all things and how to fulfill their roles.

For a time, this was enough. But something was wrong with the Sithre. They were different from the gods, but not different enough in other ways. Too close to divinity without means to reach it in full. So they were hollow in places—still lost. When they smiled, it was empty, almost like a mask. When light danced in their eyes in happiness, it was a cold and faraway thing.

It's all still the same. They carry too much of the first emptiness in them. They're not far enough removed from me to be spared that oldest pain. What to do? What to do? I must make again. Please, please let this time be different.

But now Saithaan took umbrage at what was coming to pass. Firstborn and pride of Brahm. But there is something to be said for pride. And Saithaan was more than starlight and white flame. He was a place for Brahm's loneliness and suffering to hide. A place in which to bury a lost god's pain. And now it stirred in Brahm's first child. He kept it quiet and hoped his father would cease needless creation and be content.

But it would not be, for Brahm continued to craft and shape.

And thus, another suffering took root within Brahm's firstborn. A pain that would be shared with all and all would come to lament.

Brahm took no note of this as he began a new making. He pulled from what he had made before; strands from stars, hair from gods, and the breath of the Sithre. Pieces just far enough away from himself that might come to shape something else. And for the first time, he pushed a different part of himself into creation—his passion and pride.

And so came to life what we now call the Shaen. Noble, graceful, and without flaw. Brahm handed them stewardship of our world, to watch over its stone and tide. And they took to it with a will and shaped like their creator all they saw. They raised the first cities, using knowings now unknown. Creating things that left Brahm in awe.

Oh, how they shape and make. Look at them. They need a hand to guide them. They create and fill to their want. Wild and free, making and shaping all reality.

They built kingdoms of their own under the dark and in starlight. And they went on to continue shaping and mastering all things within sight. The Shaen, perfect in form and mind, sought to create a new paradise for their kind.

And in doing so, with the passing of time, they forgot the divine. To all things Brahm and holy, the Shaen chose to grow sudden blind.

They've forgotten me, and oh so fast. But, why? Did I not give them enough? Do they not have any warmth and flame left in their souls for me? Is . . . something still wrong?

A new ache formed in Brahm's heart, but this time he would not let it overtake him—no. He would find another form of life to sow. His need to create had first come from the pain of a god left lonely. But that pursuit came only to breed more of the same. So now he turned to what remained only. A new drive to create birthed of joy, to see what next could be wrought from his mind and heavenly flame.

Too much my pain has filled my makings. This time I give something else for the taking. What joy I felt at the first star, what more I saw when I made this world, and oh, the bliss I felt when I birthed my son.

So Brahm bled excitement and joy, letting his voice now carry in his creator's craft. He did not seek to make a noble and perfect thing. But something humble—free-caring—and wild, and upon doing so, Brahm laughed. The first time that sound had been heard. A noise of triumph, for he had birthed something so unlike all that had come before.

"What did he make?" Nisha's voice jarred me in a way that I still struggle to explain. If you've ever heard a masterful melody played over strings, her question was the irreverent twang of a slipped finger. Imagine that, and you'll have an understanding of how I felt.

I cleared my throat and flashed her a look, not quite a glare, owing that I didn't want to put her on edge. She met my eyes and settled so I could get back into the performance.

The first people to walk this world of beasts and Shaen. A group forgotten in name and look, of stories no longer kept in any book. But they had a gift their own to share and bring. A gift that shone and changed things for Brahm above. They came to this world with a new magic—to sing. Twisting words and breath like none before. These people sang with a trace of Brahm's voice and something hidden—something more. They lived in the world he gave them, not shying away like the Shaen. They danced in the cold under moon and starlight, content, and remembering Brahm.

"Do you hear that, my children? Listen? Look at what they make, what sounds and songs they sing and shape? Oh, they create something I could never think of. Oh, how beautiful." *It hurts again, but this is a new kind I do not know. I'm moved to weep but no longer lonely. Oh, how beautiful.*

And all was well for the first time, or so Brahm had thought.

For his firstborn, Saithaan, was still anger fraught.

And his father's undying love and attention he still wholly sought.

Brahm turned to shaping now still from bliss. Knowing now he could make without ever feeling things amiss. Then came the second people to ever be. Those who would change things for folks for eternity.

The Ruma. Born next, under black, they struggled long and hard, keeping far from their elders first. They wandered, restless like Brahm once had done in the dark, holding to the traveler's thirst. And Brahm ached for them, but would not reach out with another gift, knowing he'd done enough.

Oh, how lost these ones are. Forced to travel and remember my long trek along the dark. But, I see something in them. Something that reminds me of a distant flame I once felt. Show me. Please. I beg you. Tell me I did not err again. Please, do not falter now. Show me. Please. He waited—watched, to see what the Ruma could and would bring as all creations before had done.

And they did, in their agitation and need for warmth, make something—hard won.

They toiled and tinkered, discontent, until one day they kindled a spark—fire-spun.

Much like Brahm had birthed a flame and by flame.

The Ruma had sought warmth and fire, and thus brought about the same.

For this, Brahm rejoiced, ready to levy another gift. "Look! Look!" he exclaimed with a child's joy. "Without one whit of shaping to their name, they sparked their own fires—they made their own flame!" *I must reward them.*

And so it was done.

One last treasure.

Brahm blew a great breath, and birthed for them, our sun.

And so the Ruma traveled like Brahm, far and wide. Passing time day and night with stories of all things; fire, beasts, stone, and tide. Stories, another gift they gave. The telling of tales we'd all came to crave. By paths in light, and nights by fireside, the Ruma would tell tales so long as those listening would abide.

And time passed, and more people came to be. Lesser folk, still children the same, all coming from that first flitting flame. The first forgotten, second passed to mystery, but now we're here—you and me—having come from those who fill history.

But for this time, Saithaan sat unwell. His pain and anger he could not quell.

And time had gone on long enough. He moved to act, and confronted his father before all the gods. "Look at what you've wrought, Father. I curse these creations and hollow beings you've made. These tired things made for a desperate being's loneliness. These empty sacks made to fill a greater void. Were we not enough? Are we not now!? Does Brahm not have care and love for his first children? What are we to you, Father? What am I? What. Am. I?"

This question struck at the heart of Brahm in a way he didn't think he could be hurt. *Oh, but what is this now? This, this pain fills my chest too much. The bands of my fire are waning. They hurt. They feel weak and cold. Please, make this pain go away. What can I do? What can I say?*

And so father and son were left at bitter odds.

Only to worsen as Saithaan made the first blow, striking at Brahm's most favorite creation, in an act of hatred's first show. Saithaan pulled of himself like his father had taught, and birthed beings best left unwrought. And with them he cursed the first humans born of Brahm. Hated, hunted, to know no peace. To know a toil and a pain, like he had felt—one that would never cease.

"Curse you and your makings, Father. I'll have them suffer by my hand or the hands of men to come. To be hated for nothing more than what they are, just as you've come to detest us for being what you made us—made me. Am I not enough? Was I ever?"

Oh, but no. Please, do not do this. They've done no harm and do not deserve your wrath. Spare them—no!

And Brahm in anguish and in panic struck back at his first son, tarnishing him in the vein of what he had done. "Do not harm them! For every dark thing you do I'll do unto you. For every step you take away from my light, I'll dim your fires—your very sight!"

And so Brahm did. He dimmed Saithaan's flame, now dark as black, leaving him something broken—hollow—now first flame's shadow. He threw down his once-shining son, but knew it would not be enough. Saithaan would work and twist things he best knew, and wring new horrors on this world so long as he could do.

So Brahm tore in anger and in fear at his eldest son, casting the pieces to parts unshown. And in this pain and sorrow, so did Brahm leave, and left the world to a fate unknown.

It hurts too much to be here and see all things from a place so high. Please, let me find somewhere to be alone again—somewhere to hide. Let me be lost and travel once again. Let me be a wanderer now and then. Let me go down low and walk among them.

"Remember me, Children. Remember what I wished to do. To make and shape. What creations to sow. The purpose of it all. Tend to them. Care for them. And if you can find it in your hearts, much like I wished to do, love them. I'm leaving now. Do not look for me for you will not ever find me. Remember what I've said. Remember for what I've sacrificed and I've bled."

The other gods took hold in their father's absence, tasking the Sithre to war with Saithaan's makings. This sent our world through many ages of pain to mirror Brahm's. Endless rises and as many breakings. But, eventually, peace was done—hard fought and won. And all things could rejoice.

And that is the story from which all creation came from and of which it sings.

That is the story of Brahm and the making of all things.

Nisha sat wide-eyed, rocking in place. She exhaled once before throwing her arms around me. "Thank you, Ari. That was . . . beautiful."

I felt my cheeks color. Had she noted the flush? I couldn't tell. So I quickly broke off a piece of bread, dabbing it in stew to stuff into my mouth. I could easily pass the coloring of my cheeks as consequence of the hot meal and the spices within.

After all, I *was* a performer. Sort of. Even if Khalim hadn't ever let me onstage, I knew it to be true. The rest of the night passed like that: Nisha and I sitting together, talking of everything two children could but for the moment that had just gone by. Eventually, we slept.

There is a quiet comfort in spending time with someone you care for without a word said. It's one of my fonder memories. A night where, even after a touch of abuse, I had the company of a friend and a good story.

Tales of Brahm and his grandeur had always inspired me, helped me wash away aches and pains. They held all the possibility of changing your world with but a binding and breath of your own. All it took was an effort of will, and you could reshape reality, your life. Be the hero. To be free of loneliness and lay claim to the powers of old tales. And from the stories, power paved the way to freedom.

Little did I know it then, but I had set myself up to chase the footsteps of a god.

And in doing so, become something of one myself, following the life and many lies and legends of Brahm.

We are all worse off for that, I fear.

ELEVEN

A Promise of Magic

I woke the next morning to find Nisha gone almost as cleanly as if she'd never been there. No trace remained of the sack she'd fashioned, nor the bowl of food. Nisha always came in the night, much like a dream, and would leave all the same. It left some things lacking as far as friendship went, but it did nothing to diminish how fondly I felt of her. My life wasn't filled with an overabundance of people I could call friends.

I cleared my thoughts and sat up, focusing on the morning ahead. Khalim had an important meeting today. One with a patron that would lead many more heads passing through our doors. All of which meant more coin.

More importantly, it meant Khalim would be working on a story to tell. One of his best, if not something new altogether. That stirred me more than anything.

It meant rehearsals.

A chance to work beyond the understage. Anything done for the first time by our troupe always needed more hands than Khalim could fetch. People tried different roles, sometimes working multiple. And sometimes the little boy relegated to a space beneath the happenings got his chance to be in a play.

I smiled to myself and clambered down my rickety bed, rushing over to a tin basin in one corner. What morning rays trickled in through the windows were pale, muted, and filled with hanging particulates. The soft light brought out the many imperfections lining the metal bin's surface.

I bent over the basin, inspecting the quality of the water inside. The level had dropped, but it still remained clean enough for my use. I grabbed a wadded knotting of fabric I kept close by. In truth, it was nothing more than once-clean strips of clothing that I'd fashioned into a scrubber. I didn't have much of a soap cake—a thing more of thinly scraped shavings squeezed tight together into a lumpy ball.

Khalim had argued I didn't need one. A night's talk with him was all it took to convince him otherwise.

I learned to sharpen my tongue at an early age. Though, last night had proved some days it could benefit from a bit of blunting.

What passed for my clothes didn't sit well on my body, hanging off me like they'd been sized for someone twice as large. It took little effort to slip out of them and lather the scrubber properly. I let the minutes pass in daydream, thinking over the many legends and tales I'd learned over the years under Khalim. I didn't know which he'd go for in the performance, but brushing up on them before would only help me in making it onto the stage. Even if I couldn't play a role, he could let me be the narrator.

Anything would have been better than working the understage.

I'd scoured myself till the light and warm wood tones of my skin flushed a bit, edging near rawness. My face and hair followed; working through the thick strands of locks, matted in places, brought about sharp pains along my scalp that showed off just how quick my tongue could be when no one was around to listen.

Never underestimate the creativity in profanity a child can come up with when under pain and duress. They're better at it than most adults. Believe me.

I cleaned myself best I could, ensuring as little grime and filth as possible made it back into my basin before turning to the matter of my clothing. With as thin and frail as my clothes were, scrubbing them harshly could turn the smaller holes into places to easily fit my head. The fragility of what little I owned made the cleaning process laborious. I took slow, long, gentle strokes, almost like petting an anxious dog. In time, I managed to make my clothes into a barely presentable and uniform gray.

The shame of the matter is that they had originally been white.

Content that I looked more young boy than a conglomeration of soot and sweat, I fetched the nearby wrappings I stored whenever excess bits of frippery came my way.

They were stretches of fabric far higher in quality than what I normally could come by, sometimes the remainders of costumes, other times the leave-behinds of the few moderately wealthy attendees. I held on to them whenever I needed to go above. They served as the closest thing to shoes once properly wrapped around my feet, and the quality of the material ensured they wouldn't tear easy if I were careful. Nor would they allow a bad day's heat to scorch my soles.

If you've never been poor, I can't explain to you the necessity of using what few bits of extravagance make their way to you for something as trivial as shoes. But in the life of one of the casteless, you make do with what you're given. A performer plays all roles with nothing but wit and wiles and charm if need be.

So, I straightened my back, ran my fingers through my hair one last time, and marched my way out of the understage.

The theater proper never ceased to steal my breath and gaze. In hindsight, it wasn't anything beyond a gaudy overcoat atop a poorly kept building. But when you've lived most of your life underground with no real furnishings, even a room of fool's gold is as good as the real thing.

Sullied weren't normally allowed to purchase property, but Khalim had managed to win the place in a high-stakes game of samtharaj, the game of kings and beggars alike. The one true thing he owned. And I'd heard him once say he'd die before losing it.

Nine rows of wooden benches faced the stage, each padded with rags sewn into the cushions at Khalim's command to offer better comfort. Excess fabric had been fitted at the ends in swooping arcs with gold thread embroidery to form flowers.

It didn't matter that it cost from tin chips to copper rounds to see us work. Appearances oft sell a thing more than the thing itself.

The stone walls had been lined with poor man's wallpaper. A mixture of wood and paper pulp set to harden over the rock until it gave a softer, smoother look. It made it easier to paint over as well.

Two balconies overlooked it all. The lower of the two had a wall painted in a mud brown that would have been unappealing to the eye had Khalim not had a portion above it painted in gold. The top row of the upper balcony stood nearly eighty feet from the floor, leaving patrons able to brush the ceiling with their fingertips should they wish.

As far as I was concerned, I'd walked into a palace. One where I'd be a king in my own right in the years to come.

The stage itself was a simple thing: a solid landing of oiled wood, catching the warmth and subtle brightness of the morning light a damn sight better than anything the understage had to offer.

"Ari?"

I spun fast enough to almost leave my loose-fitting shirt still facing the way I'd turned from.

She moved silently, half due to her bare feet, the rest a mixture of natural grace and hard-earned skill from years of performing. Kauri could have been lifted from the pages of the greatest epics—stories of bewitching beauties and princesses. She had a dancer's build and what I imagined was a Shaen's supernatural grace.

A woman in the middling years of her third decade, Kauri carried herself with the quiet confidence of someone twice her age. She earned that, bought and paid for with all she had to put up with of life in the Sullied caste. Not to mention being one of the few women of low birth to take a role in the performer's trade.

She had high cheekbones that were even more noticeable when she smiled. Her eyes reminded me of a cat's, sharp and bright; a shade of light brown, they were almost golden under the light at times. Her hair fell to her shoulders in loose ringlets of dark brown threaded with hints of warm mahogany.

"Kauri-*dishi*, I didn't hear you." I worked to slow my quickened breathing, not wanting to appear out of sorts. I knew I shouldn't have been up near the stage without Khalim's permission, but if anyone would have forgiven it, it would have been her. Kauri and I had developed a relationship like overprotective sister and younger brother.

She pursed her lips, likely already aware of what went through my mind. "You weren't supposed to hear me, Ari. Why are you up here? You know what today is. Khalim will be angry if he sees you about."

I opened my mouth to spin up an excuse but she waved me off.

"No, don't talk. You'll come up with something to get the both of us in trouble."

She ran a hand over her sari of pale gold and earthy brown, smoothing the fabric. Her gaze fell past me to the planks of the stage. A smile crept across her lips, and she bent a little at the waist to bring her face closer to mine. "You want to find a way to be here and listen in on Khalim's meeting without him paying you any mind?"

I nodded with the enthusiasm only a small boy could manage.

"Fetch a bucket and some rags. Get the wood oil."

My heart sank. I knew where she was going with this.

She must have noticed the expression on my face. "Oh, don't be like that. If you pout, your face will get stuck that way."

I scowled.

"Even worse. Don't go through life scowling or no woman will look even sideways at you."

I held the expression, drawing an exasperated sigh out of her.

"It'll put you in Khalim's good graces to see you taking care of the stage, and he won't be able to say anything to you about it while meeting with whomever he's supposed to. You think it will look good to tell you off while you're just tending to the theater?"

She had a point, but telling a young man to do drudge work and be grateful about it was one of the few ways to bring out the stubborn side of them. Stubborn . . . -er sides. Kauri balled her hands and placed them on her hips, shifting her weight and managing to shoot me a look down her nose that could have made her look even taller. "Ari . . ."

I shied away from the look and muttered something unintelligible under my breath.

She bent a little lower, cupping a hand to an ear. "What was that?" Her voice came out with the sort of sweetness that left you knowing there wasn't a drop of honey behind it, but sour cider.

I found myself stiffening my back and standing straighter regardless. "I always take care of the theater, Kauri. Always. That's *all* I do." I jabbed a finger toward the ground. "Who do you think runs everything?"

She blinked, opening her mouth to speak.

I didn't give her the chance, much like she'd done to me earlier. "I'm the one breathing in smoke so it can puff and fill the stage up here. You don't choke on it. I'm the one scraping my palms raw pulling on ropes and turning hot wheels and shoveling filth. Not you. You get to perform, Kauri. You get to be the heroine, the princess, the . . . the everything!"

I may as well have run a rod through her spine by the way she snapped straight. In retrospect, I knew I shouldn't have said those things. But hindsight is something well beyond the reach of an angry young man. Shame isn't though, and it flooded me. Only my stubbornness kept it from showing on my face.

I may not have been allowed to perform, but I'd watched enough, studied enough. I knew how to control myself and let others see what I needed them to.

She licked her lips before looking back over her shoulder like she expected Khalim to walk out any moment and chastise the pair of us. Some of the rigidness left her and she leaned forward again, resting both of her hands on my shoulders. She flashed me a smile under which men twice my age would have melted, but stubborn boys seldom shift for anything short of what they want.

I wish I could say I've changed much in that regard. It would be a lie.

"Ari, I won't be able to protect you if you get caught by Khalim out here today. But, if you trust me, maybe I can speak to him about the next time we do *Kuhl Ki Supnay,* hm?"

Some of the anger left me and I tilted my head, unsure of what to make of her offer.

"Davhim is getting older. Walking around on his knees isn't as easy as it once was, and besides, he's tired of playing the role of a little boy. No matter if he grows up to be an adventuring man, swinging swords and riding horses far and wide. That fun isn't enough to make an old man's joints stop hurting. But where else would we find someone who could play a lively young man?"

She pursed her lips again and frowned. Kauri went as far as putting a hand to her brow and turning a wide look to the empty seats of the theater.

My eyes widened. A chance to play a role of importance in *Dreams of Tomorrow.* The opportunity to be onstage. My heart soared, and in the face of the offer, I could stomach another few hours of dirty work. "I just washed myself, though." I managed a weak sniffle and made my eyes wide.

She swatted one of my arms. "No, don't try that on me. But . . . I'll also talk to Khalim about seeing you get a proper bath *after* you tend to the stage."

I sighed. It had been worth a try.

Kauri turned to leave. "I have to pick up a few things from the Soft Quarter for tonight's drama. I won't be back till evening." She gave me a look that could have peeled chips of wood from the stage. "Do *not* cause any trouble. Don't try to get back at Makham. We all heard what happened."

I put a hand over my heart and smiled.

Kauri didn't return the grin. "Ari . . ."

"I promise I won't."

Still no smile.

I puffed out a heavy breath. "I won't. I swear it. Brahm and his bloody ashes, I swear it, fine?"

She finally relented. "Good enough." Kauri wrapped me in a tight hug and placed a kiss on my forehead, one I quickly wiped away. "You know, many men would have paid a great deal for just one touch from me."

"Well, then find one of them while you're out in the Soft Quarter and make a pretty iron bunt for your trouble." I rubbed the spot she'd kissed as I pulled away from her.

She rolled her eyes and placed a hand over her chest. "*I*, little Ari, am worth silver doles. Don't you forget that or think one bit less, brat."

I stuck my tongue out at her. "Harlot."

She matched my gesture. "Imp."

We traded glares before breaking into a chorus of light laughter. Kauri ruffled my hair once and walked away, leaving me to the task of cleaning the stage.

I fetched a bucket and filled it with water, falling to my knees to begin at one end of the wooden platform. Time slipped away from the monotony of my motions.

I don't know if you've ever had to scrub an entire stage before, but it's work that doesn't differentiate between young or old, fit or feeble. It will tax you and take its due no matter what.

My knees and ankles ached by the time I'd reached the middle of the platform. The constant effort along with the exposure to water had turned my hands and fingers soft and raw.

The drum of thunder sounded overhead, reverberating twice as loud in the empty cavernous room of the stage. Seconds later, the steady hammering of heavy rain filled my ears.

Wonderful. I hadn't quite learned the lesson yet as a child, but life is filled with storms. The number never changes. It will rain as hard and often as it's wont to do. The only thing we can change is whether or not we will learn to sing in the rain. For it will rain all the same.

I never did learn how to sing.

The storm intensified in a matter of minutes, beating against the roof like it intended to drench the stage.

Movement at the far end of the room caught my eye. Khalim entered the theater with three men in tow, none of them here for performers' business.

One of the men to Khalim's right had a build like a Saluki, a thin hunting hound, all gaunt and bones with his plain clothes hanging off him. His face must have been pulled at birth, a long and pointed thing furthering his dog-like appearance. He wore his dark hair loose, hanging to his shoulders and stranded through with bands of muddy red.

Thena. A cheap dye used to cover prematurely graying hairs.

The man at Khalim's other side must have eaten double the shares his slender friend had chosen to forgo in life. He stood as wide and portly as several men, clean shaven and without a wisp of hair atop his oily scalp. The generous and blubberous mass of his face almost obscured his eyes, making them appear all the beadier in comparison. He wore an open vest, too small for his frame, showcasing a belly riddled in puckered scars and swirling marks of ink. His pants had been fashioned from canvas, loose and billowing.

But the man at the rear of the group held my attention longest. He had a neatly trimmed and full beard of coal, his mustache noticeably thicker and curled at the ends. His skin was the color of sand under the sun—light for this part of the world. He had the solid build of someone no stranger to hard work, but still ate well enough to not be only lean slabs of muscle.

He had dressed in an expensive silk shirt of rich lavender and pants the color of cloudless morning skies. A curved dagger sat fastened at his waist. The weapon's hilt had been layered in ornate brass and silver with a single striking ruby at its base.

His eyes struck me hardest. They reminded me of bright citrine, almost as if the man were sick. Far too much yellow and not close to enough brown in them. A wolf of a man if I ever saw one. The stranger took in the room with a wide and sweeping look, stopping when he caught me staring.

A weight of bricks hit me and filled my stomach. I turned my gaze down to the wooden planks and resumed scrubbing with renewed vigor.

Whatever the group discussed, they were too far out of earshot for me to catch anything. But their voices loudened by the passing second. They were drawing nearer.

"And what would I get out of it, Khalim?"

I chanced a look to see who had spoken.

The man with the yellow eyes.

Khalim bucked under the question, shying away from the man's look as if afraid of what he'd find in his eyes. "Reputation, for one."

The man with the yellow eyes laughed, the pair at his side joining in. "I have one. A good one at that."

Khalim gave the man a wan smile. "We're not thinking of the same sort of good here, Koli-*eiyah*. You mean you have a strong reputation. I hope to make you one where you're well thought of too, not just feared."

Koli. The man who ran one of the largest thuggee bands in the quarter. The one who had Nisha as one of his little thieves . . . and beat her—made her life a living hell where she feared even the touch of friends.

Something hot and ugly stirred inside me. A thing of embers and writhing snakes, pressing against my stomach. My gums ached from how hard I gritted my teeth.

I was young, lean, and more than any of that, fast and agile. I could cross the stage quick enough. Making it over to the man wouldn't be so hard. But no. It'd be too obvious.

But I'd watched many of the best performers around. I could play the harmless child, get close, grab the dagger and—

The weight returned. Koli and I locked eyes. I hadn't been aware I'd been glaring at him. In that instant, I understood a part of him I wish to this day I could forget.

Koli reveled in what he did. He enjoyed the power he wielded and lorded over others. He liked the thuggery and butchery he was party to, and the idea people would dance to his tune.

I don't know what he saw in me in that moment, but he smiled. It was a thing of all teeth and anticipation. Something reserved for a hungry wolf about to get its meal.

If Khalim caught our heated stare, he gave no sign that he had. He went on as if Koli had never broken eye contact with him. "Being a patron here, Koli-*eiyah,* will soften your image to many."

"I don't need to appear soft, Khalim-*sahm*." Koli clapped a hand to the theater runner's shoulder, squeezing it hard. "I need to be paid. I need to be respected—feared. And, if some people happen to like me through all of that, that's fine. Otherwise—" He waved a hand in the air as if to banish the thought and conversation.

Sweat beaded along the back of Khalim's head. "The theater can do a lot more than just offer you a better name. Money flows through here. Not much, true, but that could change. It's a big building with lots of room for people. And it can surely be used for other things as well as dramas, no?"

His words brought me up short, my arms stopping in the motion of scrubbing.

I wasn't as wise to the ways and workings of the world as I am today, and so I missed the greater implication in Khalim's offer. If I had known then, I might have protested, and things would be different.

Koli dragged an index finger along the length of his mustache, visibly musing over the suggestion. His mouth spread into a carnivorous smile and he extended a hand. "I made a mistake earlier, Khalim-*sahm*. This place *could* use a good patron. And maybe a name for me helping the arts wouldn't be so bad, hm? People like drama. Good. I'll give what I can . . . and you'll remember this when I come to call, hm?"

I watched the muscles along Khalim's neck to shoulders tense. His body stiffened and he managed a jerky incline of the head that I took as silent acceptance.

Koli kept the hungry expression on his face and turned to move as another figure walked into view at the far end of the room.

He wore loose and flowing robes so bright a red it was as if they'd been freshly dyed in blood. A thin veneer of road dust and grime clung to their folds but did nothing to dull the color. The man could have been Khalim's senior by a decade. More iron and chalk to his hair in places than black. He wore it long and free, flowing down past his shoulders. His beard had been cut short and tight to the face, showing not a hint of silver throughout. Despite his age, he stood tall and straight as if the years hadn't taken their toll on him.

I caught sight of the head of a staff protruding from behind his back, likely fastened in place. It could have been a walking stick. Its tip looked to be fashioned of dark stone and charred wood compressed tightly together.

He had a broad face, but not carrying any of the weight you'd expect in a man of his age. His skin had been weathered by time, but that was the worst of it. He looked like he'd been carved out of dark clay and left to harden.

Khalim and Koli regarded him, trading quiet looks between themselves.

The stranger took them both in as well before settling his attention on Khalim. "Are you the man who—" He broke off, gesturing at the surroundings.

Khalim nodded. "I am. This is my theater and I put on the finest dramas and plays in Abhar."

While it was true in terms of quality, the noble and wealthy would be hard-pressed to agree. Our caste alone prevented us from being regarded even as good, not to say anything of the best. Beyond that, the influential liked who they did based on the gossip and hearsay of others in their circle. It was a long line from us to the respectable, and our skills be damned.

The robed visitor grunted more to himself than the men around him. "I've heard your reputation for being willing to put on dramas and plays outside the norm. The ones temples and priests frown upon."

Khalim shrugged. "We read the day and times like anyone else. When we can get away with being a bit more creative, we do. I'll not lie about it. I like to take my chances and push when I can. Being Sullied has its advantages at times. We're as low as can be. Means there's already so low an opinion of me that can be had." Khalim's voice carried no trace of bitterness. He spoke a long-known and accepted truth, and one he could live with.

"I can work with that, which brings me to why I'm here. Your name has been spreading through all the right circles. If it weren't for your caste, you'd be playing for little lords and ladies. All of which makes me believe you might be the perfect person to help me get to the bottom of a mystery plaguing me." He paused, chewing over what to say next.

"Do you know what these are?" The stranger pointed to a series of braided strings looping around one of his shoulders. Each set of cords were a different color. A length of twisted white, a coiling band of yellow, and the third seemed to be a sort of muddled gray almost like it had been a different shade before but was now washed out.

Khalim nodded. "I do. But it doesn't explain why you're here."

"I'm looking for a story. One I hope you might know, and if you don't, I hope you'll help me uncover it. To that end, I'd be willing to place myself at your service for the time it takes me to dig to the bottom of this. I can add a great deal to your performances. Fire, smoke—"

Khalim waved him off. "I have something for that already. Well, someone." He gestured with a tilt of his head toward me. "Though, my help has a problem doing as he's told." Khalim turned fully, giving me a look that made it clear we'd have a long talk later about why I was up above the understage today.

I forced a smile across my face I hoped came off as innocent and charming.

Khalim's mouth pressed into a frown that told me I still needed to work on my acting.

The stranger gently laid a hand on Khalim's arm, bringing the theater owner's attention back to him. "I'm not talking about whatever tricks and stagecraft the boy can conjure. I'm talking about what you know a man like me is capable of."

A moment of silence passed between all parties, and I found myself inching closer to the edge of the stage to hear things better.

The pause was the kind in the great plays. One where you knew something big would come at the end of it—a secret, a twist, the sort that would draw the breath from you.

And I wanted to be privy to it. Call it the curiosity of a young boy, though I've not let go of the habit, or simply a human need for wanting to know, but I had to see what came next.

And I'll never forget it.

Koli reached out and grabbed the stranger's collar, shoving him toward his massive henchman. "Take this idiot away and let me finish my business with Khalim in quiet. I don't want or need other ears around." He turned to face Khalim. "We were discussing something private and I mean to finish my business." Koli pulled the dagger from his belt while his large thug worked to restrain the newcomer.

I couldn't hear what the robed man said next, his eyes narrowing as he spoke in a tone so soft only the man handling him seemed to hear him.

The wide-bellied brute turned the stranger around and bent to bring his face closer to the visitor's. He gave him a frog-like smile, wide-lipped and flabby.

The robed man's mouth moved silently and he raised a hand.

A spark. A wisp of orange thread kindled in his palm.

He spoke again.

The thread of light snapped and crackled almost as if it would wink out of existence, but something kept it flickering. It burst to life as flames large as the thug's head, dancing and threatening to grow out of the stranger's open hand.

All eyes turned and fixed on the sight.

Koli's dagger came up toward the man in red with fire in his hand, but the weapon shook visibly in his grip.

"Touch me again, and I'll bring a flame hotter than this to life inside you, searing you bone and bracken. Make any move toward me"—the man in red looked over his shoulder at Koli—"and I'll bring the stones of this entire building down on you. You'll be far lower in reputation and stature when I'm done." He turned to Koli's thin, rakish henchman and raised a hand overhead as if trying to grab a piece of the ceiling. He spoke under his breath again.

Stone shook. Dust and debris flitted down, sparkling as they hung in rogue beams of morning light.

"Begone!" The stranger's voice now echoed like it came from hundreds of men at once all in a cavern. When the stone shook again, I couldn't tell if it was under the weight of his inhuman baritone, or whatever he had done with his hand earlier. "Go, *guhli-wallah*, gutter trash." He gestured at the door Koli had come in from. "Take your dogs with you and go. If you don't, I'll lay such suffering on you that you will come to fear the merest whisper about binders." He leaned closer to Koli, the flame in his other hand still burning bright. "Go."

Koli and his trio needed no further encouragement. The thugs turned and ran.

And just like that, the stone of the theater settled. The fire died, and the robed man's posture weakened like he'd run for days on end without food.

Khalim moved to his side to support him. "Do you know what you've done—cost me?"

The stranger gave him a weary and lopsided grin. "Saved you from a troublesome man who could come back to bother you later. Trust me, I've met his sort."

Khalim grabbed hold of the binder, shaking him. "I *needed* that money. We did!" He waved a hand at the theater. "I wouldn't be dealing with the likes of Koli unless I had to."

"I'll do what I can to ease the loss."

Khalim stepped closer to the binder, bringing his nose a hair's breadth from the other man's. His eyes narrowed, and I could see the muscles along Khalim's neck tensing. "You don't have much of a choice now, binder. Welcome to my theater. Don't hurt my family. Don't tarnish my reputation. And live up to your name and trade, we will be fine, *ji-ah*?" This wasn't an offer. Khalim had lost his deal with Koli, and now made it clear to the stranger that he'd been conscripted into service. To hopefully offset the loss.

The binder extended a hand, shaking Khalim's. "*Ji.* I am Mahrab."

"Khalim." My friend and caretaker pulled away from the binder's grip. "I'm going to see if I can still smooth things over with him. Don't make trouble while I'm gone. I'll settle where you'll sleep and your duties when I get back." He turned and left in the direction Koli had gone.

The rag had gone limp in my hand, falling free of my grip a second later.

Magic. Real magic. The sort done in the stories. The kind in the tales I'd heard in the theater. Binders. Scholar magicians who could mold the world around them to do great and terrible things.

I watched Mahrab, slack-jawed, unsure what to say now that a piece of real story stood before me.

He must have known what went through my mind because he approached me. "Are you one of his, then?"

I nodded, still unable to find my words.

"What's your name?"

"Ari."

"Ari, hm?" His mouth moved like he was almost tasting my name. A moment later, he gave me his thoughts on it. "It's a good name." He smiled, holding out a hand. "I'm Mahrab."

I leapt toward him, taking his hand in the both of mine and shaking it harder than necessary.

He didn't pull away from my overly enthusiastic grip, choosing instead to look around the stage. "And you help Khalim-*sahm* around here, huh? You're his . . . magic, as he put it?"

I nodded. "I work the understage, though, I'm hoping one day he'll let me star and perform."

"Is that the height of your ambition? To be a performer? That's all there is written for Ari and his story?"

I paused. The question robbed me of my excitement, but it came crashing back an instant later as I considered something. He had birthed a flame in his hand. Called fire. Like Brahm. "You did magic."

"I did."

"Like out of the stories."

Mahrab lowered his head in what could have been a yes.

I took a breath, knowing that I didn't have the right to ask what I was about to. But I had a child's fearlessness and desire. A terrible combination at times.

And I knew what I really wanted in life. To birth my own flame. To understand fire and shape it the way it once had been eons ago. I didn't want to play in a story. I wanted to be the story. A legend in my own right.

A child's ambition knows no bounds. And a man or woman who holds to that can go on to do great or horrible things.

"Will you teach me?"

Sometimes a single word can be the most dangerous of all. And he said it.

"Yes."

It was as simple as that.

Looking back, I don't think Mahrab knew what I'd come to be and do with his teachings.

After all, I was only a child.

TWELVE

Lessons and Truths

Mahrab was everything a young boy could have wanted in a teacher. Patience came as naturally to him as breathing. He appreciated curiosity, and rewarded it.

He had energy to spare and a mind strong enough to dedicate to the rigors of dealing with me as his student.

Most of all, I remember his eyes and his voice. The first were like pieces of jade worn until nothing but a tired gray remained with the slightest tinge of green to serve as a reminder of what had been there once before.

His voice resonated strong and clear. He had a commanding air like he'd taught more than just young boys in the mystic arts. He could have led an army. But his gaze and baritone were never without a measure of kindness.

"You're asking the wrong questions, Ari." Mahrab reached into the folds of his robes and plucked free a strand of silver that could have come from his own hair.

I squinted at it, then him, waiting for him to explain.

"You're wondering how I called the fire. You should be asking yourself how I kept it burning. The first is a trick. The second is where magic comes in." He pursed his lips and fixed me with a stare. "A binding, at any rate."

The way he'd said it made it clear he wanted me to ask the obvious question. So I did. "Is there a difference?"

He held up a finger. "A fundamental one. We know how bindings work, at least." Mahrab gave me a toothy grin that I flashed back. "There are ten bindings all men must know. Man has crafted, discovered, and lost more to time than we'll ever know, but the ten are the roots of every binder, even should you fail to master them. In fact, few ever do master more than one, but you need to know how to apply them."

Ten bindings. Ten whole ways to shape the world around me like Brahm had.

"What are they?" I leaned forward, not caring if my knees scuffed against the hard and unforgiving floor of the understage.

He waggled a finger. "You don't climb a tree from the top, Ari. Listen. Be patient."

I huffed a breath of irritation.

"You'll have to work on that." His mouth twitched at one corner like he wanted to laugh. "Let's start with the binding I did with the fire, hm?" He placed the strand of fine silver into one palm. "This is really a piece of wire. Do you know what suthin is?"

I shook my head.

"It's a metal found up north in the mountains, near the Ashram in Uppar Radesh. When the metal is refined and purified from other sediment, it becomes volatile when mixed with the proper amounts of salt and water." He folded his hand over the piece of wire. "I came to you in the middle of a storm. I had enough water to set this afire, and the salt I had on me."

Then I understood. "So, the metal made the spark?"

He nodded. "It did. But I kept the fire alight. That's where the binding came in. What you need to understand is that binders cannot create things like fire, wind, water, and earth. We can manipulate them. But we cannot birth them."

"Brahm did!"

He gave me a level look. "Technically, if the stories are to be believed, he was already born of fire. He pulled it from himself. But, I'll concede that he went about creating a great many things from nothing. But neither of us are him. Unless you've been keeping a secret from me?"

I rolled my eyes at that.

The silver thread sparked in his hand and Mahrab's face went tight with concentration. "Ahl." The spark rose from his palm by a hair's breadth, continuing to rise. "Ahn." It froze, now bobbing in place. "Whent." He puffed a small breath that threatened to blow the flash of fire out of existence. "Ern." The sliver of light flashed, widening and billowing into a tendril of greater flame. It licked at the air and spread, soon fanning into a ball of fire I'd seen before.

It held me, mind and heart. I couldn't tear myself away from the fire and found myself lost in every burning coil as they snapped and waved.

Mahrab exhaled and the flames died, throwing me out of the reverie.

"How did you do that?" I went back over what he had said, committing the verbal commands to memory and spitting them aloud almost as fast as I could think.

Nothing happened.

"Ari." He placed both hands on my shoulders, one still hot from the binding. "This is about more than just some words you think are magic. This is about stories, about the ways the forces of the world work and understanding them on a level beyond scholars and priests. You cannot just spit a sentence and expect the universe to bend around you. You need to start at the roots of understanding."

I raised an eyebrow. "And where are those?"

Mahrab reached back into the folds of his robes and pulled out a pair of identical stones. He placed one in each of my hands. "Hold these."

I blinked, staring at the rocks. "And then what?"

"Keep holding them."

". . . Until?"

His face remained calm and impassive as the rocks in my hand, but his eyes sparked with subdued amusement. "Until I tell you to stop."

I frowned as Mahrab got up to leave. "Wait, you're not going to sit here and teach me while I do this?"

"I have some research to do with Khalim and—"

"I can help!"

Mahrab shook his head. "You can . . . by sitting there and holding your rocks until I say you're ready to move on."

It wasn't the answer I wanted. And, as you can imagine, being told to hold a pair of stones wasn't what I had in mind for learning magic. I wanted to call fire. To journey far and wide and meet the Shaen, to walk among the Sithre. But no.

The truth of what I wanted sat within rocks.

I stared at the stones until I lost track of time and their color blurred my thoughts. Frustration soon left me and emptiness took its place.

If I said days passed this way, it would be the hyperbole of youth. But it would be fair to say hours most certainly went by with me rooted in place until I began to question if I still had an ass or it had been flattened down from sitting.

"What are you thinking about?" Mahrab's voice shook me out of my lulled state.

I nearly fumbled the rocks as I snapped my eyes open. "Brahm's tits, you scared me!"

Mahrab's mouth twisted into a wry smile. "Of all the things in the wide universe to be thinking of, I certainly hope my first student isn't spending his time in training thinking of Brahm's tits." The hint of chagrin vanished and he stared at me like he'd caught me doing something reprehensible.

I held his look, uncertain as what to say.

His composure broke a second later, and he threw his head back in laughter.

I felt the stiff strings in my body loosen and I joined him. After a few moments, I found my voice and answered him. "I was thinking about stupid rocks."

"Good. That means you were paying attention to what I'd said after all. To be a binder, you must be able to clear your mind of everything else but what you wish to see."

". . . And a binder needs to see rocks?"

He swatted my arm. "Don't get clever. You're already too much of that for your own good."

I opened my mouth to protest but spotted the tightness around his mouth. I reconsidered my quick-witted response and swallowed it, knowing better than to push him in the moment.

"The bindings, Ari, require unshakeable conviction to manifest and maintain. Two things. It's not enough to perform one. You must hold it. That takes a strength of will and belief that cannot be weak. These are universal principles that can bend the foundations of the world around you. So, for now, you're going to think on rocks until your mind only sees rocks. We start small."

"But you're not telling me *how* this connects to performing the bindings, Mahrab?" I fidgeted in place, having my answer to whether I still possessed a semblance of an ass.

I did. And it hurt.

Mahrab paced around the understage, looking over everything it had to offer. He moved about until he came to one of the sticks I'd whittled clean and straight and left in a barrel. They were one of the few things I really had to play with down there, my makeshift swords when I had the energy to spar with my shadow.

That may have been a generous interpretation of what I thought I did. Flailing with a great risk of taking my own eye out would have hit closer to the truth. But truth seldom squares with what's in a child's heart.

Then again, I've found over the years there is more truth in a child's dreams than grown men and women seem to realize. More often than not, we forget these truths as we grow older and are stuck fishing for them blindly.

He looked it over, swinging it through the air. Each swing elicited a dull *fwop*. "This should work."

I looked at the stick, then him. "Work for what?"

"For students who get too far ahead of themselves they can't see what's right in front of them."

I paused, chewing over what he said. "And . . . what's in front of me?"

Mahrab came to sit a few inches from me. "Me. With a stick." He bounced it once in the palm of his hand before sending it out in a horizontal snap.

Thwap. It struck my arm. Not hard enough to cause serious harm, but enough that I would remember the sting and get the point. I rubbed the spot and gave him a glare sharper than nails.

"I don't like it when people hit me, Mahrab." He couldn't have known all I'd gone through, but I'd developed a particular hatred to being struck by anyone. My hands balled and my teeth clenched. "Don't do that."

Mahrab looked at where he'd struck me, then my face. "It bothers you a great deal, hm?"

I nodded, teeth still gritted hard enough to risk cracking a tooth.

"Good. A binder needs to be able to shut out all distractions. All wrong emotions. You need clarity. Impassivity." He raised the stick, this time pointing its head directly at me. "Right now you need to see nothing but these two stones in your mind." He punctuated each word with a prod of the stick.

I fixed him with a stare that could have turned the stick to cinders.

"Not me." Another jab. "The stones, boy. The stones. How badly do you want to be a binder, hm? Trust me."

Some of the heat left me and I exhaled, focusing on the rocks.

"Hold a space in your mind for each of them. Two halves, each as empty as a night with no stars or moon, but for the stone. One stone. One half of your mind dedicated to each one. Understand? They are all and everything. That is all you have space for inside you. The stones."

Wiping one's mind isn't an easy thing. It took a while of sitting still, letting myself go through the endless tumble of questions and thoughts plaguing me. Eventually, emptiness came and only I remained—floating in a sea of black. My mind stood divided into two mirrors of darkness, a stone floating on each side.

I held the image as long as I could, until two points of dull pressure built in my head. The hands holding the stones grew heavy and distant. I felt their weight fill my mind instead and I ached for reprieve.

"How does it feel?"

Mahrab's question jarred me from the calm and focused vision I'd created. The black vanished and the stones with it.

My chest heaved and I labored to breathe as easily as before I'd started the mental exercise. "Tiring, like my mind spent all day running. Why is that?"

He smiled. "Most people aren't used to ever using their mind like that. They go about their days and lives at its beck and call. Few ever task it to sit and do what they want. That's the first step to becoming a binder. Clarity of mind. From there, being able to hold the perfect image—*images* eventually—of what you want to see. That is the beginning to being able to affect the world. To employ a binding." He rose and fetched a tin cup, going over to the barrel of water I kept in the understage.

He filled the cup and returned, placing it between us. "What do you see?"

"Water?" I gave the obvious answer, but that didn't mean Mahrab was looking for that.

A patient smile crossed his face. "Yes, but what about it?" He pointed a finger at the water's surface.

After a moment of thinking, I still couldn't find anything worth saying.

"It's clean," he said.

I furrowed my brow at that and eyed him askance. "That's because you've never had to drink it. I wash with that water, Mahrab."

He snorted, pinching some of the dust and debris on the floor and sprinkling it into the cup. "That may be, but watch." He added another helping of dirt to the cup and stirred the water with a finger. "Now what?"

I watched the mixture muddle in color. "It's dirty."

He nodded. "But sit with me and now watch the water as it sits with us, huh?" He stopped stirring and folded his hands.

We sat. We watched. I'm not sure how long passed before Mahrab finally seemed satisfied, but evening light filtered through the windows of the understage in bands of warm gold and soft orange.

"And now, Ari?" He gestured to the cup.

The sediment had separated from the water, sinking to the bottom. What remained at the surface was just as clear as before he'd added the dirt.

"It's clean again. Or close to it, anyhow."

Mahrab nodded. "Remember this much, Ari: Anything—any mind—clears up if you let it sit long enough. To be a binder, you're going to need to learn to still and clear your mind no matter what's happening in the world around you. So now, we sit and clear ourselves." He pointed to the rocks again. "Back to it. Sit and think of rocks."

And we did.

All night long. Until my mind grew weary and I dreamt of damnable rocks.

Mahrab didn't know it then, but he was a finer teacher than he would have imagined. Maybe too good.

But it began with rocks.

THIRTEEN

Intermission—Questions

I slipped out of the story as Eloine tugged on my sleeve. We traded a long look and I could see the questions forming behind her eyes.

The rain had thinned, now sprinkling with the promise of dying out, yet Eloine curled against me. The warmth in her eyes could have pulled the rain's chill from my body. "So how did you do it, then?"

"Do what?"

"You called—bound—fire earlier. But you've just told me a binder can't create it." She pulled away from me and fixed me with an appraising stare.

I remained silent.

Eloine pursed her lips, chewing on one corner as if weighing what to say next. "Are you upset I caught that?"

I raised a brow. "I tipped my staff into the fire, wove a breath of air around it as a current to carry the flame and fuel it. The rest was binding them to that point."

She shook her head. "Not then. When the clergos came for me."

"Ah." She had caught that, but I didn't feel up to explaining that part of my story yet, nor the pains associated with it. "You're right. I did call fire where there was no flame in sight."

Eloine waited for more of an answer, but when it became clear that was all she'd get, she reached out and placed a hand on my shoulder.

A razor-thin line of pain, the span of a fingernail, arced through my skin. "Ow!" I leaned away from her, rubbing the spot where she'd pinched me. "What was that for?"

"You promised to be a gentleman. You're not living up to that by avoiding a lady's question." She flashed me a smile that could have almost pulled the pain from my arm.

Almost.

I kept rubbing at the sore spot.

Eloine let out a little laugh. "Come now. It wasn't that hard. Besides, you've surely endured worse over your life, no?"

I narrowed my eyes. "The mistake people often make about pain is that larger ones inure you to little ones. False. It all hurts. Big or little. And the more you endure in life, the more you become aware of it all. Pain is pain. It's all valid. It's all felt." She watched me as I spoke, and I sent one of my hands sliding along the ground until it came to her thigh. I took the moment to give her a taste of her own medicine.

"Ouch!" She reeled from me, swinging an open hand at my shoulder. Eloine's swat connected exactly where she'd pinched me.

"I'm sure you've had worse, no?" My face was impassive as the stone we sat on. "See what I mean? So, as to how I was able to call fire like that, it comes with a price. All power does. And it comes with pain, which might be small, or large, depending on who you are. But it's a pain I'm not willing to share yet. I'm not upset you caught it. I'm glad you were paying attention. It's a horrible thing when someone asks for a story and isn't willing to patiently sit through it and listen." I waggled a finger in admonishment. "But like with the stones, now is the time to sit and be still."

She crossed her arms against her chest and gave me a look that could have scoured the cobblestone streets clean.

I didn't buck under the glare, and chose to get to my feet instead.

Eloine tilted her head and made no move to get up. "And like that, we're done with your story?"

I placed a hand to my chest. "Of course not. I just think it's time we found a better place to sit. Somewhere out of the rain and with a bit more warmth."

She rolled her eyes. "Oh, I've heard this one before." She extended a hand and I took it as she pulled herself to her feet. "Let me guess, there's not many places you can think to take me now that we've raised trouble and the hour is late. What, with our clothes wet and both of us strangers in a distant land, with little coin to our name, the only place you can think of happens to be your room. Is that right?"

I shouldn't have smiled the way I did, but I couldn't help it. It was a thing half caught in wolfish hunger and a child's mischievousness. "Well, we did raise a good deal of trouble. And as you've said, the hour is in fact late. It just so happens our clothing *is* wet and we *are* strangers in a distant land. However, as fate would have it, I am performing at this establishment and have a room here. It's just inside." I turned and gestured toward the door. "Would that be all right?" I widened my grin and winked.

Her face tightened, but whatever smile she hoped to hold back was betrayed by the light in her eyes. She scoffed and hitched up her skirt as she walked through the door. "I suppose it would be."

I lowered my head in what I hoped was a dignified nod. I slipped behind her, passing her by as I led the way to my room. "For what it's worth—"

"The worth of that will be determined by what you say next." I couldn't see her expression, and I didn't bother to turn, but I had a feeling Eloine was amused.

"I meant nothing else than to give you a warm place, out of the rain, to sit and hear more of my story. As much as you can bear of it, that is."

"Mhm. I'm a woman. I can bear more than you can imagine. Though, some ladies might take it a slight that that's all you had in mind."

"And are you like these ladies?"

"I haven't decided yet. Give it time. Be patient—like you, your stones, and your story—and you might find out."

We'd reached the door to my room. I pushed it open, stepping to one side and gesturing for her to enter. "Well, I know my story is worth the wait. But, that's just my opinion. Last chance to reconsider."

She laid a hand on my cheek, leaning in until her mouth came close enough the heat of her breath washed over me. "I think I'll come in to hear more of it, then." Eloine pulled away from me and entered the room. "Consider me curious. And my curiosity's not something easily sated."

"I consider you many things." I thought I'd kept the comment under my breath, but she turned and planted her hands on her waist.

The look she flashed me promised I might suffer another pinch, or worse, at a time when I least expected it.

I suppose I earned it. Deciding to mollify her, I waved a hand to the privacy screen in the corner of the room. "Would you like me to take care of your clothes for you?"

Some of the anger left her and her posture softened. One of Eloine's brows arched. "Just like that?" She clutched part of her clothing just above the chest, pulling it tight as if I meant to snatch it from her. "No sooner than I've come into your room you're already looking for ways to have me out of my dress—really." She let out an exasperated and overly played-up sigh.

I knew she only teased, but my cheeks flushed all the same. I ignored the sensation and pulled at one of the legs of my pants. "I'm offering to warm them for you. It'll—"

She shot me a smile so hot and wicked I lost my train of thought and decided I might not need to attempt a binding of heat after all. "That's better said and done than most men. But I think you're supposed to offer to warm me"—she turned and placed a hand on her cheek, playing every bit the shy and demure woman—"and not my clothing."

My tongue twisted and struggled to undo itself. I knew I looked a proper fool, mouthing to say something clever. "No—no—"

Eloine's eyebrow rose higher. "No? Well, a woman could take offense to that too." She turned away from me. "Honestly, first you bring me here and now you're saying something like that?" Her body shook and, for the space of a breath, one would think she'd begun to cry. But the underlying chuckle drained the confusion and worry from me.

I glowered. "I'm glad you're enjoying yourself."

Eloine turned to face me, a hand on her mouth to stifle her laughter. It wasn't doing a good job. "Oh, very much."

I bit back the urge to stick my tongue out at her. "Well, if you'd rather stay cold and wet . . ."

"Mhm. Are those my options? Cold and wet or being warmed by you?"

I began to think I wouldn't win this battle of wits and wordplay, so I decided to cheat. "Let me show you." I beckoned her with a finger.

Eloine came close enough to me that our noses almost touched. "Is this good?"

I didn't risk nodding lest I bump her with my head. Instead, I reached down and took one of her hands in mine, bringing it up to rest against my chest. The old line went through my head again. "Start with whent."

"What?"

I tuned her out, retreating to the folds of my mind. My clothing had been freshly cleaned and laid out in the summer's sun to dry. The image doubled, then again. It wasn't long until the inside of my head resembled a honeycomb filled with repeated imagery of warm and dry clothing. "Then go to ern." I held the images, firm, perfect. An unshakeable faith assured me that my clothing hadn't gone through a storm. It had not been soaked through until cold racked my blood and bones. No.

My skin knew only the softness of fresh clothes and the heat of being out in a nice day.

I felt Eloine's hand shake within mine. A tug. There had been the slightest moment where she wanted to pull away, but she reined the instinct in. Her eyes widened when she placed another hand on me, rubbing my shoulder down to my sleeve. "The water's gone. How?"

I smiled. "Answers to questions like that would doubtless be the subject of a story." I gave her a knowing stare. "My story. If you're willing to sit and be patient through it all. All good stories are like sex. There's interest, a promise, teasing, but if you stay with it and build the fire properly, you get your catharsis."

Eloine rolled her eyes. "Your experience is clearly different than mine, then. A man's *catharsis* is seldom felt the same as a woman's."

I pulled at my collar, which felt tighter as we discussed this particular topic. "Enshae definitely provided . . . an *experience* . . . and then some."

"She has that reputation." Something in Eloine's voice had hardened, going brittle as kilned pottery.

It took me longer than I care to admit to catch my folly, but I addressed it. "Most people only know the stories about her. I can tell you the truth. There is a difference. But part of being a good storyteller is knowing when a demonstration might help you tell your tale all the better. So, back to my original offer, will you let me warm your clothes?" I reached out slowly, taking a fold of her skirt along the waist between a thumb and forefinger.

Eloine nodded. "Though, you'll have to tell me why you wanted me out of them when I didn't see you get out of yours?" Her mouth twisted into something practically lecherous, and I became aware of an all-too-different warmth flooding my skin.

I cleared my throat and took a moment to settle my mind, knowing I couldn't trust my tongue without first taking pause. "The . . . sensation of having that binding done to you—around you—can be unsettling. It can also be a violation of a person's space."

Eloine pulled her hand away. Her voice dropped to a whisper. "Few men ever consider what might be a violation of someone's space." She had spoken as if the comment hadn't been for my ears.

A part of me wanted to place my hands on her shoulders and reassure her, but the tightness of her posture told me it wouldn't be welcome. She stood quivering like a leaf in a storm, with the promise that the slightest touch would send her flitting away.

So I used my words instead. "We have other kinds of spaces, too. Few ever learn of them, but there are sacred spaces in and outside each of us." I stretched my arms out wide, sweeping them in a circle around me. "There's an unseen area we occupy, greater than our bodies. A part of us, which some would consider something close to our soul—but not that—takes up more space than our body does. The binding I wanted to perform touches on that space. I didn't know how you'd feel about me doing that, is all. That's why I wanted you to remove your clothes and stand behind the barrier."

I hoped my explanation was enough to put her at ease.

Eloine gave me my answer the next moment, taking two steps until she was even closer. Her chest pressed against mine, threatening to dampen my clothes. I didn't mind it one bit. "I'd like to feel it, then."

That was all I needed to hear.

I closed my eyes, slipping back into the folds of my mind.

You have a subtle awareness of that greater space you occupy. People oft dismiss it, thinking it a childish notion or something superstitious. But it's true—an extra sense if you will. It's no different than the subtle and uncanny ability any animal has when it knows it's being watched.

We are all aware when something comes into that space, even if we stand with our eyes shut, even if we're blind. We know. And we are acutely aware when something violates that. Their presence is felt.

I took in Eloine's. She thrummed like a mandolin string that had been plucked and left to vibrate until it came to a natural stop. But something else caught my attention. Another piece of her stood like an iron rod, unbent, tempered hard and hot, refusing to give under anything. Nervous. But strong. Unafraid . . . of me, or anything else.

I reached blindly to place my hands on her shoulders. She took my hands in hers, guiding them along her sides as I held up the mental picture I wanted to see. "Whent." Her clothing was without rumple. Dry just as mine and with all the warmth. "Ern."

She shuddered in my grip but stayed put. "It's odd."

I said nothing, holding the binding until I knew it had been completed. My hands slid along patches of bare skin and it felt like she'd been lounging near a fire. I wanted to hold on to her longer, to linger in the touch just for a moment more.

My mind went to the last time I held someone who felt like they'd bathed in the sun, and I instinctually pulled away from her. The collar of my cloak felt tight, and its sides weighed me down as if they'd been sewn with lead. I shook my head clear of the memory. "Sorry about that."

Eloine seemed to pay me no mind. She looked over her clothing, taking bits of it between her fingers and rubbing them like she was still trying to discover the trick behind it. "I couldn't feel it happening. Just that it had. There was no transition—no feeling the heat slowly coming on. One moment I'm soaked, the next it's like a distant dream. There's no sign I'd ever been anything other than dry and warm. I felt . . ." She trailed off, waving a hand through the air. "I felt like something around me shifted, almost like it had a current, and that it had been reshaped."

Clever. It took me a while to catch on to that.

I nodded. "That's what I meant earlier about the space around us. And we'll come to the story of that binding, eventually." I moved to the bed, easing myself down onto it. "But we won't start with that. I certainly didn't. Before that, I tried my hand at another, and that's what became the earliest piece of my legend, depending who you ask."

Eloine came to sit beside me, staring at me with wide-eyed wonder.

"So, you've asked your questions, and bear in mind I've earned the right to ask some of you"—I gave her a look that made it clear I intended to follow through with that—"but since I'm playing a gentleman tonight, I suppose those can wait." I cleared my throat and tipped my staff forward so the head rested an arm's length away.

A deep breath welled inside me and I imagined it as a current of air strong enough to move clouds and cast waves to swallow ships. "Ahn." I blew the breath and pictured it weaving around the tip of my staff, binding it into a looping band until I decided to break it. A coil of fire burned inside me and I drew on it, folding my mind like I had done earlier that evening. I pulled on the inferno and spoke. "Whent. Ern." Flames sparked to life along the racing plume of air and blossomed into a serpentine length of orange light.

"You want to know about fire? About how I can call a flame from no place and bind it thus, and keep it tame? Well, I never learned to birth it like Brahm. So I decided to be bold and steal a piece of my own. Something that burns eternal and is mine to forever hold. That piece of my story is far from where we've left off, but we can touch upon what started me down that path. The road that led me to being firecaller, Ari the Unburnt, the one who kindled everlasting flame.

"To learn it, understand it, in ways better than a man knows his own hand, and most certainly his heart and mind: there is an intimacy to be found in that—fire—if you know how and where to look. Back then, I didn't. But Mahrab set me on the path to mastering it. And I daresay I did it better than any binder before me. But to learn my story with fire, you must learn the story of fire itself, and that is a story of candle and flame."

I focused on my staff, imagining the firelight dimming from its head until it ebbed and flickered, teasing that it might wink out altogether. But it remained. It bobbed and snapped, a little orb of light, almost like that of a candle in a dark room.

FOURTEEN

Candle and Flame

"The Athir, Ari, is necessary to being a binder." Mahrab held up a stone for me to see, shaking it back and forth.

Today's lesson thankfully took place above the understage on the theater platform proper. I'd had to do another morning's scrubbing and polishing to earn the right of it, and had suffered a stiff night's sleep, but it had been worth it. Most of Khalim's performers spent their day rehearsing in private or out in the quarter. I had the open place to myself for my own studies.

A dull orb of pain flared at my forehead and something slapped into my lap. I winced and looked down to find the stone sitting there. "What was that for?"

Mahrab smiled and scooped up the stone. "You weren't paying attention."

I glowered at him but had the wisdom not to lie and argue.

"Like I was saying, the Athir, Ari"—he tapped an index and middle finger to the side of his head—"is the pillar of faith. You need that frame of mind to become a binder. Without it, you'll fail at performing one . . . or worse."

"Worse?" I quirked a brow at that.

His mouth pulled into a tight line and his face hardened. "You can perform a binding and lose control of it. That is dangerous, Ari. We are meddling with the laws and functionality of the universe. Losing your grip on those?"

He didn't need to go on; I could imagine the severity of a binding gone wrong. When I'd first met him, Mahrab had bound fire to his hand and held it there ready to let loose. What would happen if someone bound a great deal of flame only to lose control of it? They might burn down a building, a quarter, a kingdom.

"Or you can lose yourself, and I'm not sure which is worse, Ari."

I stared at Mahrab, waiting for him to elaborate.

He raised the stone again. "You remember the exercises with the rocks, yes?"

I nodded.

"Some binders can hold an image so long and well in their minds that

that's all they remain able to see. They slip into the folds of the image, lost forever. Slipping is dangerous, Ari. I've seen binders go mad, trapped within their own minds, unable to function. They end up little more than gibbering dolls. And some . . . slip . . . then break."

I opened my mouth to speak, but Mahrab held up a finger to stay me.

"Breaking is when a binder is too far stuck in their attempt. It goes wrong, their mind is in a loop of folds and tries to continually employ the binding. They can not only kill themselves from the repeated strain, but imagine someone performing a violent binding over and over without control."

I wanted to do no such thing. A binder losing their grip was one thing. A binder going mad and repeatedly performing magic without knowing what they were doing? I shuddered at the thought.

"That's why we're working on building up your mind first, Ari. The mind. The mind." He punctuated the last two sentences with a tap against his head. "That is the binder's weapon, their shield, and their pillar. Without it, you cannot perform and hold a binding. It's pointless." He dropped the stone, letting it clatter against the stage to make his point. "The mind needs to be strong enough to shape and hold the folds."

I licked my teeth, wanting to press for more information, but unsure how much Mahrab would readily divulge. He knew I was impatient, but I'd shown I could listen and dedicate myself to the pursuit of bindings. I took my chance. "What are the folds?"

He shook his head and let out a heavy sigh. "You're running too fast, too far ahead, Ari. First, the Athir, the pillar of faith. The belief that the image you choose to hold in your mind is the one true shape of things. You *need* that to be able to affect anything in this world. Without that, you might as well shout at a dog to be a cat and expect it to happen. You'd have better luck. Today, we work on that."

It wasn't what I wanted, but it was a damn sight closer than where I had been before. My mind and dreams had been plagued with two mirrors of black reflecting only a pair of stones. When I pissed, I thought of stones. When I changed—stones. A rare bath? Stones. No matter what I did for the past few weeks. Stones, stones, and more damnable stones.

If this kept up, I'd end up swooning over stones.

Mahrab seemed to see my thoughts as he pulled free a tea light from the folds of his robes. "I brought this for you. Today we learn about fire—keeping a flame in mind and in sight. If you can practice this, you should be able to begin holding the folds. Learn the story of fire. If you manage that, you may be able to learn the stories of other things in this world." The way Mahrab had said it made it clear this held particular importance, but he didn't bother explaining further.

"Everything has a story," I said. It was a fundamental truth of my world, and I believed firmly that if you understood the story behind something or someone, you could come to understand them. Easier said than done, of course. "And they're all worth learning."

Mahrab inclined his head. "And knowing that gives you a certain standard of faith in your ability to affect whatever you aim at with a binding. Not every binder feels that way, though. But I've always believed in the power of story, Ari. It's why I'm here."

The hidden tale he and Khalim discussed in private. A story I didn't know.

There are certain kinds of hunger that have nothing to do with the physical.

My hunger for stories. My hunger for magic.

And stories, like magic, can be a dangerous thing.

"What's the story about?" I looked up at Mahrab, doing my best to adopt the irresistible nature of a begging puppy. I hadn't yet learned enough in my youth about the performer's art, but I'd been able to cultivate enough skill where I needed. Moisture lined my lids and I knew Mahrab could see it.

He rolled his eyes. "Oh, stop it." He placed the tea light candle between us, pinching the wick between a thumb and forefinger. Mahrab's lips moved, and even though he sat not more than an arm's length from me, I couldn't hear a whisper of what he said. He rubbed the wick rapidly as if trying to light it with the friction between his fingers. Light sparked and Mahrab moved his hand from the candle. The little flame ebbed, snapping to one side then the other as if it couldn't decide in which direction to burn.

"Watch it. I want you to stare at that flame, Ari, until your mind holds nothing but endless black and a fire inside." He held up a hand, stopping the question I'd been holding on to. "And in your mind, the fire sits still. It doesn't bob and dance. It doesn't flicker and flit. It burns as clear and steadily—unmoving as stone."

I stared at him, then the fire. "That doesn't make sense. It *does* move."

Mahrab smiled. "It does. But your task isn't to picture it true to form. You are supposed to picture it as I tell you to. A binder controls what he sees in his mind. If you want to shape the world around you, start with being able to shape what you see in here." He reached over and tapped the side of my head.

I looked at the flame, its body swaying like a blade of grass in the wind. If there was a rhythm or sense of thoughtful motion in it, I couldn't see it. It moved almost at whim, like something else stirred the flame and it had no control over itself.

Mahrab rose to his feet and walked away from me.

"Wait, where are you going?"

"To speak with Khalim about stories."

I almost stood myself, then realized my dilemma. I could sit and attend to what Mahrab had offered, another chance to improve my mind and get closer to performing a binding, or I could harangue him about stories.

It was like choosing between air and water. A learned man would tell you that lack of air will kill you quicker than a need for water. But he's a fool. Time kills us all the same, so it's never a matter of quick or slow, but what you need to live. And I needed stories, and I needed to know about the magic I heard in them.

I decided the bindings came first. I'd always be able to pry the story out of Khalim later. Somehow.

I settled myself and stared at the fire until the mote of light burned into my mind. My eyes closed when weariness took over, but I still saw the fire, immobile and bright, in my mind. I held it firmly as I had the stones. Every ounce of my attention was fixed on keeping that fire in sight and as Mahrab had dictated. It didn't move. It didn't flit and flicker. It didn't go out.

I kept it as still as a pillar of orange, contrary to what the actual flame was doing. Pressure built in the center of my skull, quickly mirrored in my forehead. Soon, my entire head felt like a dozen hands pressed on it, working to collapse it. The temptation to give up the mental effort and dizzying pain grew. Sleep called to me, but I warded it off, redoubling my efforts to focus on the candle and the flame.

A trickle of moisture touched my upper lip. I tasted copper and salt. My eyes opened and I reeled, having released the mental image I'd been holding.

A thin stream of blood rolled down my face from one nostril. My head felt like it had been kicked down the street. And despite that, euphoria filled me.

If you've ever experienced the tranquility of your own bed after a grueling day of labor, you'll know what I mean. It was like that. I felt like I'd toiled for days as a bricklayer and my brain had done much the same.

From that effort, my mind strengthened. The space in which I could hold things grew, and if Mahrab spoke truly, what I would be able to do with that space expanded as well.

I resisted the urge to collapse on my back. The candle and flame held my attention once again and I lost myself in it.

My mind and eyes ached watching it however. It went against what I had just spent an ungodly amount of time visualizing. The little flame continued its dance, swaying as it saw fit. When it didn't do that, it bobbed in place. Between that, it fanned a bit larger before dwindling to something smaller, all before resuming the size it had been earlier. It was like watching something alive, discontent with being contained and fighting it. This fire wanted to grow—yearned to move, and all that kept it from doing so was the candle, the wick, and the tin shell in which they sat.

"Learn anything?"

I snapped straight, ice forming in my chest and stealing my breath. It took me a ten-count before I steadied my heart and cleared my head.

Mahrab made his way back onto the stage, carrying a wooden bowl in one hand. His other held on to a piece of thin and folded bread. He placed them before me and nodded at the food. "I figured you'd like something to eat."

I looked at the food. An unassuming mass of brown sludge floating in a runny liquid the same color. I sulked. "I hate lentils."

Mahrab grabbed and waved the thori—the flatbread. "Everything's better with a bit of bread, Ari." He paused for effect. "And butter."

I stared at the bread, noticing for the first time the thin gloss over its surface. My hand moved of its own accord, snatching the thori from his grip and tearing free a small piece. I folded it into something like the head of a spoon using my thumb and index finger, plunging the bread into the lentils. The first bite had more texture to it than flavor. But soon, the subtle layering of spices filled my mouth.

As much as I hated that dish, more from a mind-numbing repetition of eating it, it did the job of satisfying my hunger. I inhaled as much of it as I could before Mahrab put a hand on my shoulder to stay me.

"Easy, boy. You'll choke. As with everything else we've discussed, give yourself time." He shook his head, but it was clear the gesture was more for himself than me. "So, what did you learn?"

I gestured to the smear of blood along my upper lip. "I did it." The words came out garbled courtesy of the food I chewed through. "It was a pain, but I did it. I held the flame in my mind and kept it still."

Mahrab arched a brow and tilted his head to regard me. "Really? Just like that on the first time, hm?"

I nodded, moving slower this time as I scooped more bread and lentils.

Mahrab rubbed his chin. "Impressive. It took me a great deal longer than my first time to manage that. You've a knack for this, Ari."

I beamed under the praise, but knew I hadn't done anything special. What I had done had more to do with growing up in the theater around Khalim. My life revolved around listening to stories and internalizing their every detail. Most of my free time was spent in my head—my dreams, spinning up whatever fancies I could. That brought with it a skill when it came to shaping my thoughts and holding pictures in them. Mahrab's exercises were simply the next step in that.

"And how did you feel while doing it?" Mahrab held his examinatorial stare. I could almost see the silent calculations going on behind his eyes.

"Like all the air in the world filled my head, and if it went any longer, it would burst. At the same time, it was like all the stones of the theater were squishing my skull. I knew the fire moved, but holding it still was like wrestling the fire. It was like fighting two living things. Myself, and the idea of how fire is *really* supposed to behave."

Mahrab let out a low murmur more to himself than me. He opened his mouth, took a breath, then closed it. His face twitched, slipping into a frown before he pulled it into a neutral mask. "That's because you were fighting two living things, Ari. Fire is alive. Never forget that. What you did with your mind was impressive and foolish."

My eyes widened. I wanted to protest, but he held up a hand to stop me.

"Let me finish." He scratched one of his brows, eyes narrowing like he was lost in thought. "There are so many things in this world you can work into a binding, Ari. And understanding the nature of things makes binding them easier. Remember, to bind something, you must be able to have the faith you can enforce your will on it *and* execute the binding. There is no room for half measures. Your faith and will must be perfect—both hard as Arasmus steel. To bind fire, you must understand it, because some things will challenge your attempt to bind them.

"Fire is alive. It is hungry, it is wild, it has a will to move as it sees fit. You *must* respect that. Holding it still speaks well about your ability to hold an image as you see fit. But holding fire still is contrary to its nature to move and grow and feed. Disrespecting that can threaten the folds of your mind when you work a binding, and you will lose control of it."

I stopped midway through shoveling another bite of food into my mouth, taking in what Mahrab had said. He'd already made it clear that I would have to contend with my own mind when performing a binding, keeping it still and fixed on whatever I wanted to see. To add that I would have to sometimes understand and work with the will of something alive . . . it drove in the depth of effort and mastery bindings required. I could not form a proper response to that, so I nodded instead.

"Good." Mahrab motioned with a hand for me to resume eating. "I know you want to jump into the bindings right away. But trust me when I say I'm teaching you this way so you don't burn everything down around us. Brahm's tits, you could burn yourself from the inside out if you're not careful."

That caused me a greater deal of pause than anything he'd said previously. It's a sobering thought to realize that you could cook yourself if you weren't careful with a binding.

"These are old and powerful things, Ari, passed down by Brahm himself, it's said."

I perked up at that. I hadn't ever heard a story about him doing any such thing. "Tell me." The words were out of my mouth before I'd realized I'd spoken.

Mahrab smiled and scratched the side of his head thoughtfully. "I suppose I can do that. I'm no storyteller, mind you. I believe that's your knack for things. But I can tell it as best I can, though I'll have to bring you something to better remember it by tomorrow." He didn't elaborate on what he meant by that.

"So, it's said that when Brahm set about to create all things, he did so with bindings. Though he didn't know it then. To him, it came as naturally as breathing. But when he saw the makings man made, he decided to teach them how to follow in his steps. We didn't take as easily to it as the Shaen did. It's rumored they have bindings and ways of working them unseen and unknown to anyone or anything else but the Sithre. Hidden bindings. I'd give up a great deal to learn of those." Mahrab's eyes lit with a glow that could have matched the still-burning candle.

I kept from voicing my criticism of his narrative abilities. He'd already gone off onto a tangent, but then, not everyone could tell stories the way I believed I could.

Youth can come with a certain certainty of self that life does a good job of abrading and putting in its proper place . . .

. . . for some people at least.

"When Brahm realized people had little to no knack for performing all the bindings he knew how to do, he went about things another way. He first taught us how to dream, to picture and shape things in our mind. From there Brahm showed us how to cast those thoughts and our will onto the world. He showed how the sun and moon were anchored together, and with that, man began to understand one of the bindings. You see, she and he are eternally tethered—bound—to one another. The moon was first among Brahm's creations and she moves freely about her way. The sun came next and he's bound to her and her sway. Brahm linked them with a binding to ensure the world would never be without one of them in their sky, always changing."

A binding that could tether bodies as massive and heavenly as the sun and moon. Even at my young age I realized the implications behind that, and I understood one of the bindings. Or so I thought then.

"You can connect two things together?"

Mahrab pointed at the candle and flame. "Yes, in a manner of speaking. Keep your eyes on that and continue the exercise while I tell you the story.

Only this time I want you to try to hold the image of fire as it is. You need to see it moving in your mind without your eyes. However the flame moves in reality, it moves in your mind."

The next piece of food caught in my throat as I tried to sputter. My feeble attempt to swallow and spit failed as well.

"Perseverance is usually a suggested remedy for that, Ari."

I broke concentration and glared at Eloine for the interruption. She stared back at me, mouth twitching into a smile. I appreciate a clever bit of innuendo as much as the next person, but never when I'm in the middle of telling a story. I held my stare and picked up where I left off.

Mahrab came to my side and thumped me twice on the back, helping me dislodge my half-chewed food.

"*Bluckh*." I rubbed the back of my arm against my mouth to wipe away my spittle.

"I believe I told you something about patience?" Mahrab had the grace not to speak in a chiding tone.

"I know. Just how am I supposed to anticipate how the flame is moving if I can't see it?"

He grinned. "Exactly. Right question to ask. This is where your strength *should* come true."

I noticed his emphasis on "should." He didn't say "would." Mahrab still wasn't sure of my capabilities.

There are many reasons to exert oneself, but growing up spurned and rebuffed by others for the account of my birth and caste, I took to spite early. I abhor people assuming I cannot do a thing simply because of circumstances beyond my control.

I was not born smart and quick-witted. I earned those. I survived on those. I was not the cleverest boy around. I made myself into that. And in that moment, while I smiled to Mahrab, I resolved I would show him I could in fact be a binder.

And I would show the world.

I didn't know then that I would succeed. Only that I wanted to. But sometimes that is enough—to want, and then to have the will to persevere.

"This is where you get to be the storyteller, Ari. And being a good one of those is knowing how to listen as well as you speak, or so Khalim tells me."

Mahrab was right about that.

"So, watch the flame. Listen. And when you're ready, you should be able to keep listening and close your eyes to see it perfectly. I don't expect you to get this in one go. It took me months before I came close to anticipating how fire moves. And for me, close is good enough. I won't say I've learned the story of fire, but I can bind it."

I did as instructed, falling back to watching the candle and the flame. *Months? I'll do it in days.* I stared at the fire almost as if I could bore holes through the candle wax.

Mahrab continued his tale of Brahm while I lost myself in the flame. "Brahm came to show mankind how the rules of the world worked, you see. Every bit of creation had been bound in certain ways. Things that go up will come down. All things fall in time, whether a stone is cast into the air, or a bird is too weary to fly. Eventually, anything not placed in the sky by Brahm's hand will come down."

That wasn't exactly hidden knowledge, but I kept that thought to myself. Mahrab usually got to the heart of the matter . . . eventually. He just ambled about in how to get there and when.

"When people understood this, he was able to show them how one of the bindings worked." Mahrab pointed toward the ceiling with one finger while tapping the stage with another. "What do you see?"

I made my expression as flat as the wood we sat on. "Candle . . . and flame."

Thwap. My arm didn't sting from the light slap, but I would definitely be remembering it minutes from then.

"There are times being a clever ass is appreciated, Ari. Other times, asses like that earn slaps."

I bit my tongue to prevent myself from uttering something about asses that only a young boy would laugh about. I didn't always have a good handle on my mouth, but I was learning.

"Try again. What do you see?"

I gave the obvious answer, unsure what else Mahrab could be hinting at. "One finger pointing at the roof. Your other's hitting the wood." I inclined my head toward the stage.

Mahrab raised the hand he'd had on the ground to his waist now, waggling it. "Yes . . . and no. You see two points in the world around us. One above. One below. What if I told you I could bind the space above to the space below? At least, a point in each space to one another."

I blinked, my mind spinning too fast for me to think up the possibilities. "You could bring down the roof of the whole theater? Is that what you were doing when you raised a hand overhead and the whole building shook? Were you threatening to collapse the place on Koli?"

Mahrab gave me a feral smile that would have shamed a lion's. "In a manner, yes. Though, I didn't actually want to bring the place down."

"Because you wouldn't have gotten your story from Khalim," I said.

"Because I was standing in the building too. It's hard to get a story, much less do anything else, when you're the same height as the floor." I caught Mahrab's hand sliding along the stage toward what remained of my thori and lentils.

My attention may have been fixed on the flame, but a hungry boy's eyes see a lot. Like the hand of someone trying to snag a piece of his meal. My own hand snapped out, fingers slapping Mahrab's wrist. All the while, my gaze never left the candle.

"*Vala mouna! Daritha sathva!*" He pulled his hand back, shaking it and spitting to one side. The way he'd said that had almost sounded like a curse.

"What was that you just said? What's it mean?"

Mahrab continued rubbing the top of his hand even though the blow I'd struck fell short of a stinging slap. "Hm? Oh, just something I learned at the Ashram. There are rumors of a secret place somewhere in the compound. An unseen wall bars the way, and there is clearly something behind it, but . . ." He trailed off and held up a finger, the gesture almost making me pull my attention away from the flame.

"There is no known way past the wall. It's protected by a binding that no binder who has learned at the Ashram has been able to break. To unmake. None have been able to work a counter-binding against it either."

All of which told me you could break someone else's binding. Counter them. It sounded like something I heard in stories. Great clashes of magic with binders wielding terrible manifestations of the elements. Turning the land up and over. Felling mountains as they fought.

"What's behind it?" I caught myself from breaking away from the flame and held myself still.

"I don't know, Ari. Like I said, no one's been able to get past the wall. Eventually, the rishis prevented anyone from trying. It grew to be too dangerous when young binder-trainees got too full of themselves and ended up bringing down chunks of the cavern on their heads. There's a story of one fool trying to melt the damn wall and he ended up burning himself and his friends. And if that's not bad enough, the idiot nearly sucked all the air out of the place." Mahrab cradled his forehead in one of his hands, shaking himself.

"What I said were words I once saw in my time in the Ashram. Everyone stumped by that binding and place ends up spitting that curse. Damnable binding." He shook his head in resignation. "Who knows, maybe one day you'll be the one to undo it, ah, Ari?" A tired grin stretched across his face. "But for now, don't dwell on old magics and lost bindings."

How could I do anything but that? The promise of something greater was out there, and though I didn't know it then, Mahrab had his reasons for telling me of this.

My teacher snapped his fingers, bringing me back to my task.

I focused on the candle and the flame, losing myself once again in its rhythmic swaying.

Mahrab resumed the story. "Once Brahm was satisfied man grasped the faintest shape to bindings and how the world worked, he taught them the next steps. He taught them of the many folds a mind can make. Brahm showed them how to look within themselves and recognize the atham around them—the space which we all occupy greater than our physical selves. The second binding let man do as Brahm had done, to reach inside themselves and alter the world around them. Though, we're rather limited in the scope and scale of such things. Brahm, born of fire and light, had no such restraints in power and understanding. He saw the true shape of all things, and so binding came to him as natural as sleeping does to us."

I'd lost myself in a space past Mahrab's story as well as my own wandering thoughts. Only a wall of black remained inside me. A lone flame hung in the void, pulling all my attention. I watched it until I passed out, Mahrab's words nothing more than a distant dream.

When I slept, I thought of the candle and flame.

FIFTEEN

The Folds of the Mind

Weeks passed under Mahrab's tutelage, and soon, I could hold the candle and flame in my mind for hours on end. It floated perfectly within the black. I may as well have been holding a real fire inside of me. Every tendril flickered and bowed as if alive, and I began to see the faintest shape to how fire behaved.

It would be a stretch to say I understood it fully at that point in my life, but I grew dangerously close for someone so young.

Khalim and Mahrab spent more time together each day, discussing things behind the theater owner's locked door. My earlier attempts to listen in on their conversations had led to my discovery by passing performers, all of whom quickly ushered me away but hadn't told Khalim of my attempts.

So I avoided punishment and the likely lectures but still took the blow to my ego. No young boy likes discovering he's not the clever snoop he thinks he is.

I resolved instead to spend my free time by tearing apart every word Mahrab had uttered in regards to the bindings, trying to work them out in greater detail on my own.

One day, when I was deep in the practice of the candle and flame, another of the theater actors came to me. Hands fell on my shoulders and shook me hard enough to rouse me from the meditative exercise.

I opened my eyes, ready to spring to my feet and give them a proper tongue-lashing. I stopped when I saw who it was.

Vithum had just touched his twentieth year. Lean of body and sinewy, he had the build suited for a dancer or the slender yogis outside temples, and not for his art as a swordsman. His eyes reminded me of puddle water, a cold and almost colorless gray. A haziness filled their already muted coloring, and someone had once slipped that a snake had spat in his face, nearly blinding him. While his sight had been spared, the light of his eyes had been forever changed.

I wasn't sure if I believed that, but if you stared long enough at him, you would begin to wonder.

I didn't speak, unsure what the theater's swordsman and fight choreographer wanted with me. He'd always been kind, even if distant and absorbed in his work and conditioning. But Vithum did not waste time on anything or anyone outside of his duties. He was as sharp and to the point as his tools.

"Ari-*cha,* don't let Makham catch you sleeping about down here, ah?" His voice carried a hint of concern, but the coldness of his eyes and stillness of face served as hard counterpoint to whatever softness he tried to convey. "I've come to fetch you."

My breathing had slowed its pace and I cleared my thoughts. "For who?"

Vithum smiled, the whites of his teeth shining brighter against the complexion of his skin. The darkness of his body could hold no more black in it no matter how many days he spent under the sun. "For me, Ari-*cha*. Your new friend, the *jathu* one, with the fire in his hands, has Khalim's ear now." Vithum placed a hand on his chest. "I don't know what he's been telling to Khalim, but Khalim has it in his head now for you to be on the stage. And we are needing all the help." He frowned. "Money is bad, Ari-*cha*."

I bolted upright. My chest heaved as I spoke faster than I could think. "Really? Who do I play? What role? When? Why now? Did Mahrab tell him about my acting? I played out some scenes for him, you know? I showed him down here in the understage. I did a piece about Jadir and—"

"Oi-oi, Ari-*cha*." Vithum held up his hands to stay me before placing them on my chest. He patted the spot over my heart twice before doing the same to his own. "No *thum-thum*, yes? Too much"—he bit one corner of his lip, brow furrowed—"*uurj* bad for you." His frown deepened. "What is the word for *uurj* in Trader's Tongue?"

The Trader's Tongue was the universally spoken language along the Golden Road, the path that passed through all great countries and on which caravans carried the wealth and offerings of the world. The Mutri Empire sat squarely at its center and was home to the richest resources—from spices to precious metals—and as such, it quickly adopted the Trader's Tongue as commonplace among those who could read and write. Everyone else made do with the old tongue of Brahmthi. Or, it was reserved for the learnings of the wealthy, higher class and castes, and classicists.

"Excitement? Energy?" I didn't know which he meant, but both of them fit the context.

He made a sound like he'd spat. "*P'tch!* Crude tongue and language." Vithum nodded, mouth moving silently as if sounding out the two words I'd spoken. "Yes. That. Heart should be still for this." He patted a curved wooden sword hanging at his hip. Vithum tapped my chest again. "Heart should be like water. Still. Then when needs"—he smacked a fist into an open palm—"crash-*thump*."

I took a few breaths to steady myself. "Yes, Vithum. But what's going on? What exactly does Khalim want me to do?"

Vithum's smile stretched from ear to ear. "You are to *dakha* with me, Ari-*cha*."

Dakha, the roving bandits of the wilds and open ways along the Golden Road. Horse lords, cutthroats, pillagers, and swords for hire. Every child dreamed of being one at one point, or at least the men who brought them to justice.

"We will train you. Then, you and me will give Makham a good thumping he deserves, ah?" He turned and swatted his ass several times, grinning with nearly the same enthusiasm I held at the idea of walloping that insufferable bastard. "Come."

"What about my role here?" I got to my feet and gestured to the various contraptions and tools spread through the understage.

He waved me off. "Khalim has no more plays and stories for now."

"None?"

Vithum shook his head. "Koli is making Khalim sit on his thumbs. Only studies, only practice, but no shows . . . now. . . ." He scowled and spat on the floor. My floor.

I shot a silent rebuke at him. It may have been a filthy hole of a place to live, work, and sleep, but it was mine. And Brahm would shit fire instead of birthing it before I let someone further muck up where I slept and ate.

Vithum lowered his head and gave me an apologetic look. "Sorry, Ari-*cha*. Koli's heart is broken. He's not a man. He's something else. And his ma should have spit him up, not out."

I had no idea what he meant by that, but I understood the sentiment. Sometimes in our hatred of things or people that is enough.

"Now, come-come." And that was it.

My afternoons were spent with Vithum, drilling in the ways of the sword. I had once heard he had been a caravan guard, and that's where he picked up the art. Someone else had mentioned Vithum had made it through the ranks of Abhar's army, climbing to the height of officer before he slept with the wrong man's wife. I couldn't see either of those stories being true, but I also saw little other options for a Sullied man in caste and one with his coloring.

Abhar wasn't a place where fairness ruled. And I would come to learn that in the time to follow.

My lungs felt like rags left out in the sun and then wrung further still. Every bit of my insides ached and my body wanted me to choose between standing upright and breathing. I compromised and threw my weight against the lip of my water barrel, leaning there for a while.

Vithum clicked his tongue. "*Tch, tch,* Ari. You get tired too quick." He stood shirtless, skin shining from the sweat lining his lean muscles.

Too quick? We've been at this for damnable hours. Even the thought drained me, leaving me to heave for another few breaths. I scooped up as much water as I could fit in my palms and threw it across my face and chest. It did little to absolve the heat filling me, but I noticed its coolness for a moment. It was enough. The second plunge into the barrel brought me enough water to alleviate the dryness in my throat. "Ah-ah. I think we're done with practice now, right?"

Vithum frowned, blotting away some of the sweat from his hard abdomen with his folded shirt. "You are never done with practice, Ari-*cha,* if you use the sword. Never." But he didn't push the point or me further. He inclined his head in a measure of respect, turning to leave. As he did, his arms moved with all the liquid and serpentine grace of a snake over water. His wooden sword blurred and I found myself lost in the motions much like the candle and the flame.

Enough time passed such that I could find my breath and recognize the depth of my weariness. But life cares little for that. Mahrab found me resting on a slab of cool stone in the understage, and he prodded me with the stick he'd taken from there not so long ago.

"Dozing off, are we?"

I pushed myself up, but didn't bother to stand. "No."

His face broke into an expression of mock wonder. "Oh. So you were deep in a trance, hm? Contemplating your lessons. Wondering and working on the many things I've taught you. Maybe you've found a way to lose yourself in the folds of your mind all on your own, hm? Maybe Ari has found one of the lost bindings and is secretly working away on it all while not telling his teacher, poor Mahrab—"

"All right, all right." I raised my hands in a gesture begging him to stop. "I was resting. Vithum's left me more tired than Athwun must have been fighting off those bloody Sura."

Mahrab's face lost all humor. I would have found more life in the stone under my ass in that moment. "And what do you know of Athwun, Ari? What do you know of the Sura?"

I shrugged. "Same as anyone else, really. Khalim never told me much about them, or their stories. I know Athwun fought them. People say they were demons. Conjurings of Saithaan before he fell to get back at Brahm for making people. They're something like the Asir, only their darker counterparts. Athwun won against them."

Mahrab's face remained blank. "Did he?"

I hadn't been exaggerating when I told him Vithum left me tired, and that included being too tired for superfluous questions and games. "Didn't he?" I glared at him.

If my look fazed Mahrab, or even registered, he didn't show it. "That's a matter up for debate. But I'm not here to discuss that. Get up." Something struck me in his tone. A whip of icy brambles may as well have lashed my back with how fast I got to my feet. "Good. So, you're tired, hm?"

I decided it best not to speak lest my tongue get away from me again. So I nodded.

"Good. *That* is the perfect time for you to practice the folds."

Some of my fatigue washed away at the mention of that. Some. My muscles still ached, and my stomach promised to gnaw through to my spine if I didn't find food soon. "You'll show me how they work?" I tried to keep my voice neutral and free from excitement, but my weary state left me unable to manage.

Mahrab's expression softened. "Yes." He gestured with a thrust of his chin back to the stone. "Sit back down now."

I frowned, wondering if he'd bid me to stand only to see if he could order me around. But with the promise of learning of the folds, I didn't really care. I did as he asked.

Mahrab plopped a leather satchel down at his side, rummaging within it until he pulled free a piece of rolled parchment. He spread it wide before revealing a bottle of rich black ink. The binder unstoppered it, taking care to tilt the bottle ever so slightly until a single bead of ink struck one side of the paper. He corked the bottle and placed it back inside his bag. "Now, what do you see?"

I told him.

"Right. Parchment and ink. Not so complicated, yes?"

I nodded.

"Not so hard for someone like you to hold an image of in your mind." This time it wasn't a question.

I agreed again.

"Good. What about now?" He took one side of the parchment and folded it over until I could no longer see the ink. Within seconds, I noticed the bead blot the fold under where it had been pressed. He unfolded the paper and showed me two splotches of ink now, still carrying a slight sheen. "Can you hold two perfect images of these stains? One on each side of your mind?"

Child's play. I nodded.

Mahrab held up a finger, then folded the parchment another way. Seconds later, I stared at four ink blots. Before I could speak up, he'd repeated the action, and again. Now twelve. Soon more. "And now, Ari?"

I stared. Such a simple thing. Just blots of ink, but creating that many separate images of them, one for each smear, and all accurately in my mind? My brain ached. "Why?"

"Because, Ari, *that* is how you work the bindings. This is their foundation. The folds of the mind. It is not enough to hold a perfect picture of your subject. It's not enough to gain a good understanding of them in the case of fire. You must be able to enforce their likeness through your mind as many times over. The fewer folds you can manage, the more difficult the binding. The folds represent more than your fixation and attention. They represent your faith. You must be so resolute in your belief you can bind what you wish, Ari, that nothing can question it. Nothing." The last word fell like a weight of lead.

The air grew heavier in the moment before his next words.

"That is what the Athir truly is. The binder's faith. Pillars of faith. For each fold you muster, you are showing without a doubt you will enact your will on the world around you. The more folds you hold—shape—the greater the binding and what you can in turn bind. The average binder to perform even one of the bindings can manage four folds—"

"That sounds manageable."

He glared at me, the stick in his hand twitching. "All day, Ari."

That sobered me. I opened my mouth to speak, but instinct drove me to turn and swipe the air with an open hand. The inside of my palm stung as my fingers closed around the stick Mahrab had used to swat at me. Vithum's training had improved my reflexes and awareness. I smiled, holding the stick, and washing away any of the pain in favor of the smug satisfaction of what I had done.

Mahrab grinned as well. "Your body's learning. So do the same for your mind." He prodded the parchment with the stick. "I want you to hold those folds in your mind."

I exhaled as my weariness returned. There would be no point in arguing for a longer break. "Four of them?" I crossed my legs, leaning forward to better stare at the blots of ink.

"*All* of them, Ari."

All thought left me. And reaching for the clarity and focus of the candle and flame was more than I could manage that evening. "What? I thought you said a binder can hold four all day?"

"I did. Are you going to be *just* a binder? What's the point of one day sending you off to the Ashram then, hm? Will you only work to master one of the bindings?" One of his hands tugged at his robes where the three braided cords of different colored string looped. "I'm not wasting my time here teaching you in hopes you become *just* a binder, Ari. You're going to master them all one day if I don't miss my guess."

Master them all. A feat that would definitely put me among stories like Brahm, Athwun, and other heroes the whole world knew. And the dreamer in me reveled in the idea. Pursuing that meant going to the fabled Ashram, leaving behind a place where I was judged by my caste and trade.

I would be valued by the quickness of my mind and veracity in which I threw myself at things. I'd enter a fairer world . . . I hoped.

I looked back at the piece of parchment and counted over twenty folds. Twenty to picture perfectly in my mind, each as clear and separate as if they occupied a different mind entirely. Twenty to hold. And who knew for how long Mahrab would keep me at it.

"Right then." I blew out a breath and set to it. I began with two, like the stones. Mahrab's voice hammered into me in the background as I worked to expand the rooms of my mind to four.

Hours passed before I reached twenty, but it would be a lie to say I'd mastered holding them. I'd really only created the space and images for them in my mind. And then, hunger won out, my muscles failed me, and I collapsed.

Something warm and familiar trickled from my nose to my upper lip.

Mahrab passed me a piece of clean cloth. "Wipe that away, now!"

The harshness of his voice wrenched me free from my fatigued stupor. I acted as instructed, rubbing away the blood.

He snatched the cloth from me, muttering under his breath. The rag burst into flames and he tossed it to the dirt-layered floor. It burned there, throwing up wisps of acrid black smoke until nothing remained but ash. "Never, Ari, never let your blood be spilled and left in places where someone can get it. Do you understand me?"

"Wha—"

"Say you understand me!"

"I understand, Mahrab. I swear. I'm sorry. I don't—"

He cut me off with a gesture. "I'm sorry. I was too harsh there. Ari, there are many bindings for you to learn, some of which have been long forgotten . . . but which have been found again. I won't say I know of them myself, but I have heard whispers that others who've left the Ashram have come across them. There is a binding of blood, Ari. In the old days before the Ashram, before the Jadum laws were passed, binders did terrible things to one another." Mahrab stared long and hard at the ground, the intensity so great I wondered if he'd bore holes through it.

A deep sigh of exasperation left his mouth. "The Ashram fixed a lot of things for us, including giving us the ten bindings all men should know. Maybe it's a blessing we've lost and forgotten the others." He seemed to be talking more to himself than me at this point. "Not more than fifty men and women can be admitted to the school of binding, Ari. Do you know why?"

I shook my head, not trusting myself to speak without prying too far.

He exhaled again, resting his weight on his knees. "Time is a dangerous thing. Time makes a man better or worse. But what then if he has power? What does it do to binders over ages? When we grow too sure of ourselves and our ability to shape the world? Some of us went wrong over that passing of time. And parts of the world paid for it. The world made them pay in kind." Mahrab's face tightened into a thin smile.

"A child with a stick can be dangerous to a child without one. Do you know why?" He didn't let me answer. "He can take the other child's eye out. Maybe his own. Foolishness becomes dangerous when paired with a weapon, Ari. What happens if that child is holding a burning branch?"

"I suppose it depends on the child?" I wasn't sure of my answer, but I hoped to lighten the darkening mood.

Mahrab gave me a patient look. "There is truth in that. Fine, I don't doubt you would be responsible with such a thing. But what would happen if you passed it to a fool with no respect for it?"

I winced. "They might set something on fire."

He nodded. "And what would happen with a fool and burning branch in a village of straw and thatched roofs?"

"He'd burn the whole place down, hurting or killing countless. At the very least, he'd destroy their livelihoods. I get it, Mahrab. The bindings are dangerous. What they can be used for is dangerous. And I don't know what I don't know. I'll be more careful, and I promise to never let anyone get my blood. I won't be reckless."

He placed both his hands on my shoulders, squeezing me tight for a moment. "I know you won't, Ari. But it still is the worry of an old man. Give me that much. Let me worry. We've not begun to show you how to bind, only the folds, and there are moments I realize what dangers I'm awakening you to. Let me worry."

I couldn't think of what to say. He'd gone from an anger like the sea in storm to a weakly blown breath. I nodded, knowing we'd both be better off from it and spared an awkward conversation.

"Thank you." He closed his eyes and took a slow long breath to steady himself. Mahrab reached over, fumbling with his bag before pulling free a leather-bound book. A series of knotted cords ran over its shape, fastening it tighter than anything ought to be.

I watched him run his hands over it like he was inspecting it for the first time.

"Here." He handed it to me with a more callous push than I wagered he intended.

I hooked a finger under one of the leather straps holding the book closed. "What's inside?"

"Stories, Ari. The kind much of the world's forgotten. The ones I've been collecting. And the ones Khalim hasn't answered for you."

I paused, stopping my fussing with the book's bindings. "What do you mean?"

Mahrab laid a hand on the leather cover, tapping the surface. "I mean the truth about you and yours is in here too. Not you specifically, but when you're ready, you'll understand what I mean."

Does he mean my family? Where I come from? The blood Khalim talked about? I resumed my frantic tearing at the bindings, but they refused to budge. It was like they had been fastened in place by something unnatural.

I realized the truth the next instant. "It's bound?"

Mahrab rolled his eyes. "Obviously."

"No, I mean you sealed this with a binding."

His eyes twinkled with amusement and mischief. "Ah, yes. Well done in spotting that."

I frowned as another piece of what he had said properly registered with me. "When I'm ready has nothing to do with when you deem me to be so, does it? You mean when I can undo this binding."

The light in his eyes brightened. "Yes." Mahrab gave me a pat on one arm. "But at the rate you're learning, that time will come soon enough. Don't disappoint me, Ari. I expect you to unmake more than just this binding one day." He rose and began walking away.

"Wait, is that all? We just started the folds."

He didn't stop to look back at me. "And you did a marvelous job. Now, hold them until you sleep. Then, if you feel like impressing me, Ari, hold them *while* you sleep. Good night." Mahrab left me to my own thoughts.

I sat there, staring at the parchment, considering all that had been said. I'd held more than twenty folds in my mind by the end of the day. Even if it'd been poorly done, I had done it.

I fell back into the folds and decided I could do without a night of sleep. After all, I was young, and I was eager.

SIXTEEN

Eavesdropping

Fvip. Fvip. Vithum's wooden sword scythed through the air, betraying little as to where it would strike.

Though the various bruises across my body gave me a good idea.

My shoulders burned like I'd pressed them against a bed of hot coals. My abdomen quivered, as did my lower back, both promising to give out soon.

"You use your eyes too much, Ari-*cha*." *Fvip. Fvip.* The sword continued its blurring dance across his body as he moved through a series of steps I still struggled to follow.

"What else am I supposed to use, my nose? You want me to smell where the sword is?" I regretted my moment of anger. The shouts robbed me of breath I could ill afford to waste, and that's when Vithum's flowing movements transformed into something else.

His body became a torrential wave—a singular force barreling down on the lone stone of a battered shore.

I moved on instinct, bringing my sword to where I thought he'd strike. My arms shook and my fingers numbed as the two wooden blades met with a near-splintering crack. The impact rattled through me and into my teeth, but I held my ground.

Vithum pulled away faster than I could register. He didn't follow up with an attack to knock me on my ass, however. "Good. Good! Yes, Ari-*cha*. There is seeing more than what our eyes can do. Ah? Not with your nose. Not with ears. There is"—he gestured around himself to an invisible space only he could see—"more of us."

Like what Mahrab said. The atham. "There's a space which we all occupy greater than ourselves?"

Vithum's brows knitted together. "Mhm. Come, swing. I'll show you."

I did as instructed.

Vithum didn't move immediately, nor did he shift his weight to meet my blow. He only began his subtle and fluid steps once the tip of my sword fell into his arm's reach. Vithum's hips shifted, and my sword fell harmlessly past him. But he didn't stop there. He twisted and brought the edge of his sword clashing hard against the base of mine, knocking it from my grip.

The blow reverberated through the small bones of my hand, settling in my wrist. "Ow. *Kuth. Nahin. Thab.*"

His eyes widened before he let out a sharp bark of laughter. "Where did you learn these words, Ari-*cha*?"

I grumbled under my breath, spitting on the stage floor.

Khalim would have flown into a frothing rage had he seen me do that, but he wasn't around, and I'd be the one to clean it anyway.

"I don't know. I heard it somewhere, why?"

He shook his head, but the action carried no hint of reproach. "Nothing. Back to the space." Vithum motioned again to the area around himself. "We see with this. Sacred space. If I leave mine, no good." He lunged, thrusting the tip of his sword far outside the normal reach and space he described. "I can hit you. But look." He pointed to a leg, far outstretched, and clearly off-balance. "No good. But if you come here." Vithum regained his posture and motioned for me to attack.

I did.

He quickly batted aside my blow, moving his whole body in a single perfect movement, coming to my side. He shoved a palm against the side of my head and sent me sprawling to the ground. "I move, and I take my space with me. I do not act until you are in my space. Yes? A swordsman sees with the space around him. We know when someone comes to it. We bring it with us. Always be in your space, listen to it, and bring it with you."

I had an appreciation of what he meant now. Coupled with Mahrab's explanation, it made more sense than before. Both binder and swordsman were acutely aware of the place they occupied, and it seemed to span the reach of their arm. An invisible circle in which their spirit resided beyond the body, and a place their senses had a reach outside the conscious mind.

I filed away the lesson, reminding myself to mull over it when my body didn't feel like a reed that had been trampled on.

Vithum had clearly registered my fatigue. His posture lost its catlike grace and strength, now revealing his own weariness as he slumped. "We trained many good hours, Ari-*cha*. Go rest, *ji-ah*?" He ushered me along. "Mahrab-*sahm* will be wanting you soon enough for your magics."

I didn't have the heart to tell Vithum that I hadn't exactly learned any real magic yet. Mahrab still kept me to the folds and, occasionally, brought me all the way back to the first exercise with the stones. But despite that, I practiced another exercise in private: the candle and the flame.

I can't say why I kept to this training. Call it a feeling, a compulsion, or maybe the fire itself called to me. But while I walked away from the stage, I fell into the void and kindled that flame in my mind.

Once again its flowing tendrils drew me in, and I strengthened my ability to craft a more believable fire in my mind's eye.

My body navigated the grounds above the understage with a newfound ease and grace. It came from both the increased time I spent on the main floor as well as Vithum's training. My feet cooled noticeably as I stepped onto a portion of stone smoother than the floor of the stage room.

I opened my eyes to find myself in the hall leading to Khalim's chambers.

Voices echoed through a door up ahead, but I couldn't make out the details. I drew nearer, still holding the candle and flame—aware of everything before me as well as inside my mind.

"—do better than that, Khalim." It took me a moment of concentration to identify the voice as Mahrab's.

"—best I can. What I have here—" Khalim's voice carried no note of irritation. His words only held signs of how tired he was after a long day. Of doing what, I had no idea. But he sounded close to retiring for the night.

"My research on the Ashura—" Mahrab's voice grew heated.

"And mine of Athwun and the Sura. What of it? The story will be ready to perform when it's ready. With Koli's patronage, we'll draw most of the quarter to us each night—as many as I can stuff into these seats. Word will spread. Wealthier people will follow. So I won't peddle a half-told tale or anything less than perfect. *Perfect.*"

Mahrab sighed from the other side of the door.

I pulled myself up as I realized what I had done. I'd made my way to Khalim's chamber soundless while still in my trancelike state. Aware that no one else walked the hall, I resumed my eavesdropping.

"Do you have anything useful?" Hunger filled Mahrab's voice. The sort that takes a man when he's just been given his first taste of food after days of starvation. Mahrab *had* to know whatever Khalim had learned.

"I know pieces of their stories now, which is more than most do. It's taken me years of trading scripts and notes I've bought and bartered for. Good plays, mind you. Good histories. But I know pieces of each of the nine. I know some of their names. Athwun's story isn't what the priests and temple would have you believe. And I know something of the Sura. With all of that, I have more than any other theater in the world, I wager," said Khalim.

"I daresay you do. And if I tell you that by sharing it with me, I'd be willing to let you in on what I know? We might be able to shape something whole from the pieces we both have. Is that worth spoiling your precious perfect story?" Mahrab kept the excitement from his voice this time, but I still picked up on it.

I'm not sure how, but I felt like we were linked by strings too fine to be seen by the eye. They quivered in the air as he spoke, making me aware of their vibrating tension.

I felt like I was in the room myself, and I still held the candle and the flame.

"Give me a set and a half, and I'll put on a mock performance." Khalim exhaled in what sounded like a mixture of weariness and frustration. "A set and a half. No more prodding till then, *ji-ah*?"

"*Ji,* Khalim-*sahm*. And, thank you." Footsteps sounded as Mahrab finished speaking.

Every instinct told me to leap back and run. To suck in a breath of fear and come up with an explanation as to why I was there. Instead, the state of mind brought on by the candle and the flame brought me an unexpected clarity.

I took a series of quick, measured steps back against the wall of the hall. Confident I had made no noise, I sank to my haunches, closing my eyes. Adopting the meditative trance and posture had become second nature by now. I remained silent as I began the exercise of folding my mind.

The door opened, and my body stiffened. I reined in the shock and held my composure.

"Well, what's this?" Mahrab's voice made it clear he wasn't particularly surprised by my being there, but he found it amusing.

I opened my eyes, adopting the impassivity of stone. "I'm waiting. You said we had lessons after Vithum's swordplay. You've been teaching me to be patient."

"If you're going to eavesdrop, Ari, save me the trouble of hearing you lie. You're not the performer you wish to be yet. And a binder has little use of the stageman's art."

I scowled.

"There, better. More honest at least." He turned and moved down the hall, beckoning me with a wave of his hand. "Come."

I bolted to my feet and set after him. "You're not mad? You won't tell Khalim?"

"Tell him what? I didn't see or hear anything. I came out to find my one and only student, insufferably too clever for his own good, but not as clever as he thinks, sitting *patiently* outside."

I bristled and wanted to offer him a retort. But I knew that would only prove his point about my impatience. I bit my tongue instead, showing I could learn.

I couldn't see Mahrab's face as he walked ahead, but I could almost picture him smiling. That didn't stop me from forming a series of petulant expressions at his backside as he led the way.

We returned to the stage, making our way up the steps and sitting on the floorboards.

"How long have you been able to hold the folds, Ari?"

I thought about it. "More than twenty, you mean?"

He said nothing, simply staring.

I took a breath, weighing my next words. "More than half a day now. If I hold less, I've been able to go from morning till evening on my free days."

Mahrab's brows shot up. "Really? I hadn't expected you to take to it so quickly. How many is *less*?"

"Eighteen." I had made a note to keep track of exactly how many folds I could hold over time. Eighteen had grown to become my comfortable maximum. There were still nights where I felt like my stomach nursed a pit of violent snakes and the urge to retch threatened to overtake me. I would have the occasional nosebleed from the mental effort as well as a peculiar headache that manifested as a pebble directly behind my left eye. Being stabbed there by a needle would likely hurt less.

Mahrab's brows remained raised. "What did I say about lying?"

I held his gaze. "I'm not."

He pursed his lips, gaze going distant as if he lost himself in deep thought. "Hm. Eighteen folds. Dynamic or static?"

"Static. I can't hold the moving fire for so many folds, but I can hold the stones or something easier."

Mahrab nodded more to himself than me. "Well, that's a problem of understanding and faith, Ari. Here's a secret that's not so secret to binders. They're not any different in effort. You only think that. A lot of the bindings and how we enact them have to do with our beliefs around them, the difficulty or perceived challenges in them. It's a matter of faith."

"The Athir!" I added.

Mahrab smiled. "Exactly. This is something the first binders realized, even those who fell from true understanding. Even the Ashura."

The Ashura? A question came to my mind. I tried to hold it in my mouth, my tongue moving almost like it worked to help keep the words at bay. I failed. "Were the Ashura binders? Did they have the ability to use Brahm's teachings?"

A pause.

Mahrab exhaled, bringing a hand to his mouth. I could tell I'd asked something heavy and that he wasn't sure if he wanted to discuss it. "That's a complicated question, Ari. And part of that is behind my interest in Khalim. He knows a great deal of the old stories of this world, even if he sticks to performing the tried-and-true popular ones. He's an artist *and* a businessman. He has a duty to those under his care to earn coin, which means doing what draws in the crowds. Stories of the Ashura conjure uncertainty and unease, Ari. They arouse fear. Even the bravest man will silently wish for a piece of *hokh* to burn at the mention of their name." Something about how he said the word, oak, bothered me then—slightly different than how it should have been, but I let it go.

"But, yes. It's fair to say the Ashura know the ten bindings all men must know," said Mahrab.

"I'm glad someone does." My voice hadn't been as quiet as I had thought, and Mahrab registered my discontent.

"Oh-ho. *Arrey-arrey,* Ari thinks he's ready for all ten bindings now, eh? Not even ready to do one, but now he wants them all. Well, you should have told me you'd practiced so hard and quietly that you've mastered the folds and can tackle what no binder has done since times only remembered in stories rather than years."

I glowered at him, knowing his words were bait. "I'm ready to at least know them, no?" Turning the question back on him had a particular symmetry I knew he'd appreciate. I hadn't outright said I could take on all ten bindings, but now the onus rested on him to commit and say where he thought I rested in skill.

"There's learning, Ari, and then there is mastery. The two are different. And you are a far cry from mastery. And when concerning the ten bindings as a whole, mastery is a great deal beyond the reach of nearly any binder to enter the Ashram."

That comment dropped a weight of stone into my stomach. The ten bindings were out of reach of most binders? How that was possible when the Ashram had an entire school dedicated to the pursuit and teaching of them?

Mahrab seemed to pick up my doubts. He pointed at one of the twisted braids of string looping across his robes. His index finger trailed along the coiling yellow band. "Do you know what this is?"

I shook my head. "I wondered. . . ."

"Well, stop wondering and ask. If ever there's anything in this world you do not know—ask. For that is a surer way to find out than to simply wonder."

"Fine. What is it?"

"This is a binder's knot—"

"It's hardly a knot. More of a braid, really." I mimed the difference between the two forms of tying in the air.

Mahrab narrowed his eyes at me. "Yes, well, that's what we've come to call them at the Ashram. A tradition, mind you, ages old and *respected*. It's a shame we never had clever little boys like you to teach us these differences, hm?"

I got the point and decided to shut my mouth.

"For each of the composite bindings, there is a *braid*"—he fixed me with a hard, knowing stare—"that accompanies it should you prove sufficient skill in them."

I noted he didn't say mastery.

"To truly call oneself a binder, you must demonstrate this over one of the binding pairs. Short of the Master Binder at the Ashram, there hasn't been a single binder to leave the Ashram having accomplished this feat for all ten."

I blinked, taking a moment to swallow the meaning behind that. "So you can only perform three at what's considered sufficient?"

He gave me a wolfish smile. "*Only?* And how many can you do, Ari?"

"I'm not sure. Good Rishi Mahrab hasn't taught me any. Who's to say or know just how many I could come to do should I be shown some?" I shot him a smile so sincere I daresay it could have bluffed Brahm and a cadre of Sithre.

Except Mahrab knew me better than that. "Ari." He placed a hand on my shoulder and squeezed tight. "These are not things to rush. I am old. Very old. And I can do three bindings. Walk before you can run."

I knew the tone he took when he was particularly done with a subject, and he used it then. So I chose to bring the conversation back to safer waters. "Do you think I'll be able to make it through the Ashram?"

He squeezed my arm tighter than before. "Honestly? Yes. And that is why I'm teaching you how I am. Ari, the folds and the Athir are the crux to everything. Do not ever neglect the foundations of the bindings. I have high hopes for you. I believe in you."

Four words. And they were enough. Belief—faith—is magic in and of itself. It is the fire and steel we can lend to others to help them find their strength again. Belief is the gift you can give someone to rekindle their fire. And it is the greatest foil to doubt and fear. With faith, a person can overcome anything. Do anything. It is the buoy that keeps you afloat in a storm.

Mahrab had just given me that. And I would hold to it.

"I guess I'll work more on the folds today." No sarcasm or snide resignation hung in my voice. I'd learned my lesson. I figured I could at least set about improving my grounding further.

Mahrab pulled his hand away from me, readjusting himself until he sat cross-legged. He laid his hands where his calves met in the pose and laced his fingers together. "I applaud the thought, Ari, but I think it's time we move further back to the Athir and understanding that better, yes?"

I knew enough to not argue this either. I nodded.

"You've learned how to hold static stones and dynamic fire. Now those are the truths of those two things—their stories, if you will. I want you to subvert stone. I want you to hold an image of stone that moves and dances like fire. Then, I want you to hold the folds and cast as many as you can. If you think you're up for . . . *eighteen*, then by all means show me." He flashed me a knowing smile.

I thought about it, aware that it took me longer than I would have liked to hold the shifting image of fire in my mind. That was still within the realm of believability, even if difficult at first. Now he wanted me to visualize a scenario that could never happen in the natural world. No matter how much training I had already undergone, the idea seemed dubious at best.

Hesitation flooded my voice. "You want me . . . to make stones move like fire." I didn't phrase it as a question.

He nodded.

"Even though they don't move as such. They don't even move." My mind reached for excuses to prolong an exercise I felt would only lead me to failure and embarrassment. After so much progress, I didn't relish the idea of faltering before Mahrab. A cynical part of me considered the idea that maybe this was another lesson. One to knock me down from the perch Mahrab thought I rested high upon.

"Then make it so, Ari." He leaned forward, mouth spreading into the grin of a hungry jackal. "Do the impossible. Make stone shift and sway. Bind it in the folds of your mind to do as you wish."

I opened my mouth to protest, but he went on as if he didn't see me at all.

"The pillars of your faith—the Athir—must be the founding bedrock of the mountain. As hard and clear-bright as a piece of Arasmus steel. As deep and still as the bottom of the sea! The Athir does not rest on the quivering and quaking grounds of fear, Ari. That includes the fear of failure." He stared at me like he knew the uncertainty clouding my mind. "The Athir is rooted—firm, towering, like the Water Tree. The world around it may be barren, lifeless, and trying to squeeze the very essence of the tree from it. But the tree remains. It persists, wholly itself. Grand. Resolute. Above all things. Nothing can shake it. That must be your faith.

"Make it so. Or don't, and let the world pass you by, Ari. Which will you choose?"

It wasn't a hard choice.

So I made it and spent what remained of the day sitting with Mahrab until my mind and body discovered new anguish. It felt like countless unseen fingers raked the insides of my skull. Stones didn't just fill my vision, but they filled my body with a weight and weariness that promised me a week's worth of sleep should I fail to remain conscious.

Mahrab had been right to question my ability to hold eighteen folds of this sort.

In the end, I managed ten. And my teacher gave me a new and warier form of respect. But I found my Athir and held folds of shifting stones.

I thought myself rather talented and clever.

I thought I'd prove that I was in fact ready to tackle the bindings.

I thought I was ready to work my own grand feats and fight storybook villains like the Ashura.

I was wrong.

SEVENTEEN

A Test of Will

The curved edge of Vithum's blade scythed toward my shoulder. Not a blow that would cripple me, but I'd feel the pain of it for days if I didn't handle myself properly. I twisted at the hip and thrust up with my own wooden sword. The two weapons clattered together. The force of Vithum's strike drove the back of my blade closer to my left eye than I would have liked. His pressure ceased an instant later and the choreographer resumed a neutral pose.

He lowered the weapon to his side and inclined his head. "You are being quicker, Ari-*cha*."

I beamed under the praise, but the expression brought some of the beads of sweat along my brow down into my eyes. The sting, coupled with the afternoon sun's heat, forced me to wince through the momentary discomfort. Despite this, I still managed to voice my thanks to Vithum. "*Dhunyae.*" I'd chosen the old Brahmthi word to convey my feelings to him, knowing the swordsmaster would appreciate it.

"Let your eyes breathe, Ari-*cha*. It's better for the hurt."

It felt counterintuitive to everything my body advised, but I knew Vithum was right. I opened my eyes, letting the air wick away the moisture inside them. My eyelids fluttered for a moment before the pinpricks from the sweat faded. A low fire, more smoke than flame, had built in my lungs. They felt dry and stretched. I sucked down heavy breaths regardless, sincerely hoping training had concluded for the day.

Vithum reached out with lightning speed, sending a surge through my heart and mind.

I snapped back into the series of flowing movements I'd learned. My legs spread until I stood in a shoulder-width stance. I shifted my body and sent my sword arm into an arcing strike. I compensated for my lack of finesse with all the energy and ferocity of youth. The attack succeeded in slapping Vithum's blow away but left me off-balance. Something I knew I'd pay for.

Instead of following up with a strike, Vithum leapt back. He smiled wider than before. "Good-good. Even tired Ari-*cha* is thinking without thinking now, hm?"

It sounded like something Mahrab would say. Training myself in a fashion so that my subconscious fell into what I'd learned.

The sun had baked the surface of the theater's rooftop into a near oven, its stone floor close to scalding my bare feet. What calluses I had did little to mitigate the hot coals forming under me.

I exhaled and let my sword fall to the floor. "Why are we training up here, Vithum?" I brought the back of a hand to my forehead, wiping away my sweat. "Why not inside where it's cooler?"

If the blistering heat bothered him, he didn't show it. He shrugged his shoulders and his lean muscles shone and rippled under the sunlight. "It's good for your"—he tapped a hand to his chest before sucking in a deep breath—"body. Stronger. Ari-*cha* will fight longer."

He had a point. I'd never need his skills for a real fight, much less killing someone, but I'd be pushed to perform for hours in a play. The worse time I had of it now, the better for everyone watching. And it'd ensure Khalim noted my efforts.

Still, I didn't want to wind up ashen and charred to prove my point.

Vithum mercifully ended our training, tossing me a rag that had dried out long ago.

I took it anyway and wiped myself down. "Thank you for the lesson."

Vithum gave me what he called the Warrior's Bow, bending at the waist, but keeping his eyes on me the whole time.

I returned the gesture in equal measure.

"You're working the poor boy past exhaustion, Vithum." Mahrab's head protruded from the trapdoor leading to the roof.

Vithum bowed a shade deeper to the binder than he had me. That was all he offered in way of greeting as Mahrab climbed onto the roof. Vithum passed him silently and disappeared below.

"Rishi." I didn't bother giving Mahrab a curt nod. We didn't resort to formal custom, and Vithum's training had left me ready to find a nice cool place to sleep for the afternoon in any case.

"You look properly thrashed, Ari."

"I am. I don't think I'm up for binding training today, Rishi. I can barely stand, and the sun is cooking my feet into lumps of hot leather."

Mahrab's grin edged on predatory. "Good. That's the perfect time for training."

My eyes widened.

"What, you think life and the people of the wide world will care if you're too tired? You think those at the Ashram won't ask you to enact a binding when your mind's too weary to tell piss from water and your body too weak to hold yourself upright?"

I didn't actually know the answer to that and Mahrab knew it. So I settled for shooting him a withering glare. It must have been the sun at my back that kept him from cowering, and certainly nothing to do with my miserable state and small stature.

I was sure of it.

He moved until he stood perfectly in front of me at a distance where our shadows nearly touched at the heads. "Today, little would-be binder, we're going to learn how to oppose another man's will."

I shook my head mildly, cocking it to one side hoping he'd repeat himself. "Sorry?"

"You'll make a poor performer, Ari, if you can't hear someone so close to you."

I gritted my teeth and shot him a renewed glower.

He brushed it off. "Save the effort for our exercise. You're going to learn how to contest another man's binding."

"But you haven't even taught me *how* to do a single binding. How am I supposed to stop one?"

Mahrab held up a finger. "Ah. But you don't need to know how to perform one to stop one. This is why we've been strengthening your mind. It all begins here." He tapped his temple. "And it all falls apart there."

"Foundations." The word left me as a soft breath. "If you topple that . . ."

Mahrab clapped his hands once. "Exactly. If you can stop a binder in the folds, it all crumbles. No binding. Easier said than done, of course. You must anticipate the binder's goal. Can you read minds, Ari?"

I knew the question had been posed to set me up. But I had no clue for what. I settled for the easy way out, knowing it'd set Mahrab as much on a tilt as he'd done to me. Irritation. "Of course." I matched his earlier animalistic grin.

He frowned. "Oh, this I must see. Go on then, read my mind. What am I thinking about?"

"You're thinking I'm a clever little shit who you'll work doubly hard for being so mouthy."

Mahrab's expression slipped, leaving him blinking for a moment until he regained his composure. "It's less impressive a feat, Ari, when we both know you're being a clever little shit."

I held my smile.

"Oh stop that already before I'm tempted to stuff your face with hay and dung to shut you up. The point of this is that you must guess what kind of binding you're facing. You have to guess *how* the binder will go about it. What they're binding. Understand?"

"I do." If the fatigue from earlier hadn't completely toppled me, Mahrab's lesson threatened to do the job. The sheer mental effort of having to guess at the many ways a binder could attack me, then work to oppose them . . .

It promised to be a taxing exercise.

I sucked in a breath and steadied myself. "So, how do we begin?"

Mahrab rocked on his heels for a few seconds. "Hm. I was thinking I'd attempt to do a binding and you simply stop me." His tone betrayed nothing, but I know he held back laughter.

I readopted my earlier glare. "Just like that?"

"Oh, why not? After all, the little show-off managed to hold how many folds of shifting stones again?"

I didn't take the bait, choosing instead to play his game better than him. I wanted to be a performer, after all. So I stepped into the role he clearly saw me in.

"Sure, I guess." I rolled my shoulders with such nonchalance a cat could have taken lessons from me. "Easy enough. I already did what you and a class of binders couldn't even manage with the Ashram's teachings."

My performance got the reaction I hoped for.

One of Mahrab's brows went up. "Oh, and just like that now?"

I smiled, dusting my pants off like I had nothing else better to do. "Just like that."

"Hubris, Ari . . . is a dangerous thing."

I said nothing.

Mahrab's shoulders slumped and a weary sigh left him. "Very well. I'm too old to play this game with you. I had planned on telling you what binding I was going to execute and how exactly I'd go about it. That way all you had to do was oppose the folds I made."

Simple enough in theory. But managing it would prove to be the hard part. After everything I had learned, knowing the folds wouldn't be enough. I needed to know *how* Mahrab saw the images. Not just what he saw. And every person innately sees things differently than the next.

Mahrab reached into the folds of his robe, pulling free one of the stones he'd first shown me when I began holding images in my mind. "I'm going to toss this in the air over your head. Then, I'm going to bind it to the top of your thick skull. If you fail in stopping me, it'll come down with a startling crack. And I'll wager it's the stone that'll crack when it meets your infinitely thick skull, and not the other way around."

"That's not much to work on, Mahrab."

He motioned with a hand like he was shooing away a bird. "Oh, go on, impress me. Work with it. It ought to be enough. What happened to, 'Easy enough,' hm?"

I bit my tongue and kept my face painfully neutral. "Fine. Are you willing to give me anything else? There are over a dozen ways you can picture this going. How am I supposed to match your folds? I don't even know how many you're going to be using?"

"I'm picturing it crashing into your coconut of a head, and hopefully stirring around whatever curdled milk is in there so it's a bit less dense next time I'm teaching lessons."

I clenched my teeth hard enough to bring an ache to my gums. A second later, the tension bled out of me as I brought up the candle and the flame. I fed my anger, confusion, and doubts into the fire. "I suppose I asked too much. We can't all have an imagination. Got it. You throw the stone. Then it comes down. Hardly need a binding for that, I suppose."

Mahrab fidgeted. "You're exceptionally good at setting a fire under a man's ass, Ari."

"Then I guess I don't need a binding for that either." My voice remained as colorless as the washed-out stone of the theater rooftop.

Mahrab's lips twitched, but he said nothing. His wrist snapped and the stone went into the air.

All of my cool and enforced calm left me. I thought about the dozen ways Mahrab could work and pictured the binding.

Thwap.

A concentrated bolt of pain blossomed near the center of my skull, radiating toward my forehead. All thought left me other than the throbbing. I winced, rubbing the spot.

A sharp clap brought my attention back to Mahrab. "Look at that. The stone *didn't* crack. Maybe your coconut's not as hard as I thought, ah?"

The awful temptation to scoop up the stone and send it hurtling back toward him built inside me. I pictured the rock striking his nose and setting it askew. Nothing so gruesome as breaking the thing. An adjustment. That's all.

Mahrab seemed to guess at my thoughts and waved a finger in admonishment. "Uh-uh, Ari. A binder is never one to give in to anger. They must be cool and placid as the sea asleep. No tides. No movement. No. *Anger.*"

I didn't look up at him as I retrieved the stone, swallowing my frustration and tossing him the rock.

He snatched it out of the air with a lazy catlike grace. "Again." Mahrab lobbed it overhead before I could collect myself.

"But I don't—"

Thrack. Red lanced my vision, and a band of white streaked by just as fast before it all cleared. The stone had struck with the kind of impact I knew could leave a lump. My hands had already clamped to the top of my skull on instinct. Moisture welled along my lids. "Damn and . . . damn! Mahrab, what in Brahm's bloody shit was that?"

I grabbed the stone and hurled it at him as hard as I could. The throw had been perfect, and within a second, it would connect with Mahrab's mouth and teach him a much-needed lesson.

Except that didn't happen.

The stone stopped a hand's breadth from his face and careened toward the ground. It struck and shattered with a sound like hail on glass, bits of it scattering far to the corners of the rooftop.

I stared slack-jawed.

Mahrab released a mock sigh, reaching into his robes to remove the second of the stones I'd practiced with. "That, Ari, was not calm nor placid." He bounced the stone several times in an open palm. "That will get you into trouble at the Ashram."

He bound the stone midair. He knew I was going to throw it at him. But he couldn't have known when, or where I'd aim it. That told me enough. It had less to do with my intent, since I wasn't performing a binding. He'd known I'd throw it, and that was enough. All he had to do was envision the stone and bind it to a fixed point on the ground.

He already had the point, but how did he bind something moving so fast—unfixed? I couldn't work it out, so relied on the only measure left.

Asking.

"How did you do that?"

Mahrab grinned. "Oh, now the little prodigy is stumped?"

"Mahrab . . ."

He pursed his lips thoughtfully and tapped them several times, saying nothing.

The heat of the rooftop simmered to something considerably weaker than that building inside me. He had a point. The angrier I became, the further I moved from the folds, making it all the more difficult to counter Mahrab. I brought back the candle and the flame, feeding my fury into it. Calmness returned and I nodded more to myself than him.

"Is it the atham?" The question didn't exactly get to the heart of the matter, but I knew I'd strike close enough to get an answer.

Mahrab's mouth twitched. Not much of a tell, but after a month of hard training in the folds and then reading body signals with Vithum, it might as well have been a fox's self-satisfied smile.

So, I'd struck close to the point.

"It has to do with the understanding of that, yes. This is where the complexities of the folds and bindings come in. But you're looking at it too simply. I'm not using a binding within my atham to bind the stone. I'm relying on my awareness of my atham to know when to apply the binding and where. After a point, your instincts become attuned to all things within your atham. This is part of what we've been training you to learn. I'll show you." He tossed the stone at my face.

My hands moved of their own accord, clapping around the stone midair as it came within arm's reach.

Mahrab crossed his arms over his chest, smugness clear on his face. "That is the basest understanding someone can have of what the atham constitutes. It's painfully short of the truth, but you begin to see, yes?"

I nodded, tossing the stone back.

He caught it without taking his eyes off mine. "What I did was no different, only I focused my attention and folds on the place I felt the stone would go. My hands weren't needed."

"What if you were wrong?"

An amused light filled his eyes. "It would have hurt." Mahrab held the rock between a thumb and forefinger. "Ready?"

I had no idea what for, but I motioned for him to begin.

He threw the rock again.

I reacted, snatching it and throwing it back before realizing I'd done so. "Sorry."

"That's the point I wanted to make. You can already do this with your body. Now we're trying to get you to do this with your mind, Ari. You know what I'm doing, and you can already stop a stone with your hands. I'm going to toss it overhead now, like before. When I do, try to counter my folds and binding."

He threw the rock.

Thump. I winced, passing him the stone for another try.

Thump.

Thwack. That one would leave a mark.

Thuwp. A portion of my hair had tangled to form a poor cushion against where the stone had struck. I felt the blow, but mercifully not as hard as before.

Paft. I had moved out of the way of the rock, letting it whistle downward past my hair. My hand moved and I ended up cradling the stone in my fingers. I apologized and tossed it back to Mahrab for yet another try.

A cynical part of me had wondered whether this lesson wasn't anything more than an excuse to batter me in hopes I'd drop some of the habits he had little fondness for.

Brahm's ashes. If that rock hits me one more time, I'll pummel him until he forgets all about bindings and athams. I exhaled and pumped my fists, hoping to bleed some of the anger out of me. *Think!*

If he'd stopped my throw by enacting the same binding, it meant he'd been holding on to the folds beforehand. No one thought fast enough to go through a series of intricate imaginings at the last instance. No. The only likely explanation was that he had everything ready in his mind—all the folds—choosing only to trigger the binding once the stone had passed into his atham.

Meaning he didn't put the binding on the rock. The rock passed through where he already had a binding waiting.

Understanding struck me like a hammer on brass and I knew how to foil his following attempt.

Or so I hoped.

Mahrab had unconsciously fed me the solution with each throw. He'd been binding the stone to fall in the same spot upon my head. The only reason I nursed several other sores was due to my own subtle shifts in positioning. I didn't have to stop him at all. All I had to do was envision the normal path for the stone to take.

Easy enough.

"I'm ready." I stole a breath before he threw the stone, letting myself slip into the folds. Shutting my eyes went against all instinct, but it's how I had best conditioned myself by this point. I held a singular image: the stone sailing harmlessly overhead to clatter behind me. I saw it once.

Then it doubled. Again. And again. I held eight folds of the dynamic scene. A pressure built within my head much like that of the aching spots from the rock's impacts. I held the images regardless, working to banish my discomfort.

Another few folds. Ten. In each one, the stone passed over me instead of snapping downward.

If I'd guessed correctly, the image and folds would be enough. The stone would naturally pass the point of air on which I focused, anyhow, and once it did, my folds would contest Mahrab's for the path of the stone.

The weight of a mountain filled my skull. It threatened to crush my resolve, my folds, and me in the process. Tears formed within my eyes, and no amount of force could keep my eyelids shut tightly enough to stop the moisture trickling out. My teeth ground against each other, and I chipped one in the moment. A scream built in my lungs and I begged it to stay where it was.

The skin at the bottom of my toes felt like hot glass scraped against them. I flexed the small muscles in my feet, dragging them against the uncomfortable and burning stone. Through it all, I held to the folds of my mind.

Clack-clack. The pressure vanished and I collapsed like a puppet whose strings had been cut. The heat of the stone rooftop filled me, but it grew to be a distant discomfort against the ringing and ache of my mind.

Mahrab came to stand over me, his shadow blanketing me from the worst of the sun at my back.

I looked sideways, face still burning against the touch of stone. Tears streamed freely down my face.

I stared at the stone that had landed behind me. My head had been spared another thump.

"Well done, Ari."

EIGHTEEN

TAK AND ROH

Clattering stones and dancing plumes of fire consumed me—mind and dreams—for the following weeks. I drilled with Vithum until I moved through his choreographed motions without conscious effort, and I undertook more exercises with the folds after that.

Every part of me—muscle, mind, and bone—had been torn apart to be put back to form something new. I grew in ways I couldn't imagine. The change didn't come as a grand sweeping awareness. It came as delicate shifts in my thinking, understanding, and in my movements.

Vithum's training had given me a new grace and sense of balance. Before, I had been a jerky and skittish marionette. I had all the subtlety of a terrified alley cat. Now, a new surety flooded my every movement and step.

Mahrab's exercises made me acutely observant to all the little things I'd taken for granted in the world around me. I'd focused so much on the details of fire, memorizing its movements, that I now saw how much of my surroundings I overlooked.

Hairline cracks in the furnace of the understage stood out like gaping fissures to me. It was a wonder I hadn't noticed them before with how much time I'd spent working the contraption.

Rivulets of sweat ran down my body, now hardened and leaner than before I'd begun my work with Vithum. I had stripped down to my small clothes for today's training to avoid ruining what little I had in the way of garments.

A ring of fire burned around me. I sat at the center, doing my best to ward away the prickling heat's discomfort. Part of me knew that simple patience on my behalf would have the flames burn out as the oil fizzled . . . eventually.

But Mahrab would hardly count that as a victory on my part. He'd find another new and torturous way to continue my training.

I wondered what the scene must look like to those walking Abhar's streets in the night. Low and violent orange light blossoming from an old building's rooftop.

"You're not focusing." Mahrab lobbed a pebble the size of a fingernail at me.

I didn't move to swat it away, slipping back into the folds he'd asked of me. The flames rose higher and licked the bottom of my chest.

"Hold them where they are, Ari."

I did as ordered, envisioning the flames burning exactly as they were. My eyes remained wide and fixed on the tendrils of fire as Mahrab moved a hand slowly downward.

It was as if the simple motion were enough to bid the flames to dwindle.

I resisted, holding the flickering fire in place.

"Tak." Mahrab moved his hand lower. "Roh."

That threw me. I hadn't heard the incantations for this particular binding before. My hold on the folds faltered for a second.

The flames snapped once, lowering in height.

I resumed my efforts, resisting his attempt and holding a space in place in where the fires burned as they had moments ago.

Our wills met like opposing waves, each trying to subdue the other. Unseen force rocked my mind and promised to topple me onto my back. I clenched my teeth, digging my fingernails into the soft flesh of my palms as I held my images.

The fires would not move. They burned, tall, waving, and as I saw them.

It could have been a trick of the light, maybe the weather plus the fire's heat, but Mahrab's brow broke into thick sweat.

Or maybe it could have been that he found himself a challenge in the will of a young boy.

I'd like to believe the latter.

For a moment, his shadow swayed as if receding from mine. Then it looked to grow and loom, coming to swallow me before sinking back in place. A sign of my fatigue and how I could barely see properly. Not to mention the sun behind me baking my skull and making me delusional.

A layer of sweat coated me down to my waist. I fought for each breath now, begging my lungs to take in what air they could. And the area directly behind my eyes pulsated like it nursed a separate heartbeat.

I wouldn't be able to contend Mahrab's will much longer. The amount of folds I held may have been impressive to him, but the duration I could maintain them couldn't compete with his training. Not to mention, I wasn't battling a quick binding of a stone's strike. This was a match of endurance.

The both of us pushed and pulled against the mind of the other, forcing our utter belief and vision of the fire against the other's folds.

And our struggle happened to catch the fire in the middle of it.

Mahrab had once told me that everything has its own story—a truth in and of itself. That fire had life to it, and that it had its own destiny—a will.

To say I understood the story of fire back then would be a gross exaggeration. But I did come to learn a piece of it. A piece that will always stay with me.

Fire's purpose isn't to burn—to destroy. It's to live. Fire fights against the world to exist. For each spark, it fights. It's literally born of friction, of flint and steel striking hard and fast. To warm our hearts and light our nights. It wants to burn, and to last evermore. But its own nature consumes what sustains it. Even so, it tries to spread, to grow. It's violently passionate about living—existing. It's harder to temper and to slow.

And there's a piece of it inside us all. It just goes by other names and takes different shapes.

When I came to realize this, I relinquished my hold on the folds and let the fire burn as it wanted.

Mahrab's eyes widened when he realized what I'd done. His binding didn't compress the fire down on itself. Mahrab's efforts had been focused on combating mine more than simply binding the flames. In theory, his folds should have smothered the fire completely, or left a ring of orange inches high.

Now that my resistance had vanished, he had to adjust for the flames as they were, not as I'd tried to keep them against his own will.

The rapid correction proved too much along with the surprise.

Fire flared, sinking low before snapping violently as Mahrab's shock broke his folds. The flames hissed and burned as if neither of us had entertained our battle of minds at all.

Silence.

Mahrab watched me for a span of time I lost track of. "What were you thinking?" He spoke in a voice kept so painfully free of emotion, I couldn't find the words to reply. "Well, Ari?"

I licked my lips. "I was thinking that by releasing my folds, you'd have to contend with the will of fire and readjust your own."

Mahrab's lips moved, his words inaudible against the fire. The flames sank into the stone and died out. "That was reckless, Ari. Stupid. Dangerous. Childish." Every word came clipped and hard like each time I'd been struck with a stone. "Releasing your folds like that in the middle of a binding can send your mind slipping away, Ari. If that doesn't happen, you must still fight with the new behavior of something living—like fire. If I wasn't a proper binder, that could have harmed me in a way you do not understand. If you were holding a binding instead of just opposing one, you would have endured a horrendous backlash."

The revelation sobered me. "Mahrab, I didn't know. I'm . . . sorry."

He slapped the stone beneath us. "It's not enough to be sorry, Ari." He sighed, cradling his forehead in a palm. "This is why I haven't shown you the bindings. You're not ready."

I opened my mouth to protest, but Mahrab rose, collecting himself. His shadow towered over me, swallowing my whole small one.

Without a word, he made his way to the trapdoor and left the rooftop.

I sat there and stared at the darkened ring where the burning oil had been. Part of my mind lingered on Mahrab's chastisement and the gravity of his words. Another piece, however, clung to what I had heard.

Tak and roh. Two of the bindings he'd spoken. My thoughts tumbled into a fury like leaves caught in a gale.

Mahrab's binding had been fixed on compressing the flames from top to bottom, meaning the two bindings logically coincided with that. These were the two pieces he must have used when he threatened to bring down the roof on Koli when we'd first met.

I recited them over and over, promising myself to never let their names go.

The heat grew to be too much and I rose to follow after Mahrab. I knew confronting him so soon after what I'd done wouldn't go over well, but maybe I could find other ways to pass my time until things between us settled.

The inside of the theater brought a coolness in and over me that I gave thanks for. Several of the theater troupe mingled on the stage, garbed in a motley mix of their usual clothing and costumes. Kauri moved through exaggerated and fluid circular dances. Her wrists turned through a series of flowing movements like she was beckoning someone who refused to come no matter how hard she called.

Makham sat at the lip of the stage, legs dangling off of it. He held a series of parchments in hand and his mouth moved like he was reading.

Their efforts were obvious. Each member worked as hard as possible, likely owing to the fact Koli's money had been sunk into the theater. And he'd collect. No matter what. Failure wasn't an option. Neither was a half-decent performance. Only perfection would do.

Khalim stood within the stalls. He waved me over when he caught sight of me. "Oi."

I hurried to him, slowing my pace to a crawl as I drew near. "*Ji?*" I inclined my head a shade out of respect.

"I've been looking for you. Vithum says you've been taking to the choreography well, hm?"

I rubbed a hand against the back of my head, trying not to obviously revel in the compliment. "I think so, yes."

"Good. Good." Khalim sounded as if he were speaking more to himself than me. "And, how are things with Mahrab? I saw him go by with a wind in him. Did you two lock horns?" He gave me a knowing look like he knew the answer already.

I shied away from the stare. "It's a possibility."

"Mhm." He clapped a hand to my shoulder, giving me a gentle shake. "Give him time to stew, ah? When men get to be our age, anger turns to a funny thing. It can come quick as lightning for small things, but it passes just as fast. It goes with the storm. He'll calm. Besides, I want to talk to you about the play."

Sparks of excitement coursed through me, setting me to fidget, but I controlled them. Somewhat. Khalim picked up on this.

He smiled wide, one that set the skin under his eyes crinkling. "Ah, I thought that'd speak to you. I know Vithum told you some of this, yes?"

I nodded.

"Well, don't let it get to your head, but I know you've been working hard. And, we're going to need you." He fixed me with a long stare. "Koli's money comes with strings, Ari. It'll be owed back. *With interest.* So I mean to put on a show the people of Abhar will remember. That means all hands on deck."

I tilted my head, unsure of what he was getting at. Vithum had already explained that we would be playing bandits and cutthroats. I kept quiet, however, waiting for Khalim to clarify.

"You're not training for a piddling role, Ari. I'm not a fool. You're young, yes, but one day all of my performers will be too old to swing a sword or sing. They'll have creaks in their bones and croaks in their voices. Are you following?"

I was, but I couldn't fully take it all to heart. If I guessed right, Khalim had me in mind for a better spot than I'd imagined. Something closer to what I hoped for.

"You know of Sakhan?"

". . . Yes?" The boy rogue had been another favorite hero of mine. A runaway prince who set out on adventure to make a name of his own and escape the bondage of sheltered palace life. He sailed seas, learned swordsmanship, fought the supernatural, courted them, and even stumbled through the realm of the Shaen according to the stories. "Is that who I'm to play? Is that what you're performing?" I shook within his grip as my thoughts ran away in exhilaration.

"*Arrey-arrey,* Ari." He squeezed my shoulders, working to calm me. "Brahm's blood, boy, you're shaking harder than Makham when he's had a bad brew and gets the shits. But yes. It's part of my story with the Ashura. Sakhan, Athwun, The Nine, and a string running through them all." He stopped and rubbed his chin, looking away for a moment. "Though, I seem to still be a far bit from the end of that damn rope, no matter how much I pull on it. It feels like it's longer than I can see, and sometimes I come on pieces knotted up that I have to untangle.

"Anyway, you're too young to be Athwun, but the little pirate prince?" Khalim smiled. "That I think you can do, ah?"

I nodded hard enough to risk hurting my neck. "*Ji.*"

Khalim pulled his hands back and finally freed me from his hold. "Good boy. Now, take the day off. No stage work today." He reached down, taking one of my earlobes between a thumb and forefinger, giving it a gentle tug. "Go make some mischief somewhere, ah?" He flashed me a quick smile that slipped into a stone mask of seriousness. "Somewhere away from the stage, Ari. If I can keep peace between you and Makham until my big play, all the better. Otherwise I'll have both your asses caned till you learn to start thinking more with this." He thumped me lightly across the head.

I took the warning with grace. A thought struck me as I pulled away, and my gaze turned to one of the halls at the opposite side of the theater from me. "Do you know where Mahrab went, Khalim?"

He blew a breath out through his nostrils and his shoulders sagged. "He's probably tipping his nose through the books in my study. When we can't talk stories, he finds it comfortable to go digging on his own. Check there, but remember what I said, hm? Let an old man's anger simmer before you go tossing more hot coals at him."

He clapped me on the back, and I gave him a quick thanks as I raced to Khalim's study. The door hung open just wide enough for me to slip my fingers through. Dark mutterings came from its other side, and I knew Khalim hadn't exaggerated about Mahrab's mood. My knuckles bounced a few times off the door. "May I come in, Rishi?"

"Oh-ho, *now* I'm getting the honorific of Rishi, hm?"

I held back the scowl wanting to edge across my face. "You are my Rishi, Mahrab."

No response.

I exhaled, knowing my best course sat in swallowing my ego and apologizing. Easy enough in theory, but there's something to be said about the self-assurance and cockiness of young boys.

I was certainly no different. And after more than a month of dedicating myself to learning the folds and bettering my swordsmanship, I felt my new-found confidence well warranted.

But knowing one's audience is just as much part of performing as the act itself. So I sucked down my pride and gently pushed the door open.

Mahrab didn't look up from his book, scanning the pages as he idly thumbed them by. He adjusted his posture a shade, the only cue that he'd registered me entering the room. Another page turned with the sounds of dry paper and old worn leather creaking.

I worked some saliva through my mouth and spoke. "Mahrab—Rishi." A pause. Apologies come easy to many, but for all those who find it quick, they're also the ones that fall flat. Sincerity in the act meant a great deal more than the words chosen. And in the moment, I found myself lingering in conflict.

I recognized the wrong in what I did, but my actions had been born out of nothing but honest curiosity—a risk to explore more of the bindings. At times, Mahrab rewarded my hunger. I was smart enough to know the difference between what I'd done now versus before.

Paper scraped as the edge of one sheet slid along the flat of another piece before falling flat. Mahrab remained silent, his eyes still on the book.

"Rishi, I'm sorry."

He stopped turning the pages but didn't look up. Mahrab wanted me to do more than just apologize, then. He wanted me to explain why I was sorry—what for.

I sucked in a breath, working to remain calm and placid. "I'm sorry for what I did, trying to find clever ways around the binding and doing something as reckless as I did."

Mahrab pulled his gaze away from the pages and settled it on me. He remained quiet.

"I shouldn't have thought I knew better than you—"

"Hurmph. That's certainly a start."

I kept my voice from taking on an edge and continued. "I shouldn't have tampered with our exercise. I thought about what you said once before concerning the story of fire. I think I learned a piece of it and I wanted to test it out. I should have stopped the lesson and told you my theory. I should have been cautious. I should have probably done a dozen other things than what I did, but I didn't. I'm sorry, Rishi."

The book snapped shut with a soft thud. Mahrab placed it on a dark wooden desk behind him, steepling his fingers together as he rested his chin atop them. "And I suppose this is the part where I apologize for maybe being too quick to anger. Too hard on you, hm?"

I kept on to the momentary wisdom I'd found and decided to remain respectfully silent. Though, it would be a lie to deny that I would have appreciated a little contrition on Mahrab's part. Though I'd have had better luck wringing blood from stone.

"Ari, I was right in my anger. Maybe I voiced it too harshly, but right nonetheless. The bindings are not toys. They are not little tricks for clever children.

The bindings affect the fabric of our world—reality. They are the shaping tools within our power to walk where gods did. And the same goes for the elements. Do not presume to meddle lightly with them, especially with only a *piece* of their story."

I wanted to add another apology, but I knew it wouldn't do any good in the heat of his anger. So I lowered my head and fixed my attention on the floor as I just so happened to find it exceptionally fascinating in the moment.

A long heavy sigh left his lips and he leaned back in the chair. "Ari, I'm angry more for your safety than at you, boy. I could have handled the fire's backlash. But you could not."

That brought me back from my fixation on the ground. "What? But I didn't bind the fire?"

"Not in the way you're thinking, but you did hold it in the folds, yes?" I knew enough not to respond to that. His tone made it clear he intended to go on with the explanation. "You were caught in it just as much as I was. We were both affecting it, in a way. If I hadn't regained control, you would have suffered severely for dropping your folds so quickly. Our wills were contending, and the fire stood between us. You were just as much wrapped up in it in that moment. That is part of the price we risk as binders when battling the will of another. Neither of us are safe. Neither can easily cut that kite's cord and let it float away harmlessly."

I licked my lips, realizing what I had really done.

My folds were not simply the tool to help me shape and apply my will to the world, they were my shield as well. They kept what I wished to affect from doing the same back to me. The folds were chisel to cut, hammer to drive, and they were the guard to keep me from bludgeoning my thumb—worse, breaking it.

And fire's nature, among many things, also carried the urge to burn. I was no exception to that. Had Mahrab failed in regaining control of the situation, the connection to the flames could have sent a scorching fury through my mind. I wasn't sure at that time what the damage could have been, but I knew enough to be grateful my mentor had prevented it. And enough to know that I would never again be so reckless concerning bindings and the folds.

For a time anyway.

"Mahrab, I understand. I do. I'm—"

He rose from his seat and retrieved the book, making his way to the shelves set into the stone of the walls. Countless other books and loose papers sat there in a manner making it clear Khalim never had the time nor care to set them straight. Mahrab placed the book between others, taking a moment to right them properly. "That's the problem, Ari. You understand. You *always* understand, or think you do. You don't. Not yet. But maybe that's my fault."

The walls of the room seemed to grow farther apart and I realized how small I was. The twin candles burning atop Khalim's desk called to me, and I wanted to lose myself in them, to think only of the flames.

"Ari." His voice could have come from another room—so soft and distant.

Both bulbs of fire danced and I sank into them, then the folds. I imagined them countless times over, bobbing and flaring. The exercise came back to me. I remembered the words he'd uttered earlier, and his efforts to compress the fire. My hand moved as if pulled by strings.

"Ari?"

I paid no mind to his call. "Tak."

Something clamped hard to my wrist, pulling me away from my spot and the momentary trance.

An icy wave rolled through my spine, settling in the back of my head. The jarring transition from the candle and the flame to Mahrab holding me in a tight grip left me unable to focus. "What were you doing? What were you thinking? What did you just say?"

Clarity still eluded me.

He shook me hard enough to set my head bobbling. "Ari!"

I found a thread of focus to pull on and speak from. "What do tak and roh mean, Rishi?" The words left me before I'd realized I'd spoken. I had a good idea, but I wanted—needed—the surety of an answer now that I'd asked.

Mahrab's grip slackened until he released me completely. He walked away slowly, returning to the bookshelves. One of his forearms pressed against the stone alcove and he leaned against it. "I should have known you'd hear that and remember." Another sigh left him, one that brought his weariness out to the surface. He looked old. The lines of his face appeared deeper. And, it could have been a trick of the light, but I caught more gray in his hair than before. "You've a good ear for more than just stories, Ari."

I knew it wasn't a compliment.

He turned and rested his back against the shelves, crossing his arms over his chest. "What do you think they are, clever one?" He sounded almost like a part of him didn't want me to answer, or at least be right.

"Bindings. Two parts of the binding you were working against my folds. To bring the fire down from the tips of the flames to the stone."

Mahrab brought a hand to his face, cradling it in an open palm. "I should have foreseen this." He blew a breath through the open space between fingers. "Yes, Ari. To the point perfectly, sharp as ever. They are the two parts and points of bindings. A composite pair in fact." He lowered his hand and moved to the center of Khalim's study.

"Now watch carefully." Mahrab raised an index finger to point at the ceiling. "Tak. As above." He gestured then to a spot on the ground. "Roh. So below. *That* is the first binding and its correlation to the world around us, Ari. And, no, before your clever little mind runs away with the possibilities, stop. It's not enough to know the incantations. It's not enough to know what they do, Ari. Remember, *always,* remember the foundations, the folds, the faith."

The weight of his voice and tone made only one thought come to mind. "I will, Rishi. I promise."

He waved me off. "I'm tired. I'm just rambling old man's words and fears in my head. Leave me to sit here for a while with the books before I start spitting nonsense at you. Lessons are done for the next few days, Ari. I need to think."

I didn't argue. "Yes, Rishi." I slipped out of the room, closing the door behind me. Enough of the day remained for me to make good on Khalim's words.

Some mischief to be made. And I learned an exciting and terrible thing.

The first binding.

Though first among the ten, it wouldn't be the first I'd call. Though my legends would certainly claim it so, among many other things.

And I would learn I was far farther away from channeling one than I would have liked to believe.

More's the pity, because I still wonder what would have changed in my life had I been able to execute it properly in the days to come.

NINETEEN

Intermission—Comfort and Closeness

Something jabbed my cheek, a small point of pressure that vanished just as quickly. I turned my head to stare at Eloine as she pulled her finger back from where she'd poked me. One of my brows rose, asking a silent question.

"Oh, you were getting far too serious." She waved a hand several times.

I held my look. "I told you this was a tragedy."

She gently laid her weight against my side. "Mhm. Or, you're being mercilessly hard on yourself for falling into all the trappings of being a boy."

"*Young* boy." I added emphasis to the correction.

Eloine pulled away and eyed me askance. "Youth has little to do with it. Boys are always young, and that's part of the problem." She turned away, looking to the ceiling and pursing her lips. "They grow taller and broader by the years, but I'm not so sure things change here"—she tapped me once on my temple, then over my heart—"or here."

I had a mind to argue, but some truth hung in her words. If it hadn't, then maybe I wouldn't have come to do all the things I had, and paid their prices. With a fair few still waiting to collect from me.

I tapped the base of my staff against the floorboards several times, hoping the steady and rhythmic tapping would help my mind settle. It did little.

Eloine picked up on my momentary discomfort with what I guessed was intuition. She laid an arm on mine, pushing with just enough force to make me aware of the effort but not enough to tip me onto my back. "You're tense. You're brooding. You are—"

"I'm not brooding." I rolled my shoulder, shrugging free of her hold. "I *was* contemplating. It means to be deep in thought, something you might want to try." I knew my words were harsher than what I'd meant to say. But I'd spoken them, and I paid for it.

Eloine's eyes narrowed to slits. "Oh, is that so? Maybe, oh Storyteller, that is exactly your problem. Maybe you're so wrapped up in yourself, your misery, and your *deep thoughts* that you can't see what's right in front of you." Her words were bait to rile me.

I knew that, and yet I rose to it regardless.

I have never claimed to be a wise man.

"And what exactly is that, huh? What do you think I'm missing? Because from where I'm sitting, it's you that can't see a—"

Her finger darted out, the tip of it tapping the end of my nose twice in quick succession. "Like that."

I blinked several times, all thought leaving me. I reached for something to say but came short of even an incoherent mutter.

If you've never had a beautiful woman tap you on the nose in the middle of what some would call a tantrum, but likely would be kinder to name a fit, let me tell you what it's like.

All of the anger fled me like water tipped from a pail. Any thoughts followed in kind. I sat there, processing the ridiculousness of what had just happened while I had been about to level a tongue-lashing on her.

She bit one corner of her lip while the other side quivered slightly. Her mouth didn't tremble in trepidation. This was someone struggling to control a smile one knew was inappropriate. Her eyes, however, gave full voice to that. They shimmered with a mischievous and amused light. A moment later, her efforts failed and she burst into a torrent of giggles.

"Did you just tap my nose like I'm nothing more than a stray kitten?"

She didn't stop, now breaking into a proper laugh. "Oh, well, a kitten would have more sense." Eloine had to choke out the words in the space between her fit. "And, many women would argue they are infinitely cuter."

I scowled.

"Oh, stop that, you're sinking back to broody again."

My mouth moved to argue back, but I'd regained enough of my sense to know it would be pointless. So I adopted respectful silence.

Eloine pressed against me again, this time throwing more of her weight behind the gesture. She made it clear that she wanted me to fall flat onto the bed.

I obliged her.

I've been fortunate to learn a few important things in my life, one of them being: When a dream of a woman wants to bring you down to the bed, let her.

"Are we going to bed together now?" I kept my voice free of inflection.

She leaned on her side, staring for a long moment into my eyes without a word. "Going to bed with a man is different than taking one to bed. I trust you know the difference?"

I nodded. "I do."

She smiled. "Good. Because I figured this would take some of the stone out of your face and iron from your spine. You might find it easier to tell your tale while enjoying some comfort."

"In bed?"

"And in my company, of course."

I matched her grin. "Of course. I can't deny that I'm fond of this closeness."

She shimmied her way closer, rogue strands of our hairs overlapping. Her breath warmed the skin of my cheeks and where she'd touched my nose. The scent of juniper and sandalwood, weaker than before, still came from her.

I breathed it in deep and relaxed. My grip remained tight on my staff, however. I wouldn't risk it tipping back and setting the bedding afire.

It's a frowned-upon thing in most establishments to set the place burning, and worse still if you happen to be in the building all the while.

Eloine seemed to share my concern. She gestured to the fiery tip of my staff. "Careful with that. Many a man has ruined a great thing by losing control of his tool."

I squinted at her. "Really?"

She feigned a smile of such innocence I'd have had an easier time believing it coming from a cat looking to steal a piece of my meal than her.

"Are you worried about a little fire?" A maniacal thought seized hold of me and I let it out in the form of a crazed laugh. My staff tilted back, coming closer to us, but still hanging around arm's reach.

She flinched, but didn't move away from me. Realizing I had no intent to bring the fire any closer, she frowned and snapped an elbow to one side.

"Ow." A dull throb pulsed from where she'd jabbed me. "Careful. Another blow like that and I daresay I might lose control of this." I gave my staff a little jiggle. "And people aren't as fireproof as they wish they could be."

She snorted. "If all it takes is two blows for you to lose your grip, I daresay I'm disappointed."

A flush took me from my cheeks down to my neck, but given the proximity of my fire and the coloring of room, it's just as easily possible that it was nothing more than a trick of the light.

Eloine saw my reaction and shot me a devilish grin.

I opened my mouth to say something remarkably clever, but she beat me to it.

Her expression sobered and she reached up to trail two fingers along the length of my staff. She moved them slowly, as if trying to take in every minute detail simply from touch. Her eyes looked lost in the wood. "But the stories say you are . . . don't they?"

I didn't know what she meant by that.

"Nonflammable—unburned. That's what they call you, isn't it?"

I licked my lips and nodded. "Yes. But we're a far way from that part of my story. We'll come to it soon enough as well, if you'd like me to go on."

She turned her gaze away from the staff, pulling her hand back as well. "I would." Eloine reached out and took some of my hair that had mingled with hers between her fingers. She brushed them apart and back along the side of my head.

"Very well. I've drawn my story out a bit, I suppose. A part of me hoped we wouldn't reach this part. But let's be done with it. Yes, I came to be known as unburned. But, for all that I could wish it had been years earlier in my life, it wasn't the case. Because there was one night out of all the nights in my life where it would have truly been a gift. A night I needed it. A night of burning.

"A night I learned that stories and the monsters who lurk in them are very much real."

TWENTY
BURNING

I wobbled atop the plank, fighting both for balance and against the urge to dismount and tackle the man before me to the ground.

Vithum whirled his blunted brass scimitar overhead, catching bits of the sun along its edge. "Balance, Ari-*cha*. Balance!" He advanced with short measured steps, forcing me back.

The wooden board rested on a low foundation of bricks at either end, creating a narrow strip for us to fight on. In theory, it gave me a place to practice my balance. In actuality, it felt like I'd been forced to spend a hungry morning training under the unforgiving sun.

Occasional stinging pins pricked my eyes as sweat trickled into them from my brow. But Vithum had little care for my discomfort. The choreographer drove me farther back on the plank, promising to push me off if I couldn't find a way to counter.

The blade came toward my skull at an angle that looked to take me just above the ear. Its edge wouldn't break skin unless swung with serious force, and Vithum had far too much control to let that happen. But a nasty lump wasn't outside the realm of possibility. And a headache that would have me retching what little I had in my stomach from the previous night.

Taking the blow against my own sword would have me toppling from the plank. I didn't have the footing, skill, or size to block Vithum's attack. So I played to my strengths. I sank to my haunches, my hair tingling as the sword sailed close enough to touch the locks. It passed me by and I watched Vithum's feet readjust to keep himself steady as he fought to recover.

My chance.

I sprang forward, bulling my small bulk into his stomach. I didn't have much room to build up proper momentum. My shoulders crashed into his midsection as I wrapped my arms around him, relinquishing my grip on the sword. He'd chastise me for it later, but that would be well after I'd won the bout.

My vision faltered as a cord of white raced along it. I became acutely aware of the salmon insides of my eyelids and I reeled in place. A dull and heavy throb built at the top of my head.

Vithum eased his way out of my slackened hold, waggling his sword on his hand.

I winced through watery eyes and pain to see him tapping the weapon's curved pommel with a pinky. That explained what had happened and why a procession of drums beat in my skull . . . and the lump that would follow.

He'd bashed the base of the sword off my skull and used the moment to break free of my hold.

"Why did you drop your sword, Ari-*cha*?"

I muttered something dark under my breath.

"Eh?"

I glared at him, still rubbing the top of my head. "Because I can't beat you with the sword, and I'm having a hard enough time standing on this damnable plank!" I punctuated the statement by stomping the wood once. It wobbled, as did I.

Vithum placed a hand on my shoulder to steady me. "You should rest, Ari-*cha*. Today is rehearsal." He moved his hands to the sides of my head, holding it steady before he rubbed the spot where he'd whacked me.

I winced again, but his touch was gentle and searching.

"Not so bad." He clicked his tongue once. "Ka." Another rub. "Go rest." He moved his hand to the broad of my back and gave me a quick slap before he shoved off the platform.

The blow to my head hadn't been so bad that I couldn't keep my footing even as I stumbled off the plank. I staggered a bit but found my balance, easier than ever before courtesy of Vithum's training. He didn't need to tell me twice to excuse myself and find time to enjoy the day.

I hurried down the trapdoor, heading straight for my den in the understage.

❧

The stone walls of the theater underbelly cooled me. I leaned against the hard rock surface near the rickety scaffolding supporting my bed. After I'd relaxed and found myself steadier than before, I made my way over to my water barrel to give myself a rinse.

A tapping sounded from above.

I shook it from my mind, knowing it to be the likely impact of stone and debris kicked along the road level that met my window. If not that, a particularly determined bird had made it its goal to irritate me.

The sound loudened.

It took considerably more effort than I care to admit not to splash my hands against the water in frustration.

The tapping altered its beat to *tip-tip tap-tap tip tap tip.*

I paused, tilting my head to listen harder in case the particular rhythm repeated.

It did.

My eyes widened as I realized what it meant.

I scrambled back to my platform, clambered atop it, then up the stone wall to the window.

Nisha's face stared back at me and she waved.

I undid the window latch and beckoned her inside, and the pair of us made our way down onto my bed.

She threw her weight against me the instant we'd sat ourselves comfortably in place. "I've missed you."

I placed one arm around her and returned the sentiment. "Same. I thought you'd be by to visit more since last time. I've been learning things, and I'm an even better storyteller now. Khalim has me rehearsing tonight!" A part of that wasn't exactly true. Between my studies with Vithum and Mahrab, I had little time to read old tales and perform for my amusement and practice.

Nisha pulled away from me, and I noticed the thin splotches of road grime caked to her with sweat. "I have been coming to visit, Ari." She gave me a thin and tired smile. "You never answer."

Oh. A weight of stone settled in my core, chilling me in ways I didn't appreciate in the moment. "Nisha, I'm sorry. I didn't know. I was . . ."

I was what? Too busy to see my only friend who happened to live under the thumb of a cruel cutthroat? Too busy off learning storybook magic and training to be onstage while she had to steal, beg, and probably catch the rough side of Koli's tongue and hands?

No.

There wasn't really anything I could say to take the sting out of the truth. I had been so wrapped up in my own delusions of fantasy and adventure, I'd ignored her. And that simple truth struck home rather hard.

"I'm sorry." When dealing with the hard truths, sometimes there isn't anything better or needed more than the simple answers. I had nothing that would serve as an adequate excuse.

"It's fine, because now you're here!" Her smile shone with an honest enthusiasm that only made the stone inside me all the heavier. Simply seeing me had been enough for her to forgive all the time I'd ignored her.

Forgiveness is a powerful thing, and a child's all the more.

She didn't care about my excuses or reasons and didn't think for a second that I found her less than important. To her, all that mattered was we could be together now.

"Thank you, Nisha."

She held the smile and reached into one of the pockets of her shorts, pulling free a piece of bright orange fruit sliced in a half moon. Nisha thrust it toward me, her mouth pulling down at one corner. "Sorry, it's been in there since I picked it before midday. Some of the juices got out inside my clothes. But it's probably still good. I know you like mangos."

I did. I took it, then caught her watching me—waiting for me to bite into it.

But her lips twitched in a way I knew all too well. And the light in her eyes spoke a single word to me: hunger.

Asking her when she'd last eaten would surely turn the conversation down a street she wouldn't want to go. Nisha would seize up and I'd get nowhere.

So I tried to bolster my earlier apology and give my friend the kindness she deserved. "I'm a little full from earlier." I pretended to wince, but upon seeing the wounded look on her face, I decided to break the piece of fruit in half. "But how about we each take some?"

Her hand reached out, but stopped just before her fingertips could brush against the fruit's skin. Nisha's fingers shook, letting me know a part of her still couldn't bear to take back part of the gift she'd brought me.

I gently eased the mango into her hand. "If I eat too much of this, I'll get sick. I've been training all morning under Vithum. I'm close to retching my insides out." I tapped my piece against hers before biting into the fruit.

Sweetness burst over my tongue and I took my time consuming the rest of my portion. I followed every bite with a moment to keep my lips pressed against the spot and suck the juices greedily. "Thank you for that. I haven't had fruit in . . . well, I can't remember." I tossed the peel aside, doing the same with hers when she finished.

"I know. You never really get much of anything, Ari. Even out." She gestured to the window. "When's the last time you left?" She already knew the answer to it, so I couldn't imagine why she'd bothered to ask me.

But I felt it fair to oblige, given that I'd kept her waiting for a sight of me near to a month. "I haven't since Khalim took me in. I haven't left the theater for as long as I can remember."

She hunched over, pulling her knees close to her chest and wrapping her arms around them in a tight hug. "Why?"

A simple question. And one I had no answer for. Not a good one at any rate.

Nisha shuffled over to me, gently bumping me with her shoulder. "Why, Ari? Why do you stay here and never try to leave?"

One of my hands moved of its own accord, gesturing halfheartedly to my surroundings. "Khalim needs me to clank and pull. He needs me to shovel and smoke. I have duties." I heard my own voice grow dull and distant. "Sometimes I linger at night and watch from the high seats when there's a play. I learn. I have all the things to study here too. Khalim lets me take books from his study and—"

One of Nisha's fingers pressed against my lips, stopping me. "You can always leave in between all of that. You never do. You're scared."

She was right, of course. For all the stories of adventure I absorbed, for all I'd been learning from Vithum, from Mahrab, the truth was a simpler thing. The theater had been my home so long a time that it came to dominate all my thoughts. Until the binder had come to teach me something more. But even still, leaving the safety of the theater filled my chest and stomach with cold stone.

I was Sullied. So I would be shunned a dozen times more than the lowest of actual caste members. My years of choosing to hide in the theater had left me dangerously ignorant of the streets outside. A problem that perpetuated itself the more I indulged it, but by now, it had built up to a formidable fear of its own. And then, what would I do? Where would I go? What possible reason could I have to want to go out into the quarter?

We resided in the lowest of them, and the soft trade and silks dominated the area. It wasn't a place of safety for children. Nisha's life showed that. And I had no idea how to navigate it.

I gave voice to all these concerns and more, hoping Nisha would understand.

If she did, she didn't show it. "But you have me." Nisha took one of my hands in hers, squeezing it tight and lacing our fingers together. "I'll take care of you. I know all the best places to sneak. I know where we can watch the best clouds pass and the people and the stars, if you can stay a little bit into night?"

I wanted to tell her off. Tell her that I couldn't. Tonight would be my first step closer to making my dreams reality. Then it hit me that, no, that wasn't the truth.

Since Mahrab had come into my life, my thoughts had wandered to new imaginings. I saw distant mountains and valleys. A life of magic and wonder along the Golden Road. New countries. Channeling bindings—lost magics. Finding lost and forgotten stories, and then telling them in taverns far and wide like they'd never been told before. I could and would be able to perform alone. And for that life, I would very much need to get the hell out once in a while.

I sucked in a breath, heart hammering. "You're right." I bowed my head and gave her hand a squeeze as a silent thank-you. "You're right. *But*"—I raised an index finger from my other hand—"I have to be back by *kundhul,* before end of seventh candle. Got it? I've got nearly the whole day, but we practice when dark comes on until midnight. And I'll still have to let Khalim know."

"Let Khalim know what?" The theater owner rapped one of the rickety legs of my bed platform a few times. "Ah? That you want to sneak out for most of the day and play at being a little rat. That you want to ignore your duties? Or, maybe that you want to—"

"He has a right!" Nisha's hand left mine and she bolted to her feet. Her fingers curled, two fists balled tight as she quivered. "He works harder here than anyone. And you know it too." She pointed a finger at him in accusation. "He runs the understage and he studies."

Khalim's eyes widened for the space of several breaths. "Nisha, it's always wonderful to see you, dear." His comment seemed to drain some of the anger out of her. "You know my trade here, hm? We're all performers, sweet one. I was teasing Ari." Khalim waved a hand toward one of the halls leading out of the understage. "But if you're going to leave, don't crawl out through the windows. If that glass breaks, I'll have to replace it. And if either of you falls, you'll crack your heads open and I don't want to be cleaning that up. *Ji-ah?*"

Nisha and I thanked him in unison and scrambled down the platform. She clung to his leg in a quick hug before peeling away to join me. We raced down the halls together as Khalim's cry echoed down after us.

"Be back by—"

"*Kundhul*. I know!"

Nisha led me up over a series of wooden stalls that leaned against each other for support, making up for their shoddy construction. We climbed our way along protruding blocks of equally sloppy masonry, finally reaching the rooftop of a building well into the center of the Soft Quarter.

People thronged in the narrow streets below, kicking up plumes of dust. Watching the scene reminded me of silken bands, too many colors to count, all caught in the wind during one of Khalim's plays.

Even with all my practice in the folds, tracking the maddening hive of activity sent my mind reeling.

"How do you move and live through all of this?" I kept my gaze down on the mob filtering through side streets, shoving each other aside while a few slipped through the scant spaces between people with practiced grace.

"You just do. You think too much, Ari. That's one of your problems."

I blinked. "*One* of my problems?"

She grinned, taking one of my earlobes between her thumb and forefinger, tugging it twice before letting it go. "One. Sometimes you need to stop. Sometimes it just gets in the way, like today. You didn't want to come with me at first."

I hadn't. But that came more from fear than overthinking. It certainly didn't come from not wanting to spend time with her. Now that we sat above the buildings, watching the mingling crowds below, I couldn't think what else I'd rather be doing with my time.

A simple beauty hung in watching people go about their lives in the rush of it all. Mahrab had taught me the importance of watching things—understanding their stories. And I saw a piece of everyone's below as we stared.

My mind turned to the candle and the flame, only now I held another piece of that place in my head open to taking in the sight on the streets.

One of the men I spotted wore a robe that hung to his ankles. Its color was a rich cobalt washed in places with a clean white reserved for fresh cream. His head was covered by a wrap of the same color. The cut didn't scream extravagance, but maintaining its bright dye without the slightest hint of wear spoke volumes of the wealth behind the man.

Nisha elbowed me. "Merchant. Good one."

I blinked and lost my hold on the candle and the flame. "How do you know?"

She pointed a finger at his clothing, making the same observations I had. Nisha then gestured to his headwrap. "That means he's from the Golden Road. Not from any of the kingdoms here. Maybe Zibrath? Tikhar? I don't know, but only traveling merchants wear that to keep their faces safe from the desert sands. And then look there." She pointed to one of the man's hands and the object in it.

A small leather pouch sat comfortably in his grip, but Nisha took hold of my chin, redirecting my stare. I caught sight of what she intended for me to notice. A thin leather cord ran from the pouch into the folds of his robe.

"He's been pickpocketed before or warned a long time ago. Only smart and good merchants do that. Most of those are the ones who end up rich." She rocked in place, evening light catching her eyes and adding a twinkle to them. "Koli would be really happy with me if I plucked that from him."

The muscles along my neck knotted and my jaw tightened. "Maybe you won't have to steal for Koli anymore."

Nisha looked at me like I'd told her the sun would plummet from the sky. She ran a few fingers through her hair, twining them idly in the curls. "I'll *always* have to do that. I don't have anywhere else to go. I'm Sullied like you. Nothing I can do, Ari. Koli still takes care of me." Her posture changed.

Nothing so noticeable to anyone giving her a fleeting look, but after a month of training with Mahrab, she may as well have been doing cartwheels.

Her body stiffened for an instant before she pulled away from me. The muscles along her shoulders shuddered before she regained control. The look in her eyes grew distant as if she were looking past me rather than at me.

I knew enough to not reach out and offer her a comforting hand. It would only frighten her in the moment. I made my voice as low and calming as possible, like I was speaking to a rabbit on the verge of running. "What if you could come with me?"

"Where?" Her voice held no scorn at the suggestion, only curiosity. "Khalim wouldn't have me in the theater. What would I do?" She turned her gaze toward the skies and dimming horizon.

I could almost see the longing in her stare. The desire to be anywhere else than Abhar, and doing anything but what she absolutely had to. "What if I told you I'm planning on leaving?" I'm not sure what possessed me to say it. Maybe a part of me had already known it to be true and spoke for me. Or perhaps it was the simpler thing of telling a lie in the moment to give my friend hope for the future.

Sometimes, that's all we can do. Trade truths for lies and the comforts they offer, because not everyone needs the truth. Not always. Sometimes they need ease.

Nisha didn't turn her attention back to me, still keeping it fixed on the sky as it changed to a smear of oranges and berry reds. "Where are you going?"

My tongue spoke for me again. "North. To the Ashram Mahrab's been telling me about. He says anyone can take refuge there. There are laws all the kingdoms abide by in the Empire. And I'm going to study to be a binder."

"Mhm." Her voice grew quieter, like she'd become lost in thought. "That's far. Really far."

A journey of over six hundred miles from where I stood. At least according to Mahrab. Though the man told me he'd walked it, and had stuck to walking everywhere in life—something I couldn't fathom. But given my meager possessions and having no coin to my name, I'd likely be forced to do the same. I didn't voice my concerns to Nisha, though.

"We can figure it out, Nisha."

She smiled, but it failed to touch her eyes. Nisha didn't believe me, or her life with Koli had left her unable to do so.

A piece of me ached for her in that. I wanted nothing more than to move closer and console her, but she wasn't in a place for that. Right now, Nisha sat where most people do when they've let go of hope and turn to what solace dreams can offer.

I left her to that place for several heartbeats. Then, when it became clear she would linger there far longer, I moved closer and waited with her.

Evening passed into night, and *kundhul* hour neared.

Nisha finally slipped back from her reverie, edging over to my side until our shoulders touched. She took my hand in hers, twining our fingers together. "Will you tell me something?"

"Like what?"

"A story—anything."

Torches and braziers had been lit on the street below, throwing up enough dancing flames to draw my attention from spot to spot. The candle and the flame called to me under that much firelight. The moon had risen in full, shining like a piece of polished white glass. People still bustled through the quarter in numbers rivaling the brighter hours earlier.

"How about a game?" I jabbed toward one of the passersby below. "We take turns telling small stories about each person. Guess what they're doing out here and who they are."

Nisha let out a small giggle. "You first."

I took in a figure at the corner of an intersection. He wore a shirt of homespun that could have been cotton. The color had weathered into a muted brown, telling me it must have been white at some point and had dirtied up over time. He wore matching pants and leather sandals. His face was perfectly clean shaven short of an overly grown mustache that made me inherently distrust him.

"He's out late at night trying to get away from his wife. He probably drinks too much and does little else. Look how he's walking." The man stumbled and had to brace on a wall for support. "She nags him, but does so because of his silly little mustache, which he's too proud to shave off."

Nisha giggled louder.

"He's out here hoping to woo another woman, though I think he's in for a lonely night."

Nisha jumped in, pointing to a vendor of spices. The woman's stall was filled with tin cups carrying powders in every color imaginable. She would take a pinch and reach out to travelers, asking for their hands, giving them a sample. It may have been her broad and white smile, or something else, but she managed to get coin from most of the people she stopped. "She's a sad one."

I arched a brow, waiting for Nisha's explanation.

"She's out here morning to night, trying to save money for her children and her mother. She works twice as hard as any man, and she does it with a smile and never looking tired. But she's tired inside." Nisha pressed a hand to her chest. "She won't leave her stall and spices until the last man and woman is off the streets. And here, we know that doesn't happen. She'll be here until morning and sleep behind the stall, praying no one tries to hurt her while she rests."

My mouth dried at the description, but I managed to voice the question on my lips. "That's rather detailed. How did you come up with it?"

Nisha gave me a crooked smile that had no warmth in it. "I know her."

Oh.

The sounds of the quarter and insects took over for a while. Once the sobering revelation lost some of its weight, Nisha nudged me into returning to the game. So we did, passing the time until the bells rang for *kundhul* hour.

An owl came to rest by us, ignoring us completely.

Nisha smiled at it. "It's a good sign. They're the eyes and voices of Naathiya, you know?"

I didn't. Naathiya was the goddess of long night. Patron to orphans, the lost, the wise, the clever. Those who made use of their minds and wits to survive. And some sects of the religious believed she shepherded and tended to thieves—rogues, the ne'er-do-wells.

"It means she's looking out for us tonight."

I hadn't taken Nisha for the spiritual sort, but if my friend found solace in a little owl omen, what was wrong with it? It felt more to me as a sign that she would be fine should I leave.

I got to my feet. "I should get back now. There's still time. Khalim will just be setting the mock placeholders for stage pieces."

"Stay with me, please?" The plea in her voice carried more than just a simple request. Loneliness. Not a child wanting for a friend to idly fritter away time with. Something deeper, more painful.

This was the loneliness of someone who had nowhere else to go tonight, and wanted to have somewhere to belong with someone. Even if for just one point in time. We all want to belong somewhere. And we all wish to have someone to belong with, no matter what we tell ourselves otherwise.

Belonging is one of the oldest calls and cries our hearts make. And when they go unheard, pain fills those empty spaces. It makes that part of us go distant—grow cold. Ice forms and it's ever harder to let anyone ever come into those places again.

Nisha pulled my arm before I could think of a response and leaned forward. Her lips pressed against mine for less than a heartbeat before she pulled away.

It would have been generous to call it a kiss, especially after all I've learned to date, but then, I found myself flushing.

"Please stay."

How could I say no?

I stayed until the bells sounded an hour later that *kundhul* had passed.

And the owl stayed as well, turning its head to finally regard us.

A storm broke out.

Thunder drummed hard enough to rattle my ears. The hand of Brahm had seemingly come to whisk away the moon from its corner. And the owl hooted in a frenzy before tearing into the sky at the onset of the weather change.

It flew drunkenly, as if it had lost all sense of how to move. Other birds took to the air in similar fashion. Crows, hardly visible in the dark and stormy skies, struggled to fly proper. They should have been taking shelter, but they soon set upon themselves, clawing and pecking.

Nisha and I parted ways and I ran as hard as I could toward home, knowing the practice play couldn't have gotten too far in. At the very least, my role was safely set by, waiting for me to appear.

Khalim may have been punctual to the second, but his plays always began with speeches and pontificating. He took his time perfecting the placement of even the mock stage pieces. If they were flawless then, they'd be the same on performance night. He permitted no laziness—nothing short of perfection.

The added delays meant I'd have time to arrive and prepare before my role was called.

I neared the street leading to the theater, my eyes darting from place to place under the low light of night. This part of the quarter didn't benefit from torches or braziers.

It was home to the very softest of trades. Trades of the body: art . . . and those of an unkind nature to men and women, but which called in more coin than any theatrical performance could hope to make. At least here.

Those kinds of places also invited the kind of men who sought to negotiate unfair terms and dealings at knifepoint.

And I wasn't well-equipped to handle those sorts.

Red smoke, almost tinged the color of blood, billowed from one of the buildings ahead.

And I recognized the place.

Its worn stone exterior looked nearly colorless in the dark. Nearly. Violent tendrils of orange and red strobed as much inside the building as outside.

Fire. My home.

I raced toward the theater, making my way to its door. My hand almost touched the brass knob when I registered the heat radiating from it. My heart beat fast and hammered hard as hailstorm. Instinct screamed at me to move, and I did as the door burst apart.

Streams of fire screamed their way out of the new opening, spreading further.

The window. I ran around the corner of the theater, finding the glass pane leading to the understage. No smoke beat against it or clouded my view inside. Relief swelled in me as I noted my underground home had been spared from the fire.

For now.

I had shut the glass pane after Nisha had entered, but hadn't bothered latching it, thankfully. My fingers reflexively twitched as I reached for the window's lip. My hands remembered the near mishap with the doorknob. I took hold and opened the window, sliding through and climbing down onto my bed platform.

"Khalim! Mahrab? Kauri!" Even under the duress of the situation, I couldn't bring myself to scream for Makham. I clambered down the platform, feet hitting the hard ground as I broke into a run. "Anyone?"

No answer.

I left the understage and hurtled through one of the halls, catching sight of more red smoke filtering into the mouth of the passage ahead. I brought the collar of my shirt up against my mouth and nose.

My eyes watered as I bulled through the streams of smoke. My clothing did little to keep me from breathing it in, but I told myself I'd been spared the worst. "Khalim? Mahrab!"

Nothing.

I pressed on, making my way up to the main floor. The hall I entered led to the stage room and seating area. Light cast shadows against the end of the passage. The colors and flickering made clear where the illumination came from.

Fire.

My heart pounded harder, drumming its way into my ears.

"Mahrab!" He would know what to do. He had to be here. He, more than anyone, was keen on hearing Khalim's story. He wanted to know about the Ashura, and had been promised their story in the play.

"Mahrab!" I moved into the stage room and froze.

Sections of the floor had given way as if an earthquake had torn through the place. Stone and wooden tiles sank into the ground, shattered and splintered. Not so far as to damage the roof of the understage, but deep enough to swallow a man whole. Fire licked its way up the theater's balconies and had burned out on the floor where I stood. But the smoke lingered.

Charred remains of wood and cheap upholstery littered the ground.

Ash hung in the air in far greater quantities than it should have, almost as if the whole theater had already been burned. The stench of sulfur flooded my nostrils and nearly drove me to retching.

That's not what stilled me, mind and body, however. Talim, a fresh-faced man, lay under some of the broken wooden beams. He was in his thirties but hardly looked mature enough to pass for an adult. This, plus his stunted height, made him look more an older child at times than a younger man.

Blood matted his face and the color of his light brown eyes had paled a bit. They stared directly at me, or through me in truth. The short curls of his black hair covered part of a gash along one eye, and dust and debris matted the locks. I couldn't see his clothing, just an arm protruding from the mess of former seating. The limb was bent at a horrible angle, bone protruding from a puckered mass, and more red over his skin than I ever wanted to see on a man.

It took me a long moment before I returned to my senses and called another name—hoping she at least survived.

"Kauri?" The words came out too weak to carry, though the room was designed to amplify noise. Crackling fire, still consuming wood above, drowned any other sounds I made. Seconds of searching showed me what I looked for, but I wished I hadn't asked to find her then.

Kauri's body sat slumped against the far wall. She'd been spared the fire's wrath, but that was little comfort. Blood streamed and dried along her face, all stemming from her eyes. Some had made its way down the side of her neck. I couldn't see it from where I stood, but I wagered it had come from her ears. Her mouth had been frozen in a macabre smile, still showing her teeth, which were no longer pristine white.

Blood caked them, and had pooled from her mouth. It still fell in a few strands, thick and syrupy. Enough of it had been spilled to dye the uppermost portion of her sari a color I wish to this day I could wash from my mind.

Stone and brick were not safe from whatever oddities filled the theater that night. The very mortar of the walls bled, streaming red without promise of ending anytime soon.

My throat constricted and my voice died for reasons that had nothing to do with the smoke. It was like a hand seized the inside of my throat and resolved to keep me in forced silence.

A thread of remembrance filtered through me, telling me of another name to search for, though I usually wouldn't have. "Makham?" I could barely speak his name.

Surely if he survived, he would make it obvious. The man never let his presence go unnoticed.

But his voice didn't echo back through the theater.

It's funny what a situation like that, your home burning and friends bloodied and dead, will do to your prior beliefs. In that moment, I would have sold my voice if it meant finding Makham safe and alive. No amount of hatred could make me want him to suffer that fate.

But life is keen on teaching us this lesson: a child's wants are hardly ever considered in the greater procession of things.

At least, mine weren't.

"Khalim?" My voice had turned into a brittle thing, like bits of glass, already too small for being broken underfoot to make any further noise. "Anybody?"

"Hoo-hoo!" The call came from the stage, louder than the noise of fire and deteriorating building.

I turned toward the source of the voice.

My heartbeat loudened, now thumping so hard it threatened to drive out all thought from my mind. The pounding shook my ears and my vision blurred. I had to fight to remember how to stand properly.

The world around me squeezed in with a pressure that threatened to hold me still. Even the thought of moving seemed too far out of thought and reach.

Mahrab's training begged remembrance, and I adopted the candle and the flame. I held the bead of fire in my mind and fed it all my fear, doubt, and bodily aches. The whole of me steadied and I stared toward the voice that called me.

Koli stood there, garbed in black clothes that held tight to his frame. The firelight did strange things to his eyes. They almost looked like they burned from the inside. "It's the little rat from earlier. You were scrubbing the floors when I first came to meet Khalim, hm?" His eyes widened as if he suddenly realized something. He reached down, bending at the waist, and grabbed something in one hand.

Koli hauled up the figure with no effort, smiling as he shook the man's body like a marionette. "Oh-ho, I found Khalim. You were looking for him, ah?" He gave Khalim's body another shake. "He's not very talkative today. Not so fond of making deals and asking for favors now, it seems. Dead people are like that." His face stretched into a grin fit for a hungry wolf.

Khalim had worn his lucky robes tonight. A matching pair of silken white top and bottom. In all the years I'd known him, he kept that one set as the only piece of extravagant clothing by any of our standards. Everything else came by way of secondhand homespun. He'd kept the ensemble immaculately clean.

He would have been upset to see their state now.

Crimson stained the bulk of his torso and waist before streaming into thin bands down the legs of his clothing. The candle and the flame allowed me to hold a dull impassivity for the moment, and in it, I noticed the torn edges of fabric around the center of Khalim's chest.

Then I saw what Koli held in his other hand.

The sword looked like a needle that had been stretched and broadened, but it tapered to a single point without the hint of an edge on either side. It could have been shaped from mirrorglass, shimmering perfectly within the theater like it caught and held all light around us. Its movement drew me, even in the candle and flame, as Koli swayed it at his side.

Khalim's body thudded against the stage, jarring me, though not enough to snap me out of my state of mind.

I then noticed the other seven figures standing behind Koli. Though clarity eluded me, no matter how hard I tried to take in the features of the men and women. My eyes only had room to hold Koli's form and face.

He sank to his haunches, tilting his head. "So, what are we going to do with you, little rat? Do you want to fight? Kill me maybe? Like this one perhaps?" He gestured with the tip of his sword to another figure.

Vithum lay half-slumped over the far right edge of the stage. His sword rested on the ground, cut cleanly in half like it had been nothing more than paper. The angle at which his body lay kept me from seeing anything but the back of his head. An ichor of blood and saliva clung to his hair, matting and hanging in threads.

I swallowed.

Koli moved closer, reaching the end of the stage. "What happens now, little one, if I come down there? Will you let me send you off to join your friends? Will you fight me?"

"No, but I will!"

The voice shattered my hold over the candle and flame.

My heartbeat sounded again in my ears and the urge to retch returned. The muscles in my legs shook in a manner that had nothing to do with fatigue.

Mahrab strode through the wreckage, staff in hand. The firelight cast his shadow against the far wall, making it look a looming and twisted thing out of stories. It faced the eight figures, leaning toward them almost in challenge.

I saw their shadows stand out against the walls as well, all wrongly positioned under the red light and facing each other for a battle I knew I wanted no part of. And Mahrab's stood the tallest by far.

Koli's mouth spread again into that macabre smile. It made me think of a wolf gone mad. His eyes danced like candle flames. "Oh-ho. The binder from before. Come now to work some magic? Something to scare us off with? Brahm's little tricks?"

The crowd behind Koli laughed as if in on some joke only known to them.

"I think I'm going to shove this staff so far up your ass that you'll taste the tip of my wood against your tonsils, Ashura." Mahrab leveled the staff toward Koli.

They traded words, but they fell flat against my ears.

Ashura. Storybook demons Khalim and I had discussed in passing. All the old plays performed to date had only referenced them. They spoke of them and brought to ear their songs. But Khalim had never deigned to perform one, even in practice, until tonight.

"Ari, run!" Mahrab hadn't turned to face me, still glaring down Koli. His mouth moved and he uttered words under his breath I couldn't make out. He thrust his staff toward the Ashura group. A gout of red flame shot from the tip. His mouth moved again and the lance stretched, sailing toward the Ashura.

Koli waved a hand in contempt like swatting away an irksome fly. His mouth moved as well, and the fire turned to waning sparks of orange, vanishing midair. The pillar of light had been snuffed out by nothing more than a gesture and half-muttered words.

They had just shaped and contended wills, folds of the mind, in seconds. Fire conjured and dissolved in the space it took me to breathe.

The display of binding prowess rocked me and would have sent my imagination wild under normal circumstances.

"Ari, run, boy. Brahm's blood, run!"

My feet refused to obey, rooted in place as if by another binding.

"Your bindings need work, Mahrab." Koli spoke his name half as a curse, half in a mocking tone.

"They'll be enough to bring this building down on all of us if I have to. If you survive that, maybe I'll use my last breaths to sing the Songs. Maybe I'll scream your stories wide so people know what and who you really are. Maybe I'll call for the Sirathrae and they'll deal with you."

Koli sneered. "Try it then. Call them."

"I think I'll try burying you all first." Mahrab flashed him a more wolfish smile than anything Koli had bared earlier. His cloak billowed in a wind that was not there, and it shone bright as blood under the firelight. His shadow rippled with a movement it should not have had and I knew it a trick of my mind. "Tak." Mahrab thrust the tip of his staff toward the roof of the building. "Ari, run now, damn you! Roh!" The theater shook.

Loose stones shook free, raining down around us. Larger sections of the roof fell and formed new craters in the already broken sections of the wooden stage. Every piece happened to miss the Ashura.

"Ari!" Mahrab's voice hit me with the weight of thunder, shaking me deep to my core. His words held all the force of a tempest, promising to throw me by their power alone if I didn't obey. "Run, now! I can't protect you. Run!"

And it's to my great shame to say that I did. I listened, almost compelled by what he'd said, and turned to run.

A larger portion of roof came down, exposing the night sky. Rain filtered in and a crack of lightning cast a hellish white-blue glow over the burning theater.

"We can't die, binder. But you can." I saw Koli lunge from his position on the stage, moving with the inhuman fluidity of water, and striking hard as lightning claps. His blade buried into Mahrab's chest as the rest of the ceiling gave way.

The world behind me shook like it was torn apart. I wobbled, leaning on the hallway wall as I fought to make my way back to the understage. Entering my old safe place brought no moment of solace as the building vibrated harder. My home under the theater would be buried soon enough as well.

I ran to fetch the book Mahrab had gifted me. The tome containing the promise of my identity, stories he said would be valuable, and perhaps the mysteries around the bindings. And, something I didn't wholly appreciate in that moment—memories.

I looked to the furnace, then the contraptions littering the place. The rainmakers. The repurposed piping and rope assemblies to simulate noises and effects for the theater above. Everything I was leaving behind.

It hadn't sunk in truly yet, and I clung to that numbness to help me run. I undid a length of rope, using it to fasten the book to my back. My bed platform hadn't collapsed on itself despite the shaking. I had no time to feel pride over that as I grabbed hold of the oversized nails and climbed.

Whatever aches the metal used to bring to my hands and feet had vanished. Whether it was my mind slipping into a colder version of the candle and the flame, all to distance me from the pain, or something else, I'm not sure. But I climbed my way up to the platform and then to the window.

It may be more romantic, I suppose, to say that I turned my head to give my home and old life one last look.

But I didn't.

I crawled through the window and into the storm, giving thanks for the rain as it masked the tears upon my face.

A rumble sounded between the earth and sky that I knew couldn't have been thunder. The ground quaked and I finally looked back to see the theater crumble onto itself. Stone fell below into where the understage had been and the last of my life went with it.

I had nothing.

I had asked to see magic and wonder. I had wanted a storybook life of adventure and demons—of Ashura and bindings.

Life saw fit to give me my wish.

And no amount of unwanting would unmake that wish. A lesson I would continue to learn.

But then? I turned and ran harder, no idea where to go.

Koli's words hung in my mind. "We can't die."

I ran. And I ran. And I ran.

TWENTY-ONE

Intermission—Consolations

Eloine gripped my hand tighter and the flame at the end of my staff waned. "Oh, Ari. I'm so sorry."

I didn't meet her eyes in that moment, or I couldn't. My gaze remained on the fire and I fell back into the memory of what Mahrab had taught me. The impassivity of the candle and the flame buffered me from all that threatened to take me, heart and mind.

Eloine either had been paying better attention than I imagined, or just had a level of intuition that beggared belief. But she moved her hand to my face. "You don't have to do that here. Stop. Don't try to hide yourself from your own pain. You're allowed to feel that loss, every now and again. After all, pain is pain." She gave me a knowing look as she repeated my words.

And I gave her a smile built from more than a decade of practice. A hollow and broken thing without light on the inside. But on the surface? It carried all the charm of a prince from storybooks. Wise and full. It made use of as many white teeth as I could show. It was the kind that could set others smiling upon glancing at it.

All except Eloine apparently.

She moved a pointer finger down my cheek, trailing a path almost like a tear would follow to one edge of my mouth. "And I've made enough fake smiles to know when one's shown to me." She pinched the corner of my lip.

"Ow." I glowered at her.

"Better. You're allowed to be angry. You're allowed to be sad and hurt. Let yourself."

I held my stare. "It was a long time ago. I'm fine." The fire on my staff flickered twice, almost like it disagreed with me.

"Mhm. I've heard that before too. It hardly means anything close to the words said, though. At least in my experience." She gave me a smile much like mine. A vase of sorts in a manner—a thing of shining lacquer on the surface, hollow on the inside. "See?"

I wished I had something clever to say, but I didn't.

Eloine moved her hand down along my throat and chest, stopping over my heart. "Oh, dear. It's broken."

I squinted at her. "Now you're playing games with me."

Her mouth twitched at one end, but no smile—false or otherwise—came. "Am I wrong?"

"I think you're prying—pushing, though I don't know why?" I almost reached to pull her hand away from my chest, but I didn't.

"Have you ever considered that you are painfully stubborn, even by a man's standard, and I'm trying to help you?"

"And how are you doing that?" The flame on my staff ebbed, flashing brighter before dimming to something barely alive.

"By telling you that it's okay to hold on to pain and ignore it when you need to survive. But that you can feel it again all to let it go when you have to. Like now. Because I think there's still a piece of that boy that remembers the night he lost everything, and that child has never stopped running." She moved away, settling herself on the far side of the bed, and beckoning me. "Come here."

When asked to come closer by a wonderful woman, the obvious choice is to do exactly that. But I lingered in deliberation. "Why?"

"Because, I don't suspect you'll be willing to let yourself do what you need any other way."

I arched a brow. "And what's that?"

She flashed me a smile that carried all the brightness and light of the flame from my staff. "Just come."

I relented, extinguishing the folds of my mind and letting the fire go with it. The room slipped into darkness and I laid my staff by the bedside. I still made no move over toward Eloine.

"Listening halfway only gets you so far, Ari." I imagined her still wearing that grin as she spoke.

"How far does it get me, I wonder?"

"Out of arm's reach, sadly," she said.

I inched closer, but stopped just beyond the touch of her hand. "And is that where you want me?"

"I want you to stop fighting what you really want to do. So, come here."

Men, as a rule, are terribly stubborn. And I am no exception. But even I know when it's best to stop. At least on occasion.

I moved closer to her; well, within her reach.

She took me in her arms and pulled me with more strength than I would have imagined her capable of. "Don't talk. Don't be clever and witty for just one moment . . . please."

I had almost opened my mouth to be exactly that, too clever for my own good, like Khalim used to accuse me of being. But her plea had been enough for me to bite my tongue.

"Good." She trailed her fingers along my neck and jawline, coming to stop above my left ear. She took a few locks of my hair in her hand, stroking gently. "When was the last time?"

"Last time what?"

"You let yourself grieve over your family?"

"It was a long time ago. That's why I can tell the story as I do. All the painful truths as they are."

Her fingers tightened, balling up some of my hair, and she yanked firmly.

"Ow." I winced. "What was that for?"

"You danced around the question. If I remember correctly, and not too long ago, I asked you not to be clever. I didn't think it was this badly ingrained in you."

I knew better than to respond to that. Open my mouth and risk being clever, or prove that I was stubborn.

Eloine resumed running her fingers through my hair. "You're allowed to remember their loss, Ari, more than just as part of a story." She pulled me even closer, bringing the side of my face to her chest. "You can cry. No candles and flame tonight."

I wondered if I had failed to wipe away the rain from earlier as some moisture welled along my eyelids. A few beads had trickled down my cheek to settle along my jaw.

If Eloine noticed, she made no mention of it as she rubbed her hands against my face. She held me there until the last of the rain had been cleared away, and all I remember were her gentle whispers urging me to sleep.

She'd given me good advice on occasion, and I saw no reason not to heed her now.

I slept.

TWENTY-TWO
The Black Tap

She watches the storyteller sleep. Content that he's no longer able to see her, she moves with all the subtle silence of the night, walking far from him and his staff's fading firelight. There is little time before she is pulled back again, and so she slips from the Three Tales story den. She comes out under warmest climes and moonless skies, not so far from the teller's just traded truths—and her own lies.

Eloine notices each of the cobbles under her feet as she slips between the waning candle-cast glows—all come from nearby windows. Each space of darkness she steps into is as familiar to her as every cloud the moon may come to hide behind.

Passersby take no notice of her as she continues to an alley she'd taken when fleeing the clergos.

She cannot risk a moment's rest, as she is searching for something as old as the first breath and something which will likely take her last.

A song.

One that is a story in and of itself, and could have birthed all the ones that came after it. And she knows her search will likely lead to a song to sing about her journey after the end.

Eloine is late now, and many of Karchetta's lights wink out to find sleep of their own. But there will be little to none for her this night. She moves through the alley with all the surety of a cat down well-walked paths. There is a secret between the old walls and hidden recesses of towns such as this. For all the places of well repute and those kept well under day's own light, there are those hiding holes better left untouched and kept far out of sight. She travels to one such place now, knowing a piece of what she wants is there, but knowing too that she will be asked to offer something equal in return.

Maybe more.

For that is the shape of the world she's come to know.

"No." The word echoes down the alley from the way ahead. It is hushed, clipped, like a breath over broken glass and just as sharp. She knows there is an unspoken magic in this word—a boundary, one that many do not understand, and less so come to honor.

Eloine rushes now, one hand falling to her thigh and the slender length of metal held tightly to her skin. Some of the cobbles here have not had the time and feet to wear them low—they are uneven, and their points jab at her feet, but she has no place for the discomfort and the pain.

An oil lamp of patinated brass hangs from the face of a building along the way. Its weak glow falls over a man standing too close to a stone wall. The hem of a skirt protrudes from beyond his figure—a woman ahead of him.

He moves, arm snaking out to grab hold of her.

Eloine keeps her tongue between her teeth, though the urge to bury them into the man's throat builds. She knows this is not a place or time for fire. This is a time for the coolness and cleverness of night. Her pace slows so she will not betray her coming. She walks heel to toe first now, the muscles in her calves aching from the awkward gait, but it muffles her twice as much as before. Her hand slips between the bands of her skirt and to the leather ties along her left thigh.

She is closer now. The young woman before her lets out a breath but says nothing to give Eloine away.

The man says something under his breath that she cannot hear, but it doesn't matter. She knows the hidden meaning behind his tone. It is a thing of want, anger, and what many men think they deserve.

Eloine's fingers curl tight around the piece at her leg and she puts pressure to draw.

Another half step and she'll be in place.

The oil lamp shifts under an errant gust of wind that sets it creaking as if it is bothered by the scene below.

The woman ahead flicks her gaze to Eloine and the man's back stiffens.

He turns.

Eloine pulls. The blade catches none of the lamp's amber-gold glow, almost turning it away. But it holds all of the pale gleam along its edge of white glass and starlight. Its horn hilt rests perfectly in hand as if it were made for her. Its length is just long enough to reach someone's heart should it be set to finding it. But she has another target in mind.

She lunges.

The man sees her, his eyes widening like a hare spotting a wolf, and there is no time for him to find his voice before she is on him, tooth to throat.

Eloine presses him against the stone wall. The blade rests just along the side of his neck, close enough that she can almost feel the beat of his heart against its edge, but not so hard-held that she breaks his skin.

He is not so old that he could be someone's grandfather, but well enough along to be the father to a young woman much like the one at his side. Clean shaven and carrying all the sun-kissed looks of the Etaynians. A brush has taken some of the dark at his temples, turning them a shade of gray earlier in his life than they should have. He has a figure lean and better suited to a fox, all the features of which hang in his face as well. The pinched look, sharp of jaw and cheek, and a light in his eyes that has nothing to do with pleasantness or warmth. And with the light of the lamp he holds more yellow-gold in his stare than a man should.

She leans closer, taking care to not let the knife sink so far that she makes a mistake she cannot afford. "Leave." Eloine keeps her voice hard and sharp as her blade, but not so loud to let it trail down the alley.

He bristles but says nothing.

"Did he hurt you?" Eloine keeps her eyes on the man as she waits for the woman's answer.

The lady is somewhere in the beginning of her third decade of life. Young. Fresh-faced and fairer than most of her people. Her dark hair is half-tied into a neat braid, the rest loose as if raked free by fingers. She is a girl anyone would think pretty, even with her face flushed with fear. The woman shakes her head, lips trembling but unable to give voice to any answer. Her fingers clutch at the folds of her dress—its color a shade close to blood washed lighter to carry more pink.

"The *pattena* suffered nothing from me." The man's lips pull so thin that she likely will not be able to slip her blade between them.

Eloine's eyes narrow and she thinks to try the thing and part his mouth. But she does not. "Do not call her that." She trails the knife down his throat, turning it to rest the point just above his heart. Push, twist, and a little lean.

It doesn't break through the layers of his coat, but she knows its weight is felt against his skin, and so is the promise behind the point.

He doesn't stiffen. He doesn't even breathe. He holds still and shoots the woman a silent look as if asking for help.

The lady doesn't meet the stare and looks everywhere but back at him.

"She's no one special. What's she to you?" Each word leaves him low and soft, without the barest bit of effort behind them. His chest holds still after he speaks. And his eyes never meet Eloine's—they flick to every place but her face and come to rest on the edge of the knife.

"A person doesn't have to be anything or anyone special to be treated at least like *something*, and nobody is just *nothing. Sieta?*" Eloine leans, putting more pressure on the tip of the blade. Its point now drills through some of the man's coat but falls short of breaking flesh.

The man nods once. "*Sieta*. But . . . I've paid for her."

Her eyes narrow and, for a moment, she forgets all the coolness needed in her actions. She finds instead the storyteller's fire and the knife trails farther down the man's body until it comes to rest below his waist. "Then I suggest you forget about what you've lost in coin, and consider what more you have to lose that cannot be accounted for once gone for good." She smiles and gives him a look better fit for a wolf than a woman. A thing of all gleaming teeth—silver white despite the brass lamp's oil light.

He pales more than a man of his color should be able to, but nods again. "I swear it by Solus' grace." Though he says the words, they ring hollow. She knows he has no love for his god above and less still for his people. Eloine's seen the look before of a desperate man willing to tell any lie to ease his way from trouble.

She casts a long look to the woman he tried to force himself on.

The lady moves a hand to her stomach, grasping at the fabric there as she recoils a few steps. She clearly wishes to be away from them both.

Eloine sighs and pulls the knife away from him. She's supposed to be buying herself out of trouble, not bringing herself any more. "Leave. If I see you again . . ." She trails off and holds the blade up for him to see.

He swallows what little saliva must be in his throat. The man trades no words with her as he leaves, hands in pocket—never casting one last look back at either woman.

And the blade remains in Eloine's grip until the man passes out of sight. She watches the mouth of the alley for just a breath longer, more from long-earned and well-trusted wariness than anything else. Content she is free of him, she sheathes the blade and turns to the young lady. "What did he want with you?"

The woman shies away from Eloine's stare and mutters under her breath.

Eloine sighs and puts one hand on the woman's shoulder, another under her chin, raising it. They lock eyes. "You can speak freely now. Quietness helps no one, especially yourself. What did he want?"

A short breath leaves her nose and she looks around as if someone else will round the corner on them. "He wanted *me, sengera . . .* ?"

Eloine ignores the question after her name and pursues the heart of what she asked. "I know that much. Why was he grabbing at you like that? Why here? Why not wait till he'd gotten you back to a room?"

The woman fidgets with her dress and looks away from Eloine. "He didn't like what his money bought him. Only pewter bits. It's not enough for a full roll."

"But he wanted one anyways?" Eloine already knows the answer but asks regardless.

The young lady says nothing, but her look is enough to prove Eloine right.

"What's your name?" Eloine places an arm around the woman's shoulders and begins leading her down the alley.

"M-Marania."

Eloine smiles, one of many from an old box of tools. Something meant more for Marania, and nothing to be looked deeply into, for it is a hollow practiced thing. "It's a beautiful name. Do you have somewhere I can take you now? Somewhere you'll be safe?"

Marania scoffs and spits to one side of the alley. "I'm never safe. None of us are. It's not in our work. I'm a *whore*. Dantonyio says it's not for us, and it's more than we deserve. I think he's right some days."

Eloine stops, grabbing the woman by the shoulders and shaking her twice. "I abhor that word, more than many others when it's used like that. Listen to me." Her tone is sharp and hard as the steel she flashed just moments earlier. "*Deserve* is a terribly dangerous word. Most people don't deserve the things they get, good or ill, so be doubly careful when you use it, most especially in regard to yourself. *Sieta?*"

Marania adopts the silence that had lingered in the alley before Eloine entered it.

"*Sieta?*" she asks again.

Marania's lips tremble, but she repeats the word, acknowledging it with a quick bow of her head.

"Good. Then one more lesson for you, sweet. Be just as careful when considering whose words are right, certainly so if and when they stand to profit from you—whether through effort or through your body." This time Eloine does not ask if Marania understands. She knows her point has been made. "I'm looking for a place. It's a small tavern where people trade talk that is better left unheard by the ears of others, and a place where secrets are sold. Would you know of it?"

Marania's shoulders round and she shrinks as if wanting to hide herself in the folds of her own clothes. "Y-yes. The Black Tap. It's run by Dantonyio. He does what you say and works other things as well."

"You mean running women for the simple pleasures." Eloine is not looking for an answer, but Marania gives her one regardless.

"Yes."

"And is Dantonyio the man I'll be wanting to speak with, then?"

Marania shrugs. "For some things. But it is his place, everyone speaks to him at least once. If he's not the one you need, one of his men will be. Unless you're looking for Magael. He rents space in the Black Tap for his business. No one bothers him. You do not speak to him unless invited to."

Eloine ushers Marania to follow along as she thinks on this. "And what is Magael's business?"

Marania shakes her head. "I don't know. We're not allowed to speak to him. We barely speak to the men in the tavern unless . . ." She trails off.

"Unless Dantonyio asks you to provide them with more than talk, *sieta?*"

"Sieta."

"Then I suppose I'll need to speak to both these men. Take me to them." Eloine doesn't make this a question—it is a command.

"Sieta, sengera." Marania takes Eloine's hand and leads the way.

⁂

The Black Tap Tavern is in every way like the Three Tales in that they are nothing alike at all apart from their function. Whatever noise had filled the place before her entry now deadens to a quiet that works to convince her it has always been there. It's a sullen silence, deep-darkly held in the black of the old countertop—closer to charcoal than wood in look. The walls and support beams hold the same color, something so dark it brings with it both a story and a silence of its own.

This place has known the touch of fire, maybe several times, and yet it stands. And not a one has taken to clean it. Which says more about the men inside than the place itself.

Half a dozen sit around a table so small that they must join nearly at the elbows. They wear the hard-canvas and leather motley of men used to rough work, and harder lives. Their faces tell the rest of their stories.

Scars, now faded against the bronze of their skins to look like fishing line run across them. Their eyes track her and Marania as the pair of women cross farther into the tavern. Low mutterings are traded, and they are the sort men make when weighing coin in purchase for a thing.

Eloine bristles and, for a moment, she finds her hand slipping back toward her thigh. Five points of pressure bloom within the meat of her shoulder. Marania squeezes again, giving Eloine a wide-eyed look that needs no translation. The singer stops herself and smooths her dress.

Another look around and she knows all there is to know about the Black Tap Tavern.

A row of women, dressed like Marania, wait along an exposed balcony on the second floor. Nearly as many men ogle them from below.

And one man hangs before the bar counter, watching everything with practiced disinterest, but a clear eye for all things happening within the place.

His face belongs more to a hawk, with the pronounced and hooked nose and the sharp cheeks. His clothes are loose and comfortable and a shade of gray that seems bright in this dark place. One hand rests visibly on a knife whose edge looks sharper than bottle glass and sings a song to her that it has cut many things short in life.

This is not a place where stories are told and traded—a place for them to begin or come true. This is where many stories come to end.

Marania leans close enough that her breath blows hot against Eloine's throat and ear. "That's Dantonyio . . ." She breaks off and mutters something quieter to herself, but the shape of it catches Eloine. "*Rahome diavello, Solus.*" Marania crosses a hand over her breasts, resting it over her heart before bringing it to her lips, then overhead as if gesturing to the sun.

Spare me the devil, oh God. Eloine translates the quick prayer to herself, but doesn't have the heart to tell the other woman that this is not a place in which she'll find any sort of god. Only those who've walked away from them. "Thank you, Marania, you've done wonderfully." She leans to one side and places a kiss on the woman's cheek. "I can handle things from here. You should find a place to rest."

The woman opens her mouth to protest, but one look at the set of Eloine's jaw and she reconsiders. A curtsy, a furtive look to the owner of the Black Tap, and then she is gone as quickly as if she was never there.

Eloine steals a breath and walks with the quiet comfortable grace belonging to a dancer, and just as much the confidence of the men who frequent this place and have nothing to fear under its eaves.

Dantonyio stirs but does not quite look her way. Eloine knows he has been aware of all things within his tavern and her approach does not take him by surprise. He moves with the fluidity and surety of large cats—strong, and all too quick to pounce on the unsuspecting.

She is closer now—a few strides and she'll be just within his arms' reach. *Just a hand's breadth outside that space then.* Eloine covers the distance between them and stops just short of where he can reach. She grabs the edges of her skirt and pulls them out as she curtsies, an act she knows is as foreign as she is here. This is no place for formality and the customs of the civilized. Still, small manners go a great distance at times. "*Sengero* Dantonyio?"

He straightens, letting the right side of his long coat float open, revealing a lean abdomen crossed with scars that can only come from one thing: knives.

No stranger to fights. And he's taken cuts to the softer parts of him. No stranger to pain then, either.

"That I am, *sengera* . . ." He trails off, leaving the obvious question in the air.

She smiles and rises. "Evania. Just Evania."

Dantonyio matches her expression, but his eyes hold none of the sincerity that should be there. They take her in much like a man gauging a horse for purchase. "*Sengera* Just Evania, then. You're new here."

Eloine inclines her head and says nothing else.

"What brings you to my tavern? People seldom wander in here by accident. And those who come with purpose are better known to me *before* they step through my doors." His gaze flickers to Marania. "Especially if they come in with one of my pieces."

Her eyes narrow when he says the last word, but she readopts the neutrality the storyteller wore so perfectly at times. *A man who sees nothing as it is and only how things are in relation to him. Pieces, places, and prizes. These are the three things he can see the world through and in. And he will always be the poorer for it. For he'll never learn until the end he cannot bring any of those with him.* She keeps the thoughts to herself and turns her attention to Marania as well. "She ran into trouble out in the streets."

Dantonyio's brows rise, betraying the first hint of honest surprise. "Did she really now? I wonder what that may have been. It's not good for my pieces to cause trouble. It makes clients nervous, and too much of it may bring the clergos on them."

Eloine shakes her head. "Nothing of her own doing. A man whose taste and reach exceeded the contents of his purse."

Dantonyio clicks a tongue against his teeth, the hollow sound echoing in the space around her. "Ah. *That* is terrible business. I do not like someone trying to take liberties with my investments. And is this man still alive?"

"He is. Though I believe I made my point in a manner he won't soon forget."

Dantonyio purses his lips but doesn't pry, choosing to lean back against the counter behind him. "Then it seems I'm owing you a small thanks." He turns his head and barks short and sharp. "Marania!"

The woman snaps straight and hurries over to him. Her stare falls to the ground and she says nothing.

"This woman"—Dantonyio gestures to Eloine—"says she helped you out of a bothersome spot. In that, I caught that you seem to have been paid for a service that didn't end up occurring. I'll count that as a little blessing, and I'm sure you feel the same, *sieta*?"

Marania nods.

He holds out his hand and she fidgets, pulling free the coin she'd received earlier, placing it into his grip. "Thank you." His words hold none of the honesty needed for that gratitude. He motions her away with a simple wave. Before Marania has even left their earshot, Dantonyio offers the coin to Eloine.

She refuses. "No." Before he can ask why, Eloine pulls free a purse. "I haven't come here to take coin, but to offer it."

He lets out another bark—this time rolling and carrying just a note of true amusement in it. "Oh-ho. Someone bringing me money? This will be good." Dantonyio gestures to a stool at his side. "Sit-sit. Take a drink." He snaps his fingers and a plank-thin man shuffles toward them from behind the counter.

The bartender has the years in him she'd expect out of a tree close to falling from time, and just as many lines in his face. There is no color left in his hair and little light in his eyes. He is little else but bone and knotted tired flesh.

"No, but thank you. I'm certain you've made this offer to many young and beautiful women and . . ." Eloine lets her gaze fall on the women inside the tavern before speaking again, "those that take you on it seldom leave, yes?"

He grins, but it is as cold and sharp as the edge of his knife. "Just so. Clever. I'll remember that. So, then, to business. What is it that brings you to me, purse in hand?"

"Information. The obscure kind. The sort overlooked and little cared for by many except the peculiar, the collectors, and sometimes both."

Dantonyio's eyes lose their focus for a moment as if he is lost in thought. "And which are you?"

"The clever kind. The kind who can pay. Isn't that enough?"

He shrugs. "It depends what you're looking for. But you've come to the right place. Just not the right person." He gestures to a shut door past the end of the counter. "There is a man who rents the space back there from me. His trade is secrets—some kept even from me, but for what he pays, I don't ever need to ask. And for leaving me a coin in hand already, consider that bit of knowledge payment enough."

"Thank you." She wastes no time, turning and taking a few steps toward the door.

"Oh and, *sengera*?"

Eloine stops and regards him.

He gives her a lecherous smile. "If you have some coin left after your dickering, consider coming back and perhaps spending it on some of the other pleasures within the Black Tap." His look flits to the women on the second story. "For a dickering of another sort."

She gives him a smile then that would turn the face of any man a shade of red better found in blood. "For that, I daresay you would be paying me, mostly for what you, and every other man here would walk away having learned. Which"—she breaks off to cast a lazy look around the room—"I wager would be a great deal. Do you have enough coin in your purse for that?" She doesn't wait for an answer as a series of low chuckles break through the room.

Eloine reaches the door and pushes it open.

The room stands in a darkness not helped by the few waning candle lights—all failing to bring a better brightness to the place. Her eyes strain to adjust as she steps inside and lets the door fall closed behind her. One of her hands runs along her thighs and the other balls tight before loosening again.

The light dies in the room.

Something sharp presses against the small of her back.

TWENTY-THREE

The Price of Things

"And what do we have here?" The man's voice holds all the dry edge in it of smoke over broken glass.

Eloine doesn't stiffen despite the threat of the blade. "We must be of the same mind. I was wondering the exact thing as I felt something small press against me. Is that a knife or are you mistaking me for one of Dantonyio's women?"

The tip of the knife twists, just enough to drive a pinpoint of pain through her, but nothing to break her clothes or flesh. "You don't seem to grasp the situation well enough to be properly afraid."

"Of a little prick? Hardly something any woman is ever afraid of. Disappointed, surely." Eloine moves her left hand to return the favor to the man. "And I fear it's *you* who doesn't understand the situation fully."

The knife's point trembles against her back but doesn't pull away. "I never saw you draw your weapon, lady."

"It would have rather ruined my point if you had. Right now, my knife is resting just above the meat of your thigh. A place where your blood runs thick and deep. I'm not sure if you've ever seen what a wound there can do to a person. Let me save you the trouble of thinking. It's the sort of cut that cannot be stitched clean. It bleeds much too strongly to stay shut. Once the deed is done, you're left watching the life leave you before you can take the time to recount your regrets."

The knife pulls away from Eloine. "Excellently done. What other games do you play?"

Eloine keeps her smile to herself as she turns, never once letting her own blade fall from the man's thigh. "All sorts. What did you have in mind?"

He gestures past her to the darkened center of the room. "First, we sit. Preferably in a manner that has our knives sheathed and not pressed against each other. Then, you answer a question."

She arches a brow. "Then let's start a smaller game now, shall we? We begin with the question and, if I like the shape of it, I'll join you at the table for your other game?"

He purses his lips, then breaks into a knowing grin. "I can concede that much, though I'll say that *you* came to me, and people do not come to me unless they have questions that need answering, or favors done."

"And what kind of favors can you get done?"

He raises a hand and waggles a single finger as a silent statement. "*That, sengera,* is not the question I had intended to ask. Let's not take this little game too far, *sieta*? My question is this: Do you play *Talluv*?"

The knife falters in her grip and she takes it as a sign to finally sheathe it. She keeps the surprise from showing on her face. "I may have taken time and turn with the traveler's game, why?"

He steps away from her and stays to the shadows, making his way to the table. One of his hands reaches into a pocket and pulls free a slender stick she cannot make out properly. A snap of his wrist sends the tip of the thin rod striking against the table's surface. There is a hiss and spark that quickly kindles to a bulb of bright flame. He begins the slow and measured process of touching it to the head of every candle in the room. The man blows out the black powder match and gestures for Eloine to take a seat.

She does, lowering herself into a wooden chair opposite him at the round table, and better takes in the shape of him.

He reminds her of a grizzled hound gone too long without a trim. His hair hangs long at the sides of his face and has now gone the gray of old ash. It contrasts the deep bronze of his skin and brings out the duller shades in the soft green of his eyes. His face is sharp and pointed with a nose too large to do him any favors. He wears the clothes of a man not fit for the Black Tap and its ilk, but to better move among the gentry.

The suit holds tight to him in all the right places, betraying a lean build that promises to be quicker in form than a man of his age should manage. And she guesses him to be nearing his fiftieth.

A rectangular box rests between them. Its surface is made of polished shells in varying shades of white from driven snow to the luster of pearls. A mosaic of green glass and blue gems lines the edge of the box and black paint splits the top of the shells into segmented squares.

"This is the part where you tell me why you've come to me? What need have you? Favors, answers, a mix of both? Or are you here to buy or sell?"

"I'm looking for something—information. Dantonyio said you are the one to speak to on those matters. Though, I must confess to curiosity in what favors you can grant? What is it you buy and sell?" Eloine reaches out, her fingers wrapping around the brass knob fitted to one side of the box. She pulls, opening a compartment and revealing the stored game within: a mix of polished black-stone spires no longer than her littlest finger, some small humped discs of white stone almost smooth as marble, and others that she always struggles to name the shapes of.

The man bows his head as if accepting her earlier statement. "I am that man and more. For favors? Well, I can get you anything short of entry into a princeps' arms, or Del Soliel. Need goods, above the water or a bit below, illicit and ill-gotten? I can do that. I can get some of the clergos to sweep your floors and keep their tongues between their teeth while they do it. Or have any of the clergy right under the pontifex dance to your tune while wearing your dress, *sengera*. Little is off-limits to me. But, all for a price, of course."

Eloine grits her teeth. *Of course.* "And how do you manage all that?"

He gestures back to the door she came from. "With what I buy and sell. All the *pattena* here are mine . . . in a way at least." He doesn't wait for Eloine to ask the question now on her mind. "Ah, I see your surprise. You think this place is only Dantonyio's. No, he is the face, the muscle, the man at the door to do the work I feel better left to him. He's made for that sort of thing and enjoys the simple pleasure of it. But no, I'm the purse and the mind behind it all.

"To the question at the heart of what you mean, it's simple. The lives of all men and women under this roof dangle from the lines of string in *my* hands. And very little of what they do is left a secret from me. So, when they chat, or sleep with someone of influence, consider it a known thing to me. Those people's secrets become mine as well, and my women have a far reach and sate the appetite of many lords and ladies and, yes, even the clergy. For as close to God as they claim to be, I assure you that they are as far from him as possible." He says nothing else and gestures to the board.

She takes the quiet hint and arranges her first four pieces along each of the beginning squares. "And this?" Eloine nods down to the game.

"The only thing I require while we consider what you have to ask of me. Beat me"—he gives her a knowing look that says it is not so common a thing to best him—"and you may find yourself in even better circumstances for me to grant you your wishes."

"That sounds like the response of a man with a great deal in his life and yet not much at all besides boredom."

He spreads his arms in open acceptance of her comment, inclining his head as further acknowledgment. The man pulls free a die and sets it on the board between them. "Would you care to roll for who goes first or . . . ?"

She rolls her wrist, deferring to him.

He bows his head and sets his pieces. "Do you have a preference for rules?

Mutri? Zibrathi? Or how we play in western marches? I'll admit, I do not much care for the rules out in Laxina."

"Zibrathi, with all the tales intact," says Eloine, keeping a smile buried inside her.

He arches a brow but says nothing. The man rolls. A four. He takes a spire and moves it across the squares, then motions to her.

Her toss yields her a six. She takes one of the humped discs and moves it accordingly through an irregular set of steps.

The game continues as the candlelight flickers and the man brings his spire to the other side of the board. "Over the course of my life, I've seen many things. One, a woman with three teats. Two, a man with twice as many balls as he had in brains." He rolls the die and cups a hand to shield the result from her. "And, three, a beast with the head of a serpent, the wings of a bat, and the feet of a lion. Five."

Eloine stares at the man, her gaze falling to the hand hiding the die. "Liar."

He removes his hand and reveals the carved and polished stone to read the number two.

"The little story was a nice trick to throw me off reading you." Eloine reaches out and takes the die, then moves his spire back three paces from the end.

The candles burn lower and, in the end, the game is won.

"I confess, *sengera,* you have a better mind for the game than I'd thought. I almost feel you have lied to me." He puts a hand over his heart in mock agony.

Eloine gives him a placating smile. "Oh, I'm sure you'll heal from it. But now, to business?" She pulls the purse from before and places it on the table. "I need answers and I have the coin to pay for them." *May it be enough.*

He folds his hands and leans forward. "And what do you wish to know?"

"A song. I'm looking for a song. Something old—older than Etaynia. Older than most tongues still spoken today."

He leans back and steeples his fingers, resting his chin on their tips. "That's not much to go on. Does this song have a name?"

She shakes her head. "If it does, I don't know it. But it would be a tongue most couldn't speak, much less recognize. I've searched everywhere for it and found nothing. I haven't looked far into Etaynia, however."

He nods. "I can certainly *try* to put some ears to the task, but Etaynia is not known for its love for foreign things, be they affairs, dress"—he stops and eyes Eloine's clothing—"people, or their songs. We do, for better or worse, keep to ourselves save for the sorts of trade that bring us gold. But the royal library would be the best place to find what you're looking for. One of the princeps is an avid collector, and it is no secret he's accrued books from across the world.

Even the sorts the clergy and pontifex would frown on. He's been known to pay large sums to buy such things from other nobles, not to mention the fact no one would refuse the desires of a princeps should they wish to keep their rank . . . and head.

"If that's where your book is, then I admit I cannot help. Like I said, getting you into the arms of a princeps is beyond my measure, *sengera*. All the same for getting you into the library."

But it may not be beyond mine. Eloine keeps the thought to herself.

"If there's anything else? I would hate to have lost the game *and* a chance to ply my trade and earn good money."

She bites her lip and thinks, then pushes the purse toward him. "Yes. I have drawn the troublesome attention of a few people who could make my continued residence in this country a problem. And I have no love for being hounded."

He opens his mouth in a silent O. "And how did you manage that, if I may ask?"

"By the trouble of being myself, it seems."

He says nothing and motions for her to continue.

"I'd like to be free of it, and you mentioned something about having the clergos sweep my floors?" She opens the purse and tumbles its contents to the table. Gold catches the candlelight and it is dim compared to the sparkle in the man's eyes. "I need you to handle a problem for me . . . and inquire as to the price of one of your *pattena*. Their full price."

His eyes gleam brighter and the gold is no longer on the table.

TWENTY-FOUR
DEMONS

I woke the next morning—alone. My head ached and my skin remembered the faint lines where tears had fallen. And Eloine's touch along my face. I groaned and rolled over, grabbing my staff. It served as decent support as I got to my feet and headed toward the door. Sleeping in my clothes didn't bother me as much as it would have anyone else.

The one benefit of the bindings, I suppose.

I could have straightened out the rumples with another effort of will, but decided it was best saved for later. Another performance would be asked of me and I could afford to be a bit disheveled until then.

I made my way downstairs, staff tapping rhythmically against the steps. Pale bands of morning light washed through the tavern and bathed the place in a cold glow. A few sections of the Three Tales' taproom remained in shadow.

And three men occupied the most intense corner of the darkness.

The trio who'd been there when I'd first arrived.

One of the men, a reedy thing carved from knotted wood, adjusted the cotton cap on his head. He worked it side to side, trying to screw it in place to keep what little wispy gray hair he had in place. His face reminded me of old mountain roads, worn low and deep with lines and fissures. Nothing welcoming in it, and the sun had hardened what remained into tough leather. His eyes had gone watery, which muddled the likely once-bright browns to rum spilled in a puddle of rain.

The man worked the same foot as before against the tavern floorboards as if trying to carve a furrow into the wood. At first glance, it appeared he hadn't changed his clothing since I'd first seen him. A second told me he simply had more of the same outfit.

We locked eyes.

He shied away first, turning his gaze to the leg he continued to bounce in place.

I feigned turning my head to regard Dannil's bar.

Movement. The man shifted again to watch me under the impression I no longer paid him any mind.

My performance had done as I'd hoped. The locals now viewed me as something more than entertainment. I had enraptured them, and my reputation carried.

I only hoped it spread far enough to the right people. The ones who would offer me an invitation no sane man would ignore, and the kind that would protect me.

If the clergos didn't get me first. My run-in with them wouldn't have made them fans of mine, especially not the justice. She seemed the kind of person to remember a face, doubly so if the man behind it did her a wrong.

Whispers. The kind old men tell, and the sort they fail to keep to themselves, carried over from the far corner of the taproom.

I recalled the candle and the flame, slipping into the old clarity it offered.

Murmurs slowly turned to crisper mutterings whose shape I could get the grasp of.

"Man called something unnatural here. No-no, Tiago, don't tell me otherwise." The voice held notes of dry smoke and a strained wetness that came with age and a nasty cough. His lungs must have struggled to both hold breath and let him talk at the same time.

"I saw, same as you did. And I saw him work magic, but don't go thinking it's something special. All them peddlers and storytellers on the roads can do that sort of thing. You've heard the tales." The second speaker's voice was that of a man who'd heard the same argument many times before and had little energy left to have it again. He was too far gone to even pretend the faintest interest in the subject. He sounded like a man who wanted to spend the morning without having to hear another noise.

And no words came from the third man.

"Mark my words, Tiago, he'll bring something fouler here before soon. All them folks from far down along the Trader's Road do. They bring the demons of their lands up here to our home. We're good God-fearing people. Tell me I'm not and I'll knock you back to when you had less brains between your ears and ran by what was between your legs." The first man let out a wet cough that sounded like half of his lungs would follow in leaving his mouth.

The man called Tiago rapped his knuckles along the table. "No such things as demons, Doniyo. And who says I've stopped thinking with what Solus gave me down here?" A pair of loud slaps, like a hand on soft flesh, echoed through the taproom.

Silence filled the air in the seconds after. Then two men burst into laughter while the third held space for the quiet and stillness to return, almost bringing it in himself.

I watched him out of the corners of my eyes as he cradled his clay mug, looking deep into it as if the contents were the only thing worth his attention. His two friends were of no interest, or maybe they'd already said all that could be as far as he was concerned.

Heavy footsteps pulled me back to the bar to find Dannil striding toward me from the back room.

The barkeep inclined his head at me in what could have been a weary morning greeting.

I returned it in equal measure, figuring it best not to tax the man too early, especially if he had to deal with the three men at my back. Dannil had already gone to enough lengths in welcoming me into his home and business without even a single dented pewter bit in his purse for the trouble.

And I'd certainly brought him trouble by way of the clergos. Yet, he hadn't thrown me out. That spoke well for the man, at least in my mind. But every man has his limits for how much unrest they can bear.

Dannil faced me from the other side of the counter, one of his hands trailing idly over the spot I'd polished back to its original condition. "Didn't sleep well."

I waggled a hand in a so-so gesture. "Had better. Have had worse."

Dannil grunted and grabbed a mug, turning it over to polish its insides with a rag. "I meant me." He placed the cup back where he'd gotten it from and then turned to prop his elbows up on the counter, leaning toward me. "So?"

I arched a brow. "So?"

"You met our songstress. And then you got into a fair hand of trouble. The kind that kept me from sleeping well, mind you."

I fought the urge to wince, keeping my face as wooden and neutral as the countertop. "I did."

Dannil drummed a few fingers against the bar before scratching a fingernail against the spot I'd restored. His lips pulled into a frown as he scraped harder. The wood would not give up its renewed state no matter how fervently the barkeeper clawed. "You do good work."

"Thank you."

He grunted. "Did just as well with your storytelling. Made me the kind of money that lets a man turn his head and ears away from trouble . . . of a sort. But the clergos . . ." He shook his head and sighed. "Solus' shadow, man, you know how to bring a proper sort of trouble around. And a justice on top of it all. She could shutter this place till next year's harvest if she had a mind to, but that's if she knows I'm keeping you here. Which she don't." His words fell into the distant low muttering of a man rationalizing with himself, forgetting all about me sitting just within arm's reach of him.

I gave him the moments he needed to set his mind at ease before speaking. "And I thank you for that—keeping me here that is. And our songstress friend, at that. But I know it's not an easy thing, and you just have to say the word and I'll leave."

Dannil waved me off and fetched another mug, plunking it down between us. "Don't think on it. Rita taught me better than to put out people with no home to call their own. Solus doesn't look kindly down on those that do, and he don't share his blessing with them either. Terrible thing to be without God's blessing."

A man's life seems to be better off the further he walks away from gods and their problems. Because the blessing of gods can come more as a curse in my experience.

Rather than dismiss the man and his god, I simply nodded. "There is that."

He placed a steaming clay pot before me and nodded toward it. "Tea? Or something stronger for the morning?"

"Tea please. I don't think I can handle anything more right now." My mind swam with last night's conversation, the wounds—long buried, thought to be healed—that I'd reopened in telling Eloine my tale so far.

Dannil poured a steady stream, unwavering, not a drop faltering. The liquid fell in colors like dying autumn leaves, too far past their time to hold any brightness beyond a muddled pale brown. "Sugar? Honey? Milk?"

I bit my tongue, keeping silent at my abhorrence of adding milk to tea. A practice many east of Etaynia viewed with disgust. "Just honey, thank you."

The muttering behind my back intensified, sounding like rasping wind dragging dead twigs over stone streets. The men's voices scratched and hissed at the blanket of silence within the Three Tales that continued trying to fall over our morning.

"Unnatural things 'bout that man. I'm telling you, Tiago." The speaker, Doniyo, let out a drier cough than before. "You felt those words last night? Summin' powerful strange in them. Was like strings on my ears and heart—couldn't turn away from his story if I wanted to. That's unnatural."

"You said that already. Twice already." The man I wagered to be Tiago rapped his knuckles against the table once, then again. "Keep that talk to yourself and we'll be better off for it. These are bad times. *Efante* are gutting each other, and that's ill omens there. When princes shed their own blood, the people's will follow. Tell me I'm a liar."

No one raised a voice to object.

"So, no more talk of strangeness, unnatural things, or demons . . . *sieta,* Doniyo?"

A half murmur I couldn't make out, but the table fell silent afterward.

I guessed the men agreed under their breaths.

Dannil finished spooning in more honey than anyone back home would have asked for, but the west loved its sweetness in abundance. He pushed the mug my way. "Would be I'd charge you a pewter bit for that."

I smiled as I pulled the drink toward myself. "Would be, but most houses don't charge their entertainment for the price of a cheap tea, especially when that person happens to be me. I'm sure you'll make it back and more aplenty after tonight's tale."

He rolled his eyes.

I reached to where my purse had sat, well within the folds of my heavy cloak inside one of its many pockets. My hand fell against a piece of robe that held an uncanny flatness in its shape. My eyes widened as I grasped at the spot again. But no amount of grabbing would make my purse reappear. It had vanished as well and true as the storm from last night.

Dannil caught my expression. "What's wrong?"

I gave him a hapless and tired smile. "I guess I'll be giving you a pair of stories tonight—better than what I did for you yesterday."

He cocked a brow. "Why's that?"

"Because, good stories pay, and two pay better than one. And it seems if I'm going to be paying for drinks, I'll be in need of money." I opened my cloak, showing him the pocket I'd reached into.

It took him a few heartbeats to catch my meaning. Realization struck Dannil and he burst into a fit of laughter.

Of all the things I expected from him, his amusement hadn't been on the list.

He ground the back of a hand against one eye as he leaned against the counter for support. His shirt crinkled along the bulk of his stomach as he shook. "Oh, that's something, isn't it, Rita?" He exhaled a deep breath before steadying himself. "I guess our songstress got the better of you, hm? Seems you should have kept a hand more to yourself than to her, huh? Don't know the kind of life you lived as a storyteller, but around parts of Etaynia, a man needs to have a hand on his purse at all times. Heard it said by a wise man once that, 'A gentleman is never far from his purse.'"

I grunted, thinking back to what I'd told Eloine. *I am no gentleman.* But there had been a time my hands had found their ways into purses aplenty that belonged to the gentlemen within the Mutri Empire.

It seemed that part of me had fallen asleep, and all the cleverness and awareness of that time had slipped into slumber as well. The long-practiced motions born of survival had given way to the ones I needed to survive my new life and identity as *The* Storyteller—nameless, without a story of my own beyond the reputation of my craft and deeds done under that mantle.

"I suppose she did, but so long as man has his wits about him, money is easy enough to come by." That had been true enough for most of my life.

This was no different. Just another role to play—a performance.

And I'd play it masterfully.

A heavy thud echoed behind me, drawing the attention of all. A pair of strangers had come to the Three Tales Tavern.

The first of the two men reminded me of a grizzled fox that had gone too long without eating. He stood a head taller than me, looking like he'd been stretched to that length. His limbs were lanky, the sort a child might draw.

A thin layer of sand and road grime clung to his tight-fitting pants and sleeveless shirt. His hair fell in dark waves to frame his chin, but they'd lost any sign of healthiness over whatever journey he'd recently taken, looking thin and wiry.

He surveyed the taproom before locking eyes with me. They were the color of warm honey under foggy glass. Something had dulled his irises.

An illness?

The man moved with an odd stiffness, like he'd spent too many days on rough floors and harbored old injuries he never tended to.

I shifted without fully turning toward Dannil. "Do you know him?"

Dannil shook his head and moved to grab a mug that needed no polishing, yet he set to the task like he had eyes for nothing else but the chore.

It was the kind of measured focus actors adopted when going through well-rehearsed lines. I recognized it for that, and the sort of posture a barkeep would take who's seen one too many troubles in his establishment. It was the busyness and unconcern that would hopefully keep him out of the eyes of those who wished to cause trouble.

I couldn't blame him for that.

The second man bustled into view, though how he had hidden behind the first was a mystery no lifetime of theatricality and tricks could answer.

He had the build of longtime dockworkers, rippling muscle under generous layers of fat and the sun-darkened skin to match. He could have been molded from heaping amounts of clay that no sculptor took the time to refine. His face had the same weighty mass to it. The man's eyes were a cold gray with scant hints of a green that could have been found in old sage.

He had no hair to speak of, even on his eyebrows, save for a short beard he'd braided into a single tie no longer than his index finger. Its coloring carried a red like rust, likely from the dye men and women used along the routes from the Mutri Empire to Zibrath.

That's when it struck me. The men's appearances marked them from the regions along Zibrath's roads to the smaller countries surrounding it. A mix of features found in the Mutri Empire and nearby. Pieces plucked from all over to form their people as trade flowed through and ships set sail from there to every corner of the world.

I'd once traveled and lived among men like them. And I remembered enough of the customs to hopefully start things off on a good note.

I inclined my head, bringing my left hand over my heart. "*Sholkuh.*" The greeting may have been rather formal for the likes of the two men, but it carried enough ingrained religious significance to warrant an equal and genuine return of it.

The men made no such offering.

I took a short sharp breath in through my nose, moving my hand back to my staff and clenching it tightly.

The leaner of the two men tilted his head, giving me a look like he wasn't quite sure what he was staring at. "*Tuam? Tuam ohe wahl?*"

Whatever calmness I held to shattered, leaving me feeling like bits of cold glass. I reached for the lucidity of the candle and the flame, tipping my mind into it. All of my shock and confusion fed into the single point of fire and I found a piece of myself to hold to and act around.

An old clever smile, well-rehearsed, made its way across my face. "I'm sorry?" I kept my words to the Trader's Tongue, hoping it would force the newcomers to adopt the same language. "I didn't quite catch that."

He continued in the old and dead language. "*Teham mainye* Ari?"

My eyes widened as his were overtaken by the muddled gray I'd seen earlier. The color quickly morphed into the sort of black found in an ocean at night, flooding his sclera entirely. His arms blurred and I reeled away from him only to have my back press against the countertop. He grabbed hold of my robes with a grip strong enough to tear the fabric if I resisted.

Tiago and his elderly friends got up from their table, breaking into a clamor I wouldn't have expected given their hushed and tired voices. One of them bulled past the larger of the two newcomers only to have a hand clamp down on his shoulder.

The dockworker squeezed and hauled the old man with all the ease of handling a basket of bread. He tossed the grandfather of a man against the wall near the entrance, holding him in place with no visible effort.

The other man moved into action but I turned my mind from the scuffle as the man holding me released one hand to draw something from his waist.

A bead of light glinted along a wicked edge of silver. The knife was no longer than the tip of my smallest finger down to the end of my palm, but it would have found its way easily enough through my guts.

The candle and the flame still filled my mind, and in it, I grabbed hold of another piece of my story I'd long since left behind. My hand gripped even harder to my staff as I twisted. The head of the wooden tool clapped against the man's brow, staggering him. I turned the weapon at an angle, snapping it in a sharp and short blow. The tip smacked against the man's lips.

Blood welled all along the soft tissue from where it had broken against his teeth. He reeled, but more in shock than pain.

I seized the opening and held my staff between both hands now, stepping forward and driving the whole of my weight into a blow using the weapon's length. It struck the man across the chest and shoved him back.

He kept his footing but his balance faltered.

I shifted my grip to hold the staff along its base like a club and swung. Its mass came down on the man's neck in a blow that would have taken the light from most men's eyes. A quick repositioning of my feet put me in the stance I needed to thrust the staff's tip into the hollow of the man's throat with all the force I could muster. The strike caught him perfectly in place.

His legs buckled and I expected his eyes to lose what intensity they had. They would have had he been normal in any way. I watched his chest for a moment to see if it moved, the subtle signs of breath and life.

Nothing.

His gaze remained unflinching, however, still holding to that unnatural coal-like black.

Fade away. Just leave. The temptation to shut my own eyes, hoping that his vacant dark stare would vanish, grew in me.

A staccato of curses and tangled words pulled me from my wishful reverie, and I turned toward the commotion.

The trio of old men wrestled with the brutish dockworker, and each man ended up tumbling away to crash into bits of furniture.

None of the woodwork looked worse off from the collisions, much to Dannil's relief, I wagered.

I raced back into action, reaching for the set of movements and old techniques long hidden within my mind.

The large man seemed unperturbed by my approach. He shifted with all the lazy care of a cat stretching in the morning. His hands spread wide in anticipation, but his face held all the expression of a stone at the bottom of the sea. Smooth, empty, worn to nothingness.

I stopped short, sending the staff into a diagonal cast. The length of it slammed into the soft tissue at the side and behind the big man's left knee. His joint buckled, but not enough to have him sink as far as I'd hoped. I brought the staff down on top of his skull. A crack like a hammer on thin wood filled the taproom, but the man's eyes remained as steady as before.

I pulled my staff back to inspect it and spotted a fissure along the head as wide as my pointer finger. My grimace was short-lived as the man surged to his feet, wrapping both arms around me in a hold that could have shattered an empty oak barrel. The air fled my lungs and hot strings of aching filled them in its place. I wheezed, fighting to voice the only question on my mind.

The man's body shuddered. I heard a sound like wet fruit being torn apart. Then again—several times. He opened his mouth and I caught a faint glimpse of the insides. Where there should have been pink for his tongue was the color of soot and jet. His grip slackened and I shook myself free. I had to use my staff for balance as I teetered on the ground for a moment.

The dockworker crashed to the floor, splotches of blood tingeing his clothing. In any other place in the world, it would have been a shade of crimson. But here, in the Three Tales Tavern, it pooled dark as pitch like the other man's eyes.

One of the older men, the one I figured to be Doniyo, staggered back. A simple fisherman's knife shook in his hand. The blade looked like it had been dipped in ink, still holding a film of darkness along the edge.

A thought occurred to me and sent lightning through my body. I raced toward the man, batting his knife from him with contemptuous ease. His companions blurted protests that I had no ears for in the moment. I pressed the old man against the wall with my staff and arm, using my other hand to grab his mouth and force it open.

His feet beat against the floor.

"Look at me."

He shied away from my stare.

"Look. At. Me!"

He did. His eyes remained the same.

I took one of my fingers and ground it into his ear, drawing a sharp yelp from him. The finger came back clean. "Open your mouth. I won't ask again."

He did as I instructed and I plunged two fingers in, brushing against his tongue. No residue. His mouth was healthy and pink.

The old man mustered a show of strength I would have expected from someone half his age and shoved me back. "Hell and fire, take me from Solus' grace. What was that about? Don't go sticking your bits in my mouth like that! Dannil, you going to let this—"

"You should consider yourself lucky if any of my bits go near your mouth."

The words carried no humor, though. I couldn't bring myself to muster anything other than dry hard anger.

The man's eyes went wide before screwing tight into a glare. "Why you—"

"Shut up, Doniyo." Dannil's voice fell harder and heavier than any of the strikes I'd landed in the fight. "Shut. Up. This isn't the time for anyone's jackassery. None of it now. The way I see it, two strangers just came into my tavern—*my home*—and tried to kill my regulars and my entertainment. I saw him"—he jabbed a finger at me—"come under the same threat as you. If he wants to look you over after whatever just happened, damn well let him!" Dannil slammed a fist onto the countertop, rattling the mug he'd been polishing.

Stillness returned to the Three Tales Tavern.

This was a moment for me to lay these men's concerns to rest . . . albeit by filling them with another one altogether. But it would be worth it for some peace at last.

I exhaled and extended a hand in a gesture I hoped was calming. "I'm sorry for what I did. I got swept up in things, and I just had to be sure you weren't one of them."

The trio of men exchanged a look and huddled closer, taking to muttering under their breaths. One of them shot a look my way. "That one over there said something to you, didn't he?" He pointed to the slender man with the knife.

I nodded. "Couldn't make out what, but he did." I hoped the lie wouldn't need more than that to convince them after the drama we'd endured.

Most men will readily accept an easy falsehood from someone who helped them survive such an ordeal. Doubly so if the lie is easy—convenient. Complexity isn't sought after when it comes to understanding, neither is truth. And the truth is rarely anything but complex.

"Said a name, I think. I've heard it before," said the man I'd realized was Tiago.

"Could be." I shrugged. "Hard to think on it when he pulled a knife on me." I gave him a crooked smile.

That set him back and he matched my expression, going so far as to give me a nervous laugh. "Suppose that's true." Tiago then stared at the fallen man with the knife. "Wait, I hear you right in saying you know what these two freaks are?"

I looked to the pool of blackened blood pouring from the large man. "Demons."

TWENTY-FIVE

Son of Himself

We spent the morning barring the doors to the tavern from the inside owing to fear of more strangers coming along. Every man who'd witnessed the attack set to the task of helping Dannil carry the bodies to the garden at the back of the building. All of us worked with the quiet sobriety that comes in the aftermath of murderous attempts and the weight of what we did in return.

Taking a life is never easy—no matter how practiced you become in the art. No matter how easily the motions may come to you in the grip of fear and self-preservation. It's the lingering thorns in your mind and heart that sap you of your thoughts and cheer in the time after.

Our group dug two graves with an efficiency and single-mindedness that had us eschew any water or food Dannil offered. We labored until we completed the work.

Evening came to the tavern and the doors remained boarded, keeping us in as well as the silence that had grown between the men. And the quiet remained until evening passed into night.

I knew I'd have to be the one to break it. To bring something back to the Three Tales Tavern.

A sideways look at Dannil told me that it wouldn't be an easy task. He wore a mask of tired resignation, likely keeping deeper fatigue of the mind at bay by burying himself in his work.

The trio of old men played out the same game of cards they'd been at for hours. No amount of trying or tricks would change how it would go. They were well past the kind of thinking needed for clever plays and the wit needed to make their turns exciting.

"We should open the doors. You've turned enough people away." I kept my voice to a low and level whisper, but just strong enough to carry to the men in the corner.

Dannil didn't look up from his polishing of the counter. His stare could have burned holes into the thick wood, and I knew, if he decided to glance at me, he'd be looking right through my face. "Don't think one night will make much of a difference." His tone made it clear he didn't want to argue the point, but he'd have to hear me anyway.

"It might, and to more than just you or me or them." I hooked a thumb over my shoulder to the somber trio.

Dannil's polishing slowed, but he didn't look up at me. "Why's that?"

"Because this place might be all that others have to escape whatever troubles they have. That's what taverns do in the world. That's what places where stories and music can be freely shared offer—escape. They offer respite. Freedom. We're not the only ones who had to do and see a hard thing today." I still kept my voice softer than usual, but I let a hardness creep into it.

"How many of them do you think had to watch two men try to kill their patrons today? How many had to watch blood be spilled in their home?" Dannil finally looked up from his work and, true to my guess, he stared more through me than at me.

I didn't want to match the low anger in his voice, it wouldn't go well. He'd sounded like he held on to a bed of simmering coals, not hot enough to maim you, but plenty enough to still hurt.

"The hardest thing anyone has to go through in their lives is exactly that, Dannil. It is the hardest thing for *them*. No one can take that away from them. No one can dismiss it out of hand. We are, all of us, given the difficulties we are, and it's not our place to try to put the hardships of others into places of value. They are hard. That is enough. And they need a place to forget those hardships. And so do you."

The rag came to a stop and Dannil's hand clenched hard to it, balling the cloth up. His shoulders stiffened before he could hold no more stubbornness and frustration. They finally sagged and everything he had been holding on to bled out of him. "Rita would thump me into the next set of days if I ever gave grief to someone else having it rough."

I said nothing, letting him come out of his pit by himself.

Sometimes people don't need a hand to climb out of weariness and despair. They need an ear. Occasionally, saying the right things. But mostly, many need to be heard more than they need to be talked to.

And a storyteller's craft is more listening to his audience than it is ever speaking. Watching them. Hearing the secret tells and yearnings of their hearts.

"I suppose this place would be better off if we had people making merry and drowning sorrows with friends and the like." Dannil folded the rag and tossed it onto one of his shoulders, bustling away toward the back. "Tiago, Doniyo, Miegel, take those boards down."

A chorus of protests erupted from their table, carrying more energy than the trio had managed to exhibit through the course of the afternoon and evening together.

Dannil put them in their place without even turning around. "You three put the boards up to keep trouble out, but now I'm wondering if all you've done is keep it in. Take those down, or are you planning to drink enough to pay what needs to be paid for me to keep running this place? Maybe I should be charging more than bits for beer?"

The elderly men burst into motion and grabbed hold of the boards with their bare hands, wrenching and leaning on them with all their weight. They succeeded in prying the wood free, nails and all, after a few groaning minutes of effort.

Dannil ambled back, pleased at their progress, but a shadow of doubt tinged the corners of his smile.

And I knew the unease lingering in his mind. Giving voice to it would help steer Dannil's thoughts to calmer waters. "You're worried about more *men* like earlier." I had taken a moment to enunciate "men" as my mouth fought to call them what they really were. But talk like that didn't go over well with godly men like those in Etaynia.

The Three Tales Tavern wasn't a place for demons. Those belonged in stories, and that's what Dannil's home catered to—tall tales of wonder and magic. Of darker things and the monsters that filled them. But they were not supposed to walk in through the doors and try to knife your patrons. And once that had happened, a shadow of the event would always occupy some small corner of Dannil's mind. A piece of it would always hold to the fear of . . . what if?

Two words, and for all that, they can be dangerously powerful. In the hands of an idealist, "what if" can lead to the kind of hope that brings a man to triumph over unbelievable odds and opposition. In the hands of someone resigned to despair, they can dig them even deeper into a grave of the mind. Something nearly impossible to escape. And I have been both of those men over the course of my life.

Dannil needed the former right now.

I reached out, laying a hand on his and giving him a strong and reassuring squeeze. "I'm certain the only kinds of people that'll come through the doors tonight are drunkards and tired folk wanting food and a story. I can give them the latter . . . so long as you're willing to fill their bellies?" I arched a brow and stared.

He exhaled and clapped one of his hands over mine, shaking it gently. "I can do that." Dannil broke our hold and came around the counter to stand by me, keeping his eyes on the now opened doorway. "I'll have to leave to fetch at least one of the girls for tonight. Word's probably spread I've closed the place down, and that'll keep some from checking and showing up anyhow. But there'll still be people coming. Always is."

No sooner than he finished, a group of men and women stopped in the doorway, the head of the line peering into the tavern and fixing Dannil with a look of uncertainty.

The man was dressed in loose-fitting homespun the color of dead grass. He had a thin, knotted physique that had gone hard from a mixture of not enough food and frequent heavy labor. He looked like he could have been someone's young uncle who showed signs of premature age from a rough life. "Heard you closed up earlier today. That true or . . . ?"

Dannil put on a smile broader than anything he'd shown me of late, shining and full of enthusiasm.

Feigned enthusiasm.

"Had some trouble keeping the place open in brighter hours is all. Too much to do, not enough hands." Dannil moved back to his place behind the counter, gesturing to all corners and seats in the tavern. "Sit-sit. I'll be with you. And tonight, our storyteller's going to tell a tale that'll have you talking about it for sets to come instead of gossiping about which of your sons will marry whose daughters." Dannil fixed me with a look that made it clear I'd better deliver.

"What'll it be? Hard cheese, bread with honey? Apple, and I've got peanut rattle. Small beer? Tall beer? Ale, water, wine? Olives and fish? Maybe a stewed lamb dish? I have peach butter, rabbit rugger. All things here fresh as can be. So, so, what'll it be?" He clapped his hands, pounded a fist on the counter, and then wrung his wrists as if sheer hoping would get the growing crowd to order meals.

And his hope won out.

Cries rang of people wanting cheap and fast beers, first and foremost. Simple foods followed, hard and hearty. Cheeses and breads. A pair of men pooled coins together to treat themselves to fish. Dannil moved about as best as one man could tending to things. He didn't stop, but did slow to pass word along to the crowd to get his working girls in.

In a town like this, everyone knew each other, and sometimes a word from a pair of lips to another's ears was good enough to call who you needed.

The Three Tales Tavern had tipped from grave-like silence into a welcome commotion. It brought a different kind of warmth to the taproom that had been much needed.

As more people filtered inside, along with Dannil's serving girls, I decided to allow myself time to finally weigh on what had happened.

More importantly, what the possessed man had said. He'd asked after my name. He'd known it, and he'd spoken in a tongue older than most around. Old Brahmki, something I barely had a solid grasp of, only able to parse in slivers. The language predated the modern spoken one of Brahmthi.

The fact one of the Tainted had followed my trail to the ends of the Golden Road turned my blood to a slurry of ice. All the years of subverting my name and deeds, twisting my stories, creating a dozen other heroes and villains instead had done nothing to throw those monstrous things off my scent.

Dannil must have caught something hanging in my expression because he passed me a mug of something warm and smelling of strong spices.

I eyed the drink, then him.

"Mulled wine. A weak one—cheap one—but it'll keep you from getting lost in yourself. I know the look. And this has enough of a taste to rouse you for what you need to be doing—and soon, I'll add." He twisted to look at the spot where I'd performed before. The implication was clear: do as good a job as I did before, especially for the trouble that seemed to follow me by way of the clergos and then the two men who'd come for me.

Though, Dannil hadn't picked on the reason the Tainted had come into the tavern.

I took his advice and sipped the drink, agreeing with the barkeeper's assessment of how weak the beverage was. But it did its job in bringing warmness to my mouth and throat. It wasn't long before that same heat filled my chest and made its way to the tips of my fingers. As far as relief went, it didn't go quite that far at all, but brought me back from the errant thoughts occupying my mind.

I drained the mug quicker than proper and set it down with a barely audible thump.

The noise caught Dannil's attention over the blossoming din within the tavern. He eyed me, then a group of people getting rowdy amongst themselves. "You ready to put on a show?"

I wasn't. "Yes." The muscles in my back stiffened as I rose from my place at the counter, and I hooked a finger around a piece of my cowl, drawing it over my head. I straightened, adjusting my posture with an old trick to make myself look taller—to take up more space than I actually did. The base of my staff drummed against the floorboards in a slow and rhythmic tap, almost like distant thunder.

Some of the conversations thinned around me, then silenced. A few of the laughs finally died off.

I had their attention again, and I meant to hold it for as long as it took to drive Dannil and his trio of old patrons away from what had happened earlier. And hopefully my own mind would follow.

A stream of murmurs, barely above a whisper of passing wind, still carried through the place.

I did nothing to quell them, moving and drumming my staff until I reached the place before the fireplace. Only, it held no flame today.

I looked to the candles sitting in their metal holders, fixed to the beams supporting the ceiling. Each bulb of fire hung feet above the patrons' tables and it would only take the briefest bit of effort to change all of that. I reached out with a hand almost as if trying to pluck one of the bobbing flames between my fingers and set it elsewhere. The connection between the minute fires and the empty hearth formed easier than before, now close to second nature.

Already having a source for light made my work easier than having to kindle something from within myself. I closed my eyes and linked the two points in space, breathing the words next. "Tak. Roh."

The world went dark as all of the tiny fires seemed to be blown out at once. A keen eye would have caught what really happened. Each flame bowed and bent as if pulled by invisible strings, leaping toward the empty fireplace. They rushed to fill a singular spot, bound there and quickly took to the kindling that had been left in place.

I kept no fire for myself or staff, letting what flames took to the hearth be the sole source of light tonight. Only the fire would occupy the patrons' thoughts and sight. I would simply be a shadow telling a story and, hopefully, be further from their minds and attention. One evening of that wouldn't be so bad.

My little theatricality had done the job, and everyone's gaze fixed on the firelight.

"When I first told you a story here, I told a tale of a man known to every Etaynian's heart and tongue. I spoke of a thing well-known, old and true, to this place and all those who'd call it home." I banged the base of my staff against the floorboards once to make my point. Its hollow thud echoed through the place, commanding continued silence. "Now I take you far away to a place at the other end of the Golden Road. To a time before the path itself even existed, and no man could fathom that it would ever come to be. To when and where wild magic ran rampant and the world remained unformed to how it is today. Before the Mutri Empire grew to be rich and filled with gold and spice for trade.

"This was a time when a darkness, without true name, shape, and form, took the minds and hearts of men. A time of demons and without a way to stop them. Until *he* came to walk among us in a new aspect of himself. A son. A son of himself."

And so I slipped into the story of how a god found the courage to walk among the world he'd made . . . and all the ill that he'd let be set upon it.

The world Brahm had made was perfect and all was well. Or, that is what he would have liked to have seen of his making. But, what even a god wants does not always come to pass. And so, the things he came to shape eventually fell to an ill fate.

Impurity and shadow came to fester in the hearts of all things but for the Shaen, fairest and oldest of all creation. But the lives of mortal men are weak and fleeting, and to this, a sickness came and in them grew.

Slowly, men and women turned on one another, but not in the ways you would expect. Not by sword or axe, hammer and stave—no. They turned to subtler ways of poisoning all good things. Their tongues spoke twisted truths, blackened lies, and their ears could hear no pleasantness or heartfelt cries.

The eyes of their friends saw darker shapes where once loved ones' faces sat. People soured the waters of their own towns, leaving nothing but rot in the hearts and souls of others until they turned to harsher means, having only those turns left.

Villages fell. Out of place and time, and out of tongues and mind. We've forgotten them.

And Brahm watched in silent sadness, resigned to sit and see creation fall to what had happened between him and a child of his own. Something changed in him realizing this, and he took to course like he had not before. He set his sights upon the mortal world and to finding someone who stood beyond the dark taint taking men and women. And he found her.

Her name was Chaandi, for the silver light of the moon. And she did glow in her smile, her eyes, and in her heart. For there Brahm found a place of love and forgiveness unlike any other in this world.

Chaandi saw the twists and turnings of the minds and lives of those she loved, and she loved them still. She spent each morning, afternoon, and every night weeping for the twisted souls among her town. She wished them well, she prayed for them, hoping Brahm's own light would come to wash away the darker things that dimmed their spirits and dulled their goodness.

And so Brahm came to her one night and, in her dream, bathed her in his light. He told her the truth of things. That he heard her pleas for mercy and forgiveness for those who'd strayed from the true nature of things he'd made. That they were not themselves and should be spared his harsher judgment. Even with what wickedness was in them, it was not of their own making. She begged Brahm to look upon those she loved with his own eyes as a man, not a god. To see as they saw and walk as they did, then maybe he would understand and do something more fitting for them.

Moved by her words and the stirrings of her heart, he agreed to young Chaandi's plea.

Brahm told her to expect a new child in her village who would walk alone and be the judge of all things. He would watch and listen to Chaandi's friends and fellows, and through their deeds come to weigh the lives and future of those people. She understood and thanked Brahm for heeding her wishes and giving those she loved another chance to prove their goodness.

Before he left, Brahm asked her for one kindness in return, to which Chaandi agreed. He took her hands in his and pressed them to the place just above her heart, asking her to breathe a breath for him. She did as asked by the god above all and gave him a piece of her own air, a whisper-thin length of her love and her care.

Brahm plucked it between his fingers like it was string, wound it tight so into his own chest it he could bring. Holding it there, he turned to leave without farewell, sighing out another breath as he passed from Chaandi's view.

He stirred the two pieces of air together, bound tight a new binding of life to sow. With one last effort, he pulled free another piece of a tired old flame, rending a new part of him to leave without name.

It glistened, glowed, burned bright—this fledgling flame Brahm tossed freely into the night.

And with that, Brahm, lord of fire and of all things, vanished from sight.

The next morning, the villagers of Chaandi's home woke to the cries of a baby on the street.

Tall and broad-shouldered Amman, the local smith, frowned first at this lonely child, then passed it by. He remarked about the sad fate of the world, but did nothing to help the infant. He only spoke of it not being a time to bring children to life and that parents would struggle to feed more little ones in this place.

But the child watched and listened to Amman's thoughts unsaid. The dark whispers kept inside the deeper places of the smith's heart. Amman thought of all the many places he could sell the babe. There were trades that dealt in that even in the earliest days, before the Golden Road ran along the world. Amman thought of all the people who might have lost children of their own, eager for another, and what they'd offer for the chance. And a small part of him even considered taking the infant for himself. To raise the child and have a second hand work the bellows and shape the irons, and all to make his life easier. Nothing so much for the child's sake.

But in the end, Amman passed the baby by, thinking dark thoughts, and doing no good deeds.

Then came Mohl. She of skin like honey in the sun, and hair like dusted coal. Where Chaandi was said to be the most patient and kindest woman in the village, Mohl was surely the most beautiful. She looked on the lonely child with nothing but a face of anger. Bothered by the babe's early-morning fussing and its cries. But for the sake of her standing, she bent low and whispered to the child loud lies.

She told him she would find his parents, and short of that, a loving home for him. She told him she would bring him to a place of warmth and love. Mohl leaned close and whispered more soothing lies into this child's ear. Lies loud enough for all the folk to hear. But she had no heart to bring truth to even one of these tall tales, and so content she'd done her due, she rose and left the lonely child to his ails.

After her, Shivthe came before the child. A tired man who worked more with his mouth than ever his hands. A gossip, a talking tongue, and little else. Young, with the beard and fading hair of a man decades older. A man who talked of things to do, but could never be bothered to start to do a single one of them. He stood by the baby's side, then thought it better for his time to bide. For someone else would surely come and be this boy's pa and mum. So Shivthe left the boy alone as well, and returned to fruitless thoughts on which to dwell.

A dozen others passed the child by, and did little to soothe his tears or soothe his lonely little cry.

Then came Chaandi, knowing what must be done. She would take the little boy as hers and give him a home where she would treat him like her own born son. But when she approached the baby boy, he fixed her with a gaze not meant for children. His eyes held a power and heat that brought her heart into full fright. His look carried all the glory and fury of Brahm's own light. And then she knew from where the child came, and knew this babe had all the strength of God's own first flame.

And he spoke to her then.

"Chaandi, you asked me to give the people of your home a chance, and they squander it so. They turn away a helpless child and think darker thoughts, and that is all I need to know. I am ready to pass judgment."

She fell to her hands and knees and begged. "Oh, please, son of Brahm yourself, give them another chance—another day. If not them, then let me be the one to show you there is good." But she looked into his eyes and knew it could not be so. For she had already been judged and weighed by Brahm himself. Besides pleading, there was little else she could do.

But the child had heard her words and silent plea. And he gave the people of her home another day to show a kindness for him to see. "I will give them another chance then because you ask it of me."

And so went the day into night and a morning to follow. But Chaandi's promise soon rang hollow. For more souls passed the now older child by. But they all left the youngling there alone, without food or water, and to die.

Now the child of flame, a child without name, stood taller than before. He could balance on his own two legs and hobble in place.

People looked at the boy sideways, remarking about the oddity of his new age and behavior. But they still left him to his own. Not one of them making any honest attempt to try and save the little one and give him a roof and warmth.

And the child of Brahm took all this in. He weighed their thoughts and lack of deeds and judged them as good as any other sin.

The second day passed as had the first, and not one soul offered to feed the child or slake his thirst. But again Chaandi pled that the son of Brahm hear what she had said. "Please, Lord Brahm, son of yourself, give them another chance." Surely other souls would come to do right by this child of sunlight.

And so the third day came and passed. Then the fourth. Each morning the once-babe growing older, wiser, taller.

Soon whispers spread through the village that this was no mortal child. That this was a monstrous thing, dark, evil, and sure to be wild. Whispers turned to talks of deeds to do. Things better left unsaid, things most vile. Talks of maiming the boy, burning him, hacking him to bits. And the child of Brahm himself heard each and every one of these.

And still Chaandi begged him each night to give them just one more chance.

So he did.

Until the sixth day, when now he rivaled a young man of thirteen, when a traveling bard came along the way. He sat by the boy of Brahm and asked him for his name.

"I have none. And do not need one."

The bard sank to his knees beside the young man and said, "Everyone needs a name, especially someone without one of their own. Did your parents never see fit to give you one?"

The child of Brahm shook his head. "No. And my presence here requires no name. Nothing for anyone to call me by. It's by men and women's actions through which they live and die. Names are fleeting and empty things."

The bard fell to his bottom, sitting cross-legged. He reached around to his back and pulled free a case that looked to be made of polished glass so bright it caught every scant ray of morning light. He snapped it free and pulled out a mandolin of wood more orange than brown. Its grain held every color of the sun inside against a black as dark as night. And he played.

Passersby stopped and listened until he finished. Coins tumbled through the air to land by the bard's feet, and he plucked each one up with care, placing them into a neat pile by his side. But the people went on, sparing not a glance for the young man beside him.

Brahm's child spoke again. "Do you see? They only have eyes and ears for things that amuse them, that turn them from their thoughts, but have little care for anything else."

The bard gave him a tired smile. "Many people do. It doesn't mean they're bad. It can mean they're tired. It can mean a lot of things, but don't name something malicious so easily when it could be something else entirely."

The child of Brahm was unmoved by this. "You haven't heard their thoughts. I have. You can't see into the deeper parts of their hearts."

The bard sank his head and relented. "True. I cannot. But I know someone's heart and mind today doesn't have to be the same tomorrow." He pushed the pile of coins toward the young man.

The son of Brahm himself asked, "What for?"

The bard shrugged his shoulders. "For food? A place to sleep. For water? For anything you think of so long as there's coin enough to cover it." The bard's mouth turned into a crooked and amused grin. "Maybe there's enough to buy yourself a name."

"I need none of those things. What I need is to see some glimmer of kindness in man. To see something redeemable. And something worth forgiving."

"Forgiveness oft has to do more with you than the person to forgive." The bard idly strummed his mandolin, breaking into a low and steady hum as he did.

That day passed into night with the bard and son of Brahm entertaining conversation with one another. And that night the child held no thoughts of judgment, only honest fascination with the newfound stranger by his side.

Each morning came, and the nameless bard sang new songs, and told the young man new things for him to think on. More coin piled up by their sides. And their conversations deepened.

For more days and nights the child of Brahm staved off the bard's hunger, thirst, and need for sleep, and all so they could talk and share music.

Eleven days passed, and the son of Brahm, now a full-grown man, had seen and heard enough to finally pass his judgment.

He called all the villagers to the spot where he had been born and they gathered to hear him speak.

But some came with darker purpose and thoughts in mind. And this, the son of Brahm knew.

When he spoke, he spoke clear and loud as a brass bell being struck. "I was born eleven days ago here in this spot. When I was a babe, I cried out for your help—your love. None of you gave it to me." He turned to face Amman and held the smith's look. "Some of you held monstrous thoughts inside yourselves. But Chaandi begged me to forgive you.

"Then came the second day, and I grew. I watched some of you turn to darker thoughts still. Some of you grew to hold judgment against me. Me." He pointed a finger at several in the crowd. "That is not your place. It is mine.

"Then came the next day, and the next, and still you failed me. But Chaandi's heart continued to prove true. She begged for me to give you another chance. And then another. And yet you only proved my thoughts true over those days. Until a stranger passed through." The son of Brahm pointed to the nameless bard who had spent the remaining days at his side.

"He played his music, traded his art, and shared his coin with me for free. His heart proved out. When none could be bothered to offer me the slightest kindness, he offered me his time, his voice, and a name. He offered me means to tend to my hunger, to slake my thirst. He acted. He listened. He cared. And for his voice and deeds alone, I've come to learn, and I've come to my judgment of you all."

At this, Amman, the smith, could bear no more. He stepped forward and jabbed a finger in accusation. "And who are you to judge us? Who are you at all? You came from no one into our home. I've asked around. No one knows your parents, no one was with child close enough to birth a thing like you. You've grown in days to be a man. But you're no man or child. I call you as you are: a monster!"

The young man spoke, "Who am I, Amman, son of Danath? You ask me? You, the smith who cheats his fellow man. I know you for who you are. I know what thoughts you held in mind and heart when you saw me. And they were foul. I know you use poor iron in your works and charge twice what it is worth because people cannot go elsewhere. I know all the ways you deceive. For I am son of Brahm—son of myself. I cast a piece of myself free to be born again, free to live and watch the world among you. I know all things. And I see them. I hear them."

Amman thought to speak but could find no words.

The son of Brahm called out each one of those in the crowds by name and deeds, listing their sins and dark thoughts for all to hear. "Chaandi's words and pleas moved me to give you eleven days of chances, and in that time, I've been moved to judgment. And I am willing to forgive you all if you but meet what I ask of you."

Amman looked to the others, seeing none ready to speak—none ready to ask for forgiveness. Yet he found his mettle and stepped forward. "You say you are and are not Brahm, god of all. That you are of him, but not him. Then who are you? How can you forgive us?"

The child of Brahm thought for a moment, and then decided to give himself a name and to answer Amman's question. "I am Radhivahn, son of Brahm—son of myself—and I am the forgiver. And I will forgive you now if you but walk to me and take my hand." But before Amman could take a step, Radhivahn picked up a stick and carved a thin long furrow from the man's feet to his own. Radhivahn then blew a breath of fire along the strip of earth between the two men and it smoldered and burned like a bed of coals alight. "Remove your shoes and walk the fire to me. If you will do so—if you can—you will be forgiven."

"But it will hurt," said Amman.

Radhivahn nodded. "Yes, it will. But later it will not. And I will see to you."

Amman swallowed but did as asked. He removed his shoes and took the first step. The flames burned him. He screamed. He cried. His flesh cracked, blistered, burned. But he took the next step. Then another. He staggered. He stumbled. He fell and crawled until his fingers met the same fate: burning, blistering, cracking, bleeding. Some of the flames licked their way up to his clothing, setting them aflame.

He made his way forward until he was free, crumbling to his knees before Radhivahn. It's said when he walked clear of the fire, his feet still burned, and held to the flames. And the blood still dripped from his hands. His clothing cindered and fell from his back like feathers formed in fire—wings that quickly died. He sobbed there, at the son of God's feet.

Radhivahn knelt and placed his hands on Amman's head before moving them to his feet, rubbing them. "You were the first to ignore me when I was in need, but you were the first to come to me when I asked. For that, I will take away your pain." As he moved his hands against Amman's burned feet, the skin healed, the color returned, and soon, the man could stand again. "No longer will your story be the smith who cheats and thinks to sell babes for money. No longer will you be Amman. You are Athan, first of the bridge between me and man. First of my Asir, the hands to hold and guide my world and keep my creations safe from demons and mans' darker selves."

Next came Mohl, crying as she walked the burning ground, but she too came. When she couldn't walk, she fell to her hands and knees and began to crawl, burning them all. She curled at Radhivahn's feet, too tired and harmed to even sob.

He knelt now by her side and tended to her hurt. "You pretended to care so others would think highly of you. Now you walked in truth across the fire and are low. But I will help you rise and stand again." He soothed her pains and washed them away. "Stand now, and no longer be Mohl. You are Nahila, my Asir of truth." And so Radhivahn continued to offer forgiveness to those who would take it, but some tried to walk the fire and burned.

And when their bodies failed, something remained behind and tried to flee. Tainted, twisted things, resolved to remain free. Demons. Things of black smoke and ichor, ivy that wormed their way inside the shapings of Brahm. Things to pervert and lead people astray.

Radhivahn set after them, hounding them to all corners of the world. He brought a piece of his fire with him to keep back their dark taint, and where he could not be, he told his followers to light a flame of their own to beat back the evil. And in the end, there came a night where no corner of the world was without bright flame. On that day, Radhivahn, son of Brahm, son of himself, vanquished the last demon and gave us the world of today.

Or that is what the people of the Mutri Empire believe today. But this is the story, if you care to look for it, where the meaning behind our set days comes from. This is where the festival of light and flame finds its history and name. A great many truths are hidden in stories, and this is no different. Look closely, listeners, for you'll find many more in these tales.

I broke from the story, leaving the patrons of Three Tales Tavern to sit and ponder over my last words.

. . . After the raucous applause they broke into. A few drinkers raised themselves to a shaky stand, leaning on one another for support. They clanked their mugs together and spilled more of their ale than I wagered they cared to. The trio managed to interlink their arms in a fashion I didn't think possible, then tipped their beers into mouths, cheering more for themselves now and their feat than anything to do with my storytelling.

A fair thing. A good performer knows it's their job to set their listeners up for joy. Whether they find it outside your talent after the fact isn't a problem. So long as they're happy. So long as they're distracted from the little pains of the world around them. And the fears it can bring.

That's what good storytelling does. Or, at least tries to do.

Several tables in the taproom turned to loud gossiping. A few whispers caught my ear, talking about what little truth my story may have held. They made a fair point. This was a country of Solus. They had little love, and ears less, for another god's deeds and stories. But as far as tales could go, it was interesting enough for them to pass beyond anger and instead settle on light mockery and gentle teasing.

I let them have it, knowing no good could come of trying to set them straight.

Life's often made worse by trying to teach those with wool in their ears and more of it in the space between them.

And life's a teacher of its own. The kind that cares little for one's own thoughts and preconceptions—ready to smash them all and hand you a lesson that might be too bitter for your tastes then. But you'll learn to swallow it. Or else.

Like a lesson on cunning women, who are never quite what you expect, or where you think they will be . . . or when.

I retained my composure as best I could as I stared at Eloine standing several tables away. She held my look, giving me a smile that could have stolen all the light in the room. And it wasn't without wickedness as well.

She had changed her clothes to resemble the local style, if the local affair meant dressing as the nobility of Etaynia. Her dress was the color of dark wine, threaded with gold lace from her collar to her ankles. It had been cut low to give a view of her chest, but still high enough for what the Etaynians considered proper. The sleeves were wide and loose and flowed around her wrists. A thin belt of velvet, the color of plum, cinched the outfit around her waist.

It flattered her.

Eloine's smile deepened as she noticed me staring. She reached behind her back and pulled free a small purse, giving it a shake.

My purse.

I narrowed my eyes and kept my mouth from twisting wholly into a scowl, but I'm certain some measure of one made its way across my face.

She tilted her head toward a more secluded corner of the taproom, giving me a knowing look as she moved in that direction.

I moved through the crowd, gently brushing away the few hands that reached out to clap me or grab my arm for attention. The crowd would forget about me and my performance soon enough, turning to their drinks and food and the closer comforts.

That's the nature of things. Old and familiar comforts will always take the place of new and fanciful delights. The latter are fleeting to the minds of most men and women. The former are buried deep in us, no matter how trivial. And as the world changes, and dark things come, the old thoughts and simple pleasures oft keep us rooted to weather the storms of time and change.

I reached the end of the barroom where Eloine stood. None of the clamor and commotion at the head of the tavern reached us as intensely back here. It took me a moment to find the words to say to her, and I admit I didn't have the best of them. "You left in the morning."

She looked away. "I do that sometimes."

"But you came back tonight."

Eloine still didn't meet my eyes. "I do that too." She passed the purse over to me. "Thank you for letting me borrow this."

I took the purse and noticed a difference in its weight—lighter than before. One of my brows arched as I stowed what remained of my money in one of the folds of my robe. "Borrow is an interesting choice of words. From where I was sleeping, it seems so much so like you took it without my knowing."

She gave me an uneven grin. "From where you were sleeping, you seemed rather content whether I took the purse or not."

I frowned. "That's a very fine dress. The sort I'm certain some hefty coin could play some part in acquiring."

Her smile evened out and she gave me a curtsy fit for the nobility here. "Do you like it?"

"I do." There was no point in lying.

"And it didn't cost what you think." Eloine brushed a few locks of hair out from in front of her face. "Only a bit of coin, a hint of favor, and a lot of charm." A lascivious heat flooded her eyes and the curve of her mouth.

I blew out a breath more in resignation than frustration. "And you can be charming on occasion."

It was her turn to arch a brow now. "On occasion?" She eyed me askance.

"Theft of my purse may have dulled that a bit."

She pouted and feigned a wounded look. "Oh, dear. I'll have to remedy that, I suppose."

I finally managed a weak smile of my own. "I suppose so."

"If it helps, I was in great need of your purse, and I brought it back more or less."

"Certainly less." I patted the spot where I'd stowed my coin. "And you needed it to buy a dress."

"A woman's dress is no small thing. And, if you must know, I needed to buy myself out of something more than into something."

I waited for her to elaborate.

"Trouble is a particularly troublesome thing, especially when trying to get yourself out of it. It's easier by far to get into it. It has an odd nature."

I knew that one from experience. "And what trouble is this?" I couldn't fathom what else she could have gotten herself into in the country.

Eloine reached out and tapped the tip of my nose twice. "The kind you need not worry about any longer. I believe we can rest easy for a time on that account."

I squinted, struggling to believe she'd gotten us out of what we'd stirred up with the clergos—with a justice at that. "And I thought it was my job to tell the stories. I'd love to hear how you've done what you say you have." I smirked.

She held out a hand for me to take as she slipped away.

I quickly reached out, grabbing hold of it.

"You're quite right. Here I thought we were listening to your story, Ari." She'd done me the kindness of at least saying my name in a whisper so I could be sure no one heard a piece of it. Eloine continued leading me away, taking me to the door of the tavern, then out into the night.

The moon hung full above and the stars shadowed it, running far and wide across the sky.

"Tell me more of it as we walk?" Her voice held no command, just the honest curiosity of wanting to hear more of my story. She pulled my hand down to her side and interlaced her fingers with mine.

How could I say no?

I cleared my throat and spoke. "I'd lost my family, everything I'd ever known, and the only place I'd been able to think of as home. I'd seen and learned a piece of real magic. I watched storybook monsters come to life and take all but my life from me. But they came close enough. And I didn't know what else to do but to keep running. Eventually, I made my way into a new family. One rife with secrets, dangers, knives, and all the promise of revenge a young boy could ask for."

TWENTY-SIX

The Cost of Kindness

The streets of Abhar are not kind to lost and youthful souls. They're a maze of winding stone walls and narrow passages only the initiated can navigate—ones like Nisha. And I had no idea where she could be this night.

Any adults with a shred of sense had taken shelter during the storm, and the only ones out at this time of night were not the kind of people I'd want to cross paths with. I knew little of the world outside the understage, but I knew that much, at least.

The rough debris nestled into the dirt of the back alley paths cut into my feet, yet the pain came from a place further from me than the thunder overhead. It was more of an awareness I'd been hurt than the heat of a wound itself. My feet slapped just as hard against the ground, pushing me farther down the path.

All I could see were cold walls, nearly black themselves under the night, and they looked to narrow the farther I ran. A rod of tight agony shot through my calf down into my heel, strong enough I couldn't help but register it in my manic state. I stumbled and battered my shoulder against unforgiving stone. A small grace and bit of luck kept the impact from pulling my joint from the socket.

I rocked to one side, still unsure of what had caused the lance of pain through my leg. My mind remained in a frenzy, however, and I hobbled forward until I could continue my run. And not once did I lose the book Mahrab had gifted me.

The wet air did little to assuage the burning in my lungs. For all that, I could have been breathing the hot and dry air near a fire. My chest ached. Moisture blurred my vision, and it had nothing to do with the rain.

I ran through winding streets, colliding with odd lengths of wood jutting out from poorly constructed stalls and carts, until I couldn't run anymore. Mahrab had taught me of the folds of the mind, of the candle and the flame, of many things to distance me from the things tearing me apart.

But in that moment, I could call on none of them. And I tried.

I could kindle no flame inside me. I lay on the ground, shivering, holding myself tight, aware only of every pelting drop of rain. I took and pressed my book against my chest, clutching it like it was the only piece of fire and warmth I could find, praying it would bring some heat to my flesh and bones. I knew it couldn't, but a child's hope is an interesting thing. It can hold out against all rationale and the hard things the world throws at us. It's a trick against the harsher truths.

But sometimes there is no trick to escape the pains of the mind and heart. Sometimes there's nothing to do but to sit in them until they take their toll.

So I did.

Fatigue offers a reprieve of its own. Being too tired to think, too tired to care, too tired to feel. Eventually, even pain leaves in place of a greater weariness. And when that comes, it's welcome.

I used what little strength I had to crawl toward a small stall neighboring the mouth of the alley. It had been covered in sheets of waxed canvas to protect it from the rain, each piece fastened to the frame of the wood itself or quickly staked into the ground. I found a space where the sheets folded and forced my way through them, taking refuge inside until my thoughts grew to be too much.

I had no energy for sobbing. The rain and run had seen to that. Instead, I held myself as tight as I could, waiting. . . . Eventually, I slipped into the mercy of a deep, forgetful sleep.

A blunt tip jabbed into the meat between my ribs. I winced, flinching into a tighter ball as I awoke. The night's toll had left me too stiff to get to my feet properly under the newfound pain.

Another prod. Poke. Then a jab-twist of sharp agony.

I cried out and scrambled away from the source. Mahrab's book ended up at my back, stuffed into the space between my waistband and under the end of my shirt. I finally found myself able to gaze at the source of the jab without blurriness tingeing my vision.

The man could have been in his fifth decade of life, and a rough one at that. Even the shade offered by the stall, and the layers of clothing covering his head, didn't spare his face from the toll of constant sun. His skin was the color of well-burnt sugar, and his face held all the deep lines found in men twice his age.

The man wore a loose collarless shirt that fell to his knees and could have once been the bright color of turmeric, but now was faded and covered in a thin layer of dust. He gave me a look equal parts resignation and curiosity.

"Oi, this isn't your father's shop, *ji*? Get up." He reached to prod me again, but I kicked my legs against the ground, pushing myself up against the other side of the stall.

I raised a hand to placate him, and the man paused long enough for me to get to my feet. "I'm sorry. I—"

He waved the lacquered wooden rod in the air. "Who are you?" The man tilted his head to look me over, pursing his lips as he did. The rod remained pointed at me all the while.

I opened my mouth to speak but he spoke over me again.

"Why are you in my shop, hm? Turn out your pockets. Show me your hands. Open your mouth, thief, cur, ravel, rascal!" He spat each word in rapid staccato, barely giving me the time to process them in my dazed and tired state.

I did what I could, pointing to what served as my clothes to make it clear I didn't even have pockets to store anything in. My fingers uncurled and I showed him my opened palms. All they held were calluses and fresh scrapes from the night before. Some grime and dirt courtesy of sleeping on the ground. And if he wanted me to return that to him, I'd gladly do so.

He looked me over with greater patience than before, though still with a large degree of suspicion. "Why are you here?" The shopkeeper bounced the end of the rod in one of his palms as if waiting for another chance to use it on me.

"The storm." Each word came out through shaking lips and with just as much unsteadiness. "I didn't have anywhere else to go last night. I'll leave, I swear." I joined my hands together in a silent gesture of both plea and promise.

"Why don't you have anywhere to go?" The man stepped closer, and a smile crossed his face I'll never forget. A razor's line along a sheet of ice. Cold. Cutting. And utterly without warmth. A look filled with opportunity, hunger, and something I didn't have a word for but bothered me deep in my gut. "Are you lost—alone? Where's your family, *putre*?"

He may as well have jabbed my spine with that rod of his when he called me "son."

I shook and took a half step away from him until the edge of the stall bit into Mahrab's book, pushing an unforgiving corner into my back. "My fa—" The words died in my mouth as soon as I'd started, and I had no hope of finding them again, or anything close for a handful of seconds. "No." It was as much of an answer as I could manage, and the man seemed to take it.

He nodded to himself. "Good. Good." Nothing in his tone suggested he had anything good in mind.

I leaned away from him again, but found the stall only pressed harder into me.

Then came the question I didn't expect, but should have.

"What's your caste, boy?" His smile grew lecherous, the rod bouncing faster—harder in his hand.

"Why?" I placed my palms against the lip of the stall's frame. With a little effort, I'd be able to push myself on to the first shelf and scramble away. But acting too quickly could get me caught fighting the canvas still draped over the structure, or I could tangle my limbs scampering past the mess of small lidded crates lining the shop.

"The *ratheri* sticks together, yeah? We're the same brothers, you and I." The gleam in his eyes told me he didn't believe that to be true even if we did happen to be the same caste.

It was a lesson I may have been too young to learn then, but I learned it nonetheless. The kindness of some people in the world is conditional, and few things can be done to meet those conditions. And, in truth, those are the sort of people you shouldn't seek kindness from. For they're not offering the real thing, and they are most certainly not kind in heart.

Kindness is freely given, without the want of reciprocation, let, obligation, or lien.

And I knew telling him the truth would only buy me trouble, but I did so anyway. What worse could happen to me now? Monsters existed. I'd lost everyone I held dear. Everyone I knew. Everyone I could at the very least trust with my safety and to feed me. I wouldn't run from what little I had left. My truth.

The words clumped like hard mud in my throat, but I forced them out regardless. "*Sulhi.* I'm Sullied." Every muscle in my body tensed . . . waiting.

His shoulders sagged and he sighed. "I might have known." Then he smiled. "I can't help you, but I can help myself." He took a step closer to me, raising the rod overhead. "I suppose it's good no one will miss you at least. Koli-*eiyah* pays good prices for little ones like you no one's looking for."

Whatever cold hollowness had filled me the night before fled. Instead I found the heat I'd been praying for in the dark. It took me, fanning hot and angry in my stomach before finding its way into the tips of my fingers and the small bones inside them. I clenched my fists, seized by the fire, and screamed something I knew would carry through the street.

I threw myself at the man. Koli's name had been enough to push aside all thoughts of how much larger he was than me, enough to cast the threat of the rod out of mind. I even forgot all of what Vithum had taught me.

Much the shame.

The rod came down at an angle, striking the soft flesh over my left shoulder, but pain too had found a distant place in my mind recently. And I'd endured my fair share of beatings lately.

I dug my fingers into the folds of his clothing, grabbing tight and wrenching with all the ferocity a frenzied child could manage. The fabric didn't tear, but the man staggered. My screams would surely draw attention soon enough and he knew it to be true.

He clamped a hand over my mouth, wrestling for control of the situation.

I bit down, squeezing my jaw tight as I could. I tasted salt and copper—warmth and wetness.

He screamed.

I released my toothy hold and barreled into the man, doing little but sending him faltering back a step.

The rod came down again, this time glancing off the side of my head, though the blow carried none of the weight of the first.

My world spun, and though I had little in my stomach, I felt like heaving up whatever I could. I stumbled forward and lashed out blindly. My fingernails found purchase against the underside of the man's chin. I raked as hard as I could, knowing I'd broken his flesh.

He let out another yelp, flailing with the rod in panic.

I caught another blow against the broad of my back, then a dull thump that struck Mahrab's book, nestled under my clothing. The simple act of hitting the book roused another part of my anger.

I whirled and opened my hand, forming it like a crude blade. In the peak of my anger, I recalled what Vithum had told me about a sword being an extension of one's arm. I jabbed out with my stiffened fingers and struck the hollow of the man's throat.

In theory, the blow would have forced him to gag for air and leave him momentarily crippled. Worse if I had even had a training sword in hand.

In reality, the bones of my fingers ached and I found myself wincing from the attack nearly as much as the man.

He sputtered, a trail of spittle passing from his lips. But he made no move after me.

My chance. And I took it.

I turned and hurtled free of the opening I'd crawled through the night before. A petty part of me had the wherewithal to grab hold of the canvas sheets on my way out. I let momentum, my weight, and fury do the trick.

Several of the sheets resisted my hold, pulling against the frame of the stall and whatever boxes had been stored on top of them to hold the cloth in place.

The overall structure held firm, but not without cost. Its profile shifted. The sound of splintering wood came from inside.

Some of the boxes, I guessed.

And a few of the sheets fell to the street, giving onlookers a glance inside.

I released my grip and ran with renewed energy matching my escape from the Ashura.

Shouting filled the air behind me, and I made note of a string of obscenities I don't think I have the creativity to match to this day.

People rushed to the aid of the stall merchant—passing me by, fortunately.

I turned and raced down another alley. A few men lay slumped against the walls, letting their heads fall to the side rather than turn to follow me. They looked nearly lifeless at first glance, but they took no further action beyond staring mutely. I took that as a silent blessing as I made my way past.

One of the men locked eyes with me and I nearly stopped.

I could see no color in them beyond a milky white that showed all the signs of going further cloudy. I may as well have been looking into two balls of cotton soaked in old milk.

The man reached out with an open hand, his fingers gnarled and the nails yellowed. "Coin?" He licked his lips like he'd gone days without a taste of water.

I said nothing, looking back over my shoulder to see if anyone had followed me into the narrow street. A piece of me breathed relief to find I was alone, save for the slumped men all staring at me.

The one who'd spoken scraped against the wall for support as he got to his feet. "You have anything on you to help a poor soul?" He gave me a tired and uneven smile that showed gums nearly as white as his eyes. I could barely tell where they began from his teeth. And every other man had a smile the same.

One of them reached behind his back and pulled free a thin sliver that glinted in what little light reached the alley.

I swallowed, backing away from them. "No, nothing—sorry. I . . ." I didn't finish my thought, deciding it was better to run.

But one of the man's hands snaked out, clamping on the meat between my neck and shoulder. He squeezed hard enough that his overgrown nails nearly broke my skin. The strength of his grip surprised me as it shouldn't have come from someone as emaciated as him. His clothes hung from him and looked like another few days of rough sleeping would finish eating through the fabric completely.

His hair hung thin and lank. The lifestyle he lived had taken all the healthiness from his skin, leaving him wan in places, sallow in others.

"Let me go." I struggled, but all the strength and anger of earlier had fled. All I could hold to was weariness and the promise of pain now sinking in from the shopkeeper's beating.

"Look him over," said the white-eyed man, speaking to the others in the alley. "Maybe he has something we can sell. We can get another piece of white-joy."

I didn't know what he was talking about.

"Cheep-cheep." The noise sounded like the imitation of a small bird's call, coming from farther down the alley.

Everyone turned to regard the speaker but me, unable to twist properly under the man's hold.

The source of the disturbance now released a trilling whistle. "Cheep-cheep."

I struggled against the man, but despite his frailty he clung to me as if I were a piece of gold he couldn't risk losing.

The man gripping me squinted down the alley. "Who comes?"

"The one who has what you seek—cheep-cheep. Let the boy go, and I'll give you what you could want him for."

The white-eyed man's gaze widened. His tongue passed between his pressed lips and ran along the tissue as if he were thirsty. "You have some? How much?"

"I do. Give me the boy, and I'll give you a piece of happiness—of bliss. Enough at least for you and your friends today. Tomorrow? Tomorrow you'll have to find your own, huh?"

The man's grip slackened and I grabbed hold of his wrist, squeezing as hard as I could to break free. "N-no."

The other white-eyes now came to my side, each putting another hand on me to ensure I remained where I was.

Voices sounded at the end of the alley I'd entered through, and I had a suspicion they were spurred by my antics at the shopkeeper's stall. It looked very much like I was ill-sorted no matter which way I went.

The white-eyes who'd first grabbed me now sneered at the newcomer I still couldn't see. "We could sell the boy for more joy than that. Do you . . . have more?"

"Tch-tch. Shame. You could do that, yes. But how would you? Three little cotton-eyed birds with a small boy in hand? People would notice. People would talk. How long before kuthri come asking questions? And their questions always come at the tip of their long, long knives." I had a feeling the speaker smiled.

"Could you sell the boy? I'm not sure. But if you let him go now, you'll be sure to have a piece and promise of white-joy today."

The group of men turned toward each other, whispering among themselves.

"It's been a whole day and a half, Sashi. A. Day. And. A. Half." One of the men scratched his cheek just under one of his eyes.

"Feels longer to me. My eyes feel dry. The man has a point. We can just take the joy now. *Now.*" The final word held a note of plea that I heard echoes of in my own mind on days deep hunger plagued me.

The man who'd first spoken to me finally turned back to the stranger. "Give it here and we'll give you the boy. No tricks. Nothing funny, *ji-ah*?"

"Done. Pass me the boy and I hand you the joy at the same time."

The three men shuffled me about so I could finally make out the speaker.

His appearance made me think of stories about one's eccentric and gaudy uncle. The only hair on him sprouted from his bushy brows, threaded just enough to keep from being disastrously silly, and a mustache thick to the point it could have benefitted from a serious trim. He ran a hand over his bald head, showcasing a series of thick rings of gold and silver on most of his fingers.

His clothing spoke silently of wealth. He wore a matching set of shirt and pants the color of brilliant carmine. His shoes were pointed, clean despite the dirt road, and threaded with gold lace. And every bit of it fit him like it had been stitched solely for his body, which was lean in a way no starving man's could be. This man ate, and well, but he held on to none of the fat.

A stoppered vial sat pinched between the forefinger and thumb of his other hand. Its contents were the color of water pooled with too much milk, a cloudy white.

The men shuffled me closer, the assumed leader of the group reaching out with an unsteady hand.

The well-dressed newcomer offered the white-joy with measured patience as if he were passing along something as simple as a pinch of pepper.

The white-eyed man grabbed the vial and shoved me hard at the same time.

"No!" I used the moment of freedom to flail, swinging my arms wide to deter anyone from trying to grab hold of me again. The book Mahrab had left me slipped inside my clothing. Coldness filled my chest and I stopped my frenzied motions and reached behind me to assure my sole possession wouldn't fall free to those in the alley.

"Easy, boy." The man who'd offered up the joy extended both hands toward me, open and welcoming. "You're safe now." He tilted his head to look past me at the men he'd traded with, arching a brow. "Isn't that right?"

The men inched away from us, all whispering as they held up the vial to examine its contents.

"Come-come, little bird. Come with Mithu."

A distant bell rang in my head at the sound of his name. I knew it, but I couldn't recall where from. "Why should I?" I looked over my shoulder to the men still occupying the alley. While they paid me no mind, I didn't know how they'd react to me rushing past them.

Will they try to take me again? What happens if I get beyond them? I'm just back in the alley where I started all that trouble. That shopkeeper will beat me black and blue.

Hands clasped to my shoulders and I shook free of the reverie. The stranger had taken me in his hold, yet he didn't squeeze and try to keep me in place.

"Easy-easy, little sparrow—little bird. I just want to talk, and you'll hear me out?" At that, he released his grip.

My heart still pounded, hard and heavy. The lining of my throat felt like I'd swallowed a fistful of sand. "And that's all you want, to talk?"

He nodded.

I licked my lips, his answer doing nothing to abate the fear seizing my chest and shaking my arms. "About?" I took a half step back, hoping the action went unnoticed.

"About you, little one . . . and the kindness I just did for you." He smiled but the expression left me empty. I couldn't gauge it. All my time watching those in the theater perform had taught me the many kinds of smiles a man could make; Mithu's carried no malice, and it carried no light. It carried nothing but practiced effort—a mask of the mouth if I'd ever seen one.

I breathed in deep and slow through my nostrils, using the moment to think. "Why do you want to talk about me?" One of my feet ground against the dirt, packing it tight below me should I need to push off and break into a run.

The man named Mithu scratched the underside of his chin. "Mhm. Well, how did a young bird like you end up in this alley, away from your family and in the hands of cotton-eyes?"

I didn't answer.

Mithu took my silence as an answer. "Alone? No family?" He sighed as if that pained him. "Little birds on their own don't last long in Abhar, especially in Keshum. They need a nest. A family. If you don't have one, I can offer you that." He smiled again, wide and empty.

"I . . ." One of my hands went to my back, feeling for Mahrab's book. It was still stuck in place.

Mithu caught my movements and leaned to one side. "What do you have there, little sparrow?"

"Nothing!" I backed away, swatting at the air between us. The gesture did little to perturb the man, though.

He stood as solid and unmoving as the alley walls. "I won't take it from you. I know the worth of a little boy's possessions. You know, I still have a few of my own from when I was your age. . . ." He left the words hanging in the air like a question.

I didn't rise to the bait and tell him how old I was.

"I promise you, I'm not here to hurt you. If I wanted to do that, well"—he reached under his shirt, pulling away the waist of his pants—"I could have done that anytime I wanted." He pulled free a curved dagger longer than his palm, giving the weapon a little waggle to make his point. Mithu put the blade back where he'd taken it from.

"Then what *do* you want?"

Mithu took several long steps away from me toward the exit of the alley. "To talk, longer, in detail. To offer you something, little sparrow. It's the least you can do me, to listen, that is. The kindness I offered you has a cost, and it's a small one at that. One even a bird like you can pay. Just come and meet my family and see if there's a place for you there. And I promise you this, if you find yourself wanting to stay, I will never ever take from you that which is already yours. All I want to do is show you." He extended an open hand. "What do you say?"

I thought about the offer and all he'd told me. He had a point in that he could have done me harm had he meant it. And he hadn't done so. He could have left me to the mercy of the white-eyed men, desperate to do whatever it took to procure another bit of white-joy.

I looked back to see the men passing the vial about, carefully tipping it to allow a single drop of the liquid to fall into each of their eyes. They shuddered upon the substance's contact and went limp. Their mouths all slipped into the same expression of blissful lazy smiles. I watched their chests heave before moving so slowly and shallow you could hardly tell they were breathing.

I could take my chances out here with more men like that and who knew what else. Not to mention being found by Koli.

"What was that, little sparrow? What did you cheep-cheep?"

I hadn't realized I'd spoken at all.

"Tell Mithu that name again. What's that you're keeping between your beak? If you want a place in my home, you can't keep secrets like that, hm?"

I swallowed, finding my throat hoarse even at the thought of uttering that name. But I found what moisture I could and worked it through my gullet. "Koli." I waited. I watched. Ready for Mithu's reaction.

His eyes narrowed and his mouth thinned to a line sharper than that of his blade. "*That* is a name I am not fond of, little bird. And less so of the man it belongs to. If ever you want to see the other side of me, the one that could have done hurtful horrible things to you, speak that name again, and you will see. Better yet, bring the man to me, and I'll see to it." One of Mithu's hands balled into a fist tight enough to elicit small pops from his fingers.

I found a bit more courage at the expense of tipping my heart into a faster pace. "You hate him?"

"I'll kill him. If not today, then tomorrow. If not then, then one day. He and I are at ends over—" Mithu stopped short and gestured around us.

"The alley?"

"The streets of Keshum, little bird. The streets of Keshum. And one day I'll wrest them all from him, and more." The first hint of true emotion flooded Mithu then.

I saw a fire I knew all too well. The one from the night I'd lost my family. The one the Ashura had started in the theater and the one I kept burning low in a part of my heart. Mithu meant to see Koli die.

And so did I.

I took his hand. "Yes. Take me to your family."

That was the start of it. The beginning of how I earned my first title.

TWENTY-SEVEN

A Family of Sparrows

Mithu led me to a squat building, wider than those around it, but standing no higher. The place had been fashioned from old brick, weathered smooth and cleansed of its original deeper color. It looked like it had been washed with a paint somewhere between sand tinged with blood, and faded rust. Several arched openings ran along the third floor. Sheets of all colors blocked the view inside.

We approached the dark and solid double doors. Mithu rapped his knuckles against their hard wooden surface and trilled a bird whistle I couldn't identify.

"Where are we?" I looked up at him, then the doors, waiting to see who would answer.

Mithu didn't regard me as he spoke. "We're home, little bird. Or, I am. Whether it comes to be yours is something for me to decide. And for you, of course. But I have a feeling you're in need of a place to put your head at night and somewhere to fill your belly, hm?"

I didn't reply, but nodded. A cold practicality took hold of me now that the morning's excitement had passed. I couldn't quite grab the mindset of the candle and the flame to lend greater clarity, but there's something to be said for time, even a small amount.

One of the doors creaked open enough so a single eye could peer outside. A whistle, much like Mithu's, sounded but fell apart halfway through into wet sputtering. "*Mahl!*" The speaker of the curse didn't sound to be much older than me.

"Cheep-cheep, little bird. You'll get it." Mithu placed a hand on the door and pushed it open.

"Ah!" The person behind the door tumbled to their ass, rubbing the spot while bringing their other hand up to shield their eyes from the morning light filtering inside. At first glance, he looked like any other Sullied child.

His breeches and vest had their hems sewn up to not reveal any straggling threads that could further deteriorate the fabric. The numerous holes in his attire had long since been patched.

Mithu did nothing to help the child to his feet. "Juggi, why are you standing so close to the doors? You're to stand, listen, open . . . then move. That's it. You're no guard, no kuthri. And if that's what you want to be, you're very much in the wrong line of work, no?" Mithu smiled and the boy matched it as he sprung to his feet.

Juggi dusted himself off, then turned his attention on me. His eyes widened and he shot Mithu a look of silent question. The boy reminded me of a dozen others I'd seen in his state of poverty, and I worked to try to identify a single unique feature about him, but I struggled.

"I found this little bird today." Mithu patted me on the shoulder once. "I'm showing him our nest and seeing if he wants to join your brothers and sisters. I think he could be a very good sparrow."

Juggi's mouth tightened and his eyes flashed Mithu a look that said he didn't agree. The boy didn't voice his opinion, however. He ran a hand through his hair, which had been cut and tousled to hang just below the lobes of his ears.

Mithu moved a hand to my back and eased me inside, shutting the door behind us.

Coolness radiated from inside the dark room. It took me a handful of seconds to adjust to the low light of the ground floor.

The room was large and packed with cushions and low-standing tables. You could think of it as an organized mess of sorts.

Another child crept into the room from an opening at the far right-hand wall. They looked nearly the same as Juggi down to the color and thread of their clothing. Their hair . . . the same color and cut. Their eyes were the only things that marked them differently. Juggi's were an unforgettable brown. The new boy's, a tired green washed with gray, softening the color.

"Cheep-cheep, you're up early, little one. You don't work until the evening." Mithu made his way over to the other boy, easing him toward one of the nearby cushions.

"I had a bad dream." The boy rubbed his eyes, sinking to his knees on the soft padding. Neither of the children looked to be older than ten.

Mithu gave the boy several reassuring pats all while Juggi stared knives into the side of my head.

I avoided his gaze, focusing on my surroundings.

Nothing had been done to temper the horrid color of the brick walls. A few rugs hung from nails to mask parts of the building and bring it better to life. But apart from that, I couldn't make out what the room's function was but to sit and lounge in. A far cry from my home where every floor had a specific purpose. Even the roof had one after Mahrab and Vithum started my training.

The sound of their names came to me as I thought of them, bringing a small fist over my heart to grab it. I didn't wince, but the pain lingered.

"What do you think, little bird—cheep-cheep—about our newest find?" Mithu motioned toward me with a hand.

The child resting on the cushion gave me a look through half-shut eyes, clearly still holding on to sleep. He held the stare for a moment longer before sinking further into the soft folds of the mat below him. "S'dunno."

Mithu rubbed the boy's back before getting up and beckoning me. "Come-come. Time to meet those who can be your new family." He didn't wait for me to come to his side as he moved toward one of the archways at his right.

I quickly fell in step behind him, casting one last look over a shoulder to the two boys. Both returned my gaze with varying intensity.

Juggi maintained a look that told me I was not welcome and he would be keeping an eye on me. Likely both.

The other child's stare reminded me of a cat out to bathe in the sun, unconcerned with much beyond their own contentment. Yet, an awareness still sat in it. He weighed me with a practiced disinterest.

I reevaluated which of the two boys might come to be a problem in that instant. Juggi hadn't bothered to hide his feelings. But the other boy knew how to play pretend, and if that was the case, he could hide a great deal.

That could prove troublesome over time.

Mithu slipped a hand over my back, easing it up to a shoulder and squeezing hard. The action pulled me away from my suspicions and back to our walk as we brushed aside a rug hung to serve as a curtain in the arch.

Red walls gave way to a staircase of gray and dull stone. Simple, rough, and showing no signs of ever having been smooth. Mithu led the way, pausing halfway up. He eyed me sideways. "You're quiet."

I nodded.

"That's not what I meant." He pointed down at the stone. "Look at it."

I did, unsure what he had in mind.

A moment passed before he finally decided to explain. "I'm wearing shoes. You are not. Sometimes when I find little lost birds and bring them here, these steps tell me about them, hm. Some come from places where they were treated to honeyed milk and almonds. Places with sugar rice pudding and their hands and feet rubbed with creams. They're soft, and that's not their fault. These steps tell me so, though. You walk like you don't feel them. That tells me something else. No sounds, no faces. Nothing."

I remained silent.

"You are no stranger to walking barefoot and over hard roads." It wasn't a question. "I think Juggi is wrong about you. You will make a marvelous little sparrow."

I still didn't know what that meant, and anything I'd tried to quietly glean so far from Mithu's home told me little else but that he had two boys staying here. Notably not his sons from the way they looked. But I kept from pressing him on the subject for now.

We made our way up to the second story, walking beside each other despite the narrow width of the hall only leaving a few inches of free space on either side. The walls were of the same red brick as below, and the length of the passage had one defining trait to it: doors.

I counted nearly two dozen going down just one side of the hall, and just as many on the other.

Mithu must have picked up on the question settling in my mind, for he moved past me, knocking on one of the doors. He didn't stop for it to open, moving on and continuing the action at some of the others. The movements carried an odd and measured beat to them, almost like he performed this ritual daily. Mithu completed the little circuit, making his way back to where he'd started, not looking at me as he waited.

All of the doors clicked a few breaths later. They opened in unison and one child per room stepped out into the hall, some raising balled fists to grind the sleep away at their eyes. I could hardly tell them apart from Juggi at first glance. It was as if they'd been deliberately dressed and had their hair tailored to be copies of the young boy. All that set them apart were the small features of their faces: deviations in their noses, ears, and of course their eyes. Things not all people bother to pay attention to at first look, possibly seconds and thirds.

Children are often the ignored voices and bodies of the world.

"The little ones don't start singing and working until midday. We've woken them earlier than what they're used to, new sparrow."

I wanted to point out to Mithu that I hadn't done a thing to rouse them from their sleep, and that I certainly hadn't become one of his little birds. "And what is their work, Mithu . . . *sahm*." I caught myself in the moment forgetting to add the honorific and decided to do so. It might have gone overlooked, but something told me a man like Mithu would appreciate the touch of respect.

If he noticed my hesitation, he didn't comment on it. "Every nest of birds has their secrets, little one. If you want to know ours, you'll have to wait to find out."

The children had finally wrung themselves free of their sleep-driven stupor. All of them shot me looks without directly focusing their gazes on me.

A practiced skill, one I'd taught myself watching Khalim's tutelage of other actors. Too much a coincidence for them to have all come across that on their own.

Mithu's been teaching them stagecraft. Why?

The weight of the looks grew, and I did everything I could to appear as ordinary as possible. Quite the task considering I was a new face standing beside the only adult within the building. One who obviously held power and control over all other lives here.

Mithu whistled and gestured to the stairs at the other end of the hall. "Cheep-cheep, birds. Cheep-cheep. Let's go beyond your roost and to the canopy, hm? Time to welcome another bird and see if he wants to stay." Mithu left no room for any protest, moving first and letting everyone fall into a neat tight line behind him as he walked upstairs.

I followed at the end of the pack. Or I thought I did. The uncanny awareness one has when being watched filled me. I didn't turn fully, shifting slightly to one side as I moved up the first step. A glance out of the corners of my eyes showed me the young nameless boy I'd met after Juggi.

He moved perfectly in step with how I had, masking the sounds of his feet under my own.

Either it had been marvelous luck, something I'd lost faith in all too recently, or a deliberate effort on his part. I figured the latter, and kept it in mind that Mithu's little birds carried more secrets and odd training than I'd originally thought.

Maybe I traded one danger off the streets for another. I could have run. The two boys who'd been left at my back couldn't pose enough of a threat to bar me from escaping, no matter what little tricks they'd learned. But Mithu had dozens of children, and they moved almost like puppets on strings for him.

I didn't know Keshum's streets well enough to elude anyone, much less find a safe place to keep to myself should I get away.

The truth was, I needed him. There are few options for a penniless child of no worthy caste in the Mutri Empire. And what little there were for me usually led to early graves.

I gave the light-footed boy one last look before heading after Mithu.

The stairway led to a short hall only long enough to boast three archways along the wall, each just large enough for me to squeeze through. A pair of copper doors blocked the way ahead. They'd patinated to a color I'd later come to associate with some seas, a motley green flecked with blues and splashes of brown.

None of the children who'd first come up were in sight, and the same went for Mithu.

I went over to the doors and brought the base of a fist against them, hoping I'd done the right thing.

They opened, and two of the children from earlier moved to either side of me. Their stares remained fixed on one another like I didn't exist.

The proceeding room had been painted a deep brown that held a sparkle that seemed to move with the light as my eyes tracked it. It held all the promise of gold in that extra color. Candles flickered at the edges of the room and hanging rugs kept out the morning light from the arches along one wall. A child sat before each of the little flames—motionless, making the fire seem livelier by comparison. Mithu sat at the far end of the room, resting comfortably on thicker and more ornate cushions than those on the first floor.

A man stood to either side of him, each a shocking departure from everyone else seen in Mithu's home. Where all of the children could have been copied from a single painting, the two men did not follow that convention.

"Don't let Askar and Biloo frighten you, little bird. Come-come." Mithu beckoned me with a hand.

Askar and Biloo held all the similarities of a starveling alley cat and an overfed pig taught to walk upright. The first man's eyes contained the sharp brightness and quickness of a feline's. A brown touched with hints of gold. And his mouth held a self-satisfied smile that showed off too much of his canines.

He wore an open vest, too short to cover his torso, revealing places where his ribs pressed against his skin. His pants looked like they only held themselves up by the lengths of twine he'd fastened around his waist. A clean-shaven man with short curly hair that made him look like a skeleton upon which a furry animal had died.

It would be kind to say Biloo was twice the man Askar was when he was easily three times that. He wore no shirt, the broad of his body covered in green and russet-brown swirls of ink. Kahlri, a common skin dye made from a plant and its dried roots. Every breath took effort on the man's part as he labored in the action—loudly. His hair fell in perfectly straight lengths behind his shoulders, an oily sheen tingeing the black of his locks. His eyes seemed too small for his face, and they looked utterly unconcerned with the goings-on of the moment.

I eyed both men, not wholly believing Mithu's words about being free of fear around the pair. They had only one clear purpose: to scare people. Either away from Mithu, or into his favor.

Which means he's probably just as dangerous. He came to you alone and handled those white-eyed men without help.

"Cheep-cheep. Come-come." He motioned again, and I heeded the invitation, moving within four steps of him. Mithu smiled and nodded more to himself than me.

There are many little terrors in the world. Some come from open dangers, from things you know will hurt and things that mean to. Some come from old pains promising—threatening—to visit you again. You don't know when or how, but the thoughts are there, and they are frightening. And lastly, there is the quiet fear that comes with waiting. The unease that comes from unknown things to come. All you do know is something will happen. That it's out of your control, and that it can go entirely the wrong way for you.

And you're standing there, a young boy, alone.

I did that and silently held on to the fears of what was to come, waiting for Mithu to prove them false or true in the next moments.

He reached over to a bulb of baked clay fixed to a tube. Mithu held its flexible stem in one hand, slipping it between his lips and taking a deep puff. Smoke seeped out through his mouth and nose and brought with it a smell like dying coals and weak cinnamon. He coughed several times and leaned back, eyelids fluttering. "Mhm. What do you think of my home so far, little bird?"

My life in the theater had taught me that appearances are deceiving. A lesson as true then and there as it has been throughout my life, wherever I ended up. Mithu's home was no exception to that rule. But I kept that thought to myself.

"It's nice." The short and simple answer couldn't buy me any trouble, I figured.

"Is that all it is?" Mithu took another puff followed by a shorter cough than before. "It's a home for many lost little things like you." He waved toward the children. "Isn't that right, sparrows?"

They mimicked his earlier cheeping.

He grinned. "See? They are fed, they are clothed, and they all have spaces to themselves, which is what every little bird needs. Would you like that? I'm thinking you would." Mithu brought the stem to his mouth for another inhale, but stopped short, tipping its head toward me instead.

He wasn't wrong. A home, any safe place would have been a boon. If not for the obvious reasons of food and water, to keep me from Koli's sight and grasp. At least until I was ready to do something about him.

"It would be nice. I do need a home." At the thought of the last word, *home,* another ache filled my chest. A numbness took hold of my brain and, for a time I lost track of, I felt distant from myself, like I watched everything unfolding from over my shoulder. It was almost like being in the folds of my mind with none of the acute focus.

Mithu clapped a hand and the noise jerked me out of the slips of my mind. "You're dancing, little bird." He tapped the tip of the stem against an open palm. "Come to the point. Would you like to have a new family? To have work and purpose. To do what we do?"

And there was my opportunity to finally press him over that matter. "What exactly *do* you and your little . . . um, sparrows do?"

A small chorus of laughter broke out among the children and Mithu fixed them with a look that silenced them.

"My little sparrows pick up the excess material burdening the people in Keshum, and of course those who pass through it. Trader, traveler, wealthy dullard—squabbler. We'll take the shoes from a cobbler. Fruit and veg, bowls of stew. Whatever's to take. Whatever you can do. Some run, some sing, and all with eyes open for each and every shiny thing."

"You're thieves." The words left my mouth with a harshness I hadn't accounted for, but whatever edge my voice held, Mithu ignored it.

"We're alive. We work when and where we can. We eat what we can. And we lay our heads at night on beds of our own. Which is more than the world has ever cared to offer any of us. And it looks to be more than anyone has offered you, hm?"

I saw no point in replying to that as the truth couldn't have been more evident. Mithu and I knew my situation for what it was, and no words could clarify it any better than a simple look.

He took my silence as agreement before inhaling another puff of smoke. "So"—a thin stream of clouds filtered out through his lips—"I ask again, would you like to join my little family of sparrows?"

I thought back to what Mithu had said in the alley he'd pulled me from. "Koli took everything from me. Took my family. My home. My . . ." I trailed off before telling him of my dreams and studies under Mahrab. "Everything." My hands balled tight and the fire that filled my core pushed away any fear I held of the two men at Mithu's sides. "I want to see him pay for it. I want to hurt him—to lose everything I lost . . . and more. I want to kill him."

You would think the pain of the night before, too new and fresh, would keep a child rooted in fear and hoping for forgetfulness. That I couldn't reach for anything other than the urge to shut it all away. I'll tell you now: Few things can anger quicker than a child who's been wronged. Few things can trade fear and hopelessness in a moment for a senseless wrath than a young boy who's had everything taken from him. A child's mind and heart are wonderful . . . and terrible things at times.

Mithu held my look—unflinching. Silence built within the room, and a few of the sparrows, as well as Askar and Biloo, shot various looks at the leader of their group. He ignored them all, keeping his quiet attention on me alone. Another breath passed and he spoke. "We both want that. I wish to see it done. And I will. Will you be there for that day, little sparrow?"

A spark kindled within the folds of my mind and I grabbed hold of the candle and the flame, letting the resolution and strength flood me when I answered him. "I will."

Mithu rocked in place, throwing his head back as he burst into clear and bright laughter. "Cheep-cheep, little one. Welcome to your family of sparrows. Learn to sing and steal well and quick. You start work tomorrow."

TWENTY-EIGHT

Clutchers, Whistlers, and Speakers

No ceremony or welcome followed my admission into the ragtag family of thieves. The sparrows dispersed without any prompting from Mithu, and the man himself rose and came to my side. He placed a hand on my shoulder and eased me toward the doors. "Let's show you to your home inside home . . ."

I picked up on the meaning of his lingering quiet. "Ari. My name is Ari."

Mithu led the way without a word, guiding me back down to the floor with the row of doors. We stopped at the first one closest to the stairs up to the third story. He opened it. "This is where you'll put your head down at nights. Some of them at least. I don't know if I'll make a morning bird of you yet. Maybe you are one who sings and plucks best at night. We'll see. For now . . ." He gently pushed me through the doorway.

Light poured into the room in uneven beams, filtering through an iron lattice covering the arch high in the wall opposite me. The opening would have been just enough for one of the sparrows to crawl through whenever they saw fit were it not for the metal barrier.

A wooden frame took up most of the left-hand side of the room. Tightly woven string and hemp ran between the structure to form a solid place on which to rest. Its width could easily have slept two of Mithu's sparrows with some space between. And there was at least another full head of room for me to lie in it with relative comfort. Something I never imagined.

Mithu pointed to the foot of the bed to where a wicker trunk sat. "Your clothes will be there. We will have Small Kaya see to that later. And this is what I promised you earlier." He moved by me to the corner, kneeling by a box, the construction of which outdid anything else in the room.

It had been made of solid wood, rich and dark, oiled well and carrying the warmth of sunlight across its grain. A brass lock, just as polished as the rest of the box, pulled my attention. Mithu produced a key and clicked it open. "Every boy needs a place for his treasures, and this is yours. Here is the only key to this. My gift to you. Of whatever you take for me, some things you'll keep for yourself. This is the way and law of sparrows. But you must show me all things first, yes? Remember that. Treasures you brought from your old life are beyond this law. Build your collection well, Ari-*cha*." He moved into the doorway, quiet and watchful.

Dryness seized my mouth and lips, quickly making its way down my throat. I fumbled behind myself to free the book Mahrab had gifted me. Part of me was aware of the weight of Mithu's stare, but I didn't care. Holding the memory in hand brought back my hollow rage of that night. I eased the book into the chest, storing a promise along with it in the space within my heart.

I'd see Koli pay for it. And I'd hold Mithu to his word . . . somehow.

The man came to sit beside me, passing me the key. "Close it and keep it safe, Ari-*cha*. It's yours now."

I did as he said, gripping the key tight in hand.

Mithu rose and took hold of the door handle as he stepped outside. "Today, rest. Take in your place. Dream dreams of trinkets and treasures. Of bringing me what bright baubles and clever things the pockets of the outside world have to offer. And dream darker dreams, little sparrow, of what we'll do to Koli in time." He shut the door and left me to my own.

I spent the day shifting on the bed, finding it an oddity to my body. Years of sleeping on unforgiving and solid wood left me unsure how to align myself on something softer. It says a great deal that I found a weaving of string and hemp to be comfortable to the point of discomfort.

I eventually gave up the effort and lay flat on my back, staring at the earthen red-brown wall. My mind turned to Mithu's words, and I followed another of his instructions: I dreamed dark dreams of Koli. Of terrible bindings to one day bend and call with but a will and thought. To twist and shape the world around me so to never suffer that night again.

~

A heavy thump echoed through my room.

I blinked my eyes hard and woke from sleep, letting out a low groan.

Another knock and the door opened. The woman who entered could have been in her forties or early fifties. Threads of gray banded her temples and dulled the dark of the rest of her hair. She had all the looks of someone's tired and overworked grandmother.

Her silken drape hung from one shoulder, wrapping once around her waist before falling to her ankles. It was the color of a faded apple, losing much of the brightness of red. Despite her loose and flowing clothing, parts of her belly protruded from under the dress. When she looked at me, the browns of her eyes looked muddled—watery. "You are his new little sparrow."

I nodded.

She said nothing, inclining her head toward what she held between both hands. A small bowl, over the rim of which I couldn't see. "I am Small Kaya. You are to eat. Then you will put on your new clothes and meet Mithu-*sahm* downstairs for instruction." She spoke almost without inflection. Every word clipped. It was as if she had no breath and heart left to bother with tone.

"My new clothes?"

She gave me a long look that left me tired for having shared it with her. Then Small Kaya, who was anything but small, passed me the bowl.

I nearly fumbled it, not realizing she had held a thin piece of thori pressed against the dish. It lacked any warmth, letting me know it had been sitting for a while. I stood there holding it all, unable to process the small sequence of events.

The morning before, I'd been set upon by men in an alley, and as quick as a thought, I'd been given a new home and a meal.

"Eat. Now." Her tone brooked no argument, but it held no heat either.

I did as instructed, sinking to the bed and breaking off a piece of bread to dip into the bowl. Another meal of lentils. I thumbed one section of bread over another, creating a crude shovel before scooping up more of my breakfast, doing what I could do to savor it. A task, as it lacked any taste beyond a singular and overpowering sweet spice that brought water to my eyes. I ate it all.

Hunger does a great deal to make one appreciate any flavor you can get.

"Here." Small Kaya dropped a set of folded clothing at the head of my bed, reaching out to take the bowl back.

I passed it toward her and said my thanks for the garments.

Small Kaya huffed, but said nothing, leaving with all the emptiness and life of the stone around me.

I stared at what she'd left. The clothing matched Juggi's down to the stitch, proving me right. Mithu had every child given the same outfit. I couldn't see the reason behind it, but I kept it in mind to look out for anything that'd tell me their purpose.

I stripped and slipped into the shirt and pants, wriggling my toes before hopping back to the floor. Keeping Mithu waiting wouldn't be a good idea, so I moved toward the doorway and only stopped short of leaving it. My head turned nearly of its own accord to face the small chest housing Mahrab's book.

I'd left the key Mithu had given me under the bed, but leaving now meant the key wouldn't be safe. And bringing it with me meant the risk of losing it to others should I be set upon again. I scrambled back, tearing a strip from my old rags, tying it to the head of the key before fastening it to a strand of weaving under the bed. This way it would at least hang in place and out of immediate sight at a quick glance under the bed frame.

Assured I'd secured it well enough, I hurried out of my room and made my way downstairs.

All the sparrows had gathered below, standing in a perfect circle around Mithu. He waited for me to slip neatly into place between two young boys I didn't know. Mithu clapped his hands twice before speaking. "Cheep-cheep, sparrows."

Everyone let out a singular chirp in perfect unison. My own lingered a step behind as it took me a second to realize what had happened. If the delay bothered Mithu, he didn't show it.

"New shifts today, sparrows." Mithu moved an index finger in a lazy circle through the air. "Who ran mornings yesterday?"

A number of hands went up.

He nodded to himself. "Switch. Juggi will put you into your groups for whistlers, clutchers, and speakers. Nika will be doing the dog work today."

The silent boy who'd followed me up the stairs yesterday stepped into the circle.

"And this is Ari. He is your new brother. You will not mock him for not knowing our ways yet. You will look out for him, train him, and make him into a wondrous sparrow." Mithu turned his attention on me. "Ari, you will work the morning. Juggi and Nika will take care of you." Mithu clapped his hands, which signaled dismissal.

He left, and half of the sparrows returned to their rooms, leaving the rest to form two short lines before Juggi. The boy reached into a small drawstring bag and drew out lengths of string, varying only in the colors: blue, orange, and white. He fastened one around the wrist of the boy in front of him, then another color to the one after. He repeated the process until everyone had been given one of the strings. Finally, he turned to me.

"You're too new to be a clutcher or whistler. I don't think you have the hands or eyes for it. You'll be speaking today." Juggi motioned for me to extend a hand, which I did. He tied the white string around it in, what could have been my imagination, but a knot that looked and felt much tighter than what he'd done to the others.

I rubbed my wrist absentmindedly. "What's a speaker?"

Juggi placed a hand on my neck before sliding it down to one of my shoulders. He squeezed it hard and gave me a small shake. "Let's just show you. Let's see how well you cheep, Ari."

TWENTY-NINE

A Painful Lesson

An hour on the streets of Keshum and the first thing I'd learned among the sparrows was that begging took particular skill and practice. And that it wasn't without its risks, despite it seeming a safe way to earn coin. Few people think twice about raising a hand to a street urchin. It's twice as true when you're Sullied—obviously so.

I rubbed the side of my cheek, trying to assuage the stinging that took up most of my face. The man's slap had come across me almost like a reflex. He hadn't bothered to look my way as he'd done it, nor did he break his stride.

My first lesson of the first day of what would come to be many on those streets.

I made my way off Hadhi Street, leaving behind the stalls and carts of handmade goods and crafts—glittering trinkets, treasures, and some trash, in truth. These things held no sway to me as I shambled into an alley.

Juggi waited there for me, shaking his head. "Begging doesn't work by just asking for money."

I scowled at him. "I wouldn't have guessed that. Oh, no. Nothing could have made that obvious." I jabbed a finger at the reddening spot across my face. "Why's Mithu have people asking for money or whatever else people will spare when no one does? How do I go do something else? What do clutchers do?"

Juggi shut his eyes and blew out a breath in frustration. "Come back out with me." He clapped a hand to my back, harder than necessary, in what I took was an easy way for him to hit me without making it obvious, and led me to where I'd left. "See that?" Juggi pointed to another of the sparrows, still almost unidentifiable to me as anyone other than a perfect imitation of Juggi.

I watched as the child moved against the flow of travelers passing through, then with it as they turned their attention to someone in particular: a man in his middle years, his skin a shade lighter than the grains of wood making up several stalls. He wore a small cap, shaped like an upturned cup, on his head. His clothing was a pristine white that managed to repel grime and road dust that should have soured the color.

The sparrow followed a few paces behind the man, trading a quick look our way when they caught us watching. They flashed me a wink and smile before stumbling forward. The child crashed into the man's back, pawing for support.

The man swore, turning around and raising a hand overhead to give the boy the same treatment someone had been *kind* enough to give me. The sparrow took the blow across the head and rocked to one side. My eyes widened as I realized what had just happened. He had moved ahead of the blow, first softening it, but using the momentum to careen back into the man.

He was acting.

The boy reached out again with one hand, obviously trying to grab hold of the front of the man's clothing. His other hand went to the man's waist where a cinched piece of cloth sat. The man's purse.

The sparrow's fingers dug into the man's shirt just as his other hand plucked the purse. He released his hold and crashed to the ground, concealing the freshly picked prize under his belly as he lay flat. The man lashed out with a kick, not bothering to put his full heart and effort into it, clipping the sparrow's shoulder. Content he'd done enough, the man moved on.

And the whole sequence of events happened without any break in the traffic of the street. It was like those with money to spend and business to do simply had no time for anything else other than what already occupied their minds.

The boy got to his feet and left the throng of traders and buyers moving by, making his way over to us. He bounced the purse in his hands twice, satisfied with himself. "Not even half day's mark yet and I got one." The boy passed the coin pouch over to Juggi, not bothering to count its contents.

Juggi nodded, keeping his face empty of all emotion. He pulled out a charcoal stick and marked the pouch with a symbol I couldn't understand. "Claimed for Dabi. Done. Good job. But we're not done yet, get back out there." Juggi reached out to stay Dabi as the boy turned to leave. "Oh, and go move about to shadier places for a while? The sun's not going to help that." He pointed to the red mark along Dabi's face.

The boy inclined his head and left without a word.

Juggi waited till Dabi passed out of view before turning back to me. "*That* is a clutcher. It takes a lot of things to do it and to do it well. And all of those are things I don't think you can do."

My scowl returned, but Juggi had no eyes for it, moving his attention to the street. "If you want advice on speaking—begging, try to be the most miserable thing you can. Don't beg, be pitiful. Make someone feel good for giving you a bent tin chip. Don't *ask* for coin. *Beg.* There's a difference. And if you can't learn it, you don't belong with the sparrows." Juggi's gaze remained perfectly fixed on the street, and he gave no indication he had anything else left to say.

I took the silent cue and returned to Hadhi Street. The sheer mass of movement didn't help me orient myself, and the collection of colors through clothing and goods was like a pinwheel in motion. I could hardly track what I saw.

Dizziness seized me and set my mind tumbling. In that moment, I lost all train of thought and became a victim to what ills my mind had held on to but I'd believed buried.

I remembered their bodies. Not in the way of a memory, flashes and the pained feelings that followed. No, I saw them the way you would looking down at your own hands, acutely aware of every line and speck of dirt, the awareness of your blood pumping through them.

I remembered my stomach knotting when I stepped into the theater proper and saw the broken stones and creeping flames. I remembered the smell of smoke threatening to choke me dry and wring my eyes of what little moisture they had. And I remembered the mangled forms of everyone who had raised me.

A pain seized one of my ankles and I fell, hitting the ground hard enough to snap me out of the memory. Fire built across my knees and spread through my palms. I scraped them against the street, but not hard enough to draw blood. Splotches darkened parts of the road below me and I realized I'd been crying.

I coughed, both to clear my throat and try to find my buried voice. Nothing came but a half-choked cry. My fingers curled in the hard-packed dirt beneath me.

All the while, people moved by.

I didn't know if Juggi watched me from the alley as I fell apart, but I had no care for the world around me until a pair of feet stopped in front of me.

A hand came under my chin, cupping it. The slender fingers raised my face so I could see who stood there.

She couldn't have been into her thirtieth year, but might have been close enough. Despite this, a few strands of gray had already laced the black of her hair. It's clichéd, but a kindness did hang in her eyes. She could have been someone's older sister by the looks of her, gentle and young. "What's wrong?"

I couldn't speak. How could I tell her? *What* could I tell her? It didn't matter because I found nothing inside me to say, only more sputtering.

She rubbed a hand against my hurt cheek and wiped away my tears. "Poor boy." The young woman rubbed the skin under my eyes with her thumbs one last time. "Here, it's not much, but it can buy you something." She grabbed my hand and pressed something cool into it, folding my fingers over whatever she'd placed there. "And here, to take off some of the heat. I can't finish the last piece myself as it is." The woman placed a thin slice of mango into my other hand.

For all the words I'd learned by that point in my life, I found myself unable to pick any of them that let her know how I felt. But she hardly had the time for them, as it turned out. She got to her feet, brushing at a bit of her skirt at her waist.

"Brahm's blessing on you." She moved by me and vanished into the crowd before I could turn on my knees to say something.

"You too . . ." The words were lost among the clamor of bustling people and the cries of merchants trying to entice whatever eyes they could. I unfurled my fingers and looked at the weight in my hand, blinking away what moisture remained when I saw what the woman had left me.

Two copper rounds, or sixty-four tin chips' worth of coin. Working in the theater had been the sort of life that left me in want of money, but never need as most of my needs were handled by Khalim. Though, I always knew the value of even a few tin pieces. A starving child could get something with a handful of chips, even if only a lukewarm bowl of lentils.

But the copper pieces could buy me a week of meals, all warm, and all the bread and meat I could dream of. Something I never saw enough of in my life. I could get clothes.

Actual clothes. Not rags, not a tailored beggar's outfit handed out by Mithu. Mithu . . .

The weight in my hand grew heavy as I realized what this meant. I wouldn't be holding on to the charity coins. They'd be passed to Juggi, then Mithu.

For the moment, it was enough that I had them, and I wanted to take the time to appreciate the mild wealth and the kindness.

I moved down the street, finding a new alley to slip into as I stared at my coins. A smile broke across my face and it felt like my first smile ever.

My breakfast, or what accounted for it, hadn't left me with the fullest of stomachs, so I tore into the mango with the hungry savagery only a street urchin could muster. And it was everything I expected: sweet, cool, and an absolute sticky delight that left me to suck the juices from my fingers. Some of the meat still clung to the rind, and I brought it to my mouth to tear it free.

A low whistle filled the alley, stopping me just as what was left of the mango touched my lips. I turned to look behind me.

Two boys blocked the mouth of the alley and moved toward me with their shoulders visibly squared. Khalim had taught his actors to adopt a similar posture, accentuated greatly, when trying to send the silent message that you wanted to fight.

I swallowed and recalled another lesson I'd watched the actors employ: how to appear casual and like I belonged. My weight fell against the nearest stone wall as I leaned back. I kept my attention to the mango and resumed scraping what little flesh it still held. The fingers of my other hand moved and I slipped one of the coins into a pocket in my breeches.

"What do we have here, Thipu?" The one who'd spoken reminded me of an overfed owl. His hair was a shock of black, and his eyes seemed too wide for his face, almost like they were always in a state of surprise. His puffy cheeks let me know he'd been eating well for most of his life . . . or smuggling a palm's portion of dates in his mouth.

His clothing barely fit him, and looked to be of the state that said he wasn't new to a life on the streets. The seams left torn and open to fraying further. His vest stretched too far tight across his body and his belly promised to keep it that way.

"Looks like we got a lost bird. One of Mithu's sparrows without a dog to protect him," said the one I figured to be Thipu. He had a build almost equal to the first boy, with nearly matching clothing, almost as if it were by design. His hair was a curly mess, each lock short and matted close to his scalp.

Both of them were older than me, maybe near their fifteenth year or just shy of it.

I ignored the pair, keeping to scraping my mango clean.

"This bird doesn't know how to speak up, I guess? We're talking to you."

I said nothing and resisted the temptation to stow my other coin. My heart hammered like heavy rain on a sheet of brass, but I kept it from showing on my face. The same feelings the night my family had been murdered swelled in me. Fear; it flushed me with cold water. The heat of the fire followed, burrowing into the muscles of my arms as they flexed hard.

A part of me wanted to let out the anger and resentment that had built after that night. Something hot and feral and completely removed from my rational mind.

"Looks like Mithu's new sparrow is a rude little shit, Gabi." Thipu rubbed his hands together as he drew closer. "Maybe we should see if we can make him sing, huh? Hey, little bird, do you know how a sparrow sings with a broken beak?"

At this point I knew I had nothing to gain by ignoring them other than their increased anger. Boys like that are looking for trouble, and they mean to find it no matter what you do.

"No, I don't." I still kept from meeting their gazes as I answered them.

"Neither do we, but I think we'd like to find out. Besides, you little sparrows are good at picking up coins. Koli's always got us fixed on running the joy to people, but he doesn't mind when we stop to bother a little bird or two."

I stiffened at the mention of Koli's name and stared at the boy who'd said that—Gabi.

He met my look. "Oh? I say something that bother you? What's wrong, sparrow?"

"Koli." The word left my mouth as a half-whispered curse.

The two boys exchanged a look. "That's what I said. Are you dumb, boy? Your mom throw you out because you were too stupid to know eating dirt from eating shit?"

I said nothing. My fingers flexed around the mango and the coin until my nails dug into the flesh of my hands.

"I think we should find out if this sparrow's found anything shiny today, right, Gabi?" Thipu stepped closer.

Something else the boys had said struck something in my memory. They worked for Koli. He too ran children like Mithu.

... *Nisha. Oh, no.* In my terror during my flight from the theater and then the confusion of being adopted by Mithu, I had forgotten her being under Koli's thumb and keep. And the remembrance hit me with the weight of cold stone.

"Nisha. How is Nisha? Where is she?" I lunged toward Gabi and the world tilted as crimson streaked my vision. The ground kissed the side of my cheek, the same one that had been struck earlier, but I couldn't feel it much.

When did I decide to lie down?

"You don't talk about one of Koli's girls like that. You don't talk one word about ours, yeah?"

I couldn't pick out if it had been Gabi or Thipu who'd spoken. When your head has been rung harder than a temple's brass bell, you lose track of the subtle differences in voices.

"Hey, he *does* have something on him—look!" The voice cleared and I recognized it as Gabi. "Shit's got a copper. A whole copper."

"Nnno." I could barely articulate the word and fumbled to see where I'd lost hold of the coin, but I couldn't. My vision had stabilized and I realized the copper round had slipped through my fingers and lay just outside my grip. I reached for it more on desperate reflex and instinct than anything else.

Gabi's bare heel crunched down on my fingers.

I screamed, only to have it choked off as Thipu felt the sudden need to drive a foot into my stomach. At least, I wagered he'd aimed there, but he connected with my ribs. Bits of the mango came back up, leaving a trail of acid burning along the back of my throat. More weight from Gabi's foot came down on my hand, but not enough to break the small bones inside my fingers.

I tried to get him to stop. I tried to voice it. But nothing came out other than a weak moan. Another kick from Thipu silenced my cries.

Gabi removed the pressure from my hand and knelt by my side, reaching for the coin.

I watched him take one half of all the money I'd come to in the world. As soon as I'd had it, life saw fit to take it from me.

If I hadn't been in such pain, I'd probably have let out a dark laugh over the matter. Khalim had put on plays about men with such luck that no matter what they did Brahm's bad fortune would find a way to spit in their eyes and spike their feet.

"We could buy something for the girls with this, Thipu. You think Nisha would come alone with me to the joy rooms Koli has at home?"

Something about what Gabi said and how he said it tripped a latch in my mind. Nisha became the sole focus of my attention. I couldn't manage the folds, but I was able to conjure the candle and the flame, and I fed all my anger into it.

Pain still filled me, but I grew dull to it, pushing it away. I managed to claw my way back to all fours as the two boys gawked over the copper coin. They paid me no mind, and I used the freedom to let my hatred grow, fanning the fire until I could stand. I lunged at Gabi, forgetting everything I had learned at Vithum's hands.

There was no room for swordplay and clever movement in my footwork and hands. I fell on Gabi like an animal, like an angry sparrow.

I screamed something shrill and broken, raking my fingernails against his face. He cried out and let go of the coin. I fell on him, using my weight to keep him down for a second as my hands blurred. I scratched, pulled, and tore.

Pinpricks sparked against my scalp as I realized Thipu had grabbed hold of my hair and yanked sharply. Some of the locks tore but I stayed on Gabi. Then the world tipped the other way and I was back on the ground again.

"He scratched me? I'm bleeding. Brahm's tits and asses . . . I'm bleeding! Little shit bloodied my face. My. Face!" Gabi punctuated the two words with a kick at my sternum. Thipu, good friend that he was, joined in.

I didn't know how long they intended to keep going, but I knew I couldn't weather it much longer.

Gabi must have been able to read minds, because he decided to cut the beating shorter.

And not to my benefit.

He moved by me, retrieving a half-broken brick that could have come from the alley walls. Gabi held it up overhead, the implication clear.

Juggi was right. I would learn what it meant to be a speaker, and it was a painful lesson. The worst of which was yet to come.

Gabi smiled and brought the brick down.

THIRTY

A Dog's Gift

Gabi stumbled, eyes snapping shut. The brick never struck my head and fell harmlessly by me.

I couldn't revel in my good luck, as most of my body had forgotten how to do anything other than sit in the massive amount of pain I'd been introduced to.

Gabi and Thipu turned to see who'd thrown the small stone at the back of his head.

Nika. He stood in the mouth of the alley, bouncing another stone in his hand.

"Nika!" Gabi balled his fists. "You here to save this little shit? There's two of us. And I can get more. This isn't going—" Gabi yelped, pawing at his face as another stone fell to the ground. "Bitch hit my mouth." His T's sounded like F's, and I wagered his lips had swollen. "Get her, Thipu."

Her?

Thipu made no move toward Nika, turning his attention the other way down the alley like he wanted to run. "I'm still sore thinking about the last time, Gabi. We should go."

"I fold you to hit the bitch!" Gabi shoved the boy toward Nika.

The girl blurred into action as Thipu stumbled toward her. The flat of her foot snapped into the boy's stomach. He crumpled forward, clutching his gut, completely unaware of Nika's next move. She lashed out with a quick kick to his throat that left him choking.

Gabi spat at the ground between her and Thipu, blood making up most of his saliva. "Koli's going to do something about this one day. And when he does, he's going to make you one of his too, you know that, right?" Gabi sank to his knees, grabbing hold of the brick he'd meant to smash me with.

What little strength I had left let me wriggle forward and dig my fingers into Gabi's arm.

He shook, then froze hard as he realized I was still there. Nika took the moment to finish the fight. She rushed him, taking one of his ears in her hand. She wrenched it and hauled him to his feet.

He stammered something I didn't make out, but she silenced him with two knees to the groin. He crumpled to the ground, mewling.

A piece of copper rolled free from his clutches.

"My coin." The words scratched my throat raw as I spoke them.

Nika looked at me, then the coin. She gave Gabi another kick for good measure before retrieving the copper round. "Can you get up?"

I grunted and tried to make my way to my knees, realizing I could barely manage that much. She slipped her arms under my own and helped raise me to my feet. "We should go. Gabi's got Koli's ear. He's not worth much, but Koli might send more of his runners looking for us. Move." Nika gave me a push back toward Hadhi Street.

I paused as I passed Gabi, then figured that I should follow Nika's example and give the boy a kick. Then I remembered she'd given him several, and not one to be a poor imitator, I did the same.

Her face remained perfectly neutral as I did it, but her eyes twinkled just a bit.

We made our way back onto the street, falling in step with two other sparrows we'd seen walking ahead of us. They looked me over, then Nika. The pair easily surmised what happened to me.

"How bad they get it, Nika?" One of them grinned almost like he knew the answer.

"Same as usual." She shrugged. "I don't think Gabi's going to be spending any time looking sideways at any of Koli's girls, not that they'd even look back at him."

The two sparrows laughed, then cut it short as their eyes fell on me.

"How bad did *he* get it?"

I tried to glower at them, but my face couldn't muster even that little bit of effort.

"He did all right. He cut up Gabi's face pretty bad. And he took the beating good. He didn't lose his seed either." She held up the copper coin.

I swallowed a bit of spit, adding another layer of sting to my throat as Nika offered up my coin. And if she'd come to my rescue, it brought a pair of questions to mind.

Had she been watching when the woman had given me the coins? Did she know about the other?

I fixed her with a look, which she returned with all the expression of a wall.

"You two should go check in with Juggi if you've got seeds to hand over.

He'll tally them up." Nika motioned with a hand, urging the two sparrows ahead. They listened without further word and moved off.

Nika put a hand on my chest, stopping me. The gesture brought a dull ache to my core, as it was just close enough to where I'd been kicked. "Stay with me for a moment?" It wasn't a command.

I nodded. "Thank you . . . for . . ." I trailed off and pointed toward the alley we'd left behind.

"It's my job. I watch the sparrows so no one hurts you too badly."

Too badly. So we are expected to catch a beating. I kept that to myself and voiced the question on my mind. "How long were you watching me?" The act of speaking racked my throat harder.

"Long enough to see that lady give you *two* copper rounds. Long enough to see you eat the mango. Long enough to see you hide one of the coins." Nika's face remained impassive. She reached into one of her pockets and pulled free the remaining mango rind I'd dropped earlier and pushed it toward me. "Chew it. Some of the juice will help, and it's bitter enough to stop the hurt a bit. It'll sting first, but then just feel better."

I did as she said. The mango lived up to her words, the juices biting at my throat with a new wave of acidity as the bitterness of the peel's tissue flooded my mouth. Soon, I tasted nothing but my throat's own tiredness. "Thank you . . . again."

She ignored my gratitude, tumbling the copper round between her fingers. "You know this is more than most sparrows bring home in a day. For some, it's more than they see in a week's worth of begging, and same with some clutchers. The bad ones anyways. Mithu will be happy." She stowed the coin. "I'll tell him the coin came from you and he won't ask any questions."

I tried to arch a brow and managed an awkward half squint and tilt of the head. *"Coin?"* I emphasized the word.

She smiled. "It's your first day, and it cost you a lot. Mithu doesn't need to know. You also fought back against Gabi and Thipu. Most would have run."

A part of me wanted to point out that I had only really attacked Gabi, but I didn't see any harm in letting her run with that account of things.

"I like it when someone messes up his ugly face." Her smile widened.

Then deeper realization set in. "Wait . . . you saw them follow me into the alley. You *watched* them pummel me!"

She grabbed one of my arms tightly and hauled me further down the street. "Hsst. You're yelling. That'll get the kuthri looking for whoever's making noise. Nobody wants to trade and sell with yelling kids around." Nika led me back to our sparrow home, knocking on the door. "Yes, I watched them come after you. I had to. They couldn't know I was there." Something in the way she'd said that left me to wonder if there was another part she hadn't voiced.

Nika picked up on my silent question. "And . . . I wanted to see how you reacted. I had to know." I opened my mouth to respond with something rather uncouth when she spoke over me. "You're different than most boys. They don't like it when a girl saves them."

I shut my mouth at that, pausing to consider what that meant for Nika. It couldn't have been easy being among the sparrows, all made to look like boys, and then to be the one constantly fighting and protecting them. Especially so when many young males would hold a grudge against her over something as innocent as being who she was.

Few things are as brittle as a young boy's pride. And it's a cause for a great deal of pain. Some, fortunately, learn to grow out of it. I'd like to think I began there, on the street of Hadhi.

I smiled in earnest. "Well, if I have to expect more of that"—I gestured back to the alley where Gabi and Thipu had set on me—"you can save me anytime."

She grinned back, a strange thing given how much she could wear a face like stone, and the look was brighter than all the colors on the street. Nika leaned forward quick as a cat and pressed her lips once to my swollen cheek before pulling away. "You're sweet."

It bears pointing out that I had already been under the hot morning sun for hours, and a passerby had taken the liberty to smack me handily. Add to this that Thipu and Gabi had taken their shots as well and you'll understand that the reddening of my face had already happened. It certainly had nothing to do with being kissed on my cheek.

I stood there, half tempted to raise a hand to the spot to confirm Nika had in fact done what she did, but she brushed by me as if nothing happened.

She knocked on the door, which was answered by another sparrow on watch duty. We entered and she asked the young bird to fetch Mithu, which they ran off to do.

The leader of the sparrows came down the stairs into the common room. He looked at Nika, then me, pursing his lips as the only sign of communication.

"He's done for the day." She raised the copper round up between a thumb and index finger for him to see. "He's pulled good coin and he got a hard lesson from two of Koli's runners. He needs to rest and maybe have Small Kaya look at him. They hit him pretty hard."

I'd been hit *pretty hard* at various points in my life up until that day, and that fell remarkably short of describing how painful the thrashing the two boys gave me had been. But I kept quiet, feeling it better to let her control the conversation.

A rest did sound wonderful, and if I could make a good impression on Mithu through Nika, so be it. I would take it.

Mithu reached out and plucked the coin from her, turning it over in his grip. His lips pursed another way now—appraisal. "A full copper on your first day, hm? Maybe I didn't just find a sparrow, but a lucky sparrow." He laughed.

Nika joined in and, to my ears, it came out as the most forced thing I'd ever heard.

I didn't get the joke so I remained a silent lump of pain and confusion.

"Or maybe you have a bit of crow in you to go after such shiny, big taking." Mithu laughed again and so did Nika.

A sharp jolt lanced through my ribs from where she elbowed me, flashing me a knowing look. I resigned myself and joined in on the laughter.

It ended nearly as soon as it had begun. Mithu pocketed the coin and looked me over another time. "The beating's not *so* bad."

I had a feeling he'd never been kicked and pummeled by two boys who outweighed him by half a dozen sacks of lentils.

"But he's earned the day off. A copper round is no small pull. Good job, Ari. I'll send Small Kaya to your room with something for your face and the pains."

I thanked him with just an incline of my head and moved off.

"Wait."

I stopped, not turning fully to look at Mithu.

"Did you happen to find any treasures for yourself today? Any small trinkets a little sparrow would like to keep?" The question held an edge I couldn't make out. Something about it unnerved me, like it didn't carry the honesty of the words themselves. It was like he wanted to know if I found anything else *he* might have liked to have.

I swallowed, eyeing Nika for the space of a wink.

"I watched him get the coin and get attacked. He was only able to pull the one coin and didn't even have time to cry for a second." Nika frowned, looking to the ground in thought. "Oh, and a shopkeeper gave him a piece of mango. He's still got the rind in his mouth. I told him the bitter would help him with the pain."

I chose the moment to open my mouth fully and showcase the pulped skin.

Mithu's throat worked silently, and he looked like he regretted asking the question. I had a feeling he'd come close to retching.

And that gave me an idea I decided to hold on to for later.

Mithu nodded more to Nika than me and ushered me away with a motion of his hand.

I didn't need a second telling. I left, Nika falling in step next to me as I made my way upstairs. We stopped outside my room, and I waited for her to leave, but she didn't.

"What are you going to do with the other coin?"

"Hsst." I nearly lunged to cover her mouth but I remembered her fighting with Gabi and Thipu and reconsidered that idea. "You want to tell anyone else listening at their doors?"

She rolled her eyes, obviously not bothered by that thought.

I sighed and reached a hand into my pocket, idly running my fingers along the coin's edge. "I'm not sure. I guess I'll save it for now." In truth, nothing in the world existed that the coin would be good for.

It couldn't bring back the theater and my family. It couldn't bring back Mahrab and my lessons. It couldn't buy my dreams of being a binder and seeing the world.

I blinked as I realized what I could in fact purchase.

A way to the Ashram. It would take time, but I could slowly piece together enough money to get myself to the place of magic Mahrab had told me about. I could be safe, away from Abhar, and learn to do all that I'd dreamt of. My fingers closed tightly around the coin until an ache formed in my hand.

Mithu had told me to build a small treasure fit for a boy. And I'd do just that.

Nika remained in place like she wanted another answer from me—a better one. But I couldn't give it, so I asked her something instead. "Why did you help me?"

She pressed her lips tight, as if deep in thought. "You're not the only who's had hard first days with the sparrows. And you're not the only who's been given nice things by strangers. Maybe I know what it's like to want to have something to hold on to. Maybe I have something I'm saving for, too, and understand. And maybe I just wanted to give you a gift." Nika turned without another word and left back the way we'd come.

I knew she was heading back to her duties on the streets and would leave me be. So I slipped into my room, thinking on what she said.

Wonder what she's saving for? I couldn't figure it out, but I made a point to keep it in mind until I learned the answer.

The small box in the corner of my room called to me and I fetched the key, quickly stowing my copper round and locking it away.

Small Kaya arrived moments later with a bowl and rag. She bid me to sit with a gesture. She dipped the rag in the bowl and pressed it to my face and a corner of my lip I hadn't noticed had been cut. The sudden bands of fire across my cheeks and mouth certainly made me aware, though. I winced and nearly cried out, but she had no patience for it. She pressed the bowl to my mouth. "Drink, swish it, and spit."

I did as she instructed. The liquid brought the same heat and pain through my mouth as it did across my face, but soon, numbness flooded me. I spat back the fluid along with the masticated mango pulp.

She looked at it, then me, frowning. But Small Kaya showed no anger or anything other than an old woman's resignation. She rose and left me to lie in bed.

My mind turned to Nisha, still out there in Koli's grip. I thought of the Ashram and how far away it could be. And I wondered about how many coins it would take me to get there and bring Nisha with me.

I couldn't know the sum, but I knew it'd go a damn sight quicker the better a sparrow I became. So I set my thoughts to it and onto becoming the best beggar thief the kingdom had seen.

THIRTY-ONE

A Sparrow's Cunning

Time passed, and not a word of Nisha. No utterings of a name. Until time did what it always does. It put her in the quiet places of my heart and mind . . . to be buried, but not forgotten.

Six months on the streets of Keshum taught me much, but the more useful things came from the soft arts I'd learned from my old life. I took Juggi's words to heart and mastered becoming the most pitiful and miserable wretch one could turn their eyes on.

I chewed the peels of lime and mango, turning them into fine pulp that, at a whim, I could spew onto the ground while clutching my stomach. I'd been raised by actors, and I brought their skill to the streets.

Not everyone, of course, turned a sympathetic ear to the pained moans of a vomiting child, but you could always find a few. Sometimes a shopkeeper would pay just to get you far enough out of sight from potential customers.

After all, what's a few tin chips spent in the face of iron bunts and coppers to make?

But small prices make fine payments for a sparrow.

The agony of the night I'd lost my family had now folded into a different part of my mind—a memory, surely, but one so far back it was almost like a story I'd once heard from someone else.

Now, only Ari the Sparrow remained, and his life with his brothers and sisters.

I taught them every performer's piece I had learned. Soon, Mithu's speakers began to bring in a sum that even the clutchers took note of.

But more than sparrows made these streets their home, and those eyes soon turned on us.

I finished chewing a mix of lime peels, which I'd stripped to ribbons, and a piece of orange flesh. What precious water I had found its way into my mouth to help me break up the half spoonful of turmeric. The bitterness in my mouth could have pulled all the sweet from a mound of sugar. But I grimaced through it, mixing the heinous concoction with every bite and swish. Content I'd done a good job at turning it all to a vile, but appropriately colored mush, I stumbled onto Thippre Street.

The place was a venue to stalls and carts that sold the finer sort of appointments for oneself and one's home. A few shopkeepers had done well enough to own buildings proper on the row and use floors above for extra storage.

All of it meant this was a street of showy wealth, and that meant the customers with the coin to support it.

I crashed shoulder-first into a cart, doing nothing to destabilize it and turn the owner's wrath upon me. If his goods were in danger, all sympathy would be out the door and I'd earn more than a cuffing across the ear. "Help." I parted my lips, letting some of the artificial sick seep through.

The man took one look at the color and backed away. "Don't bring anything ill near me, *nayak—gunth.*" He'd practically called me a ne'er-do-well and filth.

I stumbled forward anyway, pressing the moment as more people watched the scene. "Please, just water. Anything. I'm sick." My stomach knotted and I tensed the muscles in my neck, helping push the vomit out as I doubled over. The mixture splattered across the ground, and I made a sound that would unsettle anyone's stomach to hear.

I knew the man wouldn't risk parting with a drop of water. One, I'd dirty his drinking skin. Two, it would keep me around his shop longer if I stopped to drink. Three, I was obviously Sullied, and giving a coin to shoo me away was easier to bear than sharing food and drink.

The little ways we spurn others say a great deal about ourselves and the world. It's a lesser sin to part with money than break bread with those you think are beneath you. I never learned why, but it's the world Brahm made and left to us all.

"Please. Anything. I can't get help." I decided to take things further and retched again, letting my tinged spittle slop over one sleeve cuff.

The man looked like he'd follow my example and vomit himself. He reached at his side and plunged his fingers into an open purse. Coins flew free with an indiscriminate toss or consideration for what he was giving. "Get . . ." He trailed off and realized what his actions could be taken as. "Get yourself some help. Medicine, anything. Please-please. Poor thing." Every word came clipped and with about as much honesty as a thief selling you back your own silk.

I fumbled for the coins, letting a few fall to the ground. "Thank you. A thousand thanks, *sahm*." I scrabbled for the few precious bits of money along the road, scooping them up into my hands and bolting away.

The metal sat comfortably in my grip, my fingers never parting to betray a hint of glint in the morning light. A Sullied child, a sparrow no less, with money to their name marked you as a fresh target for many. And counting it openly was among the most foolish things for me to do.

I bustled past a trio of men from Laxina, dressed in slim-fitting robes cinched tight along the chest and waist. They raised porcelain tiles, speaking the Trader's Tongue with the shopkeeper in hopes of using him as a money changer.

I kept my thoughts on their decision to myself. If some fools wanted to use a local vendor to break coin and porcelain, then they had the sort of easy trust that deserved for them to be taken advantage of. The shop passed from view as I turned off into an alley, making my way down it into another.

A group of men sat slumped against the walls and their legs stretched out into the path.

I swallowed a sigh, not wanting the noise to rouse them. But moving past them would be a problem.

They dressed in simple robes and cowls, long and oversized, all folded over themselves for equal measures of comfort and warmth in the night. The drawn-up hoods prevented what light made its way into the alley from reaching their eyes.

Cotton-eyes. I'd learned to stay away from them. White-joy, a drug distilled from the resin of a plant and that looked like liquid cotton, took the minds and faculties of any who abused it long enough. It turned the whole of their eyes to a uniform and milky white, leaving them hypersensitive to bright lights. Their teeth bleached to a color brighter than fresh cream, along with their gums at times.

And they were utterly ruthless in the pursuit to score more of the drug. There were stories of men and women selling anything they had to their name to get another hit. Then anything that belonged to others. Then, when all was exhausted, they'd sell whatever they could of themselves. Anything. Anyone.

Nothing was sacred. And no one was safe.

I slowed my pace, not wanting to draw undue attention to myself. A sparrow in a hurry meant one of two things: trouble behind them, or coin in hand. And both signaled an easy victim.

The cotton-eyes remained in the stupor, only one bothering to tilt his head and pay me any mind.

I ignored him and walked by as if completely unbothered by their presence.

He shuffled in place, extending a hand, palm open.

I sucked in a breath and knew that avoiding it could bring me more bother than I cared for in the moment. But giving a coin, no matter the amount, could cost me more. If the cotton-eyes knew I carried marks for Mithu, I ran the risk of being set on by them for even more money. As much as they could take.

I made myself as pitiful as I could without the aid of any props, stooping a bit lower as if my back nursed pain and I hadn't slept well in weeks. My throat shook as I rattled out a weak cough and one of my hands trembled. I let a coin slip through my fingers into the man's hand, taking care to use the quivering motions to shift a specific piece of currency into position.

I'd been on the streets long enough to know the difference between tin chips, copper rounds, and iron bunts all by feel now. And to know the subtleties of silver and gold were but just a dream to me at this point.

A single tin chip fell into the man's palm. "Brahm's blessing," I said, keeping my voice as dry and tired as the ground below us.

The man's hand closed around the coin and pulled back into the folds of his robes with a fluidity of practice that let me know he'd been a cotton-eyes for a while. The maneuver had been old and familiar to him. He said nothing in return to me, probably having only enough wits and energy to tally the new coin to whatever sum he'd already hoarded, and how much white-joy that could buy him.

The rest of the alley-dwellers left me be, thankfully.

I made my way to the end of the street and turned right, slinking deeper into darker paths off the main roads.

But if you want to keep secrets safe from sparrows and the like, you need to be willing to nest where few birds go, and where fewer still will cheep-cheep about it.

I reached halfway down the alley and stopped before a section of brickworks where the mortar had cracked and chipped away. One particular area had most of the white binding scraped and hacked away, leaving a noticeable space between the surrounding bricks. I slipped my fingers into it and wiggled the block free.

Behind it sat what treasure I could truly call my own. What I kept back in my chest in Mithu's home had been carefully tailored to not arouse suspicion. But this little hiding place had come to be where I kept the precious pieces I couldn't bear to give to the sparrows as tithe.

Two small pouches rested in the hole, and I'd amassed what could be considered a fortune to a Sullied boy and sparrow. Two copper rounds and eighteen tin chips. To many, it wasn't a great deal, but for me the sum could have bought me a month of bedding and meals outside of Mithu's home and safety.

I looked down at the sum I'd acquired from the trader, sifting the coins through my open palms. Five tin chips and a copper round. A good haul, better than most. But I'd have to keep the proper sum in hand to pass to Mithu. Too much coin would lead him to expect more of me, making it harder to set aside pieces for myself. Too little would earn me punishment and a tighter eye on my activities.

I could afford neither.

The copper round would appeal best to the sparrow patriarch, but I knew the lone coin was too clean an offering. Long gone were the days I could show up with an evenly round number of coins, especially a decent single one. I pushed two of the chips onto the copper and closed my fist.

A good-enough sum to please Mithu and not have him wondering if I'd earned anything more. The remaining three tin chips joined my small collection of coins. I returned the brick and walked toward the other end of the alley.

A sharp whistle screeched down the path from behind me.

I didn't turn to look and pocketed my coins for Mithu.

The whistle came again. "Oi, little sparrow." I knew the voice—Gabi, and Thipu would likely be joined at his hip.

Shadh. I didn't let the swear pass my lips. Nika would be patrolling streets with more sparrows on them, focusing her attention on where lay the greatest risk. My decision to beg for money in a farther part of the quarter meant she'd not get to me anytime soon. And I'd have no family members nearby to catch sight of what was going to happen and run to fetch her.

I sped up, hurrying toward the mouth of the alley.

Feet hammered against the ground loud enough to tell me the two were nearly on me.

My collar tightened around my throat and I jerked backward. Someone had closed a fist around my clothing. I gave them no chance to get in the first blow, spinning and swinging a fist into the side of a face.

My strike connected with Thipu's cheek, knuckles almost catching an eye. He reeled to one side but the hand holding me didn't let go.

Because it was Gabi's grip, and the boy wasted no time exacting the due toll for what I'd done to his friend. An open palm crashed against the side of my head, snapping it to one side.

Iron and salt, warmth and wetness, all filled my mouth.

"You don't remember what happened last time, sparrow?" Gabi sneered at me, curling his fingers into a tight fist as a clear message.

I spat a pool of blood, striking his nose and watching it splatter across bits of his face. "Do you? Nika pounded you two like the—" Violent crimson painted the world around me until I saw nothing else. Another stream of blood pooled out from a nostril and onto my lips. My nose and everything behind it felt like they'd been used as drums.

I shook in place, knowing the only thing keeping my feet beneath me was Gabi's strong hold.

He used his other hand to rub a splotch of blood from his forehead. "Think I broke your nose there, little sparrow."

I couldn't tell if he was right, but the truth of it hardly mattered in the moment. The pain radiating through my face said there was little difference between a broken and badly battered nose in how much they hurt.

"Looks like the little bird finally learned his lesson." Gabi's voice sounded like it came from inside my own head as well as down from the alley.

My vision worked its way back to some clarity and I saw what he spoke of.

Sitting on the ground by my feet were the coins I'd intended to give to Mithu. My tithe. And the only thing ensuring I'd get dinner and that he'd make good on his word about going after Koli.

"Grab them!" Gabi's bark echoed through the alley and Thipu moved on command, scooping up the coins.

"He's gotten another copper round. You pull good, huh, sparrow?"

I glowered at Gabi's lackey. Well, it would be a lie to say the face I made was anything close to that. The sheer act of contorting my mouth tweaked my nose enough to send me into another spiral of red agony. So I settled for narrowing my eyes and hacking up another globule of spit, which I launched at them with all the venom I could.

Thipu reciprocated in kind with a slap he must have learned from Gabi.

My head tilted again and the world streaked white this time. No more blood touched my tongue or my gums, so I counted that as the small blessing it was.

"Been watching you make the runs for weeks now, little shit." Gabi mimed a pair of legs walking with two fingers. "Knew you'd be coming here. Seen you do it a couple times now."

Thipu grinned. He looked like he'd like nothing more than to have an excuse to pummel me again.

I didn't feel like giving it to him.

"What's the matter, sparrow? What happened to that mouth, huh?" Gabi shoved his other hand against my lips, trying to part them and jam his thumb and index finger between my teeth.

He asked me a good question, and I felt it my sworn duty to give him a sparrow's answer. So I did.

I clamped my teeth down on Gabi's finger as hard as I could, gnashing—

thrashing, tearing flesh until I tasted hot and bitter blood. My legs kicked out as Gabi screamed something so shrill his throat must have been stripped by the effort. Something struck my gut and a rush of air left me. My hold on Gabi's hand broke and I tumbled to the ground, hitting my back hard enough to squeeze what little breath remained out of me.

I lay there, stunned, watching the two boys gawk at Gabi's mangled flesh.

Thipu let loose a string of obscenities I still can't accurately recall to this day, and Gabi howled and spat curses about what he'd do to me.

And he made good on his word.

The first kick took my lower back, sending me into a spasm. Then a kick to my stomach. Another, for good measure I assumed. One never does the job. A kick to the back of my head cut my vision and threaded it with black. Then the remaining kicks came in the darkness until I couldn't tell one sore spot of my body from another.

I still believe to this day that the two boys would have killed me in that moment, but life often has a cruel sense of humor and symmetry.

"You two really don't learn, do you?" Nika's voice warbled above me, coming from what I guessed was the mouth of the alley.

"How'd you—" I couldn't tell if it was Thipu or Gabi who'd spoken.

"There are more to the sparrows than what you see. I was told. And I came." I couldn't see Nika as she spoke, but I watched her blur by into motion. She fell on the wounded Gabi before he could register what was happening.

The sparrow's dog sent her fingers into his hair, grabbing him tight and wrenching. His head pulled to one side as she brought the base of a closed fist down on his neck. She did the same to the front of his face, and the wet crunch that followed satisfied my curiosity in knowing the difference between a beaten and broken nose.

Thipu, poor soul that he was, took a kick to the groin. And because Nika was one to always take her martial craft seriously, she introduced Thipu to another blow in the same spot. Both boys crumbled in unison.

Nika came to my side in the lull and helped raise me halfway up. "Put your arms around me."

I coughed, and another bit of blood and spittle fell from my mouth. I tried to speak, but she pressed a folded rag to my lips, silencing me.

"Don't talk. Brahm's breath and body, Ari, it's like you enjoy getting beaten."

I sputtered and managed to weakly push the cloth away. "Well . . ." I choked on some bile and blood before coughing it clear. "I did say you could save me anytime." I coughed again.

Nika smiled and helped get me to my feet.

A shame Gabi and Thipu had gotten to theirs first and ran the other way. And with my coin at that.

"Let's get you back. You're done for the day."

I made a feeble attempt to shake her free but she held me with a grip of iron and stone.

"We're going back. Whatever you have to give to Mithu will be enough, even if it's just a few chips. It's enough. Besides, you know he likes you after you got all the other sparrows to pull more coin." Her expression darkened. "Especially after some of our brothers and sisters have gone missing."

She had a point, but I couldn't afford it. Even the slightest slip and Mithu would watch me like a hawk. I couldn't have him worrying about my ability to tithe. If he wanted to, he could have me watched without my knowing, and he'd come to learn about my second collection.

That I'd been stealing from him. It was the only way I could keep the promise to myself that, somehow, I'd make it to the Ashram. To learn the ten bindings. To live up to Mahrab's vision for me.

"I'll come back, but I just need a moment alone."

"But, Ari?" Nika reached out with a hand to cup my face.

I turned from the gesture. "Please. I have an idea. A safe and decent clutch. I promise."

She bit her lip, but nodded.

I watched her leave before I limped back toward my hidden stash. Content no one else lingered at either end of the alley, watching, I pulled the brick free. It galled me to have to do this and I tasted a kind of acid in the back of the throat that had nothing to do with my beating. I pulled free one of the copper rounds and then three tin chips.

It'd appease Mithu.

I sighed and made the long trek back home, stowing my coins in a pocket and praying none of Koli's other runners decided to take a crack at me today.

My thoughts soon turned grim the closer I got to the sparrow sanctuary, and I realized I'd have to do something on my own about Gabi and Thipu. So I paid Mithu his tithe, went back to my room, and dreamed up a performance that would have the two boys at my mercy.

And then I'd take care of the problem.

THIRTY-TWO

Lime, String, and Glass

Another month passed on the city streets of Keshum, and I'd walked a narrow line to avoid any more trouble with Gabi and Thipu. That isn't to say I didn't cut things close. I'd spent a few sets of days following the pair, even at the cost of earning smaller coin from my daily work, in effort to learn their routine.

I watched Gabi and Thipu make their white-joy runs for Koli, finding out which back alleys they worked. While the two didn't seem to have much for brains between themselves, they were ruthlessly efficient in their work. Any trouble or hindrance was subdued with quick force. They didn't barter or haggle with cotton-eyes, telling them exactly how it was and how much to pay.

And they got what they asked for.

I almost lost my composure, wanting to race out and throttle the boys when I saw them pass a small vial to a man clearly down on his luck. By the looks of him, I could see he'd never tried the drug, and he was exactly in the place of his life to be willing to. They gave it to him free of charge, knowing as I did that he'd be hooked and ready to pay whatever for more joy.

The two boys worked everywhere, from Hadhi Street to places like Gadha, Thikkum, and Cathri streets. A wide and irregular run of roads to operate in, but Koli must have had his reasons.

It meant many more roads in between to lose the pair in, and I'd taken my time to memorize every corner and turn along the way. I'd grown the confidence that, if chased, I could have Gabi and Thipu lost and in my hands.

I just needed to have something ready for when I had them where I wanted. And so, as Rayaan, the festival of colors and kites, came on us, I reached into my private treasure and parted with more coins than I cared to.

I bought premade string, slathered in adhesive and lined with shards of glass. The point was to run the lines on your kites when flying beside others, and with careful control, bump and tie your lines to others. Done carefully, the friction of your line, aided by the glass, would shear someone else's and leave their kite to flit away without control. But I had another need in mind for the sharp string and an excess of bottle glass.

I'd slowly whittled away every extra tin chip I'd saved, coming down to my last copper round, but this would be worth it.

I hoped.

❧

I made my way through Gadha Street, a place that mixed its trade between the harder goods and soft. Bolts of silk and rolls of hemp filled vendors' stalls. Shirts and pants and scarves. No food, no spices, nothing of clay, marble, and stone. Only fabrics and what could be made of them. And, mummers and minstrels on the street playing for what spare coin could be thrown their way.

And the women outside a building I'd learned long ago to avoid. For a copper and your time, they'd treat you to earthly pleasures. And for something more, hard iron bunts, a joy of the body and mind that came from as much them as from Koli's goods. The men and women that frequented that place were a kind of trouble no sparrow wanted. And they were the sort that would look on a Sullied child as an opportunity for more pleasure and coin.

Two-thirds of a candlemark had burned away, meaning an hour until midday. Gabi and Thipu would shortly move down an alley where some of the regular cotton-eyes would be ready to buy more white-joy.

I placed an orange slice into my mouth, biting and sucking it clean of all juices and pulp. The rind stayed in my hand, however. I'd need it.

I slinked through another alley nearby, making my way around to the end of where they'd come to be, waiting for them to show up.

It didn't take long before harsh whispers echoed down the passage. I could make out Gabi telling the cotton-eyes ahead what to expect, what to pay, and when he'd be back next. He'd raised their prices on them and, being who and what they were, they didn't argue much. It'd be easier in their minds to sell another piece of themselves or someone else than to argue and risk losing the joy altogether.

Their transactions concluded, and Thipu's and Gabi's voices grew louder as they neared where I lurked.

I stepped out into view, bouncing the orange slice in an open palm. Neither of them paid me any mind and had their attention fixed on the coins they'd just collected. That brought a smile to my face. Time they learned what it was like to be on the other end of their hounding.

I knelt, scooping up a loose stone and folding the rind over it. A snap of my wrist sent the projectile hurtling toward Gabi's face. It struck him square in the eye, some remnants of the juice spurting out from the blow and pressure of the stone.

He yowled, pawing at the spot and dropping his coins.

Thipu, to his credit, kept his mind on the currency and quickly retrieved it before tending to his friend. It took only a second longer before both boys realized I stood ahead of them.

Gabi's chest heaved and his lips peeled away from his teeth almost like a feral dog's. "You."

I grinned, wide and rakish before breaking into a bird trill. "How's the eye?"

"I'll kill you, you little shit. I'll . . ." He seethed, his words falling to the side as he mimed wringing an imaginary neck with his hands. "I swear."

"Don't swear. Just try it. Though, I think both of those things might be too hard for you." I widened my smile and let out another whistle. "Cheep-cheep." I turned on a heel and walked away.

Gabi let loose a noise I still remember to this day. Something between an elephantine roar and the shrieking of an angry cat. It managed to be a basso bellow tinged with the high shrills only young boys going through that change into adolescence are capable of.

I sucked in a breath, steadying myself for the run to come.

Both boys took off after me.

Brahm's blood, he's angrier than I thought. I ran as hard as I could, winding through the alleys ahead. It galled me to slow my pace in places to ensure I didn't lose them. First, I kept to alleys I knew they worked, so they could track me with an ease that would lower their guard.

Then we wound down roads I'd made sure they never bothered to look twice at. We came to an alley I'd laboriously set up in, knowing it'd be clear of any other through traffic.

A series of dore strings, fine as hair, and infinitely stronger, threaded through parts of the alley. Only a keen eye that knew to look for them, aided by sunlight, would spot them at first glance.

I came to a shuddering halt and bent between some of the strings I'd fastened to anchors in the alley walls. It took me longer than I would have liked to properly contort my way through without nicking my exposed skin against the glass-lined threads.

Once through, I made my way to a section of wall that had fallen apart over the years. Pitted, broken, and offering more than enough purchase for a scrappy youth used to climbing his way up to a rickety bed in an understage.

I scampered up, the old calluses on my hands and feet, now toughened further, making it an easy task. Then, I waited on the roof of the building for the two to pass through.

Gabi came first.

He hit the strings, tumbling and tearing most of them with his weight. But they did their job.

He screamed, clutching himself randomly and rolling around, only worsening his agony. The strings caught and wormed tighter, digging into him with razor-sharp and gritty fury.

Thipu, who'd been on the heels of his friend, careened over him and met a similar fate.

Both boys were lined with bleeding ribbons and fine gashes. Nothing that would kill them, but they'd bear the scars for years. And the memories with them.

It would have been enough to leave them there, but an angry sparrow is a terrible thing. It will fight and peck at something larger than itself if there's ever enough cause to. These two had given me more than enough.

So I pulled one of the broken bottles I'd stored up on the roof, first collected from the streets over many sets. I bounced it in my hand before hurling it toward the boys. It missed, breaking on the ground between them. That hardly mattered as Gabi pressed a hand to the spot in an effort to push himself up.

He met more glass and cried out again.

Several more bottles flew, a few striking home. The boys could hardly be bothered to notice, though, so buried in their own pain.

Shame. I felt I should do something to rouse them. So I did.

I grabbed the dented pail I'd stolen earlier that month, taking care not to spill what precious liquid I'd saved inside it. I'd been buying and picking limes for sets now. Half-used, thrown away, and a few times, brand new. Every drop of juice I could get now pooled in the bucket.

I edged my way along the rooftop until I stood directly above the two squirming boys. "I hope you piss and shit blood for the next month. I hope the next time you see a sparrow you remember this before thinking about hurting one of us. I hope you burn. You, Thipu, Koli, all of you!" I tipped the bucket over.

I got my wish. They burned.

The lime juice splattered them, sending both boys into spastic fits and howls. They shook and tried to touch any part of themselves that had been cut and was now drenched in lime. But every motion and twinge set them into renewed bouts of pain.

I didn't sit to savor it, though I would have liked to. That much noise would draw the kuthri, appointed guards and peacekeepers, as well as muscle hired by wealthier merchants. They kept the main parts of the Golden Road and profitable streets clear of my kind. And they were not known for showing any kindness in that task.

I made my way down from the wall and crept closer to both boys.

One of Gabi's eyes carried more red than white, streaked through with blood and nearly as much hatred. He glared at me as I looked past him to what had fallen on the ground.

Coins. All of the coins they'd claimed that day from their runs.

Two copper rounds, and nearly two dozen tin chips. Almost another round just in tin coin. I knelt and pinched every coin up, keeping a wary eye for any sudden movements from the boys. Fortunately, they looked resigned to their crippled fate and all the pain that came with it.

Good.

I won't ever say what I did was good in any measure. I knew it had been a terrible thing. But it was necessary. And often, necessity outweighs the good of things.

I'm sure philosophers, pedants, monks—and they're often the same—feel otherwise about that, but to a small child on the street without caste to protect him and a stable family to shelter him, necessity promises you safety. Be it of food, a place to sleep, or deterring threats.

And . . . it brought me pleasure. I'll not lie about that.

I took their coin before stepping away from them. Gabi sputtered something at my back that I didn't have a care to honestly hear. I looked at the pair of them over my shoulder. "If you ever come for me again, I'll do a thousand times worse to you. I promise. I'll find a way. I'll find where you sleep and I'll burn you there. You, Koli, all his dogs, and all his white-joy. All of you." And I meant it.

The look in Gabi's one open eye told me he knew it to be true as well.

I left them in their misery and ran all the way back to my hiding hole. A small treasure of its own now sat in my hand, but the day's work meant I'd not pulled a single chip for Mithu. A moment of greed did seep into me, telling me to put both copper rounds away, bringing my total to three saved. I pushed that voice aside and deposited one round and ten of the tin chips.

Another round and ten sat in my hand as offering to Mithu, while I'd kept two rounds and ten for myself. My fortune grew.

I decided that I'd done enough running for the day and deserved to walk home, making sure to stop by a cart for a slice of mango. So Mithu would get a round and eight chips. He'd hardly know the difference.

THIRTY-THREE

PROMISES

Eight months passed as a sparrow on the streets of Keshum, and my mind grew sharp, quick, and cleverer than I thought possible. It stretched in more ways than when I studied the folds of the mind, all of which now had taken up an older room inside. A place caked in dust and cobwebs. And the candle and the flame had turned into a waning fire, mere sparks, struggling to stay alight. And somewhere, stood a locked door holding a name from my theater life.

But Ari the Sparrow had no need of those things.

Ari the Sparrow needed the simpler things: time to himself, a place to keep his treasures, and a promise to be fulfilled. A promise of vengeance.

But I came to learn that some promises are made to be broken.

I woke that morning earlier than my scheduled time to run the streets. For the past two months, Mithu had set me to learning how to be a clutcher. How to bump and hold people to send their minds elsewhere while I plucked or *snicked* a purse. He'd even given me a knife to do the job.

A piece of iron, thin and tapered, lacking any adornment. It was a good tool for a sparrow. A simple tug on bindings and one good snap, the knife would part a coin pouch from any surface with ease.

I inspected my chest at the foot of my bed more out of habit than anything else. My in-room treasure had grown to house a wooden horse with a mane from actual horsehair. I had a few glassworks—little flowers of red and green. I didn't know their value, but I liked the look of them and felt I should keep them no matter what. A stone for sharpening my knife, also given to me by Mithu. I had a piece of green stone, almost like polished moss and glass, that I hadn't a clue about in its origin, name, or anything else.

But it felt special, and to a young boy with little in the world, that alone made it special. And lastly, my book.

There had been a time where I'd tried in earnest to continue my mastery of the folds and the candle and the flame. It never came. And I still hadn't been able to open the book.

I shut the trunk and made my way out of my room, heading up to Mithu's chambers in the hope he was there. The double doors barring the way were open a crack. I leaned forward, peering through the gap.

Mithu sat cross-legged on a cushion, puffing plumes of smoke as Biloo tallied sums from what coin had already come in earlier. Askar indulged in the same pleasure as Mithu, inhaling from the pipe occasionally as the men passed it back and forth. A good enough sign they were in a good mood.

I rapped my knuckles on the door and waited.

"Who's there?" Mithu sounded dazed and distant, like he'd just woken up.

"Ari, *Abah*."

"Ahhhhh. Ari." He rolled the R's when he spoke, drawing out the rest of my name as well, which was something considering how short it is. "Come-come."

I pushed open the doors and entered, walking to within twelve steps of him—the appropriate amount we were taught to stand before our adoptive father.

He took another puff and looked me over, then thrust his chin up in a gesture that asked a silent question.

"I've been wondering about some things, *Abah*. I'm up early, I've been pulling good coin between listening and clutching, and wanted to know if we could talk?"

He tilted his head in what I knew to be a nonvocal yes, and then waved me to speak. "Ask-ask, Ari. Ask. You've earned any talk you want."

I swallowed. I could ask a lot, and Mithu would likely answer, but jumping to the heart of what I wanted could rile him. Khalim had once taught me about the art of talking to people, of inching your way to what you wanted. You had to start small, but at the heart of something important.

So I did.

"It's about the missing sparrows, my brothers and sisters."

Mithu nodded and sucked on the smoking pipe again. "Mhm. It still troubles you?"

I nodded.

"I know it's hard, Ari. But sometimes, sometimes some of the rescued birds just want to fly free. I try not to take it as a hurt on my heart. Some can't stand it here. Some can't weather the life. Some simply don't like the life I've offered them. So they run. They take what little treasures they've collected and they run." Mithu frowned and looked down at the ground. His shoulders sagged and his face followed in kind.

"Maybe it's my fault, hm? Maybe I give them a way to run. I let them keep things to sell and trade and find coin to leave. Maybe I'm not a good enough father." His face tightened, and the only thing keeping me from thinking he'd come close to crying was the fact I'd never once seen him shed a tear. I didn't think him capable of it. "What do you think, Ari, hm? Am I a bad keeper of you birds? Have I not done a good job?"

Hearing him ask that weighed my heart and chest with hot stone. He'd taken us in no matter our caste, our history, and our lack of talent in thievery and the other sparrow arts. He'd given us more than any child with nothing could ever ask for.

"You have, *Abah,* you have. All of us are grateful." I placed a hand over my breast, just above my heart. "I was just worried is all. We haven't picked up any new birds for months now."

Mithu read my concern without me having to say another word. "And you fear our numbers will keep shrinking. That you'll soon lose another family, huh?"

Lead filled my stomach, sinking deeper at that thought. The question brought back memories I'd let sit and collect sand. Another family gone. This time to a slow death. The same kind that had taken my thoughts of revenge and my promise to Mahrab.

The realization galvanized me to press on. I took a breath, steeling myself. "Yes, *Abah,* that bothers me. And . . . there's more."

The only sounds were the steady puffs and exhalations of Askar and Mithu. An occasional *clink* came from Biloo thumbing coins into neat piles.

Mithu grunted in what I took as an invitation to continue.

"Koli." I let the single word fall like a piece of gold on glass. The room quieted at the mention of the man, and all eyes fixed on me with an intensity they'd lacked before.

Mithu put the smoking stem on the ground and steepled his fingers. "*What* about him?"

I shuffled in place, thinking about the best way to get to where I wanted. The door with a name behind it. Nisha. She seemed like the place to start. "My friend, the girl I told you about?"

He leaned back, nodding more to himself than me. "Yes-yes. The one you were worried over in his care."

I inclined my head, but said nothing.

"I'm sorry, Ari-*cha*. My son. I've heard nothing. And that makes me think she's in far worse trouble than we thought. Something I can't do a thing about."

I tilted my head, waiting for an explanation.

Mithu's face grew tired and he shook his head like he didn't want to go on. "Ah, Ari, it's not a good thing at all. Are you sure you want to know this?"

I didn't in that moment, but another part of me, the part that held nothing but anger, fire, and horrible thoughts for Koli had to know. "Yes."

"I think Koli's done with her. And when Koli is done with a boy or girl . . . he finds ways to get more out of them than when they were his little runners, hm? He puts them in the soft parlors, the service houses. You understand, yes?"

I gritted my teeth and bowed my head, not trusting myself to speak. My fingers curled and I pumped my hands, trying everything to remain calm. But acid and fire seared my heart.

"I'm sorry, little bird. I am. I wouldn't know how to find her if that's her fate. And I don't have the means to get her out. Askar and Biloo are strong men, true. But this is asking too much of them. Koli is a monster."

You have no idea.

"And he keeps many dogs on his leash. He is a bloodletter. He is quick to cut and kill a man or woman who crosses him. That is not what sparrows do. That brings us too much trouble, and our purses are thin. We do not peddle and trade in joy, so I do not have the coin to spare to buy us out of deeper trouble, understand?"

I did, but I didn't like it. "There's more, *Abah*." I knew if I sat and thought deeper over Nisha's fate, I would lose myself to the anger I kept in balance at the moment. So I dropped it from my mind. It wasn't a nice thing, and it certainly wasn't easy, but it was necessary.

"It's about what you promised me with Koli. It's been eight months. I still think about him, what he cost me." I took a step closer, forgetting my place as I did. "You promised me one day we'd come for him. One day we'd take from him what he's taken from us. I don't understand why none of it has happened yet, *Abah*. Why aren't we standing over him right now with a knife to his throat?" I took another few steps, my hands still clenched into tight fists as I tried to calm myself.

"Tell me, *Abah*. Tell me." My voice never rose to anything above a hard whisper. The sharpness of it could have cut a furrow through brick and mortar, though.

Mithu exchanged a look with Askar and Biloo, almost like they had just had a private conversation without words. Then he fixed his gaze on me. "It's not as easy as that, Ari-*cha*." He rose and, for a moment, I realized how far I'd overstepped and considered backing away from him. Mithu closed the distance between us and put both hands gently on my shoulders. He shook me lightly. "Koli's resources are greater. His manpower is more. His swords and knives, dogs and puppets to use are too many. This takes time. Thought.

"And we've given it that, Ari-*cha*. Do you want to know what I've thought?"

I nodded.

"We'd have to burn all of Koli's white-joy, and the building he makes it in. We'd have to take care of the men and runners he has in that place. It's not an easy thing, Ari. Not easy at all." He squeezed my shoulders. "It will happen. I can't say when, but I want to see him burn. We both do. It'll happen. It will."

I swallowed and accepted that. What else could I do? I didn't have the resources, time, or ability to do it myself. And despite my frustrations, Mithu had lived up to all other promises he'd given.

"I'm sorry, *Abah*. I am. I just . . ." I trailed off and flexed my fingers again, wishing I had something to occupy my hands.

"I know. It's a hard thing. And the hate keeps you going. I know that too. It's a good thing to hold on to, Ari. But don't let it take you away from what you have here—a family, a home. The sparrows need you more than you might need your revenge."

A family that needs me.

I never once thought of it like that. And he had a point. When I'd returned to some of my theater arts, I'd taught the sparrows how to be more efficient. Maybe in time I could do even more.

"Are you at ease now, Ari-*cha*?"

I was. "Yes, *Abah*. Thank you."

"Good, good." He didn't sound as if he was speaking to me anymore, but more to Askar and Biloo. "You've been pulling well for the last few months." Mithu didn't phrase it as a question.

"Yes."

"Without fail. So smooth, Ari. Every tithing, perfect, measured, almost to the coin." He stared at me and I saw nothing in his eyes but cold and polished stone.

I kept from visibly swallowing. "Yes?"

Did he know I stole from him? That I'd been squirreling away extra coin to occasionally pull from on days I underperformed? Had Nika found out and passed the information on to him?

My mouth ran dry as I waited for him to go on.

"You're a good sparrow, Ari." He clapped a hand to the side of my face, giving me an affectionate pat on the cheek. "Take the day off. I'll tell Juggi and Nika not to tally a sum for you. Go on the streets, buy a sweet, hm? Maybe chase a girl." He gave me a mischievous wink. "Time off is good for the mind." Mithu motioned to Biloo, who tossed him ten tin chips in a single smooth motion. He then pressed the coins directly into my hands.

I blinked, staring at the money for several breaths, then looked at him. "*Abah?*"

"Sweets aren't free, my son." He smiled. "Go, go."

"Thank you. I . . . thank you." I clutched my fist tight around the money and all but ran from the room.

It's funny how much a handful of small coins can change a man's disposition, or a boy's, in a moment of heat, questioning, and all the feelings that come with them both. But it does. And you can distract a great deal of people with a few pieces of precious metal.

But how's a young boy to know when it's being done to him?

I had coin in my pocket, answers, and the promise of a free day. I took them all in stride.

I nearly bounced into the common room as I headed toward the door.

Nika slid up to my side, quiet as a cat when not wanting to be caught. "You're in a good mood."

I smiled. "I always am when you're around."

She rolled her eyes, but a hint of color touched her cheeks. "You can't say that so loud here. Someone else might hear and tell Mithu." Nika balled a fist and smacked my arm.

"Ow." I rubbed the spot and stared at her.

"Oh, it didn't hurt." She put her hand over where she'd struck. "What are you doing down here this early, anyway? You're not to go out until next candle change. You have a full mark before that."

I told her what happened with Mithu.

Her eyes widened when I showed her the coins. "He . . . *gave* you money? I don't believe it. I see it, but Mithu never gives coin away."

I stowed the coins in my pocket, not wanting any other sparrows passing by to see them. "He did. And he at least told me what's been happening to our missing brothers and sisters. I just can't believe it."

"Same."

I nodded.

"No, Ari, that's not what I mean. I mean I don't believe it. Why would they run? They have nowhere to go."

I reiterated what Mithu had told me, but as I said it aloud, it rang hollow.

"But where would they go, Ari? Where? How long will some saved chips last? They can't have taken more. No one's stolen from Mithu. No one does. You just . . . can't."

I ran my tongue against the back of my teeth. So, she didn't know about my stash. That was something, at least. "Right. I don't know. But why would they leave?"

"I don't know if they have. I'm worried. But we shouldn't talk about this here. I'm going out for another pass of the streets before doing dog's work on the candle change. Do you want to come with me?"

An hour alone with Nika, at least as alone as I could be on the streets of Keshum—how could I say no?

She slipped her fingers between mine and we left the house of sparrows, losing ourselves on the streets and all the chaos that came with them. Ten chips couldn't buy us a world of pleasure, but it would do us a pretty good job of feeling that way, at least. And to two rather impoverished sparrows, well, we could hardly tell the difference between the joys of spending tin and what it meant to buy with gold.

We came across a woman with a cart of polished metal. A swirling inscription I couldn't make out ran along its edges. The woman had all the looks of someone's loving grandmother, hobbled by the years. The cart looked as much her livelihood as it did her means of physical support. She bid us over with an enthusiastic wave. Smoke seeped out from the corners of the lid as she moved it aside just enough for the fume to escape.

Nika and I froze, eyeing the contraption, then her.

"No fears, dears. No fears. Just a little bit of magic."

My expression went from one of caution to suspicion. I narrowed my eyes, giving the cart another look-over in hopes of spotting the trick behind it. "What kind of magic?"

She readjusted the lid so none of the smoke continued to vent. "The little kinds done by those up at the Ashram."

I blinked. This didn't look or sound like anything to do with the bindings Mahrab had talked about. "What is it exactly?" I leaned closer.

"I don't sell secrets here, boy. I sell treats. Iced mango cream. *Quhli*. Or maybe you'd like shaved ice with rose syrup? I have them both. And for the pretty little miss, too, yes?"

I nodded, not trusting myself to speak. In truth, I did want to share something like that with Nika, but a deeper curiosity pulled me toward wanting to see how this box worked. "How much?"

"Five chips."

I sputtered. "For two treats? That's worth a meal. A full meal at some places."

She shrugged. "This isn't a cheap treat or cheap tool, boy. I paid a great deal for this box from the binders up north, in the mountains, far from here.

Very far. Do you know what that costs someone? No, you don't. You couldn't, because you've lived here in Keshum your whole life. You've never seen a different sky or even ten streets past this spot, have you?"

I glowered at her, but couldn't bite back, knowing she had a point. At least half of one. I grumbled under my breath and passed her chips. "What's it do?"

She beamed as she palmed my coins, making them disappear with almost as impressive a trick as her contraption. The old woman slid the lid back and grabbed a wooden spoon nearly as wide and thick as my hand. She jammed it into the cart's basin as more smoke escaped.

I felt a coolness and realized it wasn't smoke at all. My eyes widened as she scooped clear crystalline stone into a small bowl.

The woman read my expression. "It's ice. Water made cold and hard. There's plenty of it up north in the mountains. The box the binders sold me keeps the cold in and the heat away. And if I let water stay in there long enough, it too will turn to ice." She grabbed a vial of something that looked like red oil, thick and viscous, pouring it over the ice before passing it to Nika with a small spoon.

Nika grabbed it with equal measure of wariness and excitement. She traded me a look and I shrugged, not sure what to expect of the dish. She dove in, wincing at the first bite before shutting her eyes in pleasure. "It's cold. Sweet. So sweet." She flashed me a smile so warm that even the old lady's ice box couldn't hope to withstand it.

The woman then went about making a treat for me. Scraped and chilled mango flesh, chips of ice, and what looked like chilled milk, pistachios, and cardamom. She passed it to me in a bowl the mirror of Nika's. I followed my friend's example and tore into it.

The first bite sent a frigid wave through the roof of my mouth that felt like it settled just behind my eyes. It stung and hammered. I winced through it, deciding the pleasure against my tongue far outweighed the icy discomfort. We passed the bowls and spoons back to the woman after finishing our treats, and something struck me.

"How far is it to the Ashram?"

She cocked a brow at me as she stowed the dishes in a separate compartment of the cart. "By cart, horse, and foot? Hm. Took me more than a set and a half at least. Without stop but for sleep. Sometimes not even that. And I spent a great deal, boy. Money I'd kept for ages.

"But my sons are gone, and my daughters married, and my husband has been ashes for a time I can't count. No one is here to tend to me but me. So I spent to gain what I could. And now Athi Nan has the only ice treats for as far as you can see in Keshum and maybe Abhar. It was worth it." She said nothing further, pushing away from us and breaking into a whistle song.

Nika and I wandered farther together, leaning on one another and just enjoying companionable silence.

I spotted a pair of sparrows ahead, both catching sight of us and hurrying over our way. "So much for our private time."

Nika ribbed me with an elbow, rolling her eyes. "We'll get more." She rubbed the back of a finger along my cheek before turning her attention to the pair of sparrows. "Shipu, Moni, what's wrong? You still have time to turn in marks before the candle change?"

Shipu and Moni, like most sparrows, could hardly be told apart at first look. But if you'd been around them long enough, you'd have known both were young girls. Their black hair was really a shade of brown so dark you could only make out its true color under the brightest sunlight. Their eyes were the brown of milk tea with more of the former than the latter. Neither could have been more than ten. "It's a bad day, Nika," said Shipu.

"Bad day." Moni spoke as she always did, her sister's echo.

"We're short of a good tithe." Shipu frowned and looked around almost as if she expected Mithu to appear and scold them both on the spot.

I placed a hand on Shipu's shoulder and gave her a gentle shake. "You'll be fine. One short tithe isn't the end of everything. How bad is it?"

She held up a single chip. "Both us pulled that."

I exhaled through clenched teeth. That *was* a sort of bad I didn't think possible for a sparrow to pull in. One would either have to shirk their duties or throw away coin to bring in a single chip in the richest kingdom in all of the Mutri.

"It'll be all right. Nika and I will try to smooth things over with Mithu—"

Shipu grabbed me, followed by Moni. "It won't be. We don't want to be gone like the others."

All thought left me. My mouth may have been freshly wet from the treat, but it may as well have been washed with sand after hearing that. I could hardly pull my tongue from the base of my mouth to speak. "What do you mean?" While the words were meant for the sisters, my gaze fell on Nika.

"All the sparrows who are gone. They were the worst speakers or clutchers." Moni looked at me like I'd overlooked something painfully obvious.

In truth, I had.

"Nika . . . is that true?" If anyone knew offhand who'd brought in what sums, it'd be her or Juggi. They were the only ones Mithu trusted to tally a sparrow's daily earnings before passing them on to him for final counting.

Nika pursed her lips and her stare drifted far away. One look at her and you could tell she saw not a single person out of the hundreds bustling by. No, she looked through them all to spot only what she could see. "They're right. Every missing sparrow is someone who'd been pulling low for a while. Maybe a set at worst. I don't think anyone did that badly in a straight set, but . . . almost as many days."

Those sparrows had been the poorest among us, which said a great deal considering how poor we already were.

"And what do you think it means, Nika?" I kept my voice flat and colorless.

"I don't know. I don't know if I want to." Her answer was enough for me.

I had one of my own, and a question of what to do in the moment. "What's the worst pull for this set?"

"Three tin chips in a day."

I grimaced. We only had five left to us, but maybe it'd be enough to buy the girls out of trouble. "Here, Shipu, hold out your hand." She did as I asked. I put my remaining chips into her palm and closed her fingers over them. "Split it with your sister. You already have one coin. Keep three each. Nika, you're going to tally them for six each."

Her eyes grew owlish. "What? That's three apiece, Ari, not six. I can't lie to Mithu, he'll count it himself and know. Then we'll all be in trouble."

I pulled away from her, reaching into the collar of my shirt to pull free a scarf I'd folded beneath it. "It's only a lie now, but not for long. I'm going to get the other six chips, I promise." I hugged her tight and broke into a run, leaving the trio there to wait for me.

Mithu was right. I had a family that needed me. I hadn't been there for my old one, but I'd be here for this one.

THIRTY-FOUR
BLOODLETTER

Clutching or begging for the coin might have done the trick, but not in the time frame I needed. I ran hard as I made my way past the familiar working haunt of Hadhi Street. Reaching my destination took me longer than I would have liked as several main roads were packed tighter than usual.

Today seemed to be a day of increased foreigners off the Golden Road. All manner of outsider merchants looking to brook trade, off-load their goods—and simply get in my way, by the looks of it.

I took the back alleys and forgotten paths, making my way to my secret stash of coin. The brick sat askew like it had been pulled then hastily shoved back without someone taking the proper time to align it. My chest grew colder than the old lady's ice box and a hollowness spread through my core.

Had someone found my hiding place?

My fingers shook as I touched the brick and inched it forward. A part of me wanted to leave it firmly in place as if mortar still held it rooted.

So long as we don't see some hurtful things with our own eyes, our minds are capable of playing fantastic tricks on ourselves, and with time, those can become masterful lies that can rewrite history. So long as I didn't look, my treasure would still be there. I'd convinced myself of it.

But I did look. I pulled the brick free. It slipped from my hands as I peered inside. The brick crumbled as it struck the ground and my heart followed suit.

A bird lay inside the hole, its neck twisted at a horrible grotesque angle. A sparrow. It had been plucked in places and bled, crimson staining the walls of my treasure hole. A piece of broken string had been fastened around the bird's body. String covered in fine bits of glass.

The kind used to cut an opponent's kite free . . . or, if you were feeling particularly malicious, to tangle and tear two boys who'd beaten you.

My eyelids fluttered and the muscles of my face felt weak. Tears lined my lashes as I reached inside the hole, picking free what bits of metal remained.

Eleven chips, neatly arranged in a perfect line. As many as a set of days in the Mutri Empire. As many as it took Brahm to reach judgment.

Judgment.

They were eleven pips in truth, then.

A message. One needing little interpretation.

One set from today and something terrible very well could happen to a certain sparrow.

To me.

Imagine having everything in the world you held dear taken from you. The voices you'd heard all through memory. The faces of those who called your name, occasionally shared meals with you, and offered what spare kindness they could. I had lost that. Then imagine the promise of rebuilding that and, with it, a chance to create a treasure of your own, something outside your new family. An added assurance of sort. A new promise that, no matter what, you'd have some safety.

And it had been stolen from me.

The muscles in my arms pulsated and flexed like twisted iron. The knots hardened and I felt my limbs lock in place. A pressure built in my jaw strong enough to crush stone. If I held it any longer, I'd risk cracking my teeth. And a scream built in the core of my stomach that promised to drown out all the noise along the busy trading streets of Keshum.

But it never came.

I exhaled and pocketed the coins, pushing that from my mind. I needed to think for today, and tomorrow would come calling when it did. My family needed me first.

I left the alley behind and, with it, all plans of escaping Keshum, Abhar, and making good on my promise to Mahrab.

Gabi and Thipu had seen to that. And once I'd finished helping Shipu and Moni, I'd see to doing to those two boys what I should have in the first place.

I'd picked up a speed in my run. People moved out of my way for the first time, no longer seeing an untouchable starving sparrow. No longer eyeing me a wretch worth a quick cuff along my head or a few coins thrown to have me out of their way. No.

I kept racing, barking a curse at a cart vendor who'd decided this was the most opportune moment for him to cross the street. No other time could have sufficed. It had to be now, apparently.

The man stiffened as if a hot rod had been shoved up his rear, yelping and hauling the cart out of my way.

I reached the spot where I'd left the trio of girls earlier, relieved to find them nearby.

Nika approached me first. "I didn't think it'd be a good idea to go in and lie to Mithu, then have you make up the coin."

I managed a weak smile that faded as fast as it had come. At least she'd not harbored a single doubt I'd live up to what I said. "Here." I extended a hand, passing over all the chips. "Best you didn't lie to him, I'd have been a liar too. Looks like I managed to find a bit more than six."

Moni and Shipu eyed the coins, then me. Both their weights crashed against me and I crashed to the ground.

"Stop. Stop!" I had no breath to protest further, and the two were driving what little air I could manage to get out of me as quickly as it came. "Get. Off."

Both girls did as I asked, fishing back their coins from earlier and adding them to Nika's pile. "Thank you, Ari. Thank you." I couldn't tell their voices apart as Shipu and Moni spoke in an uncanny and perfect unison.

I rose and brushed myself as Nika took hold of one of my wrists. "You should come with me. We'll turn these in together. I want to watch how Mithu reacts." She gave me a knowing look.

I agreed. If Moni and Shipu had been performing poorly, their newfound good haul would surprise Mithu if he'd come to expect less of them. And I needed to confirm a building and lingering suspicion.

We went inside together and sent a sparrow tending the door to fetch our adoptive father. The sparrow returned, frowning. "*Abah* says come to his room to talk. He can't come downstairs." The expression was enough to know something was off.

Mithu never invited sparrows to his room for something as simple as tallying coin. The only times anyone visited were when they needed to speak privately, as I'd done.

All of us traded a look, and none had an idea of what this request meant. Resigned, we moved together, heading up the stairs until we stood outside his door.

"Hsst. You knock." Shipu nudged Moni.

Moni jabbed her sister back. "You."

Both girls settled their stares on Nika.

I exhaled at the prancing around and banged a fist against the door. "I already saw him today. It shouldn't be too bad if I—"

"Who's there?" Mithu's voice cracked like thunder in a hall of stone.

We shook at it and held a shared silence for the space of several breaths.

Licking my lips, I felt I should be the one to break the quiet, since I'd disturbed him. "Me, *Abah*. It's Ari."

Quiet.

"Again?"

"Yes . . . *Abah*. You sent Dutti down to tell us to come to you." I bit off asking if he'd remembered that given it had only been moments ago.

A ten-count of silence passed. "Ah, yes. Come-come." His words came dazed and distant, but I didn't press him. We were on uncertain footing as it was.

I pushed open the door, gesturing for the two sisters to go before me as well as Nika. She stopped at my side, giving me a look that made it clear she would walk by me instead. I thanked her silently and moved on. The doors shut behind us with a resounding *thump* that brought an unease to my stomach.

Mithu sat in his usual spot, lounging amidst his cushions. His favorite smoking vessel was nowhere to be seen, however. A lone vial sat by the side of his feet. The fluid inside resembled milky clouds trapped in glass. When Mithu stared at me, the intensity and color of his eyes had faded. Not by much, but enough that it was like looking at a gem sitting just below the surface of frothing water.

White-joy. He . . . uses it? The drug was the principal driving force of Koli's income, and a way he bribed the right people, either by cutting them in on the enterprise . . . or worse. There were stories he'd gotten people addicted to it, keeping them strung along to get what he wanted. Then, when he'd finished with them, he truly did finish with them. And those people never wanted for another taste of joy, or anything else ever again.

The sight of Mithu's clouded eyes took all thought from me, leaving me unable to do anything but stand and stare, wide-eyed, like a startled hare.

Askar and Biloo stood together, holding a child between them.

Like the rest of the sparrows, he was hardly identifiable at first glance. But a closer look showed where he was different.

His eyes were set wider apart than most. His brows grew closely together in the center, and if left unthreaded for too long, you'd begin to see the hair grow back. His lashes were shorter than most, and he'd had *kahal,* a black eye paint, applied to them to make them look longer to match the rest of his siblings. His hair held fiercely to its natural strong curls no matter how many times it had been combed through to try and match the rest of us.

"Taki?" I watched him for any sign he recognized his name, but my brother looked nearly asleep on his feet. The only thing keeping him up was the grip of Mithu's two bodyguards.

I turned my head to regard my father, finally noticing what I'd overlooked upon entering the room.

Another man sat by his side, thin and wiry as a starving hound. He had a pinched face and oiled black hair that stunk of perfume. He was dressed in matching silk pants and shirt of pastel blue, all threaded with gold. His mustache had no hope of ever filling in, remaining as narrow and frail as the rest of him. The same soft clouded color tinged his eyes, obscuring whatever real shade lay beneath them.

I licked my lips, unsure where to begin. "*Abah,* you called for us?"

Mithu shook his head as if suddenly remembering. "Yes." He exhaled, then took another breath as if winded. "I was told Moni and Shipu brought in a good sum—more than they have been of late."

I nodded. "Yes, *Abah.*" I shot a sideways look to Nika, hoping she had a better idea of what was going on.

She returned my stare with perfect flatness, betraying nothing.

"All tin chips, yes?"

Nika nodded this time, answering for me.

"Mhm." Mithu didn't move and his stare went past us before he turned it to the man at his side.

That was enough to make me ask the question welling inside me. "*Abah,* who is that?"

The man smiled, but didn't answer.

Mithu cleared his throat and rose to his feet, pacing around his broad desk before coming to stop beside it. "He is a friend. A business partner."

Business? The sparrows dealt in no business but our own. We begged, we stole, we traded or sold back what we could to the cleaners all under Mithu's orders. Our livelihoods were entirely of our own making, and no other people in the whole of the Mutri Empire involved themselves with us.

"What business, *Abah*?" I crept closer, hoping to reach my lulled brother.

"Ah, Ari. It's a sad thing. A necessary thing at times. You understand the necessary things, yes?"

I inclined my head.

"You do. You're a good sparrow. Sometimes I think too good, if there's such a thing." Mithu smiled. Askar and Biloo mimicked it near perfectly.

I didn't know what he meant, but the cold filling my chest warned me it might be better not to find out. Would that I listened to that thought.

I didn't.

"What do you mean, *Abah*?"

Mithu didn't answer. Instead, he motioned me to follow as he walked to the door at the far corner of his room, right by the arched windows. He opened it and went up the stairs, Askar, Biloo, Taki all following.

I did as asked by my adoptive father. Nika and the two sisters fell in step behind me. A knot formed between my shoulders and I made sure to watch our climb up for the man we'd left behind. The idea of him at our backs made me feel like I'd swallowed a handful of cold oil.

We arrived at the roof of our home. The top of the building lacked any walls, any stone barriers to prevent one from falling over the edge should a strong gust of wind tip them over.

"What do you see, Ari-*cha*? What do you see, my little sparrow?"

I had no words.

"Cheep-cheep, little one. Now is not the time to be so silent. Sing, bird. Sing." Mithu interlaced his thumbs and flapped his fingers like a bird taking flight.

"*Abah* . . . you're scaring me. I don't know what you want."

"I want. Ari. For you to tell me. What. Do. You. See?" He waved a hand at the Keshum skyline.

I pressed my lips tight and worked for any saliva I could to combat my quickly drying mouth. "I see our streets. The sky above it all. The place where we beg and pluck coins for you. And if I look over the edge, I'm sure I'll see my brothers and sisters working hard for you, *Abah*."

"Then come close, Ari, and stand with me here." Mithu moved to the lip of the building, and Askar and Biloo followed, bringing Taki with them.

I looked at Nika, hoping she had some silent advice for me. But she had none.

Taking a breath to calm myself, I went over by our father and stood as he'd instructed.

"Do you know what I see, Ari?" He didn't wait for me to respond. "My little kingdom. My nest inside it all. And that there are bigger birds than us out there. Hawks that can take it all from us. To live and sing and count our blessings, we must appease these hawks. And sometimes that means giving up a poor bird or two to a place where they can find new ways to sing and soar for others, hm?"

I wanted to ask him what he meant by that, but the truth hit me a moment later like stone on glass. My legs promised to give way and send me tumbling to the street below. "*Abah* . . . are you saying that—"

"What happens if a sparrow goes off this roof, Ari?" He'd spoken as if I hadn't said a word. "Would they fly, you think? Would *you*?"

"*Abah?*" I took a step back only to meet solid resistance like a wall. A look over my shoulder showed me Biloo standing behind me, having left Taki in Askar's grip.

"You've left me in tricky spots, Ari. You're a clever bird. Too clever. And too clever things are too much trouble, you know?"

I'd heard something to that effect before, and under any other circumstances, I'd have found just as clever words to make light of it all. But I could find nothing but a young boy's fear and uncertainty over what would happen next. "*Abah* . . . I . . ."

He waved me off. "You. You. You and a great many deal of things, Ari. *That* is part of the problem. You are a good speaker. Too good. You've gotten the new ones thinking and dreaming dreams of being bigger than themselves. Of this place. You've gotten the clutchers getting too wild with their pullings. Too ambitious. And that brings new eyes on us. And it's brought them on me. *Me.*" He jabbed a thumb to his chest.

"And you're too ambitious yourself. One treasure wasn't enough for you. After all I did."

An invisible hand, fresh from the old lady's ice box, gripped my heart tight and held it firm, threatening to stop it beating there. And that cold soon filled the rest of me.

"This all costs money to run, Ari." He sighed and rubbed a hand against his forehead. "And sometimes, that money isn't always brought back from the little sparrows. Some birds do too poor a job, and when they do, I must look to make my money another way. Yes? The necessary things. And so, the bad birds are given new homes."

The white-joy. The missing sparrows. The reasons and time all said and wasted without so much as the slightest effort against Koli. It all crashed into place. Mithu had hated the man, or so he said, long before I came into his life.

So why had nothing been done over all that time? Why nothing now?

Because Mithu needed Koli.

And Koli needed Mithu.

I finally found a spark of fire to push back the cold building in me, and I found the words to speak along with it. "The missing sparrows—my brothers and sisters—they didn't run away, did they?" One look at his face gave me all the answer I needed. "You've been selling the low earners to Koli." The small bones of my hands cracked as I made fists.

"And you have been stealing from me."

The open accusation and truth did nothing to drive me back to the fear that had racked me moments earlier.

"You were never going to make good on your promise." I didn't need him to answer. I knew what he would say. The heat in me grew, pushing away whatever discomfort came from the sun overhead. It couldn't match the fire burning within me. "You lied to me."

Mithu gave me a measured look that said it plain: I had lied to him as well, so as far as he was concerned, we were on even footing.

"And the pips? The eleven chips. What happens to me in eleven days, *Father*?" I put as much venom and bile as I could into the last word, nearly burning my own throat from the hatred it held.

Footsteps from behind us prompted everyone to turn. The man from earlier had come up, watching the scene. "Hurry and be done with this, Mithu. Put the boy to sleep and let me take him. And if these here"—he motioned to us—"are giving you too much trouble, give them to me too. Koli will find use for their talents or bodies." He shrugged. "Either way, you will make some coin and get more joy. And Koli will be happy. All will be well."

No. All would most certainly *not* be well. Not if I had anything to say about it.

"You never wanted him dead." My voice could have scoured stone and steel.

"Oh, Ari-*cha,* that's not wholly true. I'd have Koli dead if I could. And the bastard knows it and wishes the same of me. But, we need each other alive more than we want each other dead, yes? The necessary things, my son. Like this one." He reached out to put a hand on my shoulder.

I tried to shy away from his grip, but Biloo forced me into it. His belly pressed against my side and the hilt of his sword poked a bit into my arm.

"Ari," said Mithu. "I am sorry. You've stolen from me. You've changed my sparrows too much for my liking. And now I give you a choice like I gave you the day we met. I will push you from this roof and you can try to fly like the sparrow you are. Or I can give you to the man there and you'll get your wish. You'll be taken to see Koli, but I cannot promise you will live. And I cannot promise you will live any kind of life you ever hoped for. But I will promise you that Koli will not die by your hands. And you won't find that girl of yours, Ari-*cha*. It is how it is to be. It is the way of things."

The way of things.

I hadn't learned it until then, but some men don't give their word in the hope of keeping it. They give it in the hope of gaining something. Something from you.

Oh, the things we'll swallow and do for the promise to fulfill our deeper wishes.

And this the cruel people of the world know, and they'll leverage it, dangle it, for as long as they can—as long as it takes for us to become wise to it. If we ever do. And it's a shame many never learn this lesson: Bondage isn't done with ropes and chains. No. It's done with honeyed whispers and poisoned promises never meant to be kept. And if you follow them—believe them—you may never live long enough to realize those promises and dreams on your own.

Mithu and Koli knew this. Played both sides of the street conflict between their runners and the sparrows. They manufactured the grief between us to keep us pecking and fighting one another while they profited off our efforts, our bodies, and our blood. And they soothed our tears and aches with soft promised prisons in hopes of keeping us stuck in the game until we died.

No more.

Every dark and terrible dream I'd nursed over Koli came back to me. Seized me. The candle and the flame sparked, then burst bright inside my mind. I fed it everything. All the fear. All the hatred of a boy wronged and robbed of everything past and everything he hoped for in the future. The scream I'd kept inside at seeing my treasure stolen now escaped me, and though it seemed a world away, I bet all of Keshum heard it.

A singular focus took me the way Mahrab had taught. The folds of my mind went not to bindings, but the image of killing Mithu. They shifted through all the different ways to do it.

I hadn't realized my hand had moved and taken Biloo's thumb and first finger in my grip. I moved through things burned into me by Vithum: how to break a swordsman's hold on his sword if I ever got grip of that hand. Twist. Wrench. Pull.

The large man screamed as his thumb and index finger dislocated.

Mithu grabbed my collar and moved to make good on his threat.

We would see if a sparrow could fly.

I dropped my weight, more in fear than anything rational. At least by going to the ground I could hope to stay there. I could claw and hold on as hard as I could.

Maybe it had been the white-joy, or maybe something else, but Mithu's hold slipped. He didn't figure I'd crash to the ground.

Askar let go of Taki and raced toward me.

I scrambled to my feet, bulling into Biloo in hope of moving him aside so I could barrel past him. We collided, and my hand went to the hilt of his sword. He slammed his good palm into my chest and drove me back. And the sword came with me.

The familiarity and surety that came with gripping that weapon changed things. No longer was I a child fighting off a group of large and dangerous men. This became swordplay. A dance and drilled routine Vithum had made sure I could not forget. Something I'd given every fiber and space of my mind to learning. It was the promise I would go onto the stage, and one day, be a hero of my own for the world to see.

Askar reached for his sword and I lunged.

My weapon darted forward and the tip sank into the flesh just beneath his breast. It didn't go in far, maybe as much as the nail of my small finger, but the man yelped and stumbled back. I stepped to one side, snapping the blade wide to dissuade Biloo.

The man followed Askar's lead, staggering away from me on instinct.

I rounded, bringing the blade up against Mithu. "Where is she? Where is *she*? Tell me about Nisha! Where is she?" All the ears along the streets heard us now. "Tell me!"

I don't know if it was the effects of the white-joy or something else, but Mithu laughed. He pressed a hand to his stomach as if trying to hold it all back. "Oh, Ari-*cha*. You've done it now. There's no saving you. I offered you a chance, to fly. Koli won't be so kind—" Mithu reeled, screaming as he held up one of his hands.

Every finger had been sliced cleanly through around the second knuckle.

My sword ran red.

Biloo moved.

I glided back, remembering my footwork. No. Remember is the wrong word.

It's going to bed on the same side and in the same position after years of finding the perfect one. It's waking the exact same way once you've learned how your body responds best to those early mornings. It was like that.

The movements came before I could ask of them. Before I had any need.

Vithum had taught me, and Mahrab had given me the keys to the hidden rooms of my mind that would hold anything so long as I desired them to.

And it all came back. Only now the boy didn't have a wooden sword. He held good iron and steel.

I moved in a semicircle, casting the curved blade in a similar arc.

Biloo survived its edge—barely.

Again. I moved in, bringing the blade down, hoping to bury its length in the soft tissue over the man's kidney.

He pivoted, more in panic than any training, putting himself against the lip of the roof.

I lunged.

Biloo, it seemed, never learned the awareness Vithum had said mattered so much to a swordsman. And poor Biloo was the first to pay the price for it.

He didn't scream as he fell. The fall was too short and fast for someone of his size, but just long enough to make sure he would make no other sounds upon landing.

Apart from the ones of his body hitting the ground.

Even from the roof, the unnatural bend in his neck and arms told us that sparrows and their keepers could not, in fact, fly.

Askar, to his credit, stared at his friend's body. No anger came to him. Only the look of mourning I knew all too well. I'd worn it some quiet nights when all alone in my room until time buried the memories of my family.

And now they'd returned along with the fires of that night.

You may think me cruel. Or maybe a monster for what I did next. History has seen fit to often cast me in that role.

But Askar was no innocent man. And he'd had a hand in trading my brothers and sisters to Koli.

I screamed and charged him.

He too must have been of the school of Biloo. Another poor man without regard or awareness of footing.

I never laid a hand on him. And I never reached him.

All the same.

One sparrow had fallen earlier, showing that he could not fly. Now two had fallen, but still, none flew.

But there is an old adage about things in threes. And there was a third man who needed to show us if he could fly.

Mithu trembled, eyeing the dazed Taki, then Nika. "Nika, my dear. Sweet. My dog. Loyal dog. Please. Stop him. Your brother is crazed—mad. He's going to tear down everything I've built. *We've* built. This is your home."

Nika kept the same face I'd come to see whenever she had nothing to say or when she had too much to think on. And you would never know which one it was until she deemed it so. "You're right, Mithu. It is. *My* home. And these are my brothers and sisters. You taught us that. To live for them. Die for them. But not for you. You *never* taught us that."

His eyes widened. At a glance, it almost looked like they'd begun to shake. Something took him then, and I'll never know if it was the loss of blood, the mad twist his life had taken, or the white-joy. In all likelihood, all of them. But the man threw back his head and laughed. Good and long. He laughed so the fire in me tempered and the men and women along the street tore their eyes from the fallen men up to the roof and the king of sparrows howling over it all.

"Oh, Ari. Ari. Ari. Ari." He pressed his bloody hand to his forehead, leaving a trail of red along it. The blood dripped down over his eyes and onto his cheeks. "You leave me a choice too, huh? To fly? To die by the sword? Or to maybe run, run and take my chances with Koli."

The heat of my anger weakened and realization set in.

What had I done?

My arms nearly turned to water, as did my legs. The sword trembled in my grip and I risked losing hold of it.

"Oh, Ari. But I'll let you in on a secret." Mithu laughed louder. "Before you all, I was a sparrow too. And, I, my son, can fly." Mithu turned and made his choice. He jumped off the building.

I'd already come to know he was a liar.

The jump proved it.

He was no sparrow.

And he surely could not fly.

I raced to the edge and made it just as he struck the ground.

And thus the king of sparrows passed, and I watched him die.

If you hear the stories today, you'll hear that I butchered the three of them. That I screamed and howled demon noises as I did it. That I hollered and cheered all the while. That sparrows sang and blood spilled like rain from the rooftops.

You'll hear I did it in their sleep. Cut their throats quick and quiet and that the next day, a boy had been crowned the king of thieves and sparrows.

You might hear it was done with poison and that Small Kaya had always nursed a hatred for Mithu, and that she'd taken a special liking to me. Neither of those things were anywhere close to the truth. And Small Kaya could find no place in her heart and mind to care much for anything at all but her duties and her next breath. And I was never too certain of the latter.

But after that morning, the streets of Keshum whispered a new name for me.

Khoonee.

Bloodletter.

And while they didn't know my actual name, they'd come to learn that as well.

I'd make sure of it, as the sparrows were now mine.

And no one would hurt or sell us again.

THIRTY-FIVE

The Promise of Secrets

You would think three bodies falling from a roof would attract the kuthri to investigate, but they had better uses for their time. Usually gambling or picking up extra work for merchants outside their normal state duties. The death of three men, known to run a ring of child thieves, didn't rank too high on the concerns of officials. So long as thieving did not disrupt the more profitable trade along the Golden Road and the private businesses of those in power, the sparrows weren't anything to think on.

So the three rested where they'd fallen—undisturbed, for now.

The man who'd been with Mithu, a representative of Koli, stood fixed in place. Though his legs quaked like they would give way any second.

The sword shook just as much in my hands, but given everything that had happened, I couldn't betray my fear now. I had no idea what the man would do and if he desired to still make good on procuring our brother for Koli's business.

With the slew of memories and skills flitting through me, all courtesy of the folds of my mind, I grasped for what else I could from my past life. The thought came to me.

This was a performance. Right now my job was to convince the man before me that I had every capability of killing him with all the ease of blowing my nose. And that I had every intention of doing just that.

I exhaled and remembered the posture Makham used to adopt when playing the hero ready to mete out justice. I had all the surety and lazy confidence of a large cat ready to pounce on all-too-easy prey. The sword stilled in my grip. "If you make one move for Taki, you'll join Mithu and the others. He said he could fly. He was wrong. Can you?" I arched a brow and fell silent, using the quiet to steady my breathing.

The man licked his lips, looking at Taki like weighing a sack of rice and considering the costs. Then he glanced at the lip of the building where three men had fallen to their death. He raised his hands in a gesture of defeat. "I know too well I cannot fly. And I have no desire to try and prove it." He placed a hand to his heart before extending it toward me. "Well wishes, new King of Sparrows. I'll return to Koli and tell him of Mithu's . . . departure. I want for no trouble with you or my master."

I didn't move. The muscles along my back and shoulders ached from the effort of maintaining my stance, but I held it until the man descended the stairs he'd come from. Content he'd passed out of sight, I collapsed. The sword clattered to my side and the three girls ran over to me.

Nika slipped an arm under me and helped me to my feet.

I tried to speak but my stomach had become home to discontent worms, all twisting and undulating within. I motioned her away, and she heeded the warning just as I retched on the rooftop. My stomach squeezed tight and the lining of my throat burned. I vomited again, failing to hock up anything but hot spittle and what little water had remained in my gut.

"Make sure—"

Nika shushed me. "Don't talk. Moni, Shipu, get him water, juice, something."

The two girls ran off as ordered.

I turned to face my brother, still locked in his stupor. "Taki." My voice was barely above a croak.

The sparrow didn't regard me. His eyes were glazed and held a color almost exactly like that of Mithu's. I hadn't noticed it before.

He'd been given the white-joy. Of course. What better way to lull a frightened child and leave him out of his wits? Easier to lure, to move about, and have strung along to do whatever you wished so long as he'd get more joy.

I had no strength and fire left to muster anger at this. "Bring him down." Three words were all I could manage.

"First you. Taki doesn't look like he's going anywhere." Nika gave me a look that brooked no argument.

I opened my mouth anyway. Not my smartest moment, but then I've never been too clever when it's come to the fairer sex. "And if he decides he'd like to try flying like Mithu?" Every word hurt to voice, straining the lining of my throat.

She glowered and met me halfway. "Taki?" Her voice took on a high sweetness I hadn't heard from her except for in the rare moments we shared the awkward affection only children can.

The boy spun toward us in a slow and lazy circle as if underwater. "Huh?"

"Taki. It's Nika, your sister. Your shift is over today. It's time to go back to your room. You remember, yes?"

Taki blinked several times as if just getting his bearings. He looked around the roof before nodding. "Yes. I think so." He shambled over to us, looking like he'd trip over his own two feet any moment.

Nika took his hand in hers and gave it a tight squeeze. "Follow us. We'll get you settled and have Small Kaya bring you some food. And you too." She shot me a look that made it clear I'd accept that without a word. And if I didn't, she'd show me a sort of violence that would make what had just happened fall short in comparison.

I pressed my lips together and inclined my head.

"Good." She led us down the stairs back into Mithu's office. "Go to your room, Taki. I'll be there to check on you in a bit."

He left in silence.

Nika settled me in Mithu's chair, wiping away the sweat of my brow with the end of her shirt. She brushed away a few locks of my hair that had been matted to my face from the humidity. "You're shaking and your color doesn't look so good, Ari."

I gave her a wan smile. "I think I just killed three people."

She bit her lower lip at the corner but said nothing. Nika brought her shirt back up to wipe away more of the sweat along my face. "It was a hard thing."

I wanted to nod, but I feared my head would hang limp after the effort, so I slumped harder against the chair, using it for support. "It didn't feel hard when I was doing it. It felt right—easy." I swallowed what little spit remained in my mouth, hoping it would parch me even a bit. "What's that make me?"

I thought of Koli and that night, long ago. The ease with which he and the Ashura slaughtered my family. Is that what I'd become? It must have looked that way to the folks below on the street, watching as Mithu and his men tumbled to the ground like wet sacks of red and brown. Just like the bodies in the theater the night of the fire. Wet and red. Slumped like sacks.

I swallowed again, only no moisture came. My throat burned for it. "Does it make me a monster, Nika?"

"No, Ari. No. Shh." She pressed her hand over my mouth, keeping me from speaking further. "You did what you had to to protect us. It was necessary."

Like what Mithu had said. The necessary things.

And how long, in and of doing the necessary things, does it take until we lose sight of the path? Do we keep winding down the wrong paths only to find we're so far from where we began that we now walk those same roads as the people we tried to be so different from?

I'm not sure I've ever learned the answer to that. And I've walked a great deal since that day. Thousands of miles and thousands more still, and I still don't know.

Nika kept her hand over my mouth until content I'd not argue any further.

"I'll bring you some water. Maybe Small Kaya can bring some broth. You could use it."

I'd have made a face under normal circumstances, but I couldn't even bother with that little effort. The broths that woman made were mostly left-over lentil water, boiled again, and scraps of a meat I felt best left to mystery and the imaginary hope that it might be chicken.

"Maybe just the water. Thank you." Sand over gravel wasn't as dry as my voice.

Nika gave me one last look before leaving.

Alone, my thoughts would wander to what had just happened, and so I looked for a way to distract myself. I ran my hands along the surface of Mithu's desk, ruffling papers by accident. On a whim, I grabbed one, turning it over. A read of it told me all I needed.

Not only did he have personal correspondence with Koli, they kept each other abreast of their businesses on a regular timetable. Every second set.

Other letters revealed that Mithu had adopted the business of buying information from useful traders and merchants who passed through Keshum from the world beyond our city. Some of it proved handy in blackmailing the right people. However, he hadn't gotten too far into this endeavor.

Nika returned, cradling a wooden cup in both hands, passing it to me.

I thanked her with a nod and took a sip.

"Careful. It's like when you've been beaten. Too fast and you'll drown in it."

I eyed her.

She balled her fists and placed them on her hip. "You have been beaten that bad before."

I held my stare and she matched it until I felt my attention better served by focusing on my water. I drained half the glass in silent careful measure, taking my time. Relieved, I pushed the first letter I'd found toward her, thrusting my chin up in a gesture for her to comment.

She picked up the paper. "I can't read, Ari. What's it say?"

I blinked, remembering how something I'd taken for granted in my life was a skill so many in the Empire didn't have. "It's a letter from Koli to Mithu."

Nika stiffened as I read it aloud.

I then passed her another.

She gave me the same look as before, waiting for me to explain.

"Mithu's been buying rumors and secrets, but he couldn't get too far with it. And he wanted to blackmail people with it in the future."

Nika pursed her lips and looked down at the ground. "Makes sense, but he'd make people angry doing that."

I agreed. "But there's something there." My mind raced with the idea and potential behind his blundered scheme. "If Mithu was willing to pay people to learn their secrets, and people were willing to sell them, there might be more out there wanting to do the same."

Nika tilted her head and looked at me like I'd made a new and foreign sound.

"Maybe the sparrows don't have to beg and steal for coin. Maybe we can earn it in other ways, and maybe we can earn more."

"Ari, what are you talking about?"

I took another sip from the glass before draining it completely. "I think I can teach you all to read and write."

"And what will we do with that?"

I waved a letter. "What we do best? Listen, only now for secrets. And we'll record them. Trade them. Sell them. To anyone who has coin. Anyone with need and want. How does that sound?"

Nika grinned.

THIRTY-SIX

The Cost of Joy

Days passed and the merchants and vendors outside our home grew tired enough of the bodies disturbing traffic and paying customers to finally take things into their own hands. Or, at least through the coins that filled their palms. A group of day laborers—cart pullers, sack carriers, and more—helped haul the bodies away and out of sight.

I made sure none of the sparrows left the house during that time. We spent the days hiding, first out of the fear and unease of who might come for us. When nothing happened, we stayed in hopes the bodies would be cleared, and with them, any memories of what had happened.

For all parties. Us, and the citizens outside.

And, there had been the matter of Taki.

White-joy is not something that lets go of a person easily, whether they indulge willingly or not.

The first night Taki woke us all from our sleeps with thrashing and cries. If you've never heard another child in the grips of pure terror, unable to rouse themselves from sleep to find reprieve, it's a mix of sounds you don't forget easily.

I still can't remember just how many sparrows rushed to his room. Half of us struggled to keep him still lest he hurt us or himself in the spastic fit. The other group worked to wake him from his fitful slumber. There was no proper count of time to mark just how long passed before his eyes opened.

If you had told me a day had gone by into the next night, I would have believed it.

His eyes were wide and their color had worsened, paling further than before. He muttered names that didn't belong to any of us and his face shone with sweat under the weak candlelight.

"Taki." I clapped a hand to his cheek. "Taki."

He shook, then went still. Shudder. Shake. Thrash. Still.

"Taki!" I shook him by the collar, keeping myself from rattling him too hard.

Nika peeled me away from him. "Ari, you'll hurt him."

I didn't have the words to give voice to how I felt. I had no way of knowing what to do. My fingers curled and hands pumped into fists several times as I tried to soothe myself.

I failed.

"My chest." Taki spasmed and placed a hand over his heart. "Cold."

I ran a palm over his forehead. "He's burning. Does Small Kaya know about this? Does anyone?" I looked to the other sparrows around me.

Even Juggi, who by all accounts had been one of the earliest to come to Mithu, shook his head.

I swallowed. "I'll stay with him. Everyone else go back."

A few raised their voices in protest, but I had had enough. Recent events had left me well past taxed in patience, calmness, and eroded the walls of fear and safety of my mind.

"Out!" My voice silenced all others, and every sparrow left in a neat line. A few stopped at the door to cast looks over their shoulders at Taki and me. "You too, Nika."

She shook her head. "You stay, I stay." Her tone had none of the loudness of mine, but I'll tell you that it matched me for every ounce of stone and hardness I voiced. Maybe more.

Tired beyond any hope of relief, I curled into the bed with Taki and motioned Nika to join.

She did, moving to the other side of the bed and putting our brother between us. Nika rolled over and ran a hand through Taki's hair. "It's okay, Taki. We're here with you tonight." She wrapped an arm around him and pulled him into a fierce hug.

I said nothing and hoped my presence would be enough to calm my brother's fit.

The morning proved that wouldn't be the case.

Taki couldn't manage a few moments of peace, and neither could we. He woke the next morning shivering and spouting nonsense. His eyes hadn't worsened, but that wasn't a blessing as far as we were concerned. They hadn't returned to their normal healthy color.

Sometimes all expression vanished from his face, soon replaced by dazed bliss. His mouth hung open and his face lulled like he was in the midst of the most pleasant of dreams.

In truth, as horrible a thing as it was, I wished those moments lasted longer for him. And I wished those had been among his last.

One of the worst things about white-joy is that it is easy to make, yet extremely unstable. In that, any fool with time and eagerness can distill a batch, and it will do the job. But it runs the risks of subjecting the user to horrible side effects, and they can come as quick as the pleasure. Not all who take the drug live to fall to the addiction.

Taki taught us that.

The next day he lost most of his color and spoke of wild things. He talked of Brahm and his kingdom in the sky. He muttered words about doors that opened at false midnight. He spoke of walking the fire and of a place for all sparrows to go when we were done here. He told me of walls of stillness and breaking them. And of a place before the doors of death. Then Taki stopped speaking altogether.

He spent the night mute as a dead man. He watched us, though, with the lazy recognition of someone too tired to hope for full wakefulness, but too far gone to manage any further effort.

We let him hang there somewhere in between heavy sleep and barely awake. The sparrows had no further ideas of what to do but hope for our brother. A few offered prayers, among those who ascribed to the gods and Brahm above, and Nika and I resigned ourselves to offering him our company.

Everything halted within the house of sparrows. No begging. No clutching. We subsisted off the trove of coins Mithu left in his office, never breaking our meager and pauper's lifestyle for fear the coin would vanish as quickly as our adoptive father had.

In the end, nothing proved to be enough to keep Taki with us.

He went that night. He screamed. He thrashed. My face burned as his hands raked my cheeks in a manic fit. A bruise as large as a fist soon blossomed along Nika's thigh from where Taki's foot slammed into it.

She stumbled.

I threw myself onto Taki, using my weight to try to hold him in place.

I wished instead I'd used that time to wrap him tight in a hug. To tell him that his brother loved him. That it would be okay.

Instead, the thrashing stopped and Taki's eyes turned to glass. Spittle lined his lips as did foam.

He didn't have nightmares anymore.

And he didn't dream.

THIRTY-SEVEN

Resolutions

The days after were marked with a hollow quietness that infected every sparrow. Most of us didn't leave our rooms but to use the chamber pots on the first floor. Beyond that, Small Kaya came round with the same sullen silence to give us meals.

Nearly a set passed before my anger and bitterness finally took me in a grip of iron and hot stone.

I screamed, uncaring if the other sparrows heard me. Not giving one damn if the world outside listened to my cries.

The year had given me much to be angry about. Life had taken its due for everything I'd asked and wanted, for all the dreams. But I decided then that maybe I could pay it back in kind. I'd take things into my own hands.

I rounded up the sparrows the next day in our common room. Everyone met me with bleary eyes and wan complexions. Too much had changed in a short time, and that always leaves people out of sorts, no matter what they say.

Having your world tipped one way, then another, will take a toll. Anyone who tells you otherwise is lying. And I'll be the first to tell you it's okay. Things right themselves . . . eventually. Usually with some effort. Sometimes with a lot.

And I saw fit to make that happen now.

"Everyone knows what happened with Mithu, Askar, and Biloo." I wasn't asking a question, and the sparrows nodded or muttered a low agreement. "Everyone knows about Koli?"

Another nod. More grumbling.

"And the white-joy? Nika told everyone of Mithu buying and selling secrets?"

More agreement.

"Good. Because soon enough, that will be our new trade."

The sparrows exchanged looks with everyone in direct eyeshot. A few broke into confused muttering, not voicing their concerns at me.

I didn't let them sit muddled or question what I'd said. "We risk our lives every day we go out to listen or clutch. Nika's is at risk every day she dogs for us. No more. There's money in the things people don't want others to know, because there are those who will pay for that knowing. We can give it to them. We will. The same things that go into begging and stealing will come into here. So, we'll learn to listen to those who want to go unheard. And we'll learn to tell those things to those wanting to be told . . . for a price.

"And I'm going to teach you how. But first, we're going to look for one special secret above all others. The most important one we can come to know."

One of the sparrows, Dilu, stepped out of the ring, turning to his brothers and sisters for silent support before he turned his attention back to me. "What secret is that, Ari? How are we going to do everything you want and still make money?"

I'd expected the question, and I'd given it a day's worth of thought. "We're still going to speak and clutch, and at the end of every shift, I'll be teaching everyone how to read and write. I'll teach you how to spot easy writings out on the streets to practice on."

A few sparrows bristled at this, but Nika fixed them with a look that quickly quelled any issue they might have had with my declaration.

"As for the secret . . ." I let the words hang in the air, letting the discomfort and curiosity build in my family. "We're going to find Koli's joy house. Where he makes his drugs. We're going to find out everything about it."

Dilu cleared his throat, rubbing the tip of a foot against the ground as if he was uneasy. "And then what?"

All the anger of the year filled my voice when I stared at him and the rest of the sparrows. "We burn it. We burn it all."

THIRTY-EIGHT

A Return of Fire

It took two sets to learn what I wanted. That time had been spent running classes out of Mithu's office early in the mornings before the first shift of sparrows went out to clutch and beg. Sometimes I'd go with them, trying to help bring in more coin. Afternoons led to another session of teaching my family the fundamentals of letters and how to read and write with them.

Some of my brothers and sisters were remarkably quick-witted about it.

Others made me wonder if they had boiled eggplants between their ears instead of brains.

In addition to our usual duties, we now kept keener ears out for the goings-on within Keshum's streets. Nika hounded roads not only to dog and protect our family, but to stalk anyone we thought could have a connection to Koli.

And we were rewarded for it.

"His joy house is outside the Hard Quarter, just inside the beginning of the Soft Quarter." Nika chewed her lip and gave me a sideways look. "The bad part of the Soft Quarter."

Juggi eyed me as well, saying all he could about what a bad idea this was, and all without uttering a word.

I exhaled. "I know. The part where children like us go missing. The part where those same kids turn back up, strung on joy and clutching to the arms and legs of strange men and women who have the coin for us. I know."

"Or the places where kids like us are taken for labor. For making the joy. Or, I've heard some are strung up and bled for blood. It sells, you know?" Juggi shrugged as if reciting nothing more than commonplace talk.

I glowered at him. "You're not helping."

He cocked a brow. "I don't think there's a way to help with this besides not doing it. It's stupid, Ari. It's dangerous. You poke Koli, he'll poke us back. He can take everything from us if he really wants."

My voice never rose past a whisper in the wind. I'm certain neither Juggi nor Nika heard me. "He's already taken everything from me."

The doors to Mithu's office opened and two sparrows brought forth a small wooden crate filled with bottles. "Got some more, Ari." The pair lowered the crate and left just as fast.

Nika stared at the bottles, then me. "Why are we hoarding so much of that stuff? It stinks, even in the bottles."

"Remember what I told you about my life in the theater?"

She waggled a hand. "Not all of it. And not what it has to do with cheap liquor."

"Extremely *flammable* cheap liquor. We used it in our plays for fire theatrics. It doesn't burn as well and clean as oil, but it's not as expensive either. And, it mixes horribly well with *juur*."

Juur was a pulp-like by-product of making certain fabrics. It fell somewhere between strands of cotton and sawdust. When added to tiraq, a low-cost and foul alcohol, it thickened the drink into something like a sap. It would burn long and hot, sticking to any surface until it ran out.

"How many of his runners have you handled?" I leaned back in Mithu's chair, steepling my fingers.

"Three. At least three that I've pummeled and stripped of clothing." Her throat tightened and lips pressed together like she fought to hold back a burp. "I never want to see another naked boy again in my life."

Juggi raised both brows, then shot me a look before turning away altogether.

I ignored the expression and what she'd said. "It'll do. The clothes will be enough to get me and two others close enough to start. The house is lit until eighth candle, yes? On or after *kundhul* hour?"

She nodded.

"That's enough time for everyone to get out and only his runners and makers to stay behind."

"And then what?" asked Juggi. "You can't burn stone."

I smiled, fetching the lone remaining vial inside Mithu's desk.

Nika and Juggi stared at the little glass cylinder, then me. "Don't." They spoke in unison.

I waved them off as I handled the last of the white-joy. "Follow me." I led them over to the fireplace burning in one corner of the office. "Do you know what happens when this touches real flame? Not something hot, but fire itself?"

Both of them shook their heads.

Another secret I'd learned and hoped to profit from. At least in the form of ruining Koli. I tossed the vial into the fire.

A miniature thunderclap rang out, echoing through the stone walls of the building. Glass shattered and scattered over the floor.

"It bursts." I threw my arms up and wide, mimicking a flower unfurling. "Like black powder in stories and festivals, only without the pretty colors and gently controlled chaos. It's wild. Dangerous. And enough of it could break stone."

Juggi looked at the spot where the vial had blown apart. "Sometimes you scare me. You know that?"

Good. Let's hope I can do the same to Koli.

The candles burned low and *kundhul* hour had passed. Nika, Juggi, and I had spent most of the day hauling every bottle of tiraq we could into the part of the Soft Quarter where Koli's joy house sat. We'd watched the customers come and go and learned which of his child runners filled the building and worked their shifts.

The three of us made sure to never lock eyes with his kids lest they recognize us. We'd taken pains to dirty our faces and trim our hair to match their appearance as best we could. All in all, my years watching my family perform gave me the edge to walk and talk nearly as well as one of Koli's own.

His joy house shared a roof with another building, a long-since-closed tannery. We made our way through a place in the wall that had fallen apart to time, weather, and neglect, taking care to funnel all of the bottles with us. The next hour consisted of us doing nothing but shuffling every bit of tiraq in our possession onto the roof of Koli's house.

"Do we spill any here?" Juggi pulled a black scarf up over his mouth to obscure most of his face.

"No, not yet." I followed his lead and covered my face as well. "I want you and Nika to be able to get out over the roof. It might be too hard to go out the front. We still don't know what's inside and who."

"Another reason we *shouldn't* be doing this, Ari." Nika shrouded her face completely, staring at me through nothing more than a slit just wider than a finger.

"We have to." I left it at that, knowing in truth she was right. "If we don't, there'll be another Taki. Maybe one of ours, maybe someone else's. We can't let that happen. If we can stop Koli from spreading white-joy, we can make our lives on the streets easier too. No more worrying about cotton-eyes who might be willing to do more than just beg for coins."

Nika eyed me, weighing me with that stare. She knew my reasons went well beyond what I'd said. But if it bothered her, she didn't voice it.

I went to the rooftop door, pushing against it and hoping it hadn't been locked.

It opened and granted me a way down a narrow length of stairs.

I waited in place, watching in case anyone below had heard my entrance. No one came. I waved Nika and Juggi over, taking a few bottles of our concoctions from them.

We'd poured juur into every bottle of tiraq, stoppering them with only strips of rags and old cloth we knew would burn well. The new syrup-like liquid would catch flame easily and keep alight well through the night if we spilled enough of the substance.

I made my way down the stairs, cradling four bottles against my chest with all the care I could muster.

Orange light, faint and flickering, cast itself against the wall from a room to our left.

I looked over my shoulder and shushed my brother and sister. My heart leapt as I inched my way toward the door, peering into the space ahead.

A few of Koli's young runners tallied coins and stocked wooden shelves with countless glass vials.

Vials of a milky white substance.

Of joy.

I watched for a minute in silence, squinting in the low light to make out as many of the other children as I could.

Not one bore the slightest resemblance to Nisha.

It had been but a small hope to want for her to be here, but I'd kept to that desire regardless.

A gentle tap on my shoulder pulled me away from my watching. I looked back to Nika, arching a brow to ask her what she wanted.

She leaned close and brought her mouth to my ear. "We can't do this with them in there. We have to get them out."

I opened my mouth to protest, then thought better of it. It had seemed so easy to consider burning the building down with every one of Koli's ilk inside it. But now that we were here, all I saw were tired children working the only life they'd come to know.

The only one many of them were ever likely given a chance in.

No matter what Koli did, his runners didn't deserve to burn for his sins. Even Gabi and Thipu deserved a better fate.

. . . Somewhat.

"What do we do, then?" I looked to her, then Juggi for advice.

Nika shook her head without answer.

But my adoptive brother had one at the ready. "We need to get them out of there without making too much noise. That could let Koli know we're here." Juggi stopped short, looking around as if he expected Koli to appear at the call of his name. Content that all was still well, he went on. "We could get them to leave the room. When they do, jump them, quick and quiet. No noise."

I peered back into the room and counted four children. Taking on that many, though we nearly matched them in number, wouldn't be easy. Especially considering we'd have to adhere to silence, or as much as we could manage.

I sighed, knowing Juggi to be right. "Fine. Put the bottles down, we can't risk them breaking here. And . . . be careful."

Juggi adopted a stoic mask that I guessed was an attempt at playing off his fear. With a sigh, he moved into the doorway, letting out a low whistle just loud enough to carry inside.

Silence.

Then he waved a hand to those inside the room, motioning them toward him. Juggi moved toward us wordlessly, looking over his shoulders as if worried we'd left him alone.

Footsteps.

They sounded against the stone floor, growing louder by the second.

Two of Koli's runners exited the room and turned right after Juggi, not realizing we had been standing there until they'd come by us.

We lunged.

Nika moved with all the fluidity of water, hammering the boy's throat, then his head. Dazed, he fell.

I couldn't manage that level of finesse nor the savagery needed. My hands went out and seized the boy by his collar. My arms and back ached as I used all of my weight to haul him into the near wall. He crashed hard, but before I could finish the job, Nika threw herself against the boy's back.

She snaked her arms around his neck, holding him until he went limp. Nika let out a soft and measured breath as her chest heaved. "He's fine. Asleep. He'll wake soon, though. They all will."

I nodded, taking that in stock as both good and bad. It meant they'd be able to flee this place once we'd set it ablaze, but they could rouse in time to make matters worse for us.

Unless I came up with something clever.

I raced into the room, bottles in hand. "Help!" I kept my voice to a hard and harsh whisper that I knew wouldn't carry past the walls.

The remaining two runners froze, turning to look at me. They said nothing.

I motioned toward the doorway. "They fainted. I don't know what happened. They just fell. Come on." I made my way back to the door, breaking into a light run to inflate the sense of emergency.

Panic has an odd way of stealing people's senses. The immediacy of the moment, the fear, the adrenaline form a mixture that can rob the most cunning person of all their guile. We become nothing more than animals frantically running to save ourselves from danger. Or we run right into it.

The two runners ran with me, passing me by as I nearly reached the door.

Fleshy impacts sounded from outside as I knew Juggi and Nika dealt with the pair.

My brother and sister came into the room a moment later, carrying the bottles we'd left in the hall. We fell into the cold and measured motions of taking the rags out of the tiraq and layering them as tinder in the center of the room. From there, we poured as much of the liquor as we could.

Content the room would go up should we light a fire, we raced our way back to the roof to retrieve more of the tiraq.

None of the boys had woken from their beating, bringing me a measure of relief I sorely needed. Though, it did nothing to quell my increasing heartbeat.

We wandered to another room on the same floor and found it empty of bodies. The dying candle inside the chamber forced me to move slower than I would have liked as I tried to make sense of the place and what it held.

Rows of narrow tables, all with no place to sit, ran through the center of the room. Spread across them were wood and tin bowls and cups. A murky fluid sat inside them. It looked like the foam of a rabid dog, tinged a sickly yellow.

Unrefined white-joy.

That explained the waning candle and the empty room in such late hours.

Koli likely commanded people to stop working so late into the night. Tired minds and bodies did poorly when handling a delicate process such as this. Add in the fact they required good light, a light likely coming from an open flame, any accident where a candle fell could be catastrophic.

I tipped over every bowl and cup in sight, splashing their contents wide across the room. We'd splattered most of the room in the unrefined drug and went as far as to layer the ground in thick sappy tiraq.

"This'll burn nicely." Juggi smacked the bottom of a bottle, working to get out the last remaining drops. "We still have two more floors and I don't think we have enough tiraq left."

I bit my tongue, chewing over what Juggi had said. I knew him to be right. "Bring me the last bottles and get out. Make sure those four get out too." I hooked a thumb toward the hall where the unconscious runners rested.

Juggi opened his mouth but I waved him off.

"Just do it. Get them out."

Nika rushed over and grabbed Juggi by the arm, silently urging him to follow my orders. The pair ran out of sight.

I steeled myself with a series of breaths and reached into my pockets. Something thin and brittle rubbed against my thumb. I pulled it free, looking at the little sliver of wood and the bulbous black head atop it.

A powder match.

The material came from Laxina. In small quantities, a bit of friction could set it off and kindle a small flame no larger than a man's thumbnail. It'd burn hot and clear for a minute before winking out of existence. The powder had been mixed with something to temper its explosive nature and keep it safe for single use.

The sparrows had managed to clutch a trio of these matches over the weeks we'd worked to find out where Koli housed the white-joy before moving it out across the streets of Keshum.

I held the match in one hand as I upended the last bottle of tiraq in sight between the two rooms we'd already covered, creating a path of volatile syrup. Starting in the room with joy would give us no time to escape, and I couldn't risk harming my family.

I returned to the room we'd started in and flicked the head of the match against the stone wall, ready to introduce Koli to what he'd done to me that night.

Nothing.

I tried again, nearly snapping the fragile wood. "No, no, no."

An explosion overhead nearly pulled my heart from my chest as I feared something had gone wrong.

Had a fire already broken out? Did some of the tiraq catch flame somehow?

Another crack followed by a steady tapping I knew all too well.

Rain.

A storm had broken out.

I exhaled, cursing the poor luck that brought the weather about it, but I knew it wouldn't do a damn thing to save Koli's joy and home from the worst of what I had planned.

I struck the match again.

It hissed—snapped. Orange light flickered freely—faintly. It winked as if unable to stay alight. Then it burst into a bright bulb, holding itself steady and hot.

I smiled and tossed the match.

It struck a puddle of tiraq in the room of coins and bottled joy, spreading fast and kicking up tendrils of fire.

I turned on a heel and raced from the room as Juggi came back down the stairs. "Two bottles left." He shoved them toward me before eyeing the room I'd left.

"We can't outrun that, Ari. Leave with us." He reached out to grab my shirt but I brushed him away.

"You go. Go now!" I pushed him.

Juggi sputtered and Nika stepped out from behind him, grabbing him and hauling him away.

Thank you, Nika.

Fire screamed and raced into the hall, cutting us off had I wanted to run back over to my sister and leave with her.

Please be okay.

I ran forward to the stairs leading down. I'd made it to the bottom when a new blast of thunder roared above. The building shook and it sounded like stone had crumbled under a mighty drumming.

Brick and tile fell from the ceiling of one room to my side as I ran by. The chamber above had fallen apart as the fire had reached all the white-joy it held.

"Fire!" I let my voice carry as loud as it could, knowing it too late to do anything about the flames and my presence there. "Fire!"

Voices picked up after me, echoing the cry. I paid no attention to them however and kept running.

"Nisha! Nisha!"

No answer.

The second floor passed by without revealing anything useful or anything that has stayed with me to this day.

I reached the first floor and paused.

In many ways it had been fashioned to be near a perfect replica of the room Mithu had first brought me to in his home. Had it been intentional? Was this part of how Koli and Mithu indoctrinated children into their gangs?

Did it promote a sense of ease in kids sold off by Mithu to Koli when they finally came here? Remind them of home?

The thoughts brought something ugly and twisted to life inside me and I hurled one of the bottles at the wall. Another soon hit the carpet ahead of me.

Perfect tinder if there ever was any.

I brought out the second match, kneeling to strike it against an uncovered portion of the stone floor.

"Tsk tsk." The voice froze me to the spot.

I couldn't bring myself to drag the head of the match and summon the fire I needed.

"If I had known you'd grow to be this much trouble in less than a year, I'd have made more of an effort to kill you that night, little theater rat."

I knew that voice. I glanced up and found myself staring at Koli.

He stood on the carpet I'd tossed the bottle of tiraq onto.

Words escaped me, and any thought of vengeance left with them. The hand holding the match trembled.

"What's this?" He looked everywhere but at me, motioning to the walls of his building with both hands. "Smoke. Fire. My joy burning and stone crumbling. It almost reminds me of another fire not too long ago." He put an index finger against his lips and adopted mocking thoughtfulness. "Where could that have been?"

He clicked his tongue and widened his eyes as if realization struck him. "Ah! *Khalim*'s theater."

The sound of him speaking that name pulled the cold from me. Heat leached back into my bones and heart. My teeth ground against each other and I finally found enough strength to strike the match.

Hate has a funny nature about the many shapes it takes. Up until this point mine had been a cold and calculated passion of revenge. The act of setting fire to Koli's joy house was nothing more than payback in calculated measure for what he'd done to me earlier in the year. It was a sparrow's gambit and desire.

I wanted to take away his money and means, even if only by a small amount.

But seeing the man before me changed the rhythm of my hatred from steady strings to the discordant cries of a mandolin badly out of tune.

Hatred all too quickly shifts its shape from the recognizable to angry nameless things that take us in its grip. And it seized me whole, promising to build to something I'd lose control over.

"Don't say his name." My voice couldn't have been heard over the sounds of crumbling stone and thunder above.

"Ah?" Koli tilted his head, cupping a hand to his ear. "Khalim? You don't want me to say Khalim?"

"Stop it!" I raised the match for him to see.

"Oh-ho. And with that you'll finish burning my home, huh? Is that it?" His eyes took on an odd light. The same sort they'd carried the night he'd killed my family and took everything from me.

"Yes." I couldn't tell what shook more in that moment, my hand or my voice.

Koli spread his arms wide as if inviting me to do that very thing. "Try it and see what happens. You were there, boy, and you heard what I told the old binder. You know what I am. And you know I can't die. Only you and I know this little secret." He pursed his lips as if falling back into deep thought.

"I wonder what will happen if I let you go again. Will you try to find me after tonight? Try to burn another precious prize of mine? I wonder. I wonder." Koli tapped his temple with two fingers before breaking into a wide and wolfish grin. The lupine light in his eyes intensified, half mischief, half hunger.

"I'll find you wherever you go. However long it takes." My voice rose to drown out the sounds of the storm. "I'll chase you forever! I hate you. I'll find a way to kill you."

Koli threw back his head and laughed.

I tossed the match.

The carpet burst into flames and Koli stopped laughing.

I turned and ran toward the front doors, throwing my weight against them. They crashed open and I stumbled. Dull pain smashed into me as I tumbled down the short set of stairs leading to the ground.

"You won't find the girl, either, Ari. She's gone. Gone from where even I can see her! I sent little Nisha off long ago! See if you can find her." Koli's voice came as clear as if he stood right beside me and not in the center of a burning building.

Smoke billowed from some of the windows only to be dispersed by the rain. Firelight danced through the rooms and cast violent shadows along the walls from where I could see.

The storm would save parts of Koli's building, but we'd destroyed the stores of joy he'd had on hand. Even if he had more, even if he had a dozen more buildings, I'd paid him back in kind.

He knew I'd find a way to make good on my word and, one day, kill him for good.

That was enough for tonight.

I scrambled off my back and ignored my throbbing body. Running wasn't an option, so I limped into a weak jog, making my way far into the safety of the nearest alley.

Two questions hung in my mind as I wound my way back toward my home.

Was he truly unkillable?

And why had he let me live then . . . and now?

THIRTY-NINE

An Empty Nest

I reunited that night with Juggi and Nika inside the first floor of our home, embracing them in tight and wet hugs. The two had paled a shade under the rain while running back.

Small Kaya had stoked a fire to life in anticipation of our return and brought us bone stew and freshly warm bread. To our surprise, we found the meal flavored with more spices than the norm as well as tender strips of red meat.

I eyed her.

"It was going to be a long night. A cold night. We had the coin, and there is only enough for the three of you." She said it as if it were explanation enough. It wasn't, but that was her way. It was how she showed she cared. Small Kaya left as quietly as she came, making it clear that had been the end of any hospitality we could expect that night.

We ate in silence, sharing the warmth of our meal and fire together. And once we'd finished, we sat silent still, listening to the cacophony of rain and thunder above as much as the crackling of the flame.

"What happened?" Nika didn't look at me as she broke the quiet. "We made it to the roof and over to the next building when everything shook. And the storm came out of nowhere. What happened, Ari?"

I told them. I spoke of setting the building alight and then rushing through it in hopes of finding Nisha—one last effort to see my friend. Then I reached the part of the story where I'd encountered Koli.

Juggi and Nika watched me with perfect stillness, hanging on every word.

I told them how Koli came to the room almost as if summoned by magic, leaving out what I knew of his true identity. One of the Ashura. One of those demons and storybook nightmares meant to terrify children and the superstitious. One of those relics from old fables in which the hero fights fearsome monsters and triumphs. That's what he was, something to be conquered by the noble and the bright.

At least in the stories.

In reality, I began to suspect Koli fared better than any hero sent to kill his kind in the tales told over time.

"Then what?" Juggi leaned closer to me, wrapping his arms around himself to shake off the last of his chill.

"He mocked me. Made light of killing my family, so I felt it fair to make light of him in kind. I struck the match and threw it at the rug."

Nika let out a low whistle but said nothing else.

"So, you did it? You killed him, I mean?" Juggi inched even closer.

I shook my head. "No. I saw the carpet go up in fire, but Koli just laughed. I ran before seeing what happened next, afraid of being caught in the fire and what Koli might try to do."

Only the crackling fire and the waning storm offered any sounds for a moment.

Nika licked her lips and moved closer toward the warmth of the hearth. "Do you think he's coming for us—for you?"

I shook my head again. "No. If he wanted to, he could have done me in there. I don't know why he didn't. I don't think he'll come for us, but I don't like the idea of sitting around to find out. I say we sleep and lock the doors tonight. Tomorrow, we send some sparrows to check out his joy house and see what's left." I hadn't phrased it as a question, but I hoped Juggi and Nika would weigh in.

"I don't know if I'll feel comfortable until I see it with my own eyes. I might want to go look myself tomorrow," said Nika.

Juggi nodded in agreement.

"I feel the same." I had to see the joy house myself before I believed anything another sparrow told me.

We settled the matter and gave each other one last hug in equal parts of relief and reassurance that we would get through this.

Then, I headed up to my room for a much-needed sleep.

Nika and I pulled aside six sparrows the next morning, making it clear that they were to take breaks between their shifts through the day and stop by Koli's joy house, remaining far enough away to be able to flee if need arise. They were to report back over the day and confirm, over and over, the state of the building.

"What do you think they'll find?" Nika tore a piece of thori and wolfed it down, chewing it open-mouthed.

I shrugged. "I'm not sure, but I know a part of me hopes they tell us the whole place has burned down to dust and dirt. It can't happen, but I'd feel better knowing there's nothing left of Koli and his joy house."

A full candle change later we'd been informed the building had in fact been reduced to nothing.

Nika and I traded a look and asked the sparrow to repeat herself.

"Nothing, Ari-*sahm*."

I waved her off. "Don't call me that, just say it one last time. Describe it *clearly*."

She rubbed the back of a shirtsleeve against her nose. "Nothing there. Not one stone on the ground. It's like it was all burned and then swept away." My little sister, Ishi, pulled out a folded piece of cloth from one of her pockets. "But I plucked eight chips today." She beamed.

I tried to match her enthusiasm in earnest and fell short, but Ishi couldn't tell. "That's great." I clapped her reassuringly on the shoulder and guided her over to Juggi to tally sums.

Once she'd moved out of sight, I gave Nika a knowing look. "You heard her, but do you believe her?"

She frowned. "I want to see it."

I inclined my head. "Same. Let's go."

We made our way into the Soft Quarter where Koli's joy house had been last night. Only now, nothing remained.

True to Ishi's words, it was like the building had been swept away like dust in wind. Not a single charred or broken stone remained. It had been completely severed from the building beside it like it never existed. No bits of bottle glass from the previous night. No tinge and stains of smoke.

No sign of Koli and his runners.

Nothing.

"I don't understand," said Nika.

"Neither do I." We stood there together, staring at a place so perfectly empty it could only have been the result of intentional effort.

But how? How could one person wipe away an entire building and all trace of it?

Something struck me as I thought it over.

"Nika, how many of his runners did the sparrows run into today? How many did we see?"

She blinked several times as if not registering the question. "What?"

I repeated myself.

Nika held her look on the building before finally speaking. "None. Not a single mention today."

I heard what she'd said but it didn't sink in. Every word might as well have been as far from me and my mind as the clouds above. I walked, almost as if led by puppet strings, toward the spot the building had taken up last night.

The space itself put my hairs on end and sent bumps across my arms. I knelt to run a hand along the ground.

Empty dirt with no promise of anything else now and before. A ground that had never been anything but itself. I scooped up some of soil, watching it slip between my fingers.

"What are you doing there? Oi!" The voice tore me from my wondering.

I shuffled to regard the speaker.

A man, somewhere in his middle years, stared at me. He had dressed for the day's heat in loose and light robes, all without a hint of color but tired white that had long since lost its luster. His was wrapped in a simple length of cloth the same color with a tail of the fabric hanging openly over a shoulder.

"What happened to the building here? What of the man behind it, Koli? Where is he now?" I had spoken without thinking. The words had come to me from a part of my mind that still held to the questions no matter how dazed I'd become.

The man glanced at the spot where the building had been, then me. "The building's gone. Heard there was a fire. They do that, fires, get rid of things." He fixed me with a look that said I should have known as much, and that I may very well have been one of the dimmest boys he ever had the ill fortune to meet. "And I never heard of any Koli." He waved a hand through the air as if dismissing the name altogether.

"*Everyone* knows of Koli. Haven't you ever seen a cotton-eyes before? Who do you think gives them the drug?"

The man rolled his eyes and moved by, making it clear the conversation had ended. He'd made it a dozen paces past me before turning to address me. "If there ever was anyone in that run-down place, he'd have had the sense to leave Keshum and Abhar when his fortunes and life burned. Maybe he went far to the south. It's easier for a man to get by. This"—he jabbed a finger toward the ground—"is a city and kingdom for those with wits about them. And if he had two bits of wit to rub together, he'd be gone. That's all that there is to it." The man left with that.

That's when I got my first lesson in the terrible truth of truths themselves. Some people simply do not wish to hear and see anything beyond the simple stories spun up for their ease of answers. What people truly want is the safety of familiarity. They want the knowing that the shape of the world around them hasn't changed beyond what it has been.

People need this, you see.

Because nothing terrifies people as much as change, be the shifts subtle or great. And so, what did it matter if Koli's house of joy burned and the man himself vanished?

It was good enough that he was gone and his drugs with him.

For people not addicted to his wares or pressed into the bodily trades under his thumb, life went on as it did yesterday. And, well, for the sparrows, it meant a newfound freedom with which we could grow even further.

Maybe the man had it right?

I found myself wondering over that as Nika led me home.

A world without Koli.

What could it mean for us? For me?

I intended to find out.

So marked what would be the next year of my life in Keshum, free from thoughts and fears of the Ashura, of revenge, and the loss of things. Now was the time for me to take. For my hungry sparrow's hunger to slake.

FORTY
IDLE HANDS

Over a year had passed since Koli's disappearance from Keshum, and by the rumors, Abhar overall. A year of unbothered sparrows collecting coin and secrets, peddling the latter back to those with heavy purses willing to part with pieces of their wealth. And in all the hidden knowings, not one carried half a hint of Koli's location. Not one shred spoke of strange happenings like the night my family and home first burned.

No mention of demons. No whispers of Ashura. And not a word of Nisha, though I tried to find her. Believe me.

I did.

I spent what I could, traded what whispers I heard for any of my old friend, and was met with a silence reserved for the dead.

It was as if Koli had been nothing more than a nightmare, and now he'd gone as quickly as he'd come. And Nisha had grown to be nothing but a dream gone upon waking.

The pair had vanished so cleanly it could leave a man wondering what had ever been real.

But Koli's absence ate at me more than the year he had been running his share of Keshum's streets. At least during that time, I knew he was out there, and if I had the whim and means, I could find him.

Now without that and the clarity of anger that came with it, I'd fallen into hollow complacency.

The sparrows hardly needed my help now to run things. Chicken-scratched letters filled my desk, once Mithu's, telling me of all the things to be told within Keshum. Traders doing what they did best—not tallying sums and selling spices, but faithfully being unfaithful to their wives and children. Some had families it seemed in other kingdoms, other countries. How they managed to feed them all remained outside my understanding.

Rumors reached me of the second son of the king of Thamar. The young man, almost in his nineteenth year of life, had been said to have climbed into the trade of drugs harder than white-joy. Something subtle and secret by way of the west routes through the desert kingdoms along that way. His father, rather than make a public spectacle of the boy's punishment, sent him off to the fabled Ashram instead.

The idea of that pulled at a memory buried deep inside of me. An old promise and excitement over going there myself. A man—Mahrab—telling me of the wonders to be found there. The path to living a story of my own in the vein of Brahm himself.

Bindings. Magic. Forgotten things. Adventure and knowledge. All the things a curious young boy with the time and space for dreams could wish for.

But it had grown to be a distant dream in the face of reality and responsibility. Even if the sparrows didn't need me to manage the micro happenings of the day, they still looked to me to play a role somewhat like Mithu's.

I sighed and pushed myself up from the desk, going to the side wall where the windows sat. Two pegs of black iron had been worked into the space between a pair of the arches. On it sat a curved sword of no particular remarkability. Simple. Serviceable. And the kind of thing bought for pieces of copper—no precious coin needed, maybe a lot of tin if it came handily used or you were lucky.

The sword I'd picked up the day Mithu and his thugs had died.

My days had taken to blurring, one into the next, all without a fuel to fan my fire and keep me fixated on a goal.

What to do without Koli and Mithu?

I plucked the sword from its resting place, peering out one of the windows as I did.

The streets were countless pinwheels set spinning under the wind. Every color of the rainbow, and then dozens more you would be hard-pressed to find names for, mixed and streamed through the streets.

Today was a busy day. A bright day. People were high in spirits. Money flowed, spent and earned. And a festival hung above the streets and in the hearts of those on it.

I pulled myself away from the view, nursing a small ache to be out there with my sparrows, doing the simple things of clutching and overhearing those too talkative to know any better.

My feet moved almost of their own accord, taking me back to the rooftop where my life as a sparrow had changed. The sun still cast a pale glow from behind scant cloud cover, lighting up most of Keshum with gentle ease.

But the true and better brightness of the day came from countless shapes flitting through the sky. Serpents on strings, some simple things tailored to be basic shapes, and some such cloth cut to be strung to wooden frames to create dancing boxes.

Kites of all colors shifted and danced from nearly every flat rooftop of Keshum. They wove somewhere between the deft control of skilled hands and the mercy of the wind today. A look around showed me children to young men all partaking.

Many had their hands wrapped in bandages to spare their tender flesh what was to come.

Sharpened strings, glass-lined, ready to cut each other as much as they could the flyer of the kites.

Twist, pull.

A kite reined in short, careening toward another. Their strings met and the flyer let his grip loosen. His kite rose higher, rubbing the tethers together. They slowed. Gnawed and biting at one another, almost like two sparring swords that struck and stuck, each hoping to saw through the other's blade rather than pull away to begin the fight anew.

Twist, turn, and pull. Loosen. The black box kite wobbled as if threatening to break free first, but in the end, it held firm. The flat red diamond shuddered and sank, losing whatever wind held it high aloft.

Victory. The black kite cut through, sending the other drifting low, then far above as it caught the wind and had no line to hold it to the city skies. It sailed above and out of sight.

A whooping cheer came from a distant building, followed by a string of loud and creative profanity suggesting to the other man all manner of physically impossible things to do with his head and spine and where to put the pair of them.

I smiled, but it felt as hollow as most things did to me these days. The sword grew heavier in my palm and I stepped into the first sequence Vithum had ever shown me. Soon, I stripped out of my shirt as sweat and heat prickled my skin. The motions loosened my body and pulled my mind from the drudgery it'd been stuck in.

Faster still. I let myself become fluid, stepping with greater ease and grace. Vithum's exercises had grown to a new nature in me over the last year. Though I never had cause to use them, they were all I could think to do with what free time I now had in plenty.

More strings danced overhead and across my vision.

They were nothing but hair-thin blades to me.

I stepped with them, then across, bringing the curved sword through them as if cutting them free from the hand-held bondage of their flyers. Step. Cut. Pull. Thrust.

I moved until my calves ached and a heat hotter than Keshum's afternoon burned in my shoulders. My breath came dry and strained.

"Ari! Ari!"

I faltered, finally registering the fatigue I'd buried during my training. It swept through me and brought me to my knees. Sweat fell freely onto the roof and turned its sandy face dark in places. "What?" I turned my head to look at the sparrow who'd come.

The boy hadn't reached his twelfth summer yet, but he'd sprouted like a stalk of long squash, standing nearly six feet tall already. All lean and lanky without the unhealthy lack of weight to him. He wore a pair of white pants, loose around the thigh and knee, and an open vest that showed some of his chest and torso. His face had grown thicker and lightly squared in places, and in a few years, I daresay some girls would find him handsome.

"What, Kaesha?"

My brother shifted from foot to foot. His chest heaved and I could see him struggling to catch his breath. Though, the journey back home from the streets shouldn't have taxed him much, even if he'd been running.

I arched a brow and waited.

"Sorry, sorry. I have news." He reached into a pocket and pulled out a folded rag scrap. "Here." Kaesha pushed it toward me.

I plucked it from him and turned it over. Untidy and uneven script ran across it, following a tilted margin I guessed only Kaesha could make out, because I surely couldn't. Dark charcoal was smeared in places against the rag, maybe from the wetness I attributed to sweat, or the fact the fabric still held to traces of oil in places. "I can barely make this scratch out, Kaesha. And . . ." I trailed off as I squinted at a line that seemed out of place between the scrawls. "This bit sounds like it was copied from a story or another conversation. What am I looking at?" I waved the piece of cloth at him.

"Travelers!" He spoke the word as if I should have known at first sound what he'd meant by it.

I didn't.

I fixed him with a stare that told him so and hoped the run and excitement didn't shake loose his wits. Growth of height didn't mean growth of the mind, and I sorely wondered if he'd run out of space for that after learning how to read and write.

"I heard, down by the Hard Quarter's gold circle, you know the place with all the fancy and rich traders and buyers—"

I waved him on to get to the point.

"Right. There's a caravan coming by the end of the set. Merchants, rich ones, from way out past Zibrath. 'Desert kings' I heard someone say. They're supposed to be rich, Ari. Richer than anything and anyone we've seen or heard of short of the kings and emperor here. I heard someone say they were the ones who had the second heart of all wealth along the Golden Road. And I know where they'll be staying and keeping what they bring. Someone sold me the info for a copy of low secrets!"

My eyes widened and the corners of my mouth pulled up into a true smile. The sword fell from my grip, clattering hard against the stone as I broke into laughter. It came from deep within me, honest and rolling. "You're kidding?"

He shook his head. "Brahm is my witness and judge. May I walk the fire if I lie, Ari." He bent and brushed a hand over the soles of his feet before pressing it to his heart.

"You want me to run a grab-and-flight . . . on merchant kings?" I exhaled and rubbed the back of my head. "There are easier ways to die."

Kaesha didn't budge on the point. "We can do it. We've done small ones already. It's like when you taught us to read and write and listen. Now we make more than we ever did with Mithu, and for what?" He gestured to the rag. "We just steal secrets. And sometimes it's better when we keep them for ourselves. Remember the heavy yellow theft?"

I grinned wider. Months earlier we'd gotten word that a trader had settled on a hefty price for a sack of yellow spice we hadn't learned the name of. We'd taken to calling it by the weight it came in and the sum of its value, which came to a heavy total at that. The spice itself grew in difficult places and without much knowing of how it flourished at all. So it couldn't be cultivated. It just occurred. Harvesting it came as no easy task, and all it took was a small pinch to add vibrant color and subtle flavor to any dish.

As such, it nearly held a value close to gold. Among some, at least.

We'd spent half a set watching the building the trader had purchased space in to store his goods. Once we knew who watched the doors, we learned everything about him. It didn't take long to recognize an ambitious man with little to no talent beyond standing still and being menacing.

He longed for safer work and more stable money than a random building thug could make. But city guards' work? To be among the kuthri? That would be something.

And in our year of secrets sold and stolen, we'd learned just as easily that the kuthri could be bought into. Especially if some of those in positions of power had their own dirty little secrets they wished kept quiet.

Such as a serial adulterer with a string of wives all with tempers and quicker hands than any guard could manage.

It had taken a series of payments adding up to sixteen copper rounds or half an iron bunt. To a kuthri, as well taken care of as they were, that came to over slightly more than what one made in a year.

The sad reality of our world is that money and secrets move a great deal of pieces into play, and with them, you can shape your life and the lives of others.

For better or for worse.

And with that, we coaxed the watchman to look the other way as we walked into the building and up to the door barring the way to our prize.

The reputation the sparrows had earned over the year said all locks opened from but a kiss of our lips. Just a whisper and they'd part. Not true, but I never bothered to correct folks.

But no. Money opens doors as well as it does opportunities. A rule of business and trade I'd learned early on was this: Redundancy saves a man a lot of trouble.

What if the merchant with the key to a storage room lost it? What then was he left to do but break down his own door to get his goods? That hardly left him better off than before no matter the cost of housing his goods. He still lost something.

And so, he made sure he had spare sets of keys just in case.

With but a few coins, keys, like positions among the kuthri, can be bought.

We did just that, and with the quiet quickness of alley cats, made our way into the storage room and out, all soundless as shadows in the night.

After that, it became a matter of time.

Some merchants, friends of the one we'd stolen from, put out calls to find the thieves. If that couldn't be done, just salvaging the spice would earn a reward. The temptation did hang over us to try and return it for safer pay. But our own patience had been rewarded and we were able to sell it off ourselves to interested parties for the proper rates.

That one venture increased our wealth by a measure of silver doles that had never been accomplished under Mithu's guidance. And certainly a windfall under my own time of running the sparrows.

I thought Kaesha's idea over. "If we're caught, we'll be badly off." I let out a long low whistle, considering what various punishments could be levied on us if we were discovered. And by that I meant at the hands of officials like the kuthri. The desert merchants themselves were rumored to deal with thieves their own way. Ways that meant one never had to be worried about being found red-handed ever again.

I licked my lips, looked back at the rag, and decided against it. "It's not worth it. We're rich enough already and getting richer still. And the world is barely wise to it and what we can really do. I'd like to keep it that way. We still keep to humble places and appearances. We don't need the attention." I lifted the rag to throw it back to him when the odd script caught my attention again.

I pointed to it. "What is this from? This line about Abrahm and The Turning?"

Kaesha blinked and shied away from my gaze. He said nothing.

I asked him again.

"Don't get mad."

I glowered at him. "I don't get mad."

He eyed me askance and wore a lopsided frown. "You're getting mad right now."

I exhaled and closed my eyes, trying to recover the candle and the flame—the focus and clarity that came with it. But it didn't come. "Just tell me, Kaesha."

"I may have stopped during my route. I clutched good today, though. And I picked up that secret to sell. That's something. Even if we don't do anything with it, we can pass it on to the bahnra. They do that stuff. The robbing and skulking-sneaking and stealing."

A point of pressure built within my brow and it took considerably more patience than I thought I could muster to keep it from blossoming bigger. "Kaesha, *where* did you stop? None of that explains this?" I shook the rag again.

He exhaled. "I stopped at the Zanzikari."

I stared at him, waiting for him to give me more than that.

Kaesha's shoulders sagged and he let out a sigh in unison. "I'd heard there was a stranger come through. A traveler, not a trader."

"And? What's special enough about that to make you stop there?"

"He performs, Ari."

I rolled my eyes and bent to retrieve my sword. Nothing more than idle curiosity prompted me to ask him for more. "What does he perform?" I stepped back into position and cast the sword through a few tumbles still burned into memory.

"Stories."

And all of Vithum's training left me. The sword turned to lead-layered stone in my hands and took a different tumble not taught. It clattered as I stared at Kaesha. "What did you say?"

"Stories, Ari. He tells stories. Things of Brahm the Wanderer. Abrahm, the Binder Knight, though I didn't hear that one. He talks of Athwun, Son of Fire. Of the Farstrider and Singers. He knew of Bori and his journey into the west. And the legends of Kalathem."

All other words fell to the wayside as I took in what this meant.

Stories.

A piece of my life I'd not left behind, but had been torn from me. And now the promise of its return, and with it, the possibility of all else Mahrab had talked of.

It now thrummed in me.

When something, an art in particular, is so a part of your life that it pervades most of your memories, there's something cold and numbing in the loss of it. It's like losing a limb. It's a hollowness, and you're left empty of the space you once held for that thing. Eventually, it becomes easier to bury that spot and fill it with other distractions so as to not remember the feelings of that art.

And in turn, you're spared the pain of losing it.

My time spent as a sparrow had buried that hurt and brought me all manner of new occupying thoughts. But I remembered the art of telling tales. And I remembered the dreams that came with them. They now flowered in me, and so too did all the pain that comes with remembrance.

It took me, and I had little choice else.

I had to go see this storyteller for myself.

FORTY-ONE

Tin for Tales

That day passed in a daze, much like a morning in monsoon season. Nothing but dull gray fog held me, mind and heart. Nika and Juggi took care of tallying the daily sums and sorting secrets worth keeping, trading, and selling. They knew their way around the work and I would only get in the way.

I moved like a babe first learning to walk—no surety in my steps—as I made my way to my old room. The treasure box still sat where it had the day Mithu showed it to me, and in it sat a book that had grown to be more precious than all of the silver and iron I'd come to own as the lord of sparrows.

I slipped my fingers along the edges of the cover and pried.

Nothing. It remained as solid as stone, promising to never let go no matter how much strength came up against it. Only a binding would break it free.

A binding I couldn't hope to do.

My fingers trailed over the front of the tome before I placed it on the ground. A part of me ached at the thought of having it just in hand and putting it down without one word from it. No sight of the stories inside and the knowledge Mahrab told me of.

The truth of my family.

A year since Mithu's death had given me lots of time to devote to Vithum's swordplay, but it hadn't been enough to recover the old folds of my mind. Or rather, I hadn't made use of it to that end.

I sought to correct that. Folding my legs beneath me, I sat in a comfortable position, settling myself for what Mahrab had taught me. I summoned a singular image of a bobbing flame within. A candle flame.

Ebbing. Flickering. Growing. And up to me to make tame.

I held it firm, feeling like I watched the real thing. Every subtle motion pulled me, and its every yearning struggle to grow billowed something inside me. I kept it as it was—level and true to what I'd been taught.

I don't know how many candlemarks passed with me seated silently there, managing this state of mind, but I let it all pass and fed my thoughts to the fire.

Content I'd achieved some measure of clarity, I focused on the book. The folds of my mind came back to me. Not as easily as they once had, and nothing so close as the day I'd fought Mithu, but they came nonetheless.

I filled two folds with the thoughts of both ends of the book. I visualized them parting—opening wide to give up its secrets. Then thrice. Four times. Not long later did I hold eight folds.

A lesser effort than what I could have mustered before, but better than nothing.

What was it Mahrab had uttered?

Tak and Roh?

I spoke the words in succession, still picturing the book opening.

The room remained quiet but for my breathing. I opened my eyes to slits, peering at the cover.

Nothing. It hadn't moved in the slightest.

You would think, given my stubbornness and quickness to anger, that I would remain rooted in place until I found a way to have the book opened before me.

But no.

Time and weariness take their toll on all things. Even dreams. And some defeats simply rob us of the strength and fire needed then and there to press on.

This was one of those moments.

I picked up the book, gently laying it back within the trunk. A hollow *thunk* echoed through the room as I closed it. A sound to signal my failure.

I pushed myself to my feet and let a small sigh escape me. It had me consider that I might in fact be tired, and that was surely the real reason I couldn't muster the power and focus for a proper binding.

Little lies. They save us face. And sometimes they save us something more. Right then, I needed that to hold to the greater hope of one day chasing the bindings.

I was just tired. Let's leave it at that.

So I slept and let my thoughts turn to tales to come. The promise of something more than stories.

The answers that come with them.

Why the Ashura had killed everyone I had once known. Did the binders of the past know how to battle demons? And how to go about killing a man with yellow eyes?

A monster who claimed he couldn't die.

~

I woke to Small Kaya offering me a bowl of lukewarm lentils. The sparrows' growth in fortune allowed us better meals when we wanted, but there is something to be said of old familiarity and routine. And many of us resented the idea of squandering the larger wealth we'd built, keeping it for greater need than simply filling our bellies.

But I had no stomach for food today.

I gently turned her away, and Small Kaya left as she'd come—without a word or expression.

I dressed in my sparrow's clothes, grimacing as the shoulders of my shirt felt tight. I'd grown. Not enough to be noticeable to the everyday eyes of my family, but my clothing caught the difference and brought it to my awareness more and more of late.

I made a mental note to have my garments restitched. Content that I looked the part of unnoticeable urchin and Sullied enough to be ignored by all the right people, I headed downstairs, stopping first by Mithu's old office and treasury.

I met Nika and Juggi, preparing the morning's sparrow runs and duties. I locked eyes with the pair as I passed them by. "I'm heading out. You two are running things until I get back. I trust your judgment on what knowledge to keep and what to sell." I paused as I reached the double doors. "Oh, anything that comes in today goes to a food pot."

Juggi and Nika traded a silent look.

"I'm feeling charitable. And our treasure is plenty. We can stand a day's earnings, if it'll even take that, to get everyone a dinner that's hot and meaty."

Some of the sparrows standing in the usual ring around Nika and Juggi heard my declaration. They broke into excited clamoring as I exited the doors.

I allowed myself a smile. Let them hold to the little hope of better eating tonight. Even if no coin came in, an unlikely thing, I'd fund the dinner myself.

Because everyone could use a little hope now and again. Be they lordling high, or sparrow low. Hope gives us a promise of betterness to hold to when everything else seems bad, or when things don't change.

I knew this in my heart as I walked the streets of Keshum. Some of the sparrows would never grow to be anything beyond what they were. And that brought barbs to my chest.

No one likes the thought of knowing their brothers and sisters would live and die the way they'd always lived. It may have meant one thing if they had come to this world with privileged lives.

But there is no privilege in belonging to the lowest caste, and being a sparrow at that.

The thought made me reconsider Kaesha's idea. A desert king coming this far would not do so to trade trinkets and trash. He'd come for treasure. *Real* treasure.

The sort kept for and in storybook myths and legends. The kind told to young boys and girls to get their eyes glittering as best and bright as gold.

And if we could get a piece of it for ourselves, well, then the sparrows might not have to live as sparrows any longer.

The idea sat with me until I reached the Zanzikari.

The inn had been set up along one of Keshum's busier thoroughfares. Bathri Street. A place that did nothing but cater to the weary-worn businessman of the world passing through. And it did well for that.

The inn featured a sign in the shape of a stallion in full gallop. The building had taken its name from the kind of horse it showed, a popular and expensive breed used in races down south and beyond the more crowded areas of the Empire. The beast had been painted a black so dark no night could hope to hide it. It would stand out truer black against anything. Gold letters ran across the horse's broad body and named the inn for what it was.

I slipped through the doors as another patron opened them, owing to not wanting to make any noise of my own and attract attention. Sparrows may not have been known to all, but some of Keshum's citizens had keener eyes than others.

They knew our look. And my reputation had slowly grown among some circles, aided in part by certain letters and rumors being passed along by my brothers and sisters.

As much as I peddled truthful secrets for profit, I saw no harm then to spread a few lies to bolster our standing. And in turn, mine grew by greater measure than I expected.

According to some, I had been the son of a noble, trained from early age in my sums, letters, and speech, and of course, the soldier's art. My father had the money and the time.

And every young boy has time enough to play with things that can just as easily hurt him. In fact, it seems always we make time for that. One of our many little flaws.

I'd run away after my wealthy father died at the hands of another trader, and swearing revenge, I turned myself into a trickster thief to learn the subtler ways to exact a toll. I learned to sneak quieter than the stone lizards who scuttled without a sound over the rocks they so resembled. I learned to listen through walls and pluck men's deepest secrets, all ready and spun to be sold about to any who could offer the tidy sums I asked.

And I still held to the swordsman's skills, testing them out on the second father of mine: Mithu.

He'd wronged me badly and had taken part in my father's death, you see.

At least, that's how some of the stories took shape. Others had me more in the fashion of those told the day I'd watched Mithu fall. Demon, they called me.

Born of them with something twisted wrong and dark inside me. I craved blood and all things far from the way of Brahm. So, I killed. I stole. I sowed temptation where and when I could among the gentle folk of Keshum and Abhar whole.

It's easy for men to find scapegoats for their own misdeeds, and when you have someone so convenient at hand, why not label him for worse?

In truth, my reputation didn't suffer for it.

But it did mean I'd catch the occasional side-eye more often than I would have liked.

People wondering if I was that Ari. The one from the tiny tales told around the city.

That attention wouldn't do today. I needed someone else to be the focus of a story, and I needed their tale to give me answers I'd craved for a long time.

I searched the taproom. People bustled by, all fixed on their business with no room or mind for anything else. There was an energy of quiet purpose here. Nothing wasted down to the food, the movements of men, and their speech.

Many of them, if not all, were merchants of a sort. And while this was a place of rest, it was equally a place to continue dealings away from the loud and busy streets.

So I gave it that respect. All places have silent rules to them, and if you watch them long enough, you can begin to see the shapes of those rules.

Here, interrupting a person, even to ask an innocent question, could cost them dearly in matters of money. That would earn you more than just the sharp side of someone's tongue. It'd earn you a beating, perhaps worse when dealing with those who had the coin to bribe city officials and the kuthri.

Everything here was of solid but simple stone, and just as shineless sturdy wood. Nothing here of gaudy show or of false luxury—no. You knew what you got.

The floors were tiled in gray brick that refused to hold any dirt and grime. Every bit clumped and scraped off boots only to be swept away by cleaning hands. The wood absorbed no light from outside or from any candles. Dull.

But unmarred too.

No knives had ticked a surface of its original face. No splinters. No cracks.

This place saw no brawls or violent disagreements. And if it did, or ever had, anything broken was replaced as quickly as damaged. This place had all the signs of quiet efficiency.

Which might be why it attracted the folks it did.

I looked to the counter, another mix of hard-set stone and wood. The man behind it had gone bald long ago. He had the jowls and gentle rolls along the face and upper body you'd expect of a prosperous innkeeper.

His face shone brighter than bits of mirrorglass. Some of it came from sweat, more from the heat than anything else, and the rest owed to oily skin. It gave him a dark and healthy look, however. He held much of the sun in his skin.

He locked eyes with me and I took it as a silent cue to approach. His bushy brows, long turned gray, rose as I drew closer. "You're young."

I shrugged my shoulders. "I am."

"Too young to be here alone. I'm not selling you a thimble of spit without your mother or father by your side. Unless you've coin yourself?" He cocked his head to the side.

I pulled a copper round from my pocket, moving it through the air before fanning my fingers wide. Four tin chips sprouted from behind the larger coin due to a trick another of the sparrows had taught me. It didn't do much, but I'd learned little flourishes draw more than some men's eyes.

They take the minds as well. Even if only in small measure.

It softened his demeanor toward me and he eased his elbows off the counter. "What do you want?"

I slipped the coins back inside my pocket, tucking them away with the remaining ones I'd taken from the treasury.

Kaesha had told me the storyteller took payment. "No stories come free," he'd said. "And every story is worth something, even if not to you."

I agreed with the sentiment.

"Do you have any yogurt?" I rubbed my fingers against the coins, idly keeping count of them and wondering how many I'd need for the storyteller.

The barkeeper nodded. "Fresh this morning. Won't keep for much longer, though."

"Can you make a lushi?"

He bowed his head and moved to fetch my drink.

"Wait, with honey?"

He waved a hand in a gesture I took to mean he'd heard me. The man busied himself at the other end of the counter before vanishing to a back room out of sight. He returned minutes later with a cup, placing it before me. "Two chips."

"Two? That's a chip more than I figured." I produced the coins and passed them to him, grabbing hold of my drink just as he'd plucked the money from me. "Are mangos high in rates? Or is it the yogurt?"

The barman put a hand to the side of his head, pushing once to elicit an audible crack from his neck. "Bit of both. We pay a premium on our mangos. Fresher, not as close to ripe. Gives us more time to sit on some with business as busy as it is. And we have an ice box to keep the yogurt longer. That costs us."

I could imagine. Those contraptions let one keep things cold for longer than possible, and some could even chill the air inside far enough to turn water hard and cold. "One more thing."

The man stopped moving toward the other side of the bar, his mouth pulling to one side in a tight and lopsided frown.

"I've been hearing there's a performer here some days."

The man said nothing.

"Is that true?" I knew Kaesha had been honest with me, but I needed to hear it from someone who worked the inn.

The barkeeper rolled his shoulders, glancing down the way to a small makeshift stage of wood set on brick stands. It matched the style of the rest of the inn: simple, clean, sturdy. One could comfortably be assured it would not give way under any performance, be it a rousing dance, or feet-kicking song and step. "He comes sometimes. It's up to him. But he's been here nearly every day this set. Why?"

I ignored his question. "What's he charge for a story?"

The barkeeper took an empty glass from a young woman who'd been collecting them. He set to stacking them neatly behind himself in a basin for washing later. "Four chips. You want to spend that much, boy?"

I bristled. While he'd said it in passing, and it struck true to the mark, I'd grown to hate being called "boy." I pulled free more coins, showing I had them to spare. "I'm bored. And I can't see this place hurting from someone telling a story."

The barkeeper grunted and took another glass from one of the serving ladies. "You don't know people here, then."

I know them better than you might think, and only by first glance at that. I kept that thought to myself.

No one likes to be told their business by someone else, especially a stranger. Doubly so if that stranger is a child.

"People here like their business kept quiet and done in about as much. Understand?" He raised both brows and managed to look down the bridge of his nose at me all the while.

I nodded. "Shame. I figured he'd probably buy a drink or two, wet his whistle before speaking. Or maybe while. Storytelling parches folks. That's coin earned back to the house, right?"

The barkeeper blinked several times. "You have a head for business, but you're too young for it."

I shrugged.

"What caste are you? Are your parents merchants—nobles?"

My throat ran dry. If he knew I was Sullied, he could have me thrown from the establishment. While there weren't any laws preventing people of my caste from being here, there was enough societal disdain among certain classes of folks. That extended, by rule of thumb and trade, to merchants from outside the Empire. They knew enough not to talk and do business around undesirables.

I refused to answer and bypassed that conversation altogether by taking a sip of my lushi.

The drink consisted of mango juice and pulp folded into a mixture of water and yogurt. Cool, tangy, and sweetly refreshing. It pulled away any of the day's heat and discomfort at the first sip.

"This is good. You've got a hand for drinks, *sahm*."

The compliment hardly registered with the man, but he didn't press his earlier question. "You might have struck a truth in the storyteller wanting drinks. He might have people in a mood to order more for themselves while they listen. If business is postponed while he talks, people might get to eating and sipping to pass the time." He stroked his chin and mused under his breath for a moment.

"You have a good head on you, boy. So, yes. The storyteller will be here."

I stared at him. A moment ago he didn't sound all too sure, and now he all but said it with the surety of telling me the sun would rise tomorrow. "How do you know?"

The barkeeper gestured with an elbow down to one end of the counter. "That's him there. He's been here, drinking his first drink."

I glowered at the man. "So why bother with all the talk of shearing sheep and weighing rice? I paid." I tapped the side of my drink before taking another few sips. "I don't appreciate the useless busy talk."

The barkeeper raised his hands in placation. "Easy, boy. No need to light a fire between your brow, hm. I didn't know what someone like you would want with a storyteller. No parents? Asking after a man when I haven't seen you before? A fellow's got a right to his privacy. Especially under my roof. That, and, by a quick look at you, I'd have thunk you were Sullied. How're my customers to take it if I've got Sullied asking around after them? What's one to think?"

I held my heated stare, but let it go a moment later. There was no point in starting trouble or antagonizing the barkeeper. He'd given me what I wanted.

So I thanked him and eased away from the bar, heading toward the storyteller he pointed out.

"Oi, boy."

I stopped, looking back to the barman.

"He likes ruhah." The barkeeper winked and returned to his work.

That was good to know. Ruhah had been created long ago, well before the Mutri Empire had even become what it was. Just a series of neighboring kingdoms, all squabbling for greater power paid for with a price of blood and bodies. The drink came from brewed rice meal, sugar cane, wheat, and a mixture of fruits.

Some stories said that the god Hahn favored it. It was as bitter as it was sweet and quick to intoxicate the unwary man.

And it would probably cost me more than I would have liked for the price of a story.

I reached the place where the storyteller sat and took him in.

He couldn't have been into his thirtieth year, yet. Fresh-faced and full-bronzed. His hair had all the blackness and shine of oiled ink. He wore it down past his ears in a mix of waves and curls. His eyes had the same brown in them of wood and whisky in the sun. The cut of his jaw fell somewhere between bottle-glass sharp and as hard as cinder brick.

He had the kind of face young women pined for and every other man envied enough to want to hit. The man dressed in a sleeveless shirt as black as his hair, and pants to match. A few cords of bright red were braided around his biceps, and a series of black ink dots had been pricked into one of his muscles. They resembled a bird with large eyes and a short beak. Rounded head, and large talons. An owl, perhaps?

The man caught me staring. "Yes?"

"Are you the one telling stories here?"

He raised a finger to shush me as he took another sip of his drink.

I waited for the taste to end, but it didn't.

He held the glass to his mouth, taking longer than I'd ever seen someone take to drain a thimble's worth of alcohol. Done, he smacked his lips with more show and noise than necessary, following with an exaggerated exhale. "*That* is a drink."

I fidgeted, wanting an answer to my question.

"You're impatient." The man hadn't even looked my way this time. "A good storyteller builds anticipation. It's like feeding wood to a fire, boy. You build it." He took another sip, succeeding only in building my agitation, not anticipation. "Layers." He set the glass down, and just as I opened my mouth to press him, he brought the drink back to his mouth. Another smack of the lips and I felt soon enough I'd give him one as well, courtesy of my fist. "Like that." He set the glass down and finally looked like he had no desire to further tear the already fraying edges of my patience.

"Are you going to perform today?" One of my hands already went into my pocket, fumbling over the coins.

Silence.

I couldn't bear him dragging this out any longer, so I did the childish thing and took a long and loud sip of my own drink. The noise carried none of his subtlety and exaggerated air. It had all the annoyance of a donkey braying in the middle of a temple service. Loud, rolling, like a child slurping soup.

One of his eyes twitched, like the sound bothered him more than he'd thought it would.

It may have been a small spiteful thing to do, but I was young. And in desperate need of what he had to tell.

"You keep that up, boy, and you might make one fine storyteller yourself one day."

I smiled at that.

"The sort so fine at pissing off the right people and being tossed from any establishment worth telling and trading tales in. The sort people shoo away more than they usher in." He grinned and my own faded. "So, you want a story, is that it?"

I nodded. "I can pay."

"I should hope so." Another sip. Then he looked at me over the rim of the glass. Sip. Look. He put the drink down. "No good storyteller tells a tale for free. Remember that. It's an art. And all good art must be paid for. Anything less is a sin of two measures. First, you giving away something so special for naught. Second, the person who values something so private and precious for nothing at all." He raised the glass again and sipped.

I fidgeted again, wanting to at least know if he damned well wanted to tell a story.

"Patience is another mark of a storyteller. You might have need for it." While he didn't look at me, I had a feeling his eyes glimmered in amusement.

"I've been patient for longer than you know." I pulled coins from my pocket and slammed them by his cup. "I think this is enough for a new drink."

He turned, leaving his glass where it rested. Both his hands moved and one came to rest on my shoulder. "Ari, I know more than you think." He smiled and rose from the seat.

I blinked. I hadn't told him my name. Looking back to where I'd laid the coins only showed me a spot as clean as it had been before, like the money had never been there.

When did he palm the chips?

The storyteller whistled for the barkeeper, handing him the pieces of tin for likely another drink, then made his way over to the stage.

I visited the barman as well, fishing out a whole copper round and tossing it to him. "What did he order?"

"Same as before. Simple Uttari ale."

"Are the four chips he gave you enough for a glass of ruhah?"

The man shook his head.

"And the copper I gave you plus those four?"

The barkeeper smiled. "More than enough. Want me to make his next just that?"

I nodded. "And tell him it's from me."

He tapped the side of his head with two fingers, letting me know he'd do that.

Satisfied my bribe would do the trick, and with the man having already taken the stage, I figured it time to find myself a proper seat to enjoy what would come.

I took what remained of my lushi and sat at one of the few empty tables in the inn.

The storyteller paced around the stage, hands clasped behind his back. He didn't seem in any particular hurry to grab everyone's attention. He let it fall on him slowly, as glances passed him by only to realize he occupied a space designed to hold your focus. Then people's stares hovered back to him and held still.

He walked around the wooden platform harder now. Steps just loud enough to be heard over the drumming of hands along tables, glasses and mugs coming down like distant thunder, and the endless clamoring of men like waves breaking on shores.

Too many layers of noise to make sense of any one part. But the sounds he made were tailored to cut through it all. He cleared his throat so the men closest stopped and paid him mind.

But that cut their chatter and all the other noise that came with it.

The lull then turned the heads of other men in the taproom. They stilled their talking and took notice of the storyteller as well, adopting more leisured poses as they realized entertainment was at hand.

Soon, nothing but a rhythmic and loud tapping came from the stage as the storyteller bounced the heel of his boot against the wood. It fell in step with the beating of my heart and I couldn't turn away from him if I wanted. The simple trick held me firm in my seat and kept eyes locked on him.

The barkeeper quickly bustled by and passed the storyteller a drink I guessed to be the ruhah I'd paid for.

The teller took a sip, eyelids fluttering as he did. His mouth pulled to one side in a lopsided smile and I could see he enjoyed the beverage.

Good. He might be less of an ass after that.

He cleared his throat and paced the stage again. "Tired travelers, miscontent merchants, beggars and barmen all . . ." He let the words hang for the space of a breath before breaking back into his act. "Traders, thieves, children, men, and all others under these eaves. You are mine now. For the space it takes for me to finish, you are mine. Understand this. Forget all else. I speak. You listen. That is the way of things."

A man opened his mouth and the storyteller whirled to face him.

The patron pressed his lips tight together as he fell under the performer's glare and shrank in his seat.

"There are rules to this kind of thing. They are what separate us from the beasts of the world, and why they tell no stories of their own. First, no interruptions. Second, no thoughts of interrupting me. I'll know. Third, if you need to take a piss or shit, best you do it now or in your seat later. You don't get up. You don't leave." He waited and watched the crowd. When no one spoke or bothered to move, he nodded to himself.

"Good. Now." He extended his arms, lacing his fingers together and letting out a series of cracks like twigs breaking underfoot. "People, patrons, purveyors of trade, mercantile mercenaries all. You want a story. But what tales to tell? Stories as old as time and founding stones. Tales to stir the blood and burn deep inside your bones. I have them one; I have them all. Stories of heroes risen. And of their fall. What to tell? What to tell?" He paced around the edge of the platform now.

No one spoke. None gave voice to answer his question.

"Do we talk of demons in places long since gone? Of far back in Dinture, a kingdom forgotten past and washed away by a new dawn? Or do we hear of Brahm the Wanderer?"

A few people hissed in the crowd and the storyteller rounded on them, glaring daggers that made my skin prickle with unseen pressure and heat.

Brahm the Wanderer rankled some people's sensibilities and, worse, faith. A long divide had formed among the religious bodies throughout the Mutri Empire and wherever else Brahm's divinity was worshiped. The phase of his life where he'd apparently given up his godhood and wandered the world he'd shaped—as a mortal—was heresy to many. Adherence to that part of his story, and indeed telling it, upset certain bodies of the faith.

The storyteller went on as if the interruption hadn't happened. "What to tell? What to hear of?" He cupped a hand to his ear as if listening for a broken whisper from the crowd.

I couldn't understand why he didn't just pick. Why not just be done with it and throw us into something rousing that held us to the edge of our seats? Why the theatricality and exaggeration?

I'd come to learn and appreciate these subtle tricks later in life. But then, I was just a child. What did I really know of anything but what I thought I knew?

And what you think you know is never quite the same thing as what you actually do. The latter, in fact, is far less than what you could ever hope for it to be. This is true for all things: man, woman, child, and even those that stand outside humanity.

"Who wishes to hear a tale of the plains of Sevinter? The frozen north and people of the Hael? Roving nomads of the ice and harsh unforgiving lands. I know a few stories that will hold you to your seats so long and still you'll be hard-pressed to peel your asses free when I'm done. Or do you want to know of the paths past Zibrath? Desert kings and horse lords of the sands. Of those wraiths in black who walk the night and take life for coin. Professionals. Artisans. Death's own hands. Or something closer to home?" A drumlike beat echoed from the stage as he banged the heel of a boot against it.

I'd had enough and figured I'd give him an answer. No more talking around the matter. Now he'd talk straight through it. "The Ashura!"

The beating of his boot stopped. The storyteller stilled.

A different stillness than the one he'd commanded now filled the Zanzikari.

The quiet of men refusing to breathe. A stiff silence of everyone holding their hearts painfully frozen, not wanting to betray the sound of even a single quickened beat. Even the gentle air that had been sifting through from outside had decided it better to leave this place.

The man in the corner polishing a small statue of Beru, the god of wealth and fortune, stopped in place. No sounds of rag and oil over flawless white stone, a color so clean it could have been cast from sea-foam. The portly, nearly naked god himself seemed to add another quiet that could only come from stone.

The storyteller slowly turned to lock eyes with me. "The Ashura." It wasn't a question, no. He sounded like he chewed over both the word and whether to find a way to speak of something else.

And why not?

The last time someone had told a story about them, my family had paid the price. No, not even a proper story. Simply the rehearsal of one.

The storyteller inhaled and clicked his tongue against his teeth. Then he broke into an uneven smile. "I know just the one to tell."

I stiffened at that, and when I'd found some measure of calm again, leaned forward in anticipation.

"You want to hear a story of how stories say they came to be? You want to hear of binder kings and heroes turned against Brahm's light? Of betrayal and the start of it all?" He nodded, more to himself than anyone else. "You want the story of the fall. Of Abrahm, binder legend, in name of Brahm himself, and how he died."

I did.

And the storyteller obliged.

FORTY-TWO

A Binder Knight

Before the Mutri Empire, kings and queens of modern name, comes a tale of shadows and the greatest mortal flame. His name was Abrahm. A scholar. A binder. Wanderer.

He traveled far and wide to learn all he could of the wild bindings back before man would come to lose the many names and shapes of them all. He learned the many tongues of the world.

It was said when Abrahm had been born, the sun and moon embraced, shrouding the world in a bright dark light. A false midnight. He'd been marked for glory by Brahm himself. So both a sword and staff were placed into the babe's arms, a destiny chosen to be warrior and magician-scholar great.

And he rose to this.

This was a time when shadow and taint ran rampant in Brahm's fresh world. The Shaen had retreated to the folds of land beyond mortal eyes and means. They'd come to reside in the place between Midnight. A place of ever dark and always light, one and the same. A land far from Brahm's name and his flame.

So man remained behind to right the wrongs left in his world. And to this, they rallied.

And Abrahm led the way. He gathered eight other great binder warriors to fight against the shadow and what taint they spread. Demons, things in men's shape and form, but with ways to twist and turn all they touched.

He forged a sword, shining bright, of silver and moonbeams—a binding held fast and tight. A blade that held all the power of Brahm's first making—his first light. With strength of arm and strength of will, he cut through shadow's tainted blight. Abrahm had the mind of men many years his senior, and the cunning quickness of any Shaen in his thoughts.

With this, he led armies great and forces small against the enemy, turning them back, or to kindling.

But there was no revelry for each victory in this time before empires high. No joy after each battle fought. And no singing.

Those who held the gift of voice and song did not come to aid in this war tiresome and long. They kept their talents to protect themselves, finding safety in roaming, ever moving and away from the encroaching shadow.

And so men of meager means, weary worn, and tired of the twisting of the world around them, came to Abrahm's aid. They grew in number, born anew to be battle borne. Abrahm taught these men the bindings all men would come to know, and they turned the tide, slow but surely, with all the patience of water claiming stone.

First came the battle of Uppar Radesh. Tainted things, twisted both in mind and form, took the field. Shadowed flame took the little kingdom stone and mortar, blood and body, leaving little to reclaim. Abrahm danced with shadow, a white flame of moonlight against blackened fire. He cast them back, with strength of arm, and will of mind—held them firm in magical bind.

But shadow turned more than the minds of a few and brought worse than you could know to the hills of full white snow. Through the fire and smoke came a beast of fresh frost in color as the ice around it. A worm with a mouth large enough to swallow homes whole. Fangs as sharp and bright as Abrahm's own sword of pale frozen light.

Taken by the shadow, with dark fire in its eyes, it came after the binder knight and his men. He fought it to a single stand. Binding fire and stone to hold and burn the beast scale to bone. Abrahm shone lone and ever bright, a figure of cold white light. With his final breath, he uttered of the ten bindings all men would come to know.

He seized the peak firm, tight grip on tall ice and snow. And with but another word, he brought down the mountain low.

Shadow and demons fell to the cold wave as did the beast great. Abrahm and his binders had spared the king and his land from a twisted dark fate. Usaf Ghal, lord of all as far as the white ice stretched, thanked Abrahm and his binders for their heroism, pledging that his lands, now and always, would be home and safe haven for future binders to be.

And so Abrahm would raise his ranks greater there in the time to come. He formed a knighthood of scholar sorcerers to continue his fight against the shadow—blackened flame and those who turned from Brahm's light and name.

It's said no man could pierce his skin in battles, be it from a new binding he gleaned, or the cloak and mantle of white iron ice he'd come to wear. He was always found in the heat of the worst darkness, shining bright and wild against the black.

And always the victor was Abrahm.

The shift came in the middle years of war against these twisted shapes, all turned early by demons left unfound by Brahm who came as Radhivahn. And they came to turn more and more with time.

So Abrahm took to turning to bolster his own. He trained more binder knights, and among the greatest, came to teach the daughter of another king.

Hokh Ii Saphed, princess—pure and proud and binder-to-be. It's said she took to the ten bindings as quickly as a cat does to landing on its feet. She of Dinture, the kingdom of white stone and tree, and of old Singers' blood. She who was no longer keen to sit and watch the world be swallowed by shadow's darkened flood.

Together they waded deeper into the fight, freeing any kingdom held whole by demon and tainted grip. But through the worst of the fighting, Abrahm's fire came to pass. No longer burning bright, against the shadow, his flame could not hope to last.

Through the shadow and darkest night, another binder would take up the light.

But Abrahm's soul could not rest with the job undone, and it's said something barred his way to the place weary spirits go to lay. In this place between life and death something took his heart in hold and tried to take and turn him from Brahm true.

A mystery from behind the Doors of Death.

But Abrahm rose again, flame burning once again and better bright. Still imbued with the moon's pure white light. He roused and rallied scattered forces and once more took to fighting strong.

And shortly ended the war that had been tolling ever long. The enemy now locked forever within the Halls of Stone, and beyond the Walls of Stillness, older than the known world itself.

Even so, in victory's wake, kingdoms fell behind him. Taken and forgotten—turned to ruin and rust. No darkness spreading. No demons spawning. A quiet death like age-old stone under wind and water, soon to be naught but dust.

Finally, he came to Dinture, kingdom of Hokh, and his binder student. Abrahm approached her with warm welcome and held her in his embrace.

"How have you fared?" he asked of her.

And she told him, as always, truth in all things. "Well enough that my kingdom subsists. Heavy-hearted and hollow-chested at the fall of others. Neighboring brothers and sisters all. Some, even cousins by blood. Now all gone. If not from demons, shadow, and their taint. Now to fires burning black without constraint."

Abrahm took a step back at this. "You say you know of how those kingdoms came to fall?"

She gave him a weary smile. "Not fall, Rishi." Hokh shook her head. "Never fall. They were old and strong as stone and would hold just as long. Burned. No demons did this. Nor the work of things tainted, twisted—turned. This was done by something worse. Not so old as shadow, but of its making and its turnings. That is what I think."

Abrahm looked his student once over again. "You've grown."

"Time does that." She held her tired smile.

"And you've grown in wisdom, in the ten bindings, and how to rule a land."

She kept her smile still, now a brittle broken thing, so much like the now-fallen stone of which she spoke. "Time does that too, Rishi. But you look the same. Not aged or worn deeper with lines from the battles and even death."

Now Abrahm matched his student's face and the lines of her mouth. "Time can do that, yes, but more than that as well. And I did in fact pay. Time took its toll another way. Something else spared me of it."

Hokh took her own step back now. "And what is that, Rishi?"

Abrahm paused, turning to look over the kingdom of Dinture. White stone palace, gilded roofs of a gold so bright, they were said to catch and carry all of Brahm's own light. A white so clean, not unlike the mountains far where he'd come to make a legend of himself. A place where binders could now reside and learn the ten bindings should they have the will and their time bide.

He looked past it all to the high mountain walls of dull gray stone, in which they held another rock, white and smooth as bone. It held back any forces that wished to invade in large number, be they the kingdoms of men, or worse things beyond mortal ken.

One way through this kingdom white.

And it is through this way that Abrahm had been welcomed to pass.

He looked back at this way, holding it long in sight. He sighed a heavy breath and turned back to his student. "I've taught you many things."

She nodded.

"I've taught you the ten bindings, and then some forgotten more."

Hokh inclined her head again. "Yes, Rishi."

"And I've played a part in what seems a cycle. Athwun. Now Abrahm." His lips turned at their ends, slipping into a look weary whole. "And I've learned things that have made me rethink a great deal. Of what problems there will always be."

Hokh looked at her teacher in confusion, waiting for him to answer, but it didn't come. So she asked him for it. "What problems?"

He blew out another breath, leaning heavier on his binder's staff. "That there is no turning back the shadow. That black flame will always burn in this world. And that Brahm wrought this to be. It just took me a journey past death for me to see. That this pattern will continue, and take up many other heroes' lives, make it their curse—their destiny. I seek to break it. To unmake the ties Brahm's bound us to. To undo the bars that hold his old makings first and true. Before this world, me, and you. In that, I'll truly save this world. It will begin, bright and dark, all anew." He closed the distance between her and held her tight in his arms.

Hokh realized that Abrahm then had not returned. Not at least as he once was—no. He *had* been taken and turned by shadow's grip. She called the bindings to her mind and opened her mouth to cast them full.

But Abrahm had been born to bind and fight, and he moved as only he could. He stayed her where she stood. "Whent. By my mind and iron will, I ask you, Dinture, to fall still. Ern." The binding raced through the land and held the kingdom and all in it immobile.

Hokh stood there, able only to speak and wonder how her teacher could have fallen so far. "Do not do this, Rishi."

Abrahm drew his sword and drove it through his student's belly. "I must." With her blood on blade, did he speak, and another binding came to be laid. He knelt and pressed a hand to the white stone, staining it a red so bright. "I've kindled a fire that couldn't hope to burn forever. But with my new knowing, I've come to learn a new power and can bring about a flame that will burn for all time. I've learned how to break the bindings we thought we knew. Let me show you. Whent. Ern."

A black fire burned through the stone, spreading slowly through the kingdom. It spared only the courtyard in which Hokh and Abrahm stood.

She brought to mind all her teachings and freed herself from his hold all the while her home burned. "You'll never escape from this. I won't let you." She placed her hands to her stomach, taking her own blood and turning it to her mind's own fold. The binder's magic now bled with her Singer's gift of old. She sang a cry bright and loud, spreading through the land. She bound blood and song to bind him forever long.

"May everything that burned about you in Brahm's own light, turn away from you now to burn as dark as night. May you be blackened in flame and turn away from all things as you did Brahm. So be it too with your name! Twisted and turned away from you!

"May your cloak and mantle of white go red as my blood, all that you spilled, to always remind you of what you've done!

"May your light dim and darken, let it wane. May even your own shadow turn from you at all times so you'll know nothing and no one will walk with you forever—alone. May you never be able to set your feet to any one path, stay in any place too long. May you be set to forever wandering. Find no place safe to belong! I curse you, son of darkened flame. I bind you in blood"—she flicked drops of her own blood onto the once-binder knight—"and by song. I bind you to never be able to enter the place that bars the way to what you seek. I bind you to hold to only the bindings you've taught. Never able to create another."

It's said in that moment, Abrahm's sword of moonlight burned a color. Like smoldering coals, more black than white. The blade warped and crumpled into something like pressed wood and stone. His own shadow turned away from him to look the other way. And his cloak of white iron ice turned red as blood. Then he spoke, "I'm not alone. I've taught eight before you. And to me their hearts are now forever bound. Nine kingdoms raised heroes. And nine kingdoms have we razed in turn. Nine of us eternal. Nine of us you cannot kill or burn."

"Now you are Ashura—accursed—the nine twisted and turned from Brahm's grace and light. May you be marked by all your sins, each and all of you. May they betray you wherever you go. Now, begone!" she screamed. And to her word and at her voice in trembling song, the man once Abrahm turned away and began to walk.

It's said Hokh burned her blood in that binding in name and honor of Brahm, and in that moment, he gave her the strength to weave something new. This was a time long ago, and little else is known beyond what I've said here.

But it is believed she of Dinture watched her kingdom burn, then turned her mind and sights to where Abrahm had once made his legend. She turned to plains of snowy white, some think in thought that they reminded her of the white stones of home. There she'd come to teach future binders, and continue to bind the ways to something hidden deep there, so that none could pass and find what lay within.

Some say once her time as teacher passed, she went to teach others of the first folk how to sing the songs. How to learn bindings outside the ten never to be taught to anyone else but of that blood. Others say she went to join the Sithre. The first mortal to rise among them. And others . . .

Well they say as they've always done with stories, and twist and turn things to all manner of untrue tales. It's the way of stories told wide and far. They all turn away from themselves eventually.

But of Abrahm, this much is certain. A man born to be a binder knight, stood firm and tall against shadow's blight, until tainted and taken too, he grew to be untrue. And in this, he turned away from all things noble and brilliant bright. He became an agent of shadow, blackened flame, as dark in soul as night.

FORTY-THREE

His Name Is Maathi

The quiet that followed carried all the slow still silence of the world before a storm. Before the basso boom and break of thunder you know will come.

Then came the storm—an eruption of applause, every bit the tempest you'd expect. Mugs and fists banged against wood, drubbing a hollow drum of thunder instead. Then, the aftermath, and all the quiet that comes with that.

A silence in which to sit and appreciate what had passed. To take the moment to enjoy it without a word to disturb the now glass-smooth air and clarity within the inn. There is a pleasure in this contented quiet, and the patrons all saw fit to wrap themselves in it.

I should have let them. But, I didn't know any better. So I spoke and broke the much-needed and appreciated stillness.

"You're wrong." My voice carried through the room, drawing all the irksome attention of a shrieking cat.

Everyone's eyes turned to me, but they still respected what silence had fallen.

The storyteller raised a brow and nodded for me to come closer.

I did, dimly aware of another silence that weighed in tow with the rest. The quiet condemnation of judgment. I shrugged it free of my mind, however.

The storyteller moved to the lip of the small stage, sinking to his haunches before resting his bottom on the edge of the wood. When I neared, he motioned me closer still with a motion of his index finger. "And what, Ari, am I wrong about?"

"The Ashura." I swallowed, unsure how far I wanted to press this point, and all while everyone could listen in.

The storyteller somehow picked up on my unease. That is the only thing I can still think to this day, because he reached into his pockets and pulled free a silver dole and waved it for the barkeeper to see. "As many beers as this can buy for everyone within earshot!"

The barman bustled by to grab the coin and rush to fulfill the order as the crowd of patrons broke into cheers and shouts. And so the noise returned, and the storyteller and I gained another sort of silence.

The one of privacy. The quiet space within a world of noise.

"So, how am I wrong?"

I took a breath, and then realized something still bothered me. He'd said my name again, and all without the slightest hint of how he'd come to know it. But pushing on that matter would keep me from the heart of where I wished the conversation to be. "You said there are nine."

He nodded.

"There aren't. There are only eight." And I'd seen them all and counted them so. That night in the theater still came to me with a clarity not met by any of my other memories.

He brought the almost-empty glass to his lips, taking another sip of his ruhah. "And what makes you so sure? Because I know there are nine. I know this story the same way I know the story of every star Brahm breathed to life. I know it like the story of every stone, once larger, turned to dust out there in the deserts. There are nine. Always the lesser of one by the darkness that turned them."

I didn't know what he meant by that. I realized I couldn't answer him either. What would I say? I saw the Ashura take my home, leave it in embers and ashes. My family broken and burned, all my life a crumble of stone, blood, and bone. I saw them. They of myth and nightmares.

So, I decided to press for the other question on my mind, then. If I couldn't get one clear answer, I could hope for another. "How do you know my name?"

Another sip and he placed the glass by his side. "I looked at you. I listened. All storytellers eventually learn to do it. You can tell the shape and sum of a man by listening to his story. And you don't ever have to hear him say it if you listen and look hard enough. I know you, Ari, like I know the barman took you for the price of this ruhah. It's not worth half what you paid. It's not aged. It's not from half as far from here as it should be, and, it's honestly just not that good at all. Now, look at me."

I don't know why, but I did.

We locked eyes.

In stories, this would be the part I'd come away with some newfound knowledge. Gleaned something that forever shifted my perspective. But, no. In truth, I just saw a man. A clever one to be sure, but still a man. I saw Maathi the same as I saw Juggi, or any of the sparrows. I saw the shape of his face even though I kept my attention on the color of his eyes. I saw the subtle line, fine as hair, running from the side of one brow to the edge of an eye. An old scar, now nearly faded.

"Answer fast, boy. What's my name?"

I blinked, barely registering the question. The words left my mouth before I realized I'd spoken. "Maathi."

He smiled. "First try. Impressive."

I frowned, not understanding the trick of it. In my time with Khalim, I'd seen him feed lines in moments of need to actors who'd slipped. It happens to everyone eventually. I'd overheard him in games of subtle wordplay, doling out precious bits of secret information to see who was listening and committing things to memory, and who wasn't.

I tried to think back to my time in the inn and where I'd heard Maathi's name first spoken. The longer I thought, the cloudier my mind grew.

"Stop. You're thinking too hard. You did it right the first time. You looked, you listened. There's more magic out there in the world than the bindings, Ari. You'll figure it out if you keep to your path."

"And *what* is my path?" If Maathi knew this much of me already by first glance, I wondered what he could glean of my life-to-be. Not that I believed such a thing possible . . . but then again, I didn't believe in bindings and demons once.

And I paid the price for disbelief and ignorance.

So what harm could come from asking?

Maathi smiled, but the cheer didn't reach his eyes, painting the expression a gray and hollow thing. "Well, that's up to you, isn't it? Every man's path is his own. But the road often forks, and that is where you are. Do you stay the sparrow king? Do you steal secrets, sell them wide and far, growing your empire of whispers and coins? Or, do you remember the story inside here"—he reached out and tapped two fingers to the space above my heart—"the desire to trace Brahm's footsteps. To learn more about the Ashura.

"Each man has paths to choose, Ari. And all choose or have them chosen for them. Some through bold choice, others through inaction. They let things happen to them. Which are you: the one who decides or has it decided for him? Never forget that people often let themselves become pawns in life. You've been one for a while now. What happened to the boy who desired bindings and all the stories the world has to offer? To tell them, trade them, and perform? Where is he now?"

A good question. And a shame I couldn't find the answer no matter how hard I tried.

Maathi placed a hand on my shoulder, jostling me in what I took to be a reassuring shake. "You'll find it. And in time, if you choose the way that leads you to it, come find me. The old blood speaks strongly in both of us, and you should learn to use our gifts."

Our?

Maathi flourished a hand before I could open my mouth, the gesture stealing my attention and thoughts.

He rolled his wrist and a coin sprung from his palm as if it had sprouted from nothingness.

I stared, enraptured by the little trick.

"Ari." The use of my name pulled me from the hand, but only for the briefest of seconds.

Another roll of his hand and he spread his fingers. No coin fell. Nothing.

I stared, then arched a brow, waiting for him to explain.

"There's nothing worth saying but this, Ari. With but a few flashes of my hand, I held your attention. *That* is part of storytelling. There is a truth in tales, and a power. It resonates and holds people. Remember that. But there is something to be said for theatricality and showmanship. They go a long way in the art." He folded his hands together, spreading them a second later. The coin had reappeared. With a gentle motion, he lobbed the tin chip toward me.

My hand snaked out to grab it. I closed my fingers around the piece, opening them to find nothing but air. *How did he do that?*

I looked back to Maathi, only to find as much as I had caught in my hand.

Nothing.

And no one.

Now that was a trick. I stared at the empty spot a moment longer, catching sight of the coin I'd thought he'd thrown my way. I smiled, scooping it up and storing the lone tin chip. I may have given up a pretty piece to pay for my story, but I came out with something more. A bit of truth and the realizations that came with it.

I stowed the coin, considering it a bit of fortune that I didn't leave with empty pockets, and made my way out of the Zanzikari.

Maathi's words had filled my ears and hung heavy in my chest. I had to make a choice, and one that would shape my life to come. One I couldn't turn away from once I committed. I knew that to be true.

I stepped out of the building, letting the discordant rhythm of Keshum's streets sweep over me. A soothing familiarity nested within the disharmony of endless movement all strung with as many colors as man could imagine. The noise flooded me, but none of it was able to wash out what Maathi had asked me.

But a single voice cut through all of that. "Spare a chip, *sahm*? A piece of tin for a piece of fortune?"

I turned to regard the speaker.

She couldn't have been any older than me. Her hair hung loose and limp to just below the line of her jaw. A bandage had been wrapped over her eyes, and the color of the wraps carried too much of the street in it. Grime and dust. It hadn't been washed in a while, and even if it had, the original white had long since lost its clean. Whatever injury prompted the covering was an old one.

The young girl wore a single piece of fabric fashioned like an oversized dress. It fell to her ankles and showed the signs of being all she owned. The hem had been stitched together, shoddily. Its once-yellow color had paled to a shade found in old and worn sandstone. A slip of a thing, she couldn't have been getting much to eat with her lifestyle.

I had almost moved past her without paying a second's thought. Something about her struck a familiar note. I couldn't place where, but I thought I'd crossed paths with the girl. I knew her. At least, I thought I did. "Have we met before?"

She tilted her head like a dog hearing a sound for the first time. "*Sahm?* I don't recognize your voice."

And hers brought no memory to light either. I sighed, cradling my forehead in a hand. "Sorry. I just thought."

The young girl shook a clay mug before me. A fragment of the mug the size of a fingernail had been chipped away from its rim. Tin rattled within, striking an oddly musical series of chimes as they smacked against the clay. She didn't have a single copper to her name.

I lobbed my chip in to join the rest. "Brahm's blessing on you."

She smiled as the coin *clinked* along with the rest. "And to you. Would you like a piece of fortune, then?"

I stopped midway through leaving her, considering what she'd offered. Maathi had just given me a story about the Ashura. And with it, he gave me what I needed to hear—a choice and the remembrance of what I'd once set out to do and be.

"Please." I inclined my head, feeling a touch stupid for it as I remembered the girl couldn't see.

She rubbed her hands together. Somehow, more dirt and sweat managed to spread along her palms and fingers than I would have thought possible. "You've left a piece of yourself buried and behind. But it's not something to dig back up. You need to leave. Go north. You'll find and rekindle the flame to be at the Ashram. The place where magic and stories meet reality. If you stay here, you'll grow complacent, and the man you once wished to be will die a surer death than if you try to chase this dream and die."

I blinked, tried to swallow some moisture, but found my throat drier than all the sand and stone around me. "That is quite the fortune. And I'm not sure it's a bit fortuitous."

She shrugged. "Everyone has their gifts. This is mine. Listen, or don't." She reached to her side, picking something up and tossing it my way. "For you."

The item sailed far wide to my left, heading into the street and busy throng of people passing by.

I lunged to grab hold of the object. It fumbled through my grip a few times but I managed to finally seize it.

She had thrown a small figurine of wood, whittled to resemble an owl just large enough to sit comfortably in one palm. It had been crafted rather well, bearing a striking resemblance to the actual animal.

I looked back to where the young girl had lounged near the entrance to the Zanzikari.

Today must have been a day for tricks, advice, and disappearing acts. She'd taken a page from Maathi's book and vanished.

I let myself smile over the well-played move, though, and turned the figure over once again, giving it a better look.

Nisha had once told me something about owls and taking them as a good sign.

I ran a thumb over the carving and moved out of the way of the crowd.

Maathi and the young girl had both given me something to think on. Something that had been turning in my mind of late even without prompting. I had never been made for the sparrow's life. Though I'd taken to it, I lived the role out of necessity.

But time changes the necessities of a man's life. And it'd done so for me. Ari the Sparrow, Bloodletter, had grown out of this existence, and it was now time for another. And for an old promise to myself and Mahrab to be honored.

That meant giving up the life I'd come to know. To leave behind the sparrows. And to wipe away my worry for their lives after my departure.

A slew of fears seized me, turning all my warmth to a bundle of cold and agitated snakes writhing inside me.

What happened if the sparrows couldn't manage without me? Surely I'd done a good enough job teaching them what they needed to survive on their own. They had the wealth already and the means. What would happen if Koli somehow returned in my absence? Or Nisha? And my mind went on and on, looking for any excuse, any worry to keep me rooted in the safe existence I'd cultivated.

I'd fallen into this trap right after Mithu's death. And fear knows all too well how to keep you stuck in a place that will be the slow death of you. It's like a pit of quicksand. The frantic motions of thoughts, all promising some salvation or reason, will really be the death of you. Only in the stillness of the moment can you find the way out.

It was then I learned one of the saddest things in life is to forget what gives us breath. We get caught in the madness of life. We begin to bury our finest impulses and desires. And with them, each man kills the thing he loves.

Slowly, with timid choices and bitter rue. An old but potent poison, well tested and long true. It's never a dive or with one fell fall that we jump to kill our joys—one and all.

But bit by bit. We chip away at all that makes us whole. Till time and tide take their toll. And leave us weary worn and tattered torn.

I would not have it.

I'd rekindle my flame with what Mahrab taught me. With unbent will and rawest grit. I'd reclaim what I'd lost. Bit. By. Bit.

The thought fueled the fire I'd grown to lack of late, and I clung to that heat and all the clarity and strength it brought me.

I knew what I had to do as I headed back to the house of sparrows.

The journey north required supplies, and that meant hefty coin to spare without depleting the sparrow treasury. And whatever I could do to leave behind extra money would only aid my family after I left.

I needed to make a plan.

I had a merchant king to rob.

FORTY-FOUR

High Quarter Stakes

I found little sleep that night. All my mind's doors showed me the possibilities of another life. And I wanted them. My remaining thoughts all turned toward how to go about stealing every piece of precious wealth this visiting desert merchant had brought. But first I'd need to find out more about him.

The morning of Kindling Day greeted me after a shoddy rest. My stomach had no room for food, so I turned Small Kaya's routine visit away.

I met the morning group of sparrows in our customary ring. Juggi and Nika stood where they always did, close by my side and in position to address either half of the circle of birds.

A few of the sparrows shuffled in place, casting nervous looks to one another. No matter how many times we'd done this, a new day always brought another set of challenges and worries with it. It was the way of things.

"Today's not a listening, clutching, or secret-selling day." I let the words hang in the air for a moment.

The sparrows traded looks again, but kept their mutterings to themselves this time.

Juggi and Nika tilted their heads almost in perfect unison. My comment had gotten their attention and they wanted answers.

"Every sparrow today is going to take turns rotating through the High Quarter. Everyone is taking notes, and everyone will bring them back to Nika, Juggi, or myself to go over. Everything you see. Anything you hear. Nothing is worth ignoring. It comes across your way, you record it. *Ji?*"

"*Ji.*" The single word echoed back under the voice of every sparrow, filling the cavernous room.

"The second run of sparrows will do the same. Every sparrow goes out, and every sparrow picks up something of the High Quarter." I turned to face Juggi and Nika. "But I have a special job for the night crew. Kaesha will take them out to learn about a specific spot and person."

The pair gave me a look that made it clear they had more questions, but they wouldn't ask them in front of the rest of our family. Those would be kept for later.

The sparrows dispersed, stopping by the entry at a table nearly as long as three of us length-to-length. Stacks of scrap paper, pilfered, bought, and found, littered the surface. Every sparrow grabbed a page and broken bits of charcoal we'd taken care to whittle into usable shapes to write with. They left our hands blackened in places, but that only added to the guise of a sparrow when needed.

Once they'd left, Nika and Juggi cornered me on the way back to the second floor.

Juggi placed a hand on my shoulder and stopped me from going up the stairs. "What was that about?"

I told them of Kaesha's information and the desert trader king.

"And you want to rob him?" Juggi took two steps, like he could back away from the idea altogether if he put some distance between us.

"He's right, Ari." Nika placed a hand on Juggi's back to keep him from moving farther from us. "We barely ever get within range of the High Quarter walls to smell the air there. If we go in, people will notice."

I stared at her hard. "No. No they won't. Why? Because people *don't* want to notice us. Sparrows and Sullied and the like. We'll be thrown charity loaves by the rich wanting to appear godly. Thrown a copper, maybe an iron, by someone as if it were nothing but a chip to them. But mostly, we'll be ignored. Because those people don't want to see us. Don't want to acknowledge we exist. That this world exists in their empire. We'll be as good as ghosts. And we all know it."

Juggi and Nika frowned, and the former came closer to me. "What's this about? Just because Kaesha's got a lead on good coin . . . it's not worth this, is it?"

How to tell them I wanted to do it for them? That I could fund my journey north, resume the life I was meant to live, and leave them well enough off without me? That I meant to leave them and all without a word. I couldn't do that last part—tell them.

It was as much for them as it was for me, in truth.

"It's the kind of coin that could change our lives forever. A merchant trader of that background here on business won't be carrying a chest of tin and copper. It'll be silver and gold." I saw the effect my words had on them the second I finished speaking.

Both of their eyes widened, and I could see their minds tip to tallying the sums of what that much money meant.

"If we do this right, and the pay is there, the sparrows will never have to work again. We could buy you an appointment in court, Nika, or a ministry. You too, Juggi. We could get sparrows into the temples. We could run bigger games and trade and sell things larger than we ever thought." My heart twisted as my tongue went on, feeding them ideas I knew to be lies all. "But the sparrows could be free from even this life." And I knew that bit to be true, at least.

"I know it's a risk, but . . ."

Juggi stepped into the pause. "And if it goes wrong, we'll pay a steeper price than gold, Ari. Do you know how they punish people in the High Quarter for stealing? Do you know how these desert traders do?"

I did, but I knew Juggi would say it nonetheless.

"They take a hand, Ari. A hand!" He raised one of his own to accentuate the point. "I don't know about you, but I need my good right hand."

Nika snorted. "And we don't need to know for what, Juggi. So stop there. Do what no girl's willing to for you on your own time and away from our ears and eyes."

Juggi flushed a color I didn't think possible for someone of his complexion.

And I'd say I did the same, but in truth, it was a rather hot day. The heat in my face must have come from there and nowhere else.

Thankfully, Nika saved me from the embarrassment of the moment. "Juggi's right, though. And there's worse. Even if you go for this job, getting caught by the kuthri there will be just as bad. Maybe more."

I arched a brow, waiting for her to explain.

"They don't cut off hands, but they will whip you."

As far as punishments go, it wasn't that bad. Though, I had no desire to be whipped. My feelings must have shown on my face, because Nika shook her head.

"That's not all they do. Your hands will be branded."

I hadn't heard of that particular punishment. In truth, it might have slipped my mind during my time in Keshum as I didn't pay attention to all information that came my way. Many times I focused entirely too much on how to make a safe and quick profit for the sparrows. The severity of punishments in the High Quarter didn't come into account.

"You know what that means. No trading anywhere along the Golden Road. You'll be a thief and outcast. No lodgings at any place loyal to anyone in power to enforce the brand mark, Ari. No vittles. If you ever want to travel one day along the road and the paths it goes to, you can't. All passes taken. All ways blocked." Nika leaned forward and placed her lips against mine, keeping them there for a length of time I truly lost count of, but which I sorely wished went on forever. Finally, she broke the embrace.

I would be lying if I said my mind remained solely on the gravity of all she said. The risks and danger. But no. I had no space in my mind or any of the folds for anything other than the soft lightning-like sensation flooding my body. It came as quickly as that. And it left just as soon.

Shame.

"Please, Ari. If you do this and you're caught, it'll be the end of your life as a sparrow."

I exhaled. Little did she know it was coming to an end no matter what. I flashed her my best practiced grin, a thing meant to hide uncertainty and carry all the guile I could. "Then I better not get caught."

FORTY-FIVE

A Look Myself

One day of sparrows passing through the High Quarter quickly turned into three. Then a set. Soon enough, I almost knew the turns of the smooth stone walls and alley paths like I'd been born and raised there myself.

Almost.

But all the notes and secrets in the world cannot paint a picture as well as seeing things for yourself. So, comfortable that I had a good enough understanding of the quarter to make my own way through it, I outfitted myself for the foray.

The sparrows and I had built our trove of treasure well enough over our run of the house and daily efforts. Not to mention the money still left over from Mithu's reign. It left me a sum I could spend without fear on clothing that would better help me pass through the quarter without drawing too many eyes.

A cut too fine and I could be mistaken for someone worthy enough to bother lingering a gaze upon. Shoddy, shabby, stitched together, and I'd be overlooked with practiced ease right up until I needed to get into a place where the Sullied and poor are noticed with extreme prejudice. And acted upon.

Before that, however, I needed to bathe and scrub myself raw. The sparrow's life allowed for a certain amount of scruff and grime on our person. But for this, I needed to look like I'd never done a hard day's work with my body.

I went to the lone stone pit that Mithu had fashioned long ago for himself and sparrows to use on occasion to keep us from becoming dirty enough to risk falling ill. A small nook near the pit held enough room for a fire to burn long and low enough to heat the stone and water inside. I went through the tedium of stoking the flames to life and waiting. Sadly, I had little time to enjoy the bath itself, making it a cold affair.

The first thing I chose to wear had come off the back of a traveling trader's cart. A once-white silk shirt with threads to bind it tight to the wearer and flatter their form, should they have one worthy of that. While the top had come free to us, I'd taken the liberty of spending nearly a dozen chips having it dyed a suitable burgundy that matched some wines. Any brighter a red or purple and it would cross into noticeably extravagant. The poor and well-to-do didn't wear colors like that. The stark vibrancy drew eyes, made a show of wealth, and required the latter to keep clean in a world where road dust inevitably found its way to your clothing.

I paired the shirt with a set of loose and baggy pants of the same material and color, hoping the outfit's uniformity would help me passably blend as well. Then came the one article that gave me pause.

Shoes.

In my life in the theater, then as a sparrow under Mithu, I never owned a pair or had need of them. Years had turned my feet into calloused leather that could bear the heat of burning stone and walk over brick and almost glass. Shoes made your feet soft, they kept you from feeling the turn of the earth and land beneath you. And that meant clumsier footwork.

I stifled a mounting sigh and fetched the pair we'd purchased. They were simple in shape and form, fitting me perfectly. I'd made sure they lacked any superfluous adornment and that they were a dull but unmarred black. No lacing to keep them fastened firmly, that coming by way of their slip-on fit. It would make them just as easy to remove had I need.

Though I certainly hoped I wouldn't.

The last piece of clothing served more purpose than the rest. A thin and light scarf to drape over my shoulders, which could wrap around the top of my head and my mouth if necessary. A common-enough thing when walking some streets to protect oneself from certain smells, a few bothersome air-borne spices, and dust.

But it would ensure I could keep my face from being memorized by anyone taking a longer look at me than I liked.

Juggi and Nika met me downstairs, looking me over. "I can't tell you apart from the high-stuffed and wrapped people born in the High Quarter," said Juggi. He ran a thumb and forefinger along his chin, still in thought. "You sure you're going to come back after passing for some Brahmthin? You look as high-casted as they come."

I rolled my eyes, but didn't trust myself to speak entirely. Because, no, I would not be coming back after a fashion. Even if I returned today, it would be a temporary stay.

"Nika?" I turned to face her, stretching my arms out wide and turning in place to give her a better look.

"Juggi had it right. You look like you belong. And you can talk your way like them, so you should be fine." Her words came clipped and cold. She still held to the reservation this was a bad idea and wanted me to take no part in it. If she had her way, we'd still be peddling secrets and never think to rob a soul.

In truth, had I listened to her then, I wouldn't come to be here now. Maybe she had it right. But I didn't see it that way then.

I ignored the coolness in her voice and took her at her word only. "Good. I should be able to get a better understanding of my way through the quarter today. With that, I should be able to work out how to get to the merchant's residence and take what we need."

Juggi spat to one side and fixed me with a dubious look. "It won't be easy to just get out with silver and gold. Especially with how much someone like him will have. It could be a chest, Ari. A chest!"

I smiled and waved a hand dismissively. "That's why we have money of our own. We bribe the right folk. Not the ones on the way in, that's too dangerous. But a couple of *thuulis* won't ask any questions about hauling a load, no matter how heavy, and no matter how it looks. They lift, carry, and deliver. It's the life they lead. And all we have to do is pay them enough to not ask questions, and to not stop and try to look at what's being carried."

Juggi rolled his eyes at that, giving Nika a sidelong look that spoke volumes. "Oh, that's all, hm? Easy as that?"

I kept my smile. "Easy as that." I turned the scarf around my neck just once, leaving enough slack for me to pull it up over my mouth should I need. "Make sure no sparrows come through that way today. If I get into trouble, I don't want any of the family getting mixed into it."

Both of them nodded and traded a worried look with one another.

"I'll be fine." I still held my beaming expression, wondering how well of an actor I'd grown to be over my time as a sparrow. Not well enough to fool the two people who'd come to know me the best, but enough to clearly bother them at how good a smile I could fake.

It boded well for my jaunt into the High Quarter.

Some masks hide us from our loved ones. Others keep us safe from the world.

I hoped mine would live up to the latter.

My ass ached after a third of a candlemark, by guess, jostling around in the seat of the rickshaw. I gave silent thanks the wooden seat had at least been sanded smooth to not send a splinter deep into my bottom. It wouldn't have been a problem had the runner bothered with a cushion to spare passengers, but I knew the lives men of his sort led. And even the extra coin to invest into his work could come at the cost of a meal or two.

A serious strain, and doubly so if he had family.

So, I gritted my teeth, half in part to bear the pain, and half to keep them from shaking loose over the bouncing journey.

I would have preferred to walk into the quarter, but that long a jaunt would have easily sullied my clothing. And I had neither the means nor time to have them cleaned quick enough to be serviceable. At least not without spending more coin than I cared to.

Just when I thought I couldn't tolerate the ride any longer, relief.

"Here, *sahm*." The runner slowed to a halt, gesturing with both a bow of his head and wave of an arm toward the open gates into the High Quarter.

Pink and white marble made up two columns standing on either side of the gate. The metal barring the way hadn't been fixed to the glossy stone. It held instead to heavy pillars of more serviceable and enduring iron fixed behind the ornate obelisks. One set for show, the other to keep out those undesirables come the night.

I thanked the driver and pulled free my purse, reaching inside to fetch five tin chips. The journey in truth cost no more than two. And someone of my cut and cloth could have easily lobbed the poor man a lone chip and called him lucky to get that much after such a rough ride.

But I knew the many shapes of shame that could fill a man. And I knew the hunger and pain that came with them. A moment of second thought took me and I pulled out eight chips, hoping no one else took note of how many coins filled my hand.

"For you." My words came hollow and short as I fought against adding a *sahm* of my own. Offering him that level of respect would have turned any eyes and ears within hearing range to me, and I couldn't risk that attention.

But a part of me would have liked to offer him that little bit of extra dignity.

We could all benefit from that in life. People seldom remember it, though. The kindness of respect does great favors, more so than money, at times.

The man took the coins without looking. His gaze stayed low as I stepped out from the rickshaw. Only when I'd turned my back to him and nearly reached the marble pillars did his light exhale catch my ears.

"Thank you, *sahm*. A thousand thanks!"

I ignored him, and all the while my thoughts turned to silent prayers, hoping something would turn his luck as it had mine.

Two kuthri stood ahead, one at the foot of each stone pillar. They wore silk and velvet the color of rich clay. Sections along the shoulders, waist, and above their knees had intricate gold and indigo lacing. A steel plate, shaped into a circle, sat above the center of their chests, and a broad collar of the same metal ran below their throats. Their shoulders and shins were covered in more of the same, and I could see what looked like brass fixed over the steel. Their coifs were a shining gold, but certainly not the true metal itself, and had black curtains of lace hanging to obscure the sides of their faces. All but their eyes were invisible.

Both men stared as I passed by.

I stiffened and immediately developed interest in looking everywhere but at either of the kuthri. They paid me no further mind as I passed through the open gates and into the High Quarter proper. My sternum finally loosened and it felt like I could take my first real breath after a set of being stuffed in a small box.

Only a dozen paces inside and the difference between this quarter and the one I had just come from struck me as hard as a brick to the skull.

Every building in sight had a uniform smoothness to its construction. Oh, they differed in shape, of course. But no wasted mortar. None caked by hasty hands all too eager to finish a day's construction.

The buildings held their colors as well; some, carrying a clay red that showed no sign of ever dulling; others, white stone, so clean they may have been fashioned from hardened clouds.

I noted piping and stonework running from the second stories of most, leading to small drains at the end of any block of buildings.

Communal drains. Their baths were not on the bottom as in work quarters and among where people of lesser privilege lived. Their water and waste drained out from their homes.

I gave one building a longer look as I passed by, spotting a second set of pots buried into another recess in the ground. Its contents were what I should have expected, and it made me offer another thanks that I hadn't decided to eat just before coming to view the drain.

Not one window in sight was without a finely made shutter of fibrous latticework. The slight sheen told me they'd been oiled deep, well, and regularly. They would serve to keep out the rain when monsoon season came.

So many subtle differences that spoke of the level of consistent and high wealth in the area.

It took me longer than I would have liked to acclimate to it all.

It was as if my whole life had been spent in a single room with but a hole in the wall to peer through. That narrow band of light and color and all things passing by were what I had to shape my world with. And it had been painfully lacking.

Now I saw another layer to things, and all with more color and brightness than my eyes could handle.

We all too often think we know the true shape of the world and things. But we are often as much sorely lacking in any knowledge of these turnings and how they come to pass.

Dumbstruck, I wandered for a while, my feet needing no direction from me. My wandering brought me to another street in the High Quarter, and lingering at the edge of my vision was another tin box and cart like the one I'd encountered when Mithu still ruled the sparrows.

A man, somewhere in his forties, doled out shaved lumps of ice into wooden bowls. He wore a matching shirt and pants of white with a vest the color of slate. After handing some children their dishes, he pulled out a cup in which he dipped a small ladle. Syrup, thick and viscous as honey with all the bright colors of the sun, dripped slowly over the spoon's lip. He spilled it in artful loops over their ice before smiling. The children passed him a copper.

A whole copper piece for not more than two handfuls of ice.

That could have bought a sparrow a month of meals from the right places at the right times of day. They wouldn't have been what anyone considered fine, and would certainly have been far from luxurious, but they'd have been fed without worry.

Farther down the street stood a brick structure with an iron griddle along the top. Smoke billowed from a small stack of mortar and stone that stood angled to one side. Several men, all dressed in loose gray clothes meant for traveling, gathered around it. Leather satchels hung from their shoulders.

Traders.

A man stood over the flat iron surface pouring a batter that quickly sizzled and formed into a white bread as thick as my hand. He kneaded it while it was still pliable, pulling it with ease. One hand vanished to the side before reappearing with a spoon of what looked like clarified butter. He spilled it onto the bread, spread it thin, then flipped the piece over.

Sizzle. Snap. The griddle hissed and he pulled the bread free, its surface now carrying a bronze and lightly blackened char. He folded it into a thin cloth, passing it to one of the men. Another motion of his hands and he placed enough chickpeas to fill one's palm onto the charred flatbread.

A vendor with that much space to himself, with that level of equipment, and only three possible patrons standing around him . . .

It took whatever appreciation I could muster for his skill out of my mind.

On the busier streets of soft and hard goods, food vendors stood cramped near one another. They made do with what little they could and an ingenuity that beggared belief. But for it, they gained an endless stream of customers, all wanting something hot and fast so they could go on with their business.

Here, it seemed all luxuries were readily available. And the men and women who had to work to provide these services had just as much leisure in their jobs as the people paying them. That brought another universal truth to mind.

The Mutri Empire, my home, could have held all the wonders of the world in it, but that didn't mean every man, woman, and child could experience them. Having something did not mean all could and would come to have it. The greatest marvels of the world usually came to those with the money and ability to get them. The same city, in fact, could cradle completely different lives that would never cross paths and know the same sort of hunger and relief. Two men may share the same air in theory, but they'd never breathe the same breath.

If I lingered and watched any longer I'd run the risk of my feet turning to the same stone I walked upon.

That took another piece of my attention.

Many of the paths through the High Quarter, for as far as I could see . . . were mortar and stone. No dirt. No grime and dust tracked in from the long roads outside the city and then spread through it. I took a breath and it finally hit me the difference this all made.

The air felt light, each breath absent all the filth I'd taken in most of my life. They left me as fast as I'd sucked them in.

I needed to move and get back to the job at hand or I'd lose myself in the foreignness of the quarter.

Over the set spent in the quarter, my sparrows had taken to scribbling pieces of a rudimentary map to navigate the High Quarter's turnings. I'd made the effort to put them together and redraw them on a larger sheet of parchment. It gave me enough of an idea where to find the merchant's residence so long as he remained in Keshum.

The trick rested in how to actually get in and take a better look inside the place. I'd have to pass as something nonthreatening and easily overlooked. A servant, perhaps.

I moved through the quarter, taking care not to linger too long in any one place. People develop an odd, but understandable, territorialism about their locale. The sparrows and I had done the same, to be honest, for the streets immediately around our home. Anyone new, fresh-faced enough to warrant attention, found themselves stalked by a hidden band of sparrows. At least for a while.

It let us know who could be a threat, who could be a mark, or who could be an asset when it came to secrets and things to be told and traded.

The wealthiest quarter would surely have people of the same mind if for no reason other than curiosity and the idleness that invited people to lurk and watch passersby.

I consulted a mental list I'd formed over every key landmark I'd need to find my way to the lodgings of the merchant king. My memory faltered as I passed by a structure I had been told of, but the actual sight of it made all my sparrows' words fall short in their descriptions.

The temple had been hewn from a stone the color of raw iron. It stood higher than any building around it, looking more like a mountain had sprouted in this part of the quarter and someone had decided to tunnel through it. Maybe the mountain had been there first?

I still don't know.

The arched path through the place was tall enough to swallow some of the more opulent homes I'd passed by, and columns lined both walls. Reliefs had been worked into every inch of their surface I could see, but I hadn't the religious studies to make out what they were. I couldn't even see the end of the path.

Several priests, each clad in a single garment of flowing white, with garlands of orange flowers around their necks, flowed through the hall with near-synchronized steps.

It shouldn't have been a surprise that a quarter with this level of wealth would have a temple large enough to accommodate any and every god under Brahm, but my entire life had led me to only see the busier paths sprout places of worship. After all, what better place to line a house of prayer than where traders pass through to seek fortune and ask for as much back. You'd be sure to receive a steady stream of offerings and more from such folk.

I tore myself from staring at the gargantuan temple, reminding myself why I'd come to the High Quarter. The task at hand became a mantra I repeated to myself, ensuring that I didn't deviate again.

My diligence rewarded me with sight of the building I'd been looking for.

Two stories tall, and nearly as wide as several homes joined together in the Hard Quarter. The kind of residence that only the wealthiest of travelers, just short of nobility and the comforts provided to those, could afford.

Sloped, not flat roofing, made up of ridged tiles. Their surface caught and carried bands of the sun, letting me know the tiles had been brushed with something to do so. That, in addition to their styling, told me it had been done to keep the building as free as possible from accumulating rainfall come the rainy season.

Which we were due for.

I walked over to the high double doors and the man standing before them.

He dressed the part of attendant more than any sort of guard, but my sparrows had told me the two couldn't be told apart in this part of the city. Some men had other ways to make them dangerous than obvious armor and swords at their sides.

I inclined my head to him in respect, not meeting his eyes as I moved by him.

He stepped to block my way. The man's age escaped me at a glance, but he'd definitely passed out of his twenties. His jaw rivaled a brick in shape, and his cheeks were sharp enough to cut glass. The dark of his hair carried nearly as much shine as the tiles above. He'd slicked it with something, then. His eyes reminded me of stone; not in color, but lifelessness. He had the stare of someone so tired and worn by their work they had no energy and brightness left for anything else.

Shame they couldn't find a bit more tiredness for the rest of him to succumb to.

"I haven't seen you before? Which guest are you here to see?" His voice matched the weary emptiness of his eyes.

I almost spoke in the guise of a poor and uneducated sparrow, but that wouldn't have worked here. I cleared my throat and kept to the tone best fit for my role. "I'm not here to see anyone, *sahm,* but work. Teaboy, sweep, carry small things. That's all." I didn't linger as my words fell on his ears, trying to move by him again.

He cut me off. "You're new?"

I nodded, placing a hand over the hollow of my throat. "Please, *sahm,* if I'm late, my mother will—" I drew a hand over hand, palm open, gesturing for a slap. "She's been saying I need honest work to straighten me out. She doesn't want me being a layabout like my father. You know how mothers can be."

He grunted and the hard line of his jaw softened. "Wives are the same. Who are you to collect your wages from?"

Tch. I hadn't thought of that. My best and cleverest smile crossed my face. It was an expression as sharp as paper's edge and with all the measured curve and brightness of a crescent moon. "Ma didn't tell me that. I didn't even think about it. Maybe I'm not even to be paid. She was terribly angry at me. I might . . ." I let myself trail off, turning my gaze to the ground for a moment. "I might have been caught playing marbles for coins and she hates gambling."

The man spat to one side. "She would. Kuthri here punish open gambling, even from kids. Were you switched?"

I shook my head.

He grunted, turning that hollow stare away from me. "You should have been. If you're not being paid, don't come back later looking to be. Anything a guest gives you out of their own kindness is yours. Don't make trouble. I hear of anything, I'll give you a beating that'll make you wish your mother did her job in giving it to you first, *ji-ah*?"

I nodded and moved by him, finally slipping into the doors.

Now I just needed to find a king and find a way to steal his treasure.

Easy.

And if I told myself that enough, I'd come to believe it.

FORTY-SIX

A King's Gambit

Red clay, sectioned into irregularly shaped tiling, made up the floor of the building. I walked over it, taking in all the subtle hints of wealth apparent to anyone with the eye to spot them. Every supporting beam that ran through the hall had reliefs worked into it, much like the columns of the temple.

A runner boy came down from the other end of the passage, carrying a thick tin tray with a set of cups atop it and a pot.

"Teaboy?" I stepped in his way, hoping he'd stop to give me a second's time.

He nodded. The boy couldn't have been a year older than me, and he matched me in height and build. The cut of his outfit didn't differ from mine either, if only maybe a bit plainer in the coloring and showing more signs of wear.

"Where are you taking that?" I filled my voice with hard authority. He had no idea who I was, and I hoped to play that against him. Age aside, if I acted like my father owned the place, he may very well treat me that way.

Often the appearance of authority is enough to grant it.

He stared at me for a moment, looking like he had lost whatever words he'd been searching for.

"Well?" I took a step closer to him. "Is there cotton between your ears or a brain? Where are you taking that? Which of the guests here? They don't pay the money they do to have teaboys amble about like they have rocks instead of thoughts rattling around up here." I tapped the side of his head with a hand, smacking it harder than necessary.

The jostle shook him out of whatever stupor he'd fallen into. "Yes-s . . . *ji*?" He had no idea what honorific or title to address me by, and my performance left him thinking he needed to.

I fought to keep the smile from showing on my face. "Don't bother. Just answer my question. Where?" I sounded out the last word as if I were speaking to a particularly thick-witted child.

"Trader-*hullahs*." He shook his head, realizing that hadn't been enough information. "Merchants. A group of them have taken quarters at the far end of the hall. Largest rooms available."

I eyed him, sending a silent message that wasn't enough to answer my question.

"I don't know much else . . ." He stopped short again like he was searching for how to label me. "Foreigners. Not casted, not of Mutri anywhere that I've seen. Their dress is western. Zibrath? Maybe farther like Arakesh? All I know."

It would have to be enough. Though, what he'd said had lined up with what I knew of the merchant and his band. The odds of another group with a similar background taking residence here would be slim. Just like birds or thieves or slumlords, merchants of a certain repute and wealth didn't take to sharing close spaces.

I reached out with both hands, making it clear I intended to take the tray from him. He opened his mouth, but I cut him off before he could speak. "Don't say anything. You've said more than enough that's been less than worth hearing, to be honest. You want to keep your job."

The poor boy nodded at the statement.

"Are you paid by the day or . . . ?"

He nodded again.

"So this won't matter, then. Let me take this and do a proper job lest they get mad. Plus, you've been keeping them waiting."

He opened his mouth again, now to protest.

"It doesn't matter why. It's been done. They won't say a word to me or my father will hear of it. Besides, if they did, I'll be fine. I'm doing you a favor. You get paid and can take a short break." I fixed him with a hard stare. *"Short."*

He passed the tray to me and I took it with all the care I could muster. "Thank you. I—"

I grunted, making it clear he should stop talking and go enjoy his relief from the job.

He took my meaning and sped off with all the enthusiasm of a kid free from work.

I sucked in a breath, steadying myself and enjoying my moment of luck. *So far, so good. Now to just find out where they're hiding their coin.*

I walked down the hall, keeping the tray as steady as possible. I hadn't noticed it at first but the cups and pot were all fashioned out of bone-white and polished porcelain. The material came from Laxina, a neighbor close in proximity to the Mutri Empire, but a world apart in customs, appearances, and more. They valued the substance enough to be both currency and used in artisanal crafts.

All of which meant it was terribly expensive. Dropping or cracking even one of these cups would see me forced out of the building and promised a beating. Not to mention the possibility of the cost of the broken cup being asked of me.

I reached the end of the hall, staring at a trio of doors. The boy hadn't told me which exactly housed the man I was looking for, but I knew enough that the merchant's cadre would be behind any of the doors. I pulled back a foot to kick one of the doors in way of knocking when one of them opened to my side.

The man who stepped out towered over me, reaching well over six feet in height. Tightly bound and fitted black clothing obscured most of his body. The clothes were cut and measured to his frame, indicating they weren't cheap. But they lacked the adornment I'd expected of someone wealthy. In truth, they resembled what one might wear on long journeys. A wrap of cloth covered most of his head, hanging loose and open at the sides of his mouth to reveal some of his face.

"You're late. We've been waiting for that." He reached out to take the tea.

I didn't move or pass him the tray. "I'm supposed to bring this to the *sahm* in charge? The one who the rooms are for in all." A lump of cold stone formed in my throat, soon settling in my chest.

The man held his stare and crossed his arms. "He didn't ask you for the tea, boy. I did."

Which told me all I needed to know about these merchants. They couldn't tell one tea runner from another. To people of wealth, people like me were interchangeable. All beneath them, all not worth the bother to take notice of until we'd done the job they'd instructed.

And I know for a fact that hasn't changed in the world today.

"It's my head and hide if I don't serve everyone like good guests and get back to the others." I kept my grip firm on the tray.

The man gave me a look that made it clear he wouldn't budge on the point. "Then it's your head and hide, boy. I'll tell the next one what an idiot you were. Maybe he'll do better. Be faster." His eyes narrowed.

The temptation to hurl the tray at him, hot tea and brittle porcelain all, overwhelmed me. But that would end all my ambitions on the spot.

"At least let me set it down and serve you, then I'll leave. I have to be able to tell the *malak-sahm* I did that much."

He pursed his lips. "Who's *malak-sahm*?"

"The 'owner-sir,'" I translated. "Sorry. That much, at least, please?" My insistence obviously drained the last of the man's patience, but he'd be left with cold tea if he kept barring the way. My stubbornness wouldn't be beaten by him. Not with what was at stake for me.

Finally, he relented with a heavy sigh. He reached over and banged a fist on the door I'd been looking at first. "*Tharum!*" I didn't recognize the word. It wasn't any derivation of language spoken within the Mutri Empire, and it certainly wasn't the Trader's Tongue.

The door opened and another man dressed like the one I'd been speaking to stood in the way. He gestured me inside with the other man following at my back.

I'd made it inside with two very large gentlemen following me.

. . . Wonderful.

The room had been decorated with the opulence I expected for a group of traders with the wealth to be considered kings.

A thick rug that had more brightness in its threads than some of the clothing I'd seen High Quarter citizens wearing. I saw no signs of scuff marks despite how well-worn it must have been under the constant feet of travelers. The low table at the center of the room had been fashioned out of a black wood the name of which I couldn't recall but knew to be a weight of silver in price. And the cushions of the room were covered in silk.

A man lounged against several of the padded pillows, a smoking pipe in hand.

My first look told me he'd touched his fiftieth year of life recently. Face as hard-lined as driftwood with eyes warm and bright as honey. He too had most of his hair hidden behind a tightly fastened wrap of rich purple. His clothing matched the other men, but not the shade of plum lining his collar, breast, and cuffs. Instead he wore a sash of red so rich and deep it looked the color of ruby.

All of him reminded me of a grizzled fox. Life as a sparrow had ingrained a sense in me of which men to be wary of on the streets. Some would cause small trouble, a beating or so. Maybe a quick slap of the hand. Others would chase. Some would raise a row and get the kuthri on you. The last men were the ones who took fast and hard to settling things on their own in the most permanent of ways.

He struck me as the last. And the sword, broad and curved, resting on his hip confirmed that for me. It was no ornamental thing. Even from where I stood I could see the leather wraps were worn and stained from sweat and the oils of his hand. Sunlight and use had dampened the luster of gold on the pommel. And his hand rested on the hilt with a casual familiarity that meant he was all too accustomed to its feel in hand.

"Sit." He spoke the word with the firmness and weight that comes with years of being in charge. If you've ever been scolded by someone clearly in a position of power, you know the tone.

But no one did as asked.

The man who'd spoken locked eyes with me. "I'm not accustomed to repeating myself."

In my stupidity, I took a moment to look at the men who'd followed me in, assuming them to be the target for his command.

Neither of them moved.

I moved closer and set the tray down on the table, taking my time under the guise of not wanting to tip over a cup or spill anything from the pot. I took just as much time in pouring the tea into the first cup before the man in purple-lined robes waved me off.

"Just two cups will do. Sit, boy."

My surprise fell under the realization I'd gotten what I'd wanted, in a way. Sitting and talking with the man afforded me the time to take a good look at the room proper and commit it to memory.

He waved a hand to the pair of men who'd come with me into the room. "*Irf, thalm.*"

They bobbed their heads, hand over their hearts, and left in perfect synchrony.

The man before me took a long drag from his pipe, blowing smoke into the air that smelled like dried cherries through the dryness of the haze. "Do you know why you're here, boy?"

"Because you asked for tea?" I hadn't tried to be clever with my answer. In truth, it felt the best way to start the conversation—simple honesty.

One corner of the man's mouth twitched. "When you get to be as old as me, something I'm not yet sure you'll manage, given how clever you think you are, you come to pay attention to the little things. Things like the differences in the faces of the boys who've come and gone over the past set to serve tea. To their walks. Their voices. These things, these differences, can keep a man alive where I come from. Especially in the life I lead. Do you understand?"

I did. It was the same wariness I'd learned to adopt as a sparrow. Why he needed it still eluded me. But, I let the man go on, using the time spent talking to eye the room carefully. All done without breaking solid eye contact with him. A careful trick I'd learned long ago watching Khalim address patrons while onstage. He managed to look at all of them while looking at none of them at the same time. And many couldn't tell the difference.

"The tea tastes burnt. It's also tepid." He drained more than half the cup, though, in a single gulp.

"I'm sorry—"

He waved me off again. "It was boiled too long, too hot, and carried for just as long again." He fixed me with a knowing stare. "But I suppose that has to do with you taking the tray from whoever was carrying it, hm?"

I said nothing.

"Don't, boy. There's little point. I've had men try to poison me. Many tried to rob me. Some try under the bright sun with sword and arrow. I'm still here." He gave me a fox's own grin. Just as sharp. Just as sly.

"And where are they now?" I'm not sure what prompted me to ask, especially since I had an inkling to the answer.

His smile widened and he patted his sword.

"Oh." Sometimes all my cleverness fails me. This was one of those moments. I shifted uncomfortably on the ground, not having taken one of the cushions to ease my already tired bottom.

He noticed this and casually tossed one toward me. I caught it and alleviated my discomfort. "Most people try to rob me with less thought than you, though. For that, I'll give you the time to explain yourself." He put the pipe back to his mouth and inhaled.

I froze as I nearly touched my own cup. My head turned of its own accord, facing the doorway I'd come through. A quick spring and I could haul myself out of the room before the man could even get to his feet. I was young, fast, and sure of it.

"Don't, boy. My men are outside. You wouldn't get out of the doorway. And you wouldn't get a chance to speak, then. Maybe scream. So, why?"

My mouth dried and I eyed the cup, then him.

He nodded, catching my silent question.

I took a sip. He'd been right. The tea had been burnt. And it was cold. I drank enough to relieve the dryness in my throat. "How did you know?"

"How could I not, boy? How could you not imagine I'd find out? Better yet, think. A man in my position, a merchant with the fortune of a king, old as I am, and having kept it all. This isn't my first time here, or along any of the paths along the great Golden Road itself. Think." He tapped two fingers to the side of his head. "Do you think people only trade hard goods and that's all they have a mind for? That those without wits then peddle their bodies and soft goods? That *you* are the only one who figured out the secret turnings of a man's mind can be sold and traded."

Of course. Fool that I was. He didn't get rich just trading what he could hold in his hands. The man sold secrets as well. Which meant . . .

He smiled. "Caught on, have you?"

"Someone told you about us. The sparrows, I mean. Someone let on about my plans." There was no point in hiding it now, especially when he had me confined in his quarters with a sword nearly in hand and two men at my back. "But who?"

He shook his head, then exhaled another plume of smoke. "Almost there.

Close, boy. Close. But no. Think harder. Would someone in my position make it so easy for you to find out about me? To have such an easy time learning where I'd stay, and that I brought a small king's fortune with me?"

The truth thundered into me with the ringing loudness of metal striking metal. "Kaesha. He didn't manage to trade and pick up this secret through any wit of his own. Someone fed it to him. You *meant* for all of this to happen."

The old man nodded. "More or less. For as many secrets as you think you've traded, I've bartered off tens of thousands more over my life. And it's still not the extent of all I've come to know. In that, I still confess to having grown curious about the little boy said to run all this. The sparrows. Bloodletter. Some say you're a demon. You murdered men who ran the streets of Keshum. Stealing coins, white-joy, all before this demon boy and blood-spilling murderer burned down a drug lord's building. No one survives your wrath."

That wasn't true. Nika and Juggi did everything to ensure every child in Koli's joy house had escaped. The rest fled on account of my ruckus, and even if they hadn't, the fire hadn't been enough in the middle of a storm to raze the building to the ground. But, with the twists and turns of how stories spread to form reputations, that had come to be truth.

I *was* a demon to many. How else could I pluck and peddle people's secrets? Those were safely kept in heart and mind, of course. They never slipped a drunk man's lips or angry woman's mouth. Secrets are more easily told than ever held.

And I came to learn they made an even better hook to the greedy, the ambitious, and the childishly foolish.

I happened to be all three.

"But why?" I took another sip from the cup, still searching for any sign of the man's fortune. It had to be somewhere within the room. No man of his stature would keep it so far from where he could see it.

"Curiosity. I may have come here to trade, but there are other things far more valuable than what can be bartered for."

I waited for him to go on.

He didn't.

I relented and gave into the obvious ploy to have me ask the question. "What is that?"

"Talent, boy. Skill. I came to see what you would do. How you would go about it, and if I'd be killing a reckless fool, or maybe walking away with something else."

I licked my lips and took a series of slow and measured breaths. My heart all the while had picked up like I'd been running from the two thugs I'd encountered working the streets for Mithu all that time ago. The tension between us slowly built like a song quickening in tempo, promising a crescendo, but it refused to come and reach that cathartic break.

"Are you really a king?"

He inclined his head. "Of a different sort. It's not something you're born into where I'm from. It is, in part, by blood. Another piece is earned. We're not raised in marble and stone palaces. No gilded roofs and priests and gurus and sages. We live by and in the desert. At its mercy. By horse and shade and blood and water. Everything else is made and earned. A man's fortune is not given—passed down. It's built. Painfully.

"As I've done mine. And it's not something I mean to see taken by a child." His hand stroked the pommel of his sword again.

"So . . . what happens now?"

He arched a brow. "You tell me why. Was it greed? A boy looking to make an even larger name for himself? Robbing a merchant king from another land? A fortune large enough to never have to work another honest day in your life, or even a dishonest day. Is it just for the thrill of it? Have you fallen so far into your work you live for it now, risk and reward mean nothing? Why?"

One word. And it begged for no end of them in return to answer properly.

Should I lie to him? Would he know? A man who could set all this in motion and have me fall so neatly into his hands could easily have found a way to know the shape of my life. Would the truth earn me any sympathy?

Would it be enough?

He didn't give me the choice to think it through. The old man pulled the sword free and let the blade rest on the side of the tray, point aimed at me. He held it firmly and spoke. "Men get clever when they think they have time. Less so when they realize they have very little of it. You have until the count of five to speak, and truthfully. In my age, I've learned more than what I've said. I can tell when a man, or a boy, lies."

I bristled at him calling me a boy, but I reached for whatever words I could. "I didn't have a choice." Not wholly true, but close enough.

"One."

"It's true!" It wasn't.

"Two." He raised the sword and got to his feet.

I backed away, kicking my feet against the table. Could I make it to the door in time? Maybe past him through one of the open arched windows.

"Three."

"I needed the coin for my family. To make sure they're safe!" That was almost the truth. It certainly wasn't a lie.

"Four." He rounded the table and had me pinned against the door. "Five." He brought the sword down.

"The Ashram!"

The sword never reached my throat.

My chest heaved like I'd been starved for breath and my heart beat twice as hard as my breathing.

The old man smiled. "I knew I could make an honest man out of you, if even for a moment." He rolled his wrist in a gesture for me to continue. I noticed the sword never wavered from where he held it, the silent threat still clear.

So I told him everything. Almost everything, leaving out the Ashura. I told him of my life with the theater, of Mahrab and the night Koli and his friends came to kill my family. I told him of Mithu and my life with the sparrows, and then the day at the Zanzikari where I remembered what I wanted out of life. But the only way to get there was to follow through on what Kaesha had brought me. To rob the man before me and ensure my family would have money long after my departure, no matter what happened. And, I could use some of it myself to fund my trip to the Ashram without taking it from the sparrow treasury.

The sword still stayed steady in the air, no sign of it dipping or being pulled away. I took note of the calm strength it must have taken to hold a weapon like that for all this time without the slightest hint of wavering. He wasn't just smart, but strong.

"I can offer you a different life to studying old books and stories. A life beyond chasing and trying your hand at magics best left alone, not to mention the fact most men never manage to string half a binding together. There is a reason you rarely see a binder and the world hasn't fallen to a host of angry magicians. It's nearly an impossible thing to do. And it's why we're here."

He finally moved away from me and reached to one side, tossing another cushion out of the way.

In the space under it sat a wooden box as long as a man's face and half as thick as one's head. Not large by any means, but big enough for what it held when he lifted the lid.

Small king's fortune indeed.

The entire box shone a color I'd only seen in paint and clothing and had only ever dreamed of seeing in coins.

Gold.

Even in a box that size, the weight must have easily rivaled that of a heavy brick or two.

That much gold could buy a lifetime of comfort for every sparrow. It could buy someone a minister's appointment, a court life. Anything I could dream of.

"A life like this." He shut the lid and whatever magic had held me bound to the glittering gold faded just as fast. "We're here to make you an offer."

Both of my brows rose, but I had no words to speak.

"I'm old. My kingdom isn't the same as what you're used to, and it's old too. My mind is still sharp, but it is growing old as well. I would very much like to see what someone like you can do with me—for me.

"Ari, Bloodletter, King of Sparrows, Secret Seller of all that's whispered under Keshum. I've heard of you. Many things. And I wanted to see and learn the truth of you. If you can do these things and muster the courage to rob me, I wonder what you could do with the right man behind you. The right resources?" He patted the box of gold. "The right teacher? I'd like to find out."

And a part of me sorely would have liked the same. In fact, I burned for it in that moment. To hold that part back, then kill it, nearly broke me. A life of surety and safety beyond what I could imagine. A merchant king protecting me. A new land and the life that came with it. Travel, adventure, something of and for the stories.

And another temptation to take me away from everything that had led me here.

Not again. *Never* again.

"No."

He tilted his head at me like he couldn't believe what I'd said. I was sure a man like him didn't hear that word often, if ever. "No?"

I repeated myself.

"Why?" he asked.

"I've told you. I have to go to the Ashram. And I will." I met his stare with one sharper than the edge of his sword and far hotter than he could have ever wanted his tea to be.

"You're speaking as if you have a choice, Ari."

"Don't I?" I rose to my feet.

He waggled a hand. "Of sorts. You tried to rob me. Your choices are death or working for me. Earn back the debt you've incurred by stealing from me."

"But . . . I haven't stolen from you."

He smiled something full of mischief. "Haven't you?" He pointed the sword at me, wobbling it a bit. "Do you know the problem with reputations, Ari? Sometimes a name, or names, aren't just that. They're curses. Bondage. I know this thing, and I know how to turn it on its head. And you along with it.

"But before I show you this thing, tell you of it, and the noose that comes with it, tell me this: Even now, would you choose death over working for me?"

I looked back at the sword, knowing he'd make good on the threat if it came to it. But I also knew that among the fears I'd come to nurse and experience, death cured the fear of itself. It was the only guarantee you could have in life. And I'd already subjected myself to a series of slow sad suicides by turning away from my ambitions and dreams.

I stepped closer to the sword. "Yes."

The old man licked his lips and nodded. He sheathed his sword and fetched the box of gold in both hands. "I believe you would. Then I give you this choice to think on. You go to your Ashram, and before the end of one year from this day, finding your answers and magics or no, you come looking for me beyond the sands of Zibrath. Yes?" He reached out as if to pass me the box of gold.

My hands went for it almost on instinct. "If I take this and walk out of here, what's to keep me honoring my word?"

He smiled as if he'd been hoping I'd ask. "Your reputation and mine. And the loss of a king's wealth. You see, Ari, you *have* robbed me. When you take this gold—and it's the only way you'll leave alive—you will be bound to me. The word will spread, and I will make sure of it, that you, King of Sparrows, *did* steal from me. And I will leave it at that. No harm will befall you. But the word will spread. I will fan the fires of your name and deeds far and wide. And then, should you not return in that time, I'll hang you with them.

"This is but a piece of all I own. A piece I can afford to gamble on with you. Remember that." He passed me the box and took hold of one of the porcelain tea cups. "Do you know the cost of this?"

I shook my head, but I had an idea. And it was more than any sparrow would dare spend on nothing more than drink ware.

The cup fell from his hand, landing on the carpet to spill its tea. "This rug costs ten times that." He nodded to the fallen porcelain. It crunched underfoot a second later. His eyes never left mine as he ground the former cup to smaller pieces still. Then he repeated the process with the rest of the tea set. Piece by piece. Each breaking. Each spilling more liquid into the carpet that cost more than any laborer would earn in a year.

"You wish to keep your sparrows safe? You will never do that by breaking your word. I can spend just as much and more to have you found wherever you go, and your family as well, and then have you all killed. And I'll have my coin back then from their bodies and home. You will come to me one way or another. If not now, then later.

"*Ikthab.* It is written. It will be. This is nothing to me." He inclined his head toward the box. "A man or boy with a spark of fire, with potential, is worth infinitely more than this sum . . . or less depending on how they turn out."

I swallowed, knowing I didn't have much choice, but it bought me time. One year at the Ashram was better than dying now. My family would be safe all the while, and, yes, my reputation would grow to include robbing a king.

At the time, it seemed like a fair trade for a child with stories filling his head.

"And if I prove to be anything less than this?" I mirrored his gesture at the box of gold.

A twinkle filled the man's eyes. "Well, then I can write you off as that and afford the loss. But I am a keen gambler. One doesn't become a merchant king without knowing what to bet on. I know which of my horses will win a race, and which ones are dumb enough to die of thirst by running themselves well past what they should. I'm hoping you're to be the former."

This was it. The money in hand promised me a way to the Ashram and my family's safety. The sparrows would never go hungry again.

The box shook in my hands as I spoke. "Thank you. I'll keep my word. I'll be back. One year from now . . . I'll see you again, and I'll have done what you said can't be done, as well." My hands steadied and the weight of gold felt lighter. "I'll perform the bindings and learn those magics. And I'll show you them. I'll show you what my name and reputation can and will be. And I'll do just as much and more under you to pay this back." I raised the box to make my point.

He grinned and reached into a pocket to pull out a slender rod of horn and silver inlay with a pointed tip. A folded sheet of parchment followed and he scrawled something along it. "I expect nothing less. *Ikthab.* It is written. It will be. Come find me in one year, Ari. My name is Arfan. Find me out there along the Golden Road, past Zibrath, on shifting dunes and singing sands. If you survive that trek, it'll be the start to proving me and you right in your abilities. If not"—he shrugged—"I'll have a good deal of gold to take back, and your story ends rather early."

Like hell.

"Now go. Run. It doesn't do thieves well to linger when they've robbed someone, and make no mistake, this is a robbery." He still held that smile.

"I wonder who's the one really being robbed." I hadn't realized I'd spoken my thoughts aloud. He was losing money; I, my freedom and time of life in the future.

I didn't know it then, but there are some things gold cannot buy you, and it can serve to make a finer prison than bars of iron and walls of stone can ever do.

"I wonder the same, Ari." He drew his sword. "Run."

I did, and in doing so, brought his lie to life.

I'd robbed a merchant king, and the streets of Keshum would soon spread it to every ear willing to hear of it.

FORTY-SEVEN

LIES

There is no easy way to run with a small king's fortune in your hands. Whatever fear I had stepping into the High Quarter, then into Arfan's rooms, fell far short of that gripping my heart as I fled.

There is a certain safety in being penniless, not that it may seem like it at first. Few people see a sparrow and think to harm them for money. But put a box of gold in his hands and then watch his skin break into sweat and listen to his chest drum away.

I fought to keep my breath and body steady under the weight of coins and panic settling into me. The sight of me running did little to draw attention, fortunately, but I had no idea how long the peace would last with Arfan doing his best to raise a row behind me.

I'd nearly reached the pillars framing the entry into the quarter when I heard the cries behind me. Curses in a tongue I couldn't understand peppered the air.

The two kuthri at the entrance turned to look at the source of commotion and I slowed my pace to a walk, hunching over to conceal much of the box under the folds of my shirt.

They looked past me in what I considered to be the last bit of luck I dared to trust that day. The men didn't break into a run, falling just short of the pace as they took off in the direction of the noise.

Thanking Brahm and any other deity I could hope to remember, I made my way out of the High Quarter proper and hailed one of the nearby rickshaws. I gave the man no chance to speak and mutter the usual pleasantries. "Hard Quarter, now. Do you know where the glassmaker is on Dharum Street?"

He nodded, opening his mouth, but I cut him off again.

"No words. No nothing." I thumbed the box's lid partially open, just enough for me to sneak a coin out of it and into my palm.

The man bobbed his head, probably used to that level of treatment from other patrons out of the quarter.

I clambered onto the back and urged him go.

He did, and we traveled without exchanging a word until we reached the glassworks. The building stood not more than another half an hour from the House of Sparrows. It would be safer for me to stop here and walk. These streets had enough of my family patrolling them that no harm could befall me, and with the dissolution of Koli's band of thugs, we were the only ones who traversed the back alleys.

But in the event Arfan's words held true and people quickly came to know what I'd done, I didn't want eyewitness accounts of people spotting me near my home.

"Five chips, *sahm,*" said the driver. His voice had cracked and it hadn't come from fatigue. The way I'd spoken to him earlier had left an impression, and I got the feeling the kind of people that talked to him like that weren't keen on paying their fair share for his services. His posture shrank and he looked like he expected me to swat at him.

I held my breath for a moment, praying my own heart would finally settle. Once it had, I hopped from the rickshaw and came to the man's side. "Hold out your hand."

He did, and his shook nearly as much as my own.

I placed the gold rupai into his palm, closing his fingers over it. The man didn't let me go more than five steps before a series of choked-out words dribbled behind me.

"*Sahm.* This is . . ."

I waved him off without looking. "It's enough."

"No one will believe someone paid me in gold, *sahm.*"

I thought about what Arfan had said. If I was going to end up a thief no matter what, one with a reputation, I might as well be a famous one. A little slip of my own wouldn't hurt to feed my story, I figured. "They will when you tell them this: Someone paid you to tell them about someone you'd carried earlier. You'll tell anyone who asked that you rickshawed someone who'd stolen a king's hand of gold. His name is Ari. And he robbed a merchant king. You carried him without knowing, and for telling the right people this truth, they gave you a gold rupai. That's *if* anyone asks. Hopefully they won't."

"But, *sahm,* I never carried any such person?"

A crooked smile crossed my face. *And the truth is, you did. That's what makes this a great story.* "But you did, and you tell yourself that until you believe it. And if anyone asks about me, you tell them you brought me here, to the glassworks on this street, *ji-ah*?"

"Ji."

I made a dismissive gesture with a hand, not turning around until I heard the wheels of the cart rattle and roll away. It wasn't long until I found myself passing through some of the alleys, box still tight in hand, and came across some of my family.

Two sparrows had just broken into view, running hard and each holding a small purse in hand.

Clutchers. They'd just plucked a fresh pick from someone.

Though, not smoothly enough to go unnoticed.

I whistled, drawing their attention and flagging them down.

Both hurried after me and I led them down another path.

"Ari?" asked one of them. She was younger than me by a year or two. Her hair had streaks of a rusty red through the muddled brown and it all hung in messy curls falling to her earlobes. Her eyes were just a shade lighter than her locks.

"What is it, Bippi?"

She ran a tongue over her front two teeth and chanced a look over her shoulder—more in fear of being chased, it seemed, than anything else. "We heard you'd left for the High Quarter. Didn't think you'd be back."

I smiled. "Well, I am."

The other sparrow, a boy the same age as her, remained silent. He clutched his purse as if he expected someone to swoop down and snatch it away.

"Let's get you both back home."

"I pulled nine chips and a copper," said the boy.

I clapped him on his shoulder. "That's good. And, if I'm right about something, that's the last time you'll ever have to clutch again."

The boy fixed me with an odd look, but I didn't bother explaining. I led my brother and sister home instead.

I didn't share the contents of the box with Bippi or any of the other fledgling sparrows, especially those who'd come so newly into our care. It would have brought so many of them a great deal of ease to know, but it also would have been a risk I couldn't take. Some of the sparrows hadn't quite learned when to keep their beaks shut and from cheep-cheeping. As much as we traded secrets, Arfan had shown me we needed to work on keeping our own tightly held.

That night, I called Nika and Juggi to Mithu's old office.

"What's this about, Ari? First you spend the morning keeping us worried you won't make it out of the High Quarter, now you know what I'm hearing on the streets?" Nika leaned closer to me, somehow adopting a posture that made her look like she was looming instead. Her hands balled into fists and came to rest on her hips as she glared.

I didn't answer her, knowing well enough it was a trick that would only buy me more trouble than I could afford. And considering I'd walked away with a box of gold, I could afford quite a bit, but still not as much as that.

Some troubles are simply not worth the price you pay for them. Angering a girl like Nika was one of those.

"I'm hearing whispers from some of our sparrows our boy-king managed to rob the merchant he'd only gone to snoop on. Did he do it quietly? Did he get away without a word or sound? No. The whole High Quarter knows of it. And they know your name, Ari!" She jabbed an index finger against my chest.

"Well, if they didn't know it before, they do now. Especially with you shouting it like that," said Juggi. He gave her a sideways look that he managed to keep just short of being reproachful. It did little to spare him a withering glare in return.

Nika turned her gaze back on me, waiting for an explanation. When it didn't come, she let out a low growl that told me I should have spoken up sooner. "Well, did you?"

The best I could manage was a rakish smile that did little to improve her disposition. "You could say that."

Her eyes narrowed. "I could, and most of Abhar will be saying it too within the set, *which* is the problem. Most of Keshum already knows. Or they believe. I'm not sure which is worse."

"That depends on what answer I'm getting hit for saying." I managed to straighten out my smile a bit, but still fell short of something honest.

"I don't know if there's a way for you to get out of that, Ari. But believe me, your best chance is giving me an answer."

Juggi decided that the window had become the most fascinating thing he'd ever seen and turned his attention on it, taking several steps away from Nika and me.

Traitor.

I didn't know what to tell the two of them. The whole truth is what they deserved, and it's what I wanted to say. But doing so meant making them privy to Arfan's deal, and that meant sharing my plan to go to the Ashram. I could tell you they weren't ready for me to leave, that seeing me go would have broken their hearts.

And it was true. I knew that much.

But it was just as true that it would tear the same piece out of me to have told them, watched their faces, and then done the thing anyway. Sometimes, the lies we don't tell spare us a greater pain than what we'd put on others.

It's not the right thing, many will say. But I'm not sure I've seen any proof it's quite so wrong either.

So I sucked a breath in through my teeth and gestured to the box I'd set atop Mithu's desk. "You tell me." I walked over to the container of gold and threw back the lid.

Every coin caught the candlelight, shimmering something sunlight-bright and then some. Maybe part of it had to do with a day spent with the rumor of my deed spreading. That kind of attention and questioning always leads to a bit more splendor in moments like this. Maybe a part of it had to do with the fact that, up until then, Nika and Juggi had never seen a piece of gold, much less a box of it.

"I told you I'd do it." I left the lid open, leaving the contents to mesmerize my adoptive brother and sister. "Though, I wouldn't say I robbed him so much as alleviated him of its weight."

Juggi grinned, an uneven thing that could have matched the coins in brightness.

Nika's mouth hung open in a perfect circle as she stared at the gold, then me. "How?"

"Haven't you heard? I'm the King of Sparrows. Thief, tin taker, lie cobbler, problem maker. Steal your secrets, spin them proper, then sell the lot to king or a pauper. No one and nothing's safe from my hands." I waggled my fingers. "And nowhere's safe to hide your goods in all these lands. For my—*ow*!" I stopped and rubbed a spot on my arm just under my shoulder.

Nika held up a balled fist. "You keep talking like that and you're going to end up believing your own shit-spun stories. And then I'll pummel you again." She shook the fist, making the threat clear.

I muttered something under my breath, taking care to keep it from her ears despite the proximity.

"What was that?"

"S'nothing," I said. "Just finishing the rest of my reputation . . . under my breath where you can't hear it."

Nika raised her fist higher.

I grinned but had the smarts to back away. "Kidding-kidding." I rubbed the sore spot once again before clearing my throat and deciding to answer her question partially. "I did steal all this, but it was mostly by luck."

Both of them looked at me but preserved the quiet that had fallen after my last word. They wanted me to explain in greater detail, I suppose.

I sighed and fell into the story of how I talked my way past the doorman and the teaboy, meeting both of Arfan's pals. Then came the lie that hurt and weighed my chest with molten metal. I told them how I tricked Arfan into revealing where he'd kept the lockbox, and realizing how small it was, I decided that I could find a way out with it in hand without risking any more sparrows on a later attempt.

And how, you might wonder, I got this away from Arfan? Well, I was the best secret seller in the city, at least. It wasn't so hard for me to learn what kind of tea the man liked, when he drank it, and then it had been the simple matter of buying some herbs to mix into the batch to force him into a deep slumber while we talked.

And if there's anything I can do, it's talk.

So we did, and soon the merchant king fell asleep at my feet. Ari the Sparrow had little trouble from there making his way out of the place, but not before the guards and alarm were raised and I had to find an equally clever way out of the High Quarter.

I ran and lost people through alleys and turns that I'd come to know best in that quarter. I scrambled up walls and through homes, racing along rooftops, even managing to tip over a pot of excrement onto one of the guards. I went into great detail on this matter with Nika and Juggi.

Sometimes it's the little pieces of stories that matter. And, I knew how tales worked. No one would believe me if I had told them that Arfan had practically handed me the box, doubly so if I said he'd orchestrated most of it in order to get me to work for him.

No. Stories need their lies to become believable, sad truth that it is.

And so, satisfied my life had thoroughly been at risk, but their clever brother still prevailed, Nika and Juggi ate the story up without complaint.

A deeper throb, one promising to nearly reach the bone, blossomed in my arm. The same spot that Nika had struck earlier. "Ow. Brahm's tits, why?" I moved away from her until the edge of the desk dug into my lower back.

"You could have been killed! I warned you about this. All of this!" She stomped over to me until her chest almost touched mine, and our noses nearly met but for a hair's breadth.

"I mean, if you believe the stories, I can't be killed either. I'm a demon, remember?" I grinned, which was the wrong thing to do.

Nika's eyes turned to paper-thin slits.

"Last joke, I promise . . . on Juggi's life."

"Oi! Don't drag me into your mess."

I side-eyed him. One, for the lack of brotherly support. And second, for the fact that in matters of coins and danger, *we* shared the spoils even if *I* risked myself, and here he was ready to celebrate the gold all while leaving me to face the brunt of Nika's anger.

I raised both hands in a gesture of placation that managed to temper her anger, enough to get her to back away from me. She still stood within arm's reach, I noticed, but I figured it safer for my health not to make a comment about that. Instead, I turned my—and everyone else's—attention back to the box. I gave the container a small pat. "Look, I know you're mad. And you have every reason to be. I'm sorry."

More than any joke, crooked charming smile, those few words pulled all the anger out of her.

The wonders an honest apology can do.

Her shoulders slumped and she bent forward now, no longer looking at all like she was looming. Nika let out a heavy breath and put one hand on my side. "I know. I'm just glad you're back, and I was angry and worried that I'd lose you."

And she still would. Her words sent a knife into my stomach.

"I can't have that, Ari, not after learning about and losing Mithu."

The knife twisted.

"Don't ever leave us."

Twist.

Because I meant to.

"I won't," I lied.

She wrapped her arms around me and held me. Then, Nika brought her mouth to mine in the sort of awkward short kiss that brings a flush to every young boy.

Juggi broke the equally awkward silence that fell between us afterward. "What are we going to do with all this, Ari?"

I looked at the gold, trying to tally the sums, and I fell painfully—wonderfully short. A laugh left me and filled the room, rolling surely down into the halls below. "I don't know. Whatever you want?"

"Whatever *we* want," Nika stressed.

The knife buried deeper.

"This is enough money to take care of the sparrows forever. Sell secrets or don't. But no more clutching, no more listening—begging—asking, whimpering, or crying. No more dirt and tattered clothes. This sort of money? No more lost little kids in Keshum. The sparrows can be a family to any child that needs one."

I won't bore you with the rest of what we said. The conversation trailed to other dreams Juggi and Nika one day wondered about indulging. Maybe sailing the Rose Sea, being a pirate and wooing girls and stealing more treasure. Juggi tended to dream large.

Nika wished to journey far to Laxina and learn of their fighting arts. Maybe travel with Juggi too, and if he could be a pirate wooing girls, so would she, and trip just as many men along the way. She promised no one would be safe from her. And when she was done and to home returned, she'd tend to the sparrows and start a family of her own. But no child would go unfed and be at risk when and where she had the means to protect them.

I kept silent all the while, knowing my dreams were best left unsaid this night.

FORTY-EIGHT

LEAVINGS

To say I woke in the early hours of the morning would have been a lie. That would have implied I slept at all. Instead, I'd spent the night preparing for my journey north. A trip that could last two sets of days across nearly six hundred miles, not to mention the variance in terrain and cities and villages I'd pass through, all of which would bring their own hindrances.

I packed close to three pounds of dried chickpeas for grazing and keeping myself fed, dried apricots and dates, and a water gourd almost as full round as my head. It'd ensure that, even if water came rarely, I could store enough to be safe. A few bundles of what clothes I'd managed to purchase for myself as a sparrow, having never taken the time to indulge beyond the one nice set needed for the High Quarter. And, lastly, the bound book Mahrab had left me. The one keeping secrets of my family and quite possibly more.

The sun hadn't risen yet, but the pale promise of its coming washed part of the horizon with a muted glow, and a cockerel had taken to making an awful racket. Not what I wanted when planning to leave as quietly as possible.

I hadn't the heart to take much more than a handful of copper from our treasury. In some regards, the money would have been a great help, but given I had no idea what I'd have to deal with out on the roads, it might fall painfully short.

So I decided to palm one of the gold rupais from Arfan's chest. Two would have been one too many. Not in reality, but an old rhyme stuck in my head about greed and what befell those who took more than their fair share.

A handful of tin isn't much at all,
when a palm's worth of copper is enough on which to call,
but more so a pinch of iron on which to rely,
when you've no taels of silver with which to buy,
but one piece of gold's more than enough,
to be worth a plenty;
for only a greedy man hoards gold
like each piece a penny.

And ill fortune befalls those with eyes of greed,
for Brahm watches and judges
every call and deed,
he weighs your heart
and each and every thought,
so do not take more than your fair share in coin,
for it's not worth
the ill troubles bought.

The sum I'd taken wouldn't hurt the sparrows in the slightest. A different hurt would fill their hearts come the morning, though. Nika and Juggi would be the first to feel it.

I did my best to mollify that by writing a short letter.

To Nika & Juggi,

If you're reading this, then I'm already gone. Everything I did was to make sure you and the sparrows will be safe for the remainder of your lives. I'm sorry for the risks, sorry for the worry I put you through, and I am sorry for this. I know I promised you I wouldn't leave, but I have to go north. There are parts of me I have buried and I need to recover, and the north is the only place for me to do so. I can't stay. Take care of the others. Make sure that any lost child looking for a place has one with the sparrows—with the two of you. I know the gold won't make you any less angry with me, and it won't make this hurt any less, but it will keep you fed.

I hope to return one day, and when I do, I hope the pain will have gone from your hearts.

I love you both.

Don't follow me. Don't try to find me.

I hope even if you can't understand, that you'll forgive me. And if you can't forgive me, then at least understand this is something I have to do.

Looking back, I realize the letter was more a way to make me feel better than the brothers and sisters I left behind. An excuse I could use to say I had told them of my departure . . . but all without having to look them in their faces and see their hurt. To not have to hear them beg me to stay, or try to convince me in some other way. No, the letter was the coward's way out.

Because I knew if I had spoken to them one last time, I wouldn't have left. And I couldn't risk that.

I left the letter on Mithu's desk after clearing away all other clutter from its surface. A fleeting look around the office brought the old sword to my attention.

The weapon somehow held a faded gleam even in the mostly lightless room. It reminded me of gray stone that had been polished so smooth it could have almost been said to shine.

One of my hands spasmed upon looking at the weapon, like it wanted to bring and hold the thing as an old comfort. I dismissed the feeling. The sword, as wanted as it was by my hand, would only serve to bring *unwanted* attention. It would draw the eyes of the kuthri to see a young man of just past fourteen carrying a blade. The sword could just as easily give any carriage driver pause, leave them wondering if I was a cutthroat under the guise of a passenger—no, it would only be a trouble.

I left it hanging in its mounts, deciding that if my old life had to be left behind, it behooved me to leave as much of it in the past as I could. I did make sure, however, to fasten the knife Mithu had given me to my side. With a little effort, I ensured it'd stay put and out of sight under the waistband and hem of my shirt.

Everything had been sorted. Sack cinched tight and over my back, I made my way down the flight of stairs and through the hall housing the sparrows' bedrooms. My feet hit the floor in absolute soundlessness, more a silent shuffle than any proper steps. I hadn't grown used to wearing shoes, and as such, struggled to move with the efficiency I'd learned running barefoot or with tattered rags barely bound to my feet.

I reached the next flight of stairs and went down them, finally daring to release the breath I'd held buried deep in my chest. A part of me had nursed the fear that even an exhale would alert the softer sleepers among my family. A noise like dry bristles scraping against stone filled my ears as I stepped into the middle of the ground floor. I turned toward the source.

Small Kaya, looking as resigned as ever, stood at one side of the room, sweeping. She watched me with a careful quiet, her face betraying nothing. "You're leaving, Ari-*cha*."

I nodded.

She took a breath, giving me a longer look. "For good, yes?"

Another nod.

"Mhm. They always leave. The ones who take over the sparrow's nest. You, Mithu, and the ones before." She punctuated each word with another sweep. "And they never come back. But Small Kaya always remains. Sometimes I think I will die with this place. When the last stone is sand and it falls, then so will I. Until then, I will see to them."

More words than I'd ever heard her speak.

"Thank you. They're going to be upset when they wake up and find out."

"Yes."

"Maybe you shouldn't tell them that you saw me go. They'll be angry with you. Ask why you didn't stop me."

Small Kaya gave my words as much thought as she gave her sweeping, which was not much at all by the looks of it. Movements born more of weary repetition than any attentiveness and obligation. "They will be angry. With me. With you. Whatever. All that changes is where they put the anger. Angry men and women will find a place for that anger no matter what. I have seen enough of it in my life. And if they put that in Small Kaya, so be it. I have held enough anger for others over my years."

The sweeping stopped and her eyes grew watery, but she had stopped looking at me while speaking.

I walked over to her and wrapped her tight into a hug. "I'll miss you too."

Small Kaya didn't gaze at me when she spoke. "Same, Ari-*cha*." She patted my head twice and gave me a gentle push.

I broke the hug and went to the door, keeping my eyes fixed ahead.

There is no looking back sometimes. For looking back is the last temptation, and if taken, can lock you in place harder than if you were set in mortar. The door shut behind me with what would have been a loud thud if I had the ears to hear it. But I'd turned all my attention to the already busy streets of Keshum and the ruckus that came with them.

Light or no, coin and commerce waited for no man, and the roads were flooded with people wanting to make their fortunes—some just as eager to risk all of theirs if it meant the promise of something greater.

I walked, holding to a tunnel vision to see and pick my way through the crowd walking against me. The oddity struck me a moment later as I realized I had taken to moving with people and around them, not as a sparrow looking to clutch a purse or use them to hide, but as someone just going about his way.

All those years in the city and I never once belonged with the crowd until the day I left. Sometimes it's only when we're through and done with something that we realize we never really belonged, and in that realization, things try their hardest to convince us otherwise.

To stay. To be in places and with the people we do not truly belong.

The crowd shuffled along, jostling elbows, trading comments and insults, and I slipped through them until I reached the small travelers' circle at the end of the Hard Quarter.

Countless roads led to it and branched back out. A place for all travelers to filter through. I spent time there, looking over what the vendors ringing the circle's edge had to offer. All goods catered for travelers who'd let something slip their minds and needed to buy at the last minute. A smart practice. One I indulged.

I circled the stalls, looking at the goods on display. Nothing caught my eye and I'd almost given up on finding anything interesting or useful until I reached the final stall.

"Oi, boy."

I bristled but turned toward the speaker.

The man should have been better fed given the location of his shop, but instead he looked like he'd been carved out of a single long and gnarled piece of driftwood. Hard knots of sinew held together by bony protruding joints. His skin reminded me of old leather never once cared for, cracked and creased and barely holding to his body. His eyes, though, somehow carried a brightness in their brown that should have left him long ago. He should have been tired and weighed down simply by the effort of holding himself upright.

"Yes?"

"You look like you're going out on the roads."

I inclined my head in agreement.

"Far, I take it?"

I answered him the same way again.

"But you certainly don't have all you need for a trip. And, by the look of your face, I can tell you don't mean to be back."

I stared at him, not speaking.

"Mhm. Thought as much. I've seen many like you before, though none so badly prepared for a long journey like you."

That got me to open my mouth. "Who said I'm going anywhere for long?"

He rolled his eyes. "It's my business to spot traders and travelers from close or long off ways. And I know when a man goes and stays. You're not one for staying—anywhere. But you're not carrying all you need for the world outside." He leaned to one side and pulled up a trio of candles with a tin base to hold one in.

I raised one brow. "You think I need that?"

He gave the bundle a little waggle. "Of course. Every traveler and wanderer worth their salt and silver needs a candle. Oh, what will you do come the long and dark night? Trust me, you will be in want of candlelight. There's more than men out there, you know? And on the nights there's not, strange men in the dark can still leave a traveler worry-filled and fraught." Another jiggle of the candles. "Besides, three things each wise traveler takes: a cloak to shield him from dirt and pains, candle for when sunlight wanes, and a trusted sturdy walking cane. At least, if he's a traveler with any sense and brains."

The candles fell to the table and his hand reappeared holding a bundle of folded fabric the color of old sage blanched to almost gray with only a memory of once any shade of green. He let it fall loose between his fingers to reveal a hooded cloak. "It's old, mind you. But not a hole in sight or a thread out of stitch and line."

Before I could tell him I didn't need any of that, he moved again, pulling up another item. He placed a long cane atop the now-folded cloak.

Truthfully, it measured more than any old man's cane. It resembled more a proper traveler's staff. Long and sturdy. The walking stick had been carved from a wood the color of molasses, rich and still holding some oil in its finish. It lacked any adornment or carving. Just a simple strong length of wood.

"I'm not old enough to need a cane."

He looked at me as if I'd said something incredibly stupid.

"You wait until you need a cane, boy, then you'll be sorely out of luck and in more trouble than you'd wish for. Young men and old get humbled by long roads and hills. Especially if you're going north toward mountainous ways. If you're too dumb to know when someone's helping you—" He broke off and shrugged.

I narrowed my eyes at him. "Most vendors try to do a better job of convincing customers to buy."

He rolled his shoulders with the nonchalance reserved for a man with not a care in the world. "I have a stall in the heart of the Arban's Circle. I never hurt for coin or customer. If not you, someone else will come. I do not need to beg and plead. I will not. Some things are more important, besides. If you want to get your clothes dirty, what little I feel you own, anyway, and have your legs ache over hills, and eyes pain in the night, then go." He waved me off.

I gritted my teeth. As much as I hated to admit it, especially with how asinine the man had been, he had a point. Candles would be useful, as would the cloak. I didn't have enough clothes or the money to guarantee I'd change them for the whole trip and beyond. Not without knowing what would happen along the way. "How much?" I kept the grit and edge out of my voice, knowing full well any more antagonization from my end could lead the man to up his prices.

"Two coppers."

I choked. "Not a chance! This wood isn't anything special. It's worth maybe eight tin chips. And the cloak?" I jabbed a finger at the fabric. "I'll bet that's twelve at best new." I glared at him. "And we know that's not the case here. Candles? I can pick up a bundle for three to four tin. This is no bundle."

He didn't miss a beat. "Surely so. But, you'll have to go back outside the circle for those prices, and the morning caravans heading out will be gone by the time you're back. You'll miss your chance to leave. And by the look of you, I can tell if you don't get out now, you won't be leaving ever. No. Keshum and Abhar are too stuck in you, and you them. You need to leave now. And you'll need candle, cloak, and cane." He smiled, revealing a missing tooth to the side of his front two large ones.

I exhaled, knowing his prices were taking me and any other fool who had the dumb luck to stop at his shop. I looked over the trio of things, my gaze passing over the other small items littering the table's surface. I spotted iron and steel bracelets, cords of wrapped string, and a small figurine. The wood had been carved into a small and squat owl with an oversized head and eyes. I took it as another sign of good luck and decided to gamble on the deal.

"Done." I passed him two coppers from my purse, taking great care not to betray a glint or glimmer of gold within. Four copper pieces remained to me, and it would have to be enough, for I dared not think on having to spend the rupai.

He handed me the candles and I took good care to slip them into my pack.

The cloak fitted nicely around me and covered most of my body without being so long as to trail and track dirt and dust along with me. Surprisingly, the cane fit comfortably in the palm of my hand. The irregular shape to part of its body had almost been made for me. My fingers fit along the grooves and crevices perfectly, helping me place my weight on it without aching any part of my hand.

"Thank you."

The man finally smiled in earnest. "So, little wanderer. Where are you traveling to?"

"North. The Ashram." I took a second to look to the many caravans and carriages littering the outermost edge of the circle. Some clearly had just come in, depositing people, and others were setting to depart. I couldn't tell which ones were heading where I wanted.

The man must have caught my look and understood the meaning behind it. "Only one I know of heading that way." He pointed for me and I followed his finger. "Jaseem. He and his wife do long runs up that way. Sometimes they trade for the sort of goods and trinkets you only get outside a place full of *jathu*-doers. All that magic and mystery nonsense. But, still . . ." He rubbed his chin as if in deep thought. "There are some real wonders that come back from that way. I can never make sense of them myself. Still, good thing you were wise enough to buy what you did." He gave me a knowing look. "Boy going up that far will need those three things . . . *at least*."

I let the comment slide and kept my attention on Jaseem and the carriage. "Thank you for the information."

The man grunted. "Consider it paid for. Best of luck on your trip, and I hope you find what you're looking for. Brahm's blessing, boy."

I wasn't religious, but, having long been captivated by Brahm's stories, legends, and magic, I welcomed the bit of luck. "Ari," I said.

"Hm?"

"My name is Ari. Remember it. The world will know it one day. You should start ahead of them and know it now." I couldn't see the man's face as I walked away from him, but I had a feeling he was smiling.

"Is that so? Ari. I will remember it then."

In truth, that moment of confidence, or arrogance—it's hard for a young boy to know the difference at times—might have been the start of so many of my problems to come.

But, I couldn't have known. I'd just left my family behind, and now I acted in ways to mask the hurt, from my face, and most of all from my heart.

I figured the little boldness would help steel me for the journey to come and against the pains of missing my family I knew I'd nurse beyond its end.

FORTY-NINE

Intermission—Lamplight and Moonlight

"Leaving is never easy, is it?" Eloine didn't look at me when she spoke, but she wore a tired sympathetic look I felt was for me.

"No, and what you're never told is that you risk leaving parts of yourself behind when you do." We strolled farther down the road, passing by low-standing buildings, paying them all little mind. Some of the lanterns along the way had been lit, providing us a pleasant glow by which to walk.

"It's a hard thing." Eloine's hand found mine and squeezed. "I know that pain well enough myself." Something in her voice told me she did, and knew it as intimately as I'd come to.

"I don't suppose this is the part of our story where I get to ask about yours?" Hope filtered into my voice, and I wished for her not to hear my extra enthusiasm.

"*Our* story, hm?" She shot me a sideways look, the corners of her lips playing their way into an amused smirk. "Such a short time together and it's already ours. You certainly don't give a woman time to catch her breath, do you?"

"It's been said I do a better job at taking their breath away. Depending on how much stock you put in the stories, of course."

She rolled her eyes. "Of course. Well, we're learning just how unreliable those stories can be. And, I suppose I'll come to learn most of those women lost their breath for reasons entirely unrelated to your charms. Mayhaps from frustration or resignation?" Her face fell into a perfectly neutral mask, but her eyes betrayed her. They danced with the soft light of the lanterns shining over them.

"I suppose I'll have to settle for the fact that, no matter what, I've left women without breath—however the stories say I have. It's something."

"Mhm." She pursed her lips and touched two fingers to them. "I don't think you're one for settling, especially when it comes to stories. Doubly so with yours, otherwise . . ." She trailed off and looked me up and down. "Well, you wouldn't be like this now, would you?"

She was right, and I found myself fighting back a laugh. I screwed my face tight and flashed her a wounded look in reply. "And what's that mean? Are you implying that I'm—" I stopped short, the look falling from my face. "Wait, what are you implying?"

Eloine rolled her eyes and pulled her hand from mine to poke me with her fingers. "I'd thought I was rather clear. You *are* a bit dramatic, aren't you? Someone who dresses like this"—she pinched a piece of my cloak, letting go almost as fast—"doesn't settle when it comes to his trade."

"I'm not sure if that's a compliment or an insult."

She folded her lips tight, refusing to speak, and the light in her eyes intensified.

"Oh-ho, cute."

Her mouth parted in a self-satisfied grin that could have been pulled from the smuggest of cats. "I am. I'm glad you've noticed, though a bit disheartened it's taken you this long to say."

I blinked and reached for some words, falling short of anything worth saying.

"Well, that's certainly good to know. Some men are ever so hard to quiet. I almost had a worry, with your way and lack of want for words, you'd be one of those who never stops talking." She reached out and tapped a finger to my lips as I still searched for a riposte. "No. None of that. Maybe learn to walk with a woman without talking. There's something to be said for silence, and there's not always a need to break it."

If only she knew how true that was.

Silence is oft held to hold a value as much as gold. But, sometimes, it can hold one more than any coin can come to count. It can hold back some things that come with terrible cost, truth be told. And that sort of silence is the best kind to uphold.

Being quiet never hurt anybody. Though, I didn't learn that lesson soon enough in my life.

But, there, on the road with Eloine, I figured it better late than never to start learning.

We walked quietly for a third of a candlemark. She led the way, retaking my hand, and steering us onto a cobblestone street. The rocks were of nearly uniform height, though I figured that had more to do with the wear of frequent footfalls than meticulous design. We walked over the smoothed and less bumpy part of the way.

Eloine let out a sharp gasp and tipped toward me.

I moved without thinking, sweeping her into an arm while planting my staff against the road as a brace. Catching her came as an old reflex, reawakened then. It took me a moment to realize what had happened, in truth. "That was well done. I'd thought you'd actually fallen."

She slipped herself out of my grip. "Maybe you just left me breathless." She spoke like she'd run all the way from the Three Tales to the spot we were now. "Oh, Ari," Eloine said, still keeping to the same winded whisper.

I gave her a gentle shove. "You're funny." My voice was as flat as I wished the stones under us were.

"And you should take the time to appreciate that. You're so somber, I swear. If you keep this way, you'll reach dour in no time. That won't do you well in taking any more women's breaths away."

I arched a brow and resumed walking. "Am I supposed to? Be thinking of taking other women's wind from them? Here I thought there was only one worth trying for?" I gave her my best jaunty grin.

She huffed. "Men always say that. All the while, they're flashing a smile just as fine as yours to a handful of other women."

I knew what she said to be true, but it wasn't for me. "I'm different."

Eloine gave me a long drawn look. "They say that too."

They did.

I licked my lips, searching for something better to say as silence filled the space between us.

A universal truth I've learned over my life is this: No matter how clever the man, we are all fools when it comes to words with a woman who's taken our heart. Even if we don't realize she holds it, a part of us does, and that part, so fixated on that one thing alone, makes it ever the effort to find anything sensible to say. Especially when we put our foot in our mouth.

"The moon's full tonight," I said. Not the best of things to discuss, but I figured anything would be better than nothing.

"She is."

"I never appreciated that sight much, truth be told." I held the moon's shape full in view, taking the moment to marvel at its pristine whiteness in the sky; a better bright diamond than any star could hope to shine.

"Most people don't. They watch her sail and slip through her faces, hiding her hurt all the while."

I paused, almost catching my foot on a stone that protruded higher than the rest. "What's that?"

"There's a song I heard long ago about her." Eloine frowned and looked to the ground, her gaze growing distant as if deep in thought. "About a wolf who wanted to swallow her whole—to take the moon and make her his. She rebuffed him, and in his anger, he hurt her—scarred her, which became a reminder of his sin." Eloine rubbed a hand down her face. "That's why she changes the side of her face she shows, you know? And a night with a full moon is a special thing, for she's decided to show you all of her."

I'd never heard even a piece of that story, much less the song that spurred it. "Do you know the song?"

She nodded.

"Will you sing it for me?"

The smile she wore was no full and bright thing, unlike the moon tonight in every way. Strained, pulled thin, it made her face seem wan even under all the various light we'd been given tonight. "Not here. Maybe soon in private. Certainly not where she can hear." Eloine gestured at the sky. "Sometimes remembering hurts."

"It does." The quietness returned and we walked down the alley, though I gave silent thanks that she slipped her fingers through mine again and held me tight.

We rounded a corner and found ourselves on a wider road with larger shops and buildings. Bigger, brighter bulbs of light burned here in a longer row of lanterns.

A slender man, dressed in rough canvas clothing with a cap screwed firmly to his head, moved about one of the light poles. He held a metal rod in hand, long and thin, its end a blunted hook. He slipped it through a handle on a lantern's face and pulled open the glass pane. Then, with another rod, fully wooden, he brought a burning wick up to the flameless candle within the housing. Spark, flash, the fire flickered to life.

We passed him by, exchanging polite nods. Though, his gaze lingered for a moment longer, noticeably so, on Eloine.

"People seem to stare more at you than me. That's a bit of a hurtful thing when dressed as such." I poked at my cloak, hoping the callback to her earlier joke would draw another smile from her.

But it didn't come.

"People stare at strangers and strange things all the time. It's easier. And the stranger the stranger, the longer and harder the stares."

"Depends on the kind of stares, I suppose." I hoped the words would pull some of the sullenness from her. "I do rather stand out."

She gave me a smile, but not the one I'd been looking for. Lopsided, without any honest joy behind it. Tired and drawn. "You do, but for all the right reasons. I do as well, but for all the wrong reasons. My dress? Last night it spoke cleanly of who I was, and so long as I sang and danced, it was fine. But I belong in taverns to entertain, nothing more. At least that's what people here think." An edge crept into her voice.

"Tonight I dress like them, but they can see the shape of who's wearing it. And I'm not one of them, and for all your own difference, you play the role you're given. I do not."

I didn't know what she meant by that, and something told me asking would ruin our night. So, I did what many didn't think I could ever do, and I bit my tongue and nodded.

"I'm sorry."

I said nothing but looked at her.

"I've made things difficult—awkward. It's not your fault, and you shouldn't be the one to hear it all."

I raised a hand in a gesture I hoped was reassuring.

But she didn't have eyes for it. She looked down the way ahead.

Hooves beat on stone like clacking wood. I followed Eloine's gaze.

A four-horse carriage, with all the splendor you could imagine from the stories, came clattering toward us. The wood was as dark as night and a streak of white shimmered almost like moonlight along the frame. I noticed it for an inlay of pearl, polished and lined with a thinner trim of silver.

The owner had the sort of money that came with nobility, then. Not even wealthy merchants spent their coin on embellishments for carriages. They existed to take you from one place to another, with no use past that for those who made their fortune from work. This subtle extravagance told me the owner had never known the cost of what it took to earn a coin.

I muttered something dark under my breath and Eloine swatted me.

The driver spotted us and eased the horses to a halt a few feet from us. He paid me no mind, I noted, keeping his eyes solely on Eloine. "The Lady Etiana?"

"I am."

"You are?" I stared at her, knowing the name to be false.

I've heard my fair share of fake names, and resorted to using just as many over my life. Spotting them was easy, but how she managed to pass herself off as a lady . . . ?

A sharp elbow dug into my ribs and stifled the thought along with the words that would have followed.

"I've been instructed to take you to Del Soliel by a request from most high. It won't be but a few hours. I promise." The driver's voice made me think of a badly tuned mandolin; high, stringy, and peaking loudly at the wrong times as if he still hadn't finished adolescence.

"Then we should leave. I would hate to keep him waiting." She unlaced her fingers from mine, giving me a long look.

"Him?"

Eloine kissed me once on the cheek. "A lady has other commitments."

I grunted, wondering who in the world she was to meet. "But how?"

She raised a brow.

"From everything last night to . . ." I gestured at the cart.

"Wit, wiles, a woman's ways and her charms."

That gave me just as much by way of an answer as I had before. So, I found myself left with nothing.

"And I won't see you next until . . . ?"

Eloine stepped away from me, stopping before reaching the carriage doors. "Until the next time we meet, of course."

Of course.

I feigned a heavy sigh and shrugged. "Well, I suppose I'll have to find someone else to share my story with in the meantime."

The driver came to her side and opened the doors for her, offering a hand to assist. Eloine froze at my words.

"You can't leave a story unfinished once it's started. It's not only a shame, but a crime." I turned away and looked to the moon. "Mayhaps she'll want to hear the next piece of it. Someone will want for it I hope? I've only been keeping it buried for so long, and now, here I am sharing it all only to find you've not the ears for the rest of it." I placed a hand over my heart and squeezed.

Her lips twitched, but she took control of them, pressing them tight. But the smile reached her eyes instead. "Well, we can't have that. I suppose I'll have to find a way to make sure I won't be too long without your company."

I bowed. "Seems the likely thing if you'd like to hear the rest of the tale."

"I do." Eloine took the driver's hand and stepped up into the carriage. "Wait for me?"

"Yes."

The doors closed and the driver walked around the carriage, getting back into position all without passing me the slightest glance. I may as well have not been there.

He spurred the horses to action and kept his head so fixed ahead I knew it to be the look of someone loudly ignoring a person.

I squinted as he passed by and resisted the terrible temptation to unleash a binding on him.

Soon as the thought faded, the carriage and Eloine disappeared into the night.

I looked overhead to the moon to find clouds had taken her as well, leaving me full and truly alone on the streets of Karchetta.

FIFTY

What We Mean

The inside of the carriage is upholstered in a red so vibrant it makes the storyteller's cloak look a dull wash of blood in comparison. The cushions offer her a better respite than anything she's slept on in long memory. Eloine adjusts herself and turns a shade to regard the small panel near her head.

She pulls on the brass knob, sliding the wooden slat aside. A thin grate is revealed, and through it she makes out the back of the driver's head. "Driver?"

"Yes, Lady Etiana?"

"How is the road to Del Soliel?" It is as easy a topic to get someone to talk about. The roads of the world are always questionable to someone, and there is ever a complaint to voice. It makes the passing journey more bearable than muffled silence within the carriage.

"Ah, they are well enough, lady. No frets, no worries. Not even with the *camarani* so close by. Why, I can see their campfires and caravan from here. An ill-blotted sight on our pristine hills, but you shouldn't be able to see them from your windows, lady. Peace."

Eloine stiffens before turning fully to regard the man. "Where?"

"I'm sorry?"

"Where? The singing folk. Where are their wagons? You can see them now?" Her tone leaves no room for further questions. It is hard as the stones of ocean cliffs and just as sharp.

"Y-yes. Why, they're not more than a hundred paces from the side of the road. Not so close they violate the laws of the land by bringing themselves into the country proper. Them with uncultured music and songs . . . and their dancing, lady, so vulgar—"

"Quiet." Her voice doesn't raise by a single note. It has all the subtle weight of the world before a storm.

To the man's credit, he adopts respectful silence on command.

Eloine takes a series of breaths to better still herself before deciding what she needs to do. "Stop the carriage."

"I'm sorry?"

Eloine closes her eyes and steals a piece of patience from a better part of herself, though her tongue wishes to remind the driver of his recently enacted silence. "Stop the carriage, Driver. Immediately."

"But . . . my orders to take you to—"

"Which you will still fulfill . . . *after* I see to something. Are the roads dangerous?"

"N-no."

"Are we in danger?"

"Of course not, Lady Etiana. No one would even look on this carriage the wrong way for fear of losing—"

"Then whatever is the matter? Am I a letter to be delivered, or is my presence a request? One, I wonder if I can refuse? I do believe I can. I wonder who then will be—"

The carriage slows before she can even finish what she is saying.

"Am I permitted to ask the lady what is wrong?"

"You are. I am going for a walk. To the wandering folk, in fact—their encampment. I wish to see them—*alone*."

"I don't think—"

"Then I think it's better we continue that habit, please. And if you do, I'll be sure to tell your master what a wonderful driver you have been, and that I've felt nothing but pleasure being in your company."

The man opens his mouth, then closes it. She can see thoughts running through his mind, and they are cut short as he comes to the most appropriate answer. "Ah, yes. May you enjoy their . . . everything, Lady Etiana."

"I'm sure I will." Eloine wastes not another moment in the carriage, stepping out from it and crossing the dirt road onto the grass.

The driver spoke truly. Campfires dot the near distance, bringing to light waxed canvas canopies large enough to shelter a hundred men and women. A ring of wagons, used to carry all the materials to build the structures, surrounds the encampment like a wooden fence. She can make out no people from where she stands.

Eloine draws closer, taking her time to enjoy her freedom from the city, from the driver, and to be in an open field without the eyes of strangers on her. The stars her destination, almost, as she looks up to them and follows their glow more than the firelight ahead.

The low and lilting melody of flutes touches her ears first, then the rhythmic twang of strings. There are sounds that only come from flesh clapping flesh, and something nearing a jingle that is of silver bells.

She reaches the closest of the wagons and slips between the openings to find herself before the white tenting.

Laughter. It fills the air, and a pair of men stumble out from the makeshift home. They are locked elbow to elbow by a band of red fabric, and their steps are those taken by boys who've addled their brains. Usually from too much drink, or from introducing their fists to one another. She reasons it's a combination of both.

They stop as they realize she is there and the laughter dies. They look her over, then their faces twist in unison into the same puzzled mask. Both are young, somewhere just beyond their twentieth year. Lean, muscled, wearing open sleeveless vests and breeches rolled up to showcase their calves. Well-tanned, but not enough to hide the flush of red at their cheeks.

"Under familiar stars, and the ever-moving moon, we are one and of the same family."

The stones setting both men's backs rigid now vanish and they relax, stumbling over their tongues to repeat the familial greeting.

She eyes the ribbon binding their arms together and raises a brow.

They catch on to her silent question and break into a torrent of renewed laughter. "*Karbanti* . . . uh, the—" Both men speak over one another, leaving little clearly heard.

Eloine raises a hand, staying both their lips. "What was the bet between you two, and did the loss result in you being stuck to one another or . . . ?" She lets the question hang in the air.

Both men frown, and it is almost like a pantomime performance. "Oh, we forgot to take off the band," says the first. The second laughs and claws at the length of red, his fingers fumbling, giving clearer indication of his inebriation. "Or we forgot how?" the second man adds. "Wait, were we supposed to be stuck together?" The first's brow furrows and the second's quickly follows. "I think so? *Mamman* said it'd help our—" The first man is drowned out as the second speaks over him. "Our *brotherly* affections."

Eloine's mouth opens and she clicks her tongue against the side of her cheek. "Ah. I hope your affections are bolstered then, and do not cross well into the . . . amorous."

The brothers purse their lips with an uncanny symmetry. Then they break into grins better served for lechers. "If you so wish, we can foster that love with a third and willing participant?" The first brother barely manages to get each word out. The second looks on as if expecting her to agree.

Eloine reaches out, running the back of a hand against both of their cheeks. She rolls her wrist and takes the earlobe of the second man between her thumb and forefinger. Her smile widens and she yanks once.

The second brother yelps and staggers. His brother tries to counter the movements, but the lash at their arms is their undoing, sending the pair to the ground in a tangle of limbs.

Eloine steps over them and enters the great tent. She tallies a rough count of fifty people by the low-standing candles that are shining their glow through half-moon bulbs of glass nearly swallowing the wax pillars they sit over.

Every shirt or dress worn by the assembly is a cut that shows more skin than any Etaynian would find proper. The colors are pulled from all those found in the night and brightest mornings and across any field afar of flowers. There is no comparison in her mind to the vibrancy and life in their movements while they dance.

A man and woman sit in the middle of the tent, playing a flute and plucking a traveler's harp. Every step of the crowd brings a chime of bells, the clap of hand drums, and the rhythmic, percussive, silver-struck beat of tambourines.

She is home.

Eloine closes her eyes and breathes, less to take in the air, and all the more to take in the moment of being among singers, dancers, and musicians. The *Maghani*. The wanderers who always feel better bright and bold under the guise of darkness and moonlight.

She lets out a low hum, more born of instinct than any invitation to join the nightly festivity. Her feet drum themselves against the thick rug of the tent, drawing nothing noticeable but a dull thump her own ears can scarcely pick up.

The music never falters all the while.

A woman breaks from her performance and rushes over to her, taking Eloine's hands into hers. "Sister," she says, her chest heaving in what is both excitement and, just as much, from exertion from the dance. "What family are you from? I don't recognize you." The young girl cannot be more than sixteen.

Eloine runs a hand through the woman's hair, a color close to mahogany, but holding better the brown than red of it. "An old one. One far from here, I'm afraid. Tell me, sweet, is the *Mamman* of your family here, or is she resting?"

"She is here, but she's not watching the *sanzara*. She's been too tired of late to dance and stand in watch. She is in the Circle's tent, but none of the members are there. Just her. I can bring you?" She says the last words more as a question.

Eloine cups the girl's chin and gives it a gentle shake. "What is your name?"

"Shira."

"Thank you, Shira. Yes, please. Take me to her."

Shira barely waits for Eloine's words to fall and die against the air. The girl takes her wrist and pulls with all the strength and enthusiasm of a child, hauling her forward.

A man steps before the pair of women. He is what many a young girl might think of when their heads are filled more with cotton and dreams than sharper things. The cut of his jaw is sharp and strong—broad. His eyes hold a light plucked from candles and stars in the warmth of their brown. His hair is dark and short and curly. And the shape of him is a dancer's body with the lean muscles all out for her to see from the vest and short breeches. The sort of shape that can give many a person all manner of ideas.

He smiles, and it is wide, bright, and utterly practiced for one reason alone.

She doesn't return the expression, and both she and Shira try to step around him.

He moves ahead of them again. "I haven't seen you before."

Eloine inclines her head. "No, you haven't. And, for both our conveniences, I expect you won't see me again. If you'll excuse me." She tries once more and the man is before her as if he's set solely to the task of barring her way. She curses but keeps the words from leaving her lips. "I'm on my way to speak with the *Mamman* of the family." Her smile is thin and as cutting as wire lined with glass.

He stiffens and the earlier expression slips from his face, but not for too long. It is back across him just as quick. "I would be happy to take you to her myself. Tell me, do you wrestle?" He gestures to a length of red cord folded in his other hand.

Eloine reaches out, placing a hand on one of his arms. She squeezes the muscle there once before trailing her fingers down it until she reaches the edge of his palm—just above where the length of string sits. "I do." Eloine grips his wrist tight, slips her foot between his legs, and her heel claps against the meat of his calf. She wrenches, pulls, and twists. The man's expression slips before the rest of him and he is on the ground. She pins him there under her foot and leans forward. "Proficiently."

Shira lets out a torrent of giggles she stifles behind her hands, though not so quickly that the laughter doesn't reach the ears of those nearest by and set them off as well.

"Ah, well, I suppose there are worse places to be than under a woman like you." The man finds his smile again and she wishes he'd lost it in the fall.

Eloine says nothing and walks over him, extending a hand for Shira to take. The young girl does and leads her out of the main tent. They walk through tall-standing grass, taking the time to brush the stalks aside as she is led toward a smaller lodging.

It stands out among the simpler designs—a color between sapphires and the darker blues of night. Gold thread embroidery runs along the outside in long, large loops that take the eyes and almost ask you to continue following to complete the pattern. The circular tent is held in place with a band of flexible wood on the outside she knows is set to squeeze against more poles within. An odd design in the world, at least among folk not her own.

"How long have you lived with this family, Shira?"

The girl's face tightens, but she doesn't look at Eloine as she ponders the question. "My mum and me came here when I was little. But I wasn't alone. Our old family came too—all of us. We were a small band. It was long ago. Years."

Eloine smiles, wondering what someone still young would consider little.

They reach the tent and Shira holds up a hand, motioning for Eloine to remain in place. "You're family, but a stranger still to the *Mamman;* I need to check if she'll see you." The girl straightens, setting her hands on her hips and giving Eloine a look that makes it clear she is not to be challenged on the point.

Eloine fights to hide her amusement. "Of course, little one. Go ask her. I'll wait."

Shira slips into the tent. Hushed voices are traded and then go silent. She reappears and pulls the tent's flap aside, gesturing for Eloine to enter. "She'll see you." Shira shifts in place and looks to her feet.

"What's wrong?"

The girl's mouth twitches. "I can't stay, though." She fixes Eloine with a look full of a child's pleading and curiosity. "Can I?"

Eloine places a hand on the girl's shoulder and gives her a gentle squeeze. "Maybe next time. For now, this is a private matter." Another pat that turns to a light push sends the girl a step forward. "Go on, there's dancing to be done tonight, music to be made, and songs to be sung."

The words have their intended effect and all the enthusiasm returns to the girl. She races off like she had never cared about listening in on Eloine's meeting.

Eloine doesn't wait to watch the young girl go, though for a moment, a weight settles in her, and the yearning for the same freedom the child enjoys. She enters the tent.

A thick rug of wool, dyed to a sapphire ringed with cream, covers the floor. There is a bed better suited for a large child sitting in the corner. A small box of stone sits in the middle of the tent, its frame lined with carvings in a language she does not recognize. Sand occupies its center, and a kettle rests at the core of that, letting out its steam.

"Marvelous things that come out of the Mutri, hm?" The speaker is a woman in her fifties, though her hair holds more to black than what's turned to silver and white. The sun-kissed tone of her skin carries fewer lines than one would imagine, and those that do crease her face are along the edges of her mouth and eyes. She wears a simple dress of a brown nearly gold, and she is utterly without jewelry at her wrists or ankles.

An oddity for their kind.

She reminds Eloine of someone's loving grandmother.

"It's been a good many years since I've seen you," says the band's *Mamman.*

Eloine recognizes the voice finally and the change that time has done to the old woman's face. She says no words and nearly throws herself against the woman's chest, embracing her. "*You, Mamman* of another family? When I last saw you—"

The woman doesn't grin, but whatever could have passed for a warm smile shows in the warmth of her eyes. "As I said, many years. Things change—are bound to change. This you know. But, I give thanks your wanderings and ours have brought us to cross paths again, my sweet . . ." She trails off. "And what name are you calling yourself nowadays?" The tone is that of someone close to chiding a child.

Eloine nearly shies away from the woman's look. "A few here. But Eloine is the one I'm most fond of, *Mamman* Asha."

Asha's lips press tight together, but not so much there isn't a hint of a gap between them, and an amused note passes through that space. "Mhm. I still think of you as my Eliyana. So, Eloine." She stops and moves her mouth as if chewing over the sound of it. "Is that a name you've come up with for yourself?" The old woman's tone makes it clear she already knows the answer.

Eloine says nothing that can be discerned, keeping her voice to low muttering as she adopts the new habit of fidgeting with her fingers. A moment goes by before Eloine finds her voice again. "I'm still looking for it."

Mamman Asha nods. "The song—all this time later, and you're still after it?"

Eloine stiffens and stops playing with her hands. "You don't believe, do you?" She doesn't look up to gauge Asha's reaction.

"Oh, I believe, child. You know I do. And we all have proof of it, don't we?" Asha reaches out and cups Eloine's chin. "I'm sorry it has to be you, you know."

Eloine moves out of the old woman's gentle grip. "It has to be someone. And I think I have something. Or, someone, at least."

The old woman's brows rise at this, but she says nothing, motioning with a hand for her to continue.

"The one all the stories are about. Our theories, remember?"

Asha inclines her head. "Flower, will you get the tea. This sounds like a long conversation and I'm a touch cold."

Eloine moves before the woman has finished speaking. "I wish you'd stop calling me that. I'm grown now."

Asha chortles, placing a hand to her chest as if trying to stop herself from doing so. "And I wish I had one to put in your hair, even now." The old woman pauses, leaning on the bed to fetch a small leather bag. She digs through it before pulling free her wish. A flower as large as her palm now rests cupped between her hands. It is as white as a thing can be.

Eloine fetches two cups and pours the tea, placing one on the small wooden stand near *Mamman* Asha's bed, before holding her own in both hands. She does not take a sip, waiting for the older woman first.

Instead, the matriarch of the traveling band rises from the bed, crossing the few steps toward Eloine. "Oh, look at me, child."

Eloine does, and resists the urge to shift away from the woman as Asha takes some of Eloine's hair in hand, threading the flower into it. She doesn't know what to say, so goes for the easy question. "Jimsonweed?"

Asha shakes her head. "You know its name, though you don't want to say it. Still the stubborn young girl at heart. I've heard them call it the Goodnight flower in these parts. Though, those don't grow on a vine like this. Still, fitting, after a fashion."

Eloine keeps the frown from her face. "Yes, *Mamman.*"

"Don't pout, child. Sit with me." Asha sinks to the bed, patting a place by her side as invitation for Eloine to join her.

She does, still holding the cup in hand, slowly rotating it without much thought to do anything else. "You don't think I should be searching for it, do you?"

Asha sighs and takes a sip of her tea, not bothering to give it a cautionary breath of cooling air. "Forget the wish of the flower, for if I could have any other I'd wish you didn't have to. I know it's not a matter of things I think or want. It is. That is enough. But still . . ."

Eloine reaches out and takes one of the woman's hands in one of hers. "I know. Still, I'm getting closer."

"I've been afraid of that for years. The closer you get to it, the more you bring yourself into danger."

Eloine pulls up a side of her dress, revealing the old knife kept there. She lowers the cup and draws the blade. "I'm safe enough. I know how to move through the world, remember."

Asha looks to the knife, then Eloine. "After all this time, you've still kept that same old thing, but in those same years, I swear your face has changed."

Eloine gives her a thin smile. "It's the nature of things." She turns the knife over. The white horn grip is paler than the flower in her hair and holds a bit of yellow in its color.

"Have you ever found him again?" Asha nods to the blade.

Eloine shrugs. "He styled himself something of a merchant prince, or one in the making. A dozen other things as well. A sailor. A pirate. A wanderer of another sort." She grins to herself, but it is short-lasting. "But no, I don't think I'll see him again for quite the while. He still has to find himself first." She turns away from the subject and sheathes the knife, taking Asha's lead to sip from the tea.

It is bitter and holds no note of sweetness to save her from the bite. She swallows it regardless and settles for the warmth it brings her instead. "The Shaen roam more freely than before, you know?"

Asha nods and says nothing.

"And Amir is set to marching—banners and swords ready."

Asha takes another sip—a longer one, and the only sound is that of liquid passing through tight lips.

"I think we're finding ourselves in another story, *Mamman,* and if I don't find the song, I'm afraid this one will end terribly."

Asha stares into her cup, nearly half empty now, and her look is one of someone trying to find a measure of clarity in something they know there isn't much to glean from. "May Chaandi watch over you then." She doesn't look at Eloine as she runs the back of a hand along the woman's cheek. "What will you do now? What plan do you have?"

Eloine blows on her cup but doesn't drink. "I plan to play a game on a pair of princes. One with a castle and with secrets to pry free. The sort who may have the song I seek. The other with nothing to his name but his name itself, and in hopes he remembers all that he's once had."

Asha gives her a long and searching look. "*That* sounds a dangerous game to be playing. And do either of these tricks of yours involve robbing the poor princes."

The light that touches Eloine's eyes in the dark sets them to a dance. "I've already done one prince a turn, and I do mean to steal from the other."

Asha watches Eloine over the lip of her cup but says nothing, merely nodding.

Eloine returns the look. "Oh, and one more thing."

Asha raises one of her brows in place of voicing the question on her tongue.

"Do you have room for one more in your family? I have a woman, freshly freed, and in need of a new one."

FIFTY-ONE

Reasons Why

I made my way back to the Three Tales Tavern in a sour mood. Some of the crowd had dispersed since my performance and walk with Eloine, but not enough had left for my liking.

Dannil spotted me and waved me over to the bar.

"You have the look of a man who tried his hand and tongue with a lady only to find both tied and turned away." He gave me a toothy grin before giving me a longer look. The smile faded. "Where's our songstress . . . oh."

I flashed him a knowing look. "It was just a walk and a talk."

Dannil plucked a mug, polishing it while watching me over its rim. "Sure. Sure."

I glowered at him. "What?"

"Nothing." He resumed his cleaning, building a quiet between us I knew was intentional. The awkward silence stretched, growing inside me like an itch I knew would be better scratched than left untended.

"What? Just say it."

Dannil placed the mug down and tossed the cleaning rag over a shoulder. "She's got you all bound in knots."

I opened my mouth to protest but he didn't give me the chance.

"Don't. Older than you, seen it aplenty. Hell, there was a time I could say it was me on the other side of the counter wearing the same look as you."

I kept my dagger-sharp glare on him, but most of its edge had blunted. "She confuses me, that's all."

"Mhm."

"What's it matter anyhow?"

Dannil grabbed the mug and put it on the counter behind him, grabbing another cup to clean. "It doesn't, and it does. You're the one with the long face, friend. You're making it matter, and right now, you're performing and lodging in my tavern. That makes it matter to me." He finished cleaning that mug, then grabbed another. "This one's clean." He turned away from me and went over to a pewter pitcher, tipping its contents into the cup. Dannil returned and handed it to me.

"Thanks. What is it?"

"Something that'll make matters matter less. A small bit, at least."

I smiled. "And how much does one have to drink to make them forget?"

He laughed. "A lot. It's not that strong and you're not bringing in enough coin to earn that much drink for free plus the room."

I grunted. "Maybe I should do better, then." I took a swig. The drink tasted cool. Not in temperature, but it reminded me of the breath of spring mornings that still held to winter's chill. Something almost like the lingering taste of mint. The beer held a smoothness and something I couldn't quite bring word to. It made me think of the savoriness that came with cooking food over fire. An earthy taste.

"It's good."

Dannil nodded. "It is. But it doesn't do much for a man's mind when he's in a mood to forget. Or when he wants to set his feet to dancing but his heart's a bit shy. I'm afraid it tastes much better than what it can do for you."

"There are a lot of things like that in life. What they look like or promise fall far short of what they do for you."

He inclined his head but said nothing.

I took it as he'd had his own fair share of those relationships. He knew the shape of what I meant.

If my comment bothered him, however, he didn't show it. Dannil reached into a deep pocket stitched on to the front of his apron and pulled free an oddly shaped purse. It looked less like a squat, bulbous pouch cinched with string and more like a sock that had been stretched horizontally. A shape more like a slug, the color of old grass. Red laces ran along the top of it. He undid them and pulled out another bronze septa, placing it on the counter with two fingers holding it in place. "This is what I ought to be paying you, for your piece at least."

I nodded, knowing what would follow. I'd been party to these talks many times as a performer.

"But tonight wasn't as good as last night, and our songstress didn't give us as grand a tune as before. And last night you told a story more the kind to get people proud of who they are. An Etaynian story."

All true. I knew the excuses for what they were. He needed to justify a night with less coin, and I didn't take it personally. It's a poor performer who takes out a poor compensation on the man suffering just as much in his business.

Dannil pulled the coin away and stowed it in the oddly shaped purse, plucking something else free instead. Several pewter bits landed on the counter, each worth less than a tin chip back in the Mutri Empire. More bits joined. Then more. Nearly thirty piled up soon enough.

Not so bad a night, then. Maybe not grand enough to warrant bronze, but enough to earn almost half a septa.

I pulled the coins toward me, stopping short as I thought of something and slid half of them back.

He eyed me but took the coins regardless. That told me enough. Most tavern owners worked to stay on good terms with performers they knew would bring in more money and keep their customers happy. They'd buck at having their coin passed back, or at least make more of a show of it. Dannil did none of that.

"Times are rough."

"That they are, Storyteller." His lips were pressed thick. "Didn't think you'd notice."

It clicked in my head a moment later. "That's why you led with the septa the first night. It wasn't just a good night, it would cover me for long enough if I hadn't spent it. And it would keep me in a better mood for nights like this if things were tighter."

Dannil tapped a finger to the side of his temple. "Been around long enough to know how to treat my performers."

I thought on that. "So have I, and I know how to treat people back. The rooms and food are more than enough. Truly." It wasn't the truth, but he didn't need to hear that and feel guilty for it. Pewter bits went plenty far here, so long as I kept firm on the ones I had in hand.

While I'd come to the country with coin in my purse, I didn't know how long I'd be here before accomplishing what I set out to do. Then there came the matter of getting into the royal family's library, the best repository of stories in Etaynia I could possibly access, to see what tales they had on hand that mentioned the Ashura. Anything, even if distorted and misshapen, as happens to tales through time and over tides to new lands.

Even if the shapes of them changed, their heart would be there, and I needed that. Securing that knowledge gave me a way to spare a bit more of Dannil's pride and get what I wanted out of the situation.

"Consider the coin back payment for something you can do for me."

Dannil didn't quite side-eye me as he turned to grab the pitcher and shuffle away down the counter. He returned just as quickly after filling another customer's mug. "And what's that?"

"Information. With everything surrounding the *efantes,* I suspect they're not ones to be out and about of late, yes?"

Dannil stiffened visibly but went about his motions, tending to nearby people's needs. "Yes. They're not at the capital now. They've moved to the summer palace in Del Soliel. It's closer to the pontifex and the Vatemiyo. Makes things easier for them to go about the prince-election to king."

The Vatemiyo was a miniature town, rumored to be made of entirely white stone and scrubbed regularly to keep it that way. The whole town had been fashioned solely for Etaynia's clergy and those in their studies of religion. The pontifex carried the same authority within those stone walls as the king, maybe more.

Something else Dannil said sparked a thought. "Del Soliel?" That's where Eloine's driver had said he would take her. "How far is that by foot?"

Dannil grunted. "Take up most of your day if you walked, and then some. Tired, dirty, sweaty. Be better to hire a horse and cart if you can spare that kind of money. Might take you even longer, though, by your own two good legs. Carriages might run you off the good roads if they're busy.

"Why? Already bored and outgrown this place, eh?" He gave me a look that made it clear he didn't believe that. "You ready to mingle and make your way along with the gentry and people who eat off silver?"

I snorted. "I'd never survive long among people like that." And old truth that was. I always landed myself in trouble among royalty of any sort. "No, but it wouldn't hurt a man of my reputation to come away with a story or two of performing for nobility here."

His eyes widened. "You think you'll get an audience to perform for the *efantes* and court?"

I nodded. "I hope so." It would allow me to at least cater to one reason for why I'd come all this way, and hopefully the other.

I have a prince to kill.

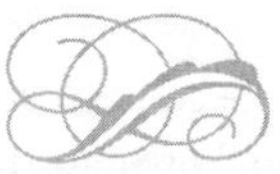

FIFTY-TWO

Road and Rumors

I had no mind or mood for dinner that night, spending the hours in my room until sleep took me. My attitude changed by morning and I headed downstairs to take a meal and speak with Dannil.

Fortunately, the Three Tales had no customers so early, not even the trio of elderly men who came to do nothing more than gossip in each other's company. And the same could thankfully be said of people wanting to kill me.

I take my blessings where I can.

Dannil left half his steamed fish untouched, turning to his cup to drain its contents in a single gulp. "You mean to head out early for Del Soliel, or do I get a chance to convince you to stay?"

I finished all of my own fish. The meat had gone flakey in parts and I found too much lemon in the seasoning for my liking. What little honey Dannil added to the dark tea performed a small wonder to remove some of its bitterness. I noted a hint of what could have been orange blossom, and I appreciated the subtle extra taste of it.

"I hope to be back soon if that's any consolation. And depending on how I return, I might have a new tale or two to tell. That might be worth the price of leaving."

"It's only worth that price if you can pay it back. And what you might get doesn't mean the same for me, *sieta*? I might not see you again. Maybe you'll grow fat and comfortable performing for the gentry. Or maybe you'll wag your tongue at the wrong lady or her lord husband and pay a different price. Either way, I lose an entertainer, though. One I stuck my neck out for when he stirred up trouble with the clergos."

I raised a finger at that, staying his argument. "*I* stirred nothing." Which wasn't wholly true. "They came looking for trouble. I merely obliged. There's something to be said for giving someone what they want."

Dannil grunted. "I was wrong. With a mouth and wit like that, you'll surely run afoul of the gentry. And worse. Noble ladies." He traced his index finger through the air in an imaginary circle before touching it to his lips. A silent gesture of the Ring of Fire, symbol of Solus. "God go with you, Storyteller."

"Better if he didn't. I've had a tricky time when gods and the like get involved with my life."

Dannil looked up from his meal, looking at me as if I'd spoken in another language.

I didn't bother explaining. People didn't take well to their gods being talked about like that, and less so the implication you've walked among them. Gods are better left off in the distance, in stories and faraway places from where you are. That's where they belong. Or so we tell ourselves.

"Thank you for the meal and everything else. I'll be back."

"I'm hoping for it." He offered his hand.

I took it and shook, then turned to begin the long walk to Del Soliel.

Dannil hadn't lied when he said the walk would take most of the day. Three carriages passed me by, none offering me the courtesy of asking if I would even like to pay for a ride. I counted eight wagons, farmers living off the king's road and probably taking it to other towns to sell their goods. They gave me the same treatment, though they at least had the decency to send a smile my way. One farmer, at the strong-handed urgings of his wife, begrudgingly passed me a piece of hard cheese the size of my fist and some bread.

I thanked him, going so far as to offer payment, but a look from his wife had the man waving me off. I gave her the widest smile I could and a greater thanks than her husband. It seemed to be more than enough.

The kindness and charity of old women is not something to be taken lightly. It can save lives. I know that much to be true.

I finished the cheese well before making it halfway to Del Soliel, resigning myself to sating my stomach's pangs with cautious sips from my waterskin.

Daylight soon turned to dusk, then to darker night by the time I stepped onto the dirt of Del Soliel proper. The city looked to be everything Karchetta wasn't. More of the paths were paved and layered in thin slates of stone. Larger portions of the streets were illuminated by lanterns. The buildings stood higher, and more of them had been fashioned of hard rock and brick rather than wood and simpler materials.

A pair of guards, not clergos, marched by and gave me a long look before passing me over.

I ignored them and fixed my stare on my surroundings, searching for the nearest inn that looked in need of a performer. And I found it within a handful of minutes.

The Leyon Dis Ario stood three stories high with a russet tile roof that sloped both ways. Its shape meant some of the higher rooms and walls would be canted—narrow. An annoyance, but a longer look at the place assured me of its quality.

The paint showed no sign of wear, still holding to all the soft warmth and invitation of sunflower petals. The wooden beams framing the landing to the door were the color of rich red clay and well cared for.

I made way into the Golden Lion Inn and took in the nightly chatter of its crowd.

The nearest conversation dulled, dimmed, then died completely. Others followed suit, falling full into silence as eyes slowly turned on the stranger in the red cloak and cowl.

A few voices carried on, but they'd become nothing more than a wisp of wind rolling through a dead and quiet field.

To say the Golden Lion was similar in any regard to the Three Tales would be like saying a butterfly and moth were the same. Not that the Three Tales was ugly by any means. It had its own charm, and one, in truth, I preferred. But the Golden Lion had an open-faced and easy-to-see beauty.

The walls had been painted to match the tawny color of the beast the tavern was named after. A soft and muted shade that brought warmth to your eyes without being jarring. The wood throughout the place had been painted a red like old brick, just as light and easy to take in. All the while the candlelight brought another subtle brightness to the place. It had all the comfort of a fire under familiar stars and the surety of good food with it.

I walked over to the counter, ignoring the silence that had followed me. I saw no reason to break the quiet and direct more attention to myself. My time was better served focusing on a room for the night and what it would take to get one. Then finding a way to the palace from here.

The barkeeper noticed my approach and gave me a look as if weighing the trouble I'd bring.

I decided it best not to give him cause to think I'd be a bother. A flick of a hand sent my cowl falling from my head, at least giving the man a better view of my face.

People generally feel more at ease when they can see the face of who they're talking to, but it did me no favors, the night being so late and me clearly marked as a foreigner.

"Do you have any rooms available? I can pay. I can also make it worth your while by performing."

The man had the build of someone who labored hard day in and out most of his life before deciding his body couldn't keep up with it. He must have been a barkeeper only for the last few years of his life, putting on some fat over still-noticeable slabs of muscle. The green shirt stretched tight around his shoulders and chest, though did little to hide what he had by way of a belly now. He looked like everyone else in Etaynia—dark of brow and eye. His beard could have nested birds with its thickness and only betrayed a speck of steel in its color.

"Might do. You play?" His voice came hard and dry as smoke over broken stone. He then settled his gaze on the mandolin case in my hand. "You sing. Don't look like a singer. Dance? No. What? Juggle? Tumble." He shook his head, each of the words having come out sharp and clipped. "What? What do you do?"

The speed of everything would have tripped me once, but now I'd come to expect people like him every now and again. "I perform. I tell tales that entertain. Stories and little magics if you have the—"

The barkeeper grunted and shuffled away from me, grabbing a pitcher to serve another patron.

I stood there, blinking several times. I could count on one hand the number of times someone ignored my offer to perform since I'd cobbled my new reputation as The Storyteller.

Whispering, not low enough to keep to itself, graced my ears.

"Heard someone like him come to Karchetta?"

Ah, word had spread. I leaned closer to the conversation happening seats down from me.

"Think he's that one? Heard he and some songstress put on a show worth sitting through in some small tavern south of here. Word came up from my cousin who heard it himself from his brother's sister."

A grunt. "Could do with a story. Things are tighter and stiffer here than my legs, especially with the *efantes* coming here. You know how things are now, everyone on edge after the . . . incident."

Another grunt, one of affirmation. "Maybe he knows somethin' of them foreign far-off tales. I heard a piece o' one long ago. How's it go?" The man speaking screwed his face tight as if thinking twice as hard as he usually did.

> *"On the mountain of ice and snow,*
> *he called to it to come down low*
> *and brought it crashing on the serpent*
> *and then something . . ."*

The man's companion snorted, then broke into snickering. "Good thing we're not paying you to tell things, huh? 'And then something,' you remember that bit and want to hear something foreign? Keep it to good tales of here, I say." He punctuated the statement by banging his mug on the counter.

That earned him a long and steady stare from the barkeeper. "You nick the wood? You pay. You spill a drink and stain the wood? You pay. You get too drunk and tip something over? You pay. You get drunk and start a fight . . . you wish you could pay."

The man sobered immediately, clearing his throat and deciding that maybe he should keep his mug just a bit out of arm's reach for the moment. "Was just talking is all, Santiyo. That's all."

"You want to talk. You talk. But you do it without banging the counters, *sieta*?"

The man nodded. "*Sieta*." He drew a circle through the air before kissing the tip of his finger. "Swear it."

"Besides," said the first man who'd tried to recite the little rhyme, "there's more story to that than what I just tried to say. Heard rumors come up long ago that the fella swallowed the whole village under that mountain. Or he buried them all. Or dropped the mountain on them. Vile thing, that. Imagine the man it takes to do something like that. Dark things. But still a story maybe worth hearing. Maybe."

The second man grunted. "Heard something of a name to go with it. Something foreign soundin' too. Aryan? Arun? One of those, just like all those eastern stories that find their way here. Half of them have someone or other with the same name. Or close enough. Maybe they all just make monsters out there. Must be." He looked deep into his mug. "Dropping a mountain on nothing but harmless village folk."

The quiet that came between the group of men was the perfect sort for me to break and win a piece of attention I could use.

"Actually, it goes like this:

"Atop the mountain // ever high
along the crest // kissing sky,
he called upon a binding old
to unleash a vengeance
most bitter cold

"and called down a fury
of all ice and snow
upon the serpent
to bring down // the mountain low

"and did so succeed
to bury this beast
in this deed,

"but too great a price was unfairly paid
for the village buried,
lost to time,
and // unmade."

The two men gossiping, as well as the barkeeper, all turned to look at me with renewed interest. But it was the barkeeper who spoke. "You did good with that little riddle rhyme. Maybe you can perform good enough to be worth something. But I have no rooms. You need a place to sleep? You can sleep with the horses, but for free."

The pressure in my gums promised to burst them as I ground my teeth. "I don't perform for a share of horse trough and hay."

It's said pride is a terrible thing, and that it may be. But it is just as tricky a thing as well, and important. It may lead us into trouble, keep us from charity that spares us hardships, but without pride, we'd hardly ever come to know our worth. And people are generally worth a great deal more than they ever give themselves credit for, in my experience.

"I've performed for kings and sultans. The duke of Tarvinter." One of my hands came up before I realized I'd moved. My mind moved through the folds and I blew a breath into my open palm. "Whent. Ern."

"What's that?" The barkeeper looked at me quizzically.

The thin current of air flew fast into the space above my hand, coiling with the sinuous grace of a snake and all the fluidity of water. I shaped it within the folds of my mind until a ball of air formed, dancing and strobing, all unseen but to my eye. Every flickering candle flame called to me, and I envisioned them all, keeping track of their every movement in my mind. I knew them to be within my reach and pulled, focusing them onto the air in my hand. "Tak. Roh."

Every minute bulb of fire winked out of existence. Streams of flame all stretched gossamer thin, burning brilliant bright, arcing through the tavern and to my palm. They coalesced and joined the currents of air to form a ball of fire. It danced and throbbed like any tiny flame, though now nearly as large as a man's head.

The whole of the tavern stilled and fell better silent than a graveyard. "Does this prove my worth? I can take the breath of every person here and hold it in hand until I feel they're best to breathe again. I can set their hearts thundering in anticipation with stories they've never heard, and tell those they have in such ways they'll sit on edge waiting to hear what happens even though they know it by heart. I can conjure magic out of myth and legend to set them all clapping and ready to tip iron and silver onto your counter."

"And for all that, he doesn't know well enough to keep his tongue from going sharp and too far past what needs to be said. Many men don't, sadly." I knew that voice.

The folds of my mind nearly vanished, the binding slipping as I realized Eloine was nearby, but shrouded in the darkness. I eased out of the binding, letting the flames return to where they had been. The breath of air dissipated with a sound like someone gently exhaling.

Light returned to the Golden Lion and I watched Eloine approach.

She'd traded her dress for a new one of emerald green, all the better to bring out the color of her eyes. Her hair held more curl in it than before and most of the gold had vanished from her arms and ankles, the only glint now coming from the hoops at her ears. "And to think, you couldn't be without me for so long that you decided to follow me here."

It wasn't the truth. I'd come for reasons of my own, and there had been no way to know she would be at this inn, of all places. I opened my mouth to voice that, but one of her fingers pressed against my lips, hushing me effectively.

"I think you've talked enough. And, you've done a good enough job making your point. I"—she placed one hand to her chest—"just so happen to have a room here. Join me." She didn't phrase it as a question.

I nodded.

She moved past me, giving no signal for me to follow, but I knew well enough by now to do so. I slipped in behind her and ignored the renewed threads of gossip that broke up as I passed folks by. Eloine led me up two flights of stairs to a narrow floor with just enough space for four small rooms.

Whatever the Golden Lion boasted in décor below it lost on this floor. Don't mistake me, the wood showed all the signs of being well cared for. The handles on the doors were brass, all without any wear. The glass of the windows were without a speck of dust. The area simply lacked the brightness and eye-drawing tricks that had been employed below.

I found the place better for it, in truth.

Eloine led me to her room, opening the door and gesturing me inside. They'd given her a better one than I'd expected. Certainly something nicer than what I had back at the Three Tales Tavern.

The bed was twice as wide as mine and thicker in padding as well. The blanket had been dyed the color of bright plum. She had her own copper washtub, full mirror, without any scuffs, and a changing screen that didn't look like it had been cobbled together out of flimsy wood.

Eloine eased herself onto the bed, lounging on her side. "Why did you follow me all the way here, Ari? Or are you going to tell me you just so happened to be in the same inn on the same night as me all by happenstance? And, I must admit, if it's the latter, my feelings will be slightly hurt."

I noted that. "Since you said only 'slightly' I suppose it won't be so bad a wound for you to hear that, yes, it was quite by accident."

She narrowed her eyes to give me a stare that could have turned stone hot in seconds, but I knew she didn't really mean it.

"Besides, with the carriage coming to get you, how could I have known you'd be here, *lady*? If anything, you ought to be in your suitor's manor—castle?"

She straightened and rose, looking me over. "Are you jealous?" Eloine leaned closer. Her eyes and mouth widened a second later. "You are!"

"Nothing of the sort." I waved her off and fell into restless pacing around the room. "I came here to get to the *efantes'* summer palace. All I needed was a room for the night. I mean to head there first thing tomorrow."

"Fine, don't tell me the truth." She let the strength out of her posture and collapsed against the bed, shifting into a position she felt comfortable in.

I stopped moving, turning slowly to face Eloine and fix her with a long look. "You should know me better by now to know that I wouldn't do that to you. I *did* come to this country in hopes of visiting the library held by the *efantes,* though I hoped to work my way into their palace proper, not their summer one. I'm sure their collection here is just as nice, though. There's something I'm looking for." *And someone.*

"And here I had hoped you were only looking for me." Her voice came light and breathy. "Foolish girl that I was to hold such a hope."

I rolled my eyes and took a place by her—well, what little corner she left free by her feet. "It's a hope well held, because I held a secret one myself."

She lifted a brow. "Oh?"

I smiled. "Yes. I was so dearly hoping to find a room tonight, and wouldn't you know it, someone was kind enough to—*ow*!" I nearly fell from the bed and my hip throbbed.

Eloine pouted and pulled her foot back, keeping it raised in the silent promise of another kick.

I laughed. "I'm glad to see you. I am. And, yes, I did hope to see you, but I couldn't know for certain whether I would."

She pursed her lips and coiled up, giving me space to sit comfortably. "So you came all this way for books, not princes and to entertain the gentry? You've already hurt my feelings, and with an attitude like that, I daresay you'll hurt the nobility's as well. They are tender people at their cores."

"You sound like you know them. But then, I suppose you would." I gave her a knowing look. "But"—I drew the word out—"if I've hurt your feelings, I suppose it would only be proper to make it up to you."

She gave me a solemn nod.

"Tell me how?" I fought to keep the smile off my face, knowing what she would ask.

"Lie with me. Tell me the rest of your story. As much as you can tonight."

I obliged her.

"I just left behind my family and took the first steps into my new life. I had a new cloak, candles, and a cane. Three things I didn't appreciate, but I'd been convinced to buy. And I'd just been told who to seek to find my way to the Ashram. That's probably the best place to pick up. The journey north."

FIFTY-THREE

The Journey North

"Oi!" Jaseem waved at me as I neared his cart. "You need a ride? You're set and dressed for traveling."

"Yes. To the Ashram in the north, or as close as you feel comfortable taking me."

"More than comfortable. How many are we taking? Where's the rest of your family, boy?"

My core tightened at the question. "Just me. No family." Those last two words sent a chill through me, but I pushed it from my mind, knowing the quicker I got on board and underway, the better and further I'd be from my pain. "How much?"

"All that way is about four. Three and twelve in truth. But if you're going to be wanting a better place to sleep at night than under the carriage, and more than broth, the remaining chips will get you some of that."

I nodded and pulled my last copper rounds from my purse. One gold piece left. It would have to do for whatever came up. "Thank you."

Jaseem hooked a thumb to the open carriage back. "Get on. We leave soon as my wife returns with vittles for the horses." At that, he walked over to the trio at the head of the carriage. He gave the one on the far right an affectionate pat. "Ay, ay, Meeta. Sshh. Calm." The horse neighed but otherwise showed no signs of agitation.

I did as Jaseem said and climbed aboard, taking a seat against one of the carriage sides.

The other passengers had already boarded and stared at me as I took my place.

One of the men wore clothing clearly from Laxina. Fine fabrics but fit tightly to his frame, not the loose and more comfortable fashion found more among the Mutri. He reminded me of a cat, round-faced and smiling with all the guile of one in his eyes. Both his eyebrows were so thin I thought them to be drawn on with charcoal. He nodded to me, a gesture I returned.

"Ari." I placed a hand to my chest.

"Lixin." He repeated my motion.

I left it at that. His voice had an odd cant to it that made it clear the Trader's Tongue wasn't native to him, and pressing him to speak in it could irritate the man.

The other two passengers were just as odd. One looked to be the same age as me. A girl whose hair had more ash gray in it than it ever should have in her youth, barely betraying any hints of rich black. Lean—willowy in body—and parts of her skin were noticeably paler in broad splotches the size of my spread hands. She dressed comfortably in the clothing needed for a long and rough journey.

The last passenger stood out the most. His robes were thin but layered and lacked any pigmentation but a tired gray. It almost looked as if they once had been a different color, but had long since let it go through time and wear. Even the few strands of braided string above his breast had all but lost their hue.

"Never seen an old man before, boy?" His voice carried just as little color and strength as his clothing.

"Sorry, I didn't mean to stare." Which was true. I hadn't. But something about him struck painfully close to a face out of my memory. I just couldn't settle on which and the name behind it. "You reminded me of someone."

His face went tight, bringing out the heavy lines along his cheeks and under his eyes. "Who?"

I told him of Mahrab without naming him or his occupation. Some people frowned on binders, thinking them devilish folk who meddled in things that ventured outside of Brahm and his path. Never mind that the bindings themselves were passed down by Brahm in some stories, they were unnatural things.

And people always fear what they find unnatural. Sadly so.

"Your teacher sounds like an interesting person." The man had a face of hard angles, well-weathered by age, leaving me to guess he was in his fifties at least. If not, he'd lived a hard forty-something years. Very hard. His hair, however, held up better for it, keeping most of its darkness, and his beard only showed faint gray instead of brighter white. "My name is Vathin." He held out his hand.

I took it and shook. "Ari."

"It's a good name. Your family must have thought highly of you to start your name like that."

I blinked and gave him a look, hoping he'd explain that.

While I didn't voice my question, he caught my stare and the meaning of it. "Your name, the first letter tells you a lot about names in the Mutri Empire. Any son of Brahm and his caste"—Vathin rolled his eyes and spat over the side of the cart—"often has a name inspired by his. Many use the letter B. But, older names, ones from a time of heroes and legend, are saved for some girls and boys. Take a guess what they start with." He smiled and gave me a wink.

"A?" I wasn't sure, but given what he'd said, I nursed a hope.

He nodded. "They didn't tell you that?"

I frowned. "I never knew them." My words brought a stillness to the passengers, which said quite a deal considering we were all resting comfortably. "It's okay. I've lived with another family for a long time, and they were good." That thankfully lightened the mood and I could see everyone visibly relax.

"Are they the ones you're leaving behind now?"

I inclined my head. "I have to. I have things to do up north."

"Such as?"

"Attend the Ashram."

Both of Vathin's brows went up. "You're going to be a student? You're young. Most don't enter until fully grown. You're not even to your sixteenth year, are you?"

I shrugged. "People always think I'm younger than I am." It wasn't an answer, but I knew deflecting would have him not weigh me with any more scrutiny. So long as I didn't admit I was, in fact, young, it couldn't be claimed as a mark against me. "And I've already learned some things that will help me there. I won't know, though, until I go."

"There is truth in that. Maybe while we journey north, you can show me some of what you learned? Maybe I can teach you something back."

A part of me bristled at the idea of sharing what Mahrab had taught me. It's not that I thought the information particularly worth keeping secret, but more that it was something special between him and me. One of the few tangible things, of a sort, I could hold on to and put into practice from my old life.

Before Koli and the Ashura took everything from me.

But I had always been a keen learner. I became obsessive over it. What I lacked in inherent genius and did not take to with the ease of some heroes out of stories, I made up for in tenacity and resolve. I could think of nothing better than to learn from Vathin on the road northward bound.

"I'd like that." I grinned in earnest and he returned it.

Jaseem came back to our side of the cart, slapping the wood with his palm. "We're setting off soon. Last rules. We have four other carts, my workers and my family ride in those. Anything happens to them, we all help. I don't care what you paid. You help, *ji-ah*?"

Everyone nodded and returned the agreement, even the man from Laxina.

"That's my wife, Thaiya." He pointed to a squat woman whose face was just as round as the rest of her. She wore her dark hair in a braid that fell to the middle of her back, and when she smiled, the extra folds in her cheeks couldn't blot out the genuine warmth in her expression. "She says she needs help with something, you do it. *Ji?*"

Another agreement.

"We eat what she cooks. If anyone wants to spend coin for more or better, we welcome it, but don't think you keep it to yourself, *ji*? Here, we are all one family going north. People thinking of themselves get left to be by themselves." He paused, letting the quiet stretch and build before turning his voice to heavy cold stone. "They don't last long on their own up that way."

Everyone nodded in solemn silence.

"At night, we unload what we can, and we share what room we have. Thaiya and my children get the tents. Everyone else, myself included, get the canvas. We set up high to cover from rain and around for the wind. That is enough. And there is always underneath the wagons."

Nobody said a thing to that.

"Good. Get comfortable and tell a tale or two, long journeys are made better with stories to pass the time. You'll get tired of watching stone and stream pass by, and just as bored by trees and skies. They all blur the same. The road is long. And it is hard."

He was right on all accounts.

FIFTY-FOUR

Stones and Stream

Pleaing Day turned into Wanting, then soon into the night of Singing Day. Each lived up to what Jaseem had warned. Hard. The roads were well-worn and rutted how you expected for paths along the Golden Road, but that didn't make them soft. No amount of constant footfall and wagon wheels could pack down and smooth these lands. Every jostle promised to shake loose my bones, and my teeth occasionally clacked together in a manner to make me wonder if I'd chipped one.

The first night left me tired and shaken enough to want to do nothing but curl into a ball and sleep like stone. The second drove home the discomforts of the journey twice as hard as the first. And the third seemed to make no other point than to find whatever taxed me most on the ride . . . and give me threefold the agony in that.

But by Waiting morning, I'd weathered the worst of it. The rest of the passengers felt the same.

No longer did low muttering and grousing fill the cart—no. Now Lixin clapped his hands, smiling all the while, all to a tune only he could hear. Vathin sat cross-legged, arms resting on his thighs and knees, breathing slow and steady, much like the pose I'd adopted when taught the folds of the mind. And the silent girl remained as quiet as when I'd first seen her, all the expression and colorlessness of Vathin's clothing in her face.

Our newfound comfort brought us a new ease that opened mouths and set tongues loose into the first real conversation I feel is worth remembering in this part of my story.

The wagons stopped and we rolled off the path onto an open field, keeping just close enough to get back onto the path and be in view of any other travelers.

Jaseem told us that our bodies would thank us for taking the time to stretch and move about properly. The first three days were always the hardest, but they were just as important to drive hard through to make the progress he desired.

We took him at his word and left the confines of the wagon, going for a stroll.

Unlike some of the others on the journey, I kept my sack over my shoulder, an old habit telling me to not let my belongings out of sight—much less out of hand.

"You hold on to that thing like it's the last piece of precious left to you in this world, boy." Vathin reached out toward the sack, hand open to likely give it a pat.

I turned, shying away from his arm, keeping doubly sure my sack remained free of his touch.

He raised a hand to calm me. "You're more skittish than a stray cat."

I held back the glower wanting to work its way across my face. The truth was Vathin had spoken accurately. My time on Keshum's streets had made me wary of those outside my family. And I still remember the first time a stranger extended a hand toward me . . . and how much it hurt.

"Sorry." I released the tension from my back and shoulders, letting the sack slump a little in my hold. "This is all I have left after leaving my family behind." Saying the words aloud ached, but noticeably less than it had back in the city. Even a few days on the road had already dulled the pain from what it had been. I gave thanks for that.

Vathin gave me a long and searching look before nodding. "Then I can see why you'd want to keep that close. I'm sorry for putting you at unease." He brought a hand to the hollow of his throat. "I swear it by my neck and my voice, sorry."

I accepted the apology.

"Would you care to show me what's inside?"

I hadn't expected that. The fact he'd asked made me inclined to oblige. I lowered the sack to the ground and undid the cinched string binding it tight. "There's not much. Mostly food and clothes. I didn't have much to my name except this." My fingers closed around the book Mahrab had left me. I pulled it out and passed it to Vathin.

He took it in both hands with as much care as I myself showed in handling it. "This is important to you. I can tell that much."

I nodded.

His fingers clipped under the covers and he pried. Then his face went through a series of expressions so fast I couldn't track them, all to settle on one of profound confusion. He stared at the book, squinting as he tried to wrench it open. "This isn't merely stuck." Before I could answer, he closed his eyes and ran another hand over it, breaking into a loud laugh that rolled through the field. "Oh, that's good. It's a binding—cleverly done, too." He passed the book back to me.

I took it, but didn't put it away. "You're not going to unbind it?"

He shook his head. "Whoever bound it did so for a reason. It's a foolish binder who unmakes another's without knowing why they made it in the first place. Better so, without knowing what undoing the binding will bring about. Only an idiot releases a binding that's sealed something, even on a book. So, can you tell me why it's shut?"

"Only if you tell me how you knew it was bound in the first place?" I waited a handful of breaths for Vathin to answer, but he didn't. "Are you a binder?"

He waggled a hand. "I'm familiar. It's a matter of discussion, a great one at that, if I'm a binder by any definition. I'm better suited to philosophy, thinking, and musing on things. They are simpler, and thus, better joys than what bindings can bring a man."

I didn't believe that.

"So, why do you have a book shut by a binder that you cannot open?"

I told him. "My teacher said it was a gift for me, and that in it were all the things I could ever hope to know about my family and more. But, he said I'd only be able to open it when I was ready to know and ready to do the binding necessary."

Vathin nodded like he understood. "Then it would be wrong for me to do it. If this man was your teacher, then he knows you better than I do, and I'm sure he has his reasons no matter your curiosity. But, thank you for showing it to me."

I sighed in resignation and stowed the book. It had been a bit much, I suppose, to hope that Vathin would have unmade the binding on the spot.

"So is that why you're heading to the Ashram, then? You wish to be a binder?"

"Yes. And they have stories and records of all the tales I could dream of, or so I've heard."

"That much is true."

My eyes went wide and I nearly fumbled in tying my sack shut. "You've been there?"

He waggled his hand again. "Another matter up for debate. Some of the rishis there think I've never set two steady steps through any part of the Ashram long enough to count as being there. No. They say I never really leave here." He tapped the side of my head. "Maybe they just don't like the talking they call arguing whenever we speak. I have a habit of making them think about their words and not everyone likes that." He gave me a mischievous smile that I found myself mirroring. "They're not fond of philosophers there."

"What's it like?" I hadn't realized the excitement that flooded my voice until I heard myself speak.

"You'll see it soon enough for yourself. Keep that in mind, hm? It's not good for a man to fix his gaze too far ahead on things his feet are far behind. Keep your eyes on where you're at, otherwise you'll be chasing a cloud on the wind. It gets farther the more you follow. You'll miss this." Vathin pointed to the ground.

I followed his gesture to spot a snake slithering through the grass between us. I yelped, leaping back.

"Nothing so bad." Vathin moved with reflexes better than a man of his age should have had, grabbing the serpent by the tip of its tail. He snapped out his other hand to take the creature by its head as well and cradled it in his hold. "It's not dangerous."

I eyed the snake. "How can you tell?"

He shrugged. "Learn to look at things and you come to see the shape of them. And, I've lived and traveled long enough to know what's harmful and what isn't." Vathin tapped a finger to the snake's head, agitating the creature slightly. "Shape of its face, and the coloring." He traced a finger along the body. "These little ones bite and swallow their food whole." Vathin moved over a dozen paces from me, setting the snake in the grass. "It'll leave us alone, and I hope you took its lesson to mind."

The blank look on my face must have told Vathin I hadn't a clue what he meant.

"Focus on things now, Ari. Not where and what they will be."

"Right now we're in the middle of nowhere somewhere between where we left and where we want to be." I grumbled something else after that under my breath, knowing he didn't catch the string of profanity.

"Then let's be here and enjoy what we can. Besides, it'll give us time to do more than be discontent in the back of a wagon, eh?"

I tilted my head and looked at him sideways. "What do you mean?"

He smiled. "I think we made offers of teaching one another before we set off. I mean to hold up my end, do you?"

I did.

Morning passed to late afternoon and I spent the time with a stick Vathin had whittled clean and straight, showing him what I'd learned at the hands of my old choreographer and swordsmanship teacher. He clapped all the while as I flowed through old and long-practiced movements.

In return, Vathin lectured me on philosophy, asking me the greater questions of the world—and, more importantly, myself. He made me think on the bindings themselves, even though I hadn't close to a full understanding how they worked or what they could do. All I knew was what I'd seen. Even still, I thought on them in as many ways as I could.

He taught me to wonder why people did the things they did, obeyed the rules they did, even though the only things making them were the arms of men strong enough to . . . and usually a few swords. He made me think on who wrote those rules and for whose benefit. I pondered on why the bindings were so hard that only a handful of people ever learned them well enough to call themselves a binder. Why not make them easier?

I thought and thought on things until my head swam and ached much like when I'd begun learning the folds.

To reciprocate, and maybe give Vathin a head of his own back, I decided to teach him what little I knew of the folds of the mind. He never asked a question, only listened. When I tried to prod him with questions of my own, well hidden within things I tried to teach, he ignored them with more cleverness than I could manage in conversation.

I soon found why the rishis at the Ashram grew weary of him and probably barred him from staying too long among them, whatever his business may have been.

But most of all, and of what I fondly remember, we traded stories. Little things, and large. He taught me why people believed all the silly things they did, and why, maybe, some of those beliefs weren't so silly at all.

Waiting Day passed, and we spent the night sleeping near each other. Well, we hardly slept, keeping in conversation and watching the stars until our eyes grew heavy. By the next morning of Listening, we'd set back out on the road, our bodies renewed from the rest. Jaseem promised us it would be the only full day's rest we'd have, so it was a good thing we made the most of it.

The evening came on us and we crested a small hill before a stream. The only way ahead came by way of a bridge too narrow for more than one wagon to take at a time. My attention drifted elsewhere while Jaseem dismounted and spoke to the other drivers about crossing.

On the banks of the stream stood a stack of stones, almost like cairns, except they arced over the water almost like miniature bridges themselves. I don't know what force held them all together, so neatly fit, but without any clear binding or mortar.

"What are those?" I pointed a finger, hoping Vathin had it within him today to give a clear answer rather than pose me a question.

"What do you think they are, Ari?"

I scowled. "I asked you."

"And I asked you. We can do this all night. It does a man well to think." He crossed his legs and lounged in the wagon.

"If I knew, I wouldn't have asked. And I thought I was asking someone smart enough to know. Maybe I was wrong." I watched him out of the corners of my eyes for any agitated shifts in posture, but he didn't take the bait.

"Maybe you were. Doesn't hurt my pride the slightest. Besides, I know when someone's trying to poke me for their own good. And, Ari, the wise man never takes a fool's bait. That makes a fool of them both."

I muttered darkly under my breath.

"They're Fhaalds."

I blinked, turning to the young girl who'd spoken. Through most of the whole set of days, she hadn't traded a single word with me. Nor Vathin, from what I'd seen. The only person I'd seen her talk to was Jaseem's wife, Thaiya. Even then, I'd been far enough away I didn't once hear a whisper.

"What?" It hadn't struck me until a moment later how stupid I sounded in saying that.

"Fhaalds." She spelled out the word, though it sounded almost like she was trying to say "Folds." "The stones. That's what they're called." She pointed to the same place I had. "They're old pieces of the world. Older than the bridges. That's what I heard, anyway." Every word of hers came breathy and light, almost like she didn't have the air to give them voice—perpetually tired and unable to speak.

"Oh."

"You see them out in the world around streams and bends in the land."

"Bends?" I looked back at the stream and noticed it ran nearly clean and straight through with barely a twist or turn in its path. "I don't see one."

She shook her head. "Not just the water but"—she motioned to the part of the hill we'd just crested—"land too. Some stories say they mark where Brahm put folds in the land, the ones we can't see."

I cocked a brow at that. "Folds we can't see?"

"I know a riddle rhyme about that," said Vathin. He finally leaned close to me and decided to join the conversation properly. He cleared his throat and spoke clearly.

"Mark the Fhaalds and heed them well,
for they have secrets
to show and tell;
these Fhaalds are more than just old stone,
they lead the path // to places lost,
and unknown,

"somewhere far,
somewhere between,

"where the moon and sun meet in close embrace;
beware the Fhaalds on a moonfull sunny night,
for they will lead you // out of sight.

"The Fhaalds are more than just old stone,
and they will open with a price,
of fresh blood,
and of bone,

"and act the way to take you in
to places lost—long-hid // den.
A place for wanderers and the wise,
to fall into and among—un // bid // den;

"A place of strange skies and stranger light.
A place hung between the doors of midnight."

I looked at Vathin as I tried to remember the riddle and recite it to myself. How could something be both full of moon and sunny during the night? "What's it mean?"

"I. Don't. Know. Ari. That's why it's a *riddle* rhyme." He smiled.

"You have an annoying habit of asking more questions than you answer."

He shrugged. "He who asks, comes to know. He who knows, knows to ask. And the one who thinks he knows, never asks enough, and so he never knows when to ask. Thus the man only asks for trouble."

I suddenly grew overwhelmed by a desire to ignore Vathin in every shape and form and speak only to the ashen-haired girl. It certainly had nothing to do with the fact he had grown increasingly insufferable and smug while the girl knew things I didn't. Not to mention she at least had the inclination to share her knowledge.

"Do you know anything else about them?" I kept my attention focused on the girl, making it clear to Vathin I had no words for him.

She shook her head. "No. Sorry." Each word came fast and whisper-soft, almost as if she were too shy to keep up the effort of speaking.

I knew that kind of timidness, especially from my first days as a sparrow. As much as I wanted to push her for more—whatever she could share—I let it be. There'd be nothing gained by making someone more uncomfortable, especially since we were to share a long ride together. Instead, I settled for offering her my name, hoping that would at least put her better at ease. "I'm Ari." I placed one hand on my chest, offering her my other.

She didn't take it, choosing to wrap her arms tightly around herself instead. "Laki," she said it as *Lucky*.

I pulled my hand back. "That's a nice name." I didn't know what else to say to warm her up to me. All her movements reminded me of someone else like her, just as thin and on edge when it came to touch.

Vathin noticed the exchange and broke in to soften the mood. "How about a story? By the looks of things, we'll have some time in the wagons tonight before we settle somewhere for sleep."

Jaseem finally finished his rounds with the other drivers, retaking his seat up front and goading the horses back into motion. We reached the edge of the bridge and crossed onto it.

"I don't know many, but I know one good tale people seem to enjoy."

I perked up at that. "Which one?"

"Do you know about Brahm's time as a wanderer?"

I had heard pieces of the stories, but in truth, Brahm the Wanderer was a collection of various tales told over time. It lacked a unifying theme—more chance adventures and details of his time traveling the wider world. So, I shook my head, feeling it best to pretend I knew nothing and follow Vathin's advice.

That way, he wouldn't try to avoid telling me something for fear I'd already heard it. I might even hear something new.

He cleared his throat, coughing hard into one balled hand. "Right, then. This is a story of when Brahm, mighty and first of all gods, decided to lose himself in our world as he'd come to feel lost himself. What better thing for a lost man to do to find himself than get even further lost? This is after the time of birthing a new piece of himself as Radhivahn, son of himself, if you believe those stories."

I almost broke in to ask if Vathin believed in Brahm's second birth, but something about the set of his face told me to keep the question to myself for now.

"Brahm, all without an idea how to go about this, decided to do what he'd not done. He cast himself down—mortal-made, no longer god of fire and sun. This is how his story starts. But, like all stories, many pieces have been lost to time, and I can only remember but a piece of the pieces. So we'll start with what I can recall."

FIFTY-FIVE
Candle, Cloak, and Cane

This is a time long after the time of demons and shapeless things that turned men against each other. This is past the point when bindings were wild and without names, and the binders who could call them became paragons—heroes. Yes. The Ashram came to stand long ago, and many things have since been lost. Only the ten bindings all men must know are taught, but we are far from mountain temples teaching men and women things.

We are out among the jungles deep and dense along the Golden Road and its paths before they came to be known by any of their current names. Wait, no, there was no Golden Road then. Just paths, all nameless, some greater than the others.

Brahm wandered westward from lands past where Laxina stands now, and all he had to his name were the three things all wanderers must keep in care: candle, cloak, and cane.

In his left hand he held a candle of waxy white: a simple thing in form, but capable of burning ever bright. A candle of endless flame and light. With it, no things could escape his sight. He wore a cloak of forest green, tattered and torn, but far more than it seemed. It's said no eyes could spot Brahm with his cloak if he had a mind to turn loose a binding that only he knew.

Lastly, he carried his cane of wood and grain. All to keep his body firm and free from greater strain. And should he need it be, it could serve as one last weapon to keep him from injury.

He wandered far, passing rural villages and taking of what kindness they would show, repaying them in fair measure for their generosity. When he could wander no more for a day, he slept, kept safe by his ever-burning candle. It kept all dark things at bay.

This story starts when Brahm came to the broken kingdom of Jadheer, king of eastern eld, the expanse of forests and jungles outside the mountain passes that neighbor what is now Laxina. His lands were vast and rich. No end of wood, water, and stone. Food? Plentiful.

So why then was his called the broken kingdom?

For jealousy and cruelty held strong in Jadheer's heart, though this was not always the case. Once a man, noble bright, and in service to Brahm's flame and his light. He'd now fallen from his former grace. And wore a greedy king's title and face. He took where and what he wanted of his people, leaving them with nothing but hateful thoughts and poorer lives. But still, his people never took up against him, for all the while, they held to the hope and memory of who he once was.

But then came Brahm the Wanderer, knowing the truth of the man. He strode into his kingdom and called the king to meet him for justice. While no longer a god above, he still held to much of his power and his binding. But now, he was a mortal man, bindings or not, and he could fall. He took this into account as he met with Jadheer.

The two fought terribly, channeling bindings lost to most men, shaking stone, stream, and trees. In the end, trickery bested Brahm.

Too afraid, and unable to see Brahm for who he really was, men came to the aid of their crooked king, hoping to earn his eye and favor. And some did.

In the end, Brahm was stripped of candle, cloak, and cane, left to rot below the castle. To be imprisoned in the Halls of Stone.

Brahm waited nine and ninety days, living off what scraps he could. All the while, he turned to what he'd never had to before. The folds of the mind. He sat in practice, deep and thoughtful, reflecting on the bindings he'd laid and shaped for all. In this, Brahm found solace and more, a way to best the king who'd beaten him.

He bound a breath bold and boisterous, sending it echoing through the Halls of Stone and all the way up to where he knew Jadheer would hear him. "Face me, crooked and corrupted king. I challenge you once again, no other men need be involved. Just you and me. I'll show you for what you are. I'll best you before all you care to bring."

And so the call went answered.

But before it did, Brahm noticed something strange among the stone walls in where he lay imprisoned.

At every seam where rock and mortar held and joined, crimson and brighter red leaked and bled. The walls streamed more blood than any body could hold.

Then came Jadheer, opening the stone door to Brahm's prison, and leveling his staff at the once-god, now mortal. His men stood by his side, eyes and mouths veiled by dark cloth. "Who are you to challenge me? To call to me so among the ears of my men?"

"I am Brahm. Born first and of myself—from nothing. I am before and will be beyond at the end itself. The end of all things, even you, Jadheer. I made myself mortal, but do not think I cannot contend with you here and now with the bindings."

Jadheer laughed. "Then do so. Best me. Show us what you who claim to be god above can do. Here in the Halls of Stone you can do nothing. Far from your candle, cloak, and cane. Here, no man can call on the folds of the mind but me. Without your candle, you've no source of flame. Without your cloak, you cannot ward off harm. And without your cane, you have nothing with which to bind and hold the fire. No sword or arm of any fashion with which to cut your way free or break through stone."

And Jadheer was right in this. No normal man could do these things in the Halls of Stone, especially without candle, cloak, and cane. But he did not goad just any man. For while he didn't believe, he did in fact challenge Brahm, first and last of all things.

And so Brahm slipped into the folds of his mind. Hand outstretched, he reached toward the ceiling almost like he sought to take a piece of the stone above in hold. "As above!" The world shook. Stone shuddered, threatening to fall apart. With his other hand, Brahm pointed to the spot between where he and Jadheer stood. "So below! I bind you stone, and bid you down to bury Jadheer. Flesh. And. Bone!"

And the world roared with Brahm like it heeded his call. Stone split and cracked with thunderous cries. Pieces larger than men fell between the two, creating craters in the ground between them, and still the world shook as if it meant to break in two from end to end.

Brahm did not relent, holding to the binding as more of the Halls of Stone shook apart.

"Enough!" Jadheer screamed. "Fine. If you wish to challenge me, then meet me in the courtyard outside. I'll even leave you your candle, cloak, and cane." At this his men and he laughed something terrible. They hauled in a chest made from the very walls of the halls around them. Seamless, sealed, and of all heavy stone, the box had no visible lid nor way to open.

Jadheer left the chest in Brahm's cell and closed the way behind him, his laughter echoing still through the halls.

But Brahm would not be bested again. He'd shown enough to prove to Jadheer that he could channel at least one of the bindings all men must know. He knew the corrupted king believed him capable of little else beyond that, leaving him the box of his belongings more as an insult than as a gift. But Brahm had done more than hone his mortal skills with just one of the bindings. He'd mastered all ten now as nothing more than a man.

And so he placed his hands upon the chest and slipped once again into the many folds of his mind. "As within, so without!" The shape and stone of the box changed within Brahm's hold and he opened it like it had never been sealed and seamless.

From it he retrieved his candle, cloak, and cane. Brahm slipped himself into the old comfort of his worn and weathered cloak, settling better with its weight around him. The candle brought a warmth to him and leached away the cold of the Halls of Stone. Even without a flame, the candle carried the memory of fire, and that was enough for Brahm to ward away the chill. Lastly came his cane, giving his legs more strength than he'd had of late from being trapped so long in his prison.

He stood better with it and cast it through a few swings, using it like a sword. Then he placed its tip against the wall and channeled another binding. "Stand firm all, then chase danger." The stones shook, then exploded with the force of thunder, hurtling forward to crash to the ground outside.

With that, Brahm stepped free of his cell, ready to wander the Halls of Stone and chase after Jadheer.

He muttered another binding, breathing a whisper-blown breath over the candlewick, pulling at what little flame remained inside him. With that, he kindled a spark of brightness, burning hot and clear. It cast away the shadows of the halls but brought a pain to his eyes, for Brahm had seen no sun nor candlelight for so long. He weathered the pain and walked through the halls.

But Jadheer had left behind other trickery, knowing, were the man who thought himself Brahm to escape, he would not be able to best him again.

So serpents, long of tooth and poisoned fang, leapt at Brahm.

But Brahm, born of himself, still had his trusty cloak. He wrapped himself in it and bound it tight, muttering another binding. Snakes bit into the fabric hanging from his legs, some reaching as high as his clothed arms, but none broke through the unseen barrier. They fell away harmless.

Then Brahm channeled something else. A binding only the greatest binders could call. He stretched a piece of fire thin, then bound it to his own breath within, blowing it over his cane and wreathing it in flame most bright. He cut through the serpents and all other monsters in the halls.

And so Brahm bested all challenges before him, leaving the Halls of Stone. But when he came above to the courtyard, he found it empty but for the bodies of those who'd attended Jadheer. All stone higher than a man could stand had now been brought down low. The castle had fallen, and so had all those in Jadheer's service. The king himself had fled, knowing he could not challenge Brahm.

And in doing so, he loosed bindings so terrible they took the heart of life from the land, sapping its color until only whiteness remained. No warmth lay in the land, and the trees could not bear the new cold. Only the mountains remained. Such a twist and turn of nature itself, the world came to weep frozen tears.

"I'll chase you, Jadheer, to every end of this world. I know its corners and its every fold. I'll find you. Even if I must wander for eternity!"

And so he meant to live up to his word.

Some say Brahm still walks among us, ever wandering the wide world, seeking to find the corrupt binder king and bring him to justice.

Night came a deeper dark than it had the nights before, and Vathin's story had kept us so well occupied I hadn't noticed it until Jaseem stopped the wagons and told us to rest. We all left our places in the cart and found comfortable spots to sleep. I kept myself close to Vathin, hoping he would bother to tell me more before dreams took us.

"Thank you for the story."

He inclined his head. "A small thing, but worth its weight if you can figure out the meanings hidden in it."

I ran my tongue against the back of my teeth, thinking on what he said. "What's the hidden meaning?"

He waggled a finger in admonishment. "*That* is cheating."

"Technically, it's asking. A philosopher I know told me to try doing that more often."

Vathin twisted and lunged, a cupped hand snapping out to cuff me.

I moved away just in time to have his hand sail harmlessly through part of my hair. I grinned and stuck out my tongue.

"Stories have grains of truths hidden within them. The problem is many pieces and things are lost to time and translation, especially when told over distance and traded through different languages. But there are always kernels to find. The wise one knows how to do so."

I fixed him with a look. "So, wise one, do you know?"

He mirrored my earlier expression, tongue peeking between his teeth. "I know one thing and that is that I am no wise man." His face told me that he'd said that more to find a way to not answer me, if anything to irritate me.

He succeeded.

Nearby, Jaseem had lit one of many fires.

I thought of the story and then fished through my pack until I found one of the candles I'd gotten from the merchant. I walked over to the fire and lit it, bringing it back, hands cupping the gentle flame to keep it from snuffing out.

When I returned to Vathin, I decided to change the topic. "Do you think it's true?"

"Mhm? What is?" Vathin shifted in the grass, folding some of his robes under him to help create a thin cushion of sorts.

"Brahm the Wanderer. Any of it. That he's still out there wandering as a man but not a man, and certainly not the god."

"All stories are true from a certain point of view. But, I know you want a clearer answer than that. To be honest, I don't. But I'd like to think so. I've often thought that might be the most important part of belief and stories, choosing to believe the pieces we want. Otherwise, what good and fun are they?"

He had a point, but I had asked for another reason. Once, I hadn't believed in the kinds of magic and monsters stories held. Then I paid the price for my ignorance. I never wanted that to be the case again.

So maybe Brahm the Wanderer was real. And if he was, I meant to find him.

I thought on that until I could think no more. The candle and the flame occupied my mind all the while and I fed it my thoughts on Brahm and the story. They filled me until my mind weighed more than stone. I went to bed dreaming of chasing after Brahm.

FIFTY-SIX

Tricks by Moonlight

The first set of days passed and we all grew more comfortable with one another. Laki finally spoke more than a few sentences with me, usually questions about myself, never really letting anything slip concerning her own life. And I never pried.

Lixin and I developed a solid-enough method of talking to one another, which involved pantomime and simple words in the Trader's Tongue. He shared with me a series of slow and gentle flowing exercises, all stretches that carried the motions of the wind within them. At first, I thought it nothing more than something to keep him active and his joints healthy in his age. After a short time though, I realized it was more than that.

The movements lent me another sort of clarity as I enacted them. A mental freedom that turned my mind almost as soft and shifting as the exercises themselves. I found myself slipping easier into the folds of the mind as I practiced with him, and that going through the old image exercises Mahrab taught me was now easier. More so, I could change and hold different ideas blindingly fast compared to before. A piece of my mind that came with the hard-won logic of living on Keshum's streets began to fade. I no longer worried about the reality of things when in this lucid mindset brought on by Lixin's training.

I simply thought.

And my mind brought the scene to life inside the folds.

Vathin and I continued our philosophy discussions. He took every chance to ask me about anything he could think of, and then poke holes wherever he could in my logic. His was a different kind of training that stretched my mind in how I looked at things and people in the world. I didn't know it then, but I would come to greatly appreciate it later in life, especially once I began to truly see the shape of the bindings and how they worked. But back then, the discussions were tiring, yet admittedly, fun.

We used them to sling mild barbs at one another when we could.

I practiced my swordsmanship with the stick Vathin had whittled for me.

I helped a wagon get unstuck. I trained on the folds, and when nights came, I relit my candle and focused on the flame like Mahrab had taught me.

The journey became a blur. I trained in every regard, not knowing what else to do, waiting for evenings to come in the hopes of a story.

Lixin had none he could properly articulate, and Laki had gone quiet on any subject close to a story since sharing what she had about the Fhaalds. That left Vathin, who usually resorted to stories I'd already heard, but I appreciated someone else saying them.

I didn't have the heart to tell any myself.

Sometimes there is a simple comfort in old stories told again, especially from someone else's mouth. It's like a favorite meal served in a new way. It tastes the same, but there is a pleasure in the different presentation.

That night, though, Vathin decided to tell us a piece of another story that stays in my memory to this day.

I'd lit my candle in preparation, holding it in its tin base, letting the glow cast itself over Vathin's face.

"This is a story about a woman, fairer than any, and the young man who chased her around the world. But he could never pry her from her sun, her first and true love. In truth, her only love. And this he knew. But he chased her all the same. Some say he still does, and that you can hear his calls some nights. Howling her name through the skies, a name no one but he can hear and make out."

This was a time before castes and kingdoms. A time when the free folk of the world wandered and moved as they would. There were the first people, then the second, the Ruma. Singers and tellers of tales. These second people made their ways through trades of their voices. And the people who came after? They toiled with their hearts, minds, and hands. They took to shaping the world after Brahm, but all without the bindings, until they too came to learn those. Though this was before the Ashram, when people had to learn the bindings on their own.

There was no code of conduct among binders, so arguments arose, some ending in violent clashes that shook mountains, carved new fissures in the world, and formed rivers in their wake. A terrible time for some. A hard time.

This was a time when demons and darker things still walked the earth, doing as they were wont to do.

In this time, a young man named Kohlri set out on an adventure. Bored of his life of meager means and lesser dreams, he wanted for something more. At first, all he could hope for was to become a carpenter like his father. To marry the local beauty, though even that seemed a far-fetched thing for him. So he set his gaze on the wider world and wandered it in the hope it would bring him something greater than what he'd come to know.

He traveled wide and far, eventually coming by an old man on the road.

The robed man looked bedraggled and starved, huddling tight within his cloak.

So Kohlri knelt by him, knowing how to treat elders in need of help. He offered the man food and water, then asked if there was anything else he could do for the man, telling him there was a limit to what he could spare.

"Thank you. You've given more than most and many." The old man pressed his hands together for a gesture of added thanks. "But perhaps I can ask something else of you, and in return, give you something back."

Kohlri, unsure of what the old man could offer, let his curiosity take hold of him. "What else do you wish to ask of me? I have little to my name, and what pieces of precious I have I brought with me. My shoes are nearly worn through from my time on the road, and my clothes are threadbare; I'll need a change soon. What food I have is enough to get me to the next village, maybe not. I have little else but my walking cane."

The old man wrapped his cloak even tighter around himself. "Not so much as that. I'd very much like a partner, someone young to keep me safe, and keep me steady. I could use your arm as much to help me up as keep danger at bay. You should be able to manage that. You and your cane."

"You want an escort?" Kohlri didn't know how the man had gotten so far without one if he needed one now. "And what will you give me in return?" He would have helped the man anyway, truth be told, but now that the man had offered, Kohlri felt it wise to seek compensation.

The old man's eyes shone and he spoke two words of power, hands moving. Earth shifted and rolled under his command. A mound formed under the man, raising him higher than Kohlri before it crumbled beneath the elderly fellow.

Kohlri caught him and eased the man to the ground. "What was that?"

The old man coughed and dusted himself clean. "One of the bindings made and left to man by Brahm. I confess, I don't know many, and I certainly don't know them all. There are too many for any one man to know, I wager, but I know a few. If you stick with me, I can teach you. I'd very much like to pass these on. All those years of life to learn them, and when I die, they'll go with me unless someone is willing to take them on."

Kohlri had spent his life wanting something more, had traveled as far from home as he could go to find it. And now he had.

Power.

The means with which to shape the world, and with it, maybe reshape his own life as well. Kohlri saw the true calling he'd been looking for and pledged himself at the feet of the old man, naming him his rishi—teacher.

Together, the two of them walked to the next town, and then the next. They traveled, traded, talked, and trained. They wandered ever wayward, chasing the sun and the moon. Walking end to end. In time, Kohlri grew to be a fine binder, growing in power greater than the man who'd trained him.

His mind was young and he'd learned the bindings early—before age took its toll on him. The folds of his mind were conditioned hard and well so as not to fall apart with the passing of years.

Kohlri found work easy in the world, making money wherever he went, his rishi in tow. They lived an easy life, but never were ones to sit still. Kohlri wondered what life waited for him back home, a place so far away and long buried in memory now. But whenever he thought of it, he could see no hope in the idea. He'd outgrown the place, and the Kohlri who once called it home could never again see it as such. It was somewhere and something too strange to him—too small.

So Kohlri sought bigger and greater things still. And what he could desire, he set to with a will. He challenged other binders to duels that redrew the face of some lands. He took up work for money to defend villagers from bandits, and sometimes, some say he turned bandit himself. Other times he went to war, full and hard, fighting for whatever cause took his heart.

Yet in all this, Kohlri's heart hung heavy and empty. Its rooms hadn't all been filled by magic and power, by wandering the wider world, or by war and fighting. All the lands under the skies traveled and searched, and yet he couldn't fill such small a thing inside him.

So what was he to do?

Then, as life often does, the answer was shown to him. Though he didn't know it for what it was.

On a lone night after a long wearying battle, Kohlri returned to his rishi and their most recent home under the stars.

"It's going to storm tonight, Rishi."

"Yes, it will. Then, like it does, it will pass. They always do. And with it, we will see a different beauty."

"Beauty?"

"Oh, yes. All things have their beauty for those that can see them. The storm. The stars. The night sky. The moon. All of them. And they have their place as much as the morning sun, clouds, and lines of trees along the top of our world."

Kohlri didn't know then what his teacher meant, so instead he set to quietly making a hovel for them, using the bindings to do so.

Then came the storm, and Kohlri found a gentle peace in listening to the thunder and the gentle susurrus of rain. It felt much like the tumult inside him had been given voice and shared with the world. It heard him. And it replied.

But like his teacher said, the storm broke. The clouds vanished. And with it, the noise of the crying world. So another came to fill the void, and in doing so, worked its way through the hollow spaces of Kohlri's heart and filled them as well.

She sang a song silver brilliant and clear as the moon on a cloudless night. Her voice called to him and everything inside his heart.

So Kohlri left his bed that night.

But his rishi told him not to. "Don't go. Don't look at her. Don't listen."

"But why, Rishi?"

He gave his student and friend a pained look. "Because it will hurt. And you will be smitten—in love. And then it will hurt more. Because your heart will break."

But Kohlri had a wolf's appetite in all things, from war to kingdoms to claim. And now that something had set his heart afire, he had a hunger for love as well. "I'll be fine. I've traveled the world and no paths can weary me or my feet. I've learned all the bindings I could, and none can dull the folds of my mind. War? I've won that too. What's love in the face of that?"

His rishi was as patient as he was wise. When he spoke, it was but a whisper, one gone unheard by Kohlri. Well, it reached his ears, but didn't sit and settle in his mind, and certainly not his heart.

"Love is the one thing that can break any man. And it will break you too, if you don't take care. For her heart already belongs to another. She's set in his ways and to follow him, just as he chases her the same. The two are never to meet, and that is why she wanders with us. But, once in a while on rarest of the days, the two meet and embrace. And will bring us a midnight in which they wander further still. Until that time, she is ours. But she will never be yours."

Kohlri didn't listen, something he regrets to this day, according to the story.

He left the hovel and saw her.

Silver bright she shone, all of moonlit glow. Hair darker than any night sky. Her eyes held all the sparkle and promise of the stars. She wore nothing and held all the curves of the world in her shape and form. And she sang as clear and enrapturing as she looked. When she fixed her gaze on Kohlri, he froze, heart and mind.

"Oh." Her voice was soft as morning wind through the trees. "I didn't know you could hear me. I'm sorry."

Kohlri found his wits seconds later. "No, it's I who am sorry. I didn't mean to startle you. To stop your singing."

She smiled and said nothing.

And now Kohlri began to see the shape of love, though he didn't know it. His heart beat in a way it never had in the midst of duels, or travel, hunger-pain, storm and rain, or in the heat of war. His heart felt larger than it ever had, hammered harder than before. It felt colder and hotter than he ever thought it could. And the hollowness in it grew more apparent to him than ever, but now he had a thought of what that space could come to hold.

"My name is Kohlri."

Her smile widened. "I know. I've watched you wander. I've heard your calls in the night when you think no one is listening. I've heard your anger and your hurt. And I've heard the hollowness ringing in your heart."

He took a step forward, and she took one back in perfect tandem. "Is that why you're here?"

Another smile, but no words.

"Because if that's what you seek, then it's yours. Take it." Kohlri pulled at the collar of his shirt, baring his breast.

"For tonight," she replied. "But then you'll take it back in the morning, and I, mine. That is the way of things. And a love for a night never lasts."

But Kohlri did not want to hear this thing. He took another step, and she, one away. "I've been looking all my life for a thing I didn't know, couldn't find, but now I think I do and have. Will you prove me right?"

Her smile turned, sinking sadly. "Follow me. Look for me. And maybe one day you'll find out. But not tonight."

At that, Kohlri's heart grew cold, but he pushed it from his mind. He clung to the little hope his heart could hold. She told him to do two things, and among all that he had done, he could do those as well. "I'll follow you forever. I'll look. I'll call for you. I'll be there for and on that day."

"And tonight?" The woman smiled again, but it was one that held no warm joy.

"What can I give you tonight to make you stay awhile? To hear one more song?"

"Just ask it of me, and sing one in return."

So he did.

She answered him and sang her song, setting his heart alight. And in turn, he sang one back, a thing of howling pain and loneliness. A call for all he wanted and did not know.

And then, when it was over, she bid him farewell.

"Wait, before you leave. Will you give me your name?"

"Shaandi. Remember it. Sing it when you see me next."

"I will," said Kohlri, and then she left.

With that, the storm in his heart returned, and the world answered in reply. The storm came, and Kohlri returned to the hovel. Now he understood what his rishi had meant. And he would only come to learn it better as time went by.

The story ended and everyone's breath sat still.

It was Laki who broke the silence, though. "Did he find her again? Shaandi? Did Kohlri find her? Did they fall in love?"

Vathin gave her a strained smile. "Only one of them did. But, like the story says, he still looks for her out there every day. He still makes his cries and sings his songs that only she can hear. But, his heart's been broken forevermore. Yet, he holds to the honest fool's hope in love."

The moon had come up overhead tonight. No clouds to hide her glow behind themselves.

Vathin leaned back and looked at it.

My candle cast an odd trick then. Its light and the glow of the moon brought an odd tinge to Vathin's eyes. The yellow-orange of the fire danced until it brushed aside the gray in him, putting golden gems in their place. Under that light, the man looked leaner and more grizzled than before. Wolfish, if I had to describe him. And it passed just as soon.

Clouds slipped through the sky, hiding the moon behind themselves.

Monsoon season decided to honor the story that night.

Thunder cracked.

Then came the storm.

My candle flickered and the trick of light faded, showing Vathin to be as gray, old, and tired as ever.

And the yellow finally left Vathin's eyes.

FIFTY-SEVEN
ARRIVAL

Vathin told no more stories after that night and I didn't have the heart to ask for more. He carried on through the trip in a sullen silence all could feel.

I spent my time instead talking with Jaseem, learning of the many places he'd visited over his travels along the Golden Road.

He told me of the villages, cities, and as well the kingdoms he'd gone through. Yet, he never once left the Mutri Empire. Something that left me rather confused.

Look at it from my perspective. Jaseem had the means and inclination to travel, and in theory, could go anywhere. He had the people, the wagons, and the skills to subsist. But he kept within one empire when there was a world to see. Why?

Then I remembered the Ari of just a few sets ago. A boy who'd kept himself safe within the familiar walls of Abhar, even more so, the city streets of Keshum. Nothing physically held me back. But I had. Whether through fear or comfort, and sometimes the pair are indistinguishable from one another. I had been the one to root myself so firmly in place. Nothing else.

Jaseem had done the same, and I couldn't blame him. As hard in some aspects as his life was, he had comfort and familiarity. And enough variation in a day's work to make it exciting. He knew the roads well and the people who lived at their ends. Knew where and when he was welcome to stop. He knew the paths to everywhere he deemed worth traveling and how to turn a coin or two of profit when he wanted.

The little things changed. The people that rode with him and the stories they traded along the way. Sometimes the weather. Other times he'd come upon a rarity in trade, or something worth nothing in tin, copper, or gold, but which intrigued him all the same. He told me these little trinkets could be a treasure to a man with imagination.

"What's it like around the Ashram?" Vathin hadn't answered that question for me. I hoped our guide would.

"Mhm. Cold, for one. It's far enough up in Ughal that it never truly gets warm, even come the summer. Sure enough, the snows melt, but not in whole, and you can feel the air still clinging to their chill. It's a cold brightness up there, if that makes any sense. Not sure if you've seen the like."

I hadn't.

Jaseem read my face and knew as much. "You'll see, then. Wouldn't hurt a man to get himself heavy robes for that kind of weather. It's beautiful, though, don't think it's not. It's clean. Calm. There's something about the place you can't put in words. You smell it in every breath up there. Special air. The food is good, maybe a touch too hot for my tastes. But then, it has to be, I suppose."

I let him continue for a while, reveling in the information and letting it take my imagination whole. I needed something to pass the final drudgery of the journey.

I'd run out of my own stores of food nearly a set back, turning to anxious munching in moments of boredom. Thankfully, Jaseem and his wife cooked decent food.

Something a mark above what Small Kaya made for us. I don't mean to imply she couldn't cook or didn't care, but the wagoner pair just did it differently. And I noticed it.

They cooked together, laughing and smiling between themselves as they did. The both of them took an honest pleasure in making things for the people they carried along the way. A true joy, and it showed. I still believe that spark made its way into the food.

"We'll be there before dark tonight, Ari." Jaseem never bothered to use any of the titles and calls based on a person's age, relation, or rank by caste. He'd once told me that he found it beyond useless. They told you nothing of the person you spoke to, only of the one speaking to them.

The true way to measure a person was to watch them on the road, far away from people who cared to use their names and proper titles. To see how they fared on paths that treated all men equally, and in places where you were uncomfortable.

"Are you going straight to the Ashram?" I kept a silent hope that he would keep me aboard the wagon until we reached the place. I had the means to find lodging with my gold rupai, but the idea of spending it so soon upon arrival knotted my stomach.

Jaseem shook his head. "No. I'll be settling down with Thaiya in the trader's circle entering the city. Ughal is a small kingdom, but well respected. It has history. And Ghal is an equally small city, but has more coin flowing through it than places many times larger. Abhar may be the wealthiest, but there are places in the world where treasures trade hands easier, and with that, a man can make himself a small fortune. So, for me, it's work as soon as we get there."

I nodded, keeping the disappointment off my face.

"It's not that far of a walk from the edge of the city to the Ashram. You'll have time. It's hard to miss that place, it's not hard to find the path to it, and there are places enough to sleep and rest. You can find a meal, hot or cold, almost anywhere in Ghal."

I didn't have the heart to give him even a fake smile as he went on telling me my many options.

You would think with so much money at my fingertips, I'd be at ease. But no. There is a comfort to have something to hold on to when you've spent most of your life with so little. Even when that changes, you know the familiar hollowness of nothingness all too well. It never truly leaves you, and that fear keeps a place in your heart and stomach. That gold coin was all I had in the world besides my book and clothes.

Could I have taken more? Of course.

But guilt and fear are tricky things, and they so often work together to plague our minds with their many ills. I worried in doing so I'd subject my brothers and sisters to a similar fear as I now suffered. And my guilt over a worry that never came to pass kept me from tending to my own needs.

To some this sounds silly, but I wonder if those people ever wondered where their next meal might come from . . . much less when? If they knew the different kinds of pains hunger fills you with. A man grown familiar enough with barely eating could tell the day by the shape of the hunger hurting him.

By the end of my time as a sparrow, I'd built us a small treasure of wealth. But before that, it would be a lie to say we ate regularly. Some of us missed meals staying out past our runs to make up for any lack in tithing. Some of us got sick or were run so ragged we couldn't keep anything down. Leftovers did not exist in the house of sparrows, so if you missed a meal, you would have to make the next. And then there were the meals themselves. Nothing Small Kaya served—not to her discredit—could be considered a meal. She did her best with what she had, occasionally trying to treat us to something better.

I say this to make clear now that I too came to know the different kinds of hungers as a sparrow under Mithu. And I never wanted to experience them again.

Something of my fear must have shown in my expression, and Jaseem, being the traveler that he was, well-acquainted with the moods of men, caught it for what it was.

"You don't have anywhere to go when you get there, hm, Ari?" He placed a hand on my shoulder.

I tensed under his touch, then relaxed. "No. I don't know anything about the place other than the word Ashram. I didn't even think to ask."

Jaseem pursed his lips and bobbed his head, adopting silence as he thought. We rode until the sun reached midday zenith. Then, Jaseem finally spoke. "You can stay with us until you need. Thaiya won't mind. You'll have to help with your hands wherever we need, but you'll have a warm place to stay for the night, and food too. In the morning, you can go off to the Ashram. We won't be able to take you ourselves, still. My business is best done with them when I'm ready to leave Ghal, not when I'm there and fresh faced. *Ji-ah?*"

Relief welled in me, untangling the twists in my stomach. "*Ji!*"

True to his word, we reached Ghal while the sky still held some blue. Most of the color had darkened to something found in sapphires dusted in coal, but still bright enough to not pass for night.

Ghal lived up to all that Jaseem tried to explain earlier. The air gnawed at what bits of me lay exposed outside of my cloak, making me doubly grateful I'd decided to buy the piece after all. The city lacked any of the walls I had lived all my life seeing within Abhar. But the thing that took my mind the most happened to be the sheer space between buildings and the land.

Keshum had been crowded. No, that word fell far short of the mark. Keshum had been packed to the point it threatened to burst at the seams. A consequence of its location. Abhar sat at the heart of the Mutri Empire, and thus, the Golden Road. And Keshum lay at the center of all that. The true and pure crossroads of all roads.

The city never had a chance to be anything but a skin filled to the point of overflowing. Buildings touched one another at times, barely leaving room for an alley to spring between them. People walked shoulder to shoulder in crowds so thick it couldn't help but birth urchins who grew to be pickpockets.

But Ghal had space I couldn't understand at first look. Homes and buildings with empty land around them. I spotted wooden posts and beams around some properties, fencing them in. The roofs were sharply canted, some in tiered rings that rose into a conical point. It took me a moment to realize why.

The design shed rain and snow easily.

And then it hit me.

The sheer brilliance of the place's color jarred me so I couldn't properly process it. And it all came from the endless sheet of white blanketing the ground and distant hills. Snow covered everything but for the trader's circle we approached. The stark white brought a brightness to everything, even the colors of the buildings that would have otherwise been darker.

And smoke rose from many of the roofs. Chimney smoke—fires. The plumes of black and gray filtered high into the air before dissipating, but they looked odd in the frigid air and against the white backdrop.

"That's what you'll be wanting to visit." Jaseem tapped two knuckles to the side of my chin before pointing far ahead of us.

I followed the gesture into the distance.

A mountain range sat just beyond the last of the city I could see. Atop it, gilded ringed spires, giant versions of the design common among the low-standing buildings near us. I saw blues bright enough to be gemstones among the gold, and reds strong enough to have been drawn from blood-made stone. The roofs caught the last rays of cold light, throwing them back at everyone in Ghal.

Among all the sights I've been fortunate in my life to see, gods and those claiming to be, monsters and magic, demons, and the things that fall between those lines, I confess my first glimpse of the Ashram still holds me, mind and heart, more than the rest.

It was like seeing an old promise, one you begin to lose faith in, come true. The Ashram may have been just out of reach, but it was close enough to see. And there is something to be said for seeing a place only kept to stories for so long.

"They build on top of and into the mountain proper there. Don't ask me how. And don't ask them." Jaseem's voice hardened and turned a sort of sour that almost had me making a face like I'd sucked a lemon. "Brahm and any other god above or under the sun knows I've asked many times how those old nutters did such a thing. They never tell me. One ass once said to me, 'The same way you build a house on the ground, but this one is on a mountain.' Can you believe that?" Jaseem didn't give me a chance to answer. He harrumphed and went on.

"Better to just deal your goods and take what little magics they make to sell off down in the south. It's better for my mind and peace that way." Then his face broke into a toothy wide grin. "Plus it's better for my purse."

I matched his expression, my mood buoyed by finally seeing the Ashram. Every ounce of me wanted to break into a run and not stop till I reached its doors and began my new life pursuing the bindings. My excitement had reached beyond me because Jaseem put a hand on my shoulder and gave me a gentle jostle.

"Let's find a spot for our wagons and get things unloaded, *ji*? After that, we'll treat you and anyone else who decides to help to some dinner. We'll haggle for rooms later. You can put up with us for the night." He didn't have to say another word.

I leapt from the wagon just as it slowed enough for me to know I wouldn't tumble and dash my brains out on the ground.

"Oi, boy. You mean to empty the wagon before we even get there?"

"If that's an option!" My pace had me fall behind Jaseem's side, bringing me to the rear of the wagon.

Vathin groaned and leaned over its edge, looking at me with bleary eyes like he'd stared at the sun first thing upon waking. "The wise man lets his elders sleep so early in the day."

"It's close to sixth candle's end. Seventh is going to start soon if the sky's any judge."

Vathin glowered at me, craning his neck to look at the sky. "The wise man knows if the sun's still up, it can be argued to be morning somewhere for someone."

I matched his look. "I'm sure the wise man happens to be the lazy man to someone somewhere too."

Vathin found enough energy to pop straight up at that, then rock in place as he realized he hadn't accounted for where he stood. The cart shook and he nearly tumbled from it. "The wise man also knows not to argue with uppity little pissants too full of themselves."

"*I've* never once claimed to be a wise man. So it stands to reason I wouldn't know these things and could never put them into practice." I made a mock bow, throwing one arm out to the side as I did. Something snapped against my head with the force of being flicked by a finger. I winced and rubbed the spot. "Ow."

I looked to the ground to find a pistachio the size of my thumbnail, still in its shell. I squinted at Vathin. "Isn't there something about the wise man doesn't throw nuts at children."

Vathin grinned. "Nothing of the sort, surprisingly."

It wasn't so much of a surprise to me. The more time we spent together, the more comfortable Vathin and I had become in spirited conversation like the one we'd just had. They usually happened when he'd taken a curmudgeonly turn . . . such as upon waking, whenever that happened to be.

He turned toward the mountains, squinting at them before his eyes widened. "Ah. There it is. I can't wait to get back there and set some of those old bastards' heads spinning."

I'm sure the rishis didn't have the same enthusiasm for Vathin and his conversations.

"There's a clearing over there!" Jaseem's voice drowned out ours as he gestured to a broad swath of empty space in the circle. "No sitting about when we get there, Ari. You help the boys get everything off the wagons and set up. Don't drop anything. Don't spill a grain. Don't tear a sack, crack a box, tip a thing, or scratch the side of my wagons. *Ji?*"

I answered him but didn't think he heard me as the noise of the trader's circle's evening haggling and banter broke over us.

Everything became a wearying blur after that. I unloaded the wagons as instructed, not taking even a wayward breath to talk to any of the men helping me with the labor. Thaiya oversaw it all, measured and patient, ever with a smile on her face. When we needed a drink, she saw to it. Some soreness in our muscles, and she found us something lighter to do until we felt back up to the task of carrying things.

Jaseem handled the rest, quickly hunting down anyone who'd requested even a bent piece of wood. He sorted his accounts and off-loaded every good he'd brought up from Keshum. "Now, let's be done with this. I'm going to settle the horses and wagons. Then we get to fill our bodies and rest our bones."

He made good on his promise.

FIFTY-EIGHT
HAGGLING

I made my farewells that morning to what remained of our traveling party. Half the workers Jaseem employed had been temporary, and had now moved on to other jobs. Lixin had left before the sun had risen, conveying that he had only come here to find the first ride across the mountain border toward his homeland. Vathin was nowhere to be found. I took it to mean he'd left without a word.

That stung after our time together, but it had been foolish to think he wouldn't want to set about his own business as soon as he could. After all, I certainly planned to.

That left the quiet Laki in my company. The pair of us dressed in what we could, both woefully underprepared for the weather in Ghal.

I left the inn with Laki by my side. We quickly took each other in arm, shuddering under the first breeze to lick its way through the openings in our clothing.

"I don't think I'll be able to make it up the mountain like this." Laki's eyes settled on the golden roofs of the Ashram's buildings.

The comment lurched me away from the immediate discomfort of the cold. "You're going there too?"

She nodded. "There's something I need to get. Then I can leave for home."

A piece of my heart sank at that. Though we didn't know each other well, I had immediately hoped she intended to stay on and study at the Ashram. I would have liked one familiar face, no matter how shortly I'd known them.

It felt like Keshum to me now. I'd again be leaving a group of people I'd become comfortable with.

"What do you need? Where's home?" I finally found the strength to walk through the cold, in search of the nearest clothier I could find. My sack weighed heavier on my shoulder, though it had in reality only grown lighter. I attributed the feeling to the fatigue of the trip finally settling in, as well as the realization I still had just a bit farther to go to get where I wanted. The weight made me thankful I had decided to buy the cane the old trader had suggested as it did alleviate some of my weariness.

Laki had nothing but the clothes on her back and whatever rested within her own tied bundle. She pointed easterly with one finger. "Home. Ampur."

I left it at that, knowing I wouldn't get more from her if she hadn't already said it. My other question went ignored and pressing it wouldn't do me any good. "Are you cold?" I knew the answer, but this would be a long walk in awkward silence if we didn't find something to talk about.

"A bit. It goes numb after a while and I can't feel much then."

That didn't sound particularly safe to me. "Let's see if we can get you something warmer?" My own cloak did a poor job of keeping me safe from the chill, but I took the blessing for what it was considering Laki didn't even have that much.

The clothier's building resembled many of the others in Ghal, low-standing, squat, and round with the spired roof. All thought of the cold left as soon as we entered. Needles pricked along the skin of my face, fingers, and toes. A stone fireplace held a healthy flame that crackled and filled the small building with a warmth that kissed my blood and bones.

I already didn't like the idea of leaving.

The shop's interior held countless layers of richly dyed wools and fabrics, all thick, set in neat bundles. One side boasted a row of overly packed robes and heavy coats, though they lacked the vivid brightness of some of the materials lying in neat stacks.

The owner piped up. "You need something warm." The man looked a hard forty, and living up here in the climate surely contributed to it. His skin was blotched in places, bringing a red I didn't think possible to his otherwise tawny color. His cheeks were thick and held more fat than seemed to be in the rest of him. A woolen cap with dangling pieces that fell over his ears hid most of his forehead.

I nodded. "We're going up into the mountains." I cut myself short before admitting I didn't know how bad the terrain and temperature would be up there. It was the truth, but I knew it could also put me in a position to be taken advantage of. I'd seen enough traders go about their art over my time in Keshum.

He pursed his lips, then looked at Laki, falling into a deep frown. "For how long?"

"Long enough. We'll need to keep warm head to toe . . . obviously."

"Obviously." He looked to one side of his shop. "Robes, at least two for the each of you. Inner and outer. It's terribly cold up there. Socks, two pairs. Your feet will sweat in good wool and you should change the socks when you get to that point. A good scarf wouldn't hurt—long, lets you wrap it around your mouth." He placed his hands over his lips. "Warms the air coming to your chest. You'll need a stick—" He broke off when I raised the cane in hand.

"Nrgh. A cap. The ears get cold easy, the forehead worse." He patted the spot. "So cold it freezes a man's thoughts and you can die from that or the stupid that comes with it. Tin tankee to take hot broth in. You can't be without that." His voice quickened. "Broth. Good knife. Flint. Tenting if you're to stay up there—wool tenting."

I could tell we'd gone past the necessary into whatever he could squeeze in with fast talking, hoping me to be every bit as thick in the head as I looked poor and from the city by dress. "How much for—"

"Six dole."

I choked. "Brahm's bloody burned ashes and tits. You're selling fur, not silk."

The man shrugged as if it made no difference. "And if silk mattered here, then I'd charge that worth to it. But leave that to the half-naked degenerates in the south, flashing and flaunting more of themselves than is necessary or decent. You want to go up to the mountains in cotton and silk—" He waved a dismissive hand. "Go. Go."

I gritted my teeth, only stopping when Laki squeezed my arm. I let go of my building anger and realized he'd stated the price for everything he'd said in one go. And we didn't need the half of it. "How much for just the clothing and not everything else."

He bristled for a fraction of a moment before stiffening. "Two dole."

I narrowed my eyes but kept short of turning it into a proper glare. The bastard wanted ninety-six iron bunts for clothes. And he knew we didn't have another option.

A step into the jungle and already leeches want to bleed me. In a way, it brought me a small comfort. Things weren't so different here from Keshum. I knew this man's kind and how to deal with them, even if he had me over a barrel here. So long as these similarities extended true to enough aspects, I would survive this place.

I had been prepared for losing what money I had left upon coming here. Actually losing it, though, brought back some of the outside cold into my belly and chest. "Two bunts." The words left my mouth before I'd realized I'd spoken.

The man rolled his eyes and turned away from us, waving one of his heavily mittened hands. "Go-go. I don't have the time to waste on you."

The shop was empty but for us. "Looks like you have nothing but time and space. No customers?"

He whirled about, glaring at me.

I met the expression in kind. "I don't like people assuming I'm stupid just because I'm young. I came from Keshum. I know a thing about coin and commerce." A "thing" was right, as I certainly hadn't become an expert. But I knew enough to spot when someone saw fit to cheat me. "You have rows of people lining up to spend in silver, huh?"

His hard stare faltered. "People spend what's necessary for what they need."

I nodded. "And what's necessary here." I gestured to the row of robes. I knew them to be of quality, and we needed them, but that hardly warranted a pair of silver pieces.

The man looked me over again. "You've not got much to your name, ah?"

The truth pricked me a bit, but I inclined my head.

"Silver's a great deal to ask of many men, a boy especially."

I let the boy comment slide.

"But you're not from here. Clear you rode up in a wagon, meaning you had coin enough to spend on that."

Also true.

"Wools and fur may be common enough up here, but they're not cheap. And they're well traded for as travelers pass through these parts. I might be steep, but two bunts is far short of the fair man's mark."

I exhaled, letting my shoulders slump a bit.

"Is that all you have to you?"

Lying wouldn't do me any favors, especially since I only had the single rupai to pay with. He'd see it eventually. "No. But I do have to be careful with what I spend. This is where I'll be for as long as I can see. That means food, a place to sleep, and anything else a person needs to get by. I can be fair." I let some of the fire's warmth fill my voice. "I *can't* be taken unfairly, though."

The man nodded. "One dole then, and I'm being honest. Pairs of clothing per person? It's not cheap. This isn't bad cotton, which would wear through after a season of hard use, or canvas, which would keep you safe from sand and stone but does nothing to keep the heart and body warm." The line of his mouth grew tired and the same fatigue reached his eyes. He'd spoken the truth and had no room left to haggle.

"Done, and thank you." Whatever force buoyed me up and held my anger fled, leaving me to put more weight on the cane and breathe in relief.

Laki caught it and offered me extra support.

The exchange had worried me more than I'd cared to show. It would have set the precedent in my mind that I'd go through all the coin I had in the world at a frenzied rate.

I fished out the gold rupai, passing it over to the man.

He grabbed hold of it before realizing what it was. He paused once it sat pinched between his fingers, turning the coin over and looking at it, then me. "How's a boy, with an old cloak, old clothes, and not dressed for this weather at all, come by a rupai? What happened to not having much money?"

I told him most of the truth. "I stole it from a group of thieves after I stole it from a merchant king of the Golden Road. It's all I have left in the world, so I'd like the twenty-three doles back, please." I kept my face and voice as level as I could.

He looked at the coin as if it would bite him. "Brahm's blood, boy, you don't make anything easy, do you?"

I grinned. "Going by my past? No."

The man grumbled. "Gold spends as well as anything, even stolen gold, but I'm not one for getting my neck cut over this if someone comes looking for every last piece of a merchant king's treasure."

"They won't." I raised a hand in assurance. "I've made sure of that."

The man looked at me sideways, weighing what the words had meant.

I'd left them vague on purpose.

"Well enough, I suppose." He returned with my change and then set about fitting us to our clothes.

It wasn't a bad start to my first proper day in Ghal. Too bad my experience with the merchant wasn't the only place I'd meet some form of rejection.

FIFTY-NINE
Rejection

The hike to the mountain took the rest of the morning, pushing us into a cold and bleak afternoon. Nearly a thousand stone stairs had been built into the mountain as a path.

I thought back to the man's offer of hot broth and the tankee to carry it in. I banished the thought and trudged up the stairs with Laki by my side.

I got one detail wrong. Nearly a thousand stairs had *not* been built. That implies a figure close to one thousand. In truth, there were thousands. I sorely regretted the miscalculation by the time we reached the top, and my strained lungs promised me that my tongue and breath would find no way to be witty and loose for the coming hours.

Possibly a day.

The Ashram had no gates to bar entry. Walls of high gray stone ran along the mountain perimeter on either side, snaking with the terrain. It had more open space in places than even parts of the city below. I didn't know what to do in it as I walked through an oddly clean courtyard.

Snow had been brushed away in certain places, leaving fresh earth and tiled paths exposed. Trees had been planted in small circles along the way, and they still flourished despite the cold. The color of the leaves reminded me of blood and fire and a night I wished I could forget.

Someone walked by, stopping as he caught me staring.

His hair had been shaved close to the skull, tight and clean, making his ears look a tad too large for his head. He wore long gray robes falling to his feet, all layered, but without any hint of fur. He had just touched his twentieth year, by my guess. "Hello. I don't remember seeing you here before."

"I'm new, or, I hope to be. I'm Ari."

"Laki." She pressed a hand to her chest and bowed her head slightly. "I need to see a *viyaka* please."

The man bobbed his head. "I can show you the way. I'm Kaja." He placed a hand on the small of her back, ushering her along. "This way." Kaja looked over his shoulder at me. "You're here for admittance to the Ashram?"

"Yes."

He nodded more to himself, then motioned quickly to a set of double doors far from where we stood. "Across the courtyard, through there. Hurry. They are taking a count of the new bodies for the season. Hurry."

I didn't need to say another word. I ran, ignoring the stiffness that formed in my knees from the cold and slow walking after reaching the Ashram. The double doors flung open under my weight as I barreled through them. I hadn't meant to drive into them with as much force as I had, but they had looked fairly heavy in my defense.

Candles lit the small room, running along a semicircular desk of stone. A young man sat there who could have only been a few years older than me. His hair had been cut and combed to the side. Clean shaven, fresh faced, and closer to boyish than grown and handsome. His eyes shone bright and clear as honeyed rum. "You should try that again."

I blinked. "Huh?"

He waved a hand at the doors, the cuffs of his oversized robes flopping as he did. "The doors. Charging through them again. If you try harder, you might be able to knock them off their sides . . . or they'll knock you into next set. Either-or."

"Oh." I realized how it must have looked, me charging in like a bull. "Sorry, they looked heavier than they are and—"

"You're new. You're late. You're looking to be admitted before the new season and they're done taking a counting. I know. Everyone knows. Everyone runs through the double doors." He rolled his eyes before settling his gaze on me again. "Who told you to run?"

I frowned and thought on the bald man. "Kaja?"

The boy exhaled and slumped in his seat. "Figures. Still doing the calm and slow-speaking monk thing?"

I didn't know what he meant by that, but after I considered it, Kaja did give me the impression of being a monk. I nodded.

"Tch. He needs to find something better to do with his time than have new bodies charging into here." The young boy got up and walked around the desk, motioning down a hall of pale stone.

Braziers lined the path, all burning bright.

"Follow that to the end and stay straight. Don't take any corridors off it. You'll come to the rishis' admittance chamber. Knock, you'll be told when you can go in. Make your case, tell them which schools of study you wish to attend, your sponsor"—he waved a hand as if bored—"they test you on what you know, so on." He motioned me off.

"Keen to return to your sitting around counting your thoughts?" I'd never seen someone so eager to sit and stew in nothingness.

The boy sat back down, kicking his feet up onto the desk. "Eager to have new blood go away, whether it's to admittance or turned away. Every moment I'm here is another I'm not in studies or gathering alms or . . . any number of brain-deadening things. Besides, there's half a chance a pretty girl walks through here." He turned and looked me over again. "And sometimes . . . not." His voice carried notes of the most profound disappointment imaginable.

I glowered and marched off down the hall. No self-respecting student of the Ashram should have wanted to spend their time lounging and shirking their pursuits. It didn't connect with me why someone would work so hard to get here then throw it away.

The path to the rishis' chamber changed as I reached the halfway point. Old gray stone gave way to newer constructions of wood laminate, oiled and shining, as well as beautiful tapestries hanging from the massive walls. The shift in architecture came with no noticeable explanation. It simply was.

I reached the doors the young man had referenced and knocked.

No answer but for the echoing thud.

I repeated the gesture, this time using the base of my fist to send a deeper noise through the room.

"Enter."

I didn't take the single word as ominous, though a part of my brain had wanted to.

The chamber consisted of a stone so dark I couldn't recognize the color. Calling it black wouldn't have been close to accurate. This was a color without name, and it pulled at any source of light but for the flickering candles lighting the room. All of which failed to bring any more clarity to the stone itself. Yet, the candle flames burned brighter than any I had ever seen, taking up more space in their glow than any fire ever could. The whole room shone under them as if they were each a sun unto themselves.

A curved desk of the same stone sat in the center of the room as the only piece of furniture. Eight people sat behind it. Well, seven. One of the men I assumed to be a rishi had taken to sitting on a plump cushion placed atop the desk. His legs were crossed and his gaze fell everywhere but on me and the other teachers by his side.

"Hello?" I wasn't sure how exactly to begin.

"Name," said the central speaker. The man was well past the middle years of his life, having traded all hint of black in his hair for a uniform steel gray. His face looked hardened by stress and long hours. He had a severe brow but kind eyes a color somewhere between shale and pine boughs. He wore robes of perfect white that pulled all attention to him in the dimness of the room.

"Ari. I'm here for admittance to the Ashram." I had wanted to go on. To tell them of the many things I hoped and dreamed of learning. To make promises of what kind of student I would be. But something in the set of the rishis' jaws told me to speak when spoken to and be as proper as possible.

Something I wasn't the most inclined to be naturally.

I fidgeted, waiting for them to speak.

"You're new. There's no record of anyone by that first name. I would remember."

I nodded, then realized I should have confirmed that. "Yes."

The man scribbled something down then stroked his tightly trimmed beard. "And your reason?"

I exhaled in relief. Holding to that answer had been bothersome. "To learn the ten bindings all men must know. I studied under a binder named Mahrab. He told me of this place and—"

The man stayed me with a raised hand, scrawling something on a sheet of parchment.

"I seem to remember a Mahrab." The man scratched the underside of his chin with a finger.

"Oh, don't spin lies like wool, Davram," said a woman at the far end of the table. She had a vulpine face with the eyes to match, a brilliant shade of brown so light they carried the promise of gold. Stark angular features and short hair cut to reach just the tips of her ears in wild dark curls. Her robes were the black of coal dust and charcoal rubbings. The same color as every other person behind the desk apart from the man in white and the person sitting atop the counter. "You remember Mahrab. You and he butted heads like goats in rut trying to show off for a woman."

Davram coughed into a fist and shot the woman who'd spoken a sideways glare. "Inappropriate comment, Rishi Bharia."

The woman rolled her eyes, but said nothing.

"Mahrab was a good student and graduated as highly as some binders could. Better than most who try. You say he was your sponsor?" Davram leaned forward, watching—weighing me.

I blinked. Mahrab had never said anything like that to me or left me with a recommendation. I swallowed, realizing I had come here woefully unprepared.

"He never told me I needed one. He did teach me of the Athir and how to counter a binder's binding . . . sort of."

Murmur broke out among the rishis before the one called Davram readdressed me. "He 'sort of' taught you how to counter a binding. And did you succeed?" The room grew noticeably silent in the aftermath of the question.

I nodded. "In a fashion." I didn't feel it best to admit I succeeded in dodging a stone meant to thump my skull. It didn't sound that impressive. As long as I left it nebulous, they could interpret it far better than it might have happened in truth.

"Can you perform any of the ten bindings?"

I shook my head, knowing it best not to push the boundaries that far. An open lie like that would have me called on it and quickly dismissed for failing. "Mahrab thought it best for me to learn that here under your tutelage and proper training."

Murmurs.

"Master Mender." Davram gestured to a lean and balding man at the other end of the table.

The man rose, his dark robes rustling. He looked to be whittled from willow, thin, springy, and hard enough in body. His nose looked too long for his face and hooked to one side like it had once been broken and never properly reset. A look I knew from young boys who'd gotten into fights when sparrows.

"Rishi Marshi." The man introduced himself, inclining his head to the other rishis but not toward me. We locked eyes. "What are the effects of *Santhya*?"

I opened my mouth, closing it just as fast. "I'm sorry? I don't know what that is." I cursed myself for admitting my lack of knowledge.

"It's also known as white-joy." Rishi Marshi laced his fingers together as the folds of his robes fell over them.

"Oh. It turns people into addled drug addicts. Their eyes eventually whiten all the way, and that's why people call them cotton-eyes. They're desperate enough to get another fix that they'll sell their mother's silver, then her kidneys, all before selling their own. Maybe yours if you cross them at the wrong time in the wrong alley."

Marshi's eyes widened at my answer and he looked at the other rishis. "That is an answer I'm not used to hearing. Truthful, accurate, but not what I was wholly looking for. How did you come by your information?"

"The streets of Keshum. I'm an orphan. One of the first times I walked an alley I didn't know I came across cotton-eyes. They wanted to take my money. The hint of taking more than that was in the air. I probably wouldn't be alive if not for someone coming to help me."

Marshi sobered at my explanation. "Ah. Well you were close enough to appease me, I suppose. Out of curiosity, why did Mahrab let you wander like that if you were his student?"

I bristled and felt the room grow colder. "He died. I didn't have anyone left. Anywhere to go."

If the candles in the room had in any way been normal, they would have let out some gentle sound of burning flame. But no. They burned ever silent and still as if their fires had no need of air and did not ebb and fan to its breath.

Silence. Stillness.

No answers. No more questions.

Every rishi looked down at the counter, then to themselves for a time I lost track of.

Finally, Marshi sat down and cast one last long look to the others at the table. "I'm done."

Davram nodded. "Master Conditioner?"

Another man stood, stretching the limits of his robes to the point I feared they'd tear and leave him fully exposed. He could not hide his build under those folds. A mountain of solid muscle, the likes that could never have come from hard labor alone. This only happened with deliberate effort and single-minded conditioning to the goal of strength and size.

"Rishi Bheru." The man's voice rivaled thunder and the deep basso pounding of drums. His thick and coarse beard did nothing to hide the solid brick line of his jaw. The little curly hair he had did nothing to soften his appearance. "What do you know of the body and the many ways it can move? Do you know how to break a man's grip when he has you in a hold like this?" He clenched his arms tight to himself in a hug no man would like to be caught in. It promised aching ribs and broken bones.

"I learned some swordsmanship under a choreographer."

The great bear of a man paused, following Marshi's suit to look at the rishis around him. My answer must have thrown him as much as it had the other master. "You learned how to use a sword from someone who does theater dances?"

I shrugged. "Yes."

"Show me."

I hadn't expected that and fumbled to speak.

He undid one of the laces holding his robes shut, and I very much worried for a moment he would undress in front of us all. Thankfully, he loosened it enough to reach inside and pull free a length of wood that could have served as a sword. It had been smoothed to a perfect cylinder with a rounded bunt of a top. The kind of rod any child would dream of in lieu of an actual weapon to knock some friend senseless with.

Bheru threw it to me in an underhanded toss.

I caught it by the hilt without thinking. Make no mistake, I was by no means close to mastery of the sword at this age. But I had the reflexes that came with excitable youth and enough proficiency from Vithum's tutelage to manage.

The weight was an old comfort in my hands and I fell into the full flow of the movements I'd been taught.

"Enough!" The rishi motioned for me to return the sword.

I was almost tempted to lob it much like he had, then reconsidered. I walked up to him, the makeshift weapon laid across both my palms as I presented it to him with more care than it warranted.

He noted that and let out a pleased harrumph as he sat down. "He moves like a dancer more than a swordsman. But I can make a good fighter out of him, a good wrestler. He's skinny though. Still too much a boy, not a man. How old are you?"

"Older than my teeth for sure. Younger than my tongue I think. Who can tell? Closer to my eighteenth year than my first by far." My theater tongue got the best of me as I rattled out the rapid answer.

The big rishi's eyes looked like they'd spin in their sockets for a moment before he grunted. "Too clever. He needs some of that knocked out of him. I'm satisfied."

But to what end he didn't say.

Davram took more notes before looking to the woman who'd spoken earlier. "Master Artisan."

She stood on command. "Rishi Bharia." She gave me a warm smile, the first bit of real welcome I'd felt since my arrival. "Do you know any of the minor bindings? How to impart your will into tools and shapings?"

I shook my head. The old knots returned to my stomach and a cold weight settled in. I knew my performance so far had left the rishis wanting for something more—better. I'd been doing poorly. "Mahrab focused on conditioning my mind for the folds and the bindings. He didn't stop until I could hold twenty—"

"How many?" The voice that cut in didn't belong to Rishi Bharia. It had come from the man sitting atop the desk on his velvet cushion. He wore what would have been robes if the sleeves hadn't been torn from them to reveal scrawny arms corded with lean muscle. The fabric itself was really countless other pieces of clothing stitched together in a horrible multicolored patchwork.

He was clean shaven with just a bloom of wild black hair atop him like dandelion seeds. Unlike the rest of the rishis, he alone looked young, perhaps somewhere in his middle twenties. His eyes shone with a light that, to this day, still makes me uncomfortable. Their brown carried something of firelight in them in their brightness and the dangerous shine.

"I'm still asking the boy questions." Rishi Bharia glared at the man who'd interrupted.

He waved her off. "You can after I'm done. The boy wanted to be a binder, no? Let me talk to him." He straightened and puffed up his chest far more than anyone would ever need to. "Master Binder." He blew out his heavy breath before pressing his lips tight over his tongue, sputtering as he did. The noise could easily have been mistaken for something one didn't do in polite company.

I shifted from foot to foot. Sweat beaded along my brow and at the nape of my neck. My breaths grew shorter—shallower. "Twenty, Rishi."

"Oh, no-no." He waggled an admonishing finger. "Not yet. Not quite. Clever boy. I'll give you that. I'm no teacher of yours yet. Twenty, you say?"

I nodded.

"Humph. Impressive. At least for someone your age. Do you know the story of fire?"

I opened my mouth to speak.

"No. Don't lie. Don't talk around it. Fine. What of stone? Do you know any of how the elements came to be? This world? Do you know the story of any one person the way you know the bottoms of your feet? No? No. You don't, do you? You're too quick. Too hot—angry. Stirred up. Excitable."

"What does any of that have to do with the damn bindings?" My voice echoed through the chamber, and only then did I realize I had shouted at the man.

The man grinned, revealing perfectly straight teeth that could have used some honest correcting.

His self-satisfied smile could also have used some fixing. The temptation crept into me, I admit. One of my hands balled while the other squeezed against my cane.

He noticed, pointing at them. "And very easy to push around. Honestly, boy." He rocked in place.

"Hardly appropriate, Master Binder." Davram glared at him. "You're antagonizing the child."

"With respect, Rishi. I'm not a child. I know I look like one, but I haven't been one for years. The way I lived . . ." I stopped short, not wanting to get into it. But it was the truth. Living as a sparrow with that responsibility, the death of your family, it robs you of pieces that make you like other children. "I've had to grow up and do things most don't have to."

The Master Binder tilted his head to one side, looking at me as if he expected to see words scrawled along the top of my head. "You have, haven't you." It wasn't a question.

I nodded.

He made the same motion, satisfied by whatever he found in my face. "No. Throw him back out to where he came from. I don't think he's a good fit. And I don't want him. He wants to be a binder? He can figure it out there." He made a shooing motion.

My heart sank and I looked to Davram at the center. "You can't—he can't!"

Davram gave me a long and sympathetic look before muttering to the other rishis, including the ones who hadn't yet spoken. "I'm sorry, young one. No sponsor, and the one field you have the most aptitude in, well, the master doesn't want you. I'm sorry—"

"You can't!" Something broke in me. All the years of pain, the choices, the shapes of hunger I'd suffered, the hurt from beatings and my daily sparrow life, and all the wounds of the heart I'd taken . . . for nothing. "The Ashram doesn't turn away anyone who needs it. I've heard that."

Davram nodded. "And if you need a place to stay warm, food—those things, we can manage. But you are denied admittance to study at the Ashram for the higher arts." He placed his pen onto the stone desk and it rang with hollow judgment.

I'd failed.

Rejected.

And now I had nothing and nowhere to go.

SIXTY

Rules and Rumors

Something hot and ugly festered in me. Or it should have. That's how it goes in the story.

I fall to my knees and scream a word that shakes the walls. My fists bang against the floor, drumming louder than thunder in that echoing chamber. And all through it, I channel a binding of fire, of wind and fury, of something great from the stories. With it, the masters are cowed into silence and admit me.

That's what the stories would suggest.

But no.

I didn't have the strength. My strings had been cut and I had no more cleverness or anger for them.

Everything loudened. The rishis and their mutterings. The sound of scratching against parchment. My heartbeat. The blood in my temple. And the edges of my vision blurred.

Then something broke through that hyperawareness.

The doors burst open behind me as if they'd been kicked in by a bull.

Vathin strode into the room, trading a quick look with me. He winked and flashed me a smile before adopting a somber look that fit his new, dark robes. The man strode over to the table. "Sorry I'm late. Bit rude, I admit. Not as rude as running admittance without me when I said I'd be back today."

Davram stood up to address him. "You missed most of admittance."

Vathin shrugged. "Well, my point still stands, doesn't it? You went through most of it without me." He shook his finger much as the Master Binder had, chastising Davram. "Right is right. And you're in the wrong. There are nine of us, we should deal with students together." He cleared his throat and leaned against an empty place at the desk to introduce himself formally. "Master Philosopher. Rishi Vruk. And I've got some questions for the boy."

The Master Binder swiveled on his cushion, staring hard at Vathin. "I already told him no. He wants to be a binder. I teach it. And. I. Said. No. Do you know what that means?"

Vathin ignored him. "How are you doing, Ari?"

I couldn't find the words to speak.

"That's all right. Don't let these old bullies bother you." Vathin sighed, leaning heavier against the desk as if winded. He cleared his throat and focused on the rishis around him. "I suppose the boy already told you I'm his sponsor, *nyeh*?" Vathin put all of his attention on Davram. "So, Master Spiritualist and Headmaster, let's run the boy through it again, hm?"

The headmaster steepled his fingers, resting his chin on them. "Most of us have already asked what we need of him, but if he has you for a sponsor—"

"He does. And the boy's shown a fine head for philosophy. At the very least, I'd expect him to be in my classes. He has an understanding of the bindings, even if he can't perform one. Then again, how many masters here can?" Vathin raised a hand, waiting to watch the others.

Four more hands rose: the Master Binder's, Artisan's, Mender's, and Spiritualist's.

"Now, that's not all of us, is it? I think we can forgive the boy's inability to do something not even all the masters of the Ashram can do." Vathin managed to sneak me a self-satisfied look.

I grinned, relief flooding me. He'd just given me a chance and I couldn't thank him enough for it.

"And the boy has proof of Mahrab's teaching. We can hardly turn away someone who's been taught by another graduate binder." Vathin motioned at me with a hand.

I faltered, unsure what proof he meant. It took me another moment to remember the book I'd been given. I dropped my walking cane, letting the long staff clatter to the ground. My travel sack joined it a second later as I fished through it. I retrieved the book, running it over to Vathin.

"Thank you, Ari." He turned it over in his hands, prying at the covers. "A book bound tight so no one can open it."

Another woman at the table scoffed. Her hair had all the color of cold blood and rust. Her skin had more of the sun in its bronze than most of the other masters. She wore similar gray robes to Vathin. High nose and cheekbones, sharp and proud features that reminded me of a bird. "It could have been sealed with an adhesive. There are plenty to bind parchment so tight it would take a binder to undo them. Even then, you risk tearing it apart."

Vathin clicked his tongue. "Exactly! Only a binder to undo them. This isn't bound by man-made means." He waggled the book before tossing it to the headmaster. "Check for yourself."

Davram ran his hands over the book, pursing his lips as he did. "It's bound. Good work. A tight binding. I couldn't undo it myself. And if I took the time to try, it'd be too tedious to be worth the effort. But this doesn't prove a student bound this book and gave it to the boy in mentorship. It just means he came across a book that happens to be bound."

Vathin sighed and I did the same on the inside.

The Master Binder leaned over on his cushion, fumbling as his reach came short of the book's spine. A loud thud filled the room as he fell against the desk in his efforts to snatch the book. "Ow."

The headmaster fixed the kooky man with a level gaze.

The Master Binder righted himself and muttered something under his breath. He held his hand out as if expecting to catch something. The book shuddered in the headmaster's grip and the man's eyes widened. Mahrab's tome hurtled out of the Master Spiritualist's hands into the grip of the waiting binder.

I stared at the ease with which the man performed that binding. I couldn't guess how it worked or which binding it had been, but seeing that proof there in the moment told me I'd done the right thing by coming here.

We all seek and hope for tangible bits of proof along the paths to our dreams. And when we get them, all fear and uncertainty are washed away for a moment. But that moment can be worth all the pain it took for us to get there.

The Master Binder took the book in both hands and flipped a thumb against the corner of the cover.

I waited for him to run into the restrictive binding holding the book together.

Except it never came.

He thumbed it open as if it had never been fastened shut at all. The man turned the pages with an idleness that could have only belonged to the profoundly bored. He snapped it shut the next instant, muttering something again under his breath that I had no hope of discerning. "It's Mahrab's."

"How can you tell?" The headmaster looked at him askance.

"He wrote his name in it." The Master Binder rolled his eyes and lobbed the book toward me without care.

I ran forward, catching it by one corner that jabbed hard into the flesh of my palms. Excitement took hold of me and I pulled at the book. It didn't budge, staying as it always did in my grip. "You rebound it?"

The Master Binder grinned, an expression that belonged to a dog too excited to even know why. "I did. If you were supposed to know what's inside it, you'd be able to open it yourself."

Despite that, I beamed at what he'd said. Was he implying he meant to teach me how to do it? I leaned forward. "You're going to teach me?"

He laughed, rocking in place, going so far as to slap a hand to a thigh. "Oh, no. Not at all. But I have no objections to your attendance here. Sponsored and mentored by another? Good enough."

The headmaster nodded. "It is. Welcome, Ari, son . . ." He stopped and frowned.

I knew why he'd stumbled. The comment I'd made about being an orphan. I thought quickly of all the stories I'd heard, and kept the grin that came to me far from showing on my face. "Son of myself."

Like Brahm the Wanderer, I thought. It would be a start. First get my foot into the Ashram door, then I could set about finding a way to have the Master Binder teach me. I refused to let the stubbornness of an odd erratic man hold me back from what I wanted.

"There's still the matter of the donation." The headmaster looked to Vathin, then me.

"I thought the Ashram was free to attend?"

"It's still customary to give something as payment. The Ashram has expenses of its own. Many are covered by the children of the wealthy who attend. Their families contribute great sums. The poorer usually go every morning for a third of a candlemark to collect alms, which they bring back. It's not much but adds up over a season. If you don't have anything to spare, that's what we would expect of you."

I'd been dismissed with all the callousness only the old and comfortable could manage upon my first attempt at admittance. I'd been questioned, passed over, and talked around rather than to. I knew it in my heart and by the scars and hardened skin of my feet and fingers that I had worked harder than any of those teachers to be at the Ashram. And now they expected me to beg.

My teeth ground and fire filled my gums from the pressure. "No."

The headmaster blinked. "I'm sorry?"

"No. I've been on the streets in Keshum. I've begged, been dismissed, beaten and battered by strangers, and worse. The kinds of people that wanted to kill me because they thought they could. You won't make a beggar out of me ever again. You want a donation? Fine. Name the sum." A wiser man would have kept his mouth shut and not antagonized the collective rishis within a candlemark of meeting them.

But as I've maintained, I'm far from a wise man.

The headmaster ducked his head and conferred in a low whisper with the others. "We're not heartless." It sounded like a way to placate me as well as justify something to come. "We sympathize with your upbringing and desire to not feel lesser than others. Three copper rounds isn't beyond your means, is it?" He gave me a thin smile not meant to be mocking or anything other than strained. "An iron bunt would be more fitting given your performance but . . ."

"I can pay." I reached into my sack, fetching three coins and walking over to the desk. I opened my hand and let each piece clatter with the ring of metal on stone.

The headmaster and others stared as the coins rattled before falling perfectly flat. Their silver shone starkly against the dark desk.

"Oh-ho." The Master Binder put a hand to his stomach and laughed. "Where's a thing like you come by three silver doles?"

I met his eye when I spoke and fixed him with a stare harder than the founding stones of the mountain the Ashram sat on. "You haven't heard the story yet, but you will. It takes time for word to reach this far up, I suppose." I paused, letting their curiosity build.

I'd learned well how rumors build and spread like fire back in Keshum after selling and taking secrets. And I knew how to build a few of my own.

"I robbed a merchant king." I kept my face as hard and flat as their desk for a count of ten before breaking into a lopsided grin.

The Master Binder laughed again. "If you say so."

My little performance softened the earlier resolution with which I spoke. They'd assumed my story to be just that, a child talking big. Young boys and girls weren't beyond that. But, a part of them would always wonder, and with time, I could fan that rumor into something more if I needed.

The headmaster pushed the coins back toward me. "This will do, though it's not what we asked for. Your generosity is noted." Something in his tone told me that wasn't actually the case. He knew I'd done it partly to spurn them for their treatment of me.

I hadn't wanted a hostile beginning to our relationship, but we had played our hands. And this was the nature of things to be.

"Take your admittance payment back out there." The headmaster gestured toward the door. "Master Philosopher, would you care to see *your* boy taken care of?"

Vathin's mouth twitched, struggling between an obvious smile and impassivity. "You don't want me here to question the stragglers coming in next candlemark?"

The headmaster gave him a look that made it clear he did not. "I think we've managed without you so far. *Arrey.*" He cradled his forehead as if it had broken into pain. "You'd do well to help settle the boy in so he can start soon."

Vathin beamed. "Excellent. Let's get to it, ah, Ari?" He all but ran from the desk, coming to my side and clapping a hand to my back. "Tut, tut. Leave the old and cranky to their stodgy practice of bullying children. You should be signed to classes quickly and set to your room." He ushered me through the door and led me back to the desk where the young boy lounged.

The student sputtered and pulled his feet down from the table when he saw us. "Rishi Vruk. I didn't know—"

Vathin waved him into silence. "What you don't know could fill the Ashram, and likely hurt both you and me, Sethi." He frowned for a moment. "But it may also keep you out of as much trouble, given the sort you are. Now, this is Ari. He just gained admittance to study the higher learnings here. See him signed up, his donation counted, and set him to classes. After that, show him to his rooms and have his robes and supplies catered for, *ji-ah*?"

"*Ji.*" Sethi scrambled to clear the desk and fetch a ledger, flipping through it. He produced a rod of wood longer than my middle finger and just thinner than my smallest. A dark and pointed tip protruded from its end that looked almost like charcoal. He scratched into the ledger, leaving a thin trail of the substance behind as it broke and smeared in clear lines. "Family and name?"

Vathin didn't give me a chance to answer. "Oh, this is a good one." He cleared his throat and announced in a baritone that would have rivaled the best stagemasters: "This is Ari, son of himself, because the little shit is born of Brahm or something much like it." He nudged me hard with an elbow.

Sethi looked between the pair of us like he expected us to tell him it was a joke. When neither Vathin nor I did, he shrugged and wrote it into the ledger. "Donation?"

I planted the coins on the table. "Three silver doles."

Sethi choked. "Did you piss on one of them or something? You're not noble, and you're certainly not rich by the looks of it." He caught himself and stared at the rishi. "Sorry, Rishi Vruk. I just meant, I mean, look at him." Sethi gestured at me.

I told him what I had told the rishis. "I came by a treasure of coin." I waited for him to take the bait.

"Where? How?"

It was Vathin who spoke, and thus added a layer to my earliest rumors I couldn't have done myself. "Haven't you heard?" He looked at Sethi as if the student should have known already. "Our young Ari, son of himself, robbed a king."

That was the start of it.

And all the trouble I'd come into at the Ashram.

As well as the sorts I'd come to make.

I excelled at both.

SIXTY-ONE

Whispers

You would think that being at the Ashram would have brought me a better sort of sleep than I'd had of late. But I couldn't find a second's span of peace, tossing and turning, more in excitement than anything. I'd done it.

Reached the Ashram, convinced my way through (in no small part due to Vathin's intervention), and managed to kick the rishis' collective shins a bit.

I woke early the next morning, washing my face in the small tin tub granted to all students in their rooms. I scoured my hands, taking time to strip and use a rag to tend to the rest of me as well. I'd been informed student baths existed, but I didn't want to waste a second of the first day on anything else. The faster I attended my studies, the quicker I could learn to call a binding and spend time speaking to the Master Lorist.

That seemed the best path to learning more about the Ashura and what to do about them.

I dressed into the robes I'd been provided. Their white reminded me of cream—soft and not as jarringly bright as the headmaster's. The theory with the customary robes revolved around their color darkening with age, signifying commitment and dedication at the Ashram. In time, they would resemble the black of the rishis and discipline masters. I hadn't discovered why the headmaster's remained white, however. My cloak had enough room to slip comfortably over the robes. I didn't need the extra layer to ward off the cold, but I'd grown accustomed to it on the ride up to Ghal, not to mention its look. Something about it felt right. The same for my walking cane, so I made sure to bring that as well.

I gathered my sack, now filled with rolls of parchment, a waterskin (that I'd taken extra care to fasten tight many times over), and my graphter.

The latter had been a new wonder to me. Upon admittance, I'd been given a dozen of these slender rods of wood and stone. The binders and students at the Ashram bought blocks of a brittle powdery stone that they bound into thin tight cores, pressing and binding a layer of pulped wood around them until they hardened in unison into small writing tools. They didn't last, but they allowed a student to scrawl notes and draw as the soft stone core whittled away over time.

All it took was the oil of a finger to smudge away an error. Barring that, a bit of saliva and some vigorous rubbing did the trick.

I raced my way out of the students' hall and down to the courtyard, trying to orient myself to find my first class.

An ashen-haired girl tore by, head whipping about as if desperately in search of something.

"Laki?"

She whirled around to face me. "Ari!"

"What are you still doing here? I thought you'd have left yesterday?"

Laki frowned and pulled her clothing tighter around herself. "It took a day for them to see me." Her mouth worked through a series of expressions, all of them tired and nearing anger, but she finally settled on simply weary. "There were others first who were hurt. Since I wasn't, they made me wait."

I nodded, not trusting myself to speak given the sensitive nature of the situation.

"The students helped me with medicine for my family but—" She broke off and rubbed her hands together. "It costs." The way she'd said the words led me to believe she meant more than simply the fact it cost coin.

"And it's a lot, isn't it?" I already knew the answer to my question.

She inclined her head.

"How much?"

"A copper round. I don't have that. I spent everything I could just getting here and—"

I dropped my sack to the ground with less care than I should have exercised, but the familiar need and tone in her voice had overtaken my cautiousness.

No one should be barred help for lack of coin. Ever.

I undid the ties and found what coins I had chosen to keep on me rather than in the pouch I'd fastened under one of the corners of my bed. "I don't have only a copper round." I pinched a whole dole between my fingers and pushed it toward her.

She raised her hands, waving them as though she tried to ward off the coin. "I can't—"

"You can. It's mine to give. Besides, you gave me a story. Consider it payment. Someone once told me you always pay for a tale well told." I pushed the coin toward her again. "And use the rest to get home. Give it to your family."

Laki reached out, hand shaking. She took it and squeezed the coin tight in her palm. "Thank you. But I didn't tell you a story, really. I just told you what the Fhaalds were called."

It was true, however that little detail prompted Vathin's little riddle rhyme. It had given me something to think over during the trip even if I couldn't figure it out. But the exaggeration let me convince Laki to take what she needed, and for that, I was okay with the stretched truth.

She threw her weight against me and nearly toppled me from the force. "Thank you." Her mouth pressed its warmth to my cheek and she pulled away just as fast.

I didn't know what to say and Laki didn't give me a chance to find the words. She turned on the ball of a foot and raced away.

Several students stood nearby, watching the scene unfold. They turned to one another and whispered. What about, I didn't know.

I smiled and decided to let them have it. I knew the shapes whispers could come to take, and if the one I'd let slip among the rishis and to Sethi took root, I'd have an interesting reputation among the crowd soon enough.

I could live with that. I broke into a whistle as I made my way to my first class.

Introduction to Binding Principles took place in an open courtyard with tiered ring seating much like in Khalim's theater back home. It brought me an odd comfort of familiarity as I searched for a place to quietly slink into, hoping to go unnoticed. I slipped into one of the tiers, avoiding bumping my waist against the fixed and raised curved stone. It ran the length of each row of seating, serving as a smooth, strong desk surface.

An empty spot called my name and I sank into it beside another student.

At first look, he could have been a few years older than me. His hair held countless tousled curls, falling far down the middle of his back. A few of his locks shone and I realized he'd clipped small copper clasps into them. His jaw had a sharpness and hardness that could cut glass and he had all the angles in his face young women swooned over. The bright brown of his eyes could have been pulled from mine. He smiled, a feline lazy and easy thing.

I returned it. "I'm Ari." I settled my sack and cane at my side.

"Oh, *you're* the one people have been whispering about, hm?" His smile widened and he stretched his arms wide, resting them against the stone back of our seating. One of his elbows jostled something at his side when he'd moved.

A mandolin the color of sunburst mornings against velvet black.

"What are they whispering about?" My eyes were fixed on the instrument.

"Oh, rumors and the sort. You got into it with rishis, not just any teachers, the masters themselves. You did it during your admittance and told them off, and when they got angry, you told them to shut up and paid them silver for their troubles. Which is quite the thing considering some said they saw you come in hardly dressed like the kind of kid who could spend silver."

I bristled at that but bit my tongue. At least the rumors had started spreading.

"I also heard you robbed a king . . . or was it a prince? Maybe some wealthy faraway merchant from off the Golden Road. The kind that don't take that loss easily. The kind that come to collect at the end of a sword."

That brought a grin to my face. "It wasn't a prince." The truth would raise more questions than it would answer and be less easily dismissed. If I told him I *had* robbed a king, he'd laugh it off. But leaving him to wonder what part was true would have him run his mouth off with others to figure it out.

While they did, the tree of the story would grow more branches.

I felt it best to change the subject so it would stew in the back of his mind. "Do you play?" I gestured to the mandolin.

His smile broadened to something foxlike. "And do I." He waggled his fingers before petting the instrument's curve. "Do you know what you can do to a woman with music?" He waggled his brows next and gave me a lecherous smile.

I didn't. "No . . . do you?"

The expression slipped from his face like I had slapped him. ". . . Well, of course, that's why I asked. Do you think I don't?" He turned his attention toward the empty courtyard and kicked a foot up onto the desk.

I shrugged. "I don't know. That's all I meant."

He grunted and silence fell between us for the space of ten breaths. Then he broke it, leaning over and extending a hand. "Radi."

I shook it. I registered his name and thought back to stories. "Like . . . Radhivahn?"

He rolled his eyes. "A bit shorter than that. Less of him and more of Radi, if you will."

I smiled at that little play with words, appreciating it. Clearly there were people here with tongues as quick as mine. "How long have you been at the Ashram?"

He waggled two fingers.

"Two seasons?"

"Two years."

I felt my eyes grow owlish. It had taken him two years to get into an introductory class on binding?

He must have read my expression. "This is the toughest class to get into. Everyone wants to be a binder. They all grow up hearing stories of the Ashram, Radhivahn, Son of Himself"—he rolled his eyes harder than before—"Brahm, Brahm the Wanderer, Brahm in this guise or that—bah. So, the class fills fast and most fail out quickly and leave to become artisans. Many don't make that work either. This class doesn't have many openings, so it takes time to get in. That's about it. But the way you hear it makes it seem like Master Binder just doesn't want new students."

I shrank in my seat at that. He *hadn't* wanted me in the class and had been quite explicit about it.

"How'd you get in so fast anyway? You just have Brahm's own luck? Maybe Saithaan's?"

I shook my head and said nothing.

The Master Binder walked into the center of the stone courtyard. His robes hung from his waist, revealing him to be in an undershirt, also betraying just the band of his breeches.

No one said a word as the man walked close to shirtless, definitely not clothed for the climate, in weather that should have chilled him to the bone. "Many of you have waited many a year to be here, and many of you will be waiting many more to get any further than this. Why? Because you'll fail. Look to your left."

We did.

"Look to your right."

We did.

"One of you three will fail."

"Shit!" came a voice.

We all turned toward the source. A young man a few rows back continued cursing under his breath. He, like everyone else, was older than me by a handful of years. Dark featured and lean. A look at the girl and boy to his either side told us all we needed to know.

She wore a confident and comfortable smile, hand already moving over paper as if deep in study. She looked easy in place sitting there awaiting instruction.

The boy on the other side was much the same.

Two likely longtime students at the Ashram who probably had some grasp of the bindings already. If not that, they were clever.

The young man must have determined himself to be the one out of three in that seating doomed to fail.

The Master Binder noted this. "Well, that was certainly fast. Most don't cull themselves as quickly as our friend here. But if you're already shitting your breeches, and I don't need to know if it's figuratively or literally, you should get up and leave now."

The boy did exactly that.

We stared in silence and watched him go.

The Master Binder clapped his hands as if clearing them of dust. "Well, that's one less hollow coconut to deal with this season." He laughed, gazing at the class before settling on me.

I shrank lower into my seat and gently tugged the cowl of my cloak over my face.

"Oh-ho-no!" The Master Binder jabbed a finger at me. "And *you* can follow right behind that-a-one." He dragged his finger through the air, pointing in the direction the other would-be student had left in. "Leave."

That had the opposite effect. Most students would have done just that at any rishi's word. I had developed a particular aversion of late to the demands of those in some position of power.

I crossed my arms and screwed myself tighter into my seat, making it abundantly clear I'd go nowhere of my own accord. "No."

The Master Binder blinked, craning his head in my direction and going so far as to put a hand to his ear. "I'm sorry, I didn't hear you."

I cupped both hands to my mouth and spoke clear as a morning bell. "No."

He stared daggers at me.

I didn't give him the chance to say anything. "I paid to be here. I want to be here. I'm going to be here." I pulled my cowl down and stared back in defiance at the Master Binder. "I have as much right as anyone. And at least I can already hold the folds."

Murmuring broke out among the crowd.

Faint whispers reached my ears that let me know not every student even knew what the folds of the mind were.

I was ahead of them, even if only in knowledge, and the Master Binder knew it.

He glowered, his mouth working in silence as if chewing through a particularly rough piece of gristle. Then his face broke into a delighted, ravenous grin. It made me think of a fox coming across untended chicks. "So . . ." He teased the word out. "You think you know enough of the bindings and their workings to be here?"

I didn't fall for the bait. "This is an introductory class, isn't it? I wouldn't be here if I thought I knew all that. But I know enough to show you I'm not a waste of your time."

"I never thought you'd be a waste of time." He wagged a finger in admonishment. "I *don't* want to teach you. There is a difference. If you can't parse that, then you'll have a harder time than you think working out the nuances of bindings."

I almost rose from my seat. Almost. Instead, I settled for a low and challenging glare, keeping my expression angry, but short of threatening.

The Master Binder smiled.

I let the look fall from my face just as fast, realizing what he'd been doing. He'd already pointed out I was quick to anger and how he could push me. I'd just proven him right again.

"Oh-ho. He can learn."

I kept my face and voice painfully level—neutral. "I can. That's why I'm here."

"What are the seven underlying principles of binding?" He had spoken so fast I barely recognized the question.

I tried to recall everything I'd gone through with Mahrab, but nothing came to mind. "I . . ."

"Too slow. So, you say you know something of the bindings, but in truth, you don't even know where to begin." His smile had the kind of self-satisfaction only old men too sure of themselves can manage.

I had the overwhelming urge to smack it from his face, but I knew even a look like that would give him another small victory. "I told you what I could and could not do during my admittance. It seemed to be enough to welcome me."

He frowned.

That much had been true. And another master had not only been my sponsor, but vouched for my tutelage in the bindings, as lacking as they may have been for the Master Binder's preference. But Vathin had also made it known I could, in theory, counter a binding.

The Master Binder paced in a small circle, leaping as he stepped on a rough stone. He broke into a stream of profanity that drained the color from most students' faces.

I'd already lived as a thief, and by rumor, cutthroat. Even so, the things leaving the Master Binder's mouth set my eyes wide and mouth nearly hanging loose.

He had quite the imagination, though I suppose that was necessary for the kind of mind it took to be a binder.

When he'd finished his creative cursing, he bent over to scoop up the rock. The crazed and mischievous look he'd once worn filled his eyes with a dangerous light. He lobbed the stone in his hand a few times. "Where will this land once I throw it?"

Everyone exchanged silent looks, but it was Radi who spoke. "Well, we can't know until you tell us where you're going to throw it."

The Master Binder gave him an honest gentle smile. "True." He lobbed the stone again and motioned to throw it in one direction. "Say I toss it thataway."

Radi shrugged. "Then I guess it'll land somewhere over there."

The Master Binder cocked a brow and fixed us with a knowing look. "Oh, will it?" He threw the rock. His mouth moved and I couldn't make out the words, not even the barest shape of them.

The rock hurtled into the air, reaching the apogee of its path before it fell. Only, it sailed back in the same arc it had left, falling into the Master Binder's hand.

Everyone stared.

"Did anyone guess that?" The Master Binder juggled the rock between his palms. He threw it in another direction, moving his mouth again. The stone stopped short of its full height and fell down a path it should never have taken naturally. The Master Binder chased after it, catching it before it hit the ground. "Or that one?" He turned his gaze on me, smiling.

I caught the gleam in his eyes in time and had an idea of what crossed his mind. My thoughts turned back to an almost similar display of binding prowess by Mahrab. A man throwing a rock overhead, binding it to fall square on the top of my skull and bring me pain and irritation in equal measure. I met the man's smile and his slipped.

He frowned. "I'm going to throw this stone over our young and eager binder-to-be's head. Then, with a binding, make it fall on his thick skull. See if it knocks what I've been trying to say through his coconut." He snapped his wrist. The stone went into the air.

My mind tumbled into the folds. I couldn't perform a binding. I knew this. But I worked up two scenarios, perfect mirrors of each other, of the stone sailing harmlessly above me. Then four. Eight. Ten. I struggled to double the folds instantly, being out of practice. Fourteen. Sixteen. I fell short of the twenty.

The Master Binder's mouth moved as the stone reached the perfect point above me for it to come crashing down.

Only, it didn't.

The stone hurtled over me.

"*Mahl!*" The source of the profanity came from behind us.

Radi and I turned to see a student clutching his forehead. A stone rattled on the surface of his desk.

I snorted.

The student pulled his hand away from a reddening spot and gave me so heated a stare it could have broken and blistered skin. "You think that's funny, do you?"

"Quite." I made a lazy turn back toward the Master Binder. "Told you I could counter a binding." Honestly, it had been equal measure of luck on my part and overconfidence on the rishi's. He'd likely assumed I couldn't do a whit of what I'd said and so he didn't commit to many folds in his binding. I'd lucked out in his lack of confidence in me and overcompensated with how many pieces of my mind I'd set to the task.

But for the rest of the class, they saw the Master Binder attempt to wallop me, and fail.

Whispers rippled through the students.

"And that wasn't all the folds I could muster." I knew I'd just started a dangerous game. I'd come close to the best I could do, falling just short of the twenty. If the Master Binder could bring more to bear, and I had a suspicion he could, he would thump me bloody with another throw.

. . . Or several more given the look on his face.

But we never got to find out. The student who'd taken the stone to the face rose from his seat, making his way over to me.

I saw all the signs of someone raised on silver spoons and trays. It wouldn't have been a stretch to wager he'd even eaten off gold at one point.

His hair was cut short and slicked back with oil, bringing a shine to the rich deep dark of it. His face had an angular sharpness and his eyes held the rare gray-green of clouded emeralds.

The student's robes were another testament to wealth. They were cut and styled to be a perfect match of what the Ashram provided us, but their material screamed of quality fur. The kind that didn't need to be as thick and heavy as lesser sorts to provide the same warmth. And it had all been dyed the deep carmine of blood and beets.

Oh, he looked, in shape, like us. But everyone knew he came from the sort of money that could buy whatever and whoever he wanted.

I'd seen his kind back in Abhar and had made a policy of staying well away from them. They brought all manner of trouble with their weight and the heft of their purse.

"Listen here, you *Sulhi* piece of trash."

I bristled and nearly rose from my seat before Radi's hand clamped to my thigh, squeezing it hard under the desk so no one could see. I shot him a sideways look and he gave me a barely perceptible shake of the head.

I relaxed, knowing I'd already stirred up enough trouble with a rishi. Antagonizing another powerful member at the Ashram would bring me more difficulty than I cared for.

The Master Binder spotted the brewing tension for what it was and quickly cut through it. "Nitham, please take your seat."

The boy faced the Master Binder. "*Kaethar* Nitham, Rishi Ibrahm. I made *Kaethar* last season with my work in artisanry."

The Master Binder rolled his eyes plain for anyone to see.

That brought a smile to me. The teacher may not have liked me, but at least he didn't suffer the pompous jackassery of the other student.

"*Kaethar* Nitham, please take your seat before I bind your ass to the stone, leaving the only way to free yourself from it by tearing the seat of your pants."

Nitham's mouth went slack and his eyes nearly followed. Something told me the young man wasn't used to people speaking to him like that. He mutely returned to his seat, giving me another sharp look.

"And our little sparrow prince. Thief. Merchant robber. And did I hear tell of him being a *khoonee*?" The Master Binder had found another stone, tumbling it over his fingers in an impressive display of dexterity I'd only seen people apply to coins.

The class took to whispering again, and I felt more desire to crawl into my cloak and cowl.

It was one thing to have them talk about my exploits in robbing a merchant king, but the thought of someone associating me with murder—bloodletting—was another.

I noticed Radi slide away from me and my heart sank. Not two days in the Ashram and I'd made an enemy, and now likely turned away any chance at friendship.

And what good would denying any of it do? None. So, I set to correcting what I could as artfully as I knew how. It wouldn't salvage much, but it might give people a different way of talking about me when they were going to anyway.

"King of Sparrows." I held up a finger. "I don't know how you heard that, but I was damn good at what I did. I robbed a *king* as well." I stressed the word. "Not some cotton peddler." My chest tightened. I took a deep breath and just as much time exhaling before addressing the final point. "And I never killed men who didn't deserve it."

A different kind of silence filled the courtyard. It came with a weight that could have rivaled the mountains in which the Ashram sat. It had all the heaviness of old stone, the cold quiet sharpness of ice.

"Those men peddled children to the kinds of monsters that put their hands on them in ways no one should ever have to know. And those people made those children live lives no one in this courtyard should ever have to imagine."

The stillness returned in the space after my last breath.

The Master Binder and I traded a long quiet look that made it feel like we were the only two men in all of the stone courtyard. Finally, he inclined his head in what I took as an acceptance of my argument.

"Very well." The Master Binder paced back and forth, lobbing another stone in his palm. "It doesn't change that you were not admitted to this class proper."

I ground my teeth, but kept the feeling from reaching my face.

The other students continued to watch me and Rishi Ibrahm.

"You're right. I wasn't. I'm still here. I *chose* to be here. I thought that would count for something in a student who wanted to learn the bindings. They're not meant for the weak of mind and will, after all."

He stared at me, still bouncing the stone in his palm. "It counts for something, though not what you want it to. It says to me that you don't listen." Rishi Ibrahm snapped his hand. The stone hurtled toward me.

But I had stayed ready. Two. Six. Ten. Fourteen folds were the most I could hold before the stone reached its peak.

The Master Binder's mouth moved.

The stone crashed behind me, never once threatening to strike me.

I leaned back, crossing my arms in satisfaction.

He huffed a breath. "You've learned one little trick, and from what I can see, it applies to just this little exercise. Mahrab thought ahead."

I realized that's exactly what had happened. My old teacher knew the Ashram's methods well, and he'd prepared me in kind to deal with it. It wouldn't win me what I wanted, but it would start me down the path I needed. That was enough for now.

"You do understand that Introduction to Binding Principles does not mean you will advance to higher studies regarding the bindings?" The Master Binder gave me a long look.

"I do. I hope you understand that no matter what you try to do, you won't stop me attending unless you do so by force."

Rishi Ibrahm smiled at that.

In the moment, I took it to mean he saw it as a challenge.

I was right after a fashion.

And I was wrong how he'd go about it.

That began our headbutting over the following seasons.

At least Radi had fortunately come back around to the friendship he'd offered after hearing my explanation about the murders.

All the while, the whispers heard and passed through that class spread through the Ashram like fire through a field of dry leaves.

SIXTY-TWO

Consequences

The first set of days passed at the Ashram, and I found myself growing in quiet notoriety. No one had the sense or desire to bring what rumors they heard to my attention. They kept those to themselves in private circles. But the one thing young students are well versed in is the stage whisper. Speaking loud enough for you to hear them talk about you.

I'd challenged the Master Binder to a contest of wills and won, taking control of the stone he'd thrown to have it pummel Nitham. Some felt the jackass deserved it. Others commented that I'd opened myself up to the sort of slow bad vengeance only the wealthy could exact.

I didn't much worry about that.

I spent that breakfast period tearing through my boiled chickpeas and lamb with rice. What free time my mouth had between mouthfuls had been spent adopting a loud whisper of my own, feeding the little lies that had come to spread.

"You know, Radi . . ." I swallowed a handful of rice, washing it down with sugarcane juice.

"I've got a feeling I do." Radi rolled his eyes and pulled the mandolin into his lap, idly fretting with parts of it I didn't know a thing about. "But, go on. I live for the drama to happen."

"I never expected the bindings to be so easy. I mean, the first time I'm challenged, I didn't even have to mutter a word. It just clicked in my head and happened. And I even took control of a rishi's connection and used it for my own purpose."

Some of the whispers at my back quieted before picking up with renewed intensity.

"And you oh-so-cleverly used it to provoke a member of nobility. *Great.*" Radi dragged out the last word, letting it drip with an acidic sarcasm that could have marred the finish of his instrument.

"You mean someone not skilled enough to protect himself in a class meant for binders, not rich shits born—"

"Oi, look here." Nitham and his coterie, a half dozen other wealthy students all keen on placing their lips firmly to his ass, passed by our table. He slowed his pace noticeably to linger by us. "*It's* talking about skill when everyone heard Master Binder reject him in front of the whole class. That says something, hm? Imagine, getting admitted, but still told you're not wanted in the class. Tells you he doesn't have a touch of talent for anything he says. Maybe the rishis just took pity on him, for being Sullied. I mean, the Ashram *does* have a reputation to keep up for charity.

"I suppose it wouldn't be a good look if the Ashram only welcomed and taught the better educated and civilized. After all, Brahm had compassion for all things and even the *animals*."

The boys and girls in his group shared an uncomfortably uniformed laugh.

A few of the other students along varying tables joined in.

I glowered at him. My hand tightened around my spoon.

Radi, to his credit, caught the action. He moved to undercut the building tension. Strum. The strings of his mandolin quivered and he sent his fingers into a blur.

"There once was a boy named Nitham,
who came to trouble in Binding class.
He rose from his seat
and gave us all a treat
when he proved to be a witless ass."

Radi let loose the strings, having them fall into a gentle thrum that quieted just as sniggering broke across the tables.

Nitham flushed and looked about. Some of his own group lacked the grace to keep their crooked smiles clean from their faces. Instead of turning his fury on Radi, Nitham glared at me. "You should have taken Rishi Ibrahm's advice and left, Sullied trash. I'll make you regret staying here."

Every man has his faults. I am no exception. And mine has long been my lack of patience with bullies and the cruel. Makham. Gabi. Koli. Mithu. It didn't matter what name and looks they came with. I hated them equally and intensely with a passion that could set a thing on fire.

And it often gets me into trouble.

"The last time someone tried to make me regret something, their body landed on the ground several floors below—broken, bleeding, and very much dead." I popped another spoonful of chickpeas into my mouth. I chewed slowly, loudly, and filled the air with every smack of my lips.

Nitham's chest heaved, but I could see the thoughts turning behind his eyes. He'd been there when Rishi Ibrahm spoke of the bloodletting—the murder. How much of it did he believe? I don't know. But the idea was there, and the fear.

He swallowed and turned, his group following as he left.

Radi exhaled beside me. "Brahm's blood and ashes, Ari. You don't settle for anything less than the most problematic trouble and drama to stir up, do you?"

I grinned and finished my food. "Is there any other kind?"

Radi plucked his mandolin. A sharp sour note twanged from it. It vibrated until a low hollow sadness hummed from it. "There are. But I think you choose the worst kinds."

The strings stopped.

"The Seven Principles of Binding are . . ." Rishi Ibrahm stopped as he caught sight of me sinking into my seat beside Radi. He rubbed the space between his brows and sighed.

A sharp elbow crashed into my shoulder, drawing a hiss from me. I glared at Radi.

"Don't antagonize him today. You've already riled Nitham. Keep pushing, and he'll start throwing his weight around. You don't want that and the Master Binder frothing mad at you."

I nodded, not wanting to draw attention to the pair of us.

"The Seven Principles of Binding. Does anyone want to take a guess?"

A young woman's hand shot into the air.

Rishi Ibrahm smiled. Not his crazed and self-indulgent thing. It was honest, warm, and welcoming. "Yes, Kaethar Eira."

"They are: One, Faith. The all is the belief it is. It is the belief to connect with and will it. The universe is faith. Two, Connection. From you to the world around you. With the world around you. Three, Resonance. Movement. Everything has a resonance to connect with. Nothing is still and immovable to the mind that understands these three things so far. Four, Duality. All things have a nature and an opposite—a way and a way they can be made to be. Five, Rhythm. There is a gentle tug and flow to all things. To bind, you must learn this and how to affect it and how it affects you." The voice stopped.

My hand had blurred all the while, turning every word I heard into a messy scrawl that no one but me could hope to decipher. I dared not let a single piece of binding knowledge go unrecorded. When her voice stopped, the writing reverie went with it, and then I looked for her.

If anyone could have been said to hold the kingdom of Ghal's beauty in them, it was her. She held all the fairness of mountain snow in her face and even her hair. A brightness touched the dark of her eyes. She chewed one corner of her lip in what could have been anxiousness.

"Very good, Kaethar Eira. You're correct." Rishi Ibrahm tapped a finger to his nose. "I'll cover the last two before explaining them in greater detail." He cleared his throat into a fist. The hand blurred.

I snapped straight, heart hammering. *Tch.* The jarring nature of attending to every one of Eira's words, to the break in her speech, and now waiting for the Master Binder to teach left me no stability in my mind.

I reached and fumbled for the folds. One came to me, and turning it into two felt like trying to count to a thousand by odds only. I managed to reach four before the stone reached the same point it always did before trying to come down on my skull.

I felt the weight of our wills finally contend. The Master Binder must have only ever attempted to come at me with four folds of his own.

If Mahrab's mind had been something like a bull crashing against the walls of mine, Rishi Ibrahm's came with the force of an avalanche. It battered mine with the fury of stone and ice propelled by the power that drives all things to the ground eventually. Nothing escaped it. And nothing weathered that kind of assault.

I refused to relent—a stupid thing in truth. And I didn't think to craft more folds and commit to them under the pressure of the moment.

"It's just . . . hanging there?" said a voice I couldn't recognize.

My gums ached and only then did I become aware of how hard I'd been clenching my teeth. Something warm trickled over the top of my lips. I tasted copper and salt a second later.

The folds snapped and my eyes opened and I slumped against my seat, breathing like I'd re-climbed the thousand steps up to the Ashram.

A hand snapped out in front of mine and caught the stone before it slammed into my face.

What little strength I had was just enough to look at Radi and give him silent thanks.

For reasons I couldn't work out, Radi tossed the stone back to the Master Binder.

The man caught it without thought. "Seems you still have a few things to learn, ah?" He grinned, tapping a finger to his nose again.

If I could have managed it, I would have scowled. Maybe spat a mixture of blood and saliva in his direction. The best I could do was double over toward my parchment, letting him know with quiet cussedness that I would still attend to his words and learn whatever I could about the bindings.

He saw it for what it was and frowned. But he went on with the lesson. "The remaining two principles, then. Six—In . . . and Out." He lobbed the stone into the air, stepping back from it. His mouth moved. The rock hurtled to the ground with the speed and force of having been dropped from the top of the world. It shattered a second later. "Everything happens in regard to something put in and something coming out of that action, be they words, actions, bindings. Love is like this."

A few people snickered.

Rishi Ibrahm added a laugh of his own, cutting it short to silence the rest of the voices. "You think I'm joking? Tell me, how many of you have been able to find love without putting your own love out there? How many of you have ever even tasted a piece of it? The touch of someone's lips? Can you? Can you without leaning forward and putting your own out there? What about affection? Kindness? Can you in fact receive it without being willing to open up to it . . . and offer your own?"

No one had an answer.

And if he expected one, he didn't show it. He left us with that thought and went on. "The last principle: Seven. Nature. All things have a nature you must come to understand, and all things have within them the nature of man and the nature of woman. No one is wholly one or the other. Without this, you can never learn to bind the great things of our world." He gestured to one of the mountain peaks. "Be it mountain, stone, ice, water, the wind, or things such as fire. They have a nature, and some have something older—stories of their own. To bind them, you must learn them."

The pain from my exercise against the Master Binder dulled and my hand moved almost with a will of its own. I wrote down every word he said, not caring if I wasted parchment in the process.

The story of fire. The possibility to bind it.

Like Brahm.

The thought stayed with me until the consequences of that afternoon caught up with me.

"We'll begin the first framing exercise in understanding how to properly visualize. A prerequisite before even thinking of binding." Master Binder picked up another stone and I tensed, wondering how many folds I'd need to employ to counter a throw.

I didn't think I had the energy after the mental pummeling from earlier.

"Ari, *Sulhi*. Son of . . ." The source of the voice cleared their throat. "Son of nobody!"

We all turned toward the new voice.

The man didn't have the age to have gone naturally bald, leaving me to think he was a monk in the Ashram. He had the customary robes, the only difference being the red sash cinching tight around his waist. Broad shouldered and lean, he stood a head taller than any of the masters and had all the severity of cold marble in the lines of his face.

"Which of you is Ari?"

I didn't even have the chance to answer.

"*That's* him." Nitham came to the bald man's side, jabbing a finger in my direction.

The man nodded, then placed a hand on Nitham's chest. He stayed him, then came over to me. "You will come with me to the Admittance Chamber."

I rose from my seat, giving Radi a short look over my shoulder.

My friend shrugged and said nothing.

I followed the bald man and Nitham, aware of all my classmates' eyes on my back as I left.

❦

The Admittance Chamber had lost none of its dark and ominous appearance since I'd last been there. I had hoped it had looked that way more due to my nerves than anything in its construction. Since then, I'd learned the students referred to it as "Mines," mostly for its deep dark look and its endlessly high ceiling.

I stood before the collective masters, separated from Nitham by the bald monk between us.

The man idly bounced the tip of a heavy wooden baton in one palm.

Is that to use on students?

We waited in silence until Rishi Ibrahm joined us and made his way to the table.

"That's everyone then?" Master Spiritualist looked to both sides before steepling his fingers and resting his chin on them. "Good. Kaethar Nitham and Accepted Ari are both called here before the masters of the Ashram to discuss a formally lodged grievance. Do either of you have anything to say before we begin?"

I didn't, and nor did Nitham.

The Master Spiritualist nodded. "Very well. Accepted Ari, you have been charged with Threats of Extreme Violence, violating the Ashram's laws."

I hadn't known the place had its own set of laws, but it explained why a monk had brought me before the masters rather than the kuthri or any other armed facet of the Empire's law.

"Do you understand this?" The Master Spiritualist gave me a long patient look.

"Not really."

"Kaethar Nitham is saying that you've threatened him with extreme harm that could go as far as his death. Do you understand now?" Nothing in his tone said he was patronizing me.

I nodded. "Yes, Headmaster."

"And is Kaethar Nitham correct? Did you in fact threaten him to this degree."

"No."

"Liar!" Nitham took two steps toward me before meeting resistance in the form of the monk's club against his chest. The man hadn't thumped Nitham, just put it in front of him so the student ran into it, getting the silent message. Nitham exhaled and composed himself. "He did, Headmaster, in fact threaten me. I can call a number of witnesses—"

"All your friends whose tongues know how to lie for you as well as they know the taste of the inside of your ass since—"

"Accepted! You will not speak like that in the presence of the masters here or any other rishis throughout this Ashram. Am I understood?" The headmaster rose, staring at me hard enough to crack stone.

I nodded. "Yes, Headmaster. I'm sorry."

That seemed to mollify him and he sank back into his seat. "Good. See that it doesn't happen again or I will add another grievance."

That blunted my tongue a bit.

"The boy raises a good point." Vathin stood up. "Master Philosopher, Rishi Vruk." Vathin waited for permission to continue after he'd introduced himself by rank and last name.

The headmaster made a lazy motion with a hand, gesturing for Vathin to go on.

"Thank you. Accepted Ari has a point regarding Kaethar Nitham's friend circle. We all know his family, and that he runs with equally blooded nobles and the wealthy. The sort of students who can buy their way out of most trouble . . . or put a student of no caste into whatever trouble their purse can manage."

A few of the masters murmured in agreement.

The headmaster cut through the chatter. "Kaethar Nitham, would you care to tell us what exactly Accepted Ari said to you?"

"He said he'd leave my body dead at the bottom of the mountain."

"I said no such thing!"

"Quiet!" The headmaster stared daggers at us before settling his attention on Nitham. "What did he say exactly?"

Nitham shifted in place, his gaze shying away from the headmaster's. "He made a comment about people he's killed before in regards to something I said that he could have taken as an offense. The implication was clear: He would kill me in a similar manner to how he's killed others."

That was a mild twist of the truth. Yes, the implication had been there, but the threat had been empty. Nothing more than to scare Nitham and his pissling band of friends away from me.

"Is that true, Accepted Ari?"

I waggled a hand. "Nitham did offend me, true. But I can't take that too much to heart since I'm certain he causes offense everywhere he goes on account of his face. I'm certainly not the last he will offend, nor am I the first. I believe that was his mother, so with that, it's not a problem."

A few of the masters stifled laughs before the headmaster glowered at them. "Accepted Ari, you are coming close to earning yourself another grievance."

I reined my tongue in better than before. "I never threatened him. Nitham and I had a heated exchange. I did at one point reference something from my past and what I was forced to do in self-defense. But I never once threatened Nitham with the same treatment. He may have taken it that way, but then it could be argued he made himself an imaginary target to bring all this about."

Vathin winked at me.

I fought to keep from smiling. His philosophy lessons were coming to my aid now.

"Oh, like hell. You damn well meant it, you filthy bloodless Sullied cur!"

I noted that the headmaster didn't come to my defense when Nitham crossed the line into indecorous.

"Ooof." Rishi Ibrahm pursed his lips. "Right in the caste."

A few of the masters turned to stare at him. He met their looks and shrugged. "What?"

The Master Artisan cradled her head in a hand.

"So, it can be taken that your words could be interpreted as a threat. No matter the stretch, there is enough truth in what you said that Kaethar Nitham could have felt himself in danger?"

I shrugged. "Only if we were in Keshum, him a criminal in possession of weapons, white-joy, and harming children. Oh, and standing at the edge of a building. Other than that, I feel Nitham's stretching things a great deal."

The headmaster sighed and rubbed the heels of his palms against his eyes. "I think I've heard enough. The rest of the masters?"

They muttered amongst each other before nodding.

"Very well. Kaethar Nitham is fined in equal measure to his family's donation to the Ashram. Two gold rupai for needless antagonization and clearly levying this complaint as a way to cause further grief to Accepted Ari."

I choked.

How wealthy must his family be to easily donate two rupai, and then him not flinch one whit when asked to pay that sum again?

"Accepted Ari will be fined in equal measure to his donation this season for—"

"What?" I felt my eyes grow owlish as I looked to Vathin more than any of the other masters, hoping he could give me some explanation.

"Ari, you threatened a member of the Ashram; no matter how clever you may have made your words, the implication was there. Enough for Nitham to feel at risk. That *cannot* be allowed to pass. As such, you will be fined three silver doles and be sentenced to a punishment." The headmaster's expression held more hard ice in it than anything in Ghal's frozen climate.

"Disciplinarian Banu, what are the punishments we can levy on Accepted Ari for this offense?"

The monk fastened a leather thong at the end of the club to a loop on his robes, clasping his hands together afterward. "The student may be whipped up to eight times. They may be placed in a cold cell for up to a set of days, missing all classes, to reflect on their misdeeds. The student will be responsible for addressing all work and studies they have missed over that time. Lastly, the student may opt to do penance that measures the severity of their transgressions."

The headmaster inclined his head. "Thank you, Banu." He turned to me. "Well, Accepted Ari. You have a choice. Which would you like?"

I managed to open my mouth even though every bit of me wanted to grind my teeth to dust. "Well, Headmaster, truth be told, I wouldn't *like* any of them."

He gave me a thin smile.

I saw Master Binder touch a finger to his nose and flash me a wink. Vathin sighed in a way that let me know I'd pushed the headmaster enough. He was probably right. "I won't be whipped." My tone had all of the masters stiffen. I hadn't meant for it to come out as hard and cold as it did, but I had meant it.

No one would put their hands on me like I was back to being a Sullied orphan on the streets.

"Very well. Cell or penance?"

It wasn't a hard choice. "Penance."

Murmurs. They silenced a second later.

"Banu, what is the penance for threats of extreme violence that can go as far as threatening death?"

"Walking the fire, Headmaster."

A deeper silence filled Mines.

Rishi Ibrahm broke it with raucous laughter. "Well, how about that. Looks like you're to be burned." He howled and rubbed a hand against one eye. "The little binder-to-be is going to get his first lesson in fire."

He wasn't exaggerating.

SIXTY-THREE
PREPARATIONS

News of what I'd done to Nitham spread through the Ashram by the time I'd reached the Financiary.

It had taken me a full set since I'd arrived to learn the Ashram served as an influx point for people coming through Ghal from other countries or on trading journeys. They had cleverly designed it to tally and dispense all manner of coins, allowing travelers to use it as a bank of sorts.

Of course, this meant it was ruthless in taking its due from students.

I came to the dark wooden table at the end of the basement hall under Admittance.

A heavy oak door, barred with bands of metal and studded with brass, stood behind a young woman at the desk. She looked up at me, frowning in confusion. "Yes?"

"I'm here to pay my fine?" I'd already dropped to nineteen doles upon running back into Laki. Losing another three wouldn't hurt, but at the rate my money fled me, I'd be chipless by the end of the season. "Three doles."

The young woman had more gold to the brown of her eyes than usual, and they brightened as realization hit her. "Oh, you're him!" She rubbed a bit of her light brown hair away from her eyes. "The one everyone's been talking about." Her voice deepened to a dramatic and poor baritone. "The *khoonee*! Bloodletter! King robber. Pigeon thief . . . or something, right?" Her face broke into a grin that made it clear she hadn't been mocking me when she'd spoken.

I'd let what anger had built up in me over the day bleed out when I realized she was being earnest. "Something like that. It's actually King of Sparrows. No pigeons."

"Oh." She seemed to think on that for a moment. "You're the one who threatened Nitham, right?"

I nodded. "The same one. And I'm here to pay for it." I planted three doles on the desk.

She scooped them up and fetched a key from within her robes. "Wait here, I'll tally this so the masters have a record you've paid." She opened the door, disappearing behind it for several minutes before reappearing. "Sorry about that. Their bookkeeping is antiquated. Takes forever to jot things down."

I didn't know how to reply to that.

An awkward silence grew between us, but she had the grace to break it. She extended a hand across the desk. "I'm Aram." She gave me a look just as easy and charming as before, something of all innocence you mostly see in children and gone soon as they reach adolescence.

I met her expression best I could, knowing I didn't have that kind of honest happiness driving it. "Ari."

We shook.

"For what it's worth, I think Nitham deserves a lot worse."

I cocked a brow. "Yeah?"

"Of course. He's the kind of ass that can only come from a king's genitals. He's got the money and the silver-spoon-fed mouth to do and say anything without thinking. You know what he did to the family of a girl that spurned him?"

I shook my head, still hung on the fact Nitham was a king's son.

"He bought her father's debt, then when he called it, the man didn't have a way to pay since he'd bought out the iron suppliers the man used as well. The man couldn't get the goods to work off even a bent chip. Nitham had the man locked up, leaving the mom and girl on the streets. He let everyone know he'd done it too."

I gawked. "And his father just lets him?"

Aram rolled her eyes. "You don't know much about nobles, do you?"

"I know how to rob them."

She laughed. "Well, don't try that on Nitham. He may be a second son, but he's his father's favorite. It's not a secret. Thamar would be worse off if Nitham were back home, mark my words. He's the sort that would find a way for his older brother's life to . . . run short. But it's just as bad he's been dropped off here at the Ashram."

"He didn't want to be here?" I found that hard to believe. Nitham had the personality of someone who'd love to be a binder for all the wrong reasons, to have the power and prestige that came with reaching the top of the Ashram's studies.

Aram shook her head. "Not really. He wanted to stay where he was a monster of a prince. I can't blame him for wanting that life, I suppose."

I nodded as I mulled over what I'd learned. If Nitham didn't want to be at the Ashram, it meant there was a way to force him from it. And if done right, he might not even protest.

"Still, his loss feels like all of ours. He's made so many people's lives hell here." Aram looked me up and down. "And he's doing the same to you, huh?"

I snorted. "This is nothing. I've dealt with far worse than him." My mind went to fires of another sort. A burning theater. And the bodies along the floor and walls, all broken and torn and bleeding. In the end, they all burned with everything else. "Much worse."

Aram looked at me like she didn't believe that. "You ever walk the fires before?"

I shook my head.

"It . . . hurts. Most end up falling, crying, a few have to be pulled. One stubborn bastard refused to get off, no matter how much he burned. He passed out from the pain and ended up with his whole front side burned." Aram gestured from her waist up to one side of her face.

I stared. "What exactly is the penance?"

She blinked. "You don't know and you agreed to it?"

"Well, it was that or be whipped or take the cold cells, and—"

"Then you take the cold cells! Brahm's blood and asses, everyone knows that. They don't try to let students die here. You'd be given enough clothing to be warm but uncomfortable. You'd get meals. You just end up doing an ungodly amount of work to catch up."

"Did . . . you mean to say, 'Asses,' or—?"

Aram frowned. "That's right, isn't it?"

I shook my head. "*Ashes.* At least, that's how it's supposed to go."

She cleared her throat like she wanted to spit. "The Trader's Tongue is a vile and vulgar language." For a second, a hint of an accent seeped into Aram's voice. Something that reminded me of Vithum's, though the student carried more of a musical note in her words.

I grinned. "I knew someone like that once. Someone who felt the same way about the Trader's Tongue. You speak Brahmthi?"

Aram nodded. "And Brahmki." She held up a finger, then another. "Zibrathi, Taghal, and a smattering of Tevintersh." Aram pressed a hand to her chest. "*Athiyia* caste. Dad's a classicist and a merchant. A good one. He's had it in mind for me to follow him." Aram rolled her eyes at this. "Says I need to know as many tongues as I can if I want to make it in the world."

I focused on what Aram had said.

She came from a casted stock well above my own. The Athiyia were the landed merchant class. While Sullied could own property through certain loopholes, it could just as easily be taken away, and we were forbidden from passing it on. Athiyia could will land to their heirs, acquire more, and few ever had to worry about having a safe place to sleep at night.

And they were only halfway up the ladder of castes. All of which showed how far down the Sullied truly were.

"Anyways, the fire. You ever hear the story of Radhivahn? I don't know if you subscribe to the whole Son of Himself school of thought. Some places in Mutri will string you up as a heretic for that."

I nodded.

"Right, so you know the part where people walk across the burning ground in penance to come to Brahm's feet?"

My stomach sank. "Yes . . ."

Aram gave me a thin smile. "I hope your feet are fireproof."

I exhaled, then drew a short sharp breath as something came to me. "You said your father's a merchant, right?"

"Yes? What's that got to do with—"

I cut her off. "So you've worked with him?"

She inclined her head.

"And you probably know a good deal about nearly anything for sale? Clothes, food, materials, metal, and herbs?" I didn't give her a chance to answer. "I know we just met, but can you do me a favor?"

Her eyes narrowed and she looked at me askance. "*Depends.*"

"It'll help me give it good to Nitham, for what it's worth."

Her suspicion vanished and she beamed. "Well, that's worth a lot. Promise it won't come back on me?" She raised a brow.

I raised a hand to the hollow of my throat, swearing by my neck.

"Then sure, what is it?"

I fished another dole from my pocket, tossing it to Aram.

She caught it with a lazy motion. "What's this for?"

"Do you know of an herb called thiplan? It's a soothing herb. Calms the nerves. Its oils can also be breathed in to help settle you." That wasn't close to the truth, and I hated lying to Aram. She seemed a decent sort. But I didn't want her wondering too deeply why I needed the herb.

"I know the name. Never knew that's what it was for. *Abah*—father—covered it in passing once when haggling for a mix of herbs. You need some?"

"As much as you can buy with that. Whatever's left, keep it."

"When do you need it by?"

I thought on that. I'd be set to walk the fire tomorrow by fifth candle's end. Between afternoon and evening.

"At least by seventh candle tonight." I worried for a moment that she would pass the coin back, maybe pocket it and not do a thing.

Instead, Aram pulled a coin pouch from her robes and dropped the silver dole inside. "Done. Are you worried your nerves will be quaky and you won't go through with it?" Aram raised both hands, shaking them a bit as if quivering.

"You mean shaky? Something like that, yes."

"Are you staying in the Ashram proper or do you have rooms down in Ghal somewhere?"

I hadn't known that was an option. "Does anyone do that?" I thought of the thousands of steps and shuddered at the idea.

She shrugged. "Nitham and his ilk do. They have palanquins bring them up daily."

"You're joking."

Her expression told me she wasn't.

"Yes, I'm up in the Rookery. All the way on the top floor." The place had earned its name for being one of the highest points in the Ashram. The local mountain birds had a particular fondness for it and could be seen making small nests on the balconies and along some students' windows. I felt it a fitting place for a former sparrow to be.

"I'll see you tonight, then."

I thanked her and left, trying to calm the acid boiling in my stomach at the thought of tomorrow.

I'd cut my classes short that day, heading up to my room early. I spent the passing time equally between poring over my binding notes as well as stewing over all the horrible things a person could do to Nitham.

After a while, I admit thoughts of the latter took over. Small surprise.

The day reached evening, touching sixth candle. I'd missed dinner a third of a candle earlier. A blessing of sorts. My stomach hadn't unknotted after learning what walking the fire meant and that it would be a public spectacle.

When Brahm had done it in the story of Radhivahn, he'd let everyone watch as those he called sought penance before him.

If it was inspired by that, then I imagined there'd be a crowd. And I'd have to give them a performance—something to remember.

Or, if things went wrong, a nightmare.

A knock came at my door and I leapt from my bed.

"Ari?"

I recognized Aram's voice and raced to unlatch my door.

She stood there when I opened it, holding up a sack the size of my head. "Got it." She gave the sack a hapless smile. "Uh, well, it turns out you can get a lot of thiplan for a dole."

I looked at the sack, doing a rough tally in my head from what I'd learned as a sparrow. We'd come across merchant ledgers from time to time in selling secrets and information. "That's not a dole's worth."

"Yeah, because no one is willing to sell that much. It's apparently poisonous in huge quantities. Did you know that?"

I had, but I hadn't wanted to alarm her.

"I've got a good bit of copper left for my troubles . . ." She trailed off and gave me an uneasy look. "Unless you want the coins back?"

I thought about it for a second, then shook my head. "No. Truth is, there was a time I would have asked for every single chip I could. But you've done me a huge favor. Thank you."

"Not a problem. So, you're still going through with this tomorrow?" She passed the sack over to me and I took it.

"I don't really have a choice, do I? I said I would."

She waved a hand like trying to brush aside what I'd said. "Of course you have a choice. You can go back to the masters anytime and ask for the cell. They don't care how you pay for your trouble so long as you do."

I watched Aram for a long moment in quiet. Everything about her face and the way she spoke had an earnestness in it. The kind that came from a good life, and more to the point, choosing to be good.

She'd never had to make the hard choices some of us had to. I wagered she didn't have a crooked bone in her body, and that whatever she had learned from her father's mercantile pursuits only reached so far into her heart. She could haggle, but it came from a place of fairness, never to dupe or cheat another. And in that, she could never understand how much of a shield someone's reputation could be to them.

If she had grown up on the streets of Keshum, she'd have known that. Sometimes the only thing keeping you safe from bullies is their fear of you. Barring that, they have to know they can't hurt you or they'll keep coming back.

And I meant to show Nitham, the masters, and any of the other rishis in the Ashram that no one could hurt me ever again.

"No, I really don't. How do you think Nitham and his friends will react if they see me back away from this?" I kept my face neutral, not wanting to give Aram a thought on how to reply, even by accident.

She pursed her lips. "Nitham's the kind of person that would see you as an easy target. He'd think he could bully you into things and wouldn't let up."

"Exactly. People like him don't leave well enough alone. I have to give him and the others a reason to weigh me differently. Maybe a threat. Maybe as someone just not worth the effort. But that means I can't show a hint of weakness, and changing my mind now on this could come across as that. No. I won't give him that satisfaction of even thinking I'm scared." I brought the sack of thiplan over to my bed and dropped it there.

"Thanks again for this."

Aram eyed the bag, then me. "Thanks for letting me keep the coin." She smiled. "And just promise me this'll be worth it. Whatever you have planned, that is."

I stared at her. "Why do you say it like that?"

"Because, you're getting a reputation here, so I have a feeling you have something planned. It fits what I've been hearing about you." Her smile finally lost its innocence and she showed the first hint of the bright cunning I'd seen in her. "And I may have bet some money that you'll surprise us. Don't let me down."

I hadn't expected that. I stood stupefied for a moment before giving her a look of iron resolution. "I won't."

"Good." She waved and I watched her go.

Once I was reasonably sure no one else would come to disturb me, I latched my door shut and returned to the sack of herbs. My fingers worked the string cinch until it opened and I upturned the contents onto the floor.

Thiplan looks like thin pale green feathers all clinging to a narrow but strong stem. I fell into the cold and dreary process of plucking everything free of the stalk until I had a pile of the herb the size of my fist.

Next I fed some water into a small bowl just larger than both of my hands cupped together. I worked bits of my own saliva into a palm's worth of the herb, then added extra moisture from the bowl as needed.

Rub. Grind. Twist. I worked my hands like a crude mortar and pestle, turning the mixture into a paste. In truth, it had more the consistency of a sticky sap when I'd gotten it to a usable point. I rubbed it onto my feet, over and over, until sure it had been absorbed as best it could.

Rub. Grind. Twist. I repeated the process, coating my feet until even the thickest and oldest of calluses had taken in the sap. Most of the night passed this way, leaving me little in the way of sleep. Satisfied I'd let as much of the herb as possible absorb into my skin, I finally gave myself permission to pass out, knowing I'd pay for the night's actions tomorrow.

One way or another.

SIXTY-FOUR

Unburned

My stomach had no room for lunch that morning. Given that I'd skipped dinner the night before, my body had several complaints to raise about my choices. And it did.

The insides of my stomach protested, having long since grown used to regular eating. A piece of me remembered my early days as a sparrow, and the days before that when I'd lived in the understage. Missing two meals wouldn't kill me, but it did make the effects of the thiplan hit me harder.

The edges of my vision blurred and the colors of the world brightened, bringing pinpricks to my eyes if I looked at the wrong thing.

Like a groundscape of pristine white snow.

I blinked several times, slow and hard, trying to use the pressure to dull me to the pain. Some of that had come from the thiplan.

Too much of the herb's oil was toxic when absorbed through the skin. It could lead to death, but often fell short of that with other varying problems. You could lose sensation in your extremities.

I knelt and brushed the tips of my fingers against some of the snow on the main grounds. My hand sat there against the cold, feeling nothing but a gentle pressure like someone squeezed some of my skin. I scooped up some of the ice and molded it into a ball, holding it there to see how long it would take for the chilly sensation to sink into me.

The snow melted before I felt a thing.

Well, that's something. It's working. Maybe too well.

My mind numbed itself soon after, leaving me in a blank puppetlike state. I marched toward my artisanry class, wondering if I'd be able to retain any piece about the minor bindings we were supposed to cover that day.

I would have liked to have learned something on the day of my punishment. It seemed fair to get that kind of balance out of things: I learn something of the magics I so desperately seek, the Ashram tries to set me on fire—at the very least, tries to maim me.

The artisanry classroom had a warmth to it that had nothing to do with the fireplaces, full of flame and crackling warmth, in three of its walls. Four rows of tables, all of cherrywood, ran from the front to the rear of the class. They carried the amber light in their brightness and color, adding another layer of warm invitation. A single script, in perfect uniform writing, ran along the edge of every desk.

The walls were fashioned from the same wood and shone just like the tables under the glow of lanterns.

Rishi Bharia stood at the head desk, the only piece of large stonework in immediate sight. It was unadorned and without any color other than its worn old gray.

My vision spun under the firelight. The edge of every flame blurred and strobed brighter than I could cope with. They cast out streaks that tinged all of what I could see, leaving me to keep my attention on my feet to find some steadiness.

The thiplan hit me worse than I had expected. I wriggled my toes, trying to rub them against the insides of my shoes to see how numb they had gone. It took me to a count of ten to realize I'd been moving them before I thought I'd started and still felt nothing. My heart should have leapt into a quicker beat at that, but I found myself too dulled in thought to care that my feet felt far away.

I sat with a mute dumbness in class, trying to focus only on Rishi Bharia's voice.

It came distorted—echoing like it was partially underwater and coming through a cave.

None of her words reached me with any coherency, so I turned to the student at my side, finally realizing who I'd been sitting next to.

Eira, the white-haired and fair-skinned girl who'd recited most of the binding principles. She caught me staring and looked back at me like I had been doing something particularly odd. Her mouth tightened and the beginnings of a frown touched her face. "Why are you staring?" She kept her voice low and hushed.

"Oh. I'm sorry. Was I?" I had to fight for each word. I hadn't noted how clipped they'd come out.

"You . . . still are." She inched away from me, moving closer to the other end of the table. "And why are you speaking so slowly?"

I hadn't known I'd been doing that either. The thiplan had dulled my mind more than I thought. My perception was off, and it affected my speech. "I'm not trying to. I think I just had a really bad night of sleep."

She gave me a look somewhere between pity and wariness. "That still doesn't explain why you're staring." Eira's voice held a note of hesitancy, as if she wasn't sure if she should have been speaking to me. "You should really be trying to pay attention."

I nodded and wondered if the action also came off as slow as my speech.

"You're blinking really slow. It's odd. Are you okay?"

I blinked faster, trying to make up for the fact I'd been sluggish. "I think so?"

Eira's face said she didn't believe me. "Maybe you should leave and go to the Mendery. Master Mender should look at you."

"I might go there after my penance. I have to walk the fire today."

She moved a bit farther from me. "I know. I heard."

I stared down at the notes she'd been taking, trying to make sense of them. Her script stretched and blurred and I had to wince hard to try to clear my vision. It did nothing.

How much damnable thiplan had I absorbed?

"Here." She understood what I'd been looking at and passed the notes my way. "I'll . . . just copy another set."

I pulled them close and made better sense of the writing. "Thank you."

She gave me a strained smile and returned to her silent note-taking.

Rishi Bharia had gone into great detail in how the minor bindings worked and what they could be used for. Artisanry applied to small laws of the universe and using those laws with certain scripts—words—to imbue objects with a permanent lesser binding would alter how they functioned.

For example: a set of bindings that moved heat slowly away from a fixed location, constantly lowering the temperature to a certain point. A box like that could be, in theory, used to store and manufacture ice.

The bindings were limited in power, falling far short of the storybook magic and bindings I'd dreamed of, but they were a small step in the right direction.

Eira's notes detailed the fundamental principles: Connection, forming a physical and mental connection between the things to be inscribed and bound. A principle of likeness came into play here. The more alike two things were, the less willpower and faith it required to make the bindings apply.

The folds of the mind weren't mentioned in this at all. I wondered if this had been overlooked.

The next principle was Formation. You had to form your belief and shape it to apply to the items you wished to impart a binding on. Projection, casting your binding to be out of yourself without losing control. This sets the intent. Inscription happens in conjunction with Projection, putting the words and actions to your thoughts for the binding. You are literally putting the words down onto the item. Impression or Imprinting involved pushing your belief and binding into the words and action you previously performed. Conjoinment followed then, where an artisan combined the inscription and impression phases as one thing, holding them together in the artisan's mind.

In theory, that effectively put the binding in place. But it wasn't enough.

The last principle remained: Containment. One must contain the binding to and within the item and a space that will not affect the outside world nor interact with it in a disastrous way. You essentially create a closed loop environment where the binding only applies to the item and its function, never able to act apart from that. It is a way to both seal the binding and prevent a backlash.

My head spun as I reread Eira's writing, impressed by how well she'd recorded the detail. But I didn't have the state of mind to make better sense of artisanry in that moment.

The rest of the class passed in as much of a blur as my eyesight. I managed to shamble my way out of the Artisanry without drawing too much attention to myself, though I overheard a smattering of whispers.

"He's walking the fire." I didn't recognize the voice.

"There's something wrong with him," said another.

"You mean how he's acting?" A third person joined the hushed conversation.

"No, I mean, yes. But I heard he got into a fight with the masters. Not just rishis, but the masters of the disciplines." A woman's voice now.

And another followed. "I heard he challenged Master Binder to a duel. Someone else told me he actually stopped a binding in class."

"I was there. I was!" This voice sounded familiar, but the odd warbling that came with it altered it too much for me to recognize, all courtesy of the thiplan. "He stopped Rishi Ibrahm's binding. A few times in fact."

The rest of the conversation drubbed my brain harder than I had the strength for. The only thing keeping me steady enough to keep from planting myself in the main yard's snow was my trusty cane. It carried more of my weight today than ever before. I almost didn't notice the dull throb building in my wrist and elbow from how hard I leaned on it.

Once most of the students had cleared from the courtyard, I set about finding a quiet place to spend the remaining candlemarks until I had to walk the fire. A small tree served as the perfect place to rest against. I pulled off my shoes and socks, wriggling my toes again to see if my bare skin would take any discomfort from the cold.

Nothing.

I frowned, knowing that wasn't a good sign, but at this point there was little else I could do. It took a considerable amount of mental effort to undo the cinch holding my bag together as I reached for more of the thiplan that I had had the forethought not to use up the previous night.

I went through the same process of plucking stalks of the herb bare and grinding the leaves with my spit between my palms. It reduced to the pulpy residue, which I slathered back on my feet. All I had to do was keep a thin layer on my soles and I should be fine.

Should.

Or I'd risk poisoning myself to a degree my body couldn't handle. I stopped short of adding another coating, deciding that I had chanced things enough. I waited till the cold air helped dry the new layer of thiplan paste and slipped back into my shoes and socks.

A whistle sounded through the courtyard.

I turned, now aware of just how slow I'd made the motion.

Radi sauntered over to me—feet light on the ground while he plucked at his mandolin. The notes carried no discernible rhythm. Just an idle fingering of chords that I didn't have the skill or inclination to make any sense of. Perhaps if I weren't brain-addled by the thiplan I'd have shown a greater appreciation for the sounds.

He sank to his knees by my side, looking me over. "You look like shit."

I tried to give him a smile but couldn't feel part of my face. "Then I look better than I feel. Stop spinning, damn you."

Radi blinked. "I'm not moving. You are. You're like . . ." He stopped talking and moved a finger through the air in a lazy circle. "You're teetering in place like a top about to fall."

That gave me pause and I considered the ground, realizing it swayed a bit. A second's thought told me that was incorrect. I was rocking in place.

"Oh. Thanks, I think."

He watched me with the expression of a cat assessing something new and unfamiliar. Equal parts suspicion and curiosity to reach out and bat me. "What did you do?"

I stared at him. Well, one of him. The blurring had intensified and his face had split into two. "S'nothing."

He narrowed his eyes. "You're drunk—no, white-joy?" He shook his head even harder at that. "No, you'd never touch the stuff after everything you've told me. Brahm's tits, Ari, what are you doing?"

I groaned, putting more weight than I probably should have on my cane. I tried to get to my feet and succeeded in making it halfway before Radi slipped his arms under mine. He helped me to a decent-enough standing position. "Thank you."

He nodded. "You ready?"

I looked at him, finally able to merge the two blurred mirrors of his face into one. "It's time?"

"Close enough. How long have you been out here?"

I thought about it. "I came here after my morning artisanry class." I had to think harder on when that had been. "A third of a mark after third candle, I think?"

"Ari, it's almost fifth candle."

I would have leapt at that, but it took longer than usual for his words to reach me, and their implication. "Oh. We should go."

He nodded and offered an arm but I shook him off.

"No, I have to do this myself."

Radi frowned. "There's a song about a stubborn pig that gets himself killed by his sheer cussedness."

I glowered at him, or tried to. I'm not sure how it came across, but Radi's face grew more concerned by the second.

"Uh, don't make that face ever again, especially around women . . . or the rishis . . . or anything that has functional eyes. Brahm's blood, Ari. Let's get this over with."

I agreed and we made the walk to the penance square.

The penance square had only some truth and accuracy in its name. While it was made of a square patch of packed dirt, it rested in a larger field much like the main grounds of the Ashram in size. Only, this field held no stone. Most of it had been resurfaced to a mixture of soft clay, set to never harden past a soft springy ground, and earth.

The swath of land was where students could engage in physical exercise and larger classes under the Master Conditioner could take place. And it's how the field earned its name as Clays. A place made of such and to shape the minds and bodies of students under the Master Conditioner's tutelage.

Or at the end of his flexible wooden staff.

It also meant there was enough space and bodies to draw a decent crowd for potential immolation.

How wonderful.

I always wanted to perform—have a stage—and now the Ashram had seen fit to give me one.

And I would give them a show to talk about.

I approached the patch of dirt, noticing a long bed of coals had been spread across every inch of it.

Two bald monks stood on either side.

Radi leaned in close to my ear. "They're to make sure you don't try to run away, and they'll catch you or tend to you if you pass out or get too hurt to go on."

I gritted my teeth, unaware of how hard I'd clenched my jaw. I couldn't even feel any pressure through my gums.

The Master Binder also stood at the end of the coal patch, smiling like a child who'd played a particularly cruel prank on another. He sank to one knee, placing his hand deep into the bed of cold coals. His mouth moved, and for once I wished my cleverness hadn't gotten the best of me. I couldn't make out his words no matter how hard I tried.

A spark. Flash. Fire kindled and spread into a wide fan of flame to swallow the coals, dying a breath later. Only smoldering ground remained. The coals glowed with a quiet soft orange that almost looked inviting, but I knew only promised me harm.

I looked to the Master Binder, then the wide crowd gathering in the distance. All of their faces blurred but for Rishi Ibrahm's. I don't know why, but I could make him out clearer than anything then and to this day still.

He hopped from foot to foot, swatting at his feet as if he'd burned them. All the while, a crazed look remained on his face.

He was mocking me.

"There's still a chance to back away from this, Ari. You haven't started." Radi stayed close to my ear.

I shook him off. "Hold my things?"

He nodded as I passed him my robes, cane, then my shoes and socks.

I tried to roughly estimate how long the patch of burning ground was, but my head didn't have the space for it. I settled on it being long enough. Maybe three times my height at best . . . or worst.

I took one breath, hoping the thiplan would serve its true purpose.

I stepped onto the first coal, feeling nothing. Another step. My left foot tingled, more like an itch through my sole.

Is the thiplan's oil burning off?

It would do that, but I had hoped my night of applying layer after layer would have left my feet caked in enough of the residue.

Another step.

I saw the crowd blur further, but their mouths moved.

They were talking about me. So I gave them something to talk about.

I turned my focus onto Master Binder, holding the best glare I could as I took another step. I reached the middle of the burning ground before stopping. My feet itched harder now. Most of the thiplan's fresh oil was close to burning away. Only fresh skin and some of my calluses would remain. The latter would protect my skin from being severely burned, but it wouldn't be enough to send the message I wanted.

I would be scarred, even if lightly, from the penance. I had to do better. And I would.

The Master Binder stared back at me, tilting his head to one side as if he couldn't quite make out what to think of me in the moment.

I stayed in place, aware the thiplan's most recent layer would burn away soon. The itch deepened and the preventative effects of the herb wouldn't spare me from this much heat. I still felt the growing touch of warmness come through my feet. If I stayed too long, I'd smell burning skin and sinew before I felt it further.

Step. Then another. I pressed my feet deep into the coals, but not so far as to let the burning ground come too high above my sole. I ground one foot against a coal hard enough to turn it to ash and extinguish the bright orange color.

Another step. Then another. My skin now felt like a rash had spread through the undersides of my feet, but I walked on.

I made it to the end of the burning coals, but I didn't step onto the cooler and safe ground of clay. Not yet.

I stared at the Master Binder, meeting and holding his eyes only. "Ari, Son of Myself." I knew the words had come out slurred and slow, but he'd heard me, and that was enough. "Have I done my penance, Master Binder?" I raised a foot for him to see.

The skin had reddened by a small measure, but nothing more. It remained unscarred, uncharred, unburned.

And soon, the redness faded.

I stepped off the burning coals and onto the cool clay, feeling more of the difference in temperature than the actual chill of the surface itself.

The Master Binder squinted, searching me for the trick of it, but whatever he saw, it wasn't what he wanted. I had almost thought he'd shout, try to bring me up on other charges, declare me a cheat, or denounce my penance, but no. He broke into that odd and bothersome grin again. The one I could never guess the meaning of. His eyes danced with a light that unsettled me. "Son of Something . . . at least." The smile widened.

"Well, well. The little shit has done a tidy little trick. Maybe you do have the mind to be a binder." The Master Binder's lips pursed and he adopted an expression that could have been thoughtful consideration.

That nearly rocked me out of my stupor. I fumbled for words but found them too far gone to grasp. "I'm sorry? Wait, Rishi—"

But the Master Binder had turned and walked away.

All around me people broke back into whispers. And I was certain I had heard the words, "Unburned."

It wouldn't be the last time either.

I smiled and headed to Radi.

SIXTY-FIVE

Favors

"Brahm's bloody ashes and bloody tits and . . ." Radi shook his head as he threw my robes around me, pushing my cane into my hand as well. "What the hell was that?"

A dull spot throbbed in my arm, and it took me a long moment to realize Radi had punched me. I stared at my biceps, then him.

Radi held a look somewhere between bewilderment and childlike glee. "Did you see old Rishi Ibrahm's face? You stumped him as much as anyone else in the crowd. And Nitham's face was something properly worth remembering. I might cobble up a song about it. He went damn near as ashen as the coals." He clapped a hand to my back. "Blood and bone, Ari. You're going to have to tell me how you did that."

He spoke too fast for me to wholly keep up with, but I managed. My voice turned weak and unsteady when I spoke. "Help me with my socks and shoes?"

Radi moved the second I finished and did as I asked. "You know everyone will be talking about this for the whole season at least?"

I found more earnest energy to reply to that. "I hope they talk about it for longer than that. I hope they never forget." I leaned harder on my cane, my breathing coming heavier than before.

Radi gave me a long look, the chagrin fading. "We should get you to the Mendery."

I didn't have the heart to disagree. "Carefully. I don't want too many to see."

He said something else but my fatigue and the bleariness of the thiplan grew too strong.

I don't remember the walk, only my clouding vision.

"Hsst!" An elbow struck my ribs, snapping me out of my drug-induced haze. "Ari."

I shook myself clear. Well, as much as was possible under the effects of the thiplan.

The Mendery had none of the warmth of the Artisanry. It held to more cold than anything the mountains or Ghal's snowy climate could offer. A place of metal and stark white-tiled floors. Only the emptiest of colors found a home here; the grays of steel, stone, and little else. Wide and spacious glass windows let in light in some areas, but just as many were shuttered.

I immediately developed a distaste for the place.

A young woman came over to us. Her red hair and brows were a shade darker than beets, likely from dye. It suited the bronze of her skin. High cheekbones and dark lashes, all of which served to make her bright eyes stand out all the more. It could have been the thiplan's effects, but her brown irises made me think of honey sprinkled with cinnamon. Warm. Inviting.

She met my eyes, then turned her attention to Radi. "What's wrong with him?"

Radi sidestepped the question. "He had to walk the fire today—penance."

Her eyes widened. "Get him to one of the slabs. I'll take a look at him, but it'll be better if we get Rishi Marshi to go over him. Tch. Get him out of his shoes and socks." She went over to a basin and scrubbed her hands vigorously with water and soap all the way up to her elbows.

Radi led me over to one of the slabs, a block of solid stone under a sheet of thick metal.

"Get him out of his robes too," said the student.

Radi did as he was asked, helping me remove my shoes first, then socks, then taking everything else from me until I sat in my shirt and pants. "Want me to stay?"

I shook my head. "You've done enough, thanks."

He frowned. "Your voice sounds like you've been singing all night and morning . . . badly so, by the way. It's cracked—dry. It wasn't before. Blood and ashes, Ari, what did you do?"

I met his eyes, but said nothing.

He glowered for a moment before letting it go. Radi raised his hands in a gesture of defeat and took a few steps back. "Fine, keep your secrets. Just promise you'll tell me eventually?"

I nodded. "Eventually."

Then he left.

The young woman returned, grabbing hold of one of my ankles and raising my foot. She looked at it for the time it takes to have ten measured breaths. "That's odd."

"Hm?" I couldn't bring myself to say anything else.

"You walked the fire and you don't have a single burn. Not a scar. No coloration of your feet." Her mouth pulled tight into a frown that deepened a second later. "Or any feeling in your feet."

"They feel fine to me."

"Liar." She didn't miss a beat and then inspected my other foot. "Because if you did, you'd have yelped."

I said nothing.

"I've been pinching the soft flesh of your soles, well, the places there aren't any calluses. How did your feet get like this?" Another frown, thoughtful this time. "They wouldn't spare you from the coals, though." Her eyes widened as she looked at my face. She traced a finger through the air, keeping its tip just shy from touching my eyelashes.

"You're slow. You've been speaking dully, but that could be shock and from the pain. Maybe a bad night's sleep too from fear, but no, your eyes are slow too. Your pupils are large. Open your mouth."

"What?"

"Open your mouth." She stared, not exactly a glare, but the sharpness in her eyes made it very clear she wouldn't ask again.

When I took no action to do as she said, her hand reached out and took one of my ears between her fingers.

"If you don't open your mouth, I will turn this until you finally do begin to feel it. That, or it'll tear free given your stupefied state. Open. Your. Mouth."

"That's enough, Fhaldar Masha." The Master Mender came toward us from the far end of the Mendery. Or as far as I could properly see with my addled vision. He looked exactly the same as the day I'd first met him. The dark robes, the balding head touched with a crown of black hair, threaded with gray, running along the sides of his scalp. And the crooked nose, of course, that had to have been earned in a fight.

Masha inclined her head. "Yes, Rishi, but you should see this."

I blinked at that. "Him, technically. I'm not a this, or a that. I'm a me—a him, if we're going to be pedantic about it."

She turned back to me, looking me over like she hadn't before. "I have a good feeling you're quite used to being pedantic, and just as used to thinking you're funny when you're far from it."

I scowled.

Masha looked like I'd suddenly decided to take a shit on the table. "And he seems to have lost control of his facial expressions. I'm not sure what that was or what he meant for it to be."

I tried to sober myself immediately, realizing my best bet sat in being quiet and still.

Something I still hadn't developed a taste for.

Rishi Marshi gently eased Masha to one side. He cupped my chin, tilting my head to one side. "Ari, would you open your mouth for me, please?"

I did as he asked.

"Mhm. Dry. Look at me."

I did.

He traced his finger through the air much like Masha had done. "You walked the fire today, didn't you?"

I nodded.

"And yet, your feet aren't burned. No scalding. No ashen skin. Nothing broken. Nothing so much as pink or red as a boy blushing after a girl's kiss. Hm, no. Some students try to be clever, you know? Little tricks like wetting their feet, running over and trying to walk in awkward ways hoping to spare themselves much of the pain. It works . . . to a degree. But this"—he shook his head—"no, is something else." He leaned close to one of my feet.

"Notice the smell?" He glanced sideways to Masha.

"Smell?" She leaned in and followed his lead. "Smells . . ." Masha trailed off, clearly in thought. "It's an earthy smell, strong. An herb? Something like incense too. Dried herbs? But what?"

Rishi Marshi smiled. "Good nose. Yes. Ari, are you in any pain?"

I shook my head. "Should I be?"

He exhaled. "Yes, considering my thumb and two fingers have been squeezing into the nerve running from your shoulder to your small fingers. Here, just inside your elbow." He nodded to the spot.

I looked down to see he spoke the truth. The Master Mender had dug into the nerve everyone cursed when they bumped their elbow into a corner and their arm went numb.

"Slowed reactions. Dulled eyes and senses. Loss of feeling, even as far as pain and registering touch. Also, strong herbal odor from the feet along with no signs of burns." He spoke like someone reciting a list of goods off a trading ledger. Measured, emotionless, matter-of-fact. "What do you make of that, Fhaldar Masha?"

"I think the Accepted here took some kind of drug that dulled his senses and spared him much of the pain from walking the fire. But I can't make sense of him not being burned."

Rishi Marshi nodded. "Very good. Close. Would you bring me a pint and a half of water, two scruples of sugar, and just as much salt. I will also need these." He leaned to one side and grabbed a thin wooden board with a piece of parchment fixed to it by a thick pin. Master Mender produced a graphter and scribbled away. "These will help purge the toxin building up in his system."

"Toxin?" She didn't eye him when she spoke, keeping her attention on the list he'd handed her.

"Oh, yes. Accepted Ari here, in his attempted cleverness, has filled his body with a low dose of toxins. He will need to urinate and sweat them out." He gave me a knowing look. "It will be miserable, and he will sleep rather poorly. Now, would you fetch those things for me, Fhaldar Masha?"

"Yes, Rishi." She hurried off as ordered.

"Now, Ari." The Master Mender leaned close. "Do you know what thiplan is?" He looked at me like he already knew the answer.

I nodded.

"I thought as much. So, my *real* question is this: Where did a city boy, child thief, and whatever other titles you've earned, learn of this? How did you know thiplan oil can be used as a mild fire repellant?"

I opened my mouth to answer but ended up dry coughing instead. My lungs felt like hot hands wrung them, and the lining of my throat had gone raw as if scratched.

Masha returned, handing the Master Mender the water. She then passed him two palm-sized dishes of glass. White powders sat in each. Then she brought over another set of dishes with varying colored powders.

"Thank you, Masha. Mix the salt and sugar into the water. Accepted Ari has a parched throat. I'm sure all the talking he's been doing to get himself into trouble is the cause." The look Rishi Marshi gave me made it apparent he knew the cause had been from my overdose of the herb.

Masha treated the water and passed it to me. "Drink slowly, or you'll choke." Her voice stayed artfully neutral in a way that made me think she might have liked to see me choke after all.

I sipped, finding instant relief.

"Accepted Ari has taken a high dose of the herb thiplan. It usually is brewed in very low doses in tea to serve as a mild relaxant. Nothing more. But it possesses another odd property. It is used to treat burns, which you know. It's soothing and can numb the skin for short periods of time. In excessive use, it absorbs into the skin and causes the severe symptoms Ari is exhibiting here. If enough is applied, it blocks the pores and coats the skin, remaining outside like sweat. What was absorbed is also sweated out. The oil is susceptible to extreme heat and fire. It will burn off slowly."

Masha nodded, scribbling on a pad of her own. The focus of her face told me she only had a mind for the rishi's words and not the implication behind them. She fixated on the medical lesson before her and not my trickery.

A little blessing for me. She wouldn't spread word of how I avoided being burned. Or even bother to remember.

"Tend to your other duties now, will you?" Rishi Marshi dismissed her and she left with a little bow.

"Now, Ari. Where did you learn of this?"

I swallowed, then took another sip of water. "My life in the theater. My adoptive father, Khalim, used to coat his hands in it before working with fire. During plays, the audience didn't really care when performers left the stage only to return just as quick. In their brief moment offstage, they'd coat exposed parts of themselves in the oil. We used it during swordfights that involved burning blades, or anything to do with fire and lightning, like out of Brahm's stories. Old binder's tales. Those things."

He grunted. "Makes sense. Did they have the sense to wash it off afterward?"

I thought about it, and then realized I had always seen Khalim's actors scrubbing themselves raw wherever they had put the oil. I never thought twice about it, believing it just an annoyance to them. "Yes, they did."

"Smart people, then. You've taken in a nearly dangerous amount. Nearly." He reached out for the skin of water and I handed it to him. Master Mender then mixed in the other powders. "These herbs will help you sweat out the rest of the thiplan. You'll feel hotter eventually and your body temperature will rise. The sugar and salt are to help your body find balance. Thiplan saps some nutrients from you when absorbed into the skin in high amounts."

I nodded and thanked him, sipping more of the water down.

"Go slow with the drinking. But when you recover, I would like a favor from you, if you would? And I would be inclined to give you one in return."

I stared, all I could really do in the moment, hoping he'd clarify.

"I'll keep this a little secret, hm? The walking the fire without so much as a burn. You're clever. And I have use for clever minds and the hands that go with them. I've heard you contested a binding from Master Binder as well. You have potential. I'd like to see what you can do with it. That's fair, *ji-ah*?"

"*Ji.*"

SIXTY-SIX

Lore and Learning

Rishi Marshi hadn't exaggerated when he said I'd be sweating. I spent the rest of the day in a feverish daze, retiring to my rooms to endure the process of detoxifying my body. The urge to lie in bed and soak clean through my clothes and sheets was overwhelming. But, I chose the smarter route of stripping and sitting on the floor, burning at a temperature that kept any of Ghal's cold from reaching me.

The occasional wipe from a rag wetted in my water basin helped keep the heat from growing to be too much.

That day passed much like the one before. I missed dinner and went to bed hot, hungry, and somewhere between clear and muddled thoughts. Enough to dredge up a renewed hatred for Nitham and what he'd dragged me through. In many ways, that night reminded me of my earlier nights of being a sparrow.

Hunger, pain, and someone to focus my hatred on.

The simple things can keep a man going.

A chill racked me, blood and bone, in the early morning. I woke before the sun had even broken over the horizon. My body had sweated through the night until all of the thiplan was purged through that or frequent urinating. Now, the heat had fled me as well as the herb's effects.

I rose, shivering and with a head of mortar and wool. It took me longer than usual to slip into my clothes and robes, and I had far more need of my cane today than yesterday. I figured that came from my further weakened state post walking the fire and sweating out most of my fluids. Missing dinner didn't help.

Dressed, I took my time going down to Clanks, the food hall. It had earned its name for the endless clanking of metal trays and cups. Someone was always banging one onto a table, clinking their drinks, or dropping one. The noise, given the number of students, could rise to deafening levels at times.

Breakfast today made me doubly miss what I had passed over the night before. Pumpkin and squash mash, salted and buttered. Roasted chickpeas, thori, and a bone broth—no meat. While it was filling, it didn't satiate me the same way. Maybe a life of poverty had made me especially appreciative, and with time, desirous of meat, but all the same, I noticed its absence.

Radi and Aram didn't join me in the morning, and more than ever, I wished they had.

Years as a sparrow taught me to know when people watched me. And now they were, intensely so.

A few whispers reached my ears.

"Saw him walk it yesterday around fifth candle. Swear I did."

Another voice then. "He didn't flinch."

"He didn't make a noise."

"I heard he stopped in the middle and just stood there, burning, but he didn't burn."

"Mhm. Saw it too. He didn't. Just walked through the fire and gave Master Binder one fierce staredown. Never seen someone look at a master like that; Brahm's ashes, swear I haven't. Not even just a lower rishi. A master!"

"I talked to Masha. She worked the Mendery when he came in. She told me his feet didn't even get red from the coals. Nothing. It's like he *can't* be burned."

I finished my mash, leaving the rest of my meal alone. The story could use some tweaking, and I saw fit to give it a good twist. I got to my feet and walked through the cramped tables. A student tried to shuffle by me, heading toward one of the groups deep in gossip. I put a hand on their shoulder and stopped them.

Lean. Whisper. Rumors. That's all it takes to pass something along and have it stick.

"Do you want to know a secret they don't know?" I looked sideways to the group he was heading toward. The promise of a secret, even untrue, is more than enough to ensnare most people. And I'd learned of their allure when dealing and trading them.

The young man looked at me, then his friends. He licked his lips and I could almost see the knot form in his throat. He and I both knew his friends were talking about me, and he probably nursed a healthy dose of concern that I had now stopped him. But he nodded in the end.

I leaned in closer—dropped my voice to a whisper. "There are three things said not to burn: Brahm, the Sithre, and demons. Which do you think I am?" I pulled away from him and gave him my best cryptic smile.

His mouth moved but he said nothing. I could see the sparks kindling behind his eyes as he thought but fell short of any answer, or at least one worth voicing. Instead, he shrugged his way clear of me and jogged over to his table. He gave me one last long searching look as he sat down.

I almost cared to wonder which of the three he'd chosen. Almost. In the end, it didn't matter, because he'd share that choice with his friends. And they'd talk and spread it wide.

I lurked in Clanks for a while, listening to the renewed whispers and chattering all about the boy who couldn't be burned. Then I left, deciding it time to finally head to a place I'd been waiting to visit ever since Mahrab first told me stories of the Ashram.

The Scriptory.

I crossed the main grounds, heading toward a building isolated from the others. No halls or stone tunnels led to it. It remained cut off from any source of noise, wind, weather, and all. A stone mausoleum without any adornment on the outside.

Two doors of bright and heavy wood, studded with brass, barred the way. I knocked on them and waited.

A slit opened at eye level and a pair of gray eyes stared back at me. "Name?"

"Ari." I didn't bother adding my family link. I had learned I was the only person with my first name at the Ashram.

"Oh." The slit closed.

I stood there for a moment, unsure of what just happened. "Hello?"

The sound of latches snapped and clicked from the other side—the seam between the two doors cracked and light filtered through.

A young woman stood there, maybe a year or two older than me. Her hair was cut short, hanging just to the middle of her ears, and was just a shade of brown darker than the doors. Heart-shaped face with cheeks that still held to a bit of child's fat. They helped offset the coldness of her eyes.

"Please don't make trouble." Her look hardened and she looked me over again. "I know who you are."

I stopped midstep. "I won't. Wait, what constitutes trouble in the Scriptory?"

She frowned. "Nothing to harm the manuscripts, the books, the tablets. Nothing. You don't fetch anything yourself. You get one of us—a lorist in training—to get it for you. No ink. No graphters too close to anything. If you take notes, you do it from a safe distance. No water. No liquids of any kind. You thaw any snow off. No noise. Speak softly. And . . ." Her voice dropped to a dangerous whisper, made all the more serious as she narrowed her eyes. ". . . nothing leaves this library without permission and a record taken by either us or Master Lorist."

"Understood." I walked into the Scriptory and the doors shut behind me with a thud I felt more than I heard.

"Also, it's not called the Scriptory. It's the library."

I inclined my head, letting her know I'd taken stock of that, but I had no intention of using the name. Everyone else had dubbed it the Scriptory for the unending spread of manuscripts in the Ashram's collection.

A thought struck me that might save me some time and not irk her any further. "Hey, actually, I am looking for something specific. Mind helping me?"

She gave me a look that said she did mind, in fact, and would rather have been doing anything else. Instead, she let out a resigned sigh. "Sure. What are you looking for?"

"Any books on the Ashura."

She stopped halfway to reaching me, her back and shoulders tightening visibly. "Monster stories and tales? Children's fantasy?"

My spirits crashed and I tried to salvage the situation. "It's for the stories. I like storytelling and was raised in a theater. I have a personal interest in folklore."

She shrugged and motioned for me to follow.

The Scriptory's inside was the opposite of its hard, stone exterior. It resembled the Artisanry in many ways from the wood-paneled walls and floors. Rolled manuscripts and bound books sat in solid shelving as far as I could see. The books were sealed safely behind layers of etched glass, likely crafted in the Artisanry. All of the light in the Scriptory came from glass orbs that radiated a warm pale glow. It made me think of the sun on a cold spring morning still too close to winter's end.

"What are those?" I gestured to the spheres.

"Hm? Binder's lights. The spheres are inscribed in the Artisanry to store sunlight and recast it. Light can't be permanently generated, so we use these and set out others during the day to alternate with the ones that fade out later in the night."

I had never seen one of these in my life. It made me reconsider the potential of the minor bindings.

"Here." She gestured to one of the glass-covered shelves. The young woman produced a key, opening the small lock that held the glass seal in place. She opened the case and handed me a leather-bound tome. "Will you be needing to take it from here?" Something in her tone told me I shouldn't.

I shook my head.

"To record anything from it? We have graphters here if you need and some parchment, though there is a fee for the pulp-paper if you take more than two sheets."

I waved her off. "No, reading will be enough, thank you."

She nodded and sealed the shelves again. "Once you're done with that, I can fetch you another." It didn't sound like she wanted to, though. "One book at a time."

I didn't believe her, but I knew well enough than to keep pushing things, especially with my reputation hovering between awing and frightening depending on who you heard the rumors from.

I took the book to a table lit by one of the binder's lights. The soft light made it easy to pore through.

If only the material had been of any use.

I learned the Ashura had been born of Brahm to punish humanity for wandering away from his path. The Ashura were men turned monsters from feeding on human flesh and were cursed for it. The Ashura came from the bad dreams of children gone untended to. Eventually, they took shape and went out to carry mayhem and mischief on the world.

The book was a collection of stories gathered by the author over decades of traveling the Mutri Empire and questioning all manner of people.

And the answers reflected that.

One story spoke of how the Ashura were the first beings in creation and resented those that followed, choosing to punish them over the long thousands of years since. That made no sense to me.

Another made a comment about how the Ashura lived in secret layers in frozen mountain ranges, far from traveling eyes, all out of fear that men would stumble across them. Absurd, considering Koli had been in, and operated out of, the heart of Abhar. A place with countless people.

The only usable piece of information in the book was this: A single entry detailed people throughout the Empire reporting odd signs that coincided with Ashura sightings. No proof existed that those people had ever seen the Ashura, but the signs stirred something buried deep in the back of my mind.

> *Of all the stories about the Ashura, there is a consensus among those that have encountered them that the demons' coming is foretold by the following signs: fires giving off red smoke; a storm breaking out; the eyes of those who look on the Ashura bleeding, as do their mouths; also stones weeping blood. Some report the local birds going mad and a disturbance among fowls on farms.*

The night my family was murdered played through my mind. I lost all sight of the Scriptory and remembered bloody walls and the eyes of those I grew up with. Red smoke billowing. Being on the roof of a building with Nisha and seeing birds go mad.

I committed these to memory. Again, and again. I went through the folds of my mind and burned the signs into those. The pages blurred before me and, for a while, all I saw were endless lenses in my head all showing flashes of the Ashura's signs.

"Find something interesting?"

The question snapped me from the folds and my vision went white. It took me a second to find some clarity, but my head reeled like I had been slapped with the strength of someone's full arm behind the blow.

I looked up at the source and found someone in rishi's clothing staring down at me.

Her hair had been dyed the same color as that of the young woman who'd admitted me into the Scriptory. She wore it short, maybe just longer than finger length. Her skin spoke of spending many hours under the sun until it had developed a healthy rich tan. Sharp features with a prominent nose that made me think of a hawk.

I remembered her from my admittance. "Rishi . . . ?" I had never gotten her name or title.

"Rishi Saira—Master Lorist." She watched me with quiet interest. Her mouth remained tight and expressionless, betraying nothing of her thoughts.

I closed the book and decided to answer her question. "Somewhat, Rishi Saira. Just studying folklore and tales about the Ashura. They've been an interest to me—"

"Since you were a child?" A thin uneven frown crossed her face. I couldn't tell if she was tired, thought poorly of the subject, or of me for wanting to study it. "Most students have that phase." Something in the way she'd said "phase" made me think she didn't see it in a positive light. "There are other stories worth studying for a young mind."

She was judging me. I needed to think of a better way to explain my interest than as childish fancy. "I thought it interesting how stories change shape and truths the more they're told, over distance, and depending on how many people speak about them. The Ashura are a great proof of that. Everyone knows of them, but no one tells the same stories about them. Why?"

She pursed her lips. "That is a good point, but that is the nature of stories. Do you know why my position is referred to as 'Master Lorist,' and not something like 'Archivist'? We have no end of knowledge here, and they're certainly not all stories and fables."

I shook my head. "I hadn't thought about it."

"Because that is where it all starts."

"Where what starts, Master Lorist?"

"Knowledge. The first things told and recorded were stories. Not great histories of man's deeds. Not facts and locations about the world. No. It started with stories—lore—and the tales those people told their families first, before letting them spread wider in the world. You eventually learn everything is a story of something. A story of empires fallen and the ones that took their place. Stories of great men . . . and the worst of them. Stories of bindings and how they came to be, or how we think they did, and stories of how coinage systems work. But they are all stories first. Before any of the facts, the first keepers of knowledge kept stories."

It made sense, and a part of me loved the idea all the more for its respect of storytelling.

"So, I understand your passion for stories and their shapes—their history, but might I recommend putting aside *these* particular ones?" Rishi Saira reached out and brushed her fingers over the tome's cover. "There are better things to tackle—more respectable stories to study regarding what you want to know, hm?"

I nodded, trying to keep the disappointment from my face. "Yes, Rishi. Thank you for the advice." My feelings must have made their way into my voice, however, because her expression softened.

"If you feel what hours you have in a normal day don't permit you enough time to learn what you need here, come see me tomorrow just after fourth candle in my office. We can discuss the possibility of you working here and being a lorist."

I shot up straight at that, close to beaming. But I kept the appropriate amount of excitement on my face and in my voice. "I will. Thank you, Rishi Saira. That would be a dream come true." I thought of the many books here and all the stories I could learn.

She smiled and walked away. The Master Lorist looked over one shoulder as she moved farther away. "Be sure to have a lorist-in-training put that away for you once you've finished."

I nodded. My hands went back to the shut tome as soon as Rishi Saira vanished from sight. While she had a point that the subject matter appeared childish, I knew what most children feared to be true.

The Ashura were real.

And now I had something to track them by, find them with. It wasn't enough, but it had been more than I had had for years. I could start to hunt them, somehow.

A part of me knew it to be as childish as the study seemed to others. Kill the Ashura?

How? They had slaughtered an incalculable number over the ages according to the stories. I witnessed them laugh off my teacher and binder's efforts to subdue them. And in the end, he died buried under rubble.

All the while Koli's words still echoed through me. "We can't be killed."

I opened the book and resumed scanning through pages, looking for anything that could prove Koli's words wrong. If there was a way to kill them, I would find it.

And I would introduce him to it.

Somehow.

SIXTY-SEVEN

What All Men Must Know

I'd spent the previous day going through every book I could find on the Ashura. All of them turned up more misleading information than anything useful, which was to be expected. But I had still nursed hope to come across something like the signs I'd committed to memory.

The thoughts stayed with me until I'd gone to bed, then brought with them the sort of nightmares I wouldn't wish on anyone save Nitham.

I woke the next morning feeling like I hadn't slept at all; something becoming a habit, it seemed. I dressed and made my way down to Clanks more driven by curiosity than hunger. Though, I certainly felt that as well.

I spotted Radi and Aram at a table along with someone I didn't know.

They waved at me and called me over.

I walked toward the table, watching pockets of students flash me short furtive glances that vanished as soon as I returned their looks.

Many of them had learned to speak softer, it seemed, as none of their whispers reached me today. I grumbled under my breath for having helped bring this about.

What good is spreading your rumors if you're not privy to how they twist and turn behind your back?

I joined Aram and Radi, setting my tray down next to the newcomer. "Morning."

Radi groaned. "Morning's a hellish construct made up by someone too giddy too early in the day, too much so for their own good." He shoved a mouthful of spiced lentils into his mouth, chewing. "And for my own good too."

Aram rolled her eyes. "Don't mind him, he's just mad his night didn't go as planned."

I grinned, wiping the expression off my face before Radi could see it. "Another night alone—spent in the company of the only person who can tolerate you . . . you?"

Radi paused, holding another bite inches from his mouth. His eyes narrowed and he glowered at me. "I'll have you know that I am irresistible, charming, and a damn pleasure to be around." His argument turned into incoherent grumbling as he chewed his lentils.

I rolled my eyes. "I'm sure women find your drama and endless preening very charming."

Radi looked up from his bowl, his expression a mix of mock injury and offense. "*Please.*" He pressed a hand to his chest, then ran the other hand through his hair. "One doesn't have to preen when you're this pretty."

That drew a chorus of low groans from Aram, me, and the other man at our table. He had quite a few years on any of us by his looks. I figured him to be somewhere in his middle twenties at least. Possibly older.

The color of his hair was somewhere between a brown so dark it would pass for black in the deep of night, yet something that would shine a better, brighter mahogany under sunlight. His short and neatly trimmed beard was much the same. His eyes were more the dark of chocolate. All of it contrasted his complexion, which was far fairer than any of ours.

He hadn't opted to wear the robes the Ashram provided students. He wore a fur-lined coat and the heavy pants of hunters that lived beyond the city of Ghal's proper limits. Tribal, nomadic people.

His face was all severe lines and had a cold hardness filling it. If Radi had all the exuberance, warmth, and prettiness to draw in a young woman, this man had all the stark lack of any of that, which would give any girl a second's hesitation in approaching him.

I inclined my head in a polite hello.

He returned it before offering a hand. "Thariq."

I shook. "Ari. Thariq? Isn't that . . ." I had to think for a moment on the origins of the name. "That's Zibrathi?"

He took a spoonful of what looked like potato and carrot soup. "No. Past that. Koshtesh. Smaller, pass-through country, really. Same people in blood and language and religion, though don't tell Zibrathi folks that." He swallowed another portion of soup.

I looked him over, noting that he had none of the features of those people in his face or coloring.

He caught me staring and smiled. "Mom's Ghalthi. Father's from Koshtesh. Mixed blood. You know how it is along the Golden Road. Dad traveled a lot and reached these parts eventually. Met her and her tribe out there in the plains beyond the kingdom. I take more after her side than any of his." Thariq frowned at that, looking down at the table as if reconsidering.

"Maybe not. I've got her brawn, and that's what got me into the Ashram. But Dad's brain . . ." He tapped the side of his temple.

"He's being modest." Aram chewed through a fist-sized chunk of bread. "He's one of the youngest admitted. Came in and impressed Master Conditioner, what, eight years ago? Had all the potential to be a great wrestler. The kind nobles and kings pay to watch in the games. Then he opened his mouth and everyone found out he had a bloody quick brain between his ears. How close are you to being a rishi?"

Thariq flushed, the red coming easier and stronger against his lighter skin. He mumbled something I couldn't catch.

Aram laughed. "Man's built like an ox with the brains of a genius and he gets shy from compliments. Come on."

"Maybe a few more seasons. My work in the Artisanry is going well." Thariq shrugged and stuffed his mouth with more soup than I thought it could fit. I figured he did it to have an excuse from talking.

"A *few* seasons." Aram sounded like she didn't believe it. "He made Kaethar in two seasons, Ari. Two! Fhaldar by the end of his second year, right?"

Thariq nodded.

"What comes after that?" I hadn't touched my food, genuinely interested in the progression of the Ashram. No one had told me how it worked yet.

Radi stopped fiddling with the pegs along his mandolin and laid it across his part of the table. "There are a few options depending on the paths of education you take. You can end up a binder of varying stripes if you show competency in any of them. Same with artisanry. You can leave as an Artisan. The last option is to become a rishi of a discipline, which is still short of being a master. You usually end up running secondary classes in the discipline you're most fit for, and being an aide for the masters proper."

I nodded. "What about the ranks, though?"

Radi smiled. "Was wondering when you'd ask that. Kaethar comes after displaying some talent and skill in any of the fields. Enough to warrant specializing in them. You get extra education—access to higher knowledge pools. Like in Master Conditioner's classes, you end up learning more advanced wrestling and fighting techniques, and spend more time in the fresh and frozen hell that only he can put you through." Radi scowled. "Am I ever glad I never have to step back onto that shit-colored clay field."

Thariq lowered his head. "It's not so bad."

"Tch." Radi waved a hand to dismiss the comment. "Give me music and arts any day. The things people shaped the world with. Love and romance are built on that. Not muscles and throwing a bunch of half-naked men to the ground."

"I seem to recall more women lining up for Thariq than you." Aram had kept her voice as close to matter-of-fact as possible, but something in the light of her eyes betrayed her mischievousness.

Radi reached out to swat her.

Aram didn't exclaim in pain, breaking out instead into a little laugh that we all joined in on. Once it died, we returned to the topic at hand.

"What about Fhaldar?" I prompted.

Radi shrugged. "It's same as Kaethar, I suppose. Just more competency, yeah?" He looked to Thariq for clarification.

The big man nodded. "Usually more advanced demonstration of skills in your focuses, really. For artisanry, it comes with layering several complex minor bindings on an item. That's one way—the most common. Another is coming up with a new use for composite bindings that hasn't been done before. Doubly so if you can tinker up some new and wondrous item they've never seen before." He gave me a knowing look. "That's easier said than done, and everyone says they'll do it. I haven't seen it happen in my eight years here."

I nodded and stored that away as well. "And to be a binder?"

Everyone stopped and exchanged looks, but no one spoke.

I finally decided that maybe it would be best for me to start my food, and I dug into my oil-fried rice and eggs.

Aram took a swig of plum juice and dragged a sleeve across her mouth. "Well . . ." She drew out the word and looked to the other two boys before going on. "No one really knows that one for sure, you know?"

I didn't and shook my head to convey that.

"Right." Aram cleared her throat. "Well, most people who ever reach that status just leave. Binders are rare, Ari. Really rare. To even get that rank you have to show competency in a magic that—well, have you seen the size of the class?"

I nodded.

"It's not large, and that's because most learn early on that it's nearly impossible. What few try, fail. And then there are the ones who—" She broke off and swallowed. "They go wrong, Ari. That's the best way to talk about it. It's not right, but something happens to their heads and they never go back on straight again."

The silence returned for the space of a few breaths.

"We've all heard stories of students who've tried to push that path hard and paid a terrible price. It changes you, that study. So, by the time you learn any binding well enough to be called a binder, you're not the same person, I hear. They just leave then and go wandering the world doing . . . well, whatever they want, I suppose."

Thariq grunted and leaned closer. "It's telling that the way to earn the title is *just* showing competency, whereas everywhere else it's near close to mastery. That says something. That's how hard it is, that just being good enough is all you need to earn the title. And to master them?" He sucked in a heavy breath.

"Look at Master Binder and tell me you think he's sharp and steady." The look on Thariq's face said enough. He believed the man to be as cracked as a dropped egg.

And I couldn't argue.

"They do terrible things to you, and I don't know if it's ever worth mastering them. And I'm more afraid of what that price is. Take my advice, Ari, and stick to artisanry. It's a safer path with more options for you in the wider world to make a name, trade, and coin." Aram gave me a long look, hoping I'd take her words to heart.

Radi spat a curse and pushed away from the table. "Oh piss on the damn bindings and minor ones. On artisanry and all the arts of Brahm." He rose from the table, the only care in his movements coming when he picked up his mandolin. Then, Radi stormed away from us all.

I waited until the silence and awkwardness had dragged on long enough. "What was that about?"

Aram gave me a weak and halfway apologetic smile. "He's . . . tetchy about the bindings. He has a history. He won't talk about it, but they bother him. Ask him about it sometime."

I blinked and almost tied my thoughts into a knot thinking about that. "But he's in my Introduction to Bindings class?"

Thariq clapped a heavy hand to my shoulder that nearly tilted me under the force. "Like she said, ask Radi about it. We learned not to long ago. Doesn't make sense to us either. He's avoided the bindings forever, until now. We don't know why, and we won't try to find out. If you want to . . ." He didn't finish speaking, shrugging instead.

I looked to where Radi had stomped off. *I guess I will then.*

Radi was nowhere to be seen, however. I spent the next third of a candlemark looking for him until time crept too close to the beginning of my next class. Resigned, I headed toward the courtyard where Master Binder taught. Some of the students had arrived early and found seats among the tiered theater-style benches.

I scanned the room to find Radi already in his typical spot, having left an opening for me to sit beside him.

He saw me approaching and flashed a brighter grin than anything he'd shown back at breakfast. I took it to mean his mood had improved. That made me reconsider asking him the questions I'd held on to since our discussion. If his spirits had improved, I'd be a terrible friend to push him into something he didn't want to talk about.

After all, he'd shown me no end of kindness ever since I'd met him. And he didn't have to. He could have easily taken Nitham's side in our squabble to earn himself favor with the rich bastard. Or he could have just turned an eye and not involved himself at all. Instead, he'd chosen to be my friend.

One of the few who ever had the option and made that choice. The sparrows were friends and family out of necessity. We had to trust each other and grow close to survive. Here, people were free to decide who they wanted to be close to.

I smiled back and took my seat next to him. An awkward silence filled the space between us and I felt Radi knew a piece of me wanted to talk about the incident at breakfast. "Are you fine?" It wasn't prying, per se. Instead, I felt it safer to simply check in on his feelings rather than prod into what had set him off.

He nodded, one of his hands falling to the mandolin resting at his side. He fidgeted with one of the pegs before realizing what he was doing. His hand snapped back to where it had been before, almost like he was embarrassed by the nervous motion. "Just got a touch warmed by the subject is all. Everyone has those things, *nyeh*?"

I grunted. "I know that one all too well."

He made a sound similar to mine, and that was as far as our conversation would go considering the topic.

The little irritating intricacies of men at times. There are some subjects, no matter how much time may come to pass, we never grow great at discussing. We struggle for a deeper depth and settle for dancing around the heart of the matter. Odd noises serve well enough to get the message across.

I let the subject go and instead turned to one I knew Radi would delight in. "Have you heard anything from Nitham's circle since my penance?"

As I thought, Radi's face split into an expression reserved for a satisfied cat. "Oh, I've heard no end." He leaned in close, dropping his voice to a conspiratorial whisper. "It comes by way of a few of the high-blooded women among his ilk." He waggled his brows and gave me a knowing look.

I took his meaning, but felt it worth poking him anyhow. It would pull him further from his sour mood and maybe draw a laugh out of him. "And what's that mean? They gossipers?"

"Everyone talks when you have them on their backs and your mouth in all the right places." Radi gave me a lecherous grin.

I played the fool still. "You had some poor girl pinned to the ground and your teeth at her throat, threatening to eat her? You monster." I kept my voice and face as deadpan as possible.

He glowered at me. "Oh come off it. You know full bloody well what I mean. Bastard."

I raised my hands in a gesture of placation. "I am. And, yes, I'm giving you a hard time of it. What did you learn?"

"That you are a marvelously clever stirrer of pots, my little friend." Radi fixed me with a sly look. "I still don't know what you did—how you did it—but you've got half of them thinking you aren't entirely human. Some whisper demonspawn. Some say you're Sithre, posing among us. One lady thinks you might be a Shaen trickster in the form of a young boy, and you know . . . I think she's very interested in finding out just how much of a boy you are." The look Radi gave me then drove all the blood to my face and neck.

I decided we'd had enough of what my reputation had grown to be, but I had one last lingering question. "And how has Nitham himself taken it?"

"About as well, or poorly, as you'd imagine. He's been sulking since. Missed a few classes, I heard. He was hoping to make a mockery of you. See you hurt, spread stories of it, then come after you while you were licking your wounds. Pulling that stunt sent his tail between his legs for now." Radi stopped and looked over my shoulder, then glowered. "Though, I guess for not long enough."

I blinked, then followed his stare.

Nitham came down the stairs leading to the ringed seating, his cadre in tow. They filtered into a tier above us and to the left. He looked straight ahead like his head had been locked in place. Actively ignoring me, it seemed.

I took that for a mild victory, but I knew men like Nitham didn't sit and tend to their hurts for too long. They were the sort to keep coming back until they got what they wanted or were put so painfully in a place they would not want to bounce back from.

A thunderclap sounded and tore the class's attention from all the little circles of gossiping.

Rishi Ibrahm stood in the stone courtyard, his hands held inches apart.

Did he do that? I watched the Master Binder for any telltale signs.

He caught me staring and grinned. His hands fell to his sides and he cleared his throat. "Would anyone care to anticipate the subject of today's lesson?"

A few students traded looks, but none spoke up.

I turned my gaze on Nitham, waiting to see if he'd say anything, but it seemed Radi had been right. My performance had drained him of his usual swagger and loose lips. He sat mute and dull as a rag doll.

"Maybe our little prodigy has something on his mind, hm? What say you, Ari? Hm. Wait, what's that the students have been chattering about? Oh-ho." The Master Binder slammed one of his fists into an open palm. "Right, Ari the Unburned, is it? What do you think?"

A loaded question, and we both knew it.

But it gave me an opportunity to turn the nature of the lesson in the direction I wanted. I would have to be careful in my wording, but I hoped to push Rishi Ibrahm into discussing a topic that had long been on my mind before I'd seen the Ashura.

I cleared my throat and kept my voice as respectful as I could. "Well, Rishi Ibrahm, walking on fire without being burned hardly makes me precognitive. There are no bindings to read the minds of men, at least as far as I know." I gave him a questioning look, but he remained just as placid as Nitham, giving me no hint in his expression. "However, given that we've already covered the Seven Principles of Binding, it only stands to reason you'd next be covering the ten things all men must know.

"That is to say, the list of verbal bindings for binders to use and shape the world around us." My mouth dried as soon as I'd finished speaking and I tried to work some saliva through it. Failing that, I grabbed my waterskin and took a sip.

Master Binder eyed me, and I could see his face twitching. He kept control of himself, however, and did nothing but hold his level look on me. The man knew what I was trying to goad him into, but I'd done a fair job leading him into it. The class now had expectations, and they had been built on something he himself had set. Or at least implied.

What good was learning the principles if we weren't going to hear the verbal bindings that they were the foundations for?

"I have a terrible sneaking suspicion, Accepted Ari, that you were not beaten sufficiently as a child." The Master Binder's face held no anger in it when he spoke. He wore the expression of someone's mischievous older brother who promised to get into trouble very soon.

I played his game, though, keeping my face as impassive as his had been earlier. The man was trying to get a rise out of me, and like hell if I'd give it to him. "Actually, I've been beaten throughout most of my life." I shrugged, playing if off like it didn't bother me. "What about you?"

That brought the man up short. He blinked and his mouth hung open as he tried to find the words to speak.

A few of the students broke back into whispering.

Radi nudged me and gave me a wide-eyed look that told me I might have gone too far.

Master Binder cleared his throat and regained his composure. But the look he gave me in the brief pause let me know there'd be a reckoning between us. Somehow. Somewhere.

And I had a feeling the teacher would be a damn sight more trouble than Nitham could hope to be.

"It seems our little boy wonder is as clever as he thinks he is, which is quite the shame. Bad things happen to boys too clever for their own good." He waggled a finger at the class, but I knew it had been specifically meant for me.

"But, yes. Today I'll be covering the ten things all men must know, as our little, and rather sadly, unburnable upstart calls them. What he is referring to are the ten verbal bindings all master binders learn. It is the next step to being able to shape and fold the world to your mind's whims. Well, all within the governance of the bindings and what they allow for."

Radi raised a hand and the Master Binder acknowledged him. "This means each binding has a specific application and execution?"

Rishi Ibrahm nodded. "Correct. But we won't be going into that much detail today."

What? I hadn't voiced the thought, wondering why the Master Binder would bother indulging me at all then if not to go further into the bindings.

"There are ten words, older than Brahmthi, Brahmki, and any proper language we still speak. These are from the time before empires and man's tongues settled on a language to connect us all, the Trader's Tongue." He held up one finger, then spoke again. "Tak." A second finger joined the first. "Roh." He waggled the pair of digits.

"They are like brother and sister." Rishi Ibrahm frowned as if reconsidering that. "Mhm, no. More like twins. No-no-no-no." He grew frustrated and stomped in place, grousing to himself.

We all traded looks.

The man finally found some measure of calm and stabilized himself. "Ah, of course." He clapped his hands together, looking at them as if seeing them for the first time—wonder across his face. "They're like left and right hands. A pair."

We waited for him to elaborate, but he didn't.

"The ten things all men"—he broke off and looked over the crowd of students—"and women, must know, are really five sets of two things." He waggled a pair of fingers again. "They are composite bindings. They work together to create the proper links for binders to change the world around them." His hand flashed.

I blinked, just managing to trip my thoughts into the folds. But how many would I need this time? Two went to four, but that wasn't enough before. Four turned to six. I struggled to tumble into them fast enough. Eight. Ten.

The stone raced toward me, keeping to a lower and sharper path this time. It wouldn't reach a point high above to come crashing down with more force than before. Now it would pass a hand's breadth overhead at most before snapping down. Less of a pain if it struck, but bothersome nonetheless.

That meant it would pass through my atham, the space I occupied larger than my physical self.

Ten folds would have to be enough. Everything in me shaped the image of the stone zipping by to strike some point behind me. I didn't know where or care. It would be enough to just keep in mind that the stone would act as it was supposed to.

No binding of Rishi Ibrahm's would wallop me today.

The stone sank and I almost broke the folds, hands fidgeting out of reflex to try and catch the rock before it struck me. Something clamped hard to one of my arms and kept me from following through. The stone sailed overhead, striking somewhere behind me.

"Ow!" I couldn't tell the student from their cry of pain.

It took me a moment to realize what had happened. Radi had taken my arm in hold, stopping me from trying to swat the stone away. I looked at him, asking a silent question.

He didn't give an answer per se. Radi pulled his hand away and just shook his head. Whatever his reason, I had succeeded in stopping the stone from striking me.

I glared at Master Binder. "So, out of curiosity, how many folds was that? Six, eight, or ten?" I realized my error after I'd finished speaking. I'd effectively let him know the maximum number of folds I'd employed.

"Nine. Seems I was one short of giving you a good lesson again." The grin he gave me made me wonder if he'd gone mad. His eyes lost their focus, but none of their shine, and his mouth pulled more to one side than the other.

"Is there a reason you're so set against me?" I felt my temper rising and, for once, didn't care so much about whether or not I proved the Master Binder right about me being quick to anger. "I've just as much right to be here as any other student. I demonstrated enough of that during my admittance. I can do a damn sight more than any in the class here, even if I don't have a rank beyond Accepted."

Rishi Ibrahm didn't take a moment to think about what I said. "Maybe I don't like your face. Maybe I think you're too clever for your own good. Maybe both of those things. Maybe I don't like city boys. Or maybe I think you need some of the hot air let out of you. Maybe a dozen things that don't matter because I'm the rishi here, and not you." His hand snapped into motion.

Eleven this time. Wait, no. That's an odd number. But he'd said nine before. How in the world had he done an odd number of folds? Pain. Sharp, concentrated in a single spot as thick as my thumb, blossomed through the top of my skull. I winced as white streaked my vision. My hands shot up in reflex to clutch the struck spot.

Rishi Ibrahm still wore the same stupid grin from moments ago. "Clever boys think too much for their own good. And that's your problem."

I glowered at him, shooting him a stare so hot it should have scalded him by all rights. But my curiosity followed the anger and helped bleed some of the heat out of me. I took a breath to further calm myself. "How many folds was that, Rishi Ibrahm?"

"Oh-ho. So polite. So smooth and calm." He waggled a finger. "Not buying it. Not. At. All. I can tell how angry you are. But, I'll answer the question. That was thirteen, my boy. Thirteen."

I frowned as he went on to cover another part of the lecture. Though I wanted to listen to what he said, I couldn't ignore the odd number of folds he'd used. The way I had been taught them made odd numbers nearly impossible. Folds by their nature broke into evens. An infinite, if you had the mind for it, pattern of lenses all reflecting the same thing. How did you tack on a single extra fold? It went against their very nature.

Then it struck me. I looked up from where I had been staring, deep in thought, and locked eyes on the Master Binder.

"Oh. Has the little prodigy figured it out?" His face had readopted the neutral mask he sometimes wore.

"You tricked me."

Rishi Ibrahm tapped a finger to his nose twice. "Got it."

"Why?"

He arched a brow. "Didn't catch that bit yet?"

I frowned, mulling it over. Then I had it. "To keep me from slipping into my own folds fast enough to counter your binding."

He nodded.

"But why? Why any of this? I've shown you I can do a piece of the bindings. At least stop them. That's enough to learn more, isn't it?"

Radi's hand landed back on my arm, squeezing harder this time.

I shook free of him, not wanting to be kept silent now. "Answer me!"

Rishi Ibrahm met and held my look for a long moment of absolute silence. The breathing of students was audible around us. Finally, he nodded. "You want an answer to that, then stay after class. We'll talk."

I hadn't expected that, but it pulled the fire out of me as I slunk back into my seat. The promise of a private talk was enough for now.

The Master Binder cleared his throat and resumed the lesson. "The bindings work together, opposite ends of a stick or a string, if you will. Without the end or beginning point, the energy channeled will have no way to be contained. So, it runs on forever. That makes it useless. So, you have the composite pairs.

"Tak and Roh. Whent and Ern. Ahn, Ahl. Wyr and Ehr." He broke off and looked away from the class, keeping his gaze on the distant mountaintops.

When he didn't bother speaking after a handful of minutes, Eira raised her hand. But she went ignored for another count of breaths. Finally, she spoke out. "Rishi Ibrahm, that's . . . um, only eight bindings total."

He turned back to look at her. "Hm? Oh, yes." His mouth twitched, but he said nothing again for the span of ten heartbeats. "The last two are ones he ought never to use."

I barely caught his words, but at that, he abruptly ended the class and dismissed us.

I had been so close to learning the ten bindings' verbal components, and now I'd only gleaned eight. But I had gotten him to meet with me in private. And I meant to get the last two from him if I could.

SIXTY-EIGHT

The Crow's Nest

I waited for the last students to filter out before approaching Rishi Ibrahm.

He paced in place, muttering to himself much in the manner I'd seen men do who were deep into white-joy.

I paused, waiting for him to stop. When he didn't, I sighed and drew closer. "Rishi Ibrahm?"

He snapped out of his odd muttering and looked at me like he hadn't realized I was there. "Hm? Oh. Right. You." The Master Binder took a deep breath and just as much time in blowing it out through his nostrils. "Yes, right. The bindings. You wanting to learn. Stubbornness. Walk with me."

I nodded and fell into step as he led me out of the courtyard and into the main field.

"You're right, you know, Ari."

"About what, Rishi Ibrahm?"

He ran a hand under his chin, scratching it. "About what you can do. You are more capable than some of the other students. Even if you haven't ever tried your hand at artisanry and the minor bindings. Managing the folds as you can, as fast as you can, is impressive. More so when knowing how to counter one of my bindings so long as I don't match you in folds. But do you know what the problem is?"

I shook my head. "No, but I have a feeling you'll tell me."

He pursed his lips and nodded more to himself than me. The whole walk so far he hadn't even looked at me, keeping his eyes ahead on a spot I couldn't figure out. "That's part of it there. You're. Too. Clever—quick, and always thinking. That's a good thing at times. But not for here, Ari. Not here. Do you know what the bindings really take? Do you know the toll? The cost?"

That brought me short. I had already been thinking of what he would say next and preparing a list of possible answers. And now I had none. "No."

"That's what I've been getting at. You cannot shape and will the world how you want without consequences. Dangerous ones. And someone like you, all too ready to jump and leap and enact them . . . can court disaster. You don't slow down. You don't think about being safe. You don't think past being right, or winning.

"Go back to the time when you learned the folds, then you might start getting the hint of what I'm speaking of."

I frowned, thinking about what he could have meant. I had nothing, though.

"What was it like when you were learning under Mahrab?"

"Slow? Frustrating. He had me sitting and doing mental exercises. I watched a candle flame burning, trying to predict how it would ebb and dance." I wasn't sure how that fit in with what Master Binder was getting at.

"Mhm. And how much time did you spend on that? Did you learn it just like that?" He snapped his fingers. "Or did you have to sit, think, and change how you thought?"

"The latter."

"And that's what I'm not seeing here. I didn't see it the day you arrived. Do you want to know what I saw?"

Part of me didn't, but I knew he wanted to give me the answer anyhow. "Yes."

"I saw a boy, running from trouble, and hoping to find something to hold on to here at the Ashram. That thing is the old stories of binders. Brahm, Abrahm, take your pick. Heroes lost to time and tales." He waved a hand as if shooing away the thought. "You want power but you're not ready to think about what that power costs—worse, what it can do. And I would like to show you. Come." He motioned me to keep in step as he picked up his pace.

We walked well past the Scriptory, reaching the far end of the main yard. A lone tower stood in the distance, resting just before the face of a nearby mountain. And the fact it stood at all was nothing short of a miracle.

It boasted odd extensions. Stone rooms that jutted from the crooked center frame of the building. They should have fallen off under their own weight, and I had no idea what kept the other rooms fixed in place. The roof sat at too sharp an angle and every tile couldn't hope to sit tightly where they were set. But they did, refusing to slide off and hammer onto the ground.

"Where are we?"

He didn't answer me. Instead, Rishi Ibrahm just raised a finger to his lips. He walked on to the pair of doors leading into the tower. "This is the Crow's Nest. Let's go inside, shall we."

It wasn't an invitation. It was a command.

I followed the Master Binder into the tower, taking stock of the room we'd entered. It defied my expectations. Bookshelves had been built into the circular room, running from the floor to the ceiling, packed to the brim with books to the point the wood should have given way. Something held it all together that had nothing to do with expert craftsmanship.

"A binding?" The words left my mouth before I realized.

Rishi Ibrahm smiled. "Mhm. A good one, too. Organization of the books is a bit messy, though. Not bad for a student, no?"

I blinked at that. *This was done by a student?* A second look gave me a deeper appreciation for its construction. Every board fit perfectly in place without a single nail in sight. None of the wood flexed under the weight of books that would have bent and bowed normal shelves. "Who did this?" I looked to Rishi Ibrahm for an answer as I realized a gentle and warm current circulated the room.

"Him." He pointed to a desk littered with loose sheets of parchment that covered nearly every inch. A cup sat perfectly balanced, tilted on its edge, leaving it a wonder it hadn't toppled, spilling its contents onto the paper.

I waited for it to fall onto its flat bottom, but it didn't. "Um, Rishi? Him-who?"

The Master Binder pursed his lips, then went over to the desk. A hollow thud echoed through the room and Rishi Ibrahm pulled his foot back, cursing as he grabbed it. "Ow . . ." The rest of his words devolved into muttering profanity I could barely pick out. "Wake up, you lazy shiftless lout." He punctuated the statement with another kick at the desk, repeating the same mistake. Another string of obscenities peppered the air.

I stared at Master Binder wondering if I'd asked to be taught by an utter madman. It wouldn't have been the first time I'd shown poor judgment in looking to someone for guidance.

A long, low groan came from the other side of the desk. One hand rose from behind it and smacked hard to the table's surface, sending papers rustling. Not a one scattered, though. The force of the blow should have sent some into the air. "*Nergh.* Brahm's buxom bosom and bloody bottom, who dares wake me at . . ." The person behind the voice hauled themselves into view.

The student wore a sleeveless shirt of dull gray. Faint lines crisscrossed his forearms—scars—that hadn't quite faded enough to lose themselves against the copper-earth tones of his skin. He had a short brush of dark hair. His eyes were the color of almonds under molasses and, while soft in their shade, they contained a jarring brightness that reminded me of something.

I looked to Rishi Ibrahm and saw the same spark and light in his eyes.

"Oh. Master Rishi." The student frowned, putting a finger to his lips. I figured he couldn't have reached his twentieth year yet. Maybe just a few short of it. "Wait, no, that's not right. Binder Brahm! No." His frown deepened and he looked down at the tilted cup. "What do you call yourself again?" The boy looked up, staring hard at the Master Binder like an intruder had just waltzed into his sacred place.

If this bothered Rishi Ibrahm, he didn't show it. His face held more care and patience than I had ever seen. "*I*. Brahm." He pressed a hand to his chest and emphasized the first letter. "It's Ibrahm."

The young man turned sideways, shooting the Master Binder a long skeptical look. "Today?"

Rishi Ibrahm nodded, but his mouth twitched before breaking into a smile. "And most days."

"Mhm, no." The young man turned back to face him and hooked a thumb to his chest. "More like Ubrahm. Get it? Like, You-Brahm. I think that's you every day."

Rishi Ibrahm's lips pressed tight together for a moment. "Well, I'd hate to think then about my bosom and . . . what was it again? Oh, my bloody bottom."

The young man laughed.

"And are you still Krisham today?" The Master Binder sounded as if he already knew the answer but decided to ask anyway.

The young man—Krisham, I presumed—shook his head. "Mostly. I did a few bindings and had to be someone else for a while. Then they needed a nap." His brows grew close, forming a wrinkle in his forehead. "Or I did. But I'm mostly back now."

I had no idea what he meant by that, but the Master Binder merely nodded his head in perfect understanding.

"I'm glad you're mostly back to being Krisham. Maybe rest for a bit longer and you'll be all the way, *ji-ah*?"

Krisham nodded. "Wouldn't be so bad, but that means I shouldn't bind for a while."

Master Binder let out an affirmative grunt.

"Oh, well, that would be annoying. I have to unbind my cup to get my drink." Krisham pointed at the cup perfectly balanced on its edge.

Rishi Ibrahm smiled, reaching out and taking hold of the cup. He closed his eyes and pulled the beverage free with no effort. "Well done. How many folds was that, out of curiosity?"

Krisham shrugged. "I don't know. You'd have to ask Sheru. He did it, not me. But I think he'd tell me to tell you that it was somewhere in the thirties."

Thirty folds at least, and he'd said it so casually. No. That wasn't what staggered me either. The young man knew the bindings and could employ them with such an ease he sounded bored talking about them. And he used them to anchor a cup. To make bookshelves?

It set my mind spinning.

Then I fixed on the name he'd spoken and turned to Master Binder. "Wait, does he mean Sheru the Thamori Tiger? The binder-warrior out of stories?" I looked from Rishi Ibrahm to Krisham, hoping one of them would clarify what they were talking about.

"The same." Master Binder's face was a solemn mask. "Krisham sometimes isn't himself. But he usually comes back sooner or later, eh?" He flashed the student a smile, which the young man returned. "How many folds did you use for these, Krisham?" Master Binder pointed to all the sheets of paper.

"Hm? Oh. Only two. I don't think anyone would want to unbind my papers and have them fly all over the place, do you?"

Master Binder shook his head. "No, I don't. Have you eaten today? Drank? Did you read any stories and have good dreams during your rest?"

Krisham nodded to each of the things. "Well enough. I think I'd like to go back to sleep, though, if that's okay?"

Rishi Ibrahm reached out and put a hand on one of Krisham's shoulders. "Of course it is."

Krisham thanked him, then turned his attention on me as if noticing me for the first time. "He doesn't look like he needs to be homed here. Who is he?"

"A student—an Accepted. He's adamant in having me teach him the ten bindings. Says he's more than ready to learn them. He *can* muster up the folds of the mind, though." Rishi Ibrahm sounded like he himself wasn't quite sure how much to weigh that in my favor.

"Mhm." Krisham focused back on his cup, setting it back at the odd angle from earlier. "He's not ready. He doesn't know why he wants to be a binder, but he thinks he does."

Rishi Ibrahm nodded but said nothing.

"He's too sure of himself too—too clever. He doesn't know what he doesn't know and that's that he doesn't know quite who he is yet." Krisham rocked the cup on its bottom, water sloshing along the lip but never breaking over it. "Ahn." He released the beverage and it stood rooted firm on an edge, refusing to topple over. "It looks nicer that way, Rishi Ubrahm."

The Master Binder inclined his head again and didn't address the improper use of his name. "It does, Krisham. I hope you have a good rest. Let me know if you need anything or if Sheru proves to be a problem, *ji-ah*?"

"*Ji.*" Krisham let out a yawn and crawled back under the desk.

Rishi Ibrahm watched the young man for a moment before motioning to a winding and narrow staircase to our side. The wooden planks were much like the shelves in their construction . . . if you discounted every bit of the clean and seamless form in which they'd been fashioned. Every step was crooked in a twisting frame that looked like it hadn't quite finished in warping its shape.

I could almost picture a gentle gust of wind twisting the wood further to leave the stairs completely unusable.

The Master Binder stepped onto the first of the planks, which should have given out under his weight. At least creaked. It did neither. "Come."

I followed, eyeing each step I took with all the care and fear that the whole staircase would fall apart any second. Once none of that happened, I finally found my voice and asked the questions on my mind. "This is another binding too?"

He nodded. "You're quick, aren't you?"

I couldn't tell if he was mocking me or just speaking matter-of-factly. We talked and ascended in silence for a minute before Master Binder cleared his throat, looking at a window that sat askew in the stone wall.

"What did you think of him, Ari?" He stared at the glass as he waited for my answer.

"Krisham? He seemed a little . . ." I chewed over what else I could say. "*Different.*"

"He is. Is that bad, though?"

I didn't have to think about that one. "No. Not at all."

Rishi Ibrahm nodded, but it didn't seem like he'd been paying me any mind really. He took a few more steps before falling into a steady walk.

I moved behind him. "What's . . . wrong with him?"

"Hm? Oh, some would say he's cracked. Others would say nothing at all. At least the ones here. Depending on the day and how many bindings he's used, Krisham will tell you that he's what's wrong with him, and Sheru is what fixes him. It happens to those who think they know what they're getting into with the bindings. Everyone thinks they know, but what people think they know is never quite the same as what they actually do.

"That's what happens with the bindings, Ari. There is a cost to magic—old magic especially. If you wish to enforce your will on the world, shape it—shift it—make it—break it, what do you think will be the cost, hm? If you wish to affect it, do you think you will be spared its effects on you? There. Are. Costs. Krisham knows this. He has paid them." The strength went out of Rishi Ibrahm's shoulders and his posture sagged, but he still continued up the stairs.

"Where are we going?"

He ignored that. "So many questions. But you're still asking the wrong ones. You should be asking, 'Why is Krisham like that?'"

I thought about it, then wondered whether I really wanted to know the answer.

"The bindings take a mental toll. You're familiar with a piece of that, aren't you? You've studied how to shape the folds and hold them. You've told me about the candle and the flame, though I'm surprised you were taught that. It's an old exercise that's fallen out of practice for over a hundred years. But the toll is still there. This isn't the place to discuss it, however. We're going higher up. Keep your footing, and keep your hands on the rails."

I looked to the sides of the stairs and realized there was nothing to hold on to. That brought me up short and I nearly fumbled. "There are no rails?"

At that, the Master Binder laughed and stopped in place.

I almost bumped into him, adjusting my weight to compensate. The action threw me off-balance and I tipped sideways. A scream hadn't even formed in my mouth, but I tried to let it out anyway.

A hand reached out and grasped my robes. "Ahn." Master Binder held me with little visible effort and none of his weight shifted as he did. He stood as firm and fixed in place as Krisham's cup. He pulled. He twisted. And he grunted.

I ended up back on my feet, perfectly in place on the step I'd tumbled from. "You . . . you ass!" My hands clamped to my mouth as I realized I'd just insulted one of the Ashram's masters.

Rishi Ibrahm took no offense, however. "I can be. Made my point, though, didn't I? You think too far ahead, and not enough of now—here." He jabbed a finger at the planks below us. "You're too fast, Ari. And never present enough, which is a part of being a binder." He said nothing else and resumed walking.

We went up in silence until we reached a landing that led onto another circular floor like where we'd come in.

Rishi Ibrahm raised a finger to his mouth, gesturing for silence.

I nodded.

He led me through the curving hall, stopping outside a room shut with a metal door.

I stared at it, wondering what warranted a door like that in the Ashram. Every one I'd seen so far had been some form of wood. A few places had sliding screens of tightly woven fabric in wooden frames, but no iron or steel.

He picked up on my curiosity. "Wood is easier to break." The Master Binder rapped a hand on the door, drawing a hollow metal clang from it. "Metal, less so."

All of which meant the doors were subject to being broken. By what and how concerned me.

The door shook and a heavy clang rang from the other side like the sounding of a gong. Then another. The door shuddered. Then, then came a noise like hail on steel—heavy, unrelenting, and hitting as hard and fast as a storm.

I looked at the door, then the Master Binder.

He exhaled and reached into the folds of his robes. Rishi Ibrahm produced a key and slipped it into the lock, opening the door. "I should go first. He might react poorly to a new face."

There's a person in there? The sounds had me thinking of stories of caged monsters and the like, all vying to break free.

The room inside had been made from a motley assembly of brick and stone. Odd sections of the walls were missing, exposing another layer of the same materials behind. Some of those had fallen as well.

A look at the floor revealed what had become of them. Shattered pieces of brick and stonework lay scattered across the ground.

Master Binder shut the door behind us. It closed with a weighty thump that almost sounded like the previous crashes against it.

It was not a reassuring sound.

I looked at the metal door and saw small imperfections in its form. Indentations, shallow, but as wide as my hand, peppered its steel frame.

In place of a proper bed, a thin mattress rested on the floor with too many blankets for any one person's needs. And that was it. Nothing else at all in the room.

A young man, maybe the same age as Krisham, sat cross-legged on the mattress, looking at Master Binder. He had the build of someone who frequently skipped his meals. His sleeveless black shirt and short-cropped breeches were more suited to the summers in the south than up here in Ghal where he should have been freezing. His dark hair had been pulled into a tight and single tail. "Master Binder."

Rishi Ibrahm lowered his head . . . slowly. Very slowly. The gesture reminded me of something not unlike acknowledging a skittish or dangerous animal. "Reppi. How are you doing today?" The Master Binder looked over his shoulder to the door, then back to the young man. "You've been tearing at your room again."

Reppi nodded. "It's slipping. I am. Everything is." He threw himself back and sprawled across the mattress. "It's there—everywhere, always there. The folds. They're filled with it, you know? You do know. Of course you do." He sighed in what could have been frustration, but I had a hard time telling with him.

"So you're taking it out on the door? And if you keep this up, you'll pull enough bricks and stones free from the extra walls you'll expose your room to the outside."

Reppi made a sound like he didn't much care.

"It'll be cold." Rishi Ibrahm's voice held a touching note of concern, but he didn't let it bleed too much into his words. It had been just enough to be heard. "How bad has it been, Reppi? Are you cold already?" He glanced to the many blankets, then back to the walls. "If you are, I'll see to having the stones replaced. This place is old, I'm sure the cold finds a way through."

Reppi shook his head and he returned to his sitting position. "It's okay. I think I'll be fine. If not, I can ask someone to share that binding from the first floor."

I waited for him to explain that one, but Rishi Ibrahm nodded as if he understood.

Catching my look, he answered me. "Did you feel the current of warm air downstairs?"

I had. "Yes."

"It's a few minor bindings together. My guess is they've been carved into the undersides of the shelving planks. You'd never look there when distracted by books. They circulate warm air while moving colder air out." Rishi Ibrahm turned his attention back to Reppi. "I'm impressed you were able to pick up on that being used while up in your room."

Reppi shrugged. "Wasn't hard. Been bored. I sat. I Listened. I felt. I knew someone had done it when I'd gotten better at Listening to the stone and the walls."

Master Binder acted like that made perfect sense.

All I took out of it was that the bindings could be detected by others clearly proficient in them. Something that remained beyond my skill set.

For now.

"Are the headaches back, or have you been spared that much?" Rishi Ibrahm drew closer to Reppi, but he still remained noticeably out of arm's reach.

The young man raised a hand and waggled it in a so-so gesture. "Sometimes. I snap out of the folds too much. But sometimes—many times, it's easier to be in them. Safer. But you can't just sit in them. You have to bind, you know? Otherwise it just sits and builds and builds. Bigger, louder, brighter. The folds grow and everything you see just . . ." He trailed off and pressed his hands to his head.

"Shh." Rishi Ibrahm finally closed the distance and came to Reppi's side. He eased the young man back onto his mattress, covering him in his blankets with the care I imagined a father would show a son. "Just rest. I'll be back later to check if you need anything."

We left the room soon after, Rishi Ibrahm locking up behind us.

"There's more to see." He moved farther down the hall, leading me to another set of stairs. We went up this faster than before and didn't stop until we reached the next floor. "This is nearly to the top but it's high enough up for your lesson." He motioned to another room.

This one had a pair of sliding doors layered in thick and padded mats. A metal latch held two slats together that prevented either door from being opened.

I saw no way for a key to fit into that contraption or for it to be undone by brute strength.

Rishi Ibrahm put his hands on it and leaned close enough his lips could have brushed the metal. He whispered something I couldn't hope to hear and the latch opened. The doors slid open and he motioned for me to follow him inside.

I did, easing the doors almost fully shut behind me.

This room had nothing in common with the last but for its dimensions and general shape. The walls had more of the cushions and padding that were on the door. A proper bed and wooden frame rested in here. The color of the walls pulled my attention back to them and away from the bedding.

The pristine white of the cushions had been marred in places by red stains that looked like they'd flake free any moment from the fabric. Then I realized what they were.

Blood.

The walls were stained with more blood along them than any one person could safely lose.

A woman sat in one corner, idly clawing at the padding. She wore a thinner set of robes much like mine. Her hair had been cut short, leaving the wild curls to fall no farther than her ears. When she looked at me, her face reminded me in some parts of a feline: sharp-featured, round in all the right places, with eyes that seemed a bit too large and with an animal brightness in them.

"I don't like him." She turned her head back to the wall and resumed the bored scratching.

Rishi Ibrahm snorted. "That makes two of us."

I glowered at the Master Binder.

"How are your fingers today, Immi?" The Master Binder walked over to her, but stopped a few steps to her side. He peered at her hands, then the walls. "That is a lot of blood." He sounded no different than someone making a comment about the weather.

She shrugged. "It is. I always heal, though." Immi raised two fingers that had been rubbed raw. The outermost surface of her skin had been sloughed away to reveal reddish pink flesh that bled. She waggled them, clearly not in pain. Then she closed her eyes. "Start with whent, then go to ern," she recited.

The skin over her fingers slowly knitted itself together. Then it looked like it had never been scratched away at all.

And I didn't even see the last transition. It was like a trick of the mind. Something out of storybooks.

Like the bindings.

One moment bloody fingers; the next, they were the fingers of someone who'd never hurt them.

Immi returned to her scratching. "I don't get hurt. Not really. Time is fluid. I'm only ever temporarily losing skin and blood, but it always comes back. So, I'm never really hurt, am I? I'm just in the process of losing and regaining. Shedding and then healing. It's like a snake. I'm growing. Sometimes I just get too old for my own skin. Or . . . it gets too old and boring for me. I can't remember."

Rishi Ibrahm swallowed. His mouth moved but he said nothing. And suddenly, the young master looked nothing like his age at all. No. He looked . . . old. Not in any sense of his appearance. His features still carried all the youth of someone in their late twenties.

His body just lost the strength to stand perfectly straight, almost like someone in their later decades having grown too tired to hold themselves up. His shoulders sank. His back hunched just enough to be noticeable. And all the brightness left his eyes.

"Have you gone any days of late without scraping at your fingers, Immi?" Rishi Ibrahm sank to his knees but still moved no closer to the woman.

She shook her head. "Technically, I never have, because every time I do, my fingers are put back right. So then, they've never been rubbed raw, right? They're just in a continuing fluctuating state. But if I end each night with them returned, does that mean I went a day without leaving them bloody? I don't know."

One of Rishi Ibrahm's eyes twitched, and it could have been my imagination, but the barest hint of moisture welled at their corner. It vanished as soon as I thought I'd seen it. The man cleared his throat and rose to his feet, motioning me with a curt gesture of his head.

I took the silent cue and stepped out of the room, shutting the door.

He didn't follow and left me to wait outside for a few moments. Eventually, Rishi Ibrahm slid the door open, stepping to my side. He dragged the back of a hand against his eyes and I pretended not to see it. "Have you ever heard and seen the pains of those closest to you? The things you can't fix and can only hope to mollify?"

I thought back to my life as a sparrow. Then to a time before that—to Nisha. I nodded.

"Then you understand sometimes the only thing a man can do is cry. And no one should see a grown man cry, Ari." Rishi Ibrahm moved past me and led the way in silence.

I had no reply. I'd known that pain when Taki passed at my side, suffering, burning, and delusional until his final breaths. And I did cry.

I finally found my voice when we reached another room. The doors ahead were an odd mix of stone and metal that I could make no sense of. Slabs of rock intermingled with sheets of bronze in a manner that should never have held together.

It took me another moment of hard concentration to recognize it for what it was. *Another binding.* I reached out almost on instinct before knowing what I was doing. My fingers brushed against the mix of stone and golden metal, feeling the cold of it more than the texture of its surface. "What binding is holding these together? Whose rooms are these?" I regretted the question as soon as I'd asked.

Rishi Ibrahm placed a hand against the metal-stone mixture, smiling almost like having seen an old friend after a long time. "Mine. At least once upon a time." He pushed on the door, then frowned. "Someone's bound it up after I left. Who would have done that?" His expression warped, growing tighter, face quivering with quiet rage. Rishi Ibrahm held his hand on the metal and stone, closing his eyes and muttering something under his breath.

The walls of the tower shook. Loose stone and dust rained down on us. And all the while, I noticed the only things that seemed immovable were the bound and crooked wooden planks of the staircase.

The door of stone and iron remained as fixed and firm as before.

Master Binder scowled and lashed out with a foot. He regretted it a moment later, pulling back and clutching the appendage much like when he'd kicked the desk. After a string of less-than-inspiring and creative cursing, he readdressed the door. "Oh, right." A sly grin spread across his face. "Ahn." He touched the center of the door, then ran his hand in a circle around the space. "Ahl. Oh, Ari, you should get down now."

"What?" I didn't have the chance to think or say anything past that.

The door vibrated with an intensity that set the surrounding frame quivering.

That was enough of a sign for me to drop to the ground.

A sound like thunder, then lightning striking stone, filled the space. Parts of the door exploded and showered the air above me, falling down the long drop of the tower. The metal pieces either fell to the ground, or hung suspended from the frame—bowed and bent. An opening of sorts filled the space between it all.

If you were willing to contort yourself, that is.

Rishi Ibrahm clapped his hands together. "Ah, good enough. Imagine that, keeping me from my old rooms." He stepped into the mangled doorway, then paused. "Wait, *I* made that door so they wouldn't try to coop me up in here again." He threw back his head and laughed as if realizing something extraordinarily funny that he'd overlooked.

I didn't see the humor in it and began reconsidering wanting to learn from the man.

"Come on in, Ari." Master Binder went into the room.

I got to my feet, knowing whatever hesitation I had was pointless now. I'd come this far and wanted my answers more than any concerns over Rishi Ibrahm's sanity. A rush of cold air struck me as I neared the door and rushed in through the openings of my robe. I knew why once I'd stepped into the room.

That was a far stretch in describing the space. It looked more like a prison than anything else, and my mind went to the story Vathin had told me about Brahm being trapped in a cell of stone.

No bed. Nothing of comfort. Just solid stone everywhere except for the place where it had been torn away from the walls much like the door Rishi Ibrahm had just unmade. Beyond that, open air and the mountains of Ghal. And monsoon season came in another shape here in the cold climate of the frozen kingdom.

Crystalline flakes of ice fell from the sky, stealing all my attention. To me, it looked like someone had sprinkled irregular chunks of salt onto the world.

I stepped closer, almost reaching the edge of the prison. "What happened here? Why is this wall . . . just gone?"

Rishi Ibrahm still kept the lopsided and clever grin on his face. "Hm? Oh. I got fed up at being locked away and unbound the mortar and stone. Well, I suppose it's better to say I bound them to places elsewhere and blew it away."

More snow fell and I stood transfixed by the mixture of its beauty and just how hard it bit at my exposed fingers.

How could something so pretty hurt so much?

I'd come to learn the answer to that many times over the course of my life.

"They locked you here? Why?" I didn't look at Rishi Ibrahm for his answer.

"Because I'd gotten to be a touch too wild for them . . . and maybe even for myself. Say, Ari, do you know why we call this place the Crow's Nest?"

I frowned and thought it over. "Because . . . it's high up?"

The Master Binder smirked. "I suppose that's one reason, yes. But no, Ari. When would-be binders lose their hold on their minds, thoughts, and reality, this is where they come to be. High, high up above the clouds, and away from others. And when they've gone full mad, this is the one place where there's no leaving, and all you can do is crow!" Rishi Ibrahm cackled before cupping both hands to his mouth and letting loose a scream that could have been more a caw. It echoed long and far, and the nature of it seemed in defiance of the Crow's Nest and what it stood for.

I could see some of the dots below that I took for people stop in their tracks. They must have heard the noise and paused to search for the source.

"That's what the bindings do to a mind, Ari." Rishi Ibrahm came to my side and put a hand on my back. "Do you know what powers them? Shapes them?"

I thought on it. "Force of will?" The exercises Mahrab had taught me revolved around impressing my will on the world and my mind. Then I remembered something else. What the Athir truly was and a line about the pillars of faith. "Faith."

He nodded again. "And faith is a tenuous thing. Tricky, nebulous, shifting. It can come to us with the clarity of the morning sun at times. Easy, believable, and in sight. With faith, strong enough faith, a man can believe anything. But that faith can shatter and be lost just as quick. Faith can make a man many things, and it can break him too. And what you believe doesn't just shape the world around you, Ari. It can come back to shape you. And when some binders slip in that, they begin to lose the shape of themselves—the who and what and why of their identities. Then they come to believe terrible things.

"And they become dangerous."

Everything grew quiet but for the gentle whistling of the cold wind. I heard the sound of ice touching stone, just that brief moment of soft subtle impact before it melts.

I thought of the students I'd met in the Crow's Nest and their proficiency with some of the bindings. With that, I started to see the shape of what Rishi Ibrahm meant in terms of the kinds of minds required for this sort of magic. And I knew the costs now.

Immi, Reppi, and Krisham. One, a girl who'd convinced herself she couldn't truly be hurt. That her pain, if she even felt that much, was temporary because she could set it back. And as a result, she came to hurt herself every day by force of habit. Reppi idly tore and hurled stone and his foundations about for reasons I still couldn't quite grasp. And lastly, Krisham. The young man had conflicts surrounding his own identity. Clearly a brilliant binder, but he spent parts of his time believing himself a figure out of legend and children's stories.

And I thought about myself. My motivation. To be like Brahm.

Was I any different? Would I follow in their steps?

"So, after seeing all of this, Ari, would you still like to try to be a binder?"

I didn't have an answer right that moment. So I worked around it instead. "Do you bring every student up here and show them this?"

He shook his head. "No. And most aren't stubborn enough to push me into it. They *listen* when I tell them this isn't for them. They go on and become nice little artisans or philosophers, dancers and wrestlers. They become arithmeticians and shape the knowledge of kingdoms and courts. Some become gurus and sages. They enlighten. *You* are particularly bullheaded about chasing this no matter my warnings.

"Do you know what it takes to be in my position—Master Binder?" He fixed me with a blank look.

"To know all ten bindings?"

"Cheap answer, Accepted Ari. But, yes, that is a part of it. And to have paid the many prices they ask. The control and faith. The mastery of it. That is what makes the difference. And the patience behind it all. And you lack that."

I gave him a challenging look.

He caught it for what it was and motioned to the drop just in front of me. "You don't believe me. Fine. Let's test it all and your faith above everything, hm?"

"How?"

"Put your bag and staff down, hm? Your cloak too. When I push you off this ledge, Ari, I want you to believe against all things and knowledge that you will not go splat to the ground. I want you to believe that you will not become a piddly puddle of formerly annoying Ari. That you will be safe. I want you to show me the faith needed to be a binder and believe this thing till it is true. Can you do that?"

I could and I would, so I set my items aside. Mahrab had taught me how to make my Athir firm as stone. Strong enough to hold the image of moving, living fire inside it. My mind and heart brought to me all the hatred and memories I'd built for Koli. The promise of finding a way to find the Ashura, learn of them—him—and then make them all pay. And I would need the bindings for that.

I paused and thought on something Master Binder had said. "Wait, did you say, '*When*' you push me off?"

A hand slammed into my back and sent me off the edge of the Crow's Nest.

SIXTY-NINE

Prices

I fell.

During it, I had only the dim awareness I had done so. There is a moment in falling, especially when not done of your own volition, where your mind simply hasn't caught up to the fact you're racing toward the ground. Everything slows while the rest of you races by. For the space of a breath, I found myself able to perfectly tally the number of snowflakes falling with me. Then I realized I'd done no such thing and merely took stock of the ones I could see as I fell. And the number constantly changed.

My mind reached for something to hold on to as it struggled to process the fall.

Faster now. The wind buffeted me so hard I couldn't feel the cold of it, just the pressure. It threatened to tear my clothing away from me. My eyes ached from the rushing of air.

I'm falling now. Faster. The world is closing onto me and I can only make out the stone of the tower. It runs on for what seems forever, and the ground feels so far away.

But it's closer now.

The dots upon the world grow larger and into clarity.

Students watch me, waiting to see what will happen.

And I do the only thing I can hope to do.

The folds.

I slip into them, and no small part of prayer, too. The folds of my mind come into view and I imagine what Rishi Ibrahm told me. *I will not fall.* But I am. And I know this thing is not true.

I will hit the ground. And I will die.

Closer now. Faster still.

I'm falling.

The wind hammers harder against me, now almost like a weight of stone against my chest and limbs.

But I try. I think of the folds and imagine the many ways I can avoid falling.

I see countless lenses, and in all of them, I do not fall but am back in the tower. I stand beside Rishi Ibrahm. I am firm. Rooted. And safely in place. I cannot fall. I will not fall.

And I tell myself this lie. Over and over again. I repeat it. I believe it as best I can, but I know the truth of things.

I will die now. But even so, I do not know what else to do, and in equal measure of panic and hope, I cling to the child's idea and belief in stories. Of Brahm.

I will stop falling now.

I will not die.

Please.

A bright light flared to life before me. My breath caught in my throat and my chest ached from the conflict of pressure inside and outside. The light took shape much like a circular doorway, and within the world inside the ring I saw something.

A curved wall of stone. Flecks of white, almost like large grains of salt. And I saw the robes of the man who'd pushed me from the Crow's Nest.

I hit the wall of light.

And everything changed.

The scream I hadn't thought to let out finally left my lungs. I snapped forward, my feet striking firm stone, but my momentum carried me farther. No purchase could be found and I staggered ahead, back toward the drop.

Rishi Ibrahm's hand thrust out and caught me by my robes.

I came to a standstill. The world spun and my stomach felt like it hadn't quite forgotten the fall, still set to tumbling and churning that morning's meal. For a moment, all I could do to steady myself was set my thoughts and gaze on the falling snow. I counted what I could and hoped that mental effort would be enough to keep me from rediscovering the contents of my belly.

"Congratulations, Accepted Ari. You didn't go splattity-splat in the courtyard!" Rishi Ibrahm slapped a hand on my back that nearly threatened to send me off the edge again. While he didn't succeed in that, he did manage to bring me closer to retching than I'd been a moment earlier. "Did you believe you were going to die? Did you have an idea of what to do in that moment? No? Mhm. Most people don't. But did you try? I bet you called on the folds, didn't you? Good—good." He spoke faster than the beats of a hummingbird's wings.

"Stop. Talking. Please, Rishi Ibrahm." I shut my eyes tight, wishing the world would stop moving for one damnable second. A series of long-drawn-out breaths were what it took to finally steady myself. I opened my eyes to find the Master Binder watching me—expressionless, like he was waiting for my next words or action to judge me.

"You pushed me off a goddamned ledge." I kept my voice flat and empty of accusation, stating a fact.

He beamed. "I did. And look, by Brahm above, and a little bit of I"—he placed a hand on his chest—"you survived. You didn't answer my question, though. Did you go into the folds? Did you believe?"

I nodded, but I also didn't see the point in lying to him about what else I did. "And I hoped—I prayed, though, not to anyone or anything in particular. I just hoped I wouldn't die."

"Most people would. And that's the problem, Ari. The bindings are not for most people. They're not even for some of the talented. And I will admit, you are talented. But right now, you are not ready."

I whirled on him, a mistake given how I felt. A pressure built behind my eyes and I wished for it to recede. It didn't, leaving me to talk through the pain. "Ready based on *what*? Tossing a student off the Crow's Nest? You really *are* cracked, Rishi! What was I supposed to do? Work my own binding to find a way out without ever being taught how?"

He stood there, silent, watching me.

"Maybe that's why students are locked up in here. Is that it, Master Binder? Are those stuck in the Crow's Nest your former students, because if so, I can see why they're in here if you were their teacher! Did you drag them up to rooftops only to tip them over and then tell them they're not ready because they can't do something you can?"

That had been the wrong thing to say, and I knew it as soon as the words had left my lips.

Rishi Ibrahm's mouth moved for the span of a breath before shutting tight. His gaze fell to the ground and grew distant. The clarity of his eyes muddled, and all of their usual brightness followed suit into dimness.

A new silence filled the air between us that not even the mountain winds and snowfall could break.

I should have offered an apology. I should have at least spoken of how that was uncalled for to say, and that I shouldn't have said it. There were any number of things I could have done and should have, but I hadn't made those choices. Instead, I'd went after the man's heart, and there are few things we ought never to do in life.

And one of those is going for the pain buried in a person's heart.

"I did teach them." The four words were enough to break the quiet between us, but for all the whispering of them, Master Binder may as well have shouted them and the mountain returned the echo. "And that is why I know the shapes and tolls the bindings can take. And I know the many ways they break people, Ari. All too well." His voice cracked. "It is better that I teach them, though, than someone else who doesn't understand this thing. And it is better that some never learn them no matter how much they wish to try."

Then it all clicked.

"You . . . don't want students to learn them, do you? You teach just enough and around the subjects to give people a taste, but never enough for them to get any further."

Rishi Ibrahm raised a hand and waggled it. "Some of that, yes. And not some of the other." Which wasn't a full answer. "Not everyone is cut out for this, and I will do my best to find those people before they hurt themselves." He fixed me with a knowing look that made me feel more like I was under inspection by Master Mender.

"And you think I'm one of those?" My breathing hadn't quite steadied yet, but it was closer than before to something I'd consider normal. "Even though I can muster up the folds. Enough to thwart some of your bindings." Another thing I shouldn't have said.

Master Binder raised a hand overhead. "Tak." He motioned to my face. "Roh."

One of the stones from the ceiling tore free, showering us in particulates and debris. It hurtled toward me with the intent to pulp my face.

I ducked, regretting the sudden motion. My body still clung to the disorientation of the fall. The rock sailed harmlessly over me and off the edge, hopefully to land somewhere that didn't have a passing student under it.

I looked at Master Binder, wide-eyed. "Are you crazy? What if someone's down there?"

He shrugged. "I very well could be. And there likely is." He'd answered both my questions with such nonchalance I didn't know what to do. "Try again, and this time, Ari, use the folds, hm?"

I didn't have an idea just how difficult a binding he'd employ. To counter, I'd need to guess at least the right number of folds to use.

"Too much thinking. Not enough doing. To be a binder, you need to just be able to act on faith at times, Ari. Training and faith. Show me. Tak."

How many do I need? In class, I think I went to ten. It was ten, wasn't it? Or had it been twelve? I couldn't remember.

"Roh." Another section of the roof, nearly as long as me in length, broke free and arced toward me.

As many folds as I could hold then. Twenty. My mind slipped into them. First two, both showing the massive slab of stone passing overhead. Now eight. I didn't have time to ease into this. I refused to accept any reality other than what I saw. Nothing existed but a world in which I stood firm and the stone did not take my head from me. Ten. Then twelve. My mind ached and I remembered the dizzying fall.

My gut churned again at that thought and I felt the urge to vomit return. Working the folds while still somewhat out of sorts wasn't easy. If I survived this, I would likely end up hurling my stomach's contents all over the Master Binder's robes.

Sixteen.

I will not be harmed. I am immovable. My faith is rooted—firm, unshakable. My Athir is as strong and in place as the very stone of this tower. Like the mountain, I will not fall. I refuse.

Twenty. I managed all the folds I could, convincing myself of one universal truth: The stone would fall past me.

And it did. The piece of ceiling pushed a current of air through my hair as it rushed by overhead, nearly close enough to brush my head. It went over the edge and out of sight.

I let out the breath I hadn't realized I'd held in my chest. The combined toll on my mind and body brought me to my knees. I sat there, panting as I tried to collect myself. Through it, I managed to eye Master Binder and give him a look that said what I couldn't bring to voice.

You cannot deter me. You will not. And no matter what you try, I will remain here, and I will pursue the bindings. With or without your blessings. I will learn them. And in time, I will master them.

There are some things you cannot hope to say with words. So looks suffice.

He caught my meaning and nodded. Then his eyes grew to owlish proportions as he ran over to me. "Brahm's blood! There could be students down there."

That twist in logic drove what little strength I had out of me. I fell flat on the ground, wondering how someone so unhinged became not only a teacher, but the master of a discipline. We had already postulated that some students walked the grounds.

"Wyr. They are all one and the same. The places are not as I see them, but as I know them to be. They are all one and the same—connected, and now conjoined by my hands and will. They are not two separate ends, but two ends of the same path. I only bring them back together. Ehr!" Rishi Ibrahm motioned far out past me to the tips of the nearby mountains. His other hand pointed to where the ceiling had fallen.

Stone of that size should have made a thunderous sound upon striking the ground. The sort that even we would be able to hear up in the heights of the Crow's Nest.

But it never came.

I waited for a moment, watching Rishi Ibrahm's face break into an expression of self-satisfaction. "What did you do?" I asked.

"Hm? Oh, I sent the little bits of stone over the mountains. Didn't want them flattening some student who didn't deserve it, mhm. It's probably well off into Sathvan. Maybe one of the small villages in the province, Tharam, Ampur, Dhural?" He shrugged as if unconcerned where it ended up.

I stared off into the mountains, picturing a slab of stone and mortar crashing down to disrupt the frozen peaks. That much mass could trigger an avalanche. I'd heard of the phenomenon from other students who'd spent years at the Ashram and heard the stories themselves from travelers and traders coming through.

"I don't think that much stone counts as little, Rishi Ibrahm." I kept my eyes on the mountains.

He snorted. "Back in the old days, proper binders could move mountaintops and bring them down with but words and will. A little stone isn't much of a thing. Though, I really do hope I didn't drop that on some poor villager going about their day. People hunt out there, you know. Some collect ice to store in cold boxes and sell off." He winced.

I turned back to gawk at the Master Binder.

"I won't train someone to do what I can unless they prove to me, without a doubt, they are capable of being a master binder. Nothing short of that will move me on the subject, Ari. If you think, for whatever cleverness and stubbornness you may have, that you can change me on that, you are wrong. I want you to think on and consider everything you have seen today and what I can do. Keep that in heart and mind, Ari. Then think on what it takes to harness the folds, and not just challenge a binding, but to enact one.

"Remember that. And weigh what that means for me. What my mind is like. Because you cannot convince me with words, Ari, to teach you. You will have to show me, and as of yet, I have not seen what I want out of you. What I see is a path to putting another student, a child, a boy, in the Crow's Nest. And I will not have that." Rishi Ibrahm's hands flexed into tight fists that he released just as quickly.

I knew the strength of resolution in his words because I'd been there myself in my life. I'd spoken like that, and I'd felt the heat and hardness of it in me at times. He was right, there'd be no getting through to him on my terms. I'd have to meet him on his. So I asked for them. "And what will that take? What do I have to do to show you, without a shadow of a doubt, that I can do this? That I will." I met him, matched him in stare and voice, and held it all for him to see.

Some of the tightness and stubbornness fled out of Master Binder. His posture loosened, shoulders sagging. "Show me you have the patience. Show me you have the strength of will and faith to not crack under the bindings. Show me you've learned what they can do—truly do, on your own. Then we will talk." He turned to leave.

"Wait, you want me to figure out the bindings on my own?" I couldn't fathom how in the world to do that.

He nodded. "You won't have to be able to perform them, just show me you've come to understand their power, how they work, and the weight of them. Do that, Ari." Rishi Ibrahm moved to the doorway he'd broken, lingering in the open space.

"Will I still be able to attend your classes?"

The Master Binder grinned. "Of course. I expect you there after signing up. Besides, I doubt I could keep you from them if I tried."

I thought back to my admittance and his refusal to take me, then the collection of masters using that as a way to shun me from the Ashram. "But you did try. When I first came in, I mean."

He frowned for a moment, his gaze going distant. The smile returned a second later, just as wide and bright as before. "Oh, that." He waved a hand to dismiss the thought. "Bit of a joke. Some of the masters, myself among them, love putting the new blood through things like that. Tests to see who really wants to be here. If you didn't end up in my classes, you could have still been admitted to others. It couldn't have stopped you from attending the Ashram and learning other things." He laughed and walked through the doorway, leaving me alone with that thought—stupefied by his nonchalance.

Rishi Ibrahm's head peeked through the opening, the grin having spread into a wider, more maniacal thing. "Oh, and Ari?"

"Yes . . . Rishi?"

"Think fast. Ahn. Ahl." He waggled the fingers of both hands at me.

I blinked just before the full weight of a man's body collided with my chest, throwing me back and over the exposed edge of the Crow's Nest.

This time I screamed first. My cries echoed around me as I rushed closer to the ground. I had no warning to think and slip into the folds, but halfway down, I figured it was better than dying while hollering.

But what to think? What to do?

I thought of the other binding Rishi Ibrahm had worked. One that somehow worked over a span of large distances. One that connected them. That was it.

My mind tipped into the folds and imagined the openings of light spawning before me. A doorway to take me from my fall, and another to safely deposit me somewhere along the Ashram grounds.

Preferably in a single piece. An unliquefied piece at that.

Eight folds sprung to mind when I realized I couldn't recall the verbal components of the bindings.

Will the folds just be enough?

The last time Rishi Ibrahm had saved me, so it stood to reason this too could have been a test. An odd one only someone as cracked as him could come up with.

Closer now.

I'd passed the halfway point of the Crow's Nest, nearly reaching the quarter mark of what remained of the tower. The next few breaths would be my last if I didn't think of something.

Twelve folds.

And the way of light sprung to life before me.

I passed through it, still screaming.

The world tipped sideways and I sailed out of another doorway, hurtling horizontally. It took me a moment to orient myself and realize I was flying across the courtyard near the Crow's Nest, heading rapidly toward the front doors of the tower.

The shut doors, which were certainly many times harder than my own body.

But my weight did the remainder of the work and spared me from a bloody collision. My feet touched the earth and I tumbled, rolling head over heels in what snow had accumulated across the grounds. Not enough to cushion me, but enough to soften the worst of the landing. The thick robes and my cloak did the rest.

I'd have bruises to show for it, but nothing serious. I lay there in the snow for a moment, letting its cold wetness seep through my clothes and numb me. It came as a relief, to be honest.

Footsteps crunched against the ice and grew louder.

I looked up to see Rishi Ibrahm standing above me.

"Well done." He bent over halfway, still peering at me. "I heard the screams, and I almost felt your folds. You did try, didn't you?"

He can pick up on someone's folds? It made me think, as out of sorts as I was, that a connection existed between the folds when concerning the same binding. A theory, yes, but one I felt comfortably sure about.

Instead of answering him, I'd decided I'd taken in enough of the soothing coolness of snow. I pushed myself to my feet, clenched a fist, twisted my torso, and sent my balled hand into the air. The blow should have landed on Rishi Ibrahm's nose, sending him into blinding pain washed with a good bit of red that I felt he should be acquainted with.

I'd overlooked how much the fall had shaken me as well as my sense of coordination. My blow went wide of the man's face, not aided by the fact Rishi

Ibrahm straightened up. I missed and my momentum drove me to overextend. The snow did its job under me and took what little remained of my poor balance. I crashed back to the ground.

"Tch. Tch. Ari, if you had done a touch better there, you would have struck a rishi—a master, in fact. *That* would have been a terrible thing. You could have been brought back up before the masters on grievances for attacking me." I could almost picture his grin while I rested in the snow. "Besides, everyone's watching. Not the sort of scene to paint, hm?"

I looked around to find he'd spoken the truth.

Students stood still in the courtyard, staring at the both of us.

A part of me wondered how long people had been watching. Could they have been there since I'd first been thrown from the Crow's Nest, hearing the screams and stopping to catch the commotion? Had they seen the stones fall and then the ceiling come partially down before vanishing?

I took that in stock before getting back up to my feet, taking a moment to brush the snow from my robes. If I played this right, I could make use of everything that had just happened, at least to better shift the story in my favor.

Because Rishi Ibrahm had been right, the last thing I needed was students talking about how I almost assaulted a master. But if I could have the story go both ways, a battle of sorts between the two of us—equals—that would change things a bit.

I kept that idea in the back of my mind as I addressed the Master Binder. "You're right, Rishi." My voice held the proper amount of respect and levelness in it for the moment. Something that required great restraint on my part, but I didn't need to feed rumors that I was at fault for whatever my interaction with Rishi Ibrahm looked like to the onlookers. "I did summon the folds of my mind. I pictured the binding you used to move the ceiling from falling near the tower off into the mountains."

He nodded and grinned. "Thought you did. You're learning, even in the midst of fear. Good job." He clapped me hard on the shoulder, sending my head into a slight spin from the impact. "Learn anything else?"

I thought back to the other bindings I'd seen him employ. "One of the composite bindings you used, it . . . involves movement. Weight?" I pursed my lips as I thought harder on it, but was unable to come up with more.

"Good. Not quite there, yet, but good. You have the cleverness for this. But we knew that. Give it time, Ari. Time. I'll see you next class, and will be awaiting your thoughts should you learn anything more about the bindings. Until then, consider thinking on everything you saw and heard today. Maybe you'll prove saner than us all and walk away from this."

I gave him a hard stare that let him know I'd do no such thing.

He offered me the same wry smile I'd seen too often on his face. "Bye." Master Binder waggled his fingers as he walked away, leaving me to stew in my anger in the snow.

I'd finally noticed what had been lying at Rishi Ibrahm's feet: my sack and cane—my binder's staff. At least to me. I retrieved them, slipping the bag over my shoulder.

Some of the students realized the confrontation had ended and quickly set about making their way wherever they were headed. Others turned to whispering, not quietly enough, about what had happened.

The price to be paid for my pursuits. People would definitely be talking about it.

So I turned to give them something better to discuss. I stomped over to the nearest student, still holding to the glower that had worked across my face after my conversation with Rishi Ibrahm.

The boy could have been a handful of years older than me, just touching his twentieth by his looks. Dark hair, unassuming, and utterly forgetful as far as his face went.

"You saw all that. Heard a piece of it." They weren't questions, and he knew that.

The boy nodded.

"Did you hear the screams? Did you see and hear the falling stones from the Crow's Nest?"

He licked his lips, turning to the woman he'd been speaking to. "Parts of it. I saw you falling."

I nodded. "That's what happens when people use the bindings. They're dangerous things, and they have prices. Sorry you had to see the struggle."

His eyes widened.

Just enough of a story to let his mind run wild with what could have happened. By tomorrow, who knew how many people he would tell? And then they'd work a little magic of their own, telling others, twisting the tale until even I'd come to barely recognize it.

But if I was going to butt heads with Rishi Ibrahm for all to see, I might as well get something for the trouble. And a bit more of reputation certainly couldn't hurt.

It would also be a lie to deny that a part of me didn't realize this would inevitably reach Nitham, probably giving the spoiled prat a touch more caution before trying to start trouble with me in the future.

Or so I thought.

Like me, he was a slow learner.

And there are prices to be paid for everything.

SEVENTY

PRINCIPLES

Despite the minor joy I felt in being able to spread more stories through the Ashram, my interaction with Rishi Ibrahm had soured my mood more than I could hope to fix.

I skipped my classes for the day, including the offers to meet with Master Mender and Master Lorist for possible work with them. My mind refused to let go of the bindings, and I felt it better to attend to that first.

So I went looking for the only other person I knew who could use them and had a favorable disposition to me.

Master Philosopher and my friend, Vathin.

I found him in his classroom, a lecture hall with raised seating and wide panes of glass running along one wall. A thickly woven rug, holding all the colors of blood and sapphires, fringed with cream white, covered the floor and steps. The desks reminded me of those in the Artisanry, clean bright wood and solid enough to withstand several hammer blows.

Students rose to their feet and began filtering out of the class as soon as I'd arrived.

Vathin caught me watching him, and waved me over.

I made my way toward him through the crowd. As I passed, I overheard several of the students whispering just loud enough to reach my ears.

"Leya saw Master Binder lead him to the Crow's Nest," said a young man.

"Think maybe he's already cracked?" The young woman by his side looked to him, then saw me watching and fell silent.

"Already? I think he came in cracked. Who walks the fire instead of taking a cold cell?" Another male in the group tapped his skull a couple of times to accentuate his point. "I think he's enjoying his last few free moments before they lock him up."

A girl who looked older than the rest of the students hadn't noticed me yet and broke into a snicker. "If he's lucky. If not, they might just let him go on as is. He'll end up like Miri, or worse."

I hadn't heard that name before, but something in the way she'd said it made me burn it into my mind.

The other students fell quiet at the name and gave the woman long looks that said more of being quiet than any words could have. She took their cue and adopted silence.

I took that as my moment to lean into their group. "He did take me to the Crow's Nest, but the interesting story is what happened afterward. If you haven't heard it yet, I guess you're too far behind the important news . . ." I paused and dropped my voice to a conspiratorial whisper. "And even further from the important circles."

That had the effect I had hoped for.

They shot me glowers so similar they must have practiced them together. But I also saw the quick nonverbal exchanges they made with one another, likely all wondering what gossip they had missed and who to go to for it.

With any luck, they'd ask different sources and hear just as many takes on what had happened between me and Rishi Ibrahm in the courtyard. The rest of the group closed in around the woman, forming a tight-knit circle to keep me from speaking to any of them with ease.

I left them to it. Their own curiosity would lead them to where I wanted them to go.

Vathin stepped off the dais he'd been lecturing from, snatching up the staff that had been resting against the stone lectern.

A binder's cane? I wasn't sure, but he was among the few rishis in the Ashram—masters even—who had a staff of any sort. And I knew from my admittance that Rishi Vruk also happened to know some of the bindings. Enough to qualify as having proficiency with them.

I gave the staff a closer look as he walked toward me.

It held all the black of night in it with an ornament of metal atop that caught what light filled the room. The crown shone of solid silver, cut and shaped to resemble a wolf's head down to the details of its fur. Quality craftsmanship that must have set the Master Philosopher back a figure measured in gold.

He tilted the staff toward me, enough for my gaze to lock with the two gemstones that served as the wolf's eyes. Golden-yellow crystals as large as the tips of my thumbs. Citrine if I had to make a guess.

"Ari!" He spread his arms wide, offering me a hug that I gladly stepped into. "How goes it, *sin*?" Vathin pulled himself out of the embrace and set a hand on my shoulder. He squeezed the muscle gently before giving me a shake. "You look a touch rough." He hadn't spoken it like a question, but one hung in his words nonetheless.

"Between nearly being burned by doing my penance, Nitham trying to piss on my candle whenever he can, and dealing with Master Binder . . . just fine." I gave him a stare that told him everything was not in fact close to fine.

Vathin frowned. "Ah. Well, when you put it that way." He gestured to one of the long wooden benches at the front of the class. "Sit?"

I nodded and muttered a thanks.

He joined me and leaned back, releasing a long, drawn-out sigh. "So, what's really eating at your liver, hm? It's not walking the fire and don't pretend it is. Oh, sure, I'm certain it irked you plenty, but don't act like you weren't a clever little shit about it. Everyone's already saying you managed it without so much as a scalded toe." Vathin stopped and eyed me sideways, then narrowed his gaze. "How did you do it anyways?"

I waggled my fingers, much like Rishi Ibrahm had. "Magic." My body lurched to one side in something close to what had happened with Master Binder. I recovered and rubbed the part of my arm where Vathin had shoved me hard.

"All right then, keep your secrets, you little shit." He let out a rolling laugh and waggled his fingers like someone pretending to cast a spell out of children's stories. "Magic, hm. May as well be if you don't let slip how you did it."

I thought back to Master Mender working it out rather quickly and felt pride well up inside me. If only one person could suss out how I'd done it, that wasn't so bad a thing.

"So, what is it then, Ari-*cha*?" I appreciated Vathin for that all the more. Out of all the rishis in the Ashram, he was the only one who treated me like a friend. No, more than that, almost like an adopted son.

First, I told him of the walls I'd hit in my research into the Ashura. It hurt to keep the whole truth from him, but I didn't need him judging me like Rishi Saira had in the Scriptory.

He stroked his chin as he mused on all I'd said. "That's a new one. The Ashura hide in mountains, huh? And all to keep people from finding them? That doesn't sound close to true. Why would they need to hide?" Vathin didn't give me a chance to answer as he went on. "If that were the case, I wager you and everyone else would catch sight of them every now and again up in the mountains of Sathvan. Maybe out in Tharam, or Ampur?"

I nodded. "Most of it was useless."

He arched a brow. "Most?" I waited for Vathin to press the point, but he didn't. "Ah, I'm sorry, Ari-*cha*. It's a hard thing when we don't get the answers we want, but I'm sure if you keep digging, you'll find something, ah?" He gave me a look filled with more hope than I felt comfortable ignoring, so I gave him a false smile.

"What's wrong? There's more going on with you, isn't there?"

I sighed, letting some of the tension flee my back and shoulders. "It's Rishi Ibrahm. Him and his cracked skull, I swear. He refuses to teach me the bindings, even though I've shown I can do the folds—something that I haven't seen any other students be able to do, by the way." I stopped and took a breath, remembering what I'd seen in the Crow's Nest and how he'd reacted when I accused him of failing the students there.

I swallowed and felt my voice weaken. "He took me to the Crow's Nest." I let my words hang in the air, hoping the implication was clear to Rishi Vruk.

He sat forward, resting his elbows on his knees. "He did, did he? Mhm. Showed you some of the former students?"

I nodded.

"Ah. It's a hard thing, Ari. I've seen some of them before, not that I make a habit of going there, mind you. And . . ." He cleared his throat and stared off to the stone lectern. "I've been there at times when some of the students crack. It's never a pretty thing, and it's something you don't forget as a rishi. Worse if you're a student at the time." He sounded more like someone talking about a close friend dying rather than going slightly mad.

I knew enough not to push for a better answer. Whatever Vathin had seen deserved to remain behind the private doors of his heart until he felt comfortable enough to open them to me. Changing the subject would be the better course, so I chose that.

"He used some of the bindings on me. Treated it like a damn test." I kept myself from telling him exactly what Rishi Ibrahm had done, though. "Master Binder told me to try to sort out the bindings myself—figure out how they work and the principles behind them. I think I have an idea on one or two, but even then, I'm not sure."

Vathin interlocked his fingers and stretched his arms to elicit a series of small pops from his joints. A pleasurable groan left his mouth. "Getting old is tiresome, and the cold here doesn't help." He took a deep breath and shut his eyes. "Principles are a tricky thing, Ari. More so with the bindings. But let's start there, *and* let's ignore the fact Rishi Ibrahm clearly told you to work these out alone, hm?"

I grinned. "Already forgotten."

He opened one eye and stared at me before shutting it. "Didn't say forget, did I? I said ignore." Vathin grunted and motioned to shove me again but I'd moved out of the way. One corner of his mouth twitched, betraying the smile he wanted to break into. "You know what the foundations of the bindings are?"

I nodded, then remembered he couldn't see me. "Yes. The Athir, the pillars of faith. The will to enforce your will on the world around you."

"Mhm. We create our own realities. Well, as much as a binder can. But yes. Faith. A nebulous thing. Tenuous at best. Brittle or as hard as diamonds. Depends on the man." He peered through two barely open slits to watch me. "Depends on what the man's been through. Principles change with time, and they change the man who holds them. But what is faith? Some might say a man's principles are tied to his faith. Defined by them."

I nudged Master Philosopher with an elbow, keeping the gesture light and short of being painful. "Someone might say a rishi could get to the point without the prancing about like a show horse."

"I suppose I could take an even longer time, hm? Since we're just talking, that is. Or are we supposed to be discussing anything important?" Vathin's face tightened to become a hard mask, but I knew the truth behind it. It was the face he wore when trying doubly hard to keep from laughing.

I played his game and relented. "Fine-fine. As you were, Master Philosopher." My head stung and a spot of white danced in front of my eyes. "Ow." I rubbed the part of my head he'd slapped with the tip of his fingers. The blow wasn't close to hard, just enough to jar me.

"Don't patronize me, Ari." He cleared his throat and crossed his arms in mock frustration. "Where was I?"

I bit my tongue and kept from giving a clever answer. On occasion, rare ones admittedly, I could keep my mouth shut.

"Right. Ari, the way the bindings work are not just based in and on faith, yes? They have principles to which they apply. But what are principles if not a sort of faith—a belief?"

I thought for a moment. "Sure, but tell Master Mender that the principles behind properly setting bone are down to faith and interpretation rather than science and practice. That would go over well." My tone dripped of a sarcasm sharp enough to cut the stone lectern.

He ignored the comment. "They are all ideas, Ari. Principles, ideas, connections. But are they ever truly set in stone?" He shrugged. "I'm not so sure. I know how the bindings work, but even then, I wonder still. Are they ever set? Are they?"

I frowned. "Aren't they?"

He rolled his shoulders in a shrug more halfhearted than the previous one. "Maybe, but they're set by and in the minds of men, no? Who says the bindings work how they do because of external principles rather than the ones men impose on them? I don't know. That's the thing about principles. Sometimes it feels like they're held together by belief more than anything else. And man can believe many terrible or amazing things. Up to the man, I suppose. And what do they do with those beliefs?

"Oh, those can change the world. For better or worse. History has shown both to be true, history and the many who lived and suffered through it." More of Vathin's strength looked to leave him as he slumped against the wooden bench. "But for the bindings? I only know of them as I've come to think of them. I know the ones I do well enough to work them as I think they're supposed to. And maybe that's my problem. I'm too old and tired to think of them any other way. Maybe if I could . . . maybe they'd be different, and maybe I would too. Who knows? But the beliefs a man holds change him too—shape him."

All things Rishi Ibrahm had implied, some clear as glass. And now looking at Vathin, I could see the strain just thinking of the bindings could put on a man. He looked years older than the already aged man I'd come to know.

"I think all this philosophy has cracked you worse than Rishi Ibrahm." I knew he'd take the comment for what it really was: a light joke to make him laugh, or at least rouse him into a petulant action. Anything to lift him out of his tiredness.

His eyes snapped open and he eyed me askance. "Cracked, am I?" He grabbed his staff and tapped it twice against an open palm. "Back in my day, we had a way of dealing with students like you." Another *thwap* of his binder's cane as it struck the flesh of his hand. "I'd crack this proper across your mouthy ass."

I grinned and adopted my most respectful tone. "That would be most improper, Master Philosopher."

He got to his feet but I'd already moved across the aisle between the benches to sit down elsewhere in the room. Notably well outside the reach of his staff. Vathin stared at me for a moment before chuckling. "Not so clever now, are you?"

I met his eyes when I spoke. "Cleverness is like faith. What is it really? Who can say what makes someone well and truly—" I broke off and yelped as he set after me, whirling his staff overhead.

"I swear I'll give you a reason to be admitted to the Crow's Nest, you little . . ." I lost sight and ear of what he'd turned to saying. Mostly because I never saw the point in remembering what string of profanities people applied to me.

I'd earned an impressive share by that time in my life.

Too many to properly recall.

He eventually gave up the chase, tiring around the last rows of seats before he sank into the nearest one.

I watched him, not entirely certain if his fatigue was a ruse to draw me closer so he could make good on his threat of thumping me. Certain that it wasn't, I went over to him and took a seat at his side. "Done trying to send me off to the Crow's Nest?"

He grunted, which I took to mean he hadn't ruled the idea out yet. "Stop bothering the elderly, Ari, and go make trouble with people your age." The words held no edge or anger.

"I've done a bit of that too and it didn't go well. Nitham?"

A thin smile spread across Vathin's face but faded just as fast. "Wrong sort to make trouble with. Aim lower. Maybe someone who doesn't have as much money and influence as he has friends."

I glowered. "He has the influence and friends he does because he has the money to buy them."

Vathin gave me a knowing look. "And *that* is all the more reason to not poke that particular bear and let him sleep. Go make trouble with women. I certainly did at your age." He winked at me and gave me far too lecherous a look for someone of his age.

I stared at him, then frowned as I brought up my fingers and began counting on them. "How long ago was that? I don't think we have a measurement system that goes back that far and—*ow*!" I clutched the top of my head.

Vathin pulled his hand back from where he'd struck me. "I barely tapped you. For a young man, you've a king's sense of high drama."

I opened my mouth to spit a retort but realized I'd prove him right if I did.

"Ah, he can learn." Vathin smiled. "So while I have you quiet and willing to listen to an old man, let me give you another piece of advice concerning the bindings and Rishi Ibrahm, hm?"

I nodded.

"As touched as he might be up here"—Vathin tapped the side of his head—"the man *is* a brilliant binder. To make master by his age is no common thing, Ari. Not at all. Consider that he might know what he's talking about and why he may not be rushing to tell every student how to work them, ah?"

I knew that to be true, but it didn't mean it was something I wanted to hear.

Vathin went on. "If he wants you to be patient and show him you're capable of learning, then do that. What do you lose in waiting sets, or seasons even?"

Time. But then, I'd lost that already. Years since Koli killed my family. Him and the Ashura. *A chance to learn the bindings faster so with what time passed after that, I could master them.* And that hardly mattered, I realized, because if I never warmed Rishi Ibrahm up to teaching me in the first place, I could hardly become proficient without knowing the basics.

I exhaled, knowing Vathin to be right. "I have to do something, though." I clenched my hands several times, trying to work through my mounting frustration.

Rishi Vruk clapped a hand to my shoulder. "I know that. But sometimes doing nothing is doing something."

I eyed him, wondering if that had been a piece of cleverly annoying philosophy, or something sincere. His stoic look told me it had been the latter and I relaxed. "Any more advice?"

He cocked a brow. "For you, I have a world of advice." His mouth twitched, but no smile. "But for now, we'll start small. Tend to your other studies. The Ashram isn't as boring a place as you might think. There is a reason people study artisanry before moving to try their hand at the bindings. Devote time there. Some find new mental clarity while working with Master Conditioner . . . or they get some sense knocked into them." He gave me a hard long look.

I grinned.

". . . And some have it knocked out. Goes either way, I suppose. Work with Master Spiritualist. Take the time to meditate and improve your mind. Master Lorist. Any of them. You have the time, Ari, and the bindings won't go anywhere. I promise you."

I sighed and accepted the argument. "You're right, Rishi Vruk."

He collapsed further in his seat, sliding so far down that his back lay against the bottom with most of his body hanging off. A hand slapped against his chest, clutching at it, and for a moment, I thought something had gone terribly wrong. Vathin gasped for air. "Oh, Brahm above, did you hear him, oh Lord? I'm right he says. Never did I ever think to hear those words from a student like him. Something must be—" He broke off and stared at me. "Ari, putting your hands on a rishi, a master no less, is an offense at the Ashram."

I pulled my staff back and raised an index finger. "Technically, good Master Philosopher, I did not put a hand on you at all. I did, however, have the tip of my staff make sharp contact with your side. Your ribs, if we're being accurate, but for a moment as short as it takes to suck in a sharp breath this chilly day."

He narrowed his eyes. "I'm beginning to think I'm a bad influence on you, Ari. Too much philosophy for an already sharp tongue can buy a man much trouble." A light sparked in his eyes, one that told me he waited eagerly to see how much trouble my tongue could buy me next.

And knowing Vathin, he would use it to teach me a lesson if he could.

I cleared my throat and got to my feet. "Thank you very much for the advice, Master Philosopher. I think I'll be going now to do my best at becoming a more diligent and attentive student."

He grunted. "I think you misspoke the word *'respectful,'* Ari. Try to become a more respectful student."

I'd made my way toward the doors, lingering in the open space. "Of course, that's what I meant." I gave him a grin that told him I'd do nothing of the sort.

He returned a rather obscene hand gesture before I stepped out of sight.

I left feeling lighter than when I had come to Vathin. He always had that effect on me. I was grateful for it. The Master Philosopher had given me a path to process everything up until now and focus myself.

Maybe he was right. In time I'd come to work my way toward impressing Rishi Ibrahm.

So I took his advice and pursued the other disciplines offered me with the same fervency I had my training of the folds and in leading the sparrows.

If I couldn't learn the bindings, I'd set about learning everything else the Ashram had to offer.

SEVENTY-ONE

BROKEN STRINGS

I took the following set of days to idle in my classes. I don't mean to imply I wasted my time and didn't pay attention. No, I let myself sift through them, absorbing information passively to see what sparked my inner fire.

Vathin's advice hadn't been wrong. The connection to the ten bindings and artisanry stood out as obvious. It pulled at me as a means of working my way toward what I wanted. So I stayed after one class and spoke with Master Artisan, discussing the possibility of apprenticing myself there.

It had been as easy as asking.

My first day in the Artisanry as an apprentice included the tedious familiarization with all the tools that went into the practice. Specialized engravers, tipped with diamonds to ensure they could carve into any surface. Chisels and mallets should you need to shape something. Ink pens, the construction of which eluded me at that point in my life but I strongly suspected were fashioned by the minor bindings. And of course, graphters.

Artisanry doesn't involve a set of bindings the way the major bindings are concerned. It involves words or characters that symbolize simple meanings and can then be combined to elicit certain effects. The complexity of those increase by the artisan's talents and understanding of them. Not to mention, their will and Athir.

To make an ice box, for example, a student would have to inscribe the characters or words for heat, direction, and movement. All of those would form a sentence of their own that funneled heat in the right direction and away from the core of the box. But that wasn't enough. You would have to put in a level of control, or you would simply circulate all possible heat the box could manage to move at once. That would do you no good and create a dangerous situation.

So you worked in words for speed, managing how quickly or slowly the bindings removed the box's heat. But how do you tell the box when to stop?

Well, if it's not supposed to, you work in a word for constancy, ensuring the box continued this slow and steady process of removing heat to maintain a certain cold temperature at all times. That means it needs a baseline to understand when to stop moving heat past a limit, otherwise the box would grow colder than needed.

So, most ice boxes—the properly made ones, at least—have a character for ice engraved. This keeps the box at a temperature needed to freeze water and maintain it. Nothing more.

Artisanry was a language all to itself, in truth. And learning it took many a proper season. I looked at it another way.

As stories. And I quickly got to wondering at the stories I could tell with it. My first began with strings.

The season wound down to its end and we found ourselves facing Tharaan, shifting season, the time of year between monsoon and winter, where and when the world changed its face and things began to die.

It also signaled the oncoming of the festival Athrayaan, sister to Rayaan. Another celebration marked with bright and colorful kites to mirror the change in hues of the mountains and trees.

I knew people back in Keshum and the greater kingdom would be taking to rooftops and streets to fly kites and engage in battle. Some would be betting coins between friends—others holding competitions for more illicit gambling to take place. Some would be going as far as using the festival to conduct black market trade and pass ill goods for clean coin.

And the Ashram, for all its wise and intelligent minds, was no better a place. After all, many students were young men and women, and the young have always been inclined to mischief, mayhem, and dirty dealings.

I'd already caught wind of rumors detailing the gambling circuits among students, as well as those who'd taken to spending their sets preparing kites and sharp string to fly in the festival.

Ghal's climate offered another sort of challenge that students took to with a will. The air carried all the sharpness and cold of the icy mountains, making it a far cry different to fly a kite here than in the more stable climate of Abhar. Clean and dry warm air offered little trouble.

I'd seen students working out how to bind glass, even shards of metal, to their strings to better cut their opponents'. One student tried to be overly clever and work in bindings to his kite to better catch and circulate wind around it, giving it an advantage to fly higher and faster.

In theory, at least.

In reality, he ended up nearly losing a finger as the kite tore off with preternatural speed, digging the string into his smallest digit with enough force to tear well into it. Master Mender had been able to repair the damage, but the poor man never did get his kite back.

It sailed far off over the mountains, and some students had a wager that it was still out there, climbing ever higher.

So, the need was obvious. Students, and even some of the rishis, wanted for good kites and properly decent string. Someone who had better cordage, however, had a distinct advantage in the fights. A good kite could only do so much if your string broke. But a decent kite with unbreakable string?

Well, you could hardly lose the competition if no one could bring your craft down.

And I had a feeling people would pay a good deal for string twice as tough as anything else. So I confronted Master Artisan one day and told her of what I wished to spend my apprenticeship on.

"You want to spend several sets working on . . . string?" She blinked and frowned, but otherwise said nothing else.

I nodded. "*Ji.*"

"Why?"

I could have told her the truth, that my aim was less than aspirational or even noble. That I simply wanted to make something that could tilt the odds in the upcoming kite festival to ones I could profit from. Not to mention the fact I intended to enter a kite of my own, knowing full well that Nitham had paid a great sum to have someone engineer his entry.

How would he react to having his prized piece fail?

I can't lie and say the thought didn't bring me a great deal of pleasure. And I would savor my winnings all the more should I be the one to beat him. But these feelings were better left unsaid to Master Artisan. So I crafted a believable-enough lie that had enough of the truth in it.

"Tougher strings would have a lot of value. They're overlooked, but how many people go through bundles in everyday use? Laborers, packagers, travelers, even clothiers? They break, fray, and rot. Stronger strings would make better bindings, have better use in mendery, and probably other things." I shrugged.

She pursed her lips, thinking it over. "I suppose so. Still, it's rather unusual for an Accepted. Most try to impress me with something bold."

I thought on that for a moment, then over what I'd learned talking to older students. First-time apprentices in any discipline rarely ascended to the rank of Kaethar in the Ashram. That meant the usual methods and creations hardly worked. "Bold doesn't mean successful, respectfully, Rishi Bharia."

She inclined her head. "True enough. But, engraving on string isn't possible. You'll tear it. You'll have to use ink—carefully at that. Most strings will blot and smear with the liquid, staining deep and ruining the characters. You'll have to be clever." Her mouth twisted into an uneven smile that told me she was curious to see what I'd do.

"Haven't you heard, Master Artisan? I *am* clever. Some would say too much so." I matched her smile.

Hers faltered and she peered at me down her nose as if weighing me. "Then I'm all the more excited to see what you fashion. Will you be needing to rent tools to use outside of the Artisanry? Or will you only be working here?"

I thought on that. If I made my efforts visible within the Artisanry, people would catch sight of what I was up to. I didn't want that. "I'll need to rent them." My gut roiled. While I had the coin to ensure a comfortable living at the Ashram, I'd been going through it quickly of late.

I'd already gone down to fifteen doles. My mind froze as I realized how far my life had changed. There had been a time when one dole would have been all the money in the world to me, and now I worried about having more than ten times that.

Still, times change us, and as they do, our worries and hopes shift with them. And every coin that left me brought me closer to becoming Ari the Sparrow again. The coinless one. The beggar, the thief, and the boy who'd forgotten his dreams.

Forgotten the promise of the bindings and what to live for.

"How much will it be?"

"You won't be needing engravers." She spoke more to herself than me. "Ink, of course. Pens, tips, strings, will you be needing or wanting a sealant?"

The Artisanry produced different liquids that dried and could even harden from contact with air. They created a lacquer-like coating for some substances, but at times, the rigidity they offered cost you flexibility. And I couldn't risk that for my strings. I'd have to come up with another solution.

I shook my head. "No. Just the strings and ink, I suppose. Oh, and a booklet on the character guides, if we have them."

She eyed me sideways. "We do, but they're not available for Accepted, even the Kaethar. Those are only available to Fhaldar ranks, Rhindar, possibly Brahmir, if they've shown some results from their study and time in artisanry."

I hadn't known there were ranks above Fhaldar. "What's a Brahmir?"

Rishi Bharia's mouth tightened. "It's not for me to tell you. If you reach the rank and impress the proper masters, you'll know. As for now, focus on your apprenticeship."

I nodded, knowing I'd get nothing else from her.

"As for the material, it will cost you a copper round. That will get you eight bundles of string, and the pens and tips and ink. The pens and tips will have to be returned when you're done, of course."

"Of course."

The line of her jaw hardened and brought a sharpness to her cheeks when she next spoke. "That will also cover the expenses should you damage the pens or the tips." Her tone could have peeled the finish from every wooden table in the Artisanry. It was clear that my health, and likely my life, would be better off returning the tools in pristine condition.

I swallowed the lump that had formed in my throat. "Of course, Master Artisan."

The cold mask left her face and she smiled. "Excellent. See Kaethar Estra in Holds. She'll see you get what you need and take accounting for it."

I left, making my way to the greater storage room that joined the Artisanry.

Holds lived up to its name and operated as a place to keep the Artisanry's stock of materials to sell and rent to students. It's also where the Ashram kept its better fabrications to sell to the world and how the place made its money in addition to serving as a bank for traders and the student donations.

The place, much like the Artisanry, was fashioned out of hard bright woods and resilient stone. Its construction ensured the walls couldn't be damaged by the various things made by students.

Some tended to be dangerous.

A young woman sat at a curved desk that barred the way into Holds proper, its counter running from one end of the room to the other. She had her hair done in half a dozen braids holding tight to her scalp. Every strand carried all the whiteness of clouds, much like Eira's. Her skin was a shade paler and her eyes reminded me of frozen puddles, more gray than holding any hint of water's blue. A rarity.

She found me staring and gave me a thin smile. "I still get that a lot." Her voice was softer than a breath of winter air.

"Sorry. I'm not used to it. Most I've seen outside my own"—I pulled a length of my dark hair—"is red. Sometimes it's dyed, sometimes it's people from outside Abhar who have that kind, you know?"

Estra nodded and touched her own hair. "It's not that uncommon past the mountains. Lots of Sathvani people look like this. There's . . ." She trailed off and bit one corner of her lip. "There's a taboo of seeing people outside our own there. It's different and they never really came into the Mutri. They don't even worship Brahm there, or any of the other gods in the Empire. Same with the Sithre."

I blinked. I didn't know what to make of that. Everywhere in the Empire people followed Brahm's path, even if they chose to focus more on one of the other gods as their personal patron.

Master Conditioner openly adhered to the practices and worship of Hahn, god of strength, champions, and wrestlers. Everyone knew that, but he believed in Brahm nonetheless.

I thought on Sathvan's name and tried to suss out its history, but couldn't recall it from any stories I'd heard. "Sathvan doesn't sound Brahmthi, or even Brahmki?"

Estra shook her head. "It's not. It's older, before the kingdoms even came under Mutri as one empire. Some say it was the language from before the kingdoms and Brahmki came about. What they spoke before Brahm ever walked the world and people started converting. They still worship the natural gods there."

I frowned. "Natural gods?"

"Nagh-lokh. The Great River Serpent. Or Tabreshu, the Mountain Shepherd and deity. There are too many for me to count, and my mother only told me about them near festivals or to keep me scared if I was misbehaving." She gave me a smirk and stare so wicked, that even after all my mischief and misdoings, I grew uncomfortable.

"I've never heard of any of those things, but I'd like to . . . if you want to tell me more about them sometime?" I gave her a sincere smile, and her cheeks flushed, though at the time, I didn't know why. The idea stories and creatures existed outside what I knew baffled and excited me. It felt like discovering a whole new kind of magic, one that was within reach so long as Estra was willing to share it with me.

Far more so than the bindings, at least.

She ran her fingers through her hair, idly picking at one of her braids. "I think I can make time for that. I work Holds most days, though. I'm here from fourth candle to sixth. I'm free day after tomorrow." She flashed me a wide smile and a hint of brightness touched the cool gray of her eyes.

"I can do that."

Her grin widened. "So what can I do for you until then?"

I rattled off the list of what I needed for my project and she jotted it down on a piece of parchment.

"It'll be a copper flat."

I fished out a single silver dole and placed it on the table. "Perfectly one copper?" I had expected it to be within a degree of that, of course, but not exactly that. Master Artisan's calculation had been uncannily accurate. Then I realized she must have familiarized herself with the pricing of everything inside Holds long ago. She may as well have been a tallier as much as an artisan.

Estra bobbed her head and took the coin. "Wait here. Will you need a bag for the materials?"

I almost waved her off, then remembered Rishi Bharia's threats, not to mention the thought of keeping ink bottles in my sack. Should one break, I'd risk my rolls of parchment, notes, and possibly Mahrab's book. I kept the latter on me more out of habit and for comfort.

I liked having it on hand. It felt right while I was at the Ashram.

Estra returned with none of the materials, but had coins in hand. She placed forty-seven iron bunts and fifteen copper rounds on the table.

I collected them and answered her question. "Yes please. But I'll keep the string bundles in my own sack. I'm worried the ink could spill and stain them before I get to working with them."

"All ink bottles out of Holds are engraved to be strong enough to resist a hammer blow. You'd really have to try to break one to make it happen, and even then, many come short."

I hadn't known that either. "Does the Ashram sell this glass?"

She waggled her hand. "In small batches, and usually fabricated to someone's specifications. Nobles use it in their homes to prevent easy breakage and just as much as a safety measure. There's a mariam in the Kingdom of Rathum who had his lordling home furnished with it. He's afraid of cutthroats breaking in and taking his life and fortune."

The mariam were local lords of provinces or cities within kingdoms helping manage the smaller pieces to alleviate the burden of governance on the higher rulers—the sort of people who could afford the Ashram's rarified goods like ice boxes or binder's lights.

"It's a good way to make simple money, but the cutting, shaping, and artisanry can be time consuming. Let me get your materials." Estra shuffled off and vanished farther into Holds.

She came back after what felt like a third of a candlemark, although I knew that not to be true. A canvas bag hung from one of her hands. In the grip of the other she held a length of twine in which were wrapped half a dozen bundles of string. She placed both on the table and gave them a gentle push in my direction. "If you change your mind about needing anything else, let me know."

I thanked her. "I will. And I'll see you the day after tomorrow, then." I grabbed the bag containing my inscription tools and stowed the bundles of string into my own sack.

Estra fidgeted with one of her braids, looking away for a moment before returning to meet my gaze. Her farewell smile was wider as she waved me off.

I headed straight to my room and set about designing the plans for teaching Nitham a sharp lesson, one he'd remember all the more when it came to the cost of the coins he was sure to lose during the upcoming festival.

SEVENTY-TWO

Tinkers, Tedium, and Time Away

Studying in class is no substitute for doing the deed itself. Let it be known. My first efforts in artisanry led me to nearly tearing my hair from my head. I understood the theory, sure. The practice? I had that down as well.

None of that made my will reality, however.

There were too many things to take into account. One, the strings. The sort of string used in kite flying was not the thick string used in wrapping packages or cinching a satchel shut.

These were fine braids of silver sliver-thin strands, no thicker than a few hairs. Sharp enough on their own, and when slicked and coated with crushed glass, they were as good as a saw to work through skin, sinew, and bone.

All of which meant they were maddeningly difficult to inscribe. The surface was too small to make any legible characters.

And I knew that before starting, meaning I could barely muster the mental focus to begin the connection part of artisanry. What point was there in trying to imprint my will on something too small to later inscribe?

I realized how difficult a task I'd chosen and gained a new appreciation for artisans who crafted something new and creative to add to the Ashram's Holds.

When I admitted to myself that I couldn't begin my project right away, I turned to working out what possibilities I had with the strings. Artisanry allowed for many alterations to material, but was limited regardless of your belief, despite that being a key component to the bindings—minor, or any of the major ten.

All things had their own inherent deficiencies and properties to take into account. And string was no different.

Mine was sharp, strong, and flexible. But it was not unbreakable by any measure. While you might lose some of your skin trying, and quite possibly risk the loss of a finger, you could snap a length of the string with your bare hands. And it fell apart as easily as anything else under the blades of shears or knives. So, what to do then?

Kite fighting worked by pitting sawlike strings against each other like gnashing teeth on flesh. Push, pull, tear, rip. The actions savagely split the strings apart until the force of the flyer and the lift of the kite finished the job. Fraying bits would give way and your kite sailed free.

So my plan had to revolve around conditioning the string to handle the sawing set against it. But I couldn't simply will the string to become unbreakable. That was not in the nature of string, and I had to work within that.

String could bend, go taut, be twisted, stretch and bind, and do a great many things all to its credit. But in the end, strings are made to be broken. *That* was their nature. To want otherwise was to wish to change its nature, and I didn't have that power. But maybe I could find another way.

I had learned in the Artisanry how basic forces of motion worked, and I had an idea of how to tackle the friction between the competing strings, which, when reduced to the basics, came down to the duality of pushing and pulling. The glass shards only served to increase that friction. But if I could transfer that friction into something else, I could in theory spare the strings.

At best, I'd buy them time.

But time was all one needed to win in kite fighting.

I laid out my ideas on a piece of parchment, still short on how to inscribe the bindings I needed on so small a surface, but at least this way I'd have the fundamentals in place when I eventually figured out the latter.

My efforts led me to the secret understanding all great Artisans must come to at one point or another. That all craftsmen and creators work better on a full stomach.

I left my parchment of messy jottings on the floor of my room, heading out to Clanks in hope of something hot, something to take my mind off strings and glass and away from schemes concerning Nitham.

Sometimes we all need time away from thoughts and things.

I reached Clanks and tried to find an open spot away from the crowds of late-night students. Many of them cast flickering gazes toward me only to turn away when I caught them. A few turned up the collars of their robes, using them to shield their faces as they spoke to one another in passing, likely about me.

I couldn't revel in that as I hadn't discerned *what* it was they were saying. That matters more than the fact that they were talking about me. To build the story around myself I wanted, I needed people to be telling the right pieces. Not just anything.

A sharp bird whistle cut through the nightly staccato-rhythm of clanking trays and cups.

I looked for the source and found Radi waving from a mostly open table. Aram sat with her back against the counter, legs crossed, and writing on parchment pressed to a board for support. I returned the wave and rushed over to them. "What are they serving tonight?"

Radi's expression slipped into the sort of glumness found in children who'd just been told to eat their vegetables instead of treats. "Sweet yams, spiced spinach, fahaan, and goat kebabs."

My mouth hung open. I couldn't decide whether to shake sense into my friend, or take advantage of his misplaced misery and eat his share as well as get my own. Those words could only have come from someone who had never known a profound hunger and how it comes to take your tongue.

Still, the distaste of some men can come to be the salivating pleasure of others . . . and just as much as salvation. My work had made me as hungry as when I'd been a young sparrow.

"I'll be back." I tapped an open hand to Radi's shoulder, giving Aram an acknowledging nod as I raced over to the still-long line of the Narrows. Aptly named for the long thin canals running through the stone counter housing all the massed quantities of food. A length of dark marble ran for nearly forty feet, tin trays occupying the channels carved into it. And within those, what I had come for.

One such row, as long as I was tall, held all the dark orange and unctuousness of the mashed and seasoned sweet yams. The surface had been dusted with cinnamon and brown sugar, still sending up steam in places. The edges of the tin basin sported symbols and words I knew to be minor bindings of heat and motion, carrying and holding the food's natural warmth and passing it along.

I jabbed a finger with more enthusiasm than necessary at the mash, and a monk working the section ladled heaping portions onto my tray. My ears naturally tuned to the renewed whispering behind me, but a second of listening told me enough.

People spoke more about the fact I'd come into no end of trouble or attention of late, but not the nature of what that was.

I ignored the poor gossip and collected the remainder of my meal, making sure to grab water as well. Radi and Aram were engaged in conversation when I returned, setting my plate deliberately down by Radi's. I had designs for his food when I'd finished with my own.

"—coin all gone by the end of the year at this rate," said Aram. She reached out to the remains of Radi's tray, tearing free a piece of the fahaan—the thin stone-baked flatbread. She folded it with a thumb and forefinger and pushed it into the spiced spinach and tossed it into her mouth.

I caught myself glaring at her before anyone else noticed. While I hadn't announced my desire to pluck through Radi's food, it had become a customary practice for me to be given the left-behinds. I turned my attention to my own food, savoring the first bite of warm sweet yams. My hunger surprised me in that I hadn't realized how fast I'd gone through most of my meal, now breaking apart my bread to take the small hunks of goat along with the remaining pieces.

It tore with some effort, coming with the slightly tough chew of the meat that I had actually grown quite fond of.

Radi and Aram continued talking around me, half aware I was even there. "Should make a racket of this, get a rate going and see how many masters he'll piss on before the year is up." Radi played a pair of notes on his mandolin that almost sounded like *chagrin,* insofar as music can sound like emotion.

Aram shrugged and took some of Radi's remaining sweet yams, spreading a spoonful of clarified butter over it. She swallowed the mouthful and spoke through chewing. "You're giving our Ari too little credit here, Radi. He has a knack for riling rishis and students alike that borders the magical." She shot me a sideways look and smiled.

I didn't return it, figuring it better to stuff my mouth with food lest I give her a side of my tongue she didn't want to hear from.

"While I'm in no serious need of money . . ." Radi plucked a few more notes from his mandolin, playing with the idleness that said he did this in every spare moment he could find. "I am curious to see how far a pair of ears Ari's antics have reached." A bright gleam entered Radi's eyes. "And what we can do with that. Because I think we can turn a hefty hand of copper from this."

"At least." Aram nodded in agreement before taking another piece of food from Radi's tray.

I finally relented, abhorring the idea of them talking about me without letting me know what they were on about. "Would either of you two like to tell me what you're talking about? Because if not, have you considered shutting the hell up?"

Radi plucked a few more strings, sending out a pair of notes that almost sounded like *complaint—sadness.* Something else hung beneath the surface of those, a tone that could have been *comical* as well. I paid it little mind, in truth.

"There's his temper. I swear, Ari, it's like you've got this fire up your ass you haven't decided what to do with. Either spit it up, or shit it out. Someone says the wrong thing—splash!" He smacked a hand to the table, drawing a loud thump from it. "Oil to flame. It goes crazy and spreads into something dangerous." He gave me a knowing look. "And someone gets burned. You too, in your case."

I narrowed my eyes but deigned it wiser to not respond lest I prove his point.

"People are talking about the fight you had with Rishi Ibrahm—high up in the Crow's Nest." Aram nudged me with an elbow, prompting me to either deny it or clarify.

I took a perverse pleasure in drawing out her anticipation as I stuffed my mouth with another spoonful of sweet yam mash. I chewed, making it clear I deliberately prolonged my answer.

She mirrored my earlier expression and turned her eyes to slits.

I swallowed. "That's certainly the take on it. Do they say why we fought?"

Aram shrugged. "Too many reasons to know, really. You confronted him about some binder's secrets, he refused, you showed him you know some of the bindings and challenged him to a duel. If you won, he would have to mentor you. If you lost, you're either kicked from his classes, or to be locked up in the Crow's Nest." Aram eyed me askance. "So, which is it?"

I refused to answer. "What else do they say?"

Radi drew another pair of notes from the mandolin. I thought of them as *thoughtful, questioning.* "They say your battle . . . or whatever it was, shook the Crow's Nest and the world around it. Stone broke and fell to the ground. Some students say they saw it themselves. And some of the fallen stones are still there, other pieces vanished midair, so I'm inclined to believe part of it." Radi, to his credit, was no fool. He fixed me with a searching stare. While he didn't know the truth, he didn't easily swallow the rumors either.

A part of me loved him for that. You would think I'd want my friend to easily swallow the gossip and help fan the flames of my reputation, but no. I appreciated that, even after everything, he still saw me first as his troublesome friend.

Even so, I met his look, betraying nothing of the truth.

He sighed and relented, rolling his wrist in a gesture to continue. "Some are saying that you performed a secret binding, one of the rumored forgotten, and doing that cracked you"—he gave me another look to let me know he found that last part believable—"and Rishi Ibrahm wanted to lock you up for everyone's safety. But you fought, and something happened that no one knows. But whatever it was, it changed his mind and you're free . . . for now. He's waiting. Watching." Three notes rang out. *Curiosity. Grinning. Danger.*

"Are you going to tell us what happened?" Aram reached out and finished the remaining food from Radi's tray.

I turned to do the same to mine, guzzling the last dregs of my water as well. "I think you have the bones of it all. But, I can tell by the look on your faces there's more. What is it?"

Aram shied away from my stare, turning to Radi in a silent request for support.

The bard finally set the mandolin down, steepling his hands and resting his chin atop them. "Ari, people are beginning to say odd things. Half man, half demon. Some are whispering things out of old stories like you're a scion of Brahm come again. Maybe a piece of him himself, or him made to walk and wander the world. The shape of these stories are changing, the way songs do, and I know the nature of those. If this goes on, people won't know the real you and only have ears for the stories. It's a dangerous game."

He was right, but I didn't know it then.

Instead, I waggled my spoon at him as if unconcerned by the consequences. "Let them think what they want. All it means is most people will spend more time talking about me and hopefully less time trying to do something to me." My thoughts turned to Nitham.

"I think most will start avoiding you, Ari. And you don't really want that." Aram rested a hand on my shoulder and jostled me lightly. "You don't exactly have many friends."

I glowered at her, but I knew she had a point. Out of the whole Ashram, the two people by my side were the only ones to actively take interest in my life and friendship. Everyone else made small talk at best.

Or, true to Aram's words, stayed away from me.

"Fine." I exhaled and let some of the tension leave my neck and shoulders. "All right, fine. You're right. I'll . . . maybe try to keep some of these things from spreading. I don't know how, but dammit, you can't deny it's been a help. Nitham, Rishi Ibrahm, there's always someone chewing at the back of my heels hoping I'll fall and dash my brains out."

Radi pulled another note. *Truth*—resonating—*agreement*. Then a pair thrummed together to say to me *sympathy*. "Point to Ari on that." The bard tipped the head of his mandolin in my direction. "If you want my advice, though, not that I hear you asking, that is . . ."

"I'm not." I kept from shooting him a mischievous smile as I spoke.

He ignored the comment and went on. "You need to take some time away from things, spend a night out with a girl." Radi waggled his brows in an impressive display of facial control. "Maybe two. Though, we should start you small and within the realm of possibility." Another note sang *wry, kidding*.

I stared at him. "Estra wants to see me day after tomorrow." I took care to say it like it wasn't anything special. In all honesty, I didn't think it was. We'd agreed to talk about her home and hear some of the stories of it. What more could it have been?

But I knew how my friends would take the news.

Radi's fingers tripped over the strings and he fumbled out something that couldn't have hoped to have a meaning, but I caught one in it nonetheless. *Confusion. Wordlessness.* "What? When? Estra? White-haired girl like Eira? *Nnngh.*" His gaze fell to the table and far away from the pair of us, and I could see his thoughts followed.

"What's with him?" I nudged Aram and kept my words to a whisper.

"Eira rebuffed his *charming* advances. He wrote her a song too." Aram flashed a hapless and apologetic smile in Radi's direction.

"Two." Radi held up a pair of fingers. "I wrote her two songs. My very best. How does that happen? Do you know what I can do with words and music? Just . . . how?"

"By saying no, I suppose?" I hadn't meant the comment to be a barb in his side, but Radi's expression worsened. But before I could apologize, he rushed to change the subject and dismissed our concerns.

"This is great, though. You've got a girl to take your thoughts away from Nitham and bindings and the things which occupy a madman. Why are you still here talking to us? Go, rest, make yourself pretty . . ." He trailed off. "Urhm, as pretty as you can manage. Take a day to think up beautiful things to tell her. Go-go!" He shooed me with such fervor I didn't know what else to do but heed his words.

Sometimes it's better to follow the advice of good friends.

It will come as no surprise that I spent the following day in a bit of a daze over my upcoming engagement with Estra and what might happen during it. My classes passed through one ear and out the other, leaving me to shuffle through the motions needed until sixth candle. I skipped a late meal and returned to my strings, staring at them with the obsessions of a madman.

As cleanly laid out as they were, all I saw were knots and tangles. Maybe more so in my own head than in reality, but nonetheless, it was a mess.

I had half a mind to burn it all and toss the ink pots away.

Nothing made sense.

My mind went to the candle and the flame in an attempt to calm myself, but it wouldn't happen. The flame flickered wildly. It fanned itself larger, hotter, threatening to wash out my mind's vision with orange and tonal reds.

It surged, spreading wider now. I could almost feel the heat within wanting to take me—sear me, and send me into a rage at the cost of my room and what bits of precious I owned.

I snapped out of it, breathing like I'd run all the thousands of stairs up to the Ashram. Radi had been right, I needed time away from my thoughts of strings and vengeance.

I let my mind wander instead. I turned to what stories Estra could have for me. Myths and legends from her folk over the mountains, a place that didn't talk of Brahm the way the rest of Mutri did.

What heroes did they have? What tales of daring and danger? What of the men and women who lived up to those trials? And the ones who lived for it?

The night passed into morning and the thoughts still kept me occupied.

Estra met me in the main yard by one of the weeping trees. They stood with their bulks bowed, hanging their limbs low to the ground with lines of red leaves that looked more like lengthy strands of hair. Against the white-powder snow of Ghal, they were strikingly vibrant. And Estra's hair had a similar effect under the brightness of the tree.

I grinned and waved my staff at her.

She returned it and embraced me in a hug I hadn't expected, taking the next words from my mouth as well as from my mind. "I'm not pulling you from classes, am I? Today's an off day for me."

I shook my head and found enough of a voice to lie. "No, I'm the same. Off day." I extended her an arm, which she took, and led the way out of the Ashram.

A season there usually did the trick in conditioning all but the worst students for taking the mountain stairs down. All the climbing towers and walking through endless yards served as constant exercise, not to mention the fact many students took time to filter back into the town below for time off.

Estra and I made our way to a lodge made of a wood the color of faded oranges. It gave the place a warmth from the outside that made it all the more inviting. Blue clay tiles, the customary color found on many roofs in Ghal, lined its top and reached a pointed peak. The Agni-thaan. Otherwise known as The Fireside.

I found it fitting.

"They have the best broths and even sweet steamed milk here." Estra tugged my arm harder, leading me inside.

The interior matched my expectations. Open spaciousness that allowed for ease of movement and huddling in groups around tables. The wood of the room lost what color the exterior had, something faded too far to have a proper name.

My eyes went to the black-stone hearth that held a crackling fire more red than orange in flame. I nodded to the spot. "Mind if we sit by that?"

She smiled and led me by the arm.

We found seats at an empty table and Estra chose to sit directly opposite me rather than by my side, which I found odd. Radi or Aram would have been within arm's reach to shove me, or glance an elbow off my ribs if I warranted that much. And I always took care to return the favor.

A serving girl came round to us seconds later. She looked to be the same age as Estra, dressed like everyone else in Ghal. Heavy robes with a collar of fur, the entire outfit lacking any adornment or nod to the popular fashions. Heavy, warm, and functional. That was it. She had her hair bound close to her skull with a simple wrap of white cloth. "What'll do for you two?"

Estra needed no further prompting, breaking right away into what she desired. "Cup of pear juice. Also apple. Do you have sweet milk in? I'd like some of that—hot, of course."

The serving girl bobbed her head as she tried to keep up with Estra's deluge of requests.

"Do you have *joshni*? I'm famished. This place has the best lamb bowls." Estra reached out and touched my hand before pulling away. "Oh, and fahaan."

The serving girl nodded then looked at me.

I hadn't brought my appetite with me, interested more in what Estra could tell me in way of stories and about her home. A part of me very much wanted to visit Sathvan between the seasons when classes slowed and others stopped altogether. "Um, I'm fine with just some juice. I don't really care which. It's all the—"

Estra reached out again, taking my hand within hers and squeezing it.

I took it as a cue to stop talking, but I wasn't sure.

"He'll have the same." She gave me a look you would expect someone to turn on a sick animal they pitied. "Ari, you really should eat more, you know?"

I didn't.

"You look like you're half-starved, and then the times you get mad—feral. It's like looking at a wild cat that's never gotten enough to eat. Girls talk about it."

I glowered at her, not knowing what she meant by that. I'd gotten my fair share of food as a sparrow. While we never ate extravagantly, even after coming into money, we never went to bed with the knots of starvation in our stomachs. At worst, all of us felt the discomfort of mild hunger.

And the Ashram offered more than I could handle in food. I told Estra this.

"And how often do you remember to eat?" She gave me a heavy stare as the serving girl moved off to fulfill our order.

I licked my lips, thinking on it. "Whenever I'm really hungry, I suppose?"

She held the look. "Most people eat when they're hungry, not really hungry. And you look like your idea of hunger is different than most. So what's that mean?"

I didn't have a good answer, knowing her to be right.

"It suits you, in some ways." She turned slightly away from me, taking in my profile out of the corners of her eyes. "It reminds me of animals—hungry, fierce, lean."

I thought about what she had said moments earlier. About the girls and what they talked about. I wondered if she knew any more of the rumors people had turned to spreading about me. "What do people say? You mentioned something just now."

"Hm? Oh." She still hadn't come back to facing me straight on. "You have a way about you. People notice. The girls do, at least. Some of the boys too." She shot me a glare so wicked pins pricked along my neck. "It's your temper; how you look, and act."

I still hadn't a clue what she meant and I pressed her for clarity.

"It's like watching a cat get its hackles up whenever you're mad. People tell stories about you and Nitham getting into it. Or you and Rishi Ibrahm. Then there's the story of you walking the fire. I can't count how many people were there for that. You don't act the way a person would."

That one drove a barb into me. I'd worked hard to be judged on my talent and skill and not on circumstances I couldn't control. Estra's words brought to mind the times I'd been seen as nothing but a sparrow. Worse. The times I'd been seen as my caste.

Which was to say not even a person by the standards of most men and women.

"And how exactly is a person supposed to act when being pushed around?" My fingernails almost dug into the wood of the table. "What would you do when some silver-spoon prat makes trouble for you? Or when a rishi who's clearly touched decides to throw stones at your head? No, wait—better. How about when the Ashram decides to punish you with mutilation? How would you act?" I noticed several people had stopped eating and turned toward our conversation.

My voice had reached a level short of anything considered loud, but far above what two people so close to one another should have been using. I hadn't realized.

Estra kept her appraising gaze from earlier, however. She should have recoiled, possibly eyed me with apprehension for losing my temper. Her mouth spread into a wide, almost hungry grin instead. "That's what I mean. See, there." Estra jabbed a finger toward me that had me leaning away from the table as a precautionary measure.

"Just now, you were . . ." She frowned and her eyes turned thoughtful. Estra avoided making eye contact for a few moments, letting her attention visibly wander. Eventually, she settled on the stone hearth at our side. "Like that. Black stone like your hair, framing this fire inside your face. You were burning and brimming with this anger." Color touched her cheeks. "Some women like that in a man. It's not always there in you, but when it is, it catches in the people around you. It does things."

My mouth dried and I didn't know how to respond to that. Thankfully, even while she may have come from a place that didn't observe Brahm and his ways, the people of Ghal did, and parts of our meals arrived with the timing of a miracle.

The serving girl set down the various juices Estra had asked for. "I'll be back with the steamed milk and food."

Estra gave her a nonverbal motion of the head as acknowledgment and I offered my thanks.

The conversation lulled into an awkward silence I had no way to smoothly break, so I did away with the conventions of pleasantries. "Tell me of your home? What's Sathvan like?"

She blinked and lowered her gaze. "Oh." The color left her cheeks, shoulders slumping. She looked like much of the wind had been taken out of her. "It's home, I suppose."

I had been looking for more than that as far as answers went. "Do you know any stories? Like the ones we tell about Brahm here. Or, ones like the heroes out of legends of Mutri?"

She shrugged and looked about as interested in the topic as if I'd asked her to tell me how much fun she had watching snow melt. "Some. They're not really interesting, though. There's one that Sathvan had another name, long ago and long forgotten, in another time when the world was a different shape. The old gods were there and people lived with them. One went mad and someone killed it. This was back when the world had more magic than it does now. And Sathvan was once a kingdom unto itself by another name." Estra made a motion with a hand as if brushing aside the conversation.

"What was the kingdom's name? What kind of old god?" I leaned closer, my hunger for the story getting the better of me.

She pursed her lips and they pulled to one side of her face like she'd sucked on something sour. "I don't know. It's long ago and long forgotten. Same with the gods. The only one I even heard stories about was the Nagh-lokh. The serpent is so wide that it carved the path through the mountains in Sathvan. They say the river follows in its wake. But, no one's seen one. They can sleep for hundreds of years at a time. Ages ago, young girls and boys would be put out before their caves as sacrifice to keep them from coming into the villages." Her tone softened and grew distant like she'd gotten bored of the subject.

I took that as a disappointing cue to not press any further, so I reached for something else. "How are your classes treating you? You're already a Kaethar, right?"

Some of her enthusiasm returned. She straightened up and leaned closer to me. "I'm almost to Fhaldar, I think. My work in the Artisanry's been going really well. I'm on my way to a breakthrough with my project." Estra's excitement flooded her eyes, bringing a light and brightness to the blue buried beneath the gray.

"That's impressive. I've heard how hard it is to even get close to being raised to Fhaldar. Not to pry, but can you tell me about your project?" Apparently that had been the right question to ask as she perked up even further.

She fidgeted, running her fingers through her hair as a smug smile spread across her face. "Well, you know I can't tell you everything. Students higher up in the Artisanry are fiercely jealous over their creations. It's one of the only ways we can guarantee being raised. Otherwise you have to be something of a prodigy like Thariq." A bit of smoke entered her voice as she said his name.

Of course, I hadn't the experience and understanding of people then that I do now, and most certainly not with women, but the way she'd spoken Thariq's name sent a knot through my spine. And I didn't know why. I'd lost interest on the subject but did my best to keep up the appearance of being an attentive listener.

Our food arrived as she continued talking. "It has to do with storing heat, though. It's a tricky thing because you have to account for the limitations of the materials used, and most things aren't made to hold heat through bindings and maintain their integrity. They warp or have their natures perverted. Some fail . . . disastrously." She gave me a long look.

I felt that was an indicator to ask more, but in truth, I didn't have the heart for it. I did it nonetheless. "How bad did they go?" I let the right amount of excitement and curiosity fill my voice.

Clearly she'd heard what she wanted. "Oh, it's unbelievable. I heard stories of a student years ago who tried it and their device burst. It blew apart at the seams, flames went everywhere. But that's not the worst of it."

The lamb had all the tang of yogurt in it along with heat from the spices. A meal perfectly suited and to be appreciated in Ghal's climate. The flatbread had developed a lightly charred crust that I found pleasant with the meat, especially so with the slathering of butter on its surface. The juices did nothing for me, but the steamed milk lived up to Estra's appraisal. Warm, with touches of cinnamon, almond, vanilla, and maybe even the slightest spark of red pepper powder. It brought a different heat to me that I enjoyed.

"What was the worst of it?" The words came from me automatically and I hoped they had enough heart to keep Estra happy. My attention wandered to the crackling flames. The dark stone hearth took me, my eyes tracking every one of the fire's tendrils until the image burned into my mind.

Within moments, I could close my eyes and perfectly reimagine the fire inside me, counting for every which way it could ever come to move. I felt the ends of the flames as if they were my own fingertips, brushing against the stone, wanting for more. Wanting to be fed, to grow, to spread and be fulfilled in a different manner than being left scraps of wood.

"Are you listening?"

The simple question tore me from the fire and my heart quickened. "Of course. I can't imagine what that must have been like."

Estra watched me for a moment but her face let me know my answer mollified her. "But how could he have known his apparatus would continue to funnel and hold heat after falling apart?"

I nodded. "Right, who'd have known?"

She went on and I finished my meal with a newfound gluttony I didn't know I'd brought with me. When Estra completed her talk, I felt complimenting her was the right thing to do for at least giving me her time, even if she'd barely shared the stories I hoped for.

"You're remarkably intelligent. I'm sure you hear it all the time, but there's something magical about a brilliant woman." I almost went on, but became acutely aware of her foot sliding up against the side of one of my ankles, rubbing the spot before gently going up to my calf. Whatever words I had seized in my throat, choked, and crumbled into nothingness.

"That's very sweet of you to say." Now she sounded almost like she had when speaking about Thariq.

I cleared the blockage keeping me from speaking. "Of course. It's only the truth. Would you like to leave and take a walk together?"

She left her seat before I'd finished the last word.

I asked the serving girl for the tally and left five copper rounds. Yes, the money was more than needed to cover the sum, but I knew the pittance the women who worked these sorts of places made. I may not have been quite used to my modest wealth yet, but I knew who deserved what bit of charity I could spare.

We left arm in arm, taking to the streets. Estra technically led the way, though you couldn't tell from our pace as we walked nearly in perfect step with each other. The only way you'd know was if it was your arm being pulled with a force you'd use to try to rein in a horse.

I confess some shame in admitting that most of what she said passed through me as we passed from place to place, occasionally stopping to stare at the vendors who found buildings unbearable and chose to hawk their wares in the open.

A few of them had set up makeshift fireplaces of gray brick that looked like miniature chimneys set into the ground. They radiated steam, and men and women would come by to warm their hands and talk, usually to the vendor's pleasure and likely their design. What better way to entice customers than with free heat in a place as cold as Ghal?

The man behind a long wooden stall noticed us and waved. Fifty, likely, and having lost most of the weight of his youth, he looked more like someone's great-grandfather than someone who should have been out in the weather. The layers of heavy clothing kept me from making out his build, but if the skin clinging to the bones of his face was any indication, the man may have been near as thin as the twigs feeding his nearby fire. "Trinkets for the lady, good-*sahm*?" He pulled at one of the tails of his thin white mustache.

"I'm not a sir, but I'll take a look." I stepped closer when movement at the corners of my vision caught me.

Estra turned before I did, keeping her hold on my arm and thus forcing me to move with her.

A pair of bulls came toward us, hauling a curved-top wagon that looked almost like it could have served as someone's small home. The beasts' horns had been painted in bright red whorls, and beads with all the colors of the rainbow looped over the bone-like protrusions, as well as their heads. Bulging sacks hung from their sides, all kept in place by thick white braided rope that looked like it could have supported the weight of several fully grown men.

The cart behind was the green found in moss with a roof of yellow from sunflowers. Brass and iron fittings were fixed to the wooden side panels, each bit of metal polished so well they reflected all nearby light in a dazzling display of brilliance.

A man sat at the front of the wagon-home, gently prodding his bulls forward. He raised one hand that held on to something in the shape of a cone. "*Gadia Lohar. Lohar-lohar.* Wagoneer, privateer. Tinker, trader, teller, merchant man am I. Come one, come all. See what I have. See what I sell. Don't be shy. Don't be shy.

"Pot mender—iron shaper, metal maker and its bender. Things to sell and things to take, give me an offer—open to all trades to make. Come-come. Rumor monger, bauble seller. I've things aplenty, trinkets, wonder, and have some treasure!" He trumpeted from his handheld apparatus with a chime of near crystalline clarity. "Knickknacks, trifle, toys, and gimcracks. I may even have a gewgaw or two. This-thats and what-nots!"

The man behind the stall fell into muttering dark curses and tried to renew our interest, but I had no mind or eyes for his wares.

The wandering wagoner had taken all my attention. The cart came to a stop in the middle of the street without any regard for passersby and the flow of the place. It was as if the driver knew he could come to rest wherever he damn well pleased and people would only welcome him for it.

And he was right.

A crowd soon flocked to him, and Estra led me in tow toward the tinker. Estra made good use of our combined presence to force a way through the crowd, most of which involved using me as a crude ram. But people moved out of our way, so I could hardly fault her technique.

The tinker spotted us and smiled, revealing a few missing teeth. His robes were dyed a blue pulled from sapphires, and he wore several scarves and wraps tied over himself like they were holding his clothing together. They were just as bright and varied in color as his cart. "What'll it be, good-sir—good-sir?"

I waved him off. "No need for the pleasantries, Tinker." I flashed him a sincere smile. "I'd just like to look for a bit if that's okay. I've never met one of your folk before."

The man raised both brows, which reminded me of bushy caterpillars. "No? Sad thing, that. Whereabouts are you from, boy?"

I bristled but the bulk of my robes and cloak atop kept him from noticing. "Keshum, Abhar."

"Ahh. I know it. Yes, not many of my kind pass through those parts. Too much traffic and too many traders in too tight a space for our lot. Besides, people in busy streets don't like boys like this coming by." He reached out and patted the flanks of one of the bulls. "If looking's to your fancy, then by all means. Look away. Just keep this in mind." He gestured me closer with a finger.

I leaned in and listened.

The tinker cupped a hand to his mouth, keeping his voice low and for our ears alone. "For all the vendors of the world, there are only three things they can truly sell: trinkets, treasure, and *trash*. Hm?" He nodded to the stall past us. "Ask yourself what most men have, then what you're looking for. Seldom do people want the last thing, but it's what they're often handed. And there's nothing wrong with a treasured trinket—not at all. But it's still not a true treasure, is it?"

I smiled and looked past him to the small double doors that led into his cart. "So, Tinker, what then have you got in your wagon? Trinkets, treasures, or trash?"

His eyes widened and he threw back his head to let loose a short barking laugh. "Oh, well said and asked of me, boy. Let us look. Let us see. And let's find out, hm?" He pulled open the doors and crawled inside, coming out with a small canvas sack. "What's a young boy like you want for, I wonder?"

I could have told him, but a part of me wanted to see how good a salesman this tinker was. Could he find something to pluck my coins from me?

He reached into the sack and pulled free a golden oil lamp that, at a closer look, might truly have been fashioned from the pure metal and not a cheap veneer. "Got this from out across the Golden Road, m'boy. Heard it said that the first man to rub it gets a wish from something old and powerful." He frowned. "Or, could just be it's an oil lamp. Still, looks wonderfully pretty, and there's a chance it's worth its weight in gold."

A chance. One I bet you're hoping I take. I bet it's worth only what you're willing to charge for it, and worth far less than that to me. But I kept the thought from showing on my face.

He held it out for me to touch and I took him on the offer. All the while, a silent thought. *I wish to be part of the greatest story ever told, like Brahm himself. To find the Ashura. To master the ten bindings all men must know.*

The lamp grew cold against my touch, Ghal's freezing climate finally taking its toll.

I pulled my hand away from the trinket. "I have no need for an oil lamp, good tinker. What else?"

The lamp vanished into the bag and his hand came out with something else. A corded string of leather around an amulet of dark green stone I didn't recognize. "Very pretty. Would go wonderful with the cool cold eyes of your lady, iffen you don't mind me saying, sir?"

He was good. Smooth. And fast and flattering with his words. They had his desired effect, drawing a light flush from Estra's cheeks.

"Who notices a stone before the beauty of the mountain whole?" I gestured to the wide spanning peaks at our backs. "A piece of green rock would only dull what Estra naturally possesses in nature and her prettiness."

The tinker met my eyes, narrowing his own to slits. His face rang of discontent but also a grudging admiration. "You're quick with your tongue and can use it."

I knew I looked smug under the praise.

"Very well. I could go through my packs for days and it seems you're almost inclined to run me through them, no?"

"Almost," I said.

"Then you tell me, boy. What is it a tinker can do for you? What can I make? Anything to fix? Maybe something to share? A story, a tale or two? Rumors, gossip, hearsay? What'll it be? I've heard a good deal of late."

I pursed my lips, wondering what stories he could possibly share that I could even come to care about. Anything worth learning was likely kept in the Scriptory. "I study at the Ashram, and there I can find almost any story, myth, or legend ever told. What does that leave you with, good tinker-*sahm*?"

He pursed his lips, running a thumb and forefinger under his chin as he thought. "Hm. Well then, guess that leaves rumors, gossip, and hearsay, huh?" He grinned. "If I tell you something worth your ears to hear, you be honest with me now and tell me so, *ji-ah*?"

"*Ji.*"

"Well, odd bit of gossip, this. I heard a story from another tinker, who's not one to lie, mind you. We don't do that to ourselves. And he heard himself off a woman come upriver from the Emperor's Cradle. Way it got told to me was a whole host of noble folk were having a party of sorts. Theater, pageantry, wrestlers, and even had a binder or two. This was off on some farmland estate, of course. You know the laws down south are strict against revelry and the like. Anyway, days later, and not one hears a peep about any of them folk. Not the performers, and certainly not the nobles. And that's a sort of thing one's to hear about, no? If a little lord disappears? What's it mean?

"Trouble, that's what I say. But, that's not the damndest bit of oddness. Farmers who worked the land came on the house to find it burning one morning. Well, smoldering ruins in places, but what's the difference? Fire, red as blood with the smoke to match, they say. They found bodies of some of the men and women, not yet turned to ash and embers. Heard everyone they found had blood coming from their eyes and mouth. But, I don't right see how that's possible."

My mouth dried but I found just enough moisture in my throat to speak. "Why's that?"

The tinker shrugged. "Only was storming the night of the big party. How's a place to catch fire under all that rain? We're not so far away from monsoon season that storms have stopped, boy."

Red smoke and flames. Bleeding. And the storm before it all. The Ashura.

Only, they were at the other end of the Empire, so near about the edge of the world from where I stood. At best I could hope to make the journey after a month of hard and fast travel. But what would I find by then?

Long-cold ashes and freshly tilled ground?

But the Ashura were still out there. And they were coming after people. But why?

"Ah, and I see by your face, boy, I've done what I set out to do. I've told you a piece of something precious enough to warrant some coin, hm?"

My hands moved automatically though my mind stayed far from the present.

I passed him three coins, an old rhyme's lesson returning to me. Though I had no gold for him, I would certainly not leave the poor tinker a sum of tin.

One copper round. An iron bunt. And a silver dole.

He accepted them with a wide smile. "Well, seems I ought to be doing more business in stories than in trinkets and trade, hm. Mighty profitable, this." He shook his hand then opened his palm to reveal it empty. He may as well have vanished the coins with magic.

"Thank you, Tinker. If you should hear any more stories like that, find me. Tell me. Please? My name is Ari, and I—"

"And you study at the Ashram. I have ears, boy, and I know how to use them. But I'll keep to what you've asked of me, and surely so for what you've paid. A good sum, and not many appreciate the news of the world. I'll be back here two sets from today. Remember that. Meet me here and I'll tell you what I've heard of the world." The tinker offered his hand.

I shook it. "I'll be here." And I meant it.

Years after Koli had vanished, the Ashura had returned.

And I wanted to know what they were up to.

SEVENTY-THREE
INTERMISSION—A SAFE HARBOR

"You didn't chase after them?" Eloine propped herself up on one elbow and watched me.

I shook my head. "No. How could I? Emperor's Cradle was so far away from me at that time that even thought of traveling there boggled my mind. Never mind the cost and distance. It would have done me no good. All it did was serve as a reminder of old wounds and a long-standing promise of revenge. A young boy's promise, yes, but all the same, one I meant to keep."

Eloine reached out and took the fold of my robes over one of my shoulders. She pinched the fabric, taking a good grip, and she pulled.

I tilted toward her and did little to resist. "What would you have had me do then?"

She frowned and the lines of her mouth accentuated her lips. "Well, if I were there, I probably would have pointed out your rather amazing thick-headedness in missing that young girl's advances. But then, I wonder, would that ignorance have served a young me better? It might have been that I would have had an eye on this young and feral Ari." She smiled, but it faded just as fast. "And for the Ashura? I would have asked you to do something I don't think you had the heart to do then, and certainly still don't now."

I perked up, wondering what she could have thought too much for me to manage. "And so what would you have asked of me?"

"To let it go. The Ashura, the anger of a young man and the fires that come with it. They're the kind that burn a person up and leave little behind." She reached out and brought the fingertips of one hand to my heart, leaving them there for the space of a second before pulling away. "I'd have asked you to take a better look at where you were and let yourself actually be there. Because from the sound of it, you were not. You were still back at the theater the night your family died. Your body may have left the House of Sparrows, but not your heart, Ari. And a part of you wanted to return to both, or why else hound the Ashura."

She was right, of course, but I couldn't let myself see it. Or, I didn't want to. "If I did all that, Eloine, where would be left for me to go? Who would I become? Ari, the meandering student? Someone content to while away my days tinkering dutifully like all the others? No."

"Of course. You had a chance to live a life after one had been stolen from you several times. Why risk squandering it? You could have made a path to anything you wanted, and you had the safety of the Ashram and its walls with which to take the time to figure that out." Her eyes smoldered, but not with invitation. It was the scalding heat of judgment if you didn't take care.

I gave her a thin broken smile. "It's sweet you believe that was possible. You'll learn that was never going to be the case, no matter if I had wanted it. But I could never forget, and I did not want to. No man can look back and not see where he's been. If he can do that, then on which path does he come to travel? Though, the world would be a better place if a younger me had heard and heeded your advice. That much is true."

I shifted to move away from her, but she grabbed my clothes again, taking them in a fiercer grip than before. The same intensity burned in her eyes, letting me know I should think carefully, and act with twice as much caution. I stopped moving and resigned myself to staying in place.

"I suppose it doesn't matter much, does it? Since you clearly survived all your foolishness and idiocy. Though, I wish men grew in heart and mind as much as they do taller in height. It seems more often than not that the child remains while the rest of you only comes to look like a man."

I glowered at her, but she remained unfazed by it. "Depending on the stories, I didn't survive at all, and I don't mean the ones I've spread of my many deaths, vanishings, and the like. Some say I died and never rightly came back." *Like Abrahm,* I thought. "What returned was only a shadow of myself—tainted, twisted, and taken by something else—something worse."

Eloine pulled away from me but only in the slightest. An imperceptible inch, but I noticed. "I don't believe you," she said, but the light dimmed in her eyes just a bit.

I shrugged. "Wouldn't be the first time someone's doubted my claims. Though, you've taken my story in fair stride so far. No protest at the Ashura at all? None at them killing a young boy's adoptive family. Or the vanishing of Koli, and all without a trace. None at the girl that had been my friend while I lived below the understage, and how she too remained too far lost from me to even catch a whisper of her."

Now it was Eloine's turn to roll her shoulder in nonchalance. "I've heard many stories about you, but this is the first coming from your mouth. I'm willing to entertain the incredible." Something in her tone made it clear her belief was more than that. Or rather, her lack of disbelief came from something else.

I probed deeper. "Most aren't willing to talk about the Ashura at all, superstition and fear or the turning of time putting them in the place of children's tales and nothing more. So, why believe me?"

Eloine inched even farther away this time. Her gaze fell to a faraway place that I couldn't hope to see. "I know of them. Or, enough to not treat them as others do. They're no stories. And I would rather hear of them from your mouth and in your past than to talk of them here and now." Her voice shook and her fingers dug into the blanket and the folds of my robes.

I almost opened my mouth to ask her. To pry and seek what knowledge she had on the Ashura. Something—anything! But, I watched how still and how distant she grew as the barely audible breaths passed between us. I let it go. I'd learned enough over the years to pursue the Ashura as I needed. It may not have gone as I had hoped, but I was still alive, and I was still after them. Even now.

"I'm sorry, Eloine. I didn't mean to pry."

She looked up, one of her brows barely arching. But it was enough for me to see. "Didn't you?"

I gave her a weak smile and raised my hands, fingers splayed. "An accident. An impulse." *Quick, fool. Think of something else to take her mind from it.* I cleared my throat and remembered an all too recent offer she'd made. "It seems you know a good many things most folk do not. And among them, I recall a song about the moon." I eyed her sideways, expectation clear on my face.

She smiled. "You do, do you? I'll sing that for you then."

I gestured for her to go.

"But not tonight. No. In a time when the moon is out and her face full. If I'm to sing that song, then it should be on a night she feels comfortable enough to listen. All of her aspects should watch from overhead. It's only proper."

I didn't know what she meant, but it did bring a new question to my mind. "And how exactly would I ensure I get to hear this song? After all, you've quite the habit of disappearing on me. I'm never certain when I'll see you again, or where, for that matter. So, what to do? What to do?"

My question dulled neither her smile nor the look in her eyes. "Say then you'll look for me. That you'll find me. That you'll set after me the way the sun always does the moon. Promise you'll find me."

I opened my mouth, not knowing how to keep that promise. "But how—"

Eloine pressed a finger to my lips and hushed me. "Just say it. Make the promise."

I nodded and spoke the words. "I promise. I'll look for you. I'll set after you like the sun does the moon. I promise I'll find you."

"Then I'll sing for you when you find me under the next moon's light. But, I think I can give you another piece with which to enjoy the evening before you set out to play with princes and politics."

"Oh?"

"Yes." Eloine fell flat against the bed, bringing me with her. She pulled me close and brought my head to rest on her shoulder. "Be quiet now and listen." Eloine went as far as placing a hand over my mouth, giving me a mischievous look as she did it.

I had half a mind to pay her back for that, but I knew she could give as good as she got. And I wasn't sure if I wanted to deal with the consequences in the moment.

She cleared her throat. "This is a song of a dark bird who came across a boy meddling with things he should not have. A child too young to know the dangers of fire and who would burn himself—maybe her as well. And worst, he could burn the world around him. For fire is a dangerous thing. It's about a boy who would grow up chasing stories and the dangerous things in the world without knowing where his own two feet stood at any given time. Someone who knew how to run after things, but never how to let himself rest and find a safe harbor."

"Sounds like quite the adventurous boy." I'd barely gotten the words out as her hand still rested over my mouth.

She shot me a look that could have quenched the hot temper of the wildest men, the ones all prone to quickly anger.

I pressed my lips tight and kept my tongue well between my teeth.

Her eyes narrowed and I wagered that, while she couldn't see the smile I wore under her hand, she could feel it. "As you've said throughout your story—and I'm now reminded again—you, Ari, can be a clever little shit."

"My heart thrums whenever you compliment me like—*urmph*." She stifled my speech by pressing harder with her hand.

"You're lucky I have an interest in hearing the rest of your story someday soon. For that, you are only being kept under my hand and not a pillow." She gave me a look that let me know she might still change her mind.

I made no motion, letting her know she could proceed.

Eloine let out a low rhythmic hum. If a single sound could be paired with the meaning to soothe, it would have been her voice. It was the gentle thrum of strings slowly coming to rest, but the noise just before they stopped altogether. It was the sound of a musician teasing out the first few notes to silence a crowd and draw their eager attention—not forcefully. It was a slow seduction.

"On one dark and so lonely // a winter's night,
did she err on wind and in midst of flight,
and thus our bird came // to lose her way,
and so did she fall far from home,
and she our // dark lady // came to stray;

and then on // a fleeting whim,
and through as much in chance,
did she come upon // a far stranger sight,
one lost under dark // and in cover of night,
through greater luck // and sheer happenstance
did she come across her treasure // and find him then;

so down the girl came
to the boy born of fire
where she felt herself drawn to him,
to his sparks
and his desire,
so closer still // onward she came
to embrace him // and feel his flame,

and on her wings // did she bring him then
to a new world now // of distant dreams,
a place where all things,
were not // what they seemed."

Eloine went on, but I lost the rhythm of her words past the opening. I only had space for the sound of her voice. The soft lull of it. And I felt my eyes grow heavy with lead, but I tried to resist.

She moved her hand from my mouth as she sang, telling me of the journeys the young boy came to take on the raven-haired girl's back. How far they'd go. And of the dangers they brought with every adventure sought. Of the folly he courted, too excited to know better. And the disaster that followed.

Eloine brought her hand to my eyes now, forcing my lids shut before turning her fingers to stroking my hair. "The lesson, Ari, is sometimes even brilliant fires can burn out—burn low. And listening to your story, there's something I've come to know."

I faded further now, barely hearing her speak.

"That your once flower-bright fire flickers. Faintly fading in its glow. I deeply wonder now what its waxing-dimming flames will come to show. Why does your fire no longer fan itself full and fill your hearth?" She placed a hand over my left breast and held it there. "I know you are tired now but do not rest. Why cannot you keep your own flame alight? Why can't you fuel your own fire? What has happened to you, Ari? Where is that dreamer's once-deep desire?"

I tried to answer her. That I was resolved and resolute as ever. That nothing had happened to my fire, and that I was certainly not tired.

She hummed and the sound of it washed away my thoughts and any protest I could mutter. "Every ship knows when to set sail. And they know when to come home. All travelers grow weary and seek respite. So, for what are you yearning? Will you let your ship come home to me tonight? Will you let me be your safe harbor? You can stop now. You can rest."

But I didn't wish to. Not entirely.

Still, as life rarely listens to our designs, I drifted further and into sleep.

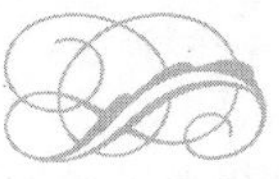

SEVENTY-FOUR

Games

My arm cradled something soft and I let out a low groan of pleasure. A gentle squeeze drove realization home and I woke quicker than any man ought to have in the early morning. My fingers dug into the body of a large pillow that had been folded into the blanket.

I frowned, looking at the empty spot next to me where Eloine had been last night. The sigh that built in me didn't find a way out as I swallowed it, having expected her absence ahead of time.

A part of me wanted to linger there and take a moment to enjoy the memory of her, but the arrival of the Tainted in Etaynia made it so I couldn't allow myself the little joys. I rose and didn't bother muttering a pair of bindings to remove the creases from my clothing. Staff in hand and sack over shoulder, the mandolin case in my other grip, I left her rooms and headed to the taproom of the Golden Lion.

The barkeeper spotted me as I passed, and he gave me the narrow-eyed glower most men reserved for the sun when it beat down on them too early in the day.

It would have been peevish and pedantic of me to have replied with a gleeful smile. So I flashed him a wide-brimming grin instead. The nuance matters.

His face drew into a more unfriendly mask and he muttered darkly to himself.

My stomach squirmed just a touch, but enough for me to recognize morning hunger's demand. The meeting with the *efantes* could wait until after breakfast.

I went over to the barkeeper, having at least enough tact to wipe the amused expression from my face before I got too close. "I don't suppose you've lit any fires in the kitchen to cook something for hungry patrons?"

"Patrons *pay.*" He'd replaced the scowl with a long-suffering stare, like he'd been waiting for something for quite the while.

"And I can." I didn't know why that had come up as an issue, especially when I'd offered to purchase a room the night before.

"Your woman couldn't."

I blinked and my mouth nearly went off without a thought, but I remembered myself and cleared my throat instead. "I'd thought the room paid for in advance."

He shook his head and kept up the weighty stare.

I knew enough of the look to get his meaning. The sigh I'd swallowed earlier returned and this time left my lips. I fetched my purse and thumbed through it, wondering how much this would cost me. "So between a room for a night and the promise of breakfast . . ." I let the question sit in the air.

"An expensive room." The man's mouth spread into the smile of a toad.

Of course it was an expensive room. "Right, and for all that?"

"Thirty pewter bits."

I nearly spat a curse but he went on.

"For the room. Meal, depends on what you get, but I've only salted fish, bread, and warm squash with butter so early in the morning. So, you get what I've got to give. That'll be another five bits."

The penalty for murder in Etaynia came in the form of public execution. However, they were a generous people and allowed the convicted a choice in how to die. You could choose between beheading or hanging.

The joys of freedom of choice.

Being fond of my neck, I reconsidered my violent urge. No easy thing considering the man's smile grew to be twice as wide and many more times that in repulsiveness.

"You charge a lot for room and food, sir."

He shrugged. "*Leyon Dis Ario* isn't some small-town tavern and inn, *sir.* The Golden Lion has catered to folk that know the true value of things, and thus, this place. They pay."

The true value of things never involves money. Anyone who thinks so is a fool who never lost something coin could not return, or had to make a bargain that cost more than any currency could come to in weight.

I fished out five Savone copper penes and pressed them to the counter. "Last I checked these are worth seven bits each." *I hope you choke on them,* but I didn't voice the thought.

He made no move to grab the coins. "Five, now. Haven't you heard?"

I hadn't, and the look must have shown clearly on my face for he explained.

"Savon's at war." The barman frowned. "Well, more like a bunch of skirmishes with Baldaen. But, it's ruined trade flow between them, and both those countries are now cut off from trade with Sevinter *and* Amir as those two are going at it."

I said nothing, knowing the state of the world was slowly growing worse. Governments tipped toward chaos as if pushed by invisible hands.

Or shadows.

I nodded in mute acceptance and pulled free two more Savone penes. My Etaynian coinage ran low, and I didn't see the point of breaking it over some dickering with an ass. "Better?"

He grunted but took the coins and shuffled away. The barkeeper returned moments later with a wooden tray atop which was everything promised: a salted cod, not my favorite thing to eat, warm squash with a pat of butter already melting at its center, golden bread with a crust that looked like it'd give me a satisfying crunch. He'd added in a dollop of soft cheese that had the consistency of thick yogurt, and a mug of something dark as my hair.

I ate in the manner of a hard and long-weary traveler, which is to say, as nearly an animal save for using cutlery. The fish had more salt in it than cod, but I appreciated the touch of lemon. The cheese had more in taste than it did in smell, and that wasn't a good thing. The only pieces of the meal one could consider satisfying were the bread and squash. The drink had bitter notes I couldn't identify and a maltiness to it I didn't care for.

The Golden Lion, it seemed, continued on prior prestige and had no worth in and of itself today.

I finished the meal and left without a word, returning to the city of Del Soliel.

The City of Sunlight lived up to its name in the morning. Despite some of the high-towering buildings of white brick and stone, golden rays filtered through every possible open space and illuminated the place with a glow reserved for springtime out of stories.

People bustled by already about their business. Vendors spoke over one another in frantic chittering that could have driven insects mad. Bright colors from clothing to vegetables and fruits were visible any side you turned to look. But I kept my gaze focused ahead to the large palace of stone that held a shade of white brighter than any other.

If you looked closely at some of the buildings, you could see where rain and age had taken their toll. Scuffs, maybe a yellowing of stone in places, and other stains closer to the ground that likely came from indecorous and indecent behavior. Like drunkards.

But the palace held all the color found in clouds out of a child's dream, or from the faraway snows you couldn't hope to see a speck of dirt in.

The way ahead was not barred, but a quartet of men stood under the archway.

They weren't garbed as clergos, bringing me a mild relief that I wouldn't have to deal with religious zealots who happened to have swords in hand.

These men wore black padded gambesons, all sporting silver accents horizontally across their torsos. Their pants were the same dark color. None of them wore helms, but they hardly needed anything else from where I stood. The broad leaf-headed spears would give any sane person pause.

My sanity had long been up for question, and by now, I was sure I tilted toward the other side of it. I smiled and waved a hand as I approached the guardsmen.

They leveled their spears at me in perfect unison.

As a performer, I could at least appreciate the coordination, even if I wasn't a fan of their choice of demonstration. I slowed my pace and brought my staff between both hands, putting more of my weight on it than necessary. My back hunched, though being so fresh in the morning, my body still had some knots from my hours of sleep. Though now I moved like a man many decades my senior, a part of my lower back began to believe the lie.

I hobbled forward, removing the tension from my shoulders and letting them slump further to give a nonthreatening impression.

The guardsmen didn't lower their spears, however. At least they were dedicated. A new figure passed through the open gap between them. He wore a brilliant red the color of poppies. His shoulders were laced with gold embroidery and it continued over his breast to form the outline of a lion pawing at a small sun. His hair had been styled in the fashion popular among the gentry: long, oiled, and hanging loose to his shoulders. His mustache and goatee were trimmed neatly: thin, and pointed at the ends.

He stopped a dozen steps from me, like his mere presence would ward me off. "Name, invitation, and reason why these fine *Alabrose* shouldn't skewer you where you stand?" The set of his eyes and jaw told me he wouldn't hesitate to turn the men and their weapons on me. Being clever could only buy me trouble.

The truth, then.

I didn't bother straightening my posture even though the cheap theatrics wouldn't fool the man. It still made me seem less of a physical threat to the guards, and sometimes, appearances in the moment matter far more than the reality. "Storyteller. I have no invitation, but I've never needed one before. A quick run-along to your masters should get you the answer you're looking for. As for your final question, the last time someone tried to put a *lansa* through me, it went poorly for that man." It wasn't a threat, but I made sure he caught the iron in my eyes when I spoke.

To his credit, the man was unmoved. "I asked you for a name and you give me a profession? Are you hard of hearing, or is it dumb, then? Should I simply tell them The Man in Red has come calling?"

I said nothing but gestured toward my staff. "I gave up my name long ago and dedicated myself to one thing. So much so, I'm known for that now more than anything else." My mind adopted the folds again, but they were still the sort I'd been using since I came to Etaynia—the only kind I really knew anymore.

The sort fit for a performer, and nothing else. Certainly not the Ari Eloine had heard stories about. "Whent. Ern." My hand moved over the head of my staff—one time it could have been considered a proper binder's cane. I threaded currents of air around the tip, then repeated the binding, pulling at an old forgotten circle of fire. Bands of flame wove around the staff's head and held, bringing a miniature sun to life before the men.

One of their spears shook, and I couldn't tell if it was in fear or anticipation of piercing me. Probably both.

I remained as stone, letting the man at the front of the group sit and stare at the fire.

His mouth twitched and I could almost see his mind turning behind his eyes. "Ah. Not a storyteller. *The* Storyteller. Yes." He nodded. "You will wait here, still, and I will go ask about what sort of welcome you are deserving, *sieta*?"

I inclined my head but didn't snuff out the flame, leaving it as a reminder and a warning to the men before me just in case any of them decided to take matters into their own hands. My posture righted itself as I maintained the folds, holding the fire in place with little effort. What I had viewed as nothing more than an entertainer's trick now brought a different feeling to me.

Comfort. Familiarity. And a fire of its own—the sort that comes with ambition, hunger, anger, and the excitement of passion.

A remembrance of what a younger Ari once saw in the flickering shapes of orange and yellow light.

My shoulders went square again and I stood proud, waiting for the man to return.

It didn't take long and I soon spotted the thin-mustachioed fellow approaching in a brisk walk. His skin shone, letting me know he'd been sweating before I could make out the streaks of moisture running down his face. He stopped closer to me than before. "Please follow closely behind, *sir,* and I would be happy to lead you to your rooms for the duration of your stay. Please." He gestured with a hand, though his tone made it abundantly clear he was anything but happy.

I also noted that he hadn't stipulated how long the duration of my stay would be. But I fell into step and kept my eyes on the men at my sides. Like most people, I had a healthy suspicion and unease around heavy bits of metal that have a pointed purpose—like impaling me.

We reached the double doors of the castle, and I slowed my pace to take them in.

I stared at the dark grain, a color between chocolate and fresh earth. Parts of it had been carved away to create the scene of a young man, lean and half-starved, standing between a host of spearmen. A crowd watched, hands on mouths in horror, as the spear-wielders stabbed the man through the flank, back, and chest.

The man remained standing, and part of the wood had been painted to resemble red tears pouring from his eyes. Not even the blood from the man's side had been colored—just what fell across his face. Despite this, he looked as if he stood outside the realm of pain, enduring this with a silent stoicism that demanded respect.

I kept the image in mind as we passed through and into the castle proper. More white tiles and stone made up the walls and floor, but I paid little attention to the rest of the details.

Men and women, all styled in the current fashion, moved by. A few of them slowed just enough to be noticeable as they cast looks my way.

I pulled my hood up before they could get a good study of my face and features, taking a small pleasure in denying them their curiosity. The more anticipation and questions I built around myself, the better. And sometimes curiosity is a safer shield among the gentry than actual armor.

For Eloine was right about these kinds of people. They were of fragile ego and prone to rash action when spurned. But, these folk loved a good mystery, enough that I knew they played a game among themselves revolving around it.

And so I needed to keep as much about myself as secret as possible.

My escort led me up a flight of wide stairs that sparkled like flecks of glass had been pressed into the marble. Under the light, they could have passed for diamond dust among a field of snow. The man eventually waved a hand at a room, motioning for me to enter.

"Your rooms. You are expected to answer any summons if called upon by the *efantes,* any of the priests, or the esteemed and honored guests currently residing here. Is that understood?"

I nodded without turning to face him, stepping inside instead.

"If you need for anything, there is a bell. Ring it, and a runner will tend to your requests."

I ignored him and shut the door.

My room, as it was, would have defied the imaginations of any of the common folk. The space could have swallowed several of my old quarters within the Three Tales Tavern. Glass windows ran along most of one wall, all the panes boasting pictures comprised of smaller irregularly shaped facets. All the colors of the world could have been found in that glass. The staining process had been developed far from Etaynia and in the place that only now knew its name as Zibrath.

To have a wall of the substance, and all set to artwork, was a staggering display of wealth. A subtle one at that. For anyone else it would have been nothing more than something pretty.

The *efantes* had a taste for the foreign from the looks of it, and I hoped that would extend to me as far as hospitality would go.

The rug lining the floor had come from the same part of the world as the windows. Thick, lush, woven with the kind of age-old craftsmanship skilled workers vied for all their lives and could still fall short of managing. The piece had been trimmed in cream, creating a border around a brilliant blood red. The center had been decorated in gold thread to show a lion pawing at a rudimentary sun.

I had more chairs than any man could know what to do with, and I guessed their only use might come if I decided to throw a party.

Too much room for any man to ever be comfortable. It was like an ill-fitting cloak—too long across the shoulders and more material than you could fill out. You would step on the fabric and find it tangled along your limbs.

I made my way to the bed, setting my belongings down at one side. My hands went to one of the journals I always carried, turning it open with a brush from my thumb. An old and familiar story flashed before me and I smiled.

It was of a red-haired boy who grew to be a man many thought a demon. Partly on account of his odd hair color, but more so for the deeds he came to be known for and by. By the end of it all, they say he killed a prince. Some say a king. Wizard. Bard. Hero. A villain.

The world saw it easier to mark him both, none, and sometimes, pick between depending on the day. Only he knew the truth.

And now I found myself understanding why he never told us the true accounting of things. I shut the book, wondered how I would find the prince I was looking for, and how best to kill him once I did.

All while still needing access to their library. Whatever stories they had here.

A knock came from the door and I went to answer it.

The boy couldn't have been past his fifteenth year. Dark of hair and eye with a complexion that said he saw little sunlight—an oddity for an Etaynian. Thin brows and just the shadow and promise of hair to come along his face. "Sir—lord?" He bit his lip as he realized his folly and thrust a plum velvet pillow toward me.

A sealed envelope rested atop it with two pieces of jewelry to the right.

"Ah, I was waiting for this." I took the items from the pillow, but made no move to open the letter. "I don't suppose you'd tell me who sent you and why?"

The boy looked at the jewelry and envelope in my hand, then me. The smile he gave me was a knife-slit in glass as he backed away. "Good day."

I almost found the words to curse him, but thought better against it. If he'd been sent by some of the gentry, whatever I said would quickly reach their ears, then it'd spread further.

If you wish the world to know a secret, tell it to nobility, for nobody has more time to gossip than them.

I shut the door and placed the letter on a nearby low-hanging shelf. The first of the items was a brooch of burnished copper that nearly reached a shade of golden red. Its bulk resembled a sun much like that on the carpet, only solid, and more detail worked into the engraving. A silver spear ran horizontally through the heavenly body to complete the piece. I turned it over and saw the pin with which to fasten it to my clothing.

The other resembled a flower I didn't recognize. Seven petals, each outlined in gold and filled with countless blood-red stones. Rubies, by my estimate. Its stem had all the curve of a serpent and held seven protrusions that could have been barbs.

Thorns, I realized. Though, I couldn't work out the meaning of either piece. I snatched up the envelope and tore it to free the letter.

To the Man in Red,

I caught sight of you moments ago in what now seems ages already. I am intrigued. I am waiting. Come to me.

The Lady Selyena

I stared at the letter, rereading it, then eyeing the brooches.

So, it's to be like that, is it?

I fastened the copper-sun brooch directly between the points of my collar, pinning the front folds of my cowl underneath the pin. The red flower sat directly above my heart.

I'd come during the Game of Families, a formal event played out among the nobility. A time for courting favor and secrets. A time for plots. And for things best left unsaid where sharper ears hid. I'd never played it, and only knew the barest shape of it, but I've always been a quick learner.

I stepped out of the room and began my search for the lady who'd summoned me.

Let the games begin.

SEVENTY-FIVE

The Man in Red

The boy who'd brought me the summons lurked just to the side of my door, rooted in place.

"I suppose you'll lead me to her?" I waved the letter to make my point.

"This way, my . . ." He let the words hang in the air, waiting for me to offer my title, status, or lack thereof.

If the nobility and their ilk wanted to learn more about me, then they could do it their damn selves instead of through a child.

I kept silent and followed the boy as he led me around the upper floor. One of my hands fell onto the bannister, running along the smooth wood as we walked.

He stopped outside a door much like mine, motioning to it with both hands. "Inside . . ." Another long pause. More waiting. He flashed me a look that held all the cunning of men decades his senior.

It gave me pause and made me reconsider the boy. I looked him over again.

The paler skin. The ease with which he dug for information. His smoothness of speech, and the smile. This was someone born and bred within the castle walls and knew of no other life than courtly politics and intrigue.

A part of me ached for him. To know no other life than what others chose for you. And in that, he was a tool by the end of the day.

No, that much wasn't true. No matter what purpose people put him to, he was a person who had his own desires and stories he dreamed of realizing. They only sat beneath the weight of others. And when that group happened to be nobility, that weight could crush the dreams of a child.

It's hard to know what to even dream of and hope for when the life you live is one you've been handed by others. Some people are molded too early in life and they never get a chance to become the person they could have been. They never know them.

And we're all the poorer for it. The world certainly is.

"What's your name, boy?"

He blinked. I could see the many thoughts spinning through him, trying to find an answer for a question I bet no one bothered to ask him. "M-Marcos."

I reached out and he flinched from my grip, eyes wide.

His breathing quickened and I saw in him the feral side of a boy who knew only two things: flight, or fight. And he was no fighter. Who could he stand up to here?

The nobility?

They'd kill him for an improper slip of the tongue if they were in the mood. At the least, they'd have him beaten further than he'd ever been.

I dropped my voice so low that he would have to lean in closer to hear it. "It's all right." I knelt, letting him be the taller man between us. "It's all right, Marcos. I didn't mean to frighten you."

Something changed in him. The wide eyes fluttered and he found clarity in the anger and stubbornness all young men can easily call on. "You didn't scare me."

"Of course. I'm sorry." I reached out and placed a hand on his shoulder.

He didn't make any attempt to brush away my hold.

"I'm obviously new here, and I'm finding it rather stuffy in my rooms. What sort of fun is there to be had around this place?"

Marcos frowned, his gaze falling to the ground as he thought over the question. "Some of the guests take to horse riding, dueling—harmless, of course—archery, there are masquerades and—"

I gave him a gentle shake. "Not what the nobles do, Marcos. What do you do for fun? The other children here as well." I knew he couldn't be the only one raised in such a lifestyle. Focusing on that would help him realize he was not as lonely as he thought. Using his name as much as I could would add to that—remind him of being more than just a runner boy, a tool and extension of the will of others.

His face tightened into a deeper mask of concentration. "Some of us try to sneak out when we can and play with wooden swords. Pretend to be the *calaberi,* sometimes we chase each other, you know?"

I smiled at that.

No matter how much the shape of the world changes over distance and time, children stay the same, and they play the games we always have.

"And are you tasked to follow me around until the lady's business with me is concluded?"

Marcos nodded.

"Then, as our little secret, consider it concluded for now. I'll meet with her and while I do, how about you go back to playing, hm? For all the things I'm sure you've overheard in your service and been told to keep quiet, I think the two of us can keep this bit just as hushed, *sieta*?"

Marcos beamed and all his cunning left him. "*Sieta!*" He produced a key and unlocked the door, opening it only a crack before announcing my arrival. "My lady, The Man in Red, answering your summons." He didn't wait for me to address her as he tore off in a full sprint that was probably improper within the castle walls.

But he was a child, and impropriety was, more often than not, the proper behavior for someone his age.

I straightened and placed the head of my staff against the door, pushing it open gently.

The Lady Selyena sat waiting for me. Her chair was the high-backed sort you expected gentry to use when entertaining guests. It lacked any supporting armrests, which made me feel it was more for show and didn't really take the person's comfort into account.

Wonderful. Especially if I had to sit in one as well.

Her face could have been the subject of paintings. High, sharp cheekbones, delicate brows, and lips that almost touched on being red without any paint. Eyes that were a golden brown and held a hint of some other shades depending on how much light shone on her face. The woman's hair hung loose and flowing in thick ringlets that spoke of having been set that way.

"You answered rather quickly." She had a voice nearly as soft and bright as her eyes, if lacking their honest honey-sweetness. What I heard spoke more of salt passing as sugar from a distance—an act.

I shut the door behind me with more care than I'd opened it, using the time to stretch out the silence and keep her waiting. Having done that, I moved closer to her, but kept far enough away that I couldn't touch her with my staff should I have wanted. "I answered. It's up to others to decide whether it was quickly or not." I hadn't lowered my hood as I spoke, still trying to make out the reason for the summons.

She smiled.

Insincere. Coy. Cunning. The three words ran through me as I read her. This wasn't a passing fancy or fleeting curiosity. She had something in mind, but I couldn't guess at what. The straightforward path then. Asking.

"I don't suppose I can inquire as to why you called me, Lady Selyena?"

She straightened, the corset doing its work under her pastel-yellow dress. "Does a lady need a reason?" The false smile grew wider, pulling more to one side than the other. It did interesting things to her cheeks and eyes, intensifying their sharpness and brightness.

This was someone used to getting her way, whether it be from position and power, or her manner. And I could tell she knew how to use both.

"Ah." I raised my left hand and put it to my breast, touching the red-flower brooch in the process. "I suppose I won't take it as too much of a blow to my ego to be only a moment's curiosity, then. Should I take my leave, Lady Selyena?"

She pouted and rose from her seat. "Don't be dramatic. Come closer and let me have a better look at you. I still haven't made up my mind."

"About what?" I made no move to do as she'd asked.

Lady Selyena clucked her tongue and stepped closer. The black frills along her dress rippled as she drew nearer, and I noticed the slit in the fabric running up one side. At first I'd thought it to allow for easy riding, then I realized it to be for show. A golden chain hung around her neck and whatever sat at the end of it fell behind the plunging neckline. "Something caught your eye?" Her smile grew wicked, sharper than bottle glass.

"Something or another usually does. Part of my trade and how my mind works, I'm afraid. My eyes flit from place to place, finding it hard to settle on any one face, unless something special comes to view."

"And is there not something special for you to fix your gaze upon now?" All false sweetness slipped away from her voice. Now that razor's edge of a smile colored her words. And it promised to cut me should I answer wrongly.

Eloine was right, the nobility were a fragile sort, and fragile things are wont to cut when they break. "There's something special everywhere for anyone with the eyes to spot it."

Another step closer now, and I found myself reminded of a cat stalking a mouse. I could guess which the Lady Selyena saw herself as. "And are you such a one, Man in Red?" She inched nearer.

I shrugged, making sure my hood didn't slip down in the process.

Closer. She reached out and brushed her fingers against the sun brooch before trailing them along my chest to rest over the red-flower pin. She tapped her fingernails against its petals to the staccato of light clicks. "Do you know how to play *Geuma des Familiya*?"

A part of me wanted to reach up to take hold of her hand and move it away from me. The other part felt it wiser to take it, fold my thumb over her fingers, and press a kiss to the back of it. Polite. Expected. And less likely to land me in trouble.

"I think you'll find me a quick study, Lady Selyena."

"Mhm." She reached out to grab hold of my hood, lowering it. "That's good to know, but it's not an answer to my question. Most men have the wherewithal to do as I ask."

Most. Men. Two very specific admissions in what she'd said.

"I'm not most men." A line I'd been using far more of late than I had a taste to. "And in that, Lady Selyena, I think you'll be disappointed. I should probably take my leave, now that you're satisfied?" I'd kept it more question than statement, just in case she was likely to take it as a slight.

"I would be most disheartened if you were to leave now." Translation: She would take it as a personal offense, and I didn't need any guest within the palace souring toward me so early into my stay. "As for satisfaction, I haven't made up my mind yet, Man in Red. But, I'm rather confident from my early appraisals of what to expect. It's why I sent my letter."

That was what I needed to steer the conversation more my way. "And to that." I tapped a finger to the sun brooch on my chest. "Consider me, for the sake of our conversation, not as clever as you in how to play the game. What would you tell me if you were to teach me?"

Another step closer and her chest nearly touched mine, though she didn't have to be as close as many women for that to be the case. "I would tell you that I could teach you a great many things." She tapped the flower on my chest again. "Do you know what this is?"

I shook my head.

"*Venesia*. The blood-red flower. They say it sprouted after our lord and savior gave his life to light the path to heaven. That's why it's as red as his blood."

My lips pressed tight as I thought on that piece of lore. I couldn't recall the story and fished for whatever memory I could, but Lady Selyena provided the answer instead.

"Your face is clouded. It's not a good look for you." Before I could say anything, she reached out and brushed a thumb against my lips, gently easing them into a smile. "Better."

One of my hands went up, taking her by the wrist with only the barest hint of force. I didn't want her thinking of me as a threat. "Touching me like that, Lady Selyena, might require a bit more acquaintance and time spent between the two of us." My voice lacked any of the stone I wanted to give it in the moment, staying neutral.

She let her hand linger on my cheek. "Then we should remedy that." Her voice dropped and picked up smoke and warmth. It stirred something in me that I quickly put back into place.

I eased her hand away from my face, lowering it. The action sent her eyes wide in shock, likely over the fact I'd taken even that much liberty. "You were saying about the flower?" I adopted all the charm then of a storybook prince.

"Not even my husband treats me like that."

"It's a good thing I'm not him, then."

She finally pulled her hand free of my gentle grip and used it to brush down her dress. "The flower, then." Her voice made it clear she hadn't let the other subject go. It would rest for now, then come back when she felt I'd least expect it. "Tell me, do you know of Jahir, Son of God Above and His Light?"

The name stirred something in me, but for all I knew of the stories of the world, I didn't know this tale. "I'm afraid not. I only know of Solus, lady, and little else. I'm a stranger here, obviously, and still learning."

Some of the heat returned to her voice. "At least he's willing to learn then." She was speaking about me, though not to me.

I inclined my head, knowing it better to keep my mouth closed.

"Jahir, Son of Himself, was born of a mortal woman. Solus visited her one night and blessed her with his touch. She was a pious and good soul. She gave birth to a boy that was Solus made flesh—Jahir."

I thought more on the name. "That's not an Etaynian name, though."

Lady Selyena shook her head. "No. It's older, and this is from before Solus returned as himself to visit Antoine and grace him as a Prince of Sunlight. This was before our land had its name and when there were fewer borders to the world."

"You're remarkably knowledgeable on this matter, my lady."

"*My* lady now, is it? Perhaps I should keep talking on this then." She tapped her lips in a thoughtful gesture. "As I was saying, Jahir was born to simple people, and he grew to be a man who traveled far and learned many wisdoms of the world. He performed the seven miracles we've all come to know—true magic that changed the shape of things. He called himself the son of god, Son of Himself. Others called it heresy."

I knew how Jahir's story ended then, but I let her say it.

"He was executed. Speared through the body after his arms and hands were bound to prevent his escape. But he did not bleed from his wounds." She shook her head. "Only from his eyes and mouth. He died without a sound of pain."

I nodded and opened my mouth to thank her for sharing that with me, but she went on.

"Then, nine days later, he rose from the shallow grave in which he'd been buried. It's said he found the ones who killed him to show them his divinity and asked them to repent. To turn over to the path of Solus and Jahir, Son of Himself. They refused. When they did, they turned to bleed and die as Jahir did."

"Thank you, Lady Selyena, for telling me that. Though, I'm still lost to the meaning of this?" I touched the red flower.

She motioned to the seat. "Sit, and I will tell you."

I did as she asked. After all, it wasn't so hard a request. I didn't expect what she did next, however.

She eased herself into my lap, adjusting herself in a manner anyone would have considered . . . indelicate given how unfamiliar we were. "Now, this"—she brushed a fingertip against the flower brooch—"represents the blood of Jahir. It's the blood of God. It represents his sacrifice."

I suddenly reconsidered why Lady Selyena might have called me to her and felt that I might have been rash in letting her pin me in place. "Ah. And this is where, like in some stories, the young and foolish man is sacrificed, no?" I gave her a smile, half-teasing, half-questioning.

She returned it and I wished she hadn't. "That would be a thing, but no. Maybe once when some in the kingdom still held to pagan beliefs. Now all that is gone and the church did their duty. Everyone adheres to Solus and his path."

I said nothing.

Lady Selyena took my silence as a sign to continue. "The red also represents a symbol of love, from God to us, and then from us to others."

I opened my mouth in a silent ah. "Hearing that makes me wonder all the more, then, if my being here is appropriate." I squirmed to move but Lady Selyena shifted her weight and made it clear that she wasn't quite done with me.

. . . How wonderful.

"Not that kind of love"—she tapped a finger to my cheek and traced it along my jaw—"but the kind that lasts for a night, an evening, or a morning. Short and enjoyable."

"All the more reason for me to—" I grunted as the lady dug her fingernails into one of my biceps hard enough to make me think she'd broken my flesh even under the layers of my clothing.

A knock came from the door. Then it opened before Lady Selyena could pull herself from me.

The man standing in the open doorway wore clothes the same shade as hers, a pale sunflower yellow accented in black. The cut of his clothing was perfectly tailored to his frame. Young, maybe half a decade older than me at best. Lean, black bearded, and short haired. His figure showed signs of there being some muscle behind the man, but not as much as someone who regularly trained or worked a physical job. The man's jaw could have been shaped from stone.

It only looked all the more severe for how hard he clenched as he stared between Lady Selyena and me.

Brahm's tits and ashes, I know how these stories go. Three guesses who he could be, and I won't need the other two.

"*Wife.*" He'd spoken the single word with more sharpness than a freshly stoned knife. "I see you're already entertaining guests and we've not been here for more than a day. How dutiful of you." Though some of his words had been about me, he had no eyes for me. The whole of his glare remained fixed on Lady Selyena.

If any of it bothered her, she didn't show it. She rose slow and languorous as if undisturbed by the situation. "Husband." Her tone lacked any of the emphasis and venom of her spouse's. "What's her name?"

The lord only raised an eyebrow but said nothing to answer.

"Already forgotten, or did you never get it? Very well. Do you know her age? How young is she, my sweet?" Lady Selyena left me behind as she neared her husband, keeping a good distance out of reach.

"You think I've . . . ?" He didn't bother finishing the question.

Lady Selyena gave him a smile that made the edge of his seem rusted and dull in comparison. It was a smile that could have cut to the bone. "I know. The bruise is still fresh just above your collar, dear. Feisty, that one. Does she know that could be seen as harming a lord? Dear." The lady raised a hand to her mouth and gasped in mock surprise. "If I recall, it's fifty lashes at least. Though, it's an easy enough thing to see her strung up and left to twist."

The lord's face colored more than I thought someone with his complexion could. "Just touched her twentieth year. Elindra. She's one of the servants here—no, I didn't bother to ask which kind. Just a passing fancy. As mine all are. Which is to say . . . not the same as yours." His eyes leveled accusation at her.

I realized how well-worn this exchange might have been between the pair, and that my poor luck had just dropped me into the middle of their newest moment of marital discontent. My best bet rested in quickly *and* quietly leaving, even if I had to break one of the large windows behind me and jump out of it.

"Mine was just as fleeting a fancy. Granted, he's only been playing the game for less than an hour. I didn't even get to have my fun. I was lacking entertainment." Lady Selyena balled her fists and placed them on her hips, still holding to the cutting edge in her voice.

Her lord husband ignored her, turning his gaze on me. No, not on me. On my chest. His stare hovered on the red-flower brooch. "And you find no entertainment I suppose in being dandled in a stranger's lap?"

If I could have made myself invisible, I would have then and there. Short of that, my best option was to admit the truth. My ignorance. "Lord, lady. I've only just arrived at the palace and, not to put too great a point on it, only come into this game of yours. Rather innocently and unaware." Which wasn't wholly true, but close enough to be the case.

The lord kept his gaze on my chest as I began walking past him. "So you have." The stare intensified on the brooch. "Red flower. Curious choice, Wife. Last I checked, our treats were given white."

I logged that piece of information for future reference. Though I didn't know what it meant, learning whatever I could about the variances in summons would go a long way to helping me keep my neck attached to the rest of me.

"A man in red, like Araiyo, no? What better than a red flower for such a one?" Lady Selyena's attention briefly flitted my way before returning to her husband.

The name she'd spoken struck me with leaden weight. But for the accent and a few superfluous letters, it could have been a name I was once better acquainted with—speaking, even. "Who?" The question left my lips before I'd realized it.

Lady Selyena turned halfway to address me, then stopped short, her attention returning to her husband. "Later, my man in red. I believe right now my husband and I must speak, then make some amends, between both of us."

I nodded, needing no further cue to take my leave. The lord's stare weighed heavy on my back as I passed them by and exited their chambers.

I hadn't quite collapsed to my bed when a knock came at my own door. I swallowed the string of curses that came to mind and checked to see who'd come.

Marcos. The same cushion as before rested upon his hands. Only now, it trembled. A single pin sat atop it with another letter. No sun brooch, however.

"What's wrong? Why are your hands shaking?"

He said nothing. One corner of his lips were swollen, almost as if they'd been close to being split. I saw the beginnings of a bruise forming under his left eye.

"Who did this to you?"

Again, nothing.

I nearly reached out and grabbed the boy, then realized that would only make matters worse. "I didn't mean to get angry, and I'm certainly not with you, Marcos. I just want to know who hurt you."

His eyes narrowed like I'd passed my rage to him. It fled just as quick and his face had all the lines and signs of tiredness men decades his senior should have worn. "Not everyone gets to keep secrets, Man in Red. And not everyone gets to play." He pushed the cushion toward me. "Your letter. Your pin." His hands shook harder.

I sighed and took them. The piece of jewelry was a perfect replica of the flower I wore now, except it lacked every bit of red. Every bit of gemstone was the perfect black of shadow.

"Thank you for bringing this to me, Marcos."

"You shouldn't. Not when you learn what it means." He didn't bother to explain, turning and leaving at that.

I placed the pin onto the bed and tore open the letter.

Man in Red,

Welcome to the game.

Lord Emeris Umbrasio

Husband to the Lady Selyena

Ps. May your heart be as hard to find as shadows in the night.

"And they say I'm melodramatic." I let the letter fall to the floor and picked up the new pin, turning it over in my hands. If the red flower was an invitation of love or for passionate exploits, then I wondered what a black one meant.

SEVENTY-SIX
The Masks We Wear

My nap lasted a few hours at best, though it felt closer to minutes from when I'd laid my head down.

Another knock, gentler than any that had come before, sounded at the door.

I rose to answer it, making sure to keep my staff in hand just in case. My welcome to the summer palace had been eventful enough as it was. I opened the door and stared into the eyes of a man whose face remained mostly hidden behind a mask.

The piece looked to be fashioned out of pearl—its body had the color at least. The outer edges were painted gold with a few bands of what could have been tendrils of fire protruding from one corner of the disguise. What was visible of the man's jaw showed something soft and youthful, probably someone still in their early twenties.

His build was lean and tight, and he dressed in clothes far beneath what I expected of other guests. Simple riding breeches in a black that refused to hold any dust and debris. And his shirt was much the same, only in a white as bright as his pants were dark.

His clothes were functional, without adornment, yet their colors so clean and fresh despite being put through frequent use given their purpose and appearance. To be all that and look new as when first made?

Whoever stood before me had more wealth than any sum of little lords conspiring quietly among themselves in the palace, which left a good bet as to who he was.

I chose my next words carefully. "Afternoon, or is it evening already?" Keeping the matter to the time of day, and a question at that, spared me from having to address the man by name or title. I'd have less chance of getting it wrong that way.

He smiled. An easy and lazy thing on his face. "Somewhere between, actually. Might I come in?" He'd said it smooth enough, but a hesitancy still hung in the words as if he wasn't accustomed to asking permission.

High enough in rank then to not worry much about the social standings of others.

I nodded, opening the door in full and gesturing a silent welcome.

The newcomer walked toward the small table close to one corner of my bed. He immediately reached out for the brooches I'd collected and left there.

I shut the door, waiting for him to speak and offer some clarity as to what he wanted.

He picked up the red-flower pin first, turning it over in his hand. "Amorous beginnings to your stay here, Storyteller."

That brought me to raise my eyebrows. He'd already heard of my arrival and who I was before many of the other guests. Someone important then. It narrowed the possibilities of his identity considerably.

"Surprised? Don't be." He set the pin down, frowning as he fixed on the black-flower one. The man didn't bother picking it up and settled for prodding it with an index finger instead. "You've been here for hours and already managed to collect a pair like this, hm? That says something. It says a pair of things, in fact. And it says a great deal more of who you've met. Let me guess, the Lady Selyena and her husband, Lord Umbrasio." The way he'd said it meant it was no guess at all.

"Quick. Accurate." That was all I'd give the man in admission.

"She moved faster than I imagined, and I'm not sure if that's impressive or terrifying. She's getting bolder, especially with the guests." He managed to eye me askance despite the mask hiding a good portion of his face. "Did she get what she wanted out of you?"

I shrugged. "At first I would have said no. But after seeing how she and her husband interacted, I'm not so sure. It could have been I was nothing more than a scene to be made and a thorn to be jabbed into that man's side."

My guest grunted as if he'd expected that possibility. "It would be very much like the pair of them, though something happened between you to warrant this." He touched the black-flower pin again.

Did I ask him what it meant and betray my lack of knowledge, or did I feign familiarity with the game?

He finally plucked up the pin and held it up, flower-face toward me. "The red one, when offered especially by a woman like Lady Selyena, is an invitation for a dalliance. The sort that often has men, young ones too at times, reconsidering their health afterward. Her appetites are said to be . . . edging on the ravenous. I'm glad she didn't have her way with you before I could, Storyteller."

All of which begged the question: What exactly did he have in mind for me?

"The black one, though, is a particular problem, given who it came from. It means animosity. *Strong* animosity. Offense given and taken with the promise to repay it in full. Bad blood—bitter blood. Hence the black." He tapped the dark flower with the inside of his thumb. "It's a promise for vengeance, and I'm rather sorry to say it doesn't always fall within the confines of the law. Emeris is a rather short-tempered man."

Not even a day in the palace and I'd already earned the hostility of another lord. It seemed, of all the curses I'd been rumored to have collected, earning the ire of the nobility still ran strong for me.

What joy.

"But *of course* you knew all of this, Storyteller, and I'm just prattling about the game as it's on my mind right now. We're at the beginning of it, though I guess for you it's already begun. Play carefully."

"Of course. And while we're just talking things we all know, I don't suppose the other flowers' meanings will come up between us?"

A crooked smile flashed across the man's face for the space of a wink. "White flowers, set with pearls, indicate a neutral meeting. Can be for personal pleasure and honest curiosity, but not the sort of entertainment Lady Selyena had in mind. An interest for conversation, learnings, perhaps to discuss mutual fancies of intellect, musings, and the like. The most common of invitations.

"The sapphire rose is an interesting one. People use it to offer favor or, if a sapphire rose has previously been granted, to call on that debt. *That* is the purpose of many players in the game. To grant and receive favors to call on. It's how gentry and lesser nobles seek to raise their stations in life."

Lesser nobles he'd said.

"Yellow set with citrines are to discuss business. Also rather common and another way some houses seek to move their way about the court and to greater fortune. Now, the pink rose is something else altogether, my friend. That is one for and of secrets." He didn't bother elaborating past that, which I took to mean was part of the flower's purpose in the game.

"It's been a while since I've seen a copper sun brooch." I hoped he'd take the meaning and explain its use as well.

"Gold, silver, copper, bronze, and wood. The first is a summons all men must heed. From the top and those closest to the sun itself—the royal family. Silver is sent to your betters along with the flower indicating what sort of meeting you desire, and copper to your peers, and bronze is sent to those less than you. The family, however, only deals in gold, and you are never to keep that brooch. Remember to return yours when you get it."

The family. And when I get one. That ended the matter for me. "Of course, Prince. And the wooden sun?"

He turned and tilted his head like a dog hearing a new sound. "I didn't know if you'd figure it out. You'd be surprised how many don't if they've never met me before. Wooden suns are for the pontifex and his people—wood, simple thing and of the earth, like Antoine. Symbolizes their connection to the common man. So, what was it?"

"The clothing. Things you've said." Revealing too much sometimes takes the trick away from the thing itself. It's often better to leave more things to mystery and the wonderings of another person's mind. They can fill in the story how they best see fit, and more likely than not, craft something just as interesting as the truth.

Sometimes better.

And it all adds to your own credit.

"Clever man. I prefer to keep the company of those more than the dithering lords and ladies currently filling up my home's many rooms." The man inclined his head a shade so slight I almost missed it. "Prince Ateine."

"The Storyteller." I offered a deeper bow than he had. As I watched the man, he showed none of the signs I'd been looking for. Smooth, controlled, and lacking any of the strangeness I'd seen in the Tainted. Many kings and leaders were already so twisted it left little doubt about their true natures. Etaynia had remained stable . . . so far, but with the murder of one *efante* already, and all done to seize power, were their princes already taken and turned? Not to mention the whispers of war on the lips of some princes.

So which prince had been taken, twisted, and turned?

Which one would I have to kill?

I didn't know, and could tell even less. But I hoped to find out.

"And the man behind the mask, I wonder?" Prince Ateine watched me with greater intensity.

Now it was my turn to cant my head at an angle and wait for him to explain.

"A man is more than his title, but often so many of us wear them for so long we forget the man under it all." He removed the mask.

Prince Ateine lived up to what I imagined. Soft faced and featured. One could consider him more beautiful than handsome. He had the dark features most Etaynians shared in hair and eye color, but his skin was more a pale gold, lacking any of the sun's warmth and shine. His hair was kept short with a few rogue locks brushing down to his eyebrows. "Being a prince is the unseen mask I wear all day, and this one"—he jiggled the disguise in his hand—"frees me to be the man I really am."

Prince Ateine donned the mask again and headed to the door. "I came to meet you and take you into account, Storyteller. You haven't disappointed. I expect good entertainment out of you—both from your trade, and your playing of the game. I wonder what mischief you'll get into." He lingered in the opening, resting against the frame. "I imagine you'll be getting other summonses soon. People have been talking, and the nobility love little else more than they do rumors." He slipped away, taking no care to shut the door behind him as he left.

My gaze slowly flitted back to the black rose resting where the prince had left it.

A promise for vengeance. It wasn't the only one I'd earned in my life, and Lord Umbrasio would have to get in line. Because a few others were already sharpening their swords, waiting for the chance to have at me.

I left instructions with one of the porters outside my door where I could be found if any party decided to take that chance to try and run me through with a blade. Then I asked for directions and headed toward the library.

Night came to the library, leaving most of it shrouded in darkness save for the parts closest to the windows that let in pale bands of moonlight to cascade over the many shelves.

I still hadn't found what I'd been looking for, but I pressed on. One of my thumbs traced along the spines of leather-bound tomes as I walked by, keeping my eyes open for anything that looked like it could hold a story instead of a history or genealogy. A book caught my eye and I stopped.

Thinner than those around it, it showed all the signs of being well worn. The title had faded nearly to nothingness as if someone had brushed the lettering away over years of heavy touch and use. A miracle held the binding together, but long knotted creases still sprouted along the book's spine as I applied just a hint of pressure to it. And the ends of the pages had been smoothed by what I knew came from years of thumbs rubbing along them.

Scholars and those obsessed with their own histories pored over books with a delicate touch and not as frequently as this. These signs spoke of something very precious inside. Something worth reading over and over again.

A story.

I smiled like greeting a long-lost friend and thumbed the book open like many before me.

Tuecanti des Nuevellos. The book's title had no Trader's Tongue translation. Reading even further revealed that the entire piece lacked any annotations I could use to parse together the story inside. All Etaynian.

I sighed, snapping it shut with a sound like a hand striking a flour sack.

Light shone through the rows of shelves, and it was not the soft nightly glimmer of the moon. Nor was it candlelight cast and holding to that weak ghostly glow that came from the edge of tiny flames. This had all the radiance of the sun in full midday bloom. It burned from rows down from me, and grew all the brighter the closer it came.

I shut my eyes, waiting for them to adapt. My ears took to the task of figuring out what was happening.

Footsteps. Soft, measured, taken with care. Whoever held the object knew how to move quietly, but not so silently that they wouldn't be heard altogether.

"I used to enjoy that book as a child. I recognized the cover," said the man holding the light source.

Most of the brightness had tempered now and no longer brought out the pink inside my eyelids. I opened my eyes and took in the stranger.

He wore an overcoat that hung to his calves. The outfit caught every bit of light around us to bring out the brightest of gold in it. A red lion pawing at a sun of the same color had been stitched into the fabric. His boots were the color of rust over clay.

Another prince, then? I'd learned long ago that the crest of a lion pawing at the sun belonged to the royal family.

Much like the *efante* I'd crossed paths with earlier, this gentleman wore a mask as well. It lacked any of the decorative nature of the previous prince's, sitting more like silvery ivy woven together in a manner that just so happened to obscure his face. A longer look at the mask led me to believe it could have been fashioned from the precious metal, much like his clothing looked to be.

"May I?" The man gestured with his free hand toward the book.

My attention went to the shining crystalline orb in his other. A lamp cut in a perfect sphere without any source of light, but which radiated it nonetheless. Unlike binder's lights, this contained all the intensity of the sun.

The man caught my stare and raised the tool. "It's a bit too bright for nights, but I've come to enjoy the little marvel. It's called a sun eater. Comes by way of your part of the world, I believe? An improvement over the binder's lights that have passed our way over the years and trade along the Golden Road. I never did learn how to temper this thing's fire, though." The masked man's lips pulled into a deep frown.

The fingers of one of my hands dug into my staff with enough force I would either crack my nails or bits of the wood. I passed the book over and resisted the urge to reach out for the sun eater.

Nonetheless, the man noticed my little gesture. "By all means, take a better look." He placed it into my hand and, for a moment, I nearly flinched away at the oncoming miniature sun.

It landed safely in my palm without any noticeable heat transference. I expected as much, but it had been a long time since I'd seen one of these, and even longer still since I was the sort of man who found any comfort in holding fire. Even a false flame.

Fire now served the role of parlor tricks and enhancing my performance.

Except for when Eloine was in danger. I thought back to when the clergos had set on us and I'd been forced to remember a shadow of what I'd once been.

The sun eater rested carefully in place and my mind went to the folds, but not to conjure a binding. I went instead for a piece of memory.

My staff slid free of my grip and struck one of the shelves as it came to rest at an angle. One of my hands held the sun eater firm while the other pressed to its curve, slowly sliding around it in a gentle caress. Some of its light dimmed, almost as if I'd created an eclipse with my palm, and soon, the fire inside the orb lessened as well.

The man I suspected to be another prince exhaled almost in reverence. "Now that is a trick, Storyteller. How did you do that?"

"Sun eaters store sunlight within them rather than a paler glow like binder's lights, but they're operated by touch. There are directional symbols carved . . ." I trailed off as I realized how deep I'd gone into a piece of my history I'd forgotten, and all the while, the possible prince watched me with an interest far beyond mild curiosity. And his look told me he had little idea how sun eaters truly worked beyond kindling one to life and snuffing it out again.

"Nothing." I shook my head. "It's just a small magic. Slide your hand one way to dim the light, then the other way to brighten it. It will keep them from burning out faster if you let them glow a little softer at times."

The man nodded, gesturing for me to set it down.

Comfortable giving silent commands and just as used to expecting them to be followed. That, and he knew who I was. If he didn't guess it at first from my appearance, then Prince Ateine could have told him. Meaning he converses with at least one prince.

"Which of the *efante* are you?"

The man gave me a lopsided smile that shifted the mask slightly. "Ateine said you were quick. Though, I suppose the clothing could have given it away, no?"

I nodded. "True, but you seem comfortable in the library in the dark. You knew the book at a glance and mentioned loving it as a child. That speaks of familiarity with it and this place. Then there's the sun eater."

The man frowned. "What about it?"

"They're expensive."

His expression deepened. "How much so?"

"Enough that any man would remember how much he'd paid for one unless he had a king's wealth to spend on trinkets. Or, a prince's purse."

The prince finally smiled. "Ah, well, there is that. Though, I never much found a handful of gold to be that shocking a sum to spend on things like this." He nudged the sun eater with a foot.

"Another point. Gold *is* expensive to nearly everyone but those who have it in abundance. And sun eaters cost a silver rose at best, depending on the seller."

"Silver's not a terrible sum for any man to pay for such a thing."

My mouth pressed tight, but not so much I couldn't voice my thoughts. "Do you think many men have silver to spare?"

That caught the prince off guard, and he knew enough to change the subject lest he look an ill-informed fool. He drummed his fingers against the cover of the book before opening it. "*Tales of the Nine.* At first I thought them like all other children's tales. Entertaining. Wondrous. Delightful." Though he'd stopped talking, the air thickened in the aftermath like he'd left something unsaid.

"But?"

"I grew older, started hearing stories sometimes from fringes of the kingdom of terrible things that had all the signs of The Nine."

"Ashura." The word left my mouth before I'd known I'd spoken it.

The prince's head slowly rose from the book to stare at me. "What word did you say?" He pursed his lips and looked back down at the book, the lines of his jaw almost saying *thoughtful* as he read on. "I haven't heard that before."

"We have stories of nine monsters—demons, more like it—back in my homeland as well. Many call them the Ashura."

"Ah. The *Nuevellos* here. The nine—nine of them." He tapped the spot of the cover where the title had been worn away. "*Tales of the Nine.*"

So the book had been what I was looking for, or at least, it could hold a piece of what I wanted in its pages. "Funny thing, that. The full name of the demons I grew up hearing about is Naushura. Nine of them. Seems we share some themes in the stories of our countries."

The prince grunted, flipping through the pages faster than any man who hoped to properly read them. "They turned to nightmares for me once I reached my tenth birthday. After that, persistent horrors every time my father got word of some unexplainable awfulness happening out in the far reaches of our world. Though, they were infrequent enough, Solus be praised." The prince's hand went to his breast, touching the sun over his heart before he moved the hand to the hollow of his throat.

I didn't mirror the gesture, though common sense told me it would have been expected of others. But my mind was elsewhere. I almost reached out to take the book from the prince, knowing the action would draw his ire.

Nobility are not fond of people taking things from their hands. It usually goes the other way around.

"In truth, as much as I hoped to come here and perform for you and your brothers, I can't deny that I hadn't hoped to also have access to your family's library."

The prince gestured to all the shelves around us. "At your leisure, Storyteller."

I bowed my head. "Thank you, Prince . . . ?"

"Artenyo. I'm sure if you continue your wanderings, Storyteller, you'll meet the rest of my brothers soon enough." He snapped the book closed, moving to put it back where I'd found it.

"The story—the tales, I mean, do you remember anything of note?"

Prince Artenyo shook his head. "I'm afraid not. But, read it yourself and you might find the answer to your question." He passed me the collection of tales.

"I'm afraid, and rather embarrassed to admit, that I can't read much in the way of Etaynian. Though, I am very interested to learn of the stories inside. And to transcribe a version in the Trader's Tongue, if that's possible and with your permission, of course."

The prince shrugged and placed the book into one of my hands. "I'll have someone sent to your rooms tomorrow to walk you through translating Etaynian to Trader's Tongue." It wasn't a question.

"That would be most kind of you."

He waved me off. "Not so much a kindness as granting a favor, Storyteller." The prince's hand went into one of the pockets of his overcoat. He then produced a flower-pin. Its color was the blue late-night skies that refused to hold blackness in them. The color of sapphires. "A favor granted is one owed, and I'm very much looking toward what I can call on you for, Storyteller. I've heard tell of your tales, and having you in my pocket for even the shortest of times will be entertaining." He placed the blue flower onto the cover of the book.

"Welcome to the game. You're off to a terrible start, from what I hear. You should really consider a mask if you want to remain in our home and make it as far as your ambitions." He tapped the side of his mask. "Good night."

Prince Artenyo left me with the book, brooch, and the dimmed sun eater.

The man hadn't outright acknowledged the existence of the Ashura, but he'd made it clear enough he still feared the thought of them.

Would a Tainted care? Was it a ruse? The seeds of paranoia promised to grow in the garden of worry I tilled, so I banished the thoughts for the moment. I'd only met two of the princes and would need to see them all before even having an idea of who to pursue further.

I placed the book under one arm and slipped the flower-pin into a pocket, not wanting to display it at all. I returned my staff to my hand and I'd nearly taken my first step to leave when I felt the late breeze filter in behind me. It rustled my cloak and brought a soothing chill to my back.

Only, the windows hadn't been open when I'd arrived hours earlier in the library. And I hadn't opened them since.

A smell struck me. One I hadn't breathed in for ages, and it brought with it a memory of singing sands and shifting dunes. A place far from Etaynia. And long ago.

The scent was of pine, lavender, orange peel, and something that could have been considered a pungent musk.

I knew it, though the men and women carrying that kind of odor were a world away from this country. They resided closer to the heart of my own, if I had any place left to call home, that is.

I licked my lips and didn't turn in case the source of the smell took me as a threat. "You're a long way from home."

"As are you, little lion." His voice was smoke over sand. Rough, a graininess to it, and all the dryness of age.

"Azrim, is that you?" I kept my gaze focused ahead of me, not behind.

"Who better to find you, lion's cub?"

My mouth dried, but I still found just enough moisture to ask the question I'd been holding in my heart after I'd first smelled him. "You're here as a Rashin tonight. Who's the target?" *Dumb question,* I realized. "One of the *efante* has already been killed. Were you the knife? And are you here for another?"

"*Chch-chch,* what's happened to you? So slow. So dull. Where is the lion now?"

I exhaled, wondering if I could round on him quick enough to bring my staff down on his skull. "Gone. That man died a long time ago. Haven't you heard the stories?"

"I was there for some, Ari. I think I still see a piece of the man that walked away from us, leaving his debts, and leaving many other things besides. You cannot hope to spurn a king and walk away without consequence. And you can do even less of that to a Rashin."

That was that, then. "You're not here for the *efante* and their succession. You're here for me."

"*Ahlm*. I've spent much-a-time looking for you. Always hearing whispers.

Listening to all the twisty truths you've left behind, seeking after the new face you wear, and the name that goes with it. You learned well, little lion. You still make the same mistakes, though."

He didn't need to tell me what they were. I knew it already. "The *clergos*. Somehow word spread of what I did there."

"*Chch. Chch.* It's one thing for many tricksters to make a little magic with fire, Ari. But for one to breathe it and be called a devil? I've only seen one man play with fire so. But I haven't heard of you doing it since, and now I am wondering why?"

Ah. Curiosity. "Like I said, Azrim. I'm not the man I once was. I . . . haven't performed the bindings like of old in a long time. What happened there was." I stopped short, not even letting the promise of more words hang in the air. I tried to find others, but couldn't. "It was." Another stop. "There was a woman, and in the moment, I didn't have a choice but to hope to remember." I shrugged.

"Same mistakes, lion. *Chch. Chch.*"

His little chastising sounds grated my ears. They were like fishhooks set into my skull, dragging and pulling at more than just the meat of me, but they brought memories to the surface. My fingers flexed against the staff, and for nearly a moment, I considered it a binder's cane again.

"Some habits die hard, I suppose. Who sent you, then? Was it Karum? No. He wouldn't care after so long." I had almost wondered if Lord Umbrasio had decided to make good on the silent threat from the pin. But Azrim had let it slip that he'd been following me longer than that. "Or is this just personal?"

"Look at me, then we can talk on this, *Ahlm*?"

I blew a breath out through my nostrils, nodding to myself before I turned.

Azrim, like any Rashin in the middle of their work, wore all the colors of night. Which is to say, he dressed in a swath of blues so varied and dark you couldn't tell where one shade ended and another began. It was all of twilight darkness in a soft cloth that could make the wearer invisible under moonlight or cloudy late skies. Only his eyes were visible through a finger-wide slit in the mask hiding his face.

"You look good. Well, as much as one can when all I can see are the wrinkles beneath your eyes. They don't look like they've worsened over the years." I couldn't manage a thin smile as I made the joke.

"Ah, you're scared. I taught you better, little cub."

"You did. And I am. Only a fool's not afraid when facing a Rashin, and for all the kinds of fool I am and have been, I'm not that kind."

"The stories say otherwise, Ari."

Now my smile turned to uneven and cutting. "They say all the things people have made them say. And as you mentioned, you were there for some of them." I swallowed before speaking my next words. "So you know what happens when people try to kill me."

Azrim produced the dagger with a fluidity and skill that made any sleight of hand I could manage seem childish. It simply appeared in his grip and its edge caught all the glint from the sun eater's light. "Look me in the eyes, cub."

I did.

Another light shone then, just barely. I caught it in the beads of water along his eyelids.

Tears.

"It brings me no pleasure to do this, cub. No pleasure at all."

"So don't." I raised one of my hands in what I hoped he'd see as a calming gesture.

"I must. You broke *araf.* There is no coming back from that."

I nodded, not accepting my death, but understanding that he couldn't walk away from trying to make it happen. Or, that he wouldn't. "I've broken more than that, Azrim—worse." I met his gaze again, and when I did, he blinked.

"I see so little of you even in your own face."

I said nothing.

"Just a Storyteller, then? All you are now."

"When I have to be, which is more often than not. But I haven't stopped my search, Azrim. I won't. You know what I'm looking for." The staff creaked in my grip and I knew my knuckles had gone white against it. "And if you try to stop me in that . . ." Some of the old fire from an Ari long forgotten filled my voice again.

"You'll kill me, little cub?"

"Worse. I'll remember. And that Ari is not the one you want to fight. Because that's the same child you once taught, and he remembers those things, even if buried now. And that's the child you once feared. Don't make me go looking for him, because if I do, I'll find him."

The knife never shook in Azrim's hand, but he lowered it and put it back in its place. "I taught you to veil yourself before doing things you never wanted to stain your eyes and heart. Maybe I taught you too well. I don't see that boy anymore, only the mask. But just now, I saw a piece of him. When you find him again, send him looking for me. Then we'll take the air together and we will dance." He snapped his hand and something flicked toward the ground.

It cracked against the floor, breaking with a violent flash like lightning in a dark room.

I shut my eyes against it out of instinct. When I opened them, smoke filled the space between us. I didn't wait for it to clear before collecting my things and leaving.

Azrim was already gone.

And he wouldn't be back until I'd removed the mask I'd grown accustomed to wearing.

SEVENTY-SEVEN
Intermission—Invitations

My encounter with Azrim kept me from a sound night's sleep. So the hours slipped by with fits of fretful turning and thoughts of daggers in the dark. They never came, of course, but the images persisted.

I managed a few winks of rest, broken up by all the things that could weigh on a man's mind, and morning arrived too soon for me to hope for anything more. The comfort of bed begged me to stay and make up for what sleep I'd lost, but I knew I couldn't afford it.

With all the princes in one place, whether for their game, or to hurry along with the succession to king, I at least had access to them all. And they, each other.

What better way to remove your rivals?

I understood then the nature of what else the game could come to mask. For all the maneuvering it allowed the gentry and nobility, it could just as easily allow princes to move around in anonymity and set in motion darker things. Exposing secrets, selling them, or clearing a path to the throne.

It seemed I'd need another mask if I wanted to move more carefully among the Etaynian upper class. Despite morning fog filling my skull, I steadied my breathing and reached for the folds. First, something familiar.

I envisioned my clothes. Not as they were now, rumpled, carrying particulates and dust from over the day. No, I saw them as they were in the minds of those that shaped each piece, better than new. I saw the dream of them.

Two folds. Then four. All one needed in honesty to affect something as simple as clothing, and my cloak and cowl refused to hold to any dirt and debris. "Whent. Ern." My Athir and will took to the task of reshaping reality within my sphere of influence. An easy enough belief to hold.

I looked down to find my clothing had been set back the way it had been. *If only I could do that for how I feel.* The mild binding left me comfortable enough to try my hand at a better one.

I took a breath, wondering if I was really up to the task. That alone should have been the answer.

An old voice went through my head. "There are no *ifs* when dealing with the bindings. Belief must be absolute."

I needed a mask and searched my room for the necessary materials. A heavy trunk rested by my bedside, offering me something sturdy with which to make the bulk of the disguise. Several candelabra sat upon a mantelpiece, and the face of the hearth was a smooth black stone that would do nicely. I reached out to brush the wood of the chest, letting my touch take in its details.

Soft, supple, and strong. All of which I could use and want for. I saw myself pulling, piece by piece and through my thoughts, to reshape a portion of its mass into the mask I sought.

Half a dozen folds filled my mind. "Whent. Ern."

Nothing happened.

"Whent. Ern."

The wood remained the same.

"Work, damn you. I believe. I do." My hand smacked against the trunk and I knew the words I'd spoken weren't true. Most of my time in Etaynia had been spent under the guise I'd spent years cultivating and convincing myself of. For one brief moment I'd let myself become my old self—all to rescue Eloine from the clergos. And I'd forgotten him just as fast, until she'd asked me to tell my story.

Even still, the Ari who could work bindings beyond showmanship and little tricks hadn't come back. So even shaping a mask, with the materials at hand, remained outside of my ability.

Fine legend I am. Cleaning my clothes and manipulating firelight for stories. Is that the breadth of what I can do now? I placed more weight on my staff than usual as I headed toward the door, deciding that maybe I'd worn enough masks of late.

The porter at my door turned to me as I stepped outside.

He reminded me of someone's portly uncle stuffed into finer clothes than he could afford. Balding, thick mustachioed, and carrying a baby's fat in his cheeks and jowls. "Would the good gentleman care for breakfast? I can have it brought to your room."

I thought on that. The more I walked around the palace, the better chance I had at learning what I wanted, but it also meant that much more exposure to the other guests. More chances for them to rope me further into their game.

"That would be appreciated." I noted he'd called me a gentleman, meaning at the very least he saw me as among the gentry, even if not a noble. "Do you know how many of the *efantes* are residing here right now?"

The porter's eyes went wide, but it might have been a moment's shock. He recovered with his next breath. "Yes. Though, some of the younger members of the family are not in Del Soliel at all. Only those in the election are here." He'd said it as if it should have been obvious.

So the game is more than what I thought. There were more ways to become king than simply murdering the other princes. Winning the election had to be the other angle the *efantes* were working.

"How long will it take for breakfast to be brought to me?" I made sure to voice the question with simple curiosity and not the impatience of a lord.

"Half mark of the hour. But it will be hot and fresh." He sounded like he was trying to reassure me.

I grunted and shut the door behind me. "I'll be back before then. If anyone asks for me, tell them I've taken to wandering the castle. My legs could use the stretching."

"And if they've sent a summons, sir?"

"Then they'll have to wait till I'm back . . . if I choose to respond at all." I didn't bother to pay attention to his reaction as I left.

My exploring led me to some of the lower halls that served no other function than boasting lengthy corridors to waste your time. If they did anything, I couldn't see it. Perhaps they were spaces to fit all the royal family's extra paintings?

One side of the walls were all of glass that let in the gray morning light. Something else hung in the sky and let me know the cause of the dimness. The moon, still lingering from the previous night. She sat there, cold and distant, no longer shining bright. Pale. Almost a shadow in white.

I bit off a curse that worked its way into my throat when I saw another figure approaching from the other end of the corridor.

They wore a coat the color of summer clouds and pants as dark as winter night skies. A longsword hung at their hip, and the ease with which their hand rested on the pommel let me know they were comfortable with the weapon.

A guard? They didn't have the look of a lord or great nobility. No mask hid their face either.

As they neared, I took in their features.

You would be hard-pressed to choose between calling them handsome or beautiful, and in truth would be better served using a term that contained both meanings. A chisel had been taken to them, providing their smooth stone face all the hard and sharp lines it needed to be striking and inviting. Skin closer to cream over tea than the well-tanned faces I'd seen more often. Their hair was near the length of mine, but tied at the back and held up by a clip if I had to guess.

"The Storyteller?" Their voice fit their face, leaving me clueless as to whether they were a man or woman.

I nodded. "And you are?"

"An arm when I need to be. A hand otherwise. Sometimes more." One of their hands tightened against the sword for the space of a heartbeat. But I'd caught the action, and that was enough.

"Ah, and what are you right now?"

"Curious," they said.

"I've been told I have that effect on men and women."

They gave me a flat smile—colorless, with no meaning for me to find in it. *A puzzle then.*

"I've heard you're a wondrous performer, not least for the magics you can conjure."

I gave them a slight bow, spreading my arms wide as I did. "That's the word, and I've done my fair share in making sure that's the sort that's spread."

"I'm sure. But I'm wondering why the *efantes* would let such a one as you enter Del Soliel at all? They can have any performers they want here. So why you? Why a foreigner?"

Ah. A good question. "I almost thought to ask the same thing when I was let in, but then decided some things are better off left unquestioned. You should consider that option."

Another empty smile. "It's my job to ask. To know."

I didn't want to linger and waste any more time, so I tried to shoulder past the person and get on with my morning.

They stepped in front of me.

I gripped my staff tighter and they noticed it, but I spoke before they decided to do anything. "Then go ask one of the princes. I'm sure they have the answer you're looking for."

More movement at the end of the hall drew my attention.

A figure, cut along the same lines as the other princes in height and general build. He wore clothing of a similar vein that had the same embroidery along his chest. A man in black from head to toe. Even his mask was a knotted wood of the same color, which covered his face from above his lips to his hairline.

The stranger in front of me turned and stepped out of the way, bowing.

That confirmed part of my theory. "Who's the little lord?"

They hissed and shot me a withering glare. "Watch your tongue in front of a prince."

And that settled it.

The prince joined us, passing a short look over me before settling his gaze on the armed stranger. "Hm. Clergos? No. Not any of the guard, especially the ones I know. And I've made it my business to know them all, especially after Eniyo passed. You're new." The prince reached out, touching the stranger's flank with two fingers and sliding them down until he reached their hips. Further still, he moved his fingers and stroked the side of their leg.

"I am, my prince."

"And who are you exactly? Did one of my brothers take you on then? What purpose, I wonder?" A lascivious grin took his face and he pinched the stranger.

They didn't squirm under it. "I'm Vanye, my prince. And I was brought on by Prince Efraine."

"To do what?" The prince's grip shifted to Vanye's rear.

I shouldn't have been surprised by the prince's forwardness. Few things, if any, were likely withheld from him, including people. Though, I still expected him to behave a bit better than that in public.

"To serve, Prince Arturo," said Vanye.

"I haven't decided, Vanye, if I find you pretty, or gorgeous. Would you help me get to the bottom of that . . . and other things?"

I had expected Vanye to rebuff the prince's advances. Barring that, I prepared myself to intervene.

"Most people find me both, before and after taking the time to ponder the differences between those terms." Vanye returned the prince's lustful look.

All of my thoughts and plans vanished with that, and I stood dumbfounded that the man's advances had worked.

"Then let's you and I work to sate my curiosity." Prince Arturo ran a hand up to Vanye's chest where he lingered, caressing the area. "Like if I were to remove your coat, what would I find?"

"A heart that bleeds for the kingdom," said Vanye.

Prince Arturo blinked, clearly at a loss over the answer. He recovered his senses and moved his hand lower, stopping just shy of Vanye's waistline. "And were I to venture further south? What would I find below?"

The curve of Vanye's mouth spoke more of sex and wickedness than anything the prince could have managed, and one look at it sent his color rising full in face. "Justice. A long night. Little mercy. And very much an entertaining time."

The prince laughed, then remembered I was standing there. "Oh. The Storyteller." All of the passion and excitement vanished from his voice.

A fair reaction, I suppose.

"I remember getting word you'd asked to pay us a visit. Good. A neutral party is most welcome during the game and election. I wonder whose favor you'll try to curry while here, and who's already done so with you?" He reached into one of his pockets and pulled free two pins. "I invite you, Storyteller."

I nearly groaned but remembered myself. I said nothing as I accepted a golden sun brooch and the white flower he'd offered alongside it. Mild relief welled in me as I realized he sought nothing more than a simple meeting.

"And for you, Vanye." The prince passed them a red flower. "Tonight?"

"I'm relieved by afternoon."

"All the better." The prince extended his hand toward me all while keeping his attention on Vanye.

We traded grips and some of the heat left me as I held on. His skin felt like he'd spent time standing naked in snow. I let go and watched as the prince stepped away from us.

"I'll see the both of you around. For now, I'm off to play and talk. I have an election to conclude and a throne to take."

I arched a brow. "You sound confident, Prince Arturo."

He shrugged with such a lack of care that I wondered if he'd ever had a single worry in his life. "I'm the eldest with Eniyo gone, the best looking"—he smiled—"as far as that can be taken into account. I'm well-liked, and I have the respect of the army. I've traveled far, studied the world. Who better? My younger brothers haven't set foot beyond our borders."

I took stock of that. "And how far would you say you've traveled, Prince?"

He rolled his shoulders again. "You know, I never kept count of the miles as they passed along the Golden Road. It was an adventure, nothing more."

Sure.

"Vanye." Prince Arturo gave them a little bow and began walking away, but not before his eyes lingered on me longer than they had before.

I knew that sort of stare and the quiet irritation it contained. My questions had bothered the prince. I didn't know why, yet, but I took it as a sign I was on the right track.

My fingers rubbed against the pearl flower as I plotted when to take my meeting with him. I'd have him alone soon enough to get whatever answers I wanted.

I hoped.

SEVENTY-EIGHT

INTERMISSION—TRANSLATIONS

True to the porter's words, breakfast arrived to my rooms hot and fresh. I'd been served a platter containing thin strips of ham, treated with a measure of salt and honey. Several small fish the size of my thumb had been cooked until a light char dulled the shine from their silver skin. They were meatier than I expected from their size, but I found it difficult to work around the thin bones clinging to every bit of their flesh. The true pleasure came from the figs and olives—fresh, and another thing Etaynia was known for.

Finishing my meal, I fished out the white flower Prince Arturo had given me. Was it too early by their customs to call on him for the meeting? The quicker I could question him, the better.

I recalled what the other prince had mentioned as well, a favor to be owed, and all for offering me help with translating the book I'd found.

Two roads to possible answers and I hadn't a clue which to pursue.

A pair of gentle knocks at the door pulled me from my thoughts and I gritted my teeth. It seemed the game had reached full swing and no soul within the palace would get rest until every possible flower had been given away and claimed.

I went to the door, wearing my best scowl. One of my hands went up on instinct and snatched my hood up to hide most of my face. I had no mood or patience for the nobility right that moment.

I opened the door and felt the words I'd been readying die away.

She'd changed her outfit to fit the company within Del Soliel. A dress of soft velvet black sequined with shimmering white like stars. It clung to her at the chest, waist, and hips. Dark, flowing, and completely complementary to her. Her hair, however, refused the traditions of Etaynia and she'd let it loose and wild, securing it partly with red bands left just as free to hang in places. A mask of whirling petals spread from her nose to cover her cheeks and around her eyes. The piece made me think of countless roses fashioned from silver and all strung together. Through it, the green of her eyes looked deeper than before—holding a better brilliance under the metallic color.

“When I asked you to look for me, Ari, I didn’t mean so soon.” Eloine smiled and moved closer.

I barred the way more out of thoughtless action than by any intent. “What are you doing here?”

She canted her head at an angle as if caught off guard by the question. “What do you mean? I’m here to help you with your translation, as requested by Prince Artenyo. He’s found me a suitable expert in tongues.”

One of my hands went tight against the doorframe, an action that did not go unnoticed by Eloine. She reached out and folded her fingers over mine, pulling my grip from where I’d fixed it. “None of that now. I thought you’d tempered that bit of your fire.”

I gently eased my hand out of hers and stepped farther back into my room, motioning for her to come in. “I didn’t realize you were courting a prince.” The words lacked any inflection and I gave thanks I could manage that much control in the moment.

“You’re pouting under that hood, and if you’re not, you’re certainly acting like you are. It’s not courting so much as spending time with him. Apparently I’m entertaining—a panacea for all the difficulties that plague a prince.”

I rolled my eyes. “Of which I’m certain there are so many. How terrible a life.” The flatness of my voice could have lulled a frenzied alley cat into a deep sleep. “Imagine the wealth of a kingdom sitting in your hands to spend on whatever whims and desires you have.”

“Stop it.” Her heart wasn’t in it as she chided me. “You know well enough money doesn’t keep one from knowing pain.”

It was true, but I also knew that having it in ample sums could certainly spare you many other problems.

“So, you’re a shoulder for him then? Someone to lean and cry on?”

She shrugged. “At times. Sometimes something else. The nature of that is between us.” Eloine’s voice didn’t carry an edge, but I could tell she wanted me to drop the matter, so I did.

“Am I permitted to ask about the nature between us, then?”

“You are.” Her mouth quirked to one side, clearly amused, but she hadn’t answered the question within the one I’d asked.

“And?”

“For now, we’re a translator and a storyteller. At other times, we’re something else—something more.”

I frowned. “And after we’re done with our work?” I’d moved over and tapped the book the prince had left to me. “Then what?”

“Then we’ll see.” Her smile broadened. “But for now, the book.”

I narrowed my eyes. “You enjoy being difficult, don’t you?”

"Absolutely. And I could say the same to you, and I have a feeling I'd get the same answer back."

I muttered something under my breath that was better left unheard.

Eloine came to my side and took one of my arms at the elbow, leading me to the bed. "Sit with me."

I did, setting the book between our laps and opening it.

She stared at the cover, mouthing words silently before her eyes went wide with recognition. "Still chasing them." Eloine sighed but she lifted the cover with a touch of her index finger. "Maybe it would have been a waste of my breath to tell young Ari all that time ago to let his demons be."

I should have ignored the comment, but I didn't. "According to the prince, the Ashura don't really care whether they're ignored or not. They still find people to take their malice out on."

"And you're going to stop them?" She hadn't meant it to be a cutting thing, but nevertheless, the question went to the heart of me and brought an ache to my chest.

I'd like to hope so. Especially after all I've done. Aloud, I gave voice to other thoughts. "I promised revenge."

"The dead care little for it."

I nodded. "But it keeps the living going."

Eloine pulled the book from our laps, holding it out of reach. "So is that it, then? This just a quest to quench a young boy's anger?"

"No, of course not." I leaned over, trying to snatch the book back, but she stayed me with a hand on my chest.

"What then?"

"They're monsters." I didn't think I had to say anything more.

"The world is filled with them. Why you? Why are you the one who has to stop them? To try? You could die just as easily as them."

I let out a bitter laugh. "*Easily?* There's no easy when it comes to the Ashura. Believe me." *And I'm still not so certain they can die, but I need to find out, so help me, Eloine.* I didn't speak those words aloud. I couldn't.

"So you're going to risk your life against monsters most men have enough sense to not even mention?"

My jaw ached from how hard I clenched it. "Most men didn't have their family killed by them. Most didn't have a friend under their thumb. Most weren't puppets on their strings and left an empire in tumult and broke things better left unbroken." The edge from earlier sharpened in my voice, now a thing of glass and jagged stone.

"So, it's not revenge, then. It's guilt? Maybe both. Maybe more." Eloine's voice had softened. The hand holding the book lowered, and her other found one of mine and took it in her grip. Her thumb stroked my knuckles. "I'll translate this for you, and I hope you find what you're looking for inside."

So do I.

"But then I have a favor to ask of you." Her eyes twinkled when she'd said that. "Are you familiar with the Game of Families, Ari?"

I grunted. "Knew of it by reputation and hoped it an easy enough thing to learn. But now I'm finding—"

"It maddeningly difficult?" She let out a little laugh. "That everyone seems to have an angle you can't quite grasp, and you never know your options until someone presents you with a pin, only to now find yourself both having more choices than you expected but that they're limited."

I made another sound.

"So, then let me give you something else to think about." Eloine pulled her hand away from mine, reaching behind her neck into her raven-dark tresses. Her fingers twined around one of the red ribbons and pulled something free.

A flower-pin that had been hidden in the thick of her hair. She pressed it into my hand and I almost groaned.

Blue. I owed her a favor now. But I had an idea of how to pay her back. I closed my hand around it. "The prince handed me one of these as well."

"It seems you're in the business of owing favors, then. Not a good place to be. See, the way it's supposed to work to your benefit is *you* being owed the favors." She gave me a teasing grin.

"Oh, is that how it's supposed to be?" I'd grumbled it low under my breath so she couldn't have heard it, but she caught it regardless.

"Maybe you'll learn to play, with time. For now . . ." She placed the book back between us. "*Tales of the Nine.*"

I rose and fetched one of my journals and the silver horn pen, opening to a blank space and waiting for her to go on.

She did, and the time passed as she read about The Nine to me, turning Etaynian into the Trader's Tongue.

Most of what I heard were things I'd learned long ago. Some of it to be true and useless, and other bits I had once hoped to be useful but which were far from true at all.

Eloine went on to read, "Of The Nine, many things can be said and believed and just as easily dismissed. But it can be agreed that their numbers total to nine. Over the collected tales, fewer than nine have been rumored to be seen, but never any more. All the stories prove this to be true. They can be known by their signs: red smoke from fires, red as the flames themselves.

Inspection of bodies found at scenes of the *Nuevellos'* crimes reveal victims with their hearts having burst inside their chests. These men and women have been found all with bleeding from their eyes and mouths."

All true. And only helpful in confirming something I've already learned, but I suppose it's good to know no matter where they go, the signs are the same. Though, those aren't all there are.

The author's notes about the tales went on to mirror my thoughts. "Other signs have been reported, however, there is inconclusive evidence on them. Some of my gatherings reveal that The Nine are known to be masters of a magic that leaves them shapeless, formless, and nameless. They are not of this world and demons truly to plague us for not bringing word of Solus to all corners under his sky. Until his light reaches every place where man lives, so we cannot drive out the shadow and its spawn. The stories of The Nine themselves are wide and varied—unknown even to me despite my best efforts to find them. They seem to have worn many faces through time and many names to go with them. With their true stories and true individual names, one might have better understanding of their natures and why they do the things they are rumored to."

My hand slipped and I nearly scribbled a long undulating line across the page. "What was that?"

Eloine repeated the passage.

In all the stories I'd collected on the Ashura over the years, I had been looking in the wrong places. I never weighed how many people they had pretended to be, and with that, the names they'd used.

Names are parts of our story. The ones we are given, the ones we choose to use, and the ones we let others call us by or gift to them. Together, they form parts of us and our identity, and with that knowing, you come to understand the heart of that person. And a heart, like many things, can be bound.

And I knew I could find the names of the Ashura. Their stories. Old ones. Forgotten ones that only existed in places no one thought to look. I now had something to look for. And once you know exactly what to seek, you can find it.

I needed their first stories. Their first and truest names.

"Your face changed." Eloine didn't shut the book, but she moved it aside for the moment. "You found something, didn't you?"

I nodded. My hand wrote on while I looked at her and answered. "Yes."

"What?"

"I can't say." All the while, I wrote the various names I could recall. The ones I suspected to be three of the Ashura.

"Then maybe for now we can stop here, if you've found a piece of what you wanted?"

I had no desire to, but giving my mind the freedom to ponder this would be better. It wasn't the whole answer, not yet, but I had gotten closer than I'd ever been over the years. A few pieces remained. And I would have them.

"Sure. Maybe I should pay you back again for this?" I reached out, bringing the blue-flower pin to her chest and fastening it in place.

"Most men would have earned a full-armed slap for presuming to touch me there."

I grinned, but didn't address the comment. "I think you're about to owe me a favor now, Eloine. Or, is it Lady Etiana here?"

She swatted me. "And why is that?"

I laughed. "Because I'm about to repay yours, but with something rather personal. So it begs reciprocation."

Eloine said nothing, but light filled her eyes.

"I think it's time we return to the story, don't you?"

The light in her eyes kindled brighter. "Yes."

"I'd just learned from a tinker that the Ashura had struck a home in Emperor's Cradle. Though he and the rest of the country thought it nothing more than a horrible pagan ritual gone wrong, the rumors of Ashura still hung on everyone's lips. Enough to spread it for a while. So while the story slipped from tongues and thoughts, I held on to it, hoping to hear of more signs to chase."

SEVENTY-NINE

SIGNS

Estra and I parted ways after returning to the Ashram. I'd like to say our outing ended with Estra wanting to see me more frequently, but I was woefully ignorant when it came to women and their subtleties. I missed what signs she'd given me during our meal, and as such, she felt it better if we didn't make any extra effort to spend more time together beyond what came natural in the Artisanry.

I took it better than most, though Radi and Aram mourned for my lost opportunity when I told them the details. While it didn't bother me, I didn't want to deprive my friends the chance to bemoan on my behalf and complain about the state of the world and loves lost as young men and women are wont to do.

The following days went by smoother than I felt fully comfortable with. Nitham and his ilk avoided me, for the most part. My classes with Rishi Vruk left me sharper than ever, much to the dismay of other teachers and students; a quicker tongue and wilder wit with which to give anyone a lashing who may have tried to get the better of me in insult or argument.

It may not have been Master Philosopher's intent, but I'm sure he would have appreciated it then if he had known: his classes made my mind ache with a euphoric rush that could be likened to what muscles go through at the end of a hard day's work—stronger, fuller, better off from the effort.

Introduction to Binding Principles continued Rishi Ibrahm's theme of throwing stones at me, testing my Athir, which proved stronger than before. I now went into class fully expecting to be tested, holding an Athir hard as Arasmus steel, and I can say that he never did succeed in striking me that season.

Maybe he had decided not to push the limits of my folds after our scene at the Crow's Nest, but it could have just as easily been something else. Whatever the reason, he threw the stones, and they always missed.

With how things had been going for me in the Ashram already, you can imagine how this further fueled my reputation.

For a while, things went as well as they could. But as with all good times, they are all meant to end.

Another set passed and I made just as much progress in my Artisanry project as I had before, which is to say none. Tangles of string sat on my floor, some knotted into balls the size of my thumb tips. Nothing I had read in the Scriptory had given me a wink of insight into how I could inscribe the all-too-thin pieces of line. I had almost debated giving the idea up, but I knew that would be worse than attempting the deed and failing.

Rishi Bharia never thought poorly of a student falling short of the mark if they truly made an effort, but she had an endless store of judgment for someone not committing to the task. Focus and dedication were paramount to anyone hoping to become a full Artisan.

I put my plans aside for the moment, knowing I had at least until the end of the season before she would ask after my workings. Another interest held my mind.

The tinker. He had said he would be back today and might have more stories to share. I know it was a childish hope to hold to the idea the tinker would have something for me, but hope is often worth keeping.

I grabbed my walking stick and left the Ashram late that morning, closer to fourth candle's end, and made my way down into Ghal.

Other students joined me as I descended the thousand-plus stairs, but all of them kept to themselves and made nearly a show of excluding me. It didn't bother me. As time passed in the Ashram, I grew comfortable with my pariah-like status. It could have been the deepening cold numbing me to people, or it could have been the weight of thoughts on my mind making me want to retreat from the world. Either way, the distance from others bothered me less than it had sets before.

I reached the street where I'd encountered the tinker before, keeping an eye for oxen-drawn carts.

Nothing in sight.

I didn't lose heart that the man hadn't arrived. One thing I'd learned was: When a tinker gave their word, they were good for it. They traded as much on that as they did from what was in their packs and wagon-homes. Whenever he came, he'd make a show of it and draw as much attention as possible, so I knew I wouldn't miss him. That freed me to wander the town and clear my head.

I walked past several street vendors, availing myself of their fireplaces, and spending twice as much energy as I wanted in convincing them I had absolutely no interest in their wares today. My stomach reminded me I had neglected it that morning, having skipped breakfast in Clanks. I headed back to the same place I'd shared a meal with Estra, feeling drawn to The Fireside for a reason I couldn't finger.

Three students left the establishment as I drew near, stopping as they passed one corner of the building. They turned to point down the way ahead.

I paused, recognizing a pair among the group.

Thalib and Qalbi, friends of Nitham. Close ones.

My feet stopped moving even though my mind screamed for me to put aside my nosiness and ignore the trio. But I found myself adopting a cat's curiosity and wanted to better make out the third person. Though I had a sinking feeling I already knew their identity.

The two boys finally moved enough to stop blocking the third as they moved down the pass between buildings.

Nitham ushered his friends ahead, a grin on his face that meant trouble for someone or something.

I waited until they all resumed walking together and then followed behind, keeping to a distance I used years ago as a sparrow trying to tail marks before clutching their purses.

The group moved unaware of me, reaching an empty space between several buildings and well away from the eyes of passersby on the main streets. I lurked at the corner, watching without rounding it.

Something bright and small skirted the edge of my vision and the trio split up to surround it.

I squinted to make out the scene better.

"What should we do with it?" Qalbi inched closer toward whatever it was they'd found.

Thalib looked around, prompting me to duck back behind the wall and hope he hadn't spotted me. "I don't know," he said. "Think it belongs to anyone?"

"Who cares? Right now, it's ours. Let's have some fun. I've got a season's worth of stress I need to get out of me. Brahm's bloody bits and ashes, I swear. The Ashram, the masters, that bloodless Sullied cur, Ari." Nitham's voice shook with a rage that must have burned his throat to voice.

"Don't take his name in vain." The voice sounded like Qalbi.

I peered past the edge again to take in the scene.

"What?" Nitham rounded on his friend. "What did you say?"

Qalbi must have been too dumb to pick up on the change in Nitham's tone. The pompous noble's anger had now changed target. "Don't say Lord Brahm and God Above's name in vain. If you do, he will weigh your ill deeds and thoughts in his flame. And if he finds a shadow on your soul, he will take his duly owed toll, with which then—"

Nitham's hand blurred, striking hard against the boy's cheek with a fleshy slap. "Oh, piss on Brahm's bloody ashes and his great flickering fucking flame. If you keep talking like that, I'll pummel you ten times over what I'll do to that scrap of fur and bones."

Those words pulled me away from the scene of quibbling boys to what they'd cornered.

A mewling sound carried through the space even as Nitham and Qalbi argued.

I looked between them and found the source of the noise.

A kitten.

The thing looked like it had more hair than its own bodily mass. Waves of orange-red that hung from it, lank with water that had likely been last night's snowfall at some point. I couldn't make out much else at this distance and from behind the wall of young men keeping the creature confined to the small area near a building wall.

Thalib, being the good lackey that he was, moved to execute Nitham's will and lunged for the kitten.

"No!" My cry echoed through the open area and brought all three boys to whip around.

Nitham's face went through a series of expressions too fast to register. His cheeks shook and I believe I saw spittle fleck his lips as he snarled. "You! Burn me and my bloody bits if you aren't like a curse from Brahm and every other pissling god. I swear, you Sullied piece of trash, why are you always there whenever I have a bit of luck go my way?"

"Because Brahm has a sense of humor and I happen to be on his good side?" I gave him a crooked smile and tried to keep the better part of the laughter welling inside me to myself.

I failed.

It rolled out and even managed to infect Thalib, who let out a low chuckle that he swallowed as soon as Nitham shot him a withering glare.

He turned to the kitten, then back to me, leveling an accusatory finger. "Walk away and I'll forget I saw you, *Quth'khoon*."

My fists balled tight without me even thinking, one of my hands squeezing hard against my cane. *Quth'khoon*, or "dogsblood," was a word few people used in public company. While no laws or even social norms kept you from using the slur, it was seen as beyond classless and even blasphemous in some circles. Especially since Brahm himself had taken to tending to Sullied folk in the stories when he became a mortal wanderer.

But men loved to lord whatever they could over others. Anything to make one feel superior to another, and if he could claim blood as that advantage, he would.

I've always maintained it says more about the man willing to use "dog" as an insult than it ever does the creature.

"Leave the kitten alone." I took a foolish step toward the trio, knowing that the odds were horribly stacked against me.

But as I've told you many times, I am nothing if not a fool.

"This is better, yeah?" Qalbi found his voice again and tapped Nitham's chest with the back of a hand. "Let's just pound him bloody, here where no one can see. The masters and other rishis won't have piss for proof and we can't be brought up for penance and punishment."

Nitham's face broke into a smile that showed all his teeth. His eyes practically danced with fire and malice. "Maybe my luck's turning for the better."

Thalib still kept half of his attention on the kitten.

My legs tensed and part of my mind went to the candle and the flame. I no longer envisioned a spark of fire, but something burning brighter, larger, and fanning greater by the second. I fed it my anger, the faces of the trio before me, letting the flame consume it all. In that moment I recalled a piece of Ari years earlier. The one who'd practiced Vithum's swordplay.

My staff was a far cry from a proper sword in length and weight, but I could manage enough. And a part of me could recall some of what I'd learned at Nika's hands when she taught me to fight.

Thalib lunged, going for the orange kitten.

I screamed, rushing toward the pair that barred the way. My staff stayed tight in grip before me as I closed in.

Qalbi bulled forward, arms wide as if hoping to grab me and take me to the ground.

I brought the stick down in a sharp arc, crashing it into where his collarbone met his left shoulder.

The thick robes softened the impact, but his eyes still shut in pain and his face twisted. His momentum stopped and he broke away from me to address his hurt.

Nitham, to his credit, didn't engage. His hands stayed opened and close in front of him. He sunk his weight, bending at the knees and keeping to the balls of his feet.

I didn't know if his newly adopted posture betrayed knowledge of how to fight, or if he had learned it from watching others. How many thrashings could a noble-born boy have gotten into?

Thalib had managed to grab the kitten by the scruff of its neck, hauling it into the air where it let out a weak cry.

The colors of its fur banded my vision in an orange-red hotness and I screamed a string of curses I can't recall. My cane went up over one shoulder and I brought it down in a diagonal arc, hoping to take Nitham across the side of the skull.

His body sank deeper as he rushed forward. He crashed into me just below the waist, arms wrapping around my lower body and taking me to the ground.

The impact drove my vision to whiteness and most of the air from me. My ribs ached, but my robes and cloak had absorbed much of the blow outside of what the light snow had already cushioned.

His hands scrabbled for better purchase on me and I squirmed, trying to shake free of him. Rishi Bheru had trained him to grapple, and while Nitham was no expert, he had a better grasp of it than I had, even with all my time on the streets of Keshum. I thrashed in Nitham's hold as one of his hands fell to my throat and squeezed. Pressure built in my neck and felt twice as heavy in my eyes. Panic seized me and I lurched forward on instinct, throwing as much of my weight into the strike as I could. He tried to move out of the way but wasn't quick enough. My forehead struck short of the mark and I felt wetness, warmth, and a hint of something hard.

We reeled away from each other and I caught sight of him moaning as he pawed his lips.

Crimson splotches peppered the white frosted ground and streaked his fingers. I saw what had happened when Nitham pulled his hands away from his mouth.

My headbutt hadn't broken his nose like I had wanted. It connected with his lips, splitting them against his teeth like he'd kissed a road of broken glass. He couldn't even scream for fear of tearing them worse.

But his eyes screwed tight in the silent rage he and I had known so well and built between ourselves. Veins pulsed visibly along the base of his neck and I could almost hear his knuckles cracking.

Qalbi had recovered while Thalib made no move to help his friends, remaining content to hold the quivering kitten firmly in his grip.

"Let it go." Enough of my breath had returned for me to get the words out through some heaving. My gaze flicked toward my cane and I saw Nitham and Qalbi make the same calculation. It was the one thing coming close to leveling the odds between us, but if they kept me from it, I couldn't hope to fight the pair of them. And if Thalib joined in, my trouncing wouldn't be one I could walk away from.

I lunged, arm outstretched, hoping to close my fingers around the cane.

Qalbi charged, Nitham right behind him.

The two boys met me first, crashing hard into my midsection and legs, throwing all three of us into the snow again.

We flailed, tangled, someone's fist struck just under my eye and I felt the hurt shake deeper into the bones of my face. My elbow hit someone, glancing off something hard and curved. Maybe a piece of one of their skulls. Nitham grabbed my collar and hauled, pulling it as one of his clenched hands slammed into my eye.

The ridge of my eyebrow took the brunt of it and I had a fleeting moment of wondering if he'd broken the bone. White-hot spots danced across part of my vision and the world tilted.

Whatever I had learned from Nika and Vithum faded and I returned to the feral boy from when two other street urchins had set upon me my first day as a sparrow. My fingers flexed and I raked the air, hoping to catch one of the pair.

My nails bit into soft flesh and I pulled.

One of them screamed and I realized it had been Qalbi.

Thin beads of blood covered my fingers and I clawed at the other, grabbing hold of Nitham's robes as he'd done mine. My other hand shot out and the open palm connected with the boy's already mangled lips.

He yowled and fell back into the snow, scooping some up and pressing it to his mouth. His body convulsed from the sudden cold, but it had to have helped numb the worst of the hot pain flooding his face.

Thalib hurled the kitten.

I scrambled halfway to my feet and jumped best I could, hoping to catch the critter. Its weight fell against my arms and I tried to clutch it tight to me in an effort to protect it.

I failed.

Thalib had already crossed the distance and drove a heavy foot into my gut. Acid flooded up my throat. Saliva and a breakfast I hadn't had still managed to fill my mouth and slop onto the ground after he kicked me again.

Nitham and Qalbi had finally gotten to their feet, but I never saw them approach as Thalib's boot connected with my skull, rocking my head back and taking my sight for a moment.

"What's happening here, ah?"

The beating stopped but I couldn't make out the trio's words.

Feet shuffled by, all lacking proper balance, like they were being driven back by force. I saw the hem of someone's robes not in the dreary colors most students were given by the Ashram. Something crossed my vision, streaking wide at one of the boys.

I heard a sound like someone beating a heavy sack. Then again.

"Leave off doing that sort of thing around here or I'll have your mothers skin your asses! Go!" A woman's voice, hard and flushed with anger.

I saw the three boys break into a run and leave the way they'd come.

My body ached in too many places for me to count, so it's better to say the whole of me had developed into a single mass of uniform agony.

The kitten mewled again, and I tried to bring it closer to my chest.

"What's that there?" The woman came toward me and I couldn't make her out.

My mouth couldn't form words properly, but I tried. "N-n-n-no." Both arms shook harder than I could control, and I failed to keep the kitten out of sight.

"Is that what all this was about, then?"

I couldn't clear the daze from my head, but I tried to right myself regardless.

"Sit still, stubborn man, I swear. If the stupidity of young boys doesn't kill you, stubbornness does eventually."

I couldn't have argued if I had wanted to. Besides, I'd have only proved her right.

She slipped an arm under mine and helped me to my feet. The woman had the build of someone's well-fed grandmother. Short, sturdy, wide, and solid. She hadn't seemed to have yet reached her thirties. Strong enough to get me up without any effort on her part, and just stressing the seams of her clothing. Soft faced and matronly in look.

I felt better already having her by my side.

"You from the Ashram?" The edge hadn't left her voice yet.

I nodded.

"They don't teach you boys any better than that?"

I opened my mouth to protest but she went on over me.

"Fighting in the streets. You're lucky I found you rather than the kuthri. They'd have strung the lot of you up for a public lashing, asses in the cold, bare as the day you were all born."

"Not likely. One of those boys is noble born. Some king's second son." I couldn't remember where Nitham hailed from but I recalled that I also didn't care.

My comment gave the woman pause. "He's trouble then." Most of the anger fled her face and she adopted a frown. "Noble boys are problems you can't really think too much on. Easy-to-bruise egos and too full of themselves. He might try to get back at me and mine for the beating he got."

That brought a different pain to me that had nothing to do with my injuries. The woman had come to my aid and her reward would be suffering under all the mayhem a wealthy noble could bring. While Nitham may not have been of a royal family in Ghal, he had the connections and money to have magistrates and government officials kowtow to his will if he wanted. Whatever the bad blood between him and his father was, he could still be a nuisance.

I didn't want that coming back to this lady. "Or he might keep it quiet if he's threatened with word of this getting out. I don't think he's the sort who wants it known an old woman knocked—"

"Old?" Her face had lost all expression, but I knew enough of her carefully measured tone of voice to know she'd bitten back some sharpness.

I raised one hand in a gesture of surrender, making sure to keep the kitten close to me with my other. "Sorry, *maem*. *Young* woman knocking him as he deserved."

She looked mollified by that and then bustled away to retrieve my cane. "Looks like you'll be needing this."

I murmured a thanks.

"Let's get you inside then, and your cat."

"Oh, no, it's not—"

She didn't have ears for my complaints. She grabbed me by the sleeve, pulling me along with more force than I had the strength to resist. The woman led me through the back of The Fireside and sat me down on the kitchen floor. "We've not much room or place for even ourselves to eat here, so you'll have to make do. I'll get Semi to see to your face and hands while I set about getting some food."

"It's not my blood." I waggled my fingers to see if they still worked after the cold had numbed them, rather than try to accentuate my point with the blood.

She ignored me. "You have coin?"

"Yes."

With that, she began barking orders to a woman I couldn't see behind her bulk. "I'm not in the mood to hear what you might want to eat. You'll get what I'm making, *ji-ah*?"

"*Ji*."

I lost track of the time that passed until she brought me a pair of wooden bowls. Warm cubed potatoes, yellowed from turmeric and spiced, filled much of the containers. She brought a broth with shredded red meat that I didn't bother to ask about, just happy for something warm. Flatbread, most of its weight seeming to be in the butter generously coating it and dripping off the edges. Its surface had been burned to a dark and crispy char that I personally preferred. Lastly, a small tin dish only as large as my palm filled with cooked spinach and a crumbly dry cheese.

"Eat." Her tone left no room for argument.

Both I and the kitten set to it with more energy than I thought either of us had left. Once we were filled, the woman returned with a young girl, no older than me, and close enough in features she could have been the lady's daughter. "Semi will tend to you."

I nodded, too tired to speak and nursing a good deal of shame for having put myself in a place to inconvenience these two.

Semi had brought a thin skin, stuffed with snow, and pressed it to my face wherever I showed signs of a bruise to come. The coolness brought out a few sharp gasps from me before the pain grew distanced and I acclimated. "Your cat's half-starved, and you look the same."

Estra had made similar comments.

"I guess we're quite the fitting pair then." My voice held enough acid and glass to scrub any surface raw. But if my words stung Semi, she didn't show it. "I'm sorry, that wasn't—"

She pushed the cold skin against my mouth, silencing me. "You're not the first to talk rudely to me, and you won't be the last."

I apologized again regardless, speaking around the obstruction held to my face. "I was hurt, and I'm angry, and I didn't mean to be a bother to you. I'm sorry."

Semi stopped and looked me over before nodding in quiet acceptance. "I didn't know they let students keep pets at the Ashram."

"They don't."

She blinked. "How are you hiding him?"

"I'm not. He's not mine. I just found him."

"You went through that beating for a stray kitten?"

I inclined my head.

"You're not very smart, are you?"

My eyes went wide, and I almost dredged up that sharper side of my tongue, but her laughter pulled me from the thought.

"But you're sweet." She reached out to scratch the kitten's head, which it enjoyed. "What are you going to do with him?"

I didn't know and decided not to answer. Once we'd been tended to, I settled the debt, feeling a whole silver dole equal measure to my life and their kind treatment.

You might think this much, but what price would you weigh your existence against? If I had a hand of gold, I would have given her that, but as I didn't have that, and only brought a few pieces of silver with me for the day, it would have to do.

Semi and the woman who had saved me tried to assure me that I didn't need to pay them that much, but I took a page from their book and suddenly developed a deafness to their complaints.

I left the way I'd come, through the back side of The Fireside, stray kitten held within my arms, and under the comfort of my robes and cloak.

The cat didn't put up any fuss as I carried it through the streets of Ghal, much to my relief, as I didn't need anything else fighting me today. I searched the trader's circle I'd seen when I'd first arrived in the kingdom off the back of a wagon.

No sign of the tinker still.

My heart sank further as I talked to some of the stall merchants and learned no tinker had passed through. I had all but given up until I sulked back toward the way to the Ashram's stairs.

A voice echoed after me. "Oi, boy!"

I recognized the call and turned to spot the tinker easing the oxen to a stop not too far from me. The morning's beating had been worth it. Even the time spent in the cold now felt a distant bother. I hobbled over to him, not wanting to chance even a light jog should it aggravate the tightness building along my ribs. Nothing had been broken, or so I hoped, but the kicks I'd received had left me a rigid knot of dull pain.

"Oi, Tinker, what news?" I managed a weak and unsteady smile.

He returned a brighter one back to me. "Oh, all sorts. The kinds of things a young boy like you would love to hear about, and just so much in way of treasure. Would you like a peek at my packs? Or do you want to trade gossip and hearsay first?"

I almost answered him, but the brass fittings and other metals fixed along his wagon-home caught my eyes again. Not for the bands of light they caught—no, something was off with them, but I couldn't figure it out. I walked by the bulls, stretching out with one hand to brush along Bathum's flank. The closest ox made no protest as I touched him.

"What's gotten into you, boy?" The tinker pulled out a small pot, its surface riddled with bumpy protrusions. A long stem jutted out from it that separated along with the lid as he lifted it to drop in a powder match he'd struck. Smoke soon filtered through the stem once he'd replaced it. The man took a deep puff before blowing most of the substance back out through his nostrils. "One look at you says you took a good beating today. You get into trouble up at the Ashram?"

I waggled my hand, only half-paying attention to the peddler. "More like it followed me down here. Or, I followed it, I suppose." My gaze fell on the knobs and short flat strips running along the wood, trying to make sense of the varied patterns.

It is a pattern, isn't it? Something in the back of my mind clawed at me, treating the fixed pieces almost like a story. My fingertips brushed along them.

"What's got you in a—oh, caught that, have you? Not many outside the traveling folk and the family notice them as any more than fanciful knick-knacks tacked to our homes."

"They're different." I looked at the arrangement, swearing they had been in another configuration the first time we'd met. But what that may have been, I couldn't fathom now.

"That they are." He took another puff, then exhaled.

I smelled something like cherries, a spice that tickled my nose, and a scent like freshly turned earth after warm rains.

"It's a language older than the Trader's Tongue, something we folk cobbled up all ourselves." He sounded proud. "The Travelers' Tongue came about as we set out on our wagons to see the wider world and deal in it and its stories. But we had to have a way to send messages to others of our family, no? And how to do that without others hearing what we want to tell? With one look, any other of the family can read where you've been, if you've had a good trade, or . . . bad reception." Something in his tone told me the traveling folk didn't get that often.

"They warn of downed trees or flooded roads ahead, banditry and other troubles, or whether you're open to meeting with more of the family for a night or two. Sometimes caravans join. Other times, we need our privacy. Or we spread messages of lost loved ones so the family can unite to mourn them proper."

I stepped back, looking at it like a system of words now. All dots and lines. Easy to overlook, but just as simple to quickly cobble together new messages to send when need arose.

A secret way to tell stories. Secret stories. And there was nothing I liked so much as that.

"Will you teach me this?"

His mouth pressed firm against the stem and I could see his jaw working, as if he'd taken to chewing on the pot and pipe. "Not something people often ask on, truthfully." But he hadn't said no.

I didn't push, knowing it to be a private decision, but I did the next best thing. I worked to make my eyes appear bigger, staring in silence and with all the hope and pleading a young half-starved-looking boy could muster. It might have helped that I looked poorly after enduring the beating I had.

"Well . . ." The tinker chewed on the pipe again, speaking around the stem. "Suppose it's possible, but I'm not in the business of giving things freely, you know?" He raised a hand, rubbing a thumb and forefinger together.

I grinned, reversing my wounded look from before. "I can live with that."

He guffawed, letting out a larger plume of smoke than before. "Don't rightly know how I'll find the time and how to teach you, but we can settle that after business. So, boy, treasures or tales?"

"The latter." I moved away from the wagon side and came closer to where the tinker sat. "Anything good—anything new?"

The ox close to me snorted and shook in what could have been discontent.

"Bathum seems bothered by something." I patted the beast, hoping to calm it.

"What's that?" The tinker pulled the pipe from his mouth and stared at me. "What'd you call him?"

I blinked. "His name?"

"Never told you his name, and it's nowhere near that. I call all my bulls, 'Bird,' on account of them being my wings." He motioned with a hand like flapping wings. "I can't fly, and it's by their backs and bodies I get around, so seemed fitting."

I nodded, not actually seeing his logic, but I'd antagonized enough people for the day. Sometimes a man needs to set a smaller quota when it comes to being a bother. "I'm not sure where I heard it then, though I could have sworn it came from you."

The tinker shook his head. "No. And it's a wonder you want me teaching you my tongue when you can already grab a piece of it yourself."

That left me speechless.

"'Bathum' means 'stubborn,' and it's not Brahmthi or Brahmki. Though, it's certainly fitting for that one. Even after two years with me and being well gentled, he's still got more mule in him some days than I know what to do with."

The bull I'd taken to think of as Bathum snorted at the tinker's comment.

"See what I mean? Thinks he's clever too." The man shot the ox a sideways glare before rounding back on me. "So, to business."

I inclined my head, wanting the moment's oddity to be ignored and out of my mind.

The kitten decided that now, of all possible times, was the perfect moment to let out a whine as it peeked its head through the folds of my robes.

"Oh, what's this then?" The tinker leaned forward. "Picked up a stray?"

I shook my head. "He's not mine. I just found him is all."

The tinker reached out a hand, wiggling an index finger at the creature.

I removed the cat from my clothing and brought it closer to the man so he could touch it.

"Ow! Little bastard nipped me." He pulled his finger back, shaking it, though for all his words, he held no anger in them. "Rescued a little flame, have we? Teach me to touch a thing like that." He put the digit in his mouth and sucked the tip before pulling it free again. "You'll do well to make a proper home for that thing."

"He's. Not. Mine." I stressed each word again, hoping that would drive the point home. Everyone had been treating the cat as if I'd taken him in already. "What of the stories, Tinker? What have you heard?" I pulled the kitten back and eased him into my robes again where he seemed content to gnaw at my clothing instead of men's fingers.

"Hm—oh, that. Ah, so, I noticed your face when last we spoke. Saw the way your eyes popped like when a young lad's learned a girl fancies him. And though for the pretty thing you had on your arm, you didn't seem half as interested in her as you did what I had to say."

That much might have been true, but hearing it aloud sent a pang to my chest that didn't come from the bruises. Had I really ignored Estra's interest and feelings that much?

"By the way, where is your lady friend?" His smile grew to something wily and mischievous. "Boy your age ought to be having as much fun with that sort as he does keeping his noses in books. Too much of one isn't good for you. A man needs balance."

"Oh, um, she's back at the Ashram."

The excitement seeped from the man's face and his shoulders slumped a little. "Ah, well, I suppose that sort of thing happens too around that age." He didn't bother explaining the meaning behind the comment. "Right then, the story. Like I was saying." He cleared his throat, coughing harder than necessary, and I realized some of the smoke had taken its toll on him. "*Ackh*. That's better. So, you seemed proper interested in what rumors there are about like what happened down south—hm?"

I gave him a silent look that made my answer obvious.

"Most won't peddle in those stories, you know?" His voice changed, and his eyes moved side to side as if he feared being overheard. "Not good things to talk about. It's one thing when far off in the Cradle so south and to nobles, you know? But even then, they're not good tales to be telling."

I nodded more to help him feel like I understood than to agree with his point.

"Something just as strange happened off past the mountain wall." He hooked his thumb over a shoulder, pointing to the snowcaps and stone the Ashram sat against. "Little village called Ampur is having the sort of trouble no one wants to go look in on. But, then, not too many places in Sathvan get much in the way of visitors. That province might as well not be part of the kingdom. People there keep to themselves more than anywhere I've seen, but this is dark news. Enough you think someone would send some kind of help."

"What's happened?"

"Quiet, boy! I'm getting to that, aren't I? Brahm's blood, you need patience. There's an order and way to telling a tale."

I gritted my teeth and busied my hands with comforting the now sleeping kitten.

"So, there I was, trading bits of precious and news a few villages over, and that's when another trader—fisherman—came from upriver. Man all but ran and shoved people aside, telling me and everyone who'd listen of what was going on up in Ampur. Houses burned, folks killed—gruesome thing. Don't know what sort of men it takes to do a horrible thing like that. Don't much know what they used to burn the place either, but all the smoke coming from the place was told to be red. Red as flame.

"Half the time I wonder how anyone's supposed to keep a fire going in that place, though. All cold and snow-touched." The tinker wrapped his arms tight around himself as if suppressing a shiver. "And then the rains." He shook his head. "Bad enough the place gets ice all the time, but freezing rain at this time of year? Hard place to live, and the folks may be just as hard, but still, can't see anyone enjoying living there like that."

My mouth dried. The Ashura had struck again, and this time so close I could almost picture ribbons of red smoke coming from over the mountains. "How far?"

"What?"

"How far to Ampur?"

He looked at me like I'd gone mad and asked him instead for the price of his own blood. "S'pose not more than a solid day and a half of travel. But you're talking riding morning and night, boy. And this ain't a place to do that with horses. You'll need something slow, sturdy, better sure-footed than those things." He reached out and patted Bathum.

"Can you take me?"

His eyes practically ballooned and I nearly expected them to burst. "What? I just got into Ghal. You're wanting me to turn around and go back where I came? That's bad business—"

I let my cane fall from my hand as I reached for my purse. My fingers brushed against a few coins and I plucked them up without discrimination. Three doles sat pinched in my grip.

A price many a man or woman would do a great deal of things for.

His eyes locked to the coins.

"How's that? How much is your trade worth against this? Is it enough?"

"Brahm's ashes, I swear." He shook his head as if he'd refuse. "You don't make things easy, do you, boy?"

I grinned. "I've heard that a lot. And, no, I don't. So, Tinker, do we have a deal?"

His hand blurred and pulled the coins from my grip. A roll of the wrist, a flash of his other hand, and a scarf across my vision that I had never seen him pull. The second went by and I lost sight of the silver doles as if they'd never been there at all. "We do. I'll need a third of a candlemark to get ready. Meet me in the square and we'll set off. Good?"

"Good." I turned and ran, not caring for the aches my body warned me of as I went up the stairs to the Ashram.

The Ashura were nearly a day from me. And I'd find them finally.

And I would confront Koli after all this time.

EIGHTY

FRIENDS

Enthusiasm can do wonders for pain and limitations. Couple that with the promise of satisfying curiosity, and maybe dreams of revenge? Then you have a recipe to push away all the things holding you back. My legs burned and I paid them little mind as I finished the journey up the Ashram's stairs. Someone had turned my lungs into thin sheets of rubber, wrung hard and left to dry. I endured the stinging through my chest with every breath, looking around the main courtyard to reorient myself.

Radi and Aram crossed a path near one of the still-blooming trees.

I willed myself to run just a bit more and make it over to them, calling out their names when I was within a reasonable distance.

Both turned to face me, first breaking into smiles, then mixed looks of apprehension and concern as they likely took in my bedraggled looks. Aram raced over first, putting her hands on my shoulders to steady me.

"Blood and ashes, Ari. What happened to you? You look like someone threw you down the stairs. What are you holding? Why are your—"

The kitten decided to cut all her questions short with an indignant *mrowl* that drew my friend to silence.

Aram gazed at my chest and arched a brow. "What's under your robes? Brahm's blood, I never thought I'd be asking you that question."

Radi let out a bark of laughter as he came within earshot. "Well, why stop there now that you've come to—"

The cat let out another sound of irritation, probably from having been woken from the slumber it had fallen into while I climbed the steps.

"Um, I guess I'll have to side with Aram here and ask why there are sounds coming from under your clothes, Ari."

I gave them a weak smile and figured I'd answer all of their questions in one go of it. "Got into a fight with Nitham and his assflies."

Aram mouthed the word "assflies" to Radi, clearly making a question out of it.

"Because they're like horseflies, only they don't stick to a steed, but a jackass instead." Radi rolled his eyes. "Really, Ari. You can do better."

I ignored that and jabbed a finger at my face. "Thanks for the concern. The fight went sour, and I paid for it with a hellish beating, but thanks."

Aram sighed. "You picked it. We've warned you not to stir trouble with him."

I parted my robes just enough so the two of them could peek into the folds. A shock of orange, still slick with some snow. "They were trying to hurt this."

My friends peered at the cat, then back at me. "Ari, please tell me you didn't adopt a kitten." Aram looked around as if she expected trouble to swoop down on us any moment.

I shook my head. "I didn't. I just stopped Nitham from hurting it. It's not mine, and I don't know what to do with it. But I need you to keep it safe for me until I get back and can figure it out."

Aram's mouth hung slack and Radi grew ashen. "What?" both said in unison.

I pulled the cat free of my clothing and handed it to Aram. "Just keep it secret. Keep it safe. No one needs to know."

Aram handled the kitten like a hot coal, shifting it from hand to hand like it would burn her. She eased the cat into her robes much like I had done and then whipped her head around, searching for a trouble that she should have known wouldn't come. The majority of students simply didn't care for anything beyond what was in front of them. "What am I supposed to do?" She kept her voice now to a low and sharp hiss.

"It's just for a few days. I'm heading over to Ampur with a tinker."

The pair of them looked at me like I'd gone mad.

Radi licked his lips and glanced at Aram. "I think he's serious. Maybe touched in the head, but also serious. He's really going to leave right in the middle of a set. And before apprenticeship exams."

I had forgotten about those. "I'll be fine." It wasn't the truth, but it wasn't a lie either. I'd have to catch up when I returned.

Radi clapped a hand to my shoulder. "I can't believe you're going to make us miss all that. Take good notes, Aram." Radi flashed her a wink.

Aram groaned and shook her head. "Yeah." She sounded like someone miserably accepting grim news that she'd expected.

I looked at them both, confused. "What the hell are you two on about?"

Radi gave me a gentle shove and readjusted the mandolin over his back. "I'm going with you, so you don't die in whatever scheme you've got in that cracked coconut of yours." He rapped a set of knuckles against my skull.

I opened my mouth to protest but he cut me off.

"Do you want to argue, because we know as sharp as your tongue can be, mine's the quicker of us three. There's not a thing I can't say faster, lines I can't spin better and leave your tongues trip-tumbling behind as you try to catch up to me. That's as plain a thing for anyone to see. So why bother with it? Let's go on, unless you'd rather be stuck here from now until it's too late to go, and what'll—"

"Fine-fine!" I put my hands to his chest, hoping to stay the verbal cascade that even I struggled to keep up with. "And . . . thank you, Radi."

He grinned something too roguish and smug, even for himself. It was a thing better suited to Aram.

We said our goodbyes, with Radi promising to have me home safe and sound. And if not, he'd at least come up with a marvel of a song over my death. Women would weep, and they would fall into his arms, all to console him of course.

Either way, he said he would come out a winner.

What are friends for?

EIGHTY-ONE

Things to Remember

By the time I'd reached the bottom stair, my knees had given up and wanted to buckle. Radi, being the friend that he was, offered me support.

"When I said I'd look out for you, I didn't think I'd have to carry you." He had actually made no move to help me physically at all. Something I pointed out.

"You're really not. Give me a hand?"

He removed his mandolin and cradled it, running one hand along its curve. "I can't, mine are otherwise occupied. It's sad when that happens." He grinned as I glowered at him. "Is that the fellow?" Radi tilted his head toward the tinker.

I doubled over, resting my hands on my thighs until my body found a hint of relief. Once I had that, I reached the tinker and introduced Radi to him.

The man didn't buck at all at the idea of carrying one more person to Ampur. Then again, no sane man would say a thing after being paid three pieces of silver for the job. He welcomed us aboard and Radi, being the creature of comfort that he was, decided that he would much rather crawl into the wagon and avail himself of the bedding there while we rode.

I let him have it, finding enough comfort in the padded seat beside the tinker. He never bothered to get Radi's name, but did do me the kindness of telling me his.

Pathar. It meant stone. Of mind, of heart, and dedication.

I decided it fit the tinker and his life.

At first, we shared few words as we trundled over Ghal's frosted terrain. Every odd bump or jostle sent aches through my already bruised body, and I slightly wished I'd seen Master Mender before leaving.

But I knew had I done that and lost any time, I could have missed the Ashura altogether, and I would never have forgiven myself for that.

Eventually, the doldrums of the first leg of our journey brought out Pathar's more talkative side. He told me the history of his people, and how they'd come about from the Ruma, who'd grown too restless to stay in place, even if for a night, to trade and tell stories. The tinkers came from a split where they could never sit still. So they took to wagons and roaming the world, the stars and skies their blankets. Grass their beds when they couldn't find enough room in their wagons.

The life held an odd romanticism for me, though at the time, I couldn't say why. Maybe it was because I'd never had a place of my own for too long where I felt I belonged. So I relished the idea of everywhere being my home.

Casteless, as far as the Empire was concerned, the tinkers kept to their ways then, choosing to make their fortunes through methods no one would lay singular claim to.

After a while, we finally got to the heart of the matter I wanted to address.

"And the horizontal lines are words?" I craned my neck to look at the side of the wagon, earning a sharp cuff to the back of my head.

"Don't do that. One bump and you're tipped off good as thrown. Or your head will smack against the wagon, and hard as that thing seems, I don't want to be replacing the wood this time of year with rains still about."

I turned and glowered at the man, but he didn't care for it.

"And, no. They're more like things you'd say altogether. Like a full telling. Maybe not the whole of it, but like what I'm doing now. It's like if you're giving someone directions and you tell them how to get from one building to another several down. It's more than a word, but it's not telling someone how to get all the way to where they want. Make sense?"

"So it's like a sentence?"

"Hm." Pathar took one hand off the reins, rubbing his chin as he thought on it. "Not sure about that. Don't know much in the way of languages. It's just what it is, and they mean more than just, 'Over there,' or, 'thataway,' see?"

I think I did. They functioned like complete thoughts, leaving little if nothing to interpretation, but that raised another question. "How do you know what they say, though? They all look the same."

"Oh, the color, metal, and arrangement. They don't mean anything by themselves. The knobs, you see, they tell you the idea of what the bars mean that come after."

Like primers then. The knobs gave you the subject and the bars would fill in part of the conversation. "And the spacing and change of knobs change the flow of conversation and the ideas you're talking about?"

He nodded.

And so we passed the first few candlemarks discussing the intricacies of the Travelers' Tongue. By our first stop, Pathar let me try my hand at rearranging some of the knobs and strips. Each had a peg or groove and slot they could be fastened into place with. It took a few tries, but I eventually managed to get the first row of the wagon side to read: Travel—coming from east, heading west. Business—good coins made behind.

It was true after a fashion, though I'd learned I was really most of the profitable business Pathar had done.

Radi rested content as a cat by a warm stone inside the wagon and didn't bother to emerge when we came to a village from which Pathar wanted to collect and maybe do a spot of quick business. He told me to remain quiet as he did and not interfere with his dealings. I could listen. I could hand him things. But one was to never cut a tinker off in speech when they bartered.

I took that piece to mind.

He never shared the place's name with me, and lived up to his word, trading with an efficiency that must have come from a lifetime of haggling and reading people's wants from their faces. He happened to pull exactly what would set a man's or woman's eyes wide with wonder or need. I admired the considerable skill that took.

A group of children played near us while this trade took place. They chased each other in a small ring and sang all the while.

"When the chimney smoke goes red as blood,
Ashura. Ashura.
When comes the storm that brings the flood,
Ashura. Ashura.
Time to pray. Do not stay.
Run away! Run away!

"When the birds and beasts all go mad,
your heart drums loud and pains sudden bad,
take to flight. Stay out of sight.

"Ashura. Ashura.
Thinkin', plottin', evil // schemin',
Time to cry. Time to fly.
Demon! Demon!"

Several of the children laughed as the three who played as the monsters caught a few of the group.

I stiffened as they finished the rhyme, but no one else seemed to mind. Just a game to every youngling and something to twist the ears of every parent with a sense of worry. To that, one woman hitched up her skirt so the hem wouldn't track against the snow, and she marched over to the boy who'd begun the chant.

She reached out and, with motherly skill, took hold of his ear between a thumb and forefinger, twisting sharp and tight to haul him away from the others. I couldn't make out what she said, but heard enough of the sharp warnings she hissed into his ear. One quick cuff to the side of his head and a last command to never speak of the Ashura aloud.

The boy, to his credit, looked properly ashamed and had the grace not to utter whatever words he'd clearly held in his mouth. The other children watched in silence, then decided maybe they'd had enough fun for the day and were better off leaving before their own parents came to teach them a similar lesson.

Pathar finished his business and handed me a separate pouch to tally what he'd earned. He told me that a tinker never counted coin where people could see. To customers, the transaction always ended with a newly bought piece of precious or wonder. It wasn't for them to see money that was better off vanished once spent. All it did was remind them of what they'd lost.

We returned to our seats and I did the simple sums. He'd made four copper rounds and even a full iron bunt. I didn't know being a tinker could lead to money like that. When taking into account that their whole lives were spent on wagon-back, it must have left him with a considerable sum of money.

Pathar told me more of the tinker's life, at least what it was like over the course of a season. He had the sort of freedom only heroes and wanderers out of stories did.

Which we decided was a fitting topic to discuss that evening. We traded what stories we each knew of the legends of the world, and when I ran out, I gave thanks that Pathar knew more than I could have dreamt of.

He told me all he could in the hours before night.

And it was a good thing I'd kept them in mind, because I would need to remember the heroes of old to help me face what was to come.

EIGHTY-TWO

What We Can Afford

The journey passed in the time Pathar had said. A day so far, with only half left to reach Ampur, all peppered with stops to ease our backs and bottoms from the nonstop riding. When we needed rest, we took shelter in a tent that Pathar carried along, leaving Radi to enjoy the comforts of the wagon.

Sathvan's terrain brought with it every difficulty one could imagine, and I realized why the trip would have been impossible on horseback. Narrow sloping roads that wound through mountain passes, still slick with snow and ice. Even the most level-footed beasts would struggle, yet Pathar's oxen managed just fine.

I attributed it to their frequent travels through the world and a likely well-honed sense of how to find their footing on whatever surface they traveled.

Snow fell harder here, blanketing everything to an almost white curtain before vanishing just as fast. Soft powder caked the ground and glimmered under the sun like diamond dust, only to thin and take to the air again when harsh winds kicked up. It felt like icy teeth gnawing at my skin until they'd left me raw.

The air felt thin and at times more like it pulled at the insides of my lungs than it filled them.

Pathar had told me to not talk or think too hard, and just to let myself breathe. That I would acclimate in a few hours as we climbed in altitude. And if I didn't, well, at least he'd gotten three doles out of me.

My head spun the higher we went up the mountain paths and I spent the time it took to reach the first village with my eyes closed and cursing every god I could think to name. Being raised in the theater, I could remember quite a few. I think I managed to burn the ears of at least seven that afternoon.

The jostling set my head hurting worse, and I nearly uttered another half dozen strings of profanity at the gods, but Pathar brought the cart to a merciful halt.

"We're stopping here before the last leg to Ampur. Little village called Volthi. Folk here still speak Brahmthi, as well as Trader's Tongue, but they're none too keen on people from the Empire proper. Don't talk too much, your accent will set folk's teeth grinding. Can't afford to have people riled before doing business."

I nodded.

"We'll let the boys rest for a bit"—Pathar reached out and patted Bathum's rear—"and I'll fetch them feed. They eat three times as much this high up, and you'll be feeling it soon enough too. Rest." He rubbed my shoulder and eased off the cart.

I heeded his advice, taking in the mountain village of Volthi. The wagon offered a good perch for me to make out most of our surroundings. Every home I could spot was much the same. All formed from snugly fit stone that did not betray a hint of open space to the cold air. That in itself was a work of art and admirable craftsmanship.

The people here didn't build too high, keeping the buildings to two floors at most. Sharp canted roofs that reached a singular peak, all to break up snowfall and keep it from accumulating. Chimneys were fixed to the sides of homes rather than coming straight through the main body. The smoke burned as gray as ashes.

Most of the buildings were built down at the base of the mountain, snaking along the winding riverway. The rest dotted the incline, all keeping close to the twisting paths that ran nearly to the crest of the mountain. As the land rose, the number of homes thinned.

The people here dressed heavier with thicker furs and layers than anyone in Ghal despite being so close to the city. Their skin was fair enough that they all held a touch of rose in their cheeks, and many of them shared the color of their hair with the snow. Some of their eyes weren't as deep-set and held distinct curves to them I'd rarely seen.

Streamers were fixed to many of the roofs, some no more than lengths of brightly dyed fabric. Others were more distinct—rows of fine line all carrying triangles of varying colors and spaced apart. When the wind picked up, they undulated like serpents in the air. The movements entranced me until Radi let out a low long groan from his place in the wagon.

The double panels leading to the bed and the rest of Pathar's goods opened. A bedraggled Radi shambled halfway through the doorway, letting most of his body hang against the frame. "Are we there yet?" He squinted at me like he'd spent the night drinking, then turned his gaze toward the sun. His eyes narrowed further. "Cursed hateful thing, that." His stare intensified at the light before he gave up and slumped his head. "I'm starving."

I snorted, then regretted it immediately as a rush of cold air sent needles up my nostrils. I coughed and cleared the pain best I could. "Pathar's gone to get us some more food. We still have some of the smoked goat strips."

Radi spat. "I hate that stuff. Dried, chewy, tough, spiced to hell."

"It's what we have." To that, I reached into the leather pouch Pathar had left next to me and pulled free a few lengths of the traveling meat. It tasted exactly as Radi had described, and I loved every bite of it.

Much as Pathar had warned us, most people avoided Radi and me, giving the wagon a wide berth. A few stared long and hard before turning back to their own business. But one man approached us. Even under the multiple layers of hide and furs, his muscles clearly made up more of his bulk than his clothing. His nose was blunted, and his eyes looked like they'd been pressed tight and thin from the harsh winds and blinding light across the snow-swept terrain.

"You with the tinker?" His voice had a guttural nature like he'd swallowed something hot and harsh. Every word sounded hard and forced.

I didn't answer immediately, chewing my dried goat.

Radi hooked a thumb in my direction. "I'm with him who's with the tinker."

The man ignored Radi's comment and settled his attention on me, stroking his mustache. It reminded me of two thin tails hanging from his face rather than facial hair. "Got news for that man. What'll he trade me for it?"

I shrugged, knowing enough that I shouldn't have been bartering on Pathar's behalf. "You'll have to wait to find out. He's gone down the slope there to buy some things. Said he'll be doing business when he gets back." I worked to keep my words simple, closer to clipped in speech after hearing how the man spoke.

Some may think it crass to match someone's accent and cadence—that I might mock them in doing it, but that wasn't why I did it. There is something to giving people the comfort of what they're used to hearing to help set them at ease. And we were strangers here. I didn't need to put people any more at guard than they already were.

The man grunted. "Then he can hear it from me when he gets back. But you might want to know." The man removed a woolen mitten, reached into a pouch at his belt, and retrieved something that resembled the goat strips I'd been snacking on, only their color had all the brightness of a peach. He bit into it and talked around his chewing. "Was fishing up farther north, going to deeper waters, stiller ones. Where the pink parthi fish spawn. Good catches there. Got cut off by another fisherman up from Ampur. Was about to come to spear and fists if he wasn't gonna let me past. Then he tells me things that's got me thinking he's been trading in that cotton juice people down south deal in.

"Crazy things. I look in his eyes and see whatever it is, it's got him true scared. So I listen. He tells me the village is mostly gone. Burned. Fires still going strong . . . in the snow. We're still getting falls every set. And he says fires burning. Tells me something foul and nasty woke up, a monster, a demon. Something that fills the river and can swallow homes whole. I tell him he's crazy. I tell him so. And you know what he does?"

I shook my head, not trusting myself to speak.

"He laughs. Tells me to go upriver myself if I want to die. Then he tells me to bring the spear and hold it close, because I'll need it. But not for any monster. Tells me it'll be for me. That better to take my own life than see what he's seen or be left with what's there. Man laughs harder. Then . . ." He stopped talking, chewing another mouthful of what I figured to be dried fish. "He tells me if I go upriver, I'll die. I'll go mad and die. Just like everyone else.

"Though, s'pose odder things have happened up there. Heard not that long back stone fell from the sky. Slab of it big enough to have come from a wall. Landed in the snow and didn't break. Folk just left it there. God's wrath or something."

I found my voice and asked everything I could think of. "What did you see? What colors were the fires? Smoke. Did you see the smoke? What kind of beast—"

The man raised a hand, silencing me with the gesture. "Whoa, boy. I didn't go up there. I'm not one for being told what to do, but if you'd've seen that man, you'd know there wasn't no good in going up that way. I'm no fool. He may have been touched, but . . ." The man bit his lip and let the words die in the air.

I didn't need him to explain. Sometimes the idea of something fearful is more than enough to stay a man's feet and his heart. It's worse when you don't know. In fact, it's often that way. When you know what to expect, you can prepare for it. But when all you have is the terror in another man's eyes and voice, that's enough to make you think twice and spare yourself a similar fate. That is the nature of fear.

"I'm no coward," said the fisherman. He puffed his chest but deflated just as fast. "It's a hard life. And few things're harder than being out there on the water year-round. Don't think otherwise. The folk that live that life know it to be a hard thing. *Hard*." He made his stare as firm and strong as the word itself. "So seeing one like that all out of sorts." He shook his head and said something under his breath I didn't catch. "Least I could do was listen to the man, no?"

I nodded, knowing he didn't want me pressing him on the matter. He needed a moment's comfort and his pride assuaged. Maybe even the guilt at leaving the man up there on the river. "Of course. All you could do. Ain't no shame in it. He asked you to leave, you did. You gave a man what he wanted when he'd probably lost a good bit. Was proper kind of you."

The man muttered something again, still too soft to reach my ears. His gaze grew distant and fell on the mountain peaks. "Yeah. That's it. I did him a kindness." He didn't sound like he believed it but wanted to convince himself of it. Something changed in his face. The color drained further and the gray of his eyes looked to pale more than possible in the moment. Maybe a trick of the light, maybe just as much due to the cold. He shook his head and spoke in a tongue I didn't understand.

Radi and I exchanged a look in silence.

"Changed my mind, boy. Tell the tinker what I said. Don't feel keen on re-telling the story myself. And if you're going up that way, maybe think not to. Be better for you. Either the man's mad and whatever did it to 'em is out there, and you'll find it, or you'll find everything he said's true. I don't right know what's worse. Not sure I can afford to find out, neither." The fisherman pulled up a hood lined in dark fur, cinching the ties tight to pull the edges of his clothes closer to his face. "Tell the tinker." He muttered again and walked off.

Radi watched him go before turning to me. "Maybe he's just as mad as the man he met."

I said nothing.

"And . . . Ampur is where we're heading, yeah?"

I kept my tongue between my teeth.

"Blood and ashes, Ari. What are you getting us into?"

"I told you I was going alone."

Radi vanished behind the doors, reappearing the next instant. "Damn cold." He fiddled with something I couldn't see, then two notes rang out from the mandolin. They seemed to say *stupid, foolish.*

I glowered at him.

"You're madder than the man in his story if you think I'm letting you go into this alone. Besides, think of the stories. Whatever is happening is the sort of thing I can turn into a song. The sort that'll make women swoon. But I'd very much like to come out of it alive." Another few notes. Together, they said, *doubtful.*

Did I tell him I was hunting the Ashura? That I'd brought my friend to chase down children's tales and nightmares the educated world consigned to fables? That I was set on revenge, and somehow meant to kill The Nine out on the frozen peaks beyond Ghal where no one would find us should things go wrong? Should I have told him we were going to challenge timeless beings from when the world was young, who had all the powers of binders out of legend?

No.

So I told him the closest truth I could, all of which still fell so far short of the mark it may as well have been a lie. "There's a chance for me to find out what happened to my family. They were taken from me years ago. And I think there's a clue out in Ampur. But I'm not going to hide this from you, Radi. It's dangerous. If you want, tell Pathar to take you back the second we get there. I won't hold it against you. You've done more than I deserve even coming this far."

His fingers tripped across the mandolin and said, *shut up. Finality. Friendship.*

I thanked him for it and we let the conversation finish, resigning ourselves to waiting for Pathar's return. When he appeared, he asked me what news he might have missed. I never told him of the fisherman and his warnings. I couldn't afford to. So once he'd completed his peddling business, we rode toward Ampur.

And toward the Ashura.

The remaining half day passed on the road, but we saw the signs I'd been looking for before coming into the village. Smoke streamed into the sky. Red. Red as blood.

Where homes had once stood now lay smoldering heaps of wood, thatching, broken tiles, and stone run just as red as the flames. All still burning even as the first signs of snowfall showed and white crystals blanketed the air.

I had been right. The Ashura had come to Ampur. And if they were still there, I'd find them.

EIGHTY-THREE

Old Gods

"Brahm's blood, boy. What is this?" Pathar pulled hard on the reins, stopping the oxen in their place. "I heard the story but . . ." He swallowed hard and let his gaze sweep across the wreckage. "There's nothing left but a few homes, and even those . . ." He shook his head and gestured toward one building that remained mostly standing.

Its roof had given way, hanging diagonally against the walls and resting across a corner of the second floor and most of the first. The stone and wood had been spared the fires at first glance, and they showed no signs of the blood I remembered seeping through the walls of the theater.

Radi watched in silence from the wagon doors, hollow-eyed and hands white from clutching the cart's frame.

I stared just the same—mind a stone tumbling down a mountain. An avalanche of thoughts took me. How long did I miss them by? Why had they come? How many people did they kill? Stories. The Ashura had spoken of stories when they'd come for my family. Had someone here told one about them? Did it hold any secrets they wished to keep silent?

Why did a few homes come to be spared their fury?

Survivors. They can tell me what happened. The thought galvanized me into action and I leapt from the wagon, my feet slipping on the near-frozen ground. I fought for balance, lashing out and striking my hand hard against a wheel. My bones and skin ached, but I gritted through it and held myself steady until I could walk.

"Boy!" Pathar hissed and tried to grab me, but I'd gone outside of his reach. "Boy, get back here."

"Ari—damn—shit—blood and . . ." Radi's voice cut short as I saw him slip and nearly crash to the ground, so close to the lip of the path that he could have slipped and rolled down the mountain. "Wait a moment, dammit." He unslung his mandolin, stowing it in the back of the wagon. "Tinker, mind staying here and watching that? It's precious to me. Only thing in the world that really matters, that mandolin. It was a gift. You do that, I'll see you paid well." Radi gave me a look that made it clear he intended for me to settle that debt.

In the moment, I hardly cared. Small price to pay for having a friend by my side right then.

"Don't need telling twice. That I don't." Pathar wound his arms tight across his chest and screwed his legs over one another just the same. "I promised you a return back, boy, but I don't think I'll be doing that if I leave my wagon. I'm fixing to head back just outside the village. You come back and find me in one night, you hear? You don't do that, I leave you here to die in this madness, you hear?"

"Two. Give me just two nights, Pathar. Please. There might be people here. They'll need help, maybe a wagon ride back to Volthi. Somewhere—anywhere, please?"

The man chewed air and likely his own tongue, fixing me with a stare that said he'd much rather leave right then than wait to find out what caused all this. He spat then relented. "Fine. Course. Don't want it said that a tinker don't know the value of life. Never have it said that we don't help folk." He sounded like he was talking to himself.

I thanked him, fixing my staff well in hand and using it to steady myself as I walked down the uneven path. My boots kept the worst of the snow and water from soaking my feet and socks, but the cold still found a way through.

The nearest building looked nothing more than a pile of stones thrown together to make the base of a shoddy fire. Tiles had shattered, and everything burned a uniform red. I watched for a moment, transfixed, thinking back to the theater until I caught sight of something in the fire.

Skin and sinew had given way to bones that hadn't quite turned to char and ash. Hands. Holding something. Clear as day to me among the flames. A clay figurine, probably painted once, sat clutched in their grip. The small size of the bones and the now-blackened toy told me enough.

A child.

Brahm's blood. I looked away, noticing the ground around me was streaked a violent crimson, which came from what stones stood just outside the fire's reach.

Everything inside me hollowed and I walked as if suspended by puppet strings, marching toward the closest of the still-standing homes.

The earth rumbled. Snow shifted around me and above.

"That's never a good sign. What in the hell was that?" Radi whipped his head around, looking for the source of the disturbance.

I didn't know or care. I hobbled onward, finding my footing and resting even more of my weight on my binder's cane. The home wasn't too far out of reach, and the door still stood straight in its frame, which was impressive considering part of the home's foundation had been hammered away. It was like a boulder had rolled by and crashed into its corner, taking a section of it along and scattering it farther down the mountain. But there was still the chance someone had survived and taken refuge.

"I'm going inside." I pointed to the home so Radi would know.

"Ashes and embers, Ari. What if whatever did this is still here? What if they're in there?" He had a point, but how could I let him know I would have almost preferred that.

Almost.

I reached the door and gently put the head of my staff against it. "Hello?"

No reply.

"Is anyone there?" I tapped the wooden cane several times in what I hoped was a polite knock to anyone still inside.

Nothing.

I swallowed and eased the door open. The cold had gotten to it, drawing sharp and pained creaks from wood and the joints as it cracked wide.

The home hadn't a drop of blood or any signs of the Ashura that I could recall. Drops of moisture had formed along the walls in places, and I could see some of the roof sinking into the room. Most of the details are still a blur to me, I only remembered what I found next.

Something creaked at one side of the home and my heart lurched. I changed my grip on the cane, holding it more like a sword. Its length and size may have been far off a proper sword's, but it was all I knew then.

Creak. Creak. Creak. The wooden floor protested any movement or micro-shift I made. Then I realized it wasn't me at all.

A section of the floor ahead of me moved. Just a hair's breadth. It rose then sank back into place.

A cellar door? I eased toward it, but it had stopped shaking. Had someone been peeping through the crack when they lifted it? I had two options, but the latter would likely lead to a confrontation I wasn't so sure I wanted. So I lowered my staff, tapping its head against the trapdoor. "Hello? I'm not here to hurt you. My name is Ari. I'm a student from—"

The door swung upward, nearly wrenching the staff from my grip. A young girl scampered out of the opening, crashing against me.

My hands went up though the breath left my body as I hit the ground. All the bruises I'd earned from my clash with Nitham flared into dull agony.

"Ari?" The voice jarred me nearly as hard as the impact had. I knew it—knew her.

My vision cleared and I found myself staring at a woman with ashen hair and blotches of uneven skin tone. I'd ridden up to Ghal with her from Keshum. "Laki?"

She nodded. "What are you doing here?"

I stammered incoherently before I found my voice. "I heard what happened and I came looking. What's going on? Did you see anything? Did you see *them*?"

She mouthed the word, "them," but her face told me enough. Laki had no idea what I meant. She shook her head. "There's no them. It's back."

"It?" I motioned for her to get off me and rose halfway to my feet, rubbing my ribs as they panged. "What are you talking about?"

Another head peered up from the cellar door. The woman had to have been in her sixties. The white of her hair had lost whatever luster it could have ever held and now resembled the tired gray of old ash. Her face looked hardened by harsh winds, her pale skin and heavy crinkles like worn and uncared-for leather. Her eyes were watery, but she held all the warmth of a close candle in her grandmotherly smile. "Laki speaks of God."

I almost barked a mad laugh at that. "You mean Brahm? Are you saying he, um, did this?" I thought of all the signs that spoke of the Ashura and wondered what these people could possibly have seen.

The woman I took to be Laki's grandmother whispered something I didn't catch. "No, not him. Nagh-lokh. The old gods. The first. God Himself."

I stared at her, then thought back to the fisherman's tale of another man he'd met who'd gone mad. Could she have suffered the same fate? Then I remembered Laki's reasoning for going to the Ashram. She'd been searching for a remedy for her grandmother. "Is she all right?" I turned my question to the young girl, trying to keep my voice all of concern and not betray my suspicion of her grandmother's mental state.

The old lady gave me a look that could have brought down stone and mountain. Caustic, withering, sharp. "I'm not mad, child. I know what I saw. The first serpent, the one who carved the mountains and riverway, and brought us water and life, is awake again. It slept for hundreds of years, and now it is angry with us. With the world that's forgotten it. Laki saw it as well."

I swallowed, then waited for her to tell me if it was true.

She nodded, but said nothing.

I asked the only question left then—the obvious one. "Then what caused the fires? The red smoke. The . . . bleeding—"

The old woman waved me off. "God. Weren't you listening? The fires started nights ago in the dark. We heard the screaming. Before we could do anything, the Nagh came. It thrashed the village, ate—" She broke off and looked at the ground. "It took people. Parts of the mountain fell in its rage, taking some of the homes with it. Others are buried. The fires. Someone used them to kill people. I don't know why. The sight of the Nagh can drive people mad. It could be that. I nearly felt it myself. I heard my own blood in my ears."

The Ashura had been here, no matter what the old woman said.

No serpent god had done this, but it seemed the Ashura had left a touch of madness on those who'd seen them or been in the village that night.

"Will you two be okay here? Do you know if anyone else survived?"

Laki made a series of expressions, all unclear. "I think so. It's cold. We're not lighting fires in case it comes back. But I don't know if there's anyone else alive." She crawled over to her grandmother, cradling the elderly woman in her arms.

I clenched my jaw, partly to steady it from the chattering it had fallen into, and just as much to give myself something to focus on while I thought. The Ashura had set the fires and the stones bleeding. But I still didn't know why, and it seemed Laki and what remained of her family didn't care for anything but the serpent. So I wouldn't get anything useful from them right now.

I headed back to the door and waited in the frame. "Stay here, I'm going to take a better look around to see if anyone else is alive." *And if the Ashura are still here.* I shut the way behind me and trudged back through the snow. Flurries fell harder now with no sign of stopping. If things continued as they were, I'd be in the full force of a blizzard before nightfall.

The homes of Ampur had been built a good deal farther apart than those in the villages I'd seen before. The terrain here left them little choice. What houses didn't line the river, rose and fell with the mounds and dips up the mountain. No area was level enough to build several buildings close together. That led to a scattered array of dwellings so few in number that Ampur was more a hamlet by definition.

Every bit of wreckage I found was much the same as the first. Bodies that I couldn't look at too long for fear of remembering. Charred flesh and broken bone. Bloody snow and stone. Wide smooth tracks ran through the frost, likely covering what were walking paths best traveled in the hotter months and all but useless now. I followed them still, using them as a poor guide to navigate my descent toward the homes at the base of the mountain.

Whoever had first laid the path must have had no knowledge how much space wagons and villagers needed to move comfortably. The way could have fit a full home inside its width as well as maybe room for a cart to eke by.

The earth rumbled again and I looked to the sky, searching for signs of a storm. Rumble-shake. Snow shifted and loose stones rolled by, shaking free of the ice that coated them. Some of the smaller debris slid away from the larger piles of former homes. I finally witnessed some of the red flames and smoke subside as they fell deeper into the cold landscape.

Radi hobbled after me, screaming for me to wait. His cries sent more of the world sliding down.

I hissed, something he couldn't hear, and then motioned him to silence himself.

He didn't get the gesture and continued shouting.

More snow and stone gave way. Thankfully, all it did was extinguish other fires and break up the smoldering ruins.

Radi finally caught up with me, chest heaving in exertion. Every labored breath he took sent plumes of fog into the air. "We should leave." He motioned to what few places still burned. "Look at this place. It's gone. There's nothing left, and if we don't leave, there'll be just as much left of us—*nothing*. It's all falling apart."

More snow.

More stone.

It fell, true to his words.

I gnashed my teeth and should have reined in the fire building in my gut, but I didn't. "Well, it might help if you stopped screaming for one bloody minute trying to bring the mountain down on us."

Radi's mouth went tight and he looked away for a moment. "Sorry."

I exhaled, rubbing the palm of a hand against my forehead. "No, I am. I'm all turned about." I pointed to the nearest ruined home. "The night my family was murdered, it was all like this. The red flame and smoke. The bloodstained brick and mortar."

Radi licked his lips, nodding, and keeping silent.

"It's a lot for me right now. I need to find something—anything. A piece that will better tell me why."

"And find the people who did it." Radi's words held no accusation. Just a hard quiet statement of fact.

"Yes. I'm sorry, I should have told you."

He waved me off and crossed the distance between us, clapping a hand to my shoulder. "You should have." His grip tightened around my joint, fingers digging in hard. He wrenched on my robe and kicked the back of one of my legs, throwing me to the ground. Radi made no other move to continue the assault. He watched me from where he stood, bending over just a bit. "But I understand. You're an ass, but you're my friend. I still think we should go—now." He smiled and offered me a hand.

I took it and he hauled me to my feet. He did me the favor of helping me brush the snow from my clothing and even returned my staff to me. I held it tight and walked down toward the river.

Radi's sigh sounded behind me. "Or I guess we die. It's not like I had a bright future ahead of me. Wine, women, song. Traveling. Seeing the wider world. Being better educated and maybe even twice as respectable as I am now. No, nothing of the sort."

I snorted. "Twice of zero is still zero, Radi." I quickened my step but wasn't quite quick enough to escape the hands that crashed into my back, nearly sending me back into the snow. I swatted at Radi with my staff, striking his lower back. The bulk of his robes took the worst of the blow, leaving him to feel little to nothing at all, I wagered.

He laughed and sank to scoop up a fistful of snow, sculpting it into a ball he threw my way.

I struck it from the air with my staff, bending to form a ball of my own to toss back. Despite the situation, we were still young boys, and in the midst of all this horror, we had a moment of fun that could take our minds away from it.

Was it right? I'm not sure.

But it was necessary. And more than that, it was fun.

Panting, we made our way down to the river, surveying the homes that had been turned to kindling. None survived, and they were in far worse shape than any of the piles far above. Smashed, battered, broken, burned, and left as nothing. No fires. Not even the smoke.

"These must have been the first." Radi sounded like he was speaking to himself. "The wood's been charred, then frozen cold. It's like glass in some places." He nudged a piece and it fell apart at the touch.

Just like the benches and floor in the theater. The thought came to me on its own.

I shook it free as the world rumbled harder.

A sound like rushing water and steam over thunder echoed from the mountain pass ahead and the riverway.

"Ari, we need to run, now!" Radi grabbed hold of my collar, trying to haul me away.

"No, I just need a moment to—"

The sound came again. Sharp, rasping, and utterly monstrous—primordial.

Radi stopped, gaping as he saw what I had.

Hurtling toward us through the river, sending up waves, was a serpent that could have swallowed homes and the mountain peak by the look of its mouth.

The Nagh-lokh.

An old god.

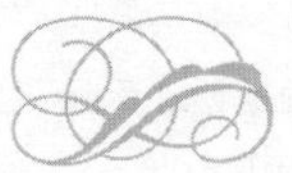

EIGHTY-FOUR

As Above, So Below

At first glance, I understood why people attributed the mountain path and river as having been forged in the serpent's wake. Its bulk easily filled the way between the valley and it had all the muscle and speed to tear aside stone as it passed through. Its scales were practically an armor of glistening white pearls among snow. I wondered what, if anything, could pierce its body, and the thought of trying to stab the beast brought a dark laugh bubbling in my core that I very nearly let out.

Only a small voice in my head, reminding me that making any noise would turn the creature's attention upon me, kept me silent.

Radi snapped out of the stupor first and grabbed me by the shoulders. "Run, Ari. Run!" He pulled me several feet up before panic broke through the paralysis that had taken me after seeing the river serpent.

God Himself.

I breathed hard, running, stumbling, using my staff to keep me from falling. Radi hooked an arm around my elbow, helping me keep balance as we reached the first house away from the river.

The serpent barreled through much of the debris. Its thrashing sent stone, snow, and broken-rubble homes into the water. It screamed again, the sound more akin to bone-deep pain than anger.

Radi faltered. Then fell. The snow took him to the waist as he accidentally stepped into a deep patch.

I toppled with him, being spared only by having landed flat. The base of my staff struck the ground and I used it to help trudge my way forward, bulling through as much of the snow as I could.

Radi recovered and followed suit.

The serpent screamed again, opening his mouth to bare fangs larger than both Radi and me standing on one another's shoulders. Flecks of white formed the back of its throat. Then they frothed, foaming into something larger, before a lance of water shot forward and struck some of the wreckage below us. The force of the blast turned wood and stone into crumble and dislodged some of the hard-packed snow. More ice fell to take its place and the mountain shifted again, noticeably.

"If we die here, I'm going to kill you!" Radi's voice barely reached my ears even though he was only feet behind me.

"If we die here, I'll kill myself. Happy?"

He swore and I took it to mean he was adequately assuaged for the moment.

The serpent reared its head, rising to a height that dwarfed the Crow's Nest tower. It lashed back and forth before diving at the ground behind us. The world shuddered as the monster burrowed through ice and earth, shaking in fury.

"Why's it so angry?" I slowed my pace, trying to take better stock of the situation.

"Who cares? Maybe it's hungry. Maybe it hates our faces. Maybe it's not a morning person. But if we stay, I'm sure we'll find out—run!" Radi grabbed the hood of my cloak and part of my robe's collar, pulling so hard they went tight around my throat until my eyes bulged.

I choked as he dragged me a few feet before I matched his awkward upward shuffle. We plowed through the snow just as the Nagh tore free of the mountain, sending another shelf of solid ice sliding down to hammer into its own body and break against its scales.

"Higher!" Radi motioned to the next ridge.

I finally understood his logic. He wasn't running away from the serpent so much as getting to a point hopefully beyond the creature's blind rage. Every motion I saw pointed to a monster rampaging without a target. Something had stirred the beast, and now that it had woken, it wouldn't stop until there was nothing left to take its anger out on.

The Nagh settled itself for a moment, letting out a low hiss, like dry leaves trailing under the wind along a gravel road. Its eyes were molten gold, glimmering with a sort of malice saved only for the worst villains out of stories.

And they reminded me of another pair I'd seen before. A color like that found in wolves and hawks. Burnished yellow-gold filled with—the only word for it—evil.

The serpent slowly turned its head from side to side, taking in the surroundings with a newfound calm. Like it searched for a better target for its destructive impulses. I wouldn't have cared so much if it hadn't squared its attention on the house Laki and her grandmother had taken refuge inside.

Something struck the side of my head with a soft *paff*, leaving my hair slicker than before and bringing a numbing cold to my cheeks. I registered what had happened and wiped away the remnants of the snowball.

Radi had climbed higher still, waving at me to follow. "What are you *doing*? Come on!"

As before. Some of the snow around him shifted. It slid. And it fell.

The serpent had gotten some semblance of control over whatever madness had gripped it. It moved slowly, sinuously toward the one home with survivors in it.

Radi hissed, forming another ball in his hand, priming to throw it.

I waved him off before motioning to Laki's home.

"What of it?"

"There are people in there."

He winced and spat a word I couldn't hear. "How many?"

I held up two fingers.

"Ai, mera lahnth koh gallao." Radi waded through the snow, coming to my side.

I didn't comment on what he'd said, asking for god to burn his ass.

"What are you thinking? Or are you not? Because that's just as likely knowing you, Ari."

"I think we're going to have to run very fast . . . and starting now."

Radi's face scrunched into a tight confused mask. "What?"

"Oi!" I scooped up snow and ice that had turned to slush, forming it into a hard-packed ball. A snap of my wrist sent it sailing toward the serpent.

It struck the creature just below the eye, doing nothing to draw its attention as it moved closer toward the house.

"Burn me, Ari. Don't antagonize the thing." Radi backpedaled from me, using his hands to climb a part of the mountain more stone than frost. He mantled the spot and trekked onward to put as much distance between the old god and himself as possible.

I searched for something better to strike the creature with, spotting bits of nearby wreckage. My staff helped me part the snow and make my way over. I bent over, the muscles in my back going tight as iron rods due to the cold and my stiffness. I gritted through the pain and grabbed hold of a stone as large as my fist.

Another throw.

This one struck the creature closer to the middle of its body, but it had the intended effect. The serpent stopped flicking its forked tongue at Laki's home. The Nagh turned and searched its surroundings, paying me little mind as if it couldn't have believed I was behind the irritation.

I grabbed a piece of wood this time, its tip splintered into something like a crude spear. The knots and throbs in my body worsened. I hadn't given my body time to heal from the beating, so it had grown rigid and unresponsive. Still, I bit down on my tongue, focusing my attention on a newfound discomfort in order to ignore the rest of my problems.

Focus.

I fed everything into the candle and the flame. It reappeared as if I'd only just been practicing it under Mahrab's guidance. I saw the folds next. A singular image flooded my mind. Striking the serpent squarely through the eye with the slender sharp piece of wood.

Laughable, true. But what else could I have dreamed and dared to do?

"Here! Here!" Radi punctuated each word with a tossed stone, striking the creature once on its snout, just where freckled pink flesh indicated its nostrils. The second blow glanced off one of the monster's fangs, instantly setting it into renewed rage.

It let out a sound like screeching mandolin strings and stones being dragged against brick walls. The Nagh dove toward Radi, looking more intent on smashing my friend with its head than swallowing him whole.

"No!" But my scream of protest did nothing.

The serpent struck hard mountain and snow, shattering rock and sending a wave of snow into the air and sliding down the way. Some of it swept over where I stood, shifting me farther away from where I'd been.

"Radi!" White clouds billowed where the beast had attacked, obscuring most of the scene from view. All I could make out was the shifting shape of the serpent. Sections of rubble had been rearranged by the snowfall and I sifted through it, searching for something that could get the Nagh away from where my friend's body might have lain. An iron rod rested among dark stone fragments that might have once been a chimney. I looked it over, realizing it to be nothing more than pig iron that had been tapered to a rough point.

Something to stoke fires with or a poor cudgel to protect oneself. I took it in hand, moving my staff and the sharp piece of wood to my other side. Tearing a length of cloth from my cloak, I fastened my binder's cane and the improvised spear to my waist, letting their bases drag against the snow.

I moved wordlessly, mustering what speed I could against the difficult terrain to reach part of the monster's bulk. Iron in hand, I reversed it in my grip to bring the point facing down.

A scream left me and echoed over all of Ampur, loosening more snow and stone. My cry came for everything: the Ashura on the night I'd lost my family, and for the people lost here. For missing them by god knows how long, and for the damage done. And for the old monster that just killed my friend.

I plunged the iron downward, striking between some of the beast's scales. A piece of its natural armor bent, buckled, and lifted. Pinkish blood welled from its flesh.

The creature screamed, filling my ears with the echoing resonance in the aftermath of a ringing bell. The whole of me vibrated and then the Nagh-lokh thrashed. Its tail and midsection snapped to one side.

My hands stayed stuck to the frozen rod, and it remained well-lodged in the Nagh's body. I sailed to one side before the momentum tore me from the weapon. A feeling of fine glass scraping against my palms filled me as parts of my skin tore from where it had touched the iron. The world tumbled and blurred into a blanket of white. I don't know how far the serpent tossed me, but I remember the landing.

You would be wrong to think that snow would cushion your fall like clouds. It spared me a certain death from impact, but the cold of it leached into my collar, sapping what little breath I had left. I struck a hardpack of ice with enough force to rattle the bones along my back and hips. All of the too-recent pains I'd collected from Nitham and his friends welled inside of me. For a moment, all I could do was blink until I remembered how to inhale again.

Someone coughed, and it wasn't me.

A hand crept out from the snow several feet ahead of me. Then another. Radi's face burst from under the frost. "Are you dead?" Each word came with a series of hard breaths after it.

"No." I barely managed the lone word.

"Too bad. I'm going to kill you now." Radi crawled over to me, but he didn't make good on his word. He grabbed hold of one of my arms and helped me halfway up. "Come on, while it's mad." Radi gestured higher up the mountain, near the peak.

"It'll take us a full candlemark to get there in this weather." I may have bemoaned the time it would take, but I didn't question Radi's wisdom in putting as much distance between us and the snake as possible. One of my hands went to my side as my ribs panged. Then I realized my staff had come loose during my short flight. And the same for the wooden stake I'd picked up.

I told Radi to help me find at least one of the two things before we went on.

He gave me a look that said I'd gone madder than before, which was impressive, especially considering he'd already made it well clear he thought I'd lost my mind. But he helped me rake through the snow, brushing it aside in the hope of finding my tools. "Got it." He grabbed hold of my staff just as I found the stake.

I took one in each hand, using the cane to ease my way up the mountain.

The Nagh wound itself tight before unleashing its mass on another part of Ampur's land. It rent stone and snow again, causing another cascade. If this continued, it would bring down the mountain whole on us. Another plunge like it wanted to dash its own brains out in its frenzy. Whip. Flail. Smash.

More rubble sailed into the air. A home that had remained halfway standing now turned to splinters, pebbles, and rained down into the river.

The cold worsened and my joints refused to work no matter how much I willed them to. We'd only made it a short way up the mountain.

And the storm worsened. Snow fell hard enough now to make me think I walked among the clouds—solid sheets of white everywhere.

"We have to go higher, Ari!" Radi's scream barely competed with the heavy wind that had stirred. It howled and moaned along the exposed rock face and over paths of hard slick ice. "If we reach the top, we'll be too far for it to pay attention in this blizzard. Reach the top, Ari. The top!"

It was rather a shame the Nagh didn't much care for Radi's plan.

The beast spat a weaker spray of water than before, drenching the ground ahead of us. Our footing went from hazardous to near impossible as snow turned to slush and soaked us worse.

The cold now reached past my blood and bone. I felt like I was hewn from a single block of ice. My teeth clacked against each other as I threw more of my weight on my binder's cane, using it to continue trudging. "We're not going to survive."

"We. Have. To." Each word took all the effort Radi could muster as we climbed on. "I still have to kill you myself."

I couldn't laugh this time, but I made him a promise, knowing the angry resolve would be our best chance of survival. "If we make it out of this, I'll let you."

Higher, then. We climbed. The Nagh's blind rage turned it from us back to the wanton destruction that had leveled most of Ampur. It hissed. It thrashed. It gnashed its jaws at empty air like wanting for something to crush—anything—but for all that, I still didn't know why.

For a moment as fleeting as an intake of sharp breath, the old god and I locked eyes.

The colors may have been the same as Koli's, but I saw none of his evil in them. One look told me enough. *Pain. Confusion. Loneliness.* Such a profound, heavy sorrow—the knowledge of being the last of your kind and that something had come to wake you from your last respite from that solitude—sleep.

The Nagh had taken to hibernating, not to conserve energy, not because the seasons and centuries mandated it. No. It had done so to slip away from the wakeful knowing that it was alone.

The longer I stared at it and listened to its noises, I came to understand it. I didn't know why or how, but I didn't question it either. I simply took it for something an old storyteller had told me about the magic of Listening.

Pins and needles racked the old god's mind. Memories it had been forced to relive that I couldn't quite glean, but they were reawakened by outsiders. A flash in its eyes told me the rest.

The Ashura had been responsible for the Nagh's awakening. And they had done something to put it into a kind of pain and madness it had no salve for. All it knew how to do and be was itself. So it took out an old god's wrath on the world, which the people of Ampur paid for.

And all the Nagh wished for was the forgetfulness of sleep.

No sooner than I'd finished the thought, movement at the end of Laki's hovel caught my eye. She and her grandmother hobbled out from under a collapsed section of the home. The Nagh-lokh's proximity must have forced them to reconsider staying put. They would have been better off remaining in the basement because the serpent slowed its spastic actions. It regained control and tasted the air.

The Nagh lowered itself to the ground, pressing itself flatter than I would have thought possible. Most of its body vanished under the snow and the rest blended so seamlessly I lost track of it under the frost.

"Laki!" My cries echoed through the storm but I had no way of knowing if she could hear them. I screamed regardless until it felt like the lining of my throat had been rubbed raw by sand and glass. "Run! It's coming for you, Laki! Run!"

She and her grandmother kept to their slow and cautious pace, almost skulking through the blizzard. It wouldn't be enough.

Mounds of snow rose and sank, showing the serpent's path.

"Radi!" I gestured toward the undulating shifts along the ground.

He heard my warning and then made out what I had pointed to. Radi nodded his head and made it to my side. "Any ideas that don't involve us dying in a horrifying way?"

I told him.

"You *are* bent on getting us killed. Brahm Above, I swear—fine." He screamed in frustration, more to get it out of himself than show any anger toward me. "Let's go."

We dropped from the low ridge onto the next bit of level ground, sinking into the snow and setting after the Nagh.

Laki and her grandmother had realized they were being followed and broke into a run.

This set the serpent to strike. It tore free from its icy cover, sending up more clouds of white. Radi and I moved through it, undeterred by the worsening blindness from the snow. The Nagh reared its head and dove after the two women, falling just short of where they stood, dashing its head into the ground. It pulled free, dazed from the repeated impacts it had done to itself.

I reached close to the creature's skull. It blinked, then its pupils shifted like they tracked me—watching me come closer. Near as I was now, I could see something deeper inside them. Something I wished I hadn't learned.

No matter what suffering it went through, it also would not stop being all it knew to be. It would continue to lash out in its crazed rage until it had nothing left. It would die this way and who knew how many others would have to pay the price for it.

"Ari!" Laki's scream pulled me from my thoughts as well as the serpent from its reverie. She stood less than a hundred feet from me.

Clarity returned to the beast and its muscles tensed.

No.

Its mouth parted and silver-white fangs flashed through the gap. The Nagh wouldn't dive after her this time. It would coil and spring, taking Laki and her grandmother in one clean swallow. The yellow eyes hardened, going a deeper gold that reminded me once again of Koli.

The Nagh shifted.

I screamed, gripped both hands to the stake, and plunged. Radi reached me and added his weight to the blow. Together, the wood drove into the creature's left eye, drawing blood.

It writhed and took us with it. Radi and I refused to release our grips. We held on, knowing that if we fell from our new height, we wouldn't recover in time to spare us from the serpent should it have the clarity to finish the job.

It sank to the ground and raced forward, dragging us through the snow. Upward—faster. It pulled us up the mountain. Stone and ice battered us. My cloak tore. My robes were not spared, suffering small gashes that let through more water than before. Some of the ice slid down my clothing and froze me in ways I hadn't known possible.

All through it, I winced and endured. I screamed when forced to. I prayed, to Brahm, to the Sithre, to Radhivahn—to anyone who would listen to me.

Fingers aching and too cold to hold on any longer, I finally let go and fell away from the creature. I tumbled fast and hard along the snowscape. Radi rolled into me, his body sending another wave of pain through me.

We were far closer to the top of the mountain. Hundreds of feet short of it. The serpent still hissed in pain, coiling itself around the narrow peak and screaming its anguish to heaven itself. The mountain here was more of stone and unsteady ice than the rest of it. Loose frozen rocks rested everywhere.

I tried to shake myself clear, unable to move much at all beside my head.

It lolled to one side, almost lifelessly. My vision blurred and the world grew distant.

Whiteness intensified.

The cold seeped past a place I didn't know it could go—far beyond the depths of me, now coming for me myself. It came for the fire inside me. It came for my hopes. My ambitions. For the piece of me that thought about what I'd do when I returned to the Ashram. The piece and the promise of tomorrow. It was talking to me now.

And telling me I would die.

The serpent's motions disrupted more of the mountain, sending it sliding farther down as snow and loose stone slipped out from under us. We now rested two-thirds of the way from the top. Through the shallow ice I could feel the various rocks beneath me.

I spotted something sticking out from the frost.

Stone. Mortared together like it had come from a building. Nearly a solid wall of it that could have weighed a ton or two. A wall that could have come from a tower.

The Crow's Nest.

If I'd had the strength to laugh, I would have.

The Nagh slithered from the peak, coming toward us, its tongue flickering and leaving no doubt as to what came next. It would end us now.

I thought of the wall. Of Rishi Ibrahm. Of the bindings I never learned. I knew the words of course. They had slipped my mind and memories over the years and hardships I'd endured. But the words were always there, like part of a story that couldn't be forgotten.

I remembered the first binding Mahrab had showed me.

I remembered the story about Brahm the Wanderer. A story about a candle, cloak, and cane. And the binding that came in it. A lesson from my old and first teacher.

How did it go?

Closer came the Nagh. Closer still.

It moved slowly, head twitching toward the side where I'd pierced its eye. Red ichor weeped from the wound and trailed along the snow. Its mouth opened and a low long rasp filled the air.

I laughed and almost tore the back of my throat. Something seized me. A madness like the one that had taken the Nagh. A dark and terrible laugh then that brought Radi back around to stare at me like I was the monster now, not the serpent.

I understood it now. And there was little else to do but die if I didn't try my hand at a binding. I knew the cost. I knew the principles. And I knew what I had to do.

I slipped into the folds, reaching out toward the mountain peak, envisioning the cap coming into my hand. I envisioned pulling it down and the rest of the mountain to follow.

Every fold I could manage now held that image. The mountain would fall. It would fall by my hand. It fell. Had fallen. It fell by my hand!

As above. So below. Tak. And. Roh.

I screamed, a wordless cry before I found the words to speak. "As above. So below! I bid you fall, all ice and snow, to bring down the mountain, and crush the serpent below. As above. So below. I bind you stone. Tak. And. Roh!" My voice shook the world, and this time, I felt the lining of my throat give way.

And the world continued to shake.

But nothing happened.

The mountain remained firm—standing still. Unshaken. Untoppled.

Radi closed his eyes, muttering something to himself.

I held the folds in my mind. I understood the binding. I knew it. A linear binding that fixed on one point above me to one below. Top to bottom. I could do it. I would.

A look at Radi's paling face told me I had to.

The serpent came closer.

My folds faltered and everything slipped away from me. I had never truly touched the mountain in my mind.

I had failed.

I scrambled for the stones beneath me. Taking one up and letting out another empty roar. No sound, just the rock tumbling through the air to strike the serpent.

It did nothing to stop its approach.

Radi prayed harder now.

I joined him but kept the words to myself. All the while, I repeated the binding in mind.

It didn't take.

Another stone throw. Desperate now. I took what little energy I had to throw one after another, uncaring what the cost would be to me. I was dead anyway.

Another. And again then.

"Fall, damn you. Fall!" My cry took the last of my voice. The next stone sailed over the serpent's head and struck the mountain.

The world rumbled back. The peak shuddered. A noise like thunder in a cavern filled the air and deafened me.

Ice and boulders slipped. The stone and snowcap crumbled. The shelf of frost holding it all in place fell to dust and rolled into a wave.

Then snow and stone rushed toward us.

And then the mountain fell.

Whiteness.

Cold.

The death-heavy weight of a closing casket came to bury us.

EIGHTY-FIVE

The Mountain Low

I remembered the color of snow and brightness but my world was black. Something shook me. I resisted the call of my name.

"Ari." It sounded a world away and in as much pain as I felt. "Ari." A whisper. Then a shake.

I resisted and lingered before the doors of death.

"Ari." Hands pressed to my face. More grabbed hold somewhere that brought my robes tight around my chest, collar, and my back. I moved, but not by my will.

An all-too-sharp heat washed over me and nearly burned, prickling my skin and bringing a soft pink to the insides of my eyelids.

I had no breath left to even groan, but I finally fluttered my eyes open. It was dark now and a fire burned before me, bringing a new brightness to my sight I had to shy away from. My heart raced at seeing the violent red flames, but when I looked again, I saw they contained just as much orange and yellow. The smoke burned black and gray.

It spoke to me almost the way the Nagh-lokh had. I watched it, each and every tendril lapping at the air for something—anything that would feed and fan it to keep it alive. In that moment, I understood a simple piece of that fire and its want. I watched it until I could do so no longer, listening to its snaps and crackles.

I sighed, letting myself slump against the person at my side. Darkness enveloped me again. But this time, there were no doors to greet me.

The fire's warmth kept me from going past a heavy sleep, and while I rested, I heard voices speak around me.

"I heard him, Tinker. I promise you. I was there, don't ever say I wasn't. If you tell this tale, you'll tell it truly. I heard him speak it. I saw him. Ari called down the mountain. He worked a binding. And he buried the Nagh-lokh."

Another voice then. "God Above. He killed Him?" The grandmother's voice.

"He studies at the Ashram. What else could it have been?" Laki, by the sound of it.

"I was there. Right by him. He screamed for it to fall. He bid it to. Bound it. He *made* it fall. When we get out of this frozen hellish hateful place, I'll write a song for it. I'll tell it in every damnable tavern in the Empire. Watch me."

I didn't have the strength to smile, but a part of me enjoyed the thought of it.

It wasn't the truth of course.

What had really happened?

Well, it's simple. The entire encounter with the Nagh-lokh had shifted the mountain more than the snow and stone could handle. Every thrash and crash. The impacts of its head striking the ground.

And the stones?

Well, they did what any stones will do to an unstable mountain already waiting to tip and tumble. My screams added to the instability.

And so, by my words, the mountain fell.

It seemed a good enough lie to let be for the moment.

I slept, wondering if Radi would make good on his tale.

⁂

Time passed, though I had no measure of it. Daylight washed over me in a paler softer light than that of the fire. Radi helped me to my feet, having somehow found my staff. I leaned on it as he and Pathar led me down from where they'd taken refuge along a part of the mountain spared the avalanche.

When they brought me to the scene, I understood the last piece of how we'd survived and what had really happened.

The Nagh-lokh, an old god, lay at the foot of the mountain. Its body rested partially on the ground and partially in the river. What remained of the serpent's skull lay a dozen feet from us. A wall of stone sat over it, crushing the jaws and fangs and bones inside it. Its scales only knew one color now, no longer the shimmering pearlescent white.

Only the color of blood.

The body twitched and Radi and Pathar let out a steady stream of cursing that rattled me.

Brains half dashed out, the Nagh-lokh still moved, but with none of its earlier fervor.

I stood there, watching the part of its face that still held one good eye. It blinked, slowly, then the pupils shifted like they had before.

Like when they had recognized me.

I stared as it lost all trace of bright burning gold like from Koli's eyes. Now, I saw a softer yellow—something tired and quickly growing gray—clouded.

Two words came to mind: *I'm sorry*. But they didn't come from me.

I spoke them back to the creature, unsure if Radi or Pathar heard me. "I'm sorry, too."

A last rush of air passed through the serpent's lips before it went off to where I thought I'd been—the doors of death.

It stopped moving then.

And an old god died.

I stared with a hollowness at the wall from the Crow's Nest. I thought of the binding that had sent it falling toward me before Rishi Ibrahm vanished it away. Far over the mountains to one of the villages beyond the crests we could see.

I could almost picture him laughing when he heard of this, if he believed a single word.

And I wondered what he would think when he learned I'd performed a binding. Even if it was a lie.

The last of my strength left me again and I dreamed of what I would say to my teacher. I thought of all that I could say to finally make him teach me.

Because I would never again be turned away from the bindings. Ever.

When I returned to the Ashram. I would learn. No matter the cost.

EIGHTY-SIX

Songs and Survivors

I drifted in and out of sleep, finding myself in the confines of a wooden frame. Pathar's wagon. The bed was nothing really remarkable: a stitched cover holding stuffed softness I couldn't figure out. The materials didn't matter much, though. For now, it felt richer and more comforting than anything I could dream of. Never mind the bundles and sacks shifting and shaking beside me. Or the cramped nature of the place.

Laki's grandmother occupied one corner of the wagon compartment. Laki sat beside her, watching me. Both women noticed me staring and leaned forward to bid me to rest.

While I wanted to, now that I had woken, questions raced through my mind. "Are you two all right?" Simple, unnecessary, but as often as not after surviving near death, our first instinct is to ask after others who had suffered alongside us.

Both women pointedly ignored the question, turning it back on me.

"Everything hurts, and I can't feel myself at the same time. I'm not sure if that's good or bad." I managed a shaky smile, then turned to my next thought. "How did you two—" A series of heavy coughs stole the words from me, leaving me unable to speak until I found my breath again. "How did you escape the avalanche?"

"We're no strangers to those. They happen often enough in Ampur." Laki's grandmother sounded like she was discussing something as common as the rising sun. "Sometimes the villagers try to make them happen after a few seasons before the snows get too heavy—too thick—and have more stones ready to fall. It keeps them small and safer."

Safer. I wasn't sure that was the word I'd use to describe how it felt to be drowned by an ocean of snow. Though it didn't answer my question, and Laki's grandmother must have seen that on my face, because she addressed the matter next.

"We kept moving while you battled the Nagh-lokh. Once everything started shaking harder, Laki and I headed down the mountain as much as we did away. We crossed the river to the other side just before everything came down. It didn't spare us, but it saved us." The old woman winced and rubbed parts of her body.

I envisioned the likely scenario. The avalanche would have broken across the mountain base and sent a weaker wave into and across the river. The blowback from that would still be enough to throw an old woman to the ground. Her only saving grace was the soft cushion of snow.

"And Pathar?" I asked, wondering how the tinker had survived.

"Smart enough to stay well far away from you and your madness, boy!" His voice warbled as it passed through the closed doors of the wagon. "Clearly left you deaf. You're shouting loud enough to bring about another fall."

I hadn't realized that, but it became apparent as my throat remembered the recent aches from when I'd screamed on the mountaintop. I rubbed my neck, but it did nothing to ease the pain.

"Here." Laki passed me a skin that warmed my palms the second I touched it. "It's not hot anymore, but it should help. *Nahne* made a needle-*chir* and lemon tea. It's for when people get coughs and bad throats up here."

I thanked her, and gave more silent thanks for the fact the drink hadn't gone completely cold. My hands shook as I freed the stopper and put the tip to my mouth. The first sip came as bitter as a thing could be and the lemon did little to temper the needle-tea's harshness. Even a scant bit of sugar would have gone a long way. Something else sent a new heat to my throat that wasn't from the drink's temperature. *Ginger?*

I knew the answer a second later when my insides burned for a moment before finally soothing.

"Sip on it. Don't guzzle." The old woman's words came clipped but lacked sternness. More the tone of a grandmother idly reminding a child for the dozenth time not to play with the sharp stick for fear of putting out their own eye.

I did as she instructed as we rode on, thinking about what Laki's grandmother had said earlier. She'd watched me battle the serpent. *Battle.* To them, I'd actually fought the beast in a manner that fit the old stories. Never mind the truth that I'd been scared, driven by a mix of panic and something else too far buried in the minds of men to know what I was doing.

But to them, they saw someone who'd slain the Nagh-lokh, and who was I to argue their truth? That's the nature of the thing. Truths often are what we make them, and never mind the reality that might be, because each of us remembers what we wish for things to have been.

We are, in the end, the greatest liars to ourselves and sometimes others.

And history?

Does it remember scared Ari futilely fighting an ancient river monster—a god? No. It remembers me for bringing down a mountain with but a word and slaying something old as time. It remembers a long and courageous battle.

History doesn't remember the truth. It remembers what we tell it to. What we tell ourselves long and hard enough. Eventually, that's all people will ever come to know unless the people there speak up—speak out. And that is one of the hardest things to do.

At that moment, though, I wanted very much to know what they saw from their perspective. So I asked them as I took another swig of the lemon-*chir* tea.

"I saw you come down and try to chase the Nagh." Laki leaned forward, beaming, her eyes wide like she couldn't wait to tell me. "You and your friend stabbed it in the eye and held on as it tried to shake you." Breathless now from how fast she spoke, but Laki still went on.

"I saw you both hang from it as it dragged you up the mountain. Then I lost you—your cloak and robes hiding you in the storm, but we heard your echoes even through the worst of it. I heard you call to the mountain. I heard you tell it to fall. And then . . ." She stopped and chewed over her next words. "And then I heard everything echo back your scream and the mountain fell."

And that's what people would remember me for. *That* truth. Laki's truth.

That is the shape of stories and how they come to be. They all have little truths within them that are the roots of what we all come to hear and know and retell, time and time again. There is truth to all tales, myths, and fables. And they all spawn from a dream, a child's wish, a want for something more—greater. And sometimes luck.

It plays as much a part in legends as anything else, though we convince ourselves otherwise.

So the truth is: I did bring down the mountain, but it was no binding, and luck certainly helped. And it is as much this: I bid and bound the mountain fall. And it did.

I killed the Nagh-lokh and buried the village of Ampur under ice and snow.

People don't remember the Ashura or the red-flame fires and smoke. No mention of the bleeding stones and the crumbling wood.

Just the serpent and the boy who slew it in the great white north high above the world.

I smiled at what Laki had told me and decided I'd earned a longer sleep in the bed until we returned.

Pathar brought us to Volthi, and by that time, the worst of my injuries had eased. That wasn't to say they'd gone away. But the tea brought better functionality back to my throat. I'd gone from a unified bruised mass that could feel nothing, to one that felt rather poorly. But at least I could feel.

Strings thrummed and Radi's voice hummed through the doors of the tinker's wagon. I hadn't realized his gift when at the Ashram. But hearing him now, I saw the appeal for songs and music.

His voice was deep and resonant, yet every note that left his mouth was just as light and buoyant when he sang. They vibrated inside you just like his strings quivered after being plucked. You felt it like the breath of a lover hot against your throat, or a kiss so deep it reached a place far deeper than any lips or tongue can press to. To the core of you.

He sang words, then, though they had grown far away. Pathar spoke to him, sounding just as distant.

I'd realized they'd left the wagon and headed into the village. My body had no wish for it, but I shook free of the covers and tried to follow suit. Everything throbbed in a single agony.

Laki moved to place a hand on my chest, gently urging me to return to bed.

I shook my head. "I'm fine." It wasn't true, but curiosity had taken the better of me. I wanted to know where the two were going.

Her grandmother put a hand on Laki's shoulder. "Men are like badgers, dear, only more stubborn and prone to anger. You mustn't try to tell them what they can and cannot do. A wise woman lets him have his way only to be around when it goes wrongly for him. Better we go with him to keep him from falling and cracking his head open than have him struggle here where there's no room for it."

I glowered at the pair of them. "I'm right here. Don't talk over me."

Laki sighed and lifted her hands from me. "*Ji, Nahne*. You're right. I'll help him walk, and maybe we can find him something for the pain."

Her grandmother nodded. "Something sweet will do as well. One for me, one for him. You can't give him bitter tea and expect him not to grow just as much. They do that, too, and a little sugar now and then takes the edge off their tongues."

My stare intensified and I could feel my eyes smoldering.

Neither of them noticed. Neither cared.

Laki moved to the back of the wagon and opened the doors while her grandmother handed me my staff—though now I knew why some binders called it a cane. I'd certainly be using it as one. Both of them helped guide me out of the compartment and to the lip of the wooden home.

I eyed the drop to the ground. Not so far. Four feet from where I sat. Nothing. Laki and her grandmother went first, then they extended their arms toward me. I waved them aside and dropped. I fell. Then I kept falling as my feet struck the ground and my knees thought it better to buckle and send me crashing into the snow.

For a moment, I welcomed the coolness across me. It dulled more of the pain and the shock brought me a sharp clarity. Then anger took its place and I felt hot enough to melt the frost away.

"See, dear. It won't do him much in the long of it. He'll still make the same mistakes until he stops growing taller and learns to grow older. Until then, all we can do is this. Help him up."

I grumbled in the snow and pushed myself to half a stand, using my binder's cane to do the rest. "I'm fine."

Her grandmother gave me a look that said she would pretend to believe me for the sake of saving time.

Laki didn't bother with that courtesy at all. "You can't even stand straight. Your legs are shaking. Here." She came to my side, throwing my other arm around her and forcing me to lean on her.

"This is embarrassing." I continued my grousing under my breath.

"And eating snow isn't?"

I knew enough to not argue that one and nodded to where Radi and Pathar had gone off to.

Both of them stood outside the largest building in sight. A whole two stories, which may have been laughable back in Keshum, but in a place like Volthi? It might have been the center of their little world. The pair entered together, and I caught sight of the case Radi kept his mandolin in.

Is he here to perform? Even though I hadn't developed a keenness for music at that point in my life, I wanted to see my friend in the heart of what he loved most. It was right, and more than that, I owed it to him. But, there is a simpler reason as well—a better one.

He was my friend.

And that is always reason enough.

So Laki and her grandmother helped me toward the building I later learned was the village hall, the men's gathering spot for discussing everything from the weather to whose son would marry whose daughter, and a place to complain about the luck of late. Nothing more than coincidence, of course, when I learned the local women used it for similar purposes. But for today, it was most importantly the place where folk would be singing songs and making music.

In a place as small as Volthi, people didn't have much in the way of entertainment. So Radi's arrival turned more than a few heads and tipped just as many ears toward him as he took the stage.

The place looked much like you'd imagine a hall in a rural village. Wood and stone with a single hearth that did a well-enough job at bringing warmth to everyone nearby. And for those it failed, a single counter offered all manner of drinks to make up for it.

A second story sat above with wooden railings people could lean over to get a decent view below. Men and women sat in their own groups, kept tight to round tables with barely enough room for four people, made all the worse by locals crowding around them in up to twice that number.

I caught Pathar talking to a man behind the bar and hobbled over to him. Laki and her grandmother at least did me the small courtesy of letting me make that effort without their aid. The tinker noted my approach and turned back to the man he'd been speaking to, gesturing toward me. Pathar stopped me as I got within arm's reach of him, handing me a mug of something warm and smelling of spices. I arched a brow at him.

"Spice wine—warm wine, winter wine, and all the things you can think to call it." His tongue hadn't lost any of its quickness, it seemed. He spoke fast enough to trip even me. "They got all sorts of names for it up in these parts, but it'll take your aches away, boy, and then some. Can make you light on your feet and your heart. And, after all that snow and what I saw, I have to say I don't mind drinking enough of this till I forget it all." He took a long, slow sip, lids closing halfway as he savored it.

I took the mug he offered and eased onto a seat, following his lead and taking a taste. It lived up to what he'd said. It struck me with star anise, cinnamon, sugar, and an acid taste I hadn't come across too much in my life. But the warmth it brought soothed away all my pains and, for a moment, I cared for little else in the world besides the heat radiating from the cup and the next sip. "Thank you, Pathar."

He grunted. "S'nothin', boy. Though, suppose I ought not to be calling you that much longer. Not after what I saw." He took a deeper taste of the drink. "Been traveling long and hard over my life—many miles, you know? In all that time, I've seen some right wondrous things—as close to magical as a man can come to find. But *that*?" He shook his head, then sipped again. "That was something for the storybooks, Ari."

I grinned when he used my name, raising my mug in a salute. He met it, tipping his against mine, and we took our next sip in unison. Once I cleared my throat from the wine's acid bite, I asked him the question on my mind. "You mean to tell the story, then? Of what you saw, I mean."

He nodded. "Already started, truth be told. No choice to it. Fishermen venture up that way every now and then. Pair of them went up thataway and saw what's left of Ampur . . . and the serpent. Them two turned back right round fast as two men can and came here tellin' folk afore we showed up. Didn't need much more than that telling me to tell them the thing true and proper of what happened. So I did." He took a longer sip. "Why do you think we're drinking free?"

I blinked, looking down at my mug and then to the man who'd served us.

He stood at the other end of the counter, talking with a woman well into her later years and just as plump as he was. When he caught me staring, he inclined his head in what could have been a respectful bow.

I returned it, unsure what else to do.

So, people had already got to talking about the Nagh-lokh and what had happened high on the mountaintop.

"Your friend's got a good mind to him. Already knew the nature of how this would go. Boy's been tinkering up a song from there to here—no time at all, and he's got something worth lending an ear to, or so I think. He'll make a pretty piece of copper or two I wager by the time the day's done. First song about you. Smart. They'll be telling it all through Ghal if he does this right."

Radi knew his cue. Strum. His fingers brushed against the strings and teased out a thrumming chord that set everyone at their ease. People turned to face him, their conversations dimming—not quite dying yet.

He plucked a low strong note—something that sounded almost like a heavy man's baritone. If it were a word, it would have said, *listen. Attend.*

And the crowd did. They waited for the last of the vibrations to end, leaving a silence in the aftermath that stretched as Radi positioned himself. I developed a new appreciation for him and his craft in that moment.

"This is a song about Ampur, the brilliant mountain village among the white-frosted crests of Ghal. A kingdom unto its own in the old stories by another name. A place of hard living and harder folks. A sister to you, and that hardiness is in your blood—I see it here well and true." Another strum, but no song yet. He teased them—pulling on their strings just as much as he plucked his own. Making them wait. Making them savor his words more than their wine.

"This is a tale you've already heard whispers of. But this isn't the place for low voices. No, this is a place for songs. One about the young binder who roused and found a sleeping vengeful god and what happened after. Of the battle. The fires. And the mountain coming down low. Of Ampur, lost to stream, stone, and snow.

"Of red smoke and flame and blood-run slopes and homes. This is the song of how one man killed an old god." He strummed, slow and soft—lilting and lulling us into a dream.

No one whispered or turned an eye and ear away from Radi then. He had them sure as if he'd bound them in place with the strings of his mandolin.

"High, oh high, on the mountaintop
high, oh high, where earth kisses sky
onward he climbed,
and would not stop,
high, oh high, our savior climbed;

"he roared to the serpent,
and challenged the beast,
high, oh high, our savior climbed,
he screamed to the heavens,
hear, oh hear, our savior's cry,

"he lured the serpent,
up to the clouds,
where the man met a monster,
and a god was bowed.

"High, oh high, up in the snow,
where the mountain rises
and kisses the sky,
did our hero bind heaven,
and it heard his cry.

"High, oh high, up in the snow,
did our hero bind heaven,
and bring down the mountain // low!"

Radi played harder then—fast and heavy—whipping like a storm. His hands blurred, the tempo increased. Soon my own heart hammered faster than it knew what to do with itself. My head spun and all I had the space for was Radi's song. Quicker now, and my blood was set to thrumming to a thunder I didn't know was in me. No longer was the storm outside, but within me. I shook and drummed at my core as he played.

Sweat broke out along his forehead. He sang of red flame and smoke, filling the battleground. Of hail and thunder that were never there, but I didn't care. There were no words but Radi's then. The only words that mattered. The ones that had rooted us in place and fixed our minds to each and every note he pulled from the mandolin.

Faster then. Harder now. He sang and played until even the thought of taking a breath seemed an affront to the performance.

He played the piece now to be a song of shaking worlds and shuddering stone. Of my words and screams as things to be seen. A magic that spread from me to grip the mountain in unseen hands, which were my own. And with a final word and cry of protest I wrenched the top free and set a world of stone and ice falling upon the old god, leaving it dead.

My fury and power too great to spare the village. Nothing remained but us in the end—victorious.

I had heard many storms in my life. I'd heard drumming in stone halls—a thing so loud it could deafen a man. But I will never forget the thunder that broke out when Radi finished his song.

It ended with a final note that did not linger. It came and died as fast as the avalanche that buried us. No vibrations. A cold hard stop.

Silence.

No one dared let out a breath and be the first to make a noise in the song's aftermath.

For once, I didn't break the quiet.

Pathar had that distinction. He clapped his hands, jarring us from the reverie that kept everyone to a hush. "Brahm's blood, boy. *That* was a song. And I'll tell it true to all of you!" He jabbed a finger at one man at random, then slowly turned in place and made sure to take in everyone with his pointing—addressing the crowd. "Was there myself. I saw it with my own two eyes—don't say I didn't. And you all know what a tinker's word is worth. Might peddle in tales, some surely so tall, but we also tell truths and tell you lot the difference between them."

Some of the patrons grumbled in agreement among themselves.

"I was there, in my wagon—a-watchin'. I saw it. I saw the boy head out there into the snow. Into a storm of frost I'll need many more a drink to pull the chill from my heart. And there I saw it then. The Nagh-lokh. Serpent big enough to swallow a mountain to the last stone. Mark my words. Some of you went up that way and turned round right as quick and brought your boats back home. I know it. You saw that monster's body."

Another smattering of people nodded in agreement and made low murmurs.

They must have been the fishermen who'd gone up that way and came back to spread the story of what they'd found.

Pathar turned his finger onto me, touching my chest lightly. "This boy here worked an old magic—*true* magic. He bound the mountain. And by Brahm's name, may he burn me for telling lies, the mountain fell. He called it. And he brought it down."

Another quiet. Then the world broke into screaming and thunderous clapping—boots stomping, and hands hammering on tables that could have drowned out the sounds of a mountain falling.

⁂

A better man might never have let that song take place. He might have stood up, told everyone the truth of what had happened, and refused their applause. But I was a young boy, and after a season of Nitham's antagonization, butting heads with Rishi Ibrahm, and failing to find anything useful on the Ashura, I didn't see the harm in it.

How far could a song spread if told in a small village like Volthi?

That evening was spent taking in more mulled wine than any young man should ever imbibe. Pathar was right, however.

It did ease my aches and pains and set me lighter on my feet than I knew was possible.

I couldn't manage a dance, but many a girl tried, and I gave them all the simple steps I could. Red rosy cheeks, others sun-kissed and warm, they all found a way or two to have my lips press to them, or bring theirs to the sides of my face. By the end of that night, the warmth I felt had nothing to do with my wine.

People congratulated me.

And I learned just how bad the day after that much alcohol can be.

⁂

My head spun the morning after worse than it had after Nitham and his friend had beaten me. I left the room I'd been granted, grating my teeth as the sounds of my own footsteps set my skull into another set of panging.

The village hall hadn't been set up to function as an inn, but it still boasted a few rooms for that purpose just in case Volthi had more than its usual infrequent travelers. The proprietor had generously offered me and my party rooms to share for what we had done. Though, one could argue we really hadn't done anything to the village's benefit.

But the way people had spoken, they'd sounded like I'd stopped the serpent from coming their way to do to Volthi what it had to Ampur. I'm not sure that would have happened, but it didn't stop them from believing it. And so, they'd treated me like a little lord.

If only they had a lord's cure to my headache.

I made my way toward the counter I'd been at last night, relieved the rooms had been on the first floor and I hadn't had to climb down any stairs. It would have been a difficult task even with my cane. My injuries hadn't come close to healing, and I knew I'd still have bruises for a set at least.

A crowd of a dozen people or so lingered in the hall, their eyes all turning to me as I approached. None of them rushed me, having noticed my bedraggled state and likely the sour-faced glower I knew I wore.

A woman in her forties came over to me, offering her hands. When I refused, she placed them on my shoulders anyway and led me to the counter. I thanked her but she waved me off. "You saved our home. It's no trouble to help you."

I opened my mouth to protest but she talked over me.

"Ampur is all we have. When the Nagh woke, I thought it would swallow us all, then the land itself. Some stories talk of that. Of its wrath and hunger and spewing a storm from its mouth that can wash away a mountain."

I *had* wondered about that, still unsure how the creature had shot a torrent of water, but it hardly had the force to wear down that much stone. My brain still moved at a sluggish pace, so I only realized what she had said far later than I should have. "Wait, you're from Ampur?"

She gave me a kind and sympathetic look instead of one better suited for my slow-witted idiocy in the moment. "We left when the fires started. At first, I thought of the children's rhymes. When the chimney smoke goes red as blood." Her smile faded and she didn't say the words, but I knew what was on her mind.

The Ashura.

"But when I left our home, little one in hand, I heard it. The Nagh-lokh. It came down the river, mad as a thing could be. I ran that very night with our child. My husband went to the hall to rally the other men to help whoever needed to flee." Her eyelids twitched and I knew what would come. They watered, then tears streamed down her face. "I haven't seen him since."

I didn't know what to say. I'd survived demons, streets as an urchin—a sparrow—killed my adoptive father—a criminal and abuser. I'd robbed a merchant king and owed him a debt I had no idea how to pay. And I'd killed an old god. None of it prepared me to console a mother and potentially a widow.

I placed a hand on her shoulder much like she had done to me. When she looked up, I spread my arms wide and gave her the only thing I could think of. A hug.

Sometimes, when we think we've lost the world, the only thing for it—for us—is the closeness of another person to let us know we're not alone in our suffering. Pain is hard, but it is infinitely more the burden alone. But loneliness has a cure, and the kindness of a hug can be that salve.

"I don't know if I'll find him."

Every part of me wanted to tell her the truth then. That she probably wouldn't. But there are times when the truth is not what people need. They need hope. "You will," I lied. "Ampur is still there. The land, at least. It can be rebuilt. I don't know what lives you'll have after this, but . . ."

She didn't give me the chance to finish. The woman wrapped me back in the hug, tight enough to cause me worry over my ribs and aching back. She kissed my forehead as if I was still a child in need of swaddling and not a young man taller than her. "You've given us our home. That is enough."

I nodded, finding no more words to speak.

She then introduced me to the others. All runaways from Ampur—survivors with similar tales. News of the fires had spread quickly through the night, and instead of helping, the villagers took to running. Some for fear of the Ashura, most after seeing the Nagh.

I learned the serpent came after the first bell had rung through the village to warn people of the flames. It left them little time to tend to those in trouble, and then they could see only to surviving themselves.

One boy, no older than ten, flagged me down as Pathar left the hall and told everyone we'd be leaving soon as he'd finished feeding his oxen.

"What is it?" I couldn't manage a smile. All the pain and unease from the drinking plagued me and made me want to snap at anyone who made too much noise.

"You was askin' 'bout ta fires?" he said. The boy shouldn't have been able to stand upright, reedy as he was, and in heavy layers to ward off the cold. The bulk of his clothing looked like they weighed nearly as much as he did, maybe more. His hair hung long and lanky, lacking the stark rich whiteness of the other people in the mountains. The locks instead reminded me of snow weathered by road dust, not turning darker per se, but losing its luster.

I nodded.

He pressed his lips tight and one of his cheeks sunk inward as if he'd started chewing on its inside. "Suppose'n I saw'it somethin'? You'n thinkin' t'would help findin' out t'what started t'fires?"

I already knew in my heart what had been behind them, no matter what the locals thought, but I inclined my head again. "It would . . ."

"Rapu." He dragged the back of a hand against his nose, leaving a thin line of snot against it. Then he rubbed that against the underside of a sleeve, looking around as if worried his mother would catch him in the act. "Name's Rapu. Where's am I suppose'n ta find you iffun I have summin?"

I told him of the Ashram and how to send me a letter, ensuring it would reach my hands. When he wondered about the cost, I set him at his ease and told him that if he had anything to tell me, I'd pay whoever brought it to me for the trouble.

Hope in heart that I might finally learn something of the Ashura, and cane in hand, I left the hall, and soon, Pathar led us back on the trip to the Ashram.

To home.

EIGHTY-SEVEN

TRUE FLAME

It took us two days to return to the Ashram rather than the day and a half it should have. We moved at a slower pace to give me more time to heal, and Pathar stopped twice as often as on the way up to trade his tale of my heroism against the serpent with any who'd hear it. We met another tinker along the way and he promised he'd spread word of what happened as well.

Radi played his song from the head of the wagon for all passersby. And while I didn't hear the reactions, I made out whistling on occasion from those who'd listened, now carrying on the tune.

Laki and her grandmother stayed in the back of the wagon-home, having chosen to visit the Ashram and make a case before the masters for hospitality until they could return to Ampur. They also made sure to feed me as much as possible from the supplies we'd picked up in Volthi. Endless dried meats that left me wondering at times if they had more spice in them than substance. Mercifully, they didn't give me any more of that bitter tea, choosing instead to make a broth of bone marrow and fat that tasted of salt and heavy butter.

By the time we arrived at the foot of the Ashram's stairs, most of my pains had dulled enough that I could move fairly well. Though, maybe not so well enough to handle thousands of steps without aid.

Pathar said farewell and thanked me for bringing him a story he'd be able to trade for a long while and make more in coin than anything I'd paid him. Though, he warned me to never again drag him into another mess like that.

I told him I couldn't make any promises.

We shared a laugh and he left me with a promise of his own: that he'd come back and share any news he picked up along the way which I might want to hear of.

I thanked him, and he left.

Laki, her grandmother, and Radi all helped me up to the Ashram's courtyard.

I won't lie and tell you that by the end my legs didn't burn. My knees felt like they'd been ground to fine powder and I knew I'd need another few days of bed rest if possible.

Radi left me to stand with the aid of my cane while he flagged down one of the passing Ashram monks, instructing him to bring Laki and her grandmother before the masters.

The monk bowed his head, hands clasped, and led the women away.

"Think you'll be able to make it to your room?" Radi nudged my elbows, and while it didn't hurt as much as it would have days ago, I stared at him like a cat who'd just had its tail pulled. He raised both his hands, palms out, to stay me. "Sorry-sorry." His lopsided smile told me that wasn't wholly true, but I let it go.

"I'll manage. It's not so many stairs to my room as the climb up here. Besides, if I need help, I can ask Aram." Realization came thundering into me. "Brahm's breath and blood . . . Aram!"

Radi's eyes widened and he looked around as if expecting trouble. "What? What about her?"

In my haste to leave the Ashram and chase after the Ashura, I'd foisted the stray kitten I'd found on her. I'd forgotten, and Radi had as well. I told him what I remembered and he, lacking any sympathy for our friend, doubled over and burst into a laughter that echoed through the main courtyard.

I twisted just enough to spare my body from a sharp twinge and snapped out with my staff, bringing most of its length across Radi's rear.

"Brahm's blood, Ari. Give a man warning before you touch wood like that to his ass." He rubbed the spot.

I gave him a level look and he returned it with the same uneven grin as before, letting me know he knew exactly what he'd said. "It's a wonder no woman will spend time with you for long, Radi. Truly. A great mystery. I can't fathom why. . . ." I stumbled as his hand crashed into my shoulder, not with enough force to topple me, but even so, my weakness led me to falter.

He reached out and caught me, keeping me from going full into the snow. "Says the man who couldn't see what was right in front of him with Estra." Radi shook his head in a mixture of regret and disbelief. "He can bring down a mountain and slay a serpent out of stories, but bring the girl back for more than a meal. Honestly, Ari." He rubbed his face and walked off, giving me one last grin. "If I see Aram I'll send her your way, *ji-ah*?"

I nodded and thanked him, making my own way toward the tower my room was in.

By the last stair, I'd developed a dozen new curses for whoever decided to put student lodging in a place so high up, and then decided that, no, twelve wasn't nearly enough. So I came up with another ten by the time I fell into bed.

Nothing had changed while I'd been gone and it brought me a sense of comforting familiarity. Strings still rested over my desk and across the floor along with my notes on how to make them unbreakable. And after riding with Pathar, I now had an idea. Though, a bit more rest called to me first.

A knock at my door kept me from indulging in that.

I grumbled and bit off another curse. When I made my way over to see who'd come, I found Aram standing there with a thick bundle of blankets in her arms.

Her eyes were ringed with shadow and her color had waned. She pushed the bundle toward me. "Brahm's blood, Ari. You know how long you've been gone?" Her voice lacked the energy I thought it would have. She sounded like she'd missed a few good nights of sleep.

I did the math and tried to count the number in my head. I failed and had to guess instead. "Nearly a set?"

She groused under her breath. "Yeah, nearly a set. And you left me this little monstrosity."

I looked down at the bundle to see the kitten I'd rescued resting soundlessly. "Looks like he's no trouble at all."

Aram gave me a hard look that made it clear that had not been the case. "You'd think the little devil would be happy to be saved and fed and kept warm. No. He's torn through two of my good shirts, Ari. *Two.* One wasn't enough, I suppose. I've been bringing him extra rations from Clanks whenever I can. He's been eating twice his weight from what I gather. Oh, he also has no concept of personal space, keeping quiet . . . even in the night, and worst of all, how to defecate like a civilized person!"

I gave the cat another look, then my friend. "I think that last one might have to do with the fact he's not a civilized person."

Aram made a choking sound and pushed the bundle into my arms. "I'm glad you're back and safe, which means now you can care for this thing. Might want to remember animals are prohibited by the Ashram's laws. I'll see you tomorrow." She stifled a yawn and her eyelids fluttered. "By the way, what do you plan to do with it?"

The kitten still slept, unaware of our discussing his fate. As I watched him, I thought back to when and where I'd found him.

Alone. Half-starved and just as much frozen in the cold. All at the mercy of whatever cruelty Nitham and his friends would have taken out on him.

I know what it is to be orphaned, alone and confused on unfamiliar streets that I may have been born to, lived beneath, but which were never mine. Which were never a home. No. It was more like being surrounded by a place rather than ever being a part of it. Than feeling safe there.

There is a different kind of loneliness in that. In being in a place that is all you've ever known, but which still is not yours, and where you are not wholly welcome as well. You are only ever tolerated at best. This kitten had lived and learned a similar thing.

I had a home now, in a way, at the Ashram.

It seemed the least I could do was give another orphan the same.

A sparrow looking after a cat, it was all I could do not to break out in laughter.

Aram watched us, waiting for an answer.

"I think I'll keep him. At least for now." I knew the Ashram's laws and what could happen if I were caught. I'd stirred up more than enough trouble to be cut any more leniency. "Don't tell anyone?"

She snorted and gave me a look that said I should have known better. "You know I won't. Just . . . maybe get a bucket or a tray for the thing. I'm not sure how you're supposed to take care of one of those. My father has dogs. They're sensible and can be trained."

I smiled. "I'm not sure either, but I'll keep that in mind." I wished my friend a good night and a nice sleep before heading back to my own bed to set the kitten down.

The blankets unraveled easily, and I rearranged them to form a cushion below the cat's body so he could rest in better comfort beside me. As I looked at him, I noticed I hadn't taken in his true color.

Or maybe it had to do with nearly a set of good food, a warm safe climate, and rest that had brought out a healthier look to his fur. But it was red, red as true flame.

His eyes opened and he stared at me unblinking as I watched him. They were the color of emeralds over sage. As much bright strong green in them as the softer faded tones. As our stare continued, they looked to lour and take on more the gray of storm clouds and ash.

He mewled once and shifted, almost inching away from me before coming back.

Shy little thing. While his long hair curled and waved much like tendrils of fire, he didn't seem to have much of that in his heart. A skittish little boy.

I knew of that too. A younger Ari had been much like him.

I smiled and thought of a name. Shola. The shy one. It wasn't a Brahmthi name, coming from Zibrathi. I'd picked up a smattering of the language back in Keshum and heard the word uttered once.

Shola reached out and touched the tip of his nose to one of my fingers before falling and smacking his head against my hand in what could have been a headbutt.

I didn't know if I should laugh or be concerned. A bit of both felt best. I scratched him just behind the ears before swaddling him again. "Rest here. I'll be back with some things."

If Aram had spent that much effort in caring for the kitten, then I figured her advice well worth considering.

So I headed out to grab some food, and stop by the Holds to see if I could find any spare materials to make Shola's life easier.

I returned from Clanks with a tray laden down with sweet yams, saffron rice, a bowl of buttered goat stew, and a spinach mash with cubed soft cheese inside. Shola needed no instruction, fighting me for any piece of meat he could get. Never mind that I'd given him a fair portion of food in one corner of the tray.

"No." I swatted his hand away with a soft touch.

He persisted.

"No."

He didn't seem to get the message.

"Shola. *No* means . . . well, no. Do not. Stop." I picked him up with one hand and set him back to his corner of the tray, making it harder for him to come after my portion.

The adjustment did little to dissuade him.

"Brahm's tits, cat, I need just as much food as you do. Maybe more."

He didn't think so, apparently.

I relented and gave him one of the pieces of goat I was about to put into my mouth.

Satisfied, he took my charity as meaning I would be more than happy to give him more.

I was not.

I glowered at the kitten but decided maybe one more would get him to leave me alone.

For a while, it did.

He then developed a sudden interest in my spinach and cheese, something he just as quickly lost all taste for after a mild lick, deigning it well beneath his refined palate.

I grew up in the theater, and I have never met a more finicky and dramatic being.

Content that he'd eaten his fill, and some of mine, Shola came over to run his head into my thigh before deciding that it was the perfect place to sleep.

I let him rest for a short while, before fetching what I'd brought up from Holds. One deep tin tray that I could layer blankets in to give Shola something close to a proper bed. Two bowls of the same metal I could fill with food and water. I had wondered what to do about Shola's need to relieve himself, but he answered the question before I could give it further thought.

He bounded to the window, batting at the glass in frustration.

I frowned but opened it only to have him leap onto the roof and scurry away from me. He moved to a ledge farther than I could have hoped to climb to if I had set out after him, turned, and proceeded to . . . give a demonstration of why I might not need to worry about his bathroom habits.

Thankfully, window frames in the Ashram, as well as any seams that could let in or out air, had all been inscribed with minor bindings to improve their ability to retain room temperatures. Though, they couldn't do much if you were forced to open the damn things.

So I was left with the conundrum of how to make it so Shola could come and go as he pleased. Being from the streets, he must have had no issue wandering on his own, and likely just needed the opportunity to do so.

Content with his work, he set out to bury his leavings under a mound of snow that had accumulated on the rooftops and sauntered back to me. I took him with both arms and brought him back to his new bed.

And of course, he decided he had no desire to rest and would rather race across the floor, which sent all of my strings into a tangle and into the air.

"No!" I lunged, grabbing the kitten and slowly unraveling the mess of strings, taking care that they didn't cut into his flesh. "Brahm's tits and ashes, Shola, you're more likely to kill me than the Nagh if you keep like this." I freed him from his self-inflicted bondage and set him into his bed, refusing his struggles for freedom until he decided that, yes, he would rather like a good sleep.

Merciful gods above.

EIGHTY-EIGHT
Things to Tell

Early next morning Shola informed me of his need to return to the rooftop, so I obliged him before even having my wits set straight. I may have bemoaned being up at that time, but he didn't give me much choice. He finished his jaunt and came back within a few minutes. Then he decided to avail himself of another nap.

I left him to it, fetching my bag and supplies, grabbing my staff as well as I headed to my classes.

A burly student spotted me heading toward Rishi Vruk's philosophy class. He had the thick neck muscles, broad shoulders, and wide back that screamed of him being one of Master Conditioner's wrestlers. The fact these were visible under the thin robe he'd chosen to wear only spoke more of the student's considerable bulk. So, when he placed a hand on my chest to stop me, I didn't give him the sharp side of my tongue.

"Rishi Vruk isn't here right now and he didn't leave a *thaina* behind to cover for him."

That gave me pause. I hadn't known he'd left, and the idea of not leaving a left hand to continue his lectures was odder still. "Why haven't any of the other rishis stepped in?"

The student shrugged, running a hand through his short-cropped hair. "He's been gone for nearly a set and left instructions that his classes were suspended—no work. Only instructions for assistants to revise lesson plans he did up for his return."

"Are you one of his then?"

He nodded.

I frowned, having wanted to see my friend and tell him everything that had happened in Ampur. If anyone would have believed me, no matter how ridiculous the story, it would have been Vathin. Even if the story strained credulity, he would have at least listened without judgment. "Thank you." I walked away since I knew I hadn't missed anything and therefore had no work to catch up on.

My next visit led me to Rishi Ibrahm, who had just finished up an Introduction to Binding Principles lesson.

He saw me and flashed a toothy grin. Whatever tiredness hung in his eyes a moment earlier vanished, and all I saw was the manic bright gleam of mischief.

It set me on edge and I approached slower. "Rishi?"

"Last time I checked, Accepted Ari. Why, was that a question?"

I didn't give him the satisfaction of glowering, keeping my expression painfully neutral. "I came to see what I missed while on my leave of absence, Master Binder. I'd like to make up any—"

He snorted. "You didn't miss much here. More students are full of dust and dreams between their ears, thinking to be like legends and binders of old. Tch. I bet you half of them couldn't piss in the dark without a candle to help them figure out how. But"—he waved a hand dismissing the topic—"what might you have need of in this class, hm?"

I tried to answer but he gave me no chance.

"*And he brought down the mountain . . . lllooooow!*" Rishi Ibrahm's voice had none of the smoothness, vibrancy, and depth of Radi's. When he sang, I almost wished the mountain fall had deafened me.

And I told him so.

"Tch. Singing's not my gift. If I ever have a son of myself, may that be his. Now, little binder, tell me of the mountain."

I licked my lips, almost answering before I realized he shouldn't have known about that so soon. "How did you . . ." I trailed off, *of course.* "The song. Where did you hear it? We've only been back a day."

"Radi played it in Stones last night. Boy had a decent turnout. I wouldn't be surprised if the story's caught a good spark by now. It will fan into a fire soon enough. Catchy tune. Parts of it anyway." Rishi Ibrahm tugged his ear.

"Stones?" I knew how stupid my question sounded, but I hadn't heard of the place yet.

"Mhm." He nodded. "There's a section of the catacombs beneath the Ashram all of black stone, smooth as glass. Wonderful sounds down there. A man with a cracking voice could sing and sound all the sweeter than he could aboveground. For someone like Radi, it's close to a magical place. Students go down there for all the young and wrong reasons: to cavort away from masters' eyes, for the thrill of going where it is forbidden, as well as for music and drinking." He rolled his eyes. "As if we don't know students do all that. The nature of children, I suppose." He shrugged.

"Wait . . . that means you had to have been there to hear him play, though."

He grinned. "Of course. I'm a proponent of the arts, even if I don't have a touch of talent for them. Do you know how hard I've tried to get a Master Rhythmist position made at the Ashram? There is a secret rhythm to all things, and musicians and storytellers have it. They need that nurturing from an expert. Besides, if those arts were better catered to, I'd likely have less of you airheaded simpering idiots chasing my hems to learn binding. The world would be a better place . . . for me." He let out a forlorn sigh and slumped a little.

Rishi Ibrahm then moved to take a seat, gesturing at me to stand at the other side of his table.

I did, waiting.

"So, out with it. What happened? I heard the song. A binding, hm? Linear. Figure it out yet?"

I nodded, not wholly trusting myself to speak. I had known the pieces of it all along when I looked back through my memories, but I hadn't performed it. Still, this felt like a test—a chance to show the Master Binder I was ready. "As above, so below. First part of the paired binding is tak. The second is roh. They link two vertically opposed points in space." I gestured above myself, then to a spot on the ground.

"Like if someone throws a rock over a student's head that should by all rights sail over it. Mutter the binding and impose your will—have the faith—and you can command it to move against its nature to strike the student's head."

He smiled, lacing his fingers together and resting his chin on the steeple they formed. "Well, well. Good job. Seems you don't need me at all then, hm?" Something about his crooked smile and the new light in his eyes told me I was playing a dangerous game now.

"I wouldn't say that." I kept my voice as nonchalant as possible. "I'd like to learn better control, not to mention the other bindings."

"Oh-ho. But you slayed the mighty Nagh, didn't you? Most go their entire lives without ever even hearing a peep about a beast like that, and I can't recall the last time anyone's been heard to have seen one. But killing one?"

"You don't seem to have a hard time believing that, Rishi." I didn't frown, but I did eye him sideways, unsure why he'd taken so quickly to the story without seeing a shred of proof.

"Hm? Oh, no. I popped over to Ampur with a pair of bindings to see the place myself. I had no idea that's where I sent that piece of the Crow's Nest. Odd bit of luck that, no?" He laughed as if he'd told a particularly funny joke.

I didn't think it was.

"Though, honestly, bringing down the whole mountain was reckless. You're lucky you survived. And, I suppose the serpent's body will be a boon to the survivors that go back to rebuild. It's worth a good deal, and I know menders across the Empire will pay a pretty sum for its parts. And Master Artisan might give an arm and a leg, possibly more, to get its scales and teeth." He gave me an appreciative nod. "Good work."

I said nothing and remained as still as possible, not wanting to betray the discomfort I felt at the praise I knew I didn't deserve. "So, will you teach me?"

He burst into laughter. "What? Oh, no. Ari, you were terribly stupid there. Triggering an avalanche to bury a creature regarded by some as an old god. Reckless—tch. Not showing the good judgment yet I've hoped for. What happens if you lose control of a binding like that? Will you bring down the Crow's Nest on the heads of everyone in it? Play with fire, you get burned. Will you set the Ashram ablaze and burn us to ash and cinder?" He wagged a finger in admonishment.

"No, you're not ready. Maybe you'll never be." Rishi Ibrahm made a shooing motion with one hand. "Pay another visit to the Crow's Nest if you've forgotten the lesson from earlier." Something went hard in his voice. Hard as cold iron, and brittle as sheet ice. "Remember the costs, and that whatever you may think of me, I will not let such a fate fall on anyone ever again. Even you."

I swallowed when his eyes turned hot and lost all touches of their whimsical mischief. The childlike instructor vanished, replaced by someone older, tired, and who had an anger I didn't want to see. I nodded and left without another word, deciding still to take his advice to visit the Crow's Nest. Though, I had my own reasons for it.

❧

I stepped through the doors of the Crow's Nest, greeting Krisham as he lounged across the desk.

He jumped to his feet, pointing a wooden rod at me like a sword. "Hold, demon—twisted turned and monstrous thing. I bar the way, and you shall not pass!"

I blinked, raising both hands in a mixture of defense and to hopefully put him at his ease. "Whoa, Krisham. It's me, Ari."

"You sound so sure, but I am not Krisham. You stand before Sheru. So stand all the firmer and be ready." He let out a shrill scream, leaping off the desk and bringing the wooden stick down to where I'd been standing a moment earlier. It clacked hard, almost loud enough I wondered if he'd cracked the stone ground.

"Brahm's tits, Krisham!" I staggered farther away, lashing out with my own staff, but not aiming to hit him with it. The strike had the intended effect, driving him back. Though, I'd forgotten one dangerous detail about the once-student.

"Stay for wyr, and travel ehr!"

What?

At his command a film of prismatic light pooled between us. It grew transparent and reflected a figure, dressed in robes and a cloak that looked familiar. Only, I stared at the figure's back.

Krisham stepped into the prismatic way and vanished, collapsing in his wake.

"Now fall!" His voice came from behind me.

I didn't turn in time as his makeshift sword struck the back of my legs, taking the world out from under me and sending me hard to the ground. The air left my lungs. Everything spun. And for a moment, I sorely did wish I could bring the Crow's Nest down on the burned idiot's head.

Krisham pointed the rod at my face, blinking hard and shaking his head. "You're that student Rishi Brahm brought here not so long ago. Ari?"

I said yes, though it may have come out more an incoherent and pained wheeze. And I saw no point to correct his misspeaking of the Master Binder's name.

"Well, why are you on the floor? That is a terrible place to sleep. Trust me, I know."

I glowered, which took all the effort I could muster. "Well, it's sort of where one ends up after having their legs swept out from under them."

He looked at me as if I didn't make sense. "Why would your legs give out like that? If you're sick, you should see Master Mender."

I stared at him harder, finally catching the subtle shifts in how he spoke. He'd lost the harshness of voice, the loudness, and now spoke near a gentle whisper—distant. "Krisham?"

"Obviously." He offered me a hand and helped me to my feet. "Wait, was I someone else?" He looked down to the wooden stick in his hand. "Oh. Sheru showed up, didn't he?" Krisham chuckled. "He's problematic, that one."

I'll say. I didn't see a point in trying to antagonize Krisham, though. I dusted myself off instead and saw an opportunity to ask about something more important. "Krisham, why is it that you have other people in your head?" I kept my voice neutral and filled only with honest curiosity, hoping my hunger for knowledge of the bindings didn't seep into it.

"Hm? Oh, *that*. Well, it's kind of hard to do some things, you know? So, you get other people to help you out. I can't do all the work by myself, so I thought, well, who could? Some of the heroes out of stories certainly! So, I asked them. Eventually they showed up in here"—he rapped a fist to the side of his head—"and decided to stay. Binding's been *pretty* easy after that." He grinned. "Though, sometimes they get pushy and take up more space in my head than they should."

They. Plural. I didn't know what to say to that, and had no desire to appear insensitive to his state, so I swallowed my tongue and nodded.

"And did they teach you the bindings and how to go about them?" I still kept my tone as level as I could.

"They did."

"And what did they teach you exactly, Krisham?"

He whirled around, tapping the tip of the wooden rod to my chest. "Oh, no. Ah-ah. Clever. *Very* clever, Ari. I can't go telling you secrets before you're ready to learn them. If you want to know that, you'll have to find and ask those heroes yourself. I did." He tipped onto one foot, careening close to the desk as if he'd fall any moment—but no, he didn't. He fell the other way, staggering before pirouetting with more grace than I'd thought he had. Krisham fell into his chair and threw his legs up onto the desk. "Why are you here?"

"Oh, Rishi Ibrahm told me to take another look around, see what the bindings can do to a person." That much was true at least, and I felt it would calm Krisham just enough after he caught on to my prying.

"That makes sense." He reached out for the cup that sat in the same spot as when I'd seen it last, still resting tilted on its side. Krisham's brows knotted together and he grabbed the beverage. He took one sip before setting it back askew. "Ahn." It remained in place. Anchored.

I thought back to what had happened when Rishi Ibrahm had thrown the invisible weight at me that sent me off the Crow's Nest. One binding rooted things in place—kept him firmly fixed. The other led to an unseen force crashing into me.

Ahn and ahl. To anchor and to throw? I shook my head, knowing I didn't have it wholly right. There was no need to lock himself in place if he had merely thrown a weight against me. *Unless it was his weight?* But it didn't explain how.

I kept that in mind, hoping to delve into that pair of bindings later. And Krisham wouldn't be of willing help. I'd have to visit someone else. "Is it okay if I go see Immi?"

"Sure. I'll take you."

"Oh, that's not—"

Krisham ignored my protest. "I'll take you. Come with me." He got back to his feet, rocking like he himself would topple. The makeshift sword hung loose in his grip and he swung it through the air as he led the way.

We walked up in silence and he opened the door for me as promised.

I thanked him and he told me he'd wait outside until I was done.

Immi sat cross-legged before the padded walls, though tonight, there were no red stains. Her hands did not press and drag against anything. They rested folded and neat in her lap, thumbs set to twiddling.

"Immi, how are you doing?"

She turned halfway to regard me. "I've seen you before."

I nodded, sinking to one knee but not getting any closer. "I was here before with Rishi Ibrahm when you were, um . . ." I couldn't finish the sentence and resorted to miming with my fingers.

"Oh, continuing my tests." She wiggled her fingers to mirror my own motions. "I remember. Are you well?"

I blinked, taken aback by the question. "I suppose as well as I can be. I've had it rough of late. But I'm alive. That counts for something."

"For now." There was no malice in her voice. It was distant and low, almost like she'd recited a boring fact from memory.

"*Right.* For now." I licked my lips, uncertain if I should ask her anything else. "Immi, may I come closer and sit by you?"

She patted the ground by her side, welcoming me. "Of course."

I smiled. "Thank you." Then I joined her.

For a while, we sat in complete silence, neither of us saying a word.

Immi idly picked at her fingernails, then the flesh around them, but not breaking skin. "What's on your mind, Ari?"

I hadn't expected that and almost didn't have an answer. But something had been weighing on me, and who better to tell about it than the girl who rarely saw anyone at all?

So I went into the story of Ampur, of my feud with Nitham, of finding Shola and taking him in. It's odd. These were things close to my heart—secrets in a way, and yet, I felt perfectly at ease with her in the quiet padded room away from the world.

When I finished, Immi pursed her lips and fidgeted. She looked more like a little girl than the woman she was in that moment. Someone who wanted terribly to ask a question that she shouldn't. ". . . Can I see it?"

I frowned. "See what?"

"The kitten? Can you bring it to me one day? I know you're not supposed to have it, but I'll keep it secret, I promise. Please?"

I thought it over, not sure how I'd sneak Shola over to see Immi, but a second look at her face convinced me. "Yes. I can do that. *But,* can you make me a promise in return?"

She pursed her lips but nodded.

"I don't have a right to ask you this, but for one set, can you maybe not . . ." I stopped short again and scratched the air before the walls.

Her face pulled into a deep frown, but it wasn't one of sadness or disappointment. More a thing of serious consideration. After another moment, she nodded. "I can. It'll be hard, but you have to bring the kitten."

I laughed. "I will."

Then Immi did something I didn't expect at all. She lunged from her place and threw her weight against me, arms going wide around me. "Thank you, Ari."

"You're most welcome." I eased out of her hold and we returned to our conversation.

She was everything you could want in an audience. Attentive. Hanging off every word. Enthusiastic when I detailed the Nagh-lokh. Furious at Nitham so much she wished she could be the one to set him aflame. And sad for the loss of Ampur. Most of all, she understood the heart of my failure that I'd kept from everyone else and why it bothered me.

Immi was the first person I told the secret of what really happened high atop the mountain. She didn't judge me for it. Instead, she laid a hand on mine and squeezed. "It's hard not being able to do them. It's really hard not having any power. Especially if it can help people." Something in her voice changed. A heaviness. A distance. Almost like she wasn't talking to me at all.

Regret.

But she didn't elaborate, and I knew enough not to ask about it.

"It took me a long time to figure out the bindings, but the riddle story really helped."

"What story?" I asked.

And she answered.

> *"There are ten bindings all men must know,*
> *one for tak,*
> *another for roh.*
> *Ten bindings for the enlightened to learn.*
> *Start with whent,*
> *then go to ern.*
> *Ten bindings to answer the wise man's call.*
> *Stand firm with ahn,*
> *push danger with ahl.*
> *Ten bindings given to man's care.*
> *Begin with wyr,*
> *end over ehr.*

There are only eight bindings for man to choose.
The last two are ones he ought never to use."

The same list Rishi Ibrahm had given, but it didn't tell me what they did. My mouth ran dry. I knew what I was going to ask might push the boundaries of Immi's comfort. But I'd come so close.

"Will you show me?"

"Yes."

Looking back, I suppose that moment with Immi was the true start of coming to know what I could really do. To my understanding the breadth of the bindings and my path pursuing them.

That moment, for better or worse, became the tipping moment for me to go out and change history.

And she told me of one. She taught me things.

❧

"I'm only really proficient with one pair. Whent and ern."

I nodded, making sure I spoke as little as possible to keep from disrupting her flow.

"These two have to do with the principle of, 'As within, so without.' Are you familiar with that?"

I shook my head.

"There's a space within us and the same outside. A space we all occupy larger than our physical bodies, but doesn't expand for forever, but it does touch to everything else?"

I agreed in silence, knowing she spoke of the atham.

"You can shape that space inside yourself, the folds, really, and project it to the space around you, making it take that shape, after a fashion. And to an extent. Certain things can't be affected the same as others, like the elements. You can't conjure them out of nothing. They can be manipulated in that space with your control if you have the strength of will and belief, which isn't easy.

"Many first-timers find it better to work with something they're already close to or have an affinity for, maybe something that's occupied their minds a lot. For me . . ." Immi motioned scratching at the wall, but fell short of actually doing it. "I used to get hurt a lot as a child, and always wished I'd somehow find a way to stop. I wished and willed until I learned to make that true. Now?" She put a finger to her mouth, and before I could protest, she bit off a piece of her fingernail.

Her eyes closed and she murmured the binding. "Whent. Ern." Her fingernail looked like it hadn't been broken at all—ever. "It helps that it's my body and I understand it. I also know fingernails and tissue can grow back, so that helps the belief as well. That makes it easier for me to convince myself I can affect the process how I want—enact the bindings."

I processed this, realizing the depth of power it worked with. "You're talking about shaping reality, Immi. Changing it within a fixed space? That's the power of . . ."

"God? Brahm? The Sithre?"

I nodded.

"To a point. You can't create something from nothing. You can't conjure fire out of thin air like Brahm. But you could manipulate it. That's something too complex to make. It's almost alive. You have to consider its motions, the fact it grows and dims, and it has to be fed or can be overfed. Fire is hard. Elements are *hard*. But watch." She leaned forward, placing her mouth against a piece of the padded walls, and ripped a section clean.

Immi then placed her hand against it and repeated the binding. A moment later and the wall had reverted, no sign of being repaired, but like that chunk had never been torn free at all. "I'm good at mending things. It's what I did before. I was a student in the Mendery, and Master Mender is proficient with this use of the paired bindings."

I blinked, unaware he had that skill. "Is that how he fixes people?"

She waggled a hand. "Sometimes, if things are really bad and there aren't normal ways. But even then, there are dangers."

"Like what?"

She frowned. "Fixing your own body is one thing. You know it, intimately. You can believe easier about it and not resist. Touching someone else's and trying to shape it? It's an invasion of sorts. Their own body and beliefs will resist you. If they're conscious, sometimes it's harder. Try convincing someone's body it's not dying when the mind behind it is certain they are. To mend a leg that someone is sure is broken no matter how much you soothe them and say can be set straight. It's a contest of wills.

"And in moments like that, fear and pain are powerful motivators for belief. They can twist and poison it, but make it really strong in negative ways. That's what makes the bindings so hard, Ari. You have to go against everything you've ever been taught to think, to believe, and belief is . . ." She trailed off, frowning as if looking for a word.

"Belief is squishy. It can change like this." Immi snapped her fingers. "Sometimes in a panic you can believe wonderful and dangerous things because there's no other choice, or you've gone mad, and you can employ a terrifyingly powerful binding. But sometimes . . . things break in people and they can't bind anymore. They lose that belief or a part of themselves. Trauma does it too."

I thought on how I'd first encountered her, stuck in the pattern of abrading her fingers into bloody bits. *I wonder what happened to you, Immi?* But I knew she'd never answer me. I still hoped to learn, one day.

"But these two bindings let you bring about what's in your mind and place it in the physical world. If you're working with something that won't resist or change too much, it's easier for a beginner. Some practice with cleaning their own clothes. Maybe cleaning a countertop or removing a stain or chip. You can heal. Or . . . hurt. You can break stone or fix it. But all it takes is the belief you can." She gave me a lopsided smile that had none of the warmth I'd recently seen in her.

No.

It had all the mischievous bright light and cleverness, and maybe a touch of madness, I'd seen in Rishi Ibrahm.

"Believing is easy. And it's the hardest thing ever. Just forget everything you've learned about how the world works, and believe it works how you want it to, no matter what. And no matter the cost."

The Crow's Nest had showed me those costs. Even so, I deemed them worth the price I might have to pay to get revenge. To learn the bindings.

We spent a whole candlemark together, going over the two bindings and how they paired together. Halfway through the lesson, my mind wandered and I found myself returning to the candle and the flame. I fed it everything. Every word.

It helped me keep a center, a focal point, while we chatted.

Immi finally told me she'd grown tired, and one of her hands reached out to the wall.

I placed one of my own on top of hers, gently easing it back. "I think for one day you can let it go."

She listened, then smiled at me. "Because you're going to bring the cat?"

I smiled back. "Because I'm going to bring the cat."

EIGHTY-NINE

Practice and Preparations

Days passed, and I spent the time sitting in my room when not in classes. The candle on my desk burned low and the image of the flame had imprinted onto my mind. I'd laid the strings across my table, holding my hand steady with my pen firmly in my grip.

Dot. A stroke to form a dash. Another touch for a dot. My fingers ached as I brought the tip to the first string, taking all the care I could to imprint the symbols across the narrow surface. My lessons with Pathar had paid off and I'd devised a language of my own. A way to put the bindings I needed into my kite.

I'd held a dozen folds, projecting my will and thoughts into the string. It would absorb friction from other bands rubbing against it and distribute down along the line into the spool I'd use, diluting the stress. If it worked, my strings would survive any encounter with glass-lined ones, as well as other damage short of directly cutting them with shears.

The dots and dashes served as the inscribed commands to tether my will and minor bindings. The spool, something I'd gotten for free from Holds, had enough weight and mass that it should be able to endure all of the energy transference from strings rubbing against each other. Not to mention the fact some of that energy would be absorbed along the string and dispersed before reaching the last point.

All in theory, of course. I wouldn't know until the festival. And it was just around the corner.

Another line, then. I repeated the minor bindings and artisanry process, holding my will firm as Mahrab had taught me.

The desk shook and Shola sauntered over a few of my strings.

"No! Shola . . . *hsst*. Stop. Brahm's bloody tits, cat. I swear." The folds slipped and my mind ached as the dissonance of what I'd been holding in belief versus the reality of what things were crashed into me. Shola firmly in hand, I looked down to see the fate of the second string I'd been working on. I'd projected my will, begun inscribing, but never finished the process. The kitten's disturbance forced me to snap out of my focus.

And a broken string lay before me. It had been snipped cleanly in several places. Twelve points to be exact. One for each fold I'd held.

My first lesson by my own hands what the price for failing to hold the folds and Athir really was.

Shola had other concerns than my immediate failure and possibly dangerous mishap. The flickering candle flame upset him for a reason I couldn't fathom and he decided to rectify this by batting a paw at it. He let out a high *mrow* of displeasure as he learned a painful lesson. The look he gave the candle almost drew a laugh from me. It spoke of centuries of offense given to his ancestors and that, the next time, he would visit nine kinds of hell upon the flame.

"Brahm burn me, cat." I shook my head and took Shola back into my arms, holding him there until he calmed. He took that as a sign that I was to be his new and current bed and fell asleep. I got little work done that afternoon.

Later that night, I headed down to Clanks, letting Radi and Aram know I couldn't stay. I'd planned to forgo a meal myself, but knew I couldn't subject Shola to that hunger. I returned with a meal for both of us and set back to my minor bindings. I'd gone through two candles.

One had burned completely down to its inevitable end. The second earned Shola's renewed wrath and had been batted away at its base, revealing my cat had learned quickly. Once on the ground, he decided he would subject it to endless torment at his hands, swiping it along the floor for a time still to be determined.

I fetched a third candle and went back to it, repeating the minor binding process. The extra strings only served test purposes, and I fully expected them to break eventually. But I needed to know how far they could be pushed. The spool had been inscribed to accept the incoming energy from the friction and heat of rubbing strings and also hold it. Eventually it would fail, but hopefully after a great many kites fell to mine.

Though, only one really mattered to me.

Nitham's.

Radi and Aram had done what good friends do and already set to spreading rumors I had something to put the rich tit out of the fights. A decent gambling pool had sprung up to see our clash and weigh in on the winner.

I stood to make a good bit of coin if I won.

And I had no intention of losing.

Once I'd finished both my meal and work for the night, I shuffled my way to bed, still feeling some of the aches from my sojourn to Ampur. Shola and I settled ourselves in place and I fell deep into my old teachings.

The candle and the flame came first.

Occasionally I'd break the closed-eyes trance and cast a look at the fire burning in the corner. Its tiny bead ebbed and danced much like I'd been taught to imagine. I smiled at the fact I could still hold a moving object like that in mind.

Soon, I moved into the folds.

I eventually fell to sleep, my last thoughts on the two bindings Immi had taught me. Whent and ern.

That night when I dreamed, I dreamed of flame.

NINETY

Kites and Coins

I woke early on the morning of Athrayaan, dressing myself and running down to Clanks for Shola and myself. Once I'd tended to the little tyrant, I went over my designs one last time. The kite itself was nothing remarkable. A solid bamboo spine and bow to allow for rigidity and flexibility. The skin was fashioned from a thin paper I could quickly mend should it develop any tears. All it would take was some paste and sticking another thin layer of the material to it.

I'd painted mine a brilliant red—the color found in fresh blood—and lined the edges with bright bands of orange and yellow. All the colors of the sun, and it would stand out wonderfully against the white backdrop of the mountains.

The strings had been coated in a starchy pulp made from corn, mixed with ground glass and shards of scrap metal. It was then baked into a pliable putty I gently spread over the line. It took hours of slow work, and even still, I'd nearly torn my hands to shreds in the preparation. The only thing that saved me was the leather gloves I'd borrowed from Holds. They were forbidden from the actual fighting festival, however.

So I took the only preventative measures we were allowed. I wrapped my fingers and palms in thick bandages. It took time as I worked to ensure I still had a good bit of dexterity so I could maneuver my kite. The bandages would still tear eventually, but I hoped it would be well after I sent Nitham's entry sinking to the ground—or better yet, sailing unstringed over the mountains never to be seen again.

My efforts would hopefully lighten his purse as well.

Content everything was as it should have been, and Shola had eaten his fair share, I let my cat out for a few moments before bringing him back in for a morning nap. I settled him down and then left with my strings wound to my spool and my kite slung over one shoulder. Binder's cane in my other hand, I made the long trek down the Rookery and went to Clays.

The field had been prepared for the festival, cleared and marked with poles banded with bright ribbons. Entrants would stand between the six-foot-distanced posts, giving limited room to work within, and be tasked with taking out their neighbors' kites first. After that, the posts would be removed to grant a fighter more space in which to tackle and cut other contestants' strings.

I made my way toward the throng of students that crowded the outermost edge of Clays. Radi and Aram waved to me and I picked up my pace to join them. They both clapped a hand to my shoulders, giving me a gentle shake.

"Didn't know if you'd actually show up." Aram meant no offense by it, her tone soft and jovial as always. "Thought you might have gotten busy with some other scheme or cleverness that we'll all be hearing about." She leaned to one side and elbowed Radi in the ribs. "Still can't believe the serpent thing."

Radi, to his credit, didn't take offense. "I sang what I saw, Aram. I was there. Don't believe me if you don't want to, but don't call me a liar either. And Ari did call down the mountain."

By now other students had noticed me and broke into low whispers. I caught the ends of sentences, making out some of what they said.

". . . out in Ampur, I heard," said one boy.

". . . family near there said it's true," said another girl.

"I heard he did a binding." I didn't recognize that voice—too distant and hushed, but it just touched my ears.

I smiled. And why shouldn't I have? I had nearly died in Ampur, not to mention the fact I'd been ostracized in many ways since coming to the Ashram. A little notoriety didn't seem so bad a thing.

"So, what are the odds? They in my favor or Nitham's?"

Radi's lips pressed tight. "Still his. You know how it is. He's got the money and that means he can buy the time of someone poorer and arguably smarter. His kite's come close to winning several times over the last three years. Mostly dumb luck he hasn't, or because a group of students move in to take him out first."

Aram winced. "*And* that's never a good idea. Anyone who's come after him usually finds themselves suffering a new kind of trouble off the field. Always odd, that." Her voice said it wasn't odd at all. "Some students find themselves mugged the next time they leave the Ashram grounds and venture into the city proper. One had his mother's debts bought and her imprisoned. Didn't Jathi end up dead?"

Radi shook his head. "No, just arrested by the kuthri for illegal possession of illicit substances. They never did say what. He was just whisked away and locked up."

I chewed on that, wondering why Nitham hadn't played a card like that against me yet. "He can really do that?"

They both nodded in synchrony. "King's second son. He has the clout and money, though he's careful in using it. Never too many students a year. Definitely not in a season, and not if it'll make him look bad or be obviously tied to him."

Radi shot Aram a long look over what she'd just said. "You know that's not true. Everyone can tell when Nitham gets a student in trouble. Every rishi knows it too." Radi looked at me and then smacked a hand hard to my back. "But don't worry, you'll be fine."

"Why's that?"

"Because, you've already made him look a fool several times over and it's no secret to anyone in the school. If you beat him here and anything happens to you, it will so obviously be Nitham's work the masters would have to get involved. And if they didn't, it'd still be a black eye to his pride, and he's careful about that. He'd rather swallow sand and shit than let his ego get too bruised in public. Letting people know he had to do something like that to you after being embarrassed?" Radi shook his head. "He wouldn't be able to live with it."

It wasn't as convincing an argument as Radi may have thought it was. "Thanks, I think? I'm really reassured now. Truly." Each word came as lifeless and without color as gray clouds.

Radi scowled. "Oh, just get in the pool and thrash him, will you? I stand to win iron if you do."

I cocked a brow. "You already bet on me?"

He grinned. "Of course. You killed a monster serpent out of stories and toppled a mountain! What's a kite fight compared to that?"

Right. What's a kite fight compared to all that? I took a breath. "And you, Aram?"

She raised her hands in defense. "Don't look at me. I'm not gambling on this one. It's against Ashram rules, and you two know it. If you're caught, it's grievances. *And* they confiscate your coins."

I tensed at that. I may have had the money to burn, but I didn't like the idea of someone taking it from me at their own whims. Especially under the guise of "rules." Those were invented by those in power to loot the powerless more often than not.

I may have been a thief, but I thought of myself as an honest one. One who stole from those who could afford it.

And Nitham certainly could.

"Odds?" I kept my eyebrow raised, eyeing the rest of Clays as I did.

"Six to one in his favor." Aram recited the numbers as if she'd memorized them and had been waiting to rattle them off.

I grunted and thought it over. "Anyone know if he's in the pool?"

Both of them nodded.

"How much?"

They frowned in unison and spoke in just as much. "Gold."

I winced. "How many pieces?"

Radi answered. "Whole rupai, so not as bad as he can do, but he knows that's too rich for many to risk in gambling."

I didn't hesitate and pulled out my purse. "I can't match that, but I'm in. I'm playing for silver, and if I'm the underdog, no one should have a problem with that."

Radi palmed the two pieces I'd held out and then looked down to the ground.

"What's wrong?" I asked.

"It's Valhum." Radi rubbed a hand against the back of his neck. "He got in deep in the betting, at least for him, and his kite was found today mysteriously thrashed to the point there's no hope for him flying."

I spat. "Blood and ashes, that's bad luck."

Radi and Aram fixed me with knowing looks.

"Oh. Nitham?"

Another pair of the same stares.

"He's afraid of Valhum?" I barely knew the student myself, but I'd seen him in passing. Quiet, bumbling, but intelligent. Many of the rishis liked him and thought well of the boy. He excelled in nearly every discipline, but didn't show much ambition. But a good guy.

"Nitham's using him to make a point." Radi didn't meet my eyes when he spoke.

"What's that? That he can cheat and steal money?" I snorted. "No one needs that pointed out."

"No, it's a message to you."

I blinked, not getting the underlying hint.

"Valhum's Sullied too. One of the few other ones in the Ashram. Most Sullied never get the kind of money it takes to get up here, and you know . . ." He trailed off.

A glass-sharp and brittle-hard edge bled into my voice. "No. I don't. Tell me."

He shrugged and looked away again like he'd rather not discuss it. "Most of you all come from the south, the warmer cities. Not really so many Sullied up in Ghal. And he couldn't go after you, or hasn't yet, so he went after Valhum."

"Is this speculation, or . . . ?" I tried to keep the anger deep down inside me and not let it reach my friend. He didn't deserve it. Though, I noted his use of, "You all."

Radi shook his head. "It's pretty obvious." And Aram nodded in agreement.

I sighed and rubbed a hand against my brow. "How much is he out?"

"Sixteen iron bunts."

I sputtered. "He spent that much on the pool?"

My musician friend rolled his wrist, flashing two silver doles before vanishing them just as fast. "Says the guy who just put down a pair of doles, and all to bleed as much as you can out of the pool."

I glowered at him. "That's different and you know it. I can afford it, and I mean to win. But Valhum? Brahm's blood, I swear. He's straight as an arrow and blunt as a rock when it comes to this kind of stuff. He's not cut out to play these games with someone like Nitham."

Aram gave Radi a sideways look. "Is it just me, or does it bother you too that he thinks of this as a game?"

"No, it bothers me too. Only he would poke a snake in hopes of antagonizing it." Radi wore a wry smile.

Aram matched it and responded in kind. "Oh, you know that's not true. He'd poke it then drop a mountain on it, and damn whatever else may be below." They laughed together.

I narrowed my eyes and fixed them with a stare they ignored. "Are you two done, or what?"

"Yes, yes, *sahm*." Radi bowed at the waist, placing one hand to his chest as he did. "Will *sahm* be needing me to carry his kite to the pitch? *Sahm*'s hands must be sore from winding his spool, will he need a massage? Maybe *sahm* will need this humble one to fly his *athan* for him so as not to cut his fingers. *Ji-ah?*"

I swatted at Radi. "Just go put my money into the pool and collect for me when I win."

He put two fingers to his forehead, tipping them in a salute. "*Ji, sahm*. This one will do."

I lunged, raising my staff just a bit.

Radi laughed and darted out of reach, but I stopped him before he left.

"Wait. About Valhum." I reached back into my purse, pulling free twenty-four iron bunts. I won't lie and say it didn't bring a small icy hand to my heart. A piece of me still remembered when even a bunt would have been all the money in the world to me. And I knew just how much this would have meant to me then, to any Sullied and sparrow.

I pressed the coins into Radi's hands. "Bring them straight to Valhum, then put my doles into the pool, please?"

Radi didn't flinch. He closed his fist tight and gave me a look that let me know he'd do just as I said.

"And . . . don't tell him where they came from."

He chewed one corner of his lip, but nodded. Aram followed behind him.

I took a few deep breaths to steady myself once they left. After I had, I headed toward one of the open pole positions and took my place. My staff had been jammed into the ground, serving less as a marker and more a reminder to myself what I set out to be. A binder. And today, I would at least be a minor one.

Time to find out if this works. And to rob a prince of his purse.

I decided to be a sparrow for one more day.

The wind picked up. Both a boon and a curse. If a kite picked up too much speed too quickly, your string could cut deep and fast into your fingers. I flexed them in equal amounts agitation and concern. I didn't much like the idea of losing a digit over this, but pride and a young boy's pettiness were powerful motivators.

Too much of me wanted to see Nitham lose. Enough that I was willing to pay a steep price. Maybe not the loss of a finger, but I could afford to bleed a bit.

The wind blew harder.

Or bleed a lot.

A few braziers had been placed along Clays and their flames bowed and bent under every gust. I watched them until they flooded my mind.

Master Artisan took to the field, a horn in hand. She placed two fingers to her throat and murmured something that I guessed was a binding. Her voice boomed then, echoing far and wide to reach everyone's ears. "Students, Athrayaan begins! Take your positions and remember the rules." She then recited them and left the field.

I shifted my feet, let out one last breath, and unwound my string. A shard of glass bit into one of my bandages and dragged, tearing it to a frayed mess. I ignored it as it didn't break skin. Then, nearly one hundred kites took to the sky and a prism of colors dotted the mountaintops.

The person next to me, whom I paid no mind to in face and body, brought their kite closer to mine. It was a horrid thing—a bamboo skeleton that formed a rough box with a paper frame. It swerved with a snap force as if taken more by strong wind than under the student's guidance.

Our strings met, not tangling. They pressed against each other like swords, then they turned to saws. Grind. Pull. They fought and sought to tear.

That's when I felt it. My string quivered, then tightened. The spool shook under something not from force, but a gentle vibration from its core. I smiled. My bindings worked and transferred the friction from the motion of the fighting strings along the body and into the spool.

Wood can hold a good deal of heat and force. It doesn't snap and break if it's the right sort and treated well. It flexes—bends. And it would take more energy than one fighting kite could generate to push this spool to its limits. Not to mention that some of that energy would be lost along the string's path to the wood.

I took a step away from the field, using the back of my thumb to press on the string and guide it south. It pulled against my opponent's string, sawing just as much. Pull, twist, shift. We continued our fight.

They tugged hard then. A long, sharp pull that dragged their length of string against mine.

The spool warmed a touch. It could have been me noticing my own body heat and tension due to my hyperaware state. Or, it was more likely the first notes of friction and energy building in the spool. Just a hint. But it had been enough to let me know to end this battle quickly to buy a reprieve.

I pulled back hard. The long sharp saw that fells a tree. The final cut.

A bright blue box sailed away, flitting toward the mountaintops.

I grinned and heard a sullen curse from my side. The edges of my vision showed me a robed figure leaving their six-foot-wide space.

A monk came between us to remove the pole that separated us, giving me twice as much room to function in.

I shifted, moving away from the person to my left. The few moments I bought were enough to dissipate the vibrations and minor warmth from the spool. Once it calmed, I took the initiative and led it toward my new neighbors. First fighting the one on my right, slowly working my way in the direction of a garish purple-and-gold kite with frills of silver. As bright as could be and made clearly of a mix of cloths that screamed expense.

It had to be Nitham.

Going for him now would be pure folly. Other kites still flew around and could tackle the pair of us in group and cut through us all. But saving him for last would let his string take enough strain that I would have an easy time of it. Not to mention it would make a wonderful show for everyone to see.

Me against him. And our rivalry settled before the Ashram.

So I worked through the posts at my sides, taking out the next person, then the next. I whittled them down, taking time to fly deftly away as much as setting after a target. Attack, flee. Let my string and spool recover.

Nearly a candlemark passed and my bandages had been cut through. I could try to leave my kite and spool fixed in place, tending to protect my hands, but only six kites remained. Remaining immobile made me a target. My spool could unwind and let me drift too far from the field, disqualifying me. I could end up taking too much damage if they came at me together.

And then the one oversight I'd made. The kite itself.

My last exchange brought someone's entry above mine, dragging a sharp line through my kite's body. It hadn't severed enough to hamper me, but I realized if done again, I could lose a whole section, leaving my kite to fall to the ground before I could reel it in to patch.

As sure a loss as any other option.

My hands shook as I recognized what I had to do. Risk them to go after Nitham.

If nothing else speaks to my seething hatred of that pompous ass, let it be that. I would see myself bloody and torn to give him a piece of the same, even if it only hurt his ego.

I used the hard bone of my wrist to angle my kite one way. Bite, slide, cut. A shallow one, but my skin finally broke. The razor-line of pain brought a different heat with it. What salt and sweat built along my arms through effort and time trickled into the wound, bringing me a new sting above the other.

I gritted my teeth, but the pain remained. So I brought up the candle and the flame, using the shifting fires of the braziers to feed my imagery. The pain found its place there and left me behind.

Twist, pull, shift. I eased the kite toward another opponent.

Their entry was a traditional diamond shape in a solid color of sunflower yellow.

I sawed through theirs at the expense of a gash along the meat of my right palm. Nothing serious, and mercifully, a clean cut. No ragged edges that would leave me worrying about what stitches I'd need.

Then the game changed.

Two came at me together and tangled their lines in mine. Harder pulls. Yank and tear. Careening to one side before another. They didn't aim to cut my line but break it by force.

I grinned, having anticipated this technique at least. If only I'd taken into account the transfer of force from it. The spool rattled in my grip as if trying to shake free. I gripped it harder, wrestling back just as much. If they sought to tear me free, it would come at the cost of my hands. I refused to lose.

I leaned back and pulled. A clean sharp yank that snapped one string. It remained tangled as his kite sailed away, leaving me to wrestle their remaining partner. We sawed and retreated, then clashed again. Two kites dove toward each other like hawks after the same mouse.

Our entries crashed, bending their frames visibly before righting themselves. I let out more line, and my kite rose, letting the string drag along my opponent's kite. A new row of knives slid along the space over the back of my thumbs. Then the meat of my thumbs. Then, the knuckles of my index fingers.

Tears welled in my eyes and blurred my vision.

The candle and the flame were not enough.

I burned and hurt.

But I bit my tongue and brought a new pain for me to fix on, as I'd done before.

A few more kites. And I tackled them with a ruthless efficiency.

One remained. The one that proved me right. Nitham's. He stared at me from across Clays with a narrow-eyed hatred that told me he would rather drag the line of his razor string along my throat and not my kite.

I would be lying to say I didn't feel the same.

Our kites hovered in place, almost matching the stares we shot each other.

The wind stilled compared to what it had been, though our entries stayed aloft.

Two kites. One prize. A sparrow and a hawk.

His kite had been built to be twice the width of mine, carrying more air under its body and able to soar faster—higher with the right winds. But it brought all that extra weight with it as well.

The wind picked up, but we did not move.

A harder gust then.

And we broke into it.

I loosed some string and let mine soar farther, forward, higher.

He came to meet me, crashing his frame against mine. Our strings met and sawed. His held, mine fought back. Pull and release. Pull. And. Release.

Every motion set my hands ablaze. New burning bands and threads formed along my fingers. But nothing had been cut so bad I lost feeling or mobility.

The candle and the flame grew in me as the braziers outside dimmed. I only had eyes and thoughts for Nitham.

Pull. Tear, but not the strings. Only the cords of me. The pain grew sharper, brighter, and my sight blurred.

Red ran along my fingers and the spaces between them now like little streams. Drops fell to the dark brown of Clays and turned to black.

It grew too much and I could no longer hold my jaw clenched shut. I screamed, and in it, I pulled one last time.

And the kite broke.

The crowd went quiet and the wind stilled. The braziers burned brighter—larger.

Then they cheered.

I had won.

NINETY-ONE

Payback

The crowd swarmed me, pulling me from my kite, and I had to fight to keep it and reel it in. They gave me that much, at least. One of the Mendery students came to my side, shooting me a glare that forced me to shy away from her eyes. She stripped the shredded bandages from me and set about tending to my wounds.

"This'll hurt." She had more smoke in her voice than all the burning fires and less brightness in it than a dying candle.

"It hurt making them."

Another glare and I shut up.

I wouldn't sully my win this quickly.

She cleaned the wounds with a red ichor that burned worse than all the cuts together, then set to rubbing a cooling salve over them before rebandaging them. "Don't tear these. You don't need stitches, thankfully. Your cuts are many, but shallow. If you change your bandages and come in for another two or three applications of the salve, they'll heal. Though, you might still have scars."

I gave her a warm grin, buoyed by my win. "I've heard women like those—*ackh*!" I winced as she squeezed my hands just enough to reignite all their pillars of pain.

She turned and walked away.

A piece of me cursed Radi and his damnable advice when it came to women. *Idiot.* I flexed my fingers and regretted it instantly when they burned again.

A moment later, my friends bulled their way through the crowd and took hold of me. Aram shook me hard enough to rattle my brain. Radi screamed incoherently and in triumph.

"You crafty bastard, you did it. You *actually* did it? I thought your string would have broken by the final six. How?" Aram tried to take a look at my rolled string and spool.

I hate to admit it, but I shifted it away from good view, letting the kite's bulk hide what she wanted to see. No one had known I'd inscribed the strings and spool with minor bindings.

Radi held out a purse. "Guess who's made thirty silver doles."

My eyes almost bulged and the world spun. "How much?" I may have come to the Ashram with nearly as much as that, but the idea I'd won that in a morning and through a game? My fingers shook as I reached out to take the coins. *How large was the pool purse to leave me that much?*

I didn't get the answer to my question, and I never would, as Nitham wasted no time in getting his revenge.

Two monks, built broader than any men had a right to be, pushed through the crowd. They pointed to me. "Accepted Ari."

I nodded, unable to speak.

"A grievance of cheating and improper use of bindings has been levied against you. You're to report to the Admittance Chamber to stand before the masters. Your accuser will face you there."

The crowd broke into murmurs and everyone kept from saying the one name we all knew had been behind this.

I cursed Nitham and my own stupidity for not running my string along his throat as I'd wished. One of my hands clenched hard to my staff, building a pressure that set blood flowing free of the salve.

The crowd parted, providing a path I had no wish to walk. I'd stowed the purse and kept the kite and spool under my other arm. Whispers reached my ears as I followed the monks.

"Cheater."

"It's true, then. He *can* do the bindings."

"But how?"

"What did he do?"

I ignored them, keeping my head held high.

Soon, I'd returned to the room where I'd first encountered the masters. All of them sat in attendance, even Vathin.

A quick look showed his face to be leaner than usual. Grizzled, nearly wolfish. His posture had lost its strength and the easy amused smile had faded as well. He looked like he'd taken ill. The lights in Mines gave his eyes a sickly yellow tinge.

Tired, I thought.

Master Spiritualist did not acknowledge me as the monks took positions by my sides.

Footsteps behind me caused me to turn my head to see who came.

Nitham, unescorted of course.

Master Spiritualist and headmaster put a closed fist to his mouth and coughed. "Now that everyone is here, we can begin. Accepted Ari, Kaethar Nitham has brought grievances against you that you employed a binding to cheat during Athrayaan. What do you have to say to this?"

I shifted and became more aware of the itches forming in my hands and wounds. My mind turned to my old stage training and what I'd learned from listening and watching others. I kept my voice as flat and level as possible. "I wasn't aware alterations to your entries were prohibited. And to that point, what about the well-known fact Nitham had someone else build his?"

"Oh, Brahm's blood and ashes, you're avoiding his question, Sullied." Nitham practically vibrated, chest heaving as he glared at me.

"Kaethar Nitham!" Master Spiritualist's voice cut through us both and echoed through the chamber. "You will permit him to speak and keep your curses to yourself."

I ground my teeth, noting the headmaster's umbrage was directed at Nitham cursing Brahm's name but not at his coming after my caste.

"Well, Accepted Ari, what of the question I asked?" His tone had calmed and now the headmaster rested a chin on steepled fingers as he watched me.

I licked my lips, thinking. "I thought the burden of proof rested on the accuser? Kaethar Nitham accused me, so what is his proof? He says I used a binding, and because I won?" I held up a hand, taking the liberty to shake it just enough to make it look like I'd lost control of it during the pain. "I certainly paid a price. But these didn't come from any bindings."

Some of the masters exchanged looks.

The headmaster turned his head back to address Nitham. "Accepted Ari makes a good point. What is your proof, Kaethar Nitham?"

He took to shuffling in place much like I had, looking to the masters for silent support, but finding none. "Well, you've heard the stories by now I'm sure." He didn't phrase it as a true question. In truth, he made it a weak fact. "People are saying he's already done a binding so powerful he buried Ampur. So, let's cast aside the fact he's a murderer, he's clearly capable of cheating and keeping his kite afloat."

I wanted to reach out and throttle him then and there. The thing keeping me from that was not the punishment I would face afterward. It was the dull deep aches that came from the pain in my hands. I'd set myself to bleeding worse and never let my wounds heal. But, the temptation still burned in me.

"If anyone had ears to hear the story I think he's referencing, they'd have heard I didn't murder a soul, save the serpent. Which, as far as stories go, isn't so bad a thing. Now, to his other point, did any of the masters see or feel me employ a binding that kept my kite soaring? My string didn't break, but nothing kept the kite in the air besides the wind."

Muttering. The masters lowered their heads and conferred.

"Point. Accepted Ari is telling the truth in that, Kaethar Nitham. And Master Binder tells me he did not feel anyone channeling one of the ten bindings or a pair during the festival. Your grievance—"

"Hold." Master Artisan rose, bidding Master Spiritualist to yield the floor to her. He inclined his head in silent agreement and she introduced herself. "Rishi Bharia. Something has come to my mind."

Sweat built along my neck, collar, and along my armpits.

"Accepted Ari came to me before Athrayaan with the idea of making unbreakable strings. He indicated their possible purpose, but I have yet to see a display from him on them. He has paid for the materials and borrowed others. So, Ari, have you put any time and work into this project?"

I nodded, unable to answer verbally.

"And, did you use these strings today?"

Nothing. No words would come. And I gave no indication.

"I would very much like to see your kite and string. Is that it under your arms?"

She knew that it was, and I couldn't refuse her, so I nodded again.

"Bring them to me." Her words were addressed to the two monks who moved to wrest it from my grip.

I waved them off, sending a drop of blood flying through the air as it seeped through my new bandages. "Don't damage it. Here." I handed it over with as much care as I could.

They passed it to Rishi Bharia and she unspooled it with slow and measured control, taking precautions not to cut herself on the glass-starch-encrusted string. "Mhm." She used a fingernail to scrape a section free of the cover and reveal the string below. "Ah. Ink. Interesting. Master Binder, would you do me the favor of stripping this coating?"

He nodded and reached out, placing a hand over the string. Rishi Ibrahm's mouth moved and as soon as he stopped, the string was laid bare.

"There we are. Symbols. I'm not familiar with them, but the strings have been inscribed with what I'm taking to be minor bindings. Ah, so is the spool. Here along the sides and on the inner wheels as well. Look." She showed some of the other masters. "Accepted Ari, could you tell me what these are and why your strings show no sign at all of fraying?"

The sweat built and my mouth ran dry. When I spoke, though, my voice remained hard and level. "I learned the markings from a tinker, inspired by their silent language of knobs and bars running along their wagon-homes. They form sentences instead of symbols that carry the inscribed meanings to take the incoming friction and impact of other strings, passing them along its length to be stored and dispersed through the spool. The spool's bindings are to accept, hold, and bleed out the energy over time. Eventually it will fail, but wood's nature is to bend and flex before breaking. Strings are meant to break, so I couldn't will them to be unbreakable. But they can pass energy through vibrations, being loose or going taut. I worked with that."

She looked over the assembly of kite, string, and spool again. "Very well thought out. You considered the properties of each item and their natures, never seeking to pervert them. You used them in conjunction to play off their strengths and create string that, to someone unaware of bindings, seemed unbreakable."

I smiled at the praise. It faded just as fast as her face pulled into a deep frown.

"But, Accepted Ari, *this is cheating.* The use of bindings, even minor ones applied to your kite, violates the rules of the Ashram in participation with Athrayaan. Then there is the other grievance Headmaster and Master Spiritualist neglected to mention."

Everything below my neck sank and grew distant from me. The hollow of my chest grew cold and my heart followed. I had an idea of what she'd say next.

"It has been brought to our attention that you ran a gambling pool over the winner of Athrayaan, and that, having won, you profited a great deal. This in concert with the fact you set out to cheat from the start is a rather large grievance that cannot be overlooked. To that effect, your winnings will be confiscated and given to the monastery for charity, continuing our monks' education, clothing, and helping those in need within Ghal."

That stung. Especially after not only putting in two of my own doles and not seeing a piece of them returned, but also the fact I'd spent twenty-four bunts helping Valhum. While I didn't regret giving to someone in need, especially another Sullied, it did burn me that my reward came in the form of growing all the poorer the longer I stayed at the Ashram.

I came in with the wealth of a little lord as far as I'd been concerned, and by year's end, I looked to be on a pauper's path if things continued as they were.

"Your kite will be taken to be studied in the Artisanry, and I propose a motion to suspend you from studies for a season." The Master Artisan looked around to her peers, waiting for a quiet judgment.

"Oh, come off it." Vathin sounded like he'd swallowed a fistful of ice and breathed in smoke. "You're looking to whip the boy after he's already been beaten and you've robbed his purse."

"There *are* rules, Master Philosopher." Rishi Bharia's stare could cut as sharp as any kite string.

Vathin rolled his eyes, visible even from where we stood. "He's been punished enough, not to mention the fact his hands are torn and he's been given no rest. We're talking of stories? Well, the boy just survived something for the history books and set himself to a binding so well he took a win in front of the whole damn Ashram. So what if he cheated? Look at what he demonstrated. Are we going to push talent like that out because of our rules? What does he gain by being out on the streets with nowhere to go for a season? No, better yet, what do *we* gain from turning away a student who duped us all and is said to have performed a composite binding?"

Rishi Vruk, Vathin, Master Philosopher, and most importantly my friend, then rose and fixed a challenging stare upon each master.

None met his glare. Knowing that he'd won, he sat back down and waited for the headmaster to take control.

Master Spiritualist needlessly reintroduced himself, sticking to the rigid and old protocol of the Ashram I'd come to hate. "Master Spiritualist and Headmaster. Rishi Vruk—Master Philosopher, makes a fair point. Though there have been *several* contentious callings with Accepted Ari before, having his winnings taken and the winning kite seems punishment enough. It was, after all, a festival and children's game. We have no way of knowing who the winner would have been without the bindings.

"And, on that note." He cleared his throat again and turned to Rishi Bharia. "Master Artisan, does Ari's example of skills here move you to raise his rank to Kaethar? Did he display enough skill?"

"He did," she said.

My heart soared.

"But not sound judgment. Even if he didn't know this would be a violation of the rules, he could have asked, and that much forethought means more to me than what he can do with his cleverness. So, no. I feel he deserves to remain an Accepted until he can learn to temper his other impulses."

Rishi Ibrahm took this opportunity to finally draw attention to himself, spreading his mouth into a wide and mischievous grin. His eyes danced and he touched a finger to his nose while giving me a knowing and self-satisfied look.

I knew the meaning behind it: I told you, too clever for your own good. I told you, you're not ready. A thousand different I-told-yous and all the excuses and jackassery one could come up with.

I swallowed my impulse to sneer at him and took whatever win I could. Doing my best to appear appropriately chastised, I bowed my head and uttered my apologies. "I'm sorry for breaking the rules, Masters. I'll do better to both apprise myself of them and never violate them again. Thank you for not suspending my studies nor subjecting me to walking the fire again."

The headmaster dismissed the grievance council and Nitham walked away, smiling to himself a grin so smug I wanted to slap it from his face. And never mind how bad it would set my hand in pain.

I left the chambers and the hall, heading toward my rooms, too sullen to want to see anyone. But Rishi Vruk caught up with me as I crossed the main courtyard, heading to the tower I slept in.

"Ari, wait." He coughed several times, placing a hand to his throat. Now that I looked at him in the paler, better light of outdoors, the murkiness I'd seen in his eyes had gone. While their color wasn't perfect, they weren't oddly tinged either. Just the fog of tiredness in them. "Are you fine?"

I grumbled something under my breath.

"Either say it so I can hear it or don't say it at all, clever shit. Now's not the time." The lack of humor and empathy in his voice brought me to a pause. He never grew that short with me so quickly. Something had set its teeth in him and left him on edge.

"Sorry, Rishi Vruk."

"Oh, don't start that now either. I suppose I can be just as much sorry for snapping. Just answer the question. I'm wound tight is all."

"I'm . . . I don't know." I placed a hand against my face, not feeling the wounds as the cold air outside numbed them a bit. "I was happy I won. Doubly so for pricking Nitham over it. I was proud of my bindings. I didn't think this would happen. And I'm angry it did."

He placed a hand on one of my shoulders to comfort me. "I know. It's a terrible business. I did what I could to spare you worse. I'd hate to see you miss a season of studies over their combined old asses." He flashed a toothy lopsided grin that didn't have all of his usual charm behind it, but it held enough to lighten my dour mood.

"Thank you."

He waved me off. "Don't think on it. Take the day to rest, *ji-ah*?"

I nodded. "*Ji*." But before I left, a question came to mind. "Vathin . . . I came to your class when I got back from my trip to Ampur. A student said you were gone. May I ask where you went?"

He grinned again. "You may." But he made no move to answer me.

I finally gave in and pressed. "Where?"

"Oh, chasing a story, I suppose. Always interesting things in those. Curious truths and lies to sort through, great stuff for a philosopher. Not to mention the lessons or lack of them, and what people flood to fill them with. Stories tell you a great deal about the person telling them as much as they do the story itself, the people listening, and the ones who came up with them. Powerful things, those. Sometimes more powerful than truths."

I saw a point in his thought process. "Even love." I'd said the comment as an offhand aside, but he stiffened at that.

"No, Ari. Not at all. Even that is a story, and probably the most powerful one of all. One day, I might tell you how I know that. One day." An old glimmer returned to his eyes. "Maybe." He raised his own cane, tapping the silver wolf's head to my chest just once. "Behave for the rest of the season, please? I can't always be around to save you."

I snorted. "No promises."

He placed a hand on his heart in mock agony and walked away.

I bid him a farewell and headed back to my room.

"Shola, what in Brahm's bloody ashes have you done?" I gawked at my room. What strings I'd left behind as duplicates had been knotted so well that nothing short of magic could unbind them. My candles, all of which had been left unlit, had been scattered, clawed, or crushed. My walls bore a few scratch marks that left little mystery as to what, or who, was behind them.

And then there was the mess of leavings on my floor.

Shola sauntered over to me, steps as light as if he were walking on clouds. His head smacked against one of my shins and he let out a little *mrowl,* sounding rather pleased with his work.

"Brahm above, I swear. If Nitham doesn't kill me one of these days, you will." I scooped him up, wincing at the pain in my hands under his weight. I bore it, however, and set to petting him until I could address the various messes.

Once those had been handled, the worst of which I fought to do without retching over my floor and worsening my cleaning load, I fetched my travel sack.

Shola, more out of curiosity than my urgings, dove into it and made himself cozy.

"Ssh. I need you to stay inside and be quiet, hm? We're going on a little trip to see a friend."

He meowed in what I could only hope was agreement, though so far in our relationship, I nursed a healthy concern he'd told me he would only consider it as far as his fleeting and changeable mood would allow.

With that, I cinched up the top of my bag just enough to keep his head from popping out and made my way down the tower and across the courtyard to the Crow's Nest.

I entered and spotted Krisham resting atop his desk. His head hung off the side, poorly supported, and one of his legs did the same. He'd wake with powerful soreness and aches through his neck and lower back. A piece of me wanted to leave him like that, still burned after our last encounter. I chose to be the better person.

Sort of.

I crept over to him, kneeling until my lips were just by his ears. He should have felt the warmth of my breath across his skin, but he didn't. I cleared my throat then screamed. "Oi, dakha! Bandits! Quick, wake and stand ready!"

Krisham scrambled, falling from the table to a hard landing. A sharp yowl left his lips and he whipped around to look for his wooden sword. He came to his senses seconds later and fixed on me. "Ari, what are you standing there for? Didn't you hear—bandits . . . wait, why are you here?" He frowned, his eyes growing distant as he fell into thought. "Wait, were you the one who woke me?"

I nodded and grinned.

He showed no signs of getting the prank. "But where are the bandits? I was about to go looking for Sheru."

I swallowed a sigh and shook my head instead. "I guess you scared them off." My voice held little amusement as his denseness deflated any pleasure I'd gotten from it. "I'm here to see Immi. Is that okay?"

He nodded. "I'll take you." The excitement had left him as well, and he'd returned to speaking in those odd distant tones. "She's been on rather good behavior of late, you know?"

I followed after him as we stepped onto the stairs. "Really?"

"Oh yes. Not a day of scratching her fingers into stumps. Not sure what's gotten into her. I sent for Rishi Ibrahm to tell him about it. He's most pleased. He went to see her too. Don't know what they talked about, but he came out looking as mad as he did happy."

Huh. I hadn't known about that visit and a part of me wondered if Immi had reneged on our deal to keep Shola's visit a secret. I clenched tighter to my sack's strap, wishing I could hold the kitten instead.

We made our way to Immi's door and Krisham unlocked it, bidding me a good visit before he left. "Remember, knock so I can let you out."

I nodded. "Just make sure it's you who opens and not Sheru. No offense, but I'm not a big fan of the fellow."

Krisham shrugged off my opinion. "He's not to everyone's tastes. Still, he's useful to have around. You should see what he gets up to when he wants to walk atop the Crow's Nest. Tricky binding that. But he has no problem bringing himself right up the walls to the roof."

I blinked several times, not knowing if Krisham spoke literally. *A binding that lets you walk up walls?* I hadn't seen a single one which demonstrated that possibility. Then again, what I knew of the bindings couldn't fill a thimble yet. And there were moments when I began to ponder Rishi Ibrahm's warnings, thinking maybe he wasn't so wrong after all. Maybe I should let them go, especially the more I spoke to him and Krisham.

The door slowly fell open and Immi sat inside, waiting for me. She beamed after catching my face and waved. "Ari!"

I took that as my cue to step inside and shut the door behind me, letting my doubts fade. "Hello, Immi." I matched her grin and warmth. "Krisham's been telling me that you've been very good and not hurting your fingers. Is that true?"

She nodded. "I have. Besides, you promised a special visit. Is that why you're here?"

"It is."

At that, she scrambled toward me, coming to sit in the center of the room, still in her favorite cross-legged position. She rocked from side to side in anticipation as I set my bag down between us.

"Be very still and quiet for a moment, *ji-ah*? He can be shy. He's had it rough by my take of things." I uncinched the top and coaxed the lump in my bag I knew to be Shola.

A discontented *mrowl* filtered through the sack.

Immi stiffened, eyes wide, before leaning forward. Her mouth twitched and I saw the makings of a smile on it. The light I'd seen so often in her eyes that reminded me of Rishi Ibrahm had now left, replaced by a brighter, clearer sort. The kind that came from children, far younger than her, who were experiencing their first sense of wonder and awe.

Shola crept out of the sack, looking back at me with a squint that told me he was thoroughly disappointed for being woken from what was apparently the most important rest he'd ever taken.

I gave him a look back that conveyed my sincerest apologies, and maybe held a light mocking note in it as well.

He sniffed the air, above my sarcastic reply, then took to observing his new surroundings. Shola didn't seem too appreciative of them. However, he instantly took to Immi, to her great delight.

She squealed but kept from reaching out for him as I'd advised.

His nose twitched as he smelled her once. Then again. A third time decided the matter for him and he crept closer, still slow and cautious. Satisfied she wasn't a threat or something to ignore, he rubbed his head along her shin.

Immi looked at me in quiet questioning.

I motioned for her to go ahead.

Her smile widened further, and she reached out to stroke the top of Shola's head down to the middle of his back. He shifted under the touch, but gave her a pleased and throaty purr that only encouraged her more.

"What do you think, Immi? Is this worth it?" I already knew the answer before I asked.

Shola finally helped himself into her lap where she picked him up and cradled him. The look of silent adoration on her face was more than enough to know I'd been right.

I let her enjoy the quiet time with the kitten, using it myself to let my thoughts wander from the loss I'd suffered at Nitham's doing, not to mention the pain that still coursed over my hands. One of them shook for a moment before I got it back under control.

The motion didn't go unnoticed by Immi, who'd snapped out of her reverie with Shola. "Why are your hands bandaged, Ari?"

I told her what had happened.

"That bastard!" Her tone could have stripped my skin better than my own strings.

I nearly choked hearing that. Immi had never used profanity, and certainly not with that kind of hatred. Before I could ask why, she went into it.

"Nitham's always been a horrid person. Absolutely the worst." Immi rarely talked about herself unless discussing what she knew of the bindings, and even then, she never mentioned how exactly she learned what she had. She always danced around it.

I knew asking what I wanted would get me a wall instead of an answer, but I had to try. "Immi . . . did Nitham do something to you?"

She fell silent and returned to petting my cat.

After a few more moments of awkward silence, I broke it to apologize. "I'm sorry. I didn't mean to pry."

"Yes you did."

My stomach sank. "Yes, I did. I'm sorry."

She took in a short sharp breath through her nose. "It's fine. It's not something I talk about. We should tend to your hands instead."

"Hm?" I didn't even have a chance to speak before she let go of Shola and took my fingers in her grip. Her touch reignited some of the hot bands of pain but I gritted through them.

"Do you trust me?" Her voice had gone soft as a morning breath of wind along the grass—distant, hollow, almost like Krisham's.

"I do."

She nodded. "Mhm. Don't resist. Don't worry. Just breathe and clear your mind. Think on anything you want that won't resist me. It helps if you focus on something—just one thing."

I immediately fell into the candle and the flame, not wanting to question her now even though a great part of me screamed at me to do so.

Then I felt it.

An unseen weight around my hands, almost like the air on cold mountains. Then an awareness of pressure, like warm fire. A tingling, but above my own skin, and I could just feel the edges of it. I felt the weight of the folds of the mind pressing against me, but they were not mine. I felt a silent desire to will, to ask, and to shape. And she had been right. It came as so foreign a thing my natural instinct begged me to resist it.

I sank deeper into the candle and the flame as I realized what she was doing.

"There. All better." She grinned and proceeded to undo my bandages.

My hands looked like they'd never been cut at all. They felt the same. And a part of me grew colder than when I'd been up in Ampur.

Immi had performed a pair of the major bindings on someone else with as much effort as it took to breathe. In the space of a few moments, she'd healed what would have taken days through modern medicine and diligent attention to my wounds. A wonder.

Or, more accurately, magic. Storybook magic.

The kind I still sought.

"I felt it when you did the bindings, Immi?" My own voice came out as a barely audible breath.

She grinned. "That's good. It means you're learning, if you can pick up on that feeling from someone who has as much practice as me. It means you can feel when someone's folds weigh on you."

Something finally occurred to me. "Immi . . . when you scratch your fingers down every day, and then bind them back to how they were, does it make it easier each time?"

"Yes. Though it's really like breathing by now. I've done it so much I don't have to think anymore. Just bind. Especially with bodily bindings under the second pairing. As within, so without. Start with whent, then go to ern. I understand the body really well, so it's natural for me to bind it. Some binders use the second two to restore things. Others use them to shape things within their personal space, so as—"

"They're not creating something from nothing, I know. You can't do that."

She nodded. "Mhm. Though, in old stories, there are mentions of early binders binding the elements with the second pairing. But it's hard. They're too . . ."

I searched for the possible words and chimed in. "Complex? Nebulous?"

Immi shook her head then waved her arms like a bird in flight. "Troublesome, lively, stubborn, and willful. It's like trying to bind someone's mind or heart. There's too much going on there. It's maddening and there are too many things to take into account. Your own mind and will know this. Even if you don't think you have to worry about all that, you do. Your mind will still try to juggle all those things, and it will fail.

"Water, for example. It's too fluid. It's so changeable. It can be anything depending on what you do with it, or the temperature, and what you put it into. How do you shape and bind something shapeless? How do you take that into your mind and make it what you will, all while keeping its nature in mind? It's . . ." She didn't bother finishing.

I got her point, though. "Yeah, that's understandable." She may have used water to make her argument, but my mind turned to something else just as unstable and lively. Something I knew all too well from dreams and nightmares and having chased its smoke to find my family's killers.

Fire.

So that afternoon, Immi and I continued discussing the second pair of bindings. I tackled them every which way I could until Immi decided we'd talked enough and felt it a better use of both our time to indulge Shola.

So we did.

I'd like to say that's how most of my visits went after that point.

But it would be a lie.

I returned once a day every set until the end of the season. Immi noted the progress in my understanding of the bindings and felt I might soon be ready to finally employ one. I agreed.

We were both terribly wrong.

And the whole Ashram was about to learn that.

NINETY-TWO

The Flame Itself

Radhvahni. Festival of fire and light. End of the year and celebration of the new one to come. Students filtered through the halls weary of their intensifying classes and relieved for the seasonal break. Not to mention the spectacle tonight.

The whole of the Ashram had been decorated with elaborate constructs fashioned of bright metals and glass. The Artisanry's top students spared no expense or time in crafting fantastical beasts and creatures out of mythology, all painted in dazzling colors. I'd been told many had been packed with powdered compounds that would ignite to shower the sky in colorful fire.

I'd heard of such things, fireworks, but hadn't seen anything like them save for black powder.

Shola rode in my backpack as I went for my final visit to Immi for the season. The kitten now weighed noticeably more than before, sometimes requiring me to use both hands to wrangle him into my arms. And yet, he still managed to adopt all the properties of liquid when it suited him, making it impossible to lift his ass when I wanted him out of the way.

The wife of a tinker stood before one of the main courtyard trees that had now gone completely barren. She waved a large fan the red of poppies and directed students to take the long stairs down. The woman promised all manner of trinkets and treasures in her wagon to be sold and dickered over by her husband.

A few jugglers made the climb to the grounds as well, spitting fire and tossing odd mallets of which the heads had been set ablaze. I had no idea how they kept the flames from spreading down the tools or their hands spared. They tossed their hammers so fast that burning rings formed in the air, leaving dizzying bands of orange to entrance passing students. Many tipped them in tin.

Having a better appreciation for performers, I produced one of the nine copper rounds I still owned and tossed it to them.

One of the men caught a mallet, spun, and bowed his head in silent thanks.

I smiled and bowed back before continuing toward the Crow's Nest.

Krisham greeted me inside, wooden sword in hand. He whirled and leveled at me. "Stop there, thug, thief—ne'er-do-well! You come before Athram, wielder of fire and the sword that bars the way. State your business and I shall judge whether or not you will pass."

I rolled my eyes, not in the mood for Krisham's oddities today. "I'm just here to see Immi, Krisham. Relax." I raised a hand, palm facing out.

It did nothing to calm him. "And what says you deserve to see her, hm? Should you find this Krisham, tell him who sent you off to meet Brahm."

I blinked at that. He'd never once taken umbrage with my requests. "Are . . . you all right?" I never got the answer as he jumped toward me, screaming.

"Aiiieeeee!"

I yelped, leaping to one side, lashing out with my binder's cane. Staff and sword met with the hard clack of heavy wood against stone. The impact rattled through my fingers and settled in my wrist with an ache I knew I'd feel a candlemark later. "Brahm's blood, Krisham, what's gotten into you? Who the bloody hell is Athram?"

"I told you! Wielder of fire and the sword that bars the way." He swung his blade in a horizontal cut meant to strike me across the broad of my chest.

I raised my staff to block, once again absorbing the vibration. There had been moments where Krisham had fallen too deeply into the folds and consequences of his bindings. And when he did, he'd adopted the personality of Sheru, a figure out of legend. I'd managed to coax him out of these spells with humor at times. It felt worth a shot, I just needed to set him up for a painful pun that would draw a smile out of him.

"I don't see any fire at the moment." I waited for him to take the bait.

But he never did. He pulled away from me, looking down at his sword. "True. Well spotted. Let me remedy that."

"What?" I hadn't expected him to respond like that.

Krisham ran his hand along the length of wood, muttering to himself, but I heard the word. "Burn!"

I flinched, leaping away, but nothing happened.

He looked down at the weapon, frowning. "Oh, right. I need fire. Wait there so I can find some, then I'll burn you proper."

"Why would I wait here for that?" I lunged, trying to jab him with the head of my staff.

He batted it aside and moved toward the lone candle burning on his desk. Krisham touched the tip of his blade to it and muttered again. The bulb of fire flickered fast then bled onto the weapon, racing along it until flames engulfed the whole sword.

My eyes widened and I lost all the breath in me.

He whirled around. "Now, ashes to ashes, cinders and embers. Let me give you one last sight to remember!" Krisham yowled, bringing his flaming sword overhead with the clear intent of bringing it down on my skull.

Only, that didn't happen.

The wood gave way and charred, turning black as coal until it crumbled and the flames extinguished.

Krisham blinked, looking up at the soot and debris slowly falling on his face like tar-colored flurries. "Huh. Maybe I made the binding too strong for the wood to hold it. Hrm." He turned his attention back to me. "Ari, why didn't you stop me? Do you know what I'll have to do now to get another sword?"

". . . Buy one?" I didn't know if he wanted me to answer.

"No. I can't do that. Rishi Ibrahm yelled at me the last time he saw me with a weapon, even a wooden one. I'll have to bind and shape one again, but I can't take the wood from the Crow's Nest." His voice dropped to a conspiratorial whisper. "Someone would know. Also, no one answers a rhetorical question. It's asinine, Ari."

"So is attacking me for the hundredth time, Krisham." I narrowed my eyes. "You are back to being yourself, aren't you?"

"Of course. Wait, did I go somewhere? I don't recall." He put a thumb and forefinger to his chin. "Oh, I suppose I borrowed trouble from someone else. I thought I'd snuck out and had forgotten again."

My mouth nearly fell open. "You leave the Crow's Nest . . . without permission?"

He put a finger up to his lips. "Sometimes. I make sure to come back before Rishi Ibrahm's check-ins."

"Where do you go? How do you go?"

He grinned—full of gleaming teeth and a boy's mischief. "With bindings, and on adventures. There's a whole wide world out there to see. Sometimes I'm a pirate. Other times I'm saving princesses from wild hungry ghouls." Krisham shrugged and returned to his desk. "It's whatever I feel like."

Some of the tension finally left my back and jaw as I realized he was lying. Or, more accurately, probably suffering another delusion. I left him to it and decided it better to focus on seeing Immi. "I'm here for my visit. Can I go see her?"

"Hm? Oh, yes." He led me back to Immi's room and left once I stepped inside.

Immi sat against the far wall, facing it. She heard me enter but didn't turn toward me.

"Hello, Immi. How are you doing today? I brought Shola, are you . . ." I trailed off when I saw rows of red stains against the wall. "Immi." The next words caught in my throat and I couldn't get them out. I raced over and fell by her side, eyes going to her hands. They were covered in the same shade of red. I looked back to the wall. "Did you . . . ?" The question died in the air.

She shook her head. "No. But yes." Each word sounded strained, like the cords of a mandolin strung too tight and close to breaking. Like glass under a weight too great, just about to crack.

I took her fingers in mine and rubbed them, unsure what else to do. "What happened?"

"Promise you won't be mad."

I nodded. "Promise."

"I was just thinking about it, I swear. But then I remembered Shola's visits. All I did was put my hands on the wall and let them sit there. Just touching, I swear it. Then, then my mind went to the bindings, but not to heal. I just thought about what my fingers are like after I claw with them. Just thoughts, Ari, I promise."

"I believe you." I rubbed faster, but kept a gentle touch, doing more to bring a modicum of warmth to her hands than anything else. And, maybe, just give her contact with someone else so she knew she wasn't alone.

Sometimes the comfort of someone else's hand can take away much of our pains.

Immi used the moment to whisper a binding, too quiet for me to hear despite how close I sat. Her hands soon looked as if they'd never been rubbed raw and to bleeding.

"It's fine. You're fine. That's what matters. And you didn't break our agreement from the way I see it. It was an accident."

She finally turned to better regard me. "You're not upset?"

I shook my head. "No." But words wouldn't be enough to assuage, so I did the best thing I could think of. I removed my pack and opened it to let Shola loose.

He did a better job than I could have imagined. The fiery kitten leapt out of the sack, throwing most of his weight against one of Immi's thighs. She let out a little laugh before he climbed into her lap and smacked his head against her belly. Content with his new resting spot, he purred and settled down to sleep. She sat there, petting him, mouthing a silent thanks.

I smiled back and let her enjoy the quiet time with the cat.

Eventually, Shola woke and let us know he wanted to prowl the room with a sharp and warbly *meow*. This let Immi and I speak without disturbing his rest.

"How is your practice going, Ari?"

I waggled a hand. "Haven't been able to make a binding still, but I'm trying."

"Have you figured out which you want to try and how? Remember the talk about the Mendery and fingers?" She waggled her own to make her point.

I inclined my head. "I do. I don't think that's for me, so that only makes it harder, right?"

"Right. It should be something you feel connected to, interested in, and know very well."

I frowned. "That doesn't make things easier."

She picked up on my frustration, turning our conversation elsewhere. "Are you excited for the festival? It starts soon, I think. It's hard to tell time in the Crow's Nest, but my body remembers. You can hear the noises from the fireworks even up here in the tower. Sometimes I picture the lights coming through the walls. I can still remember the colors from when I was a student. You should be out there watching it."

"I'd rather be here with you—a friend."

She smiled, but it lacked warmth. "That's sweet. *You're* sweet. But I can hear you want to be there. You're here because you're worried about me."

It was the truth and I saw no point in lying. "I am."

She took my hand in hers and squeezed it. "It's fine. *I'm* fine. We'll finish our talk, then promise me you'll go see Radhvahni, yes?"

"Yes."

"Good. Besides, it might be good for you. Some students need to snap to do a binding, others need fear, some need excitement and wonder to finally see the secret shape of things. Maybe this will open your mind. It certainly needs to open." Immi leaned forward and tapped two fingers to my skull, striking just hard enough to elicit a light sound.

I gently swatted her hand away. "Har. Har. Very funny. I think my mind's pretty open. I mean, I only battled a serpent out of myth and legend near the beginning of the season. But I'll take your wise and considerable knowledge into consideration, Immi." I thought about how easily I could leave the Crow's Nest to attend the festival all while she remained stuck here with only the memories of it.

"Immi, is there anything you'd like from outside? Out on the Ashram's grounds or from the festival?"

She pursed her lips and looked at the wall instead of me. A moment passed in silence. Then two . . . then three. "Mhm. Two things, if you can."

"Name them."

"There are these little sticks of crystalized sugar. They bake it hard and sweet, like rocks. I've always loved them, but they're only down in Ghal proper and not the Ashram. Sometimes vendors come up during the festival with the Masters' permission and sell them here. The other is a glass token."

I arched a brow, but didn't speak.

"It's like a copper round, about this big." She gestured with a thumb and index finger, forming a small circle. "They're colored glass and etched with beautiful art. In the sun, they catch all the light and almost sparkle. Some merchants bring them to the Artisanry for minor bindings. To either hold small amounts of sunlight or set them with a glow that is even prettier than their own shine. Some even hold warmth for a while and can restore it if you leave them out on hot days. It's like a little piece of sparkling fire inside glass."

"I think I can manage that." I rose to head out and set to the task of getting Immi her gifts.

"Thank you, Ari."

"Don't mention it."

One of her hands closed around one of my ankles and she squeezed. "No, really. Nobody comes to visit me besides Rishi Ibrahm and sometimes Krisham. I haven't seen Reppi in over a year. It's been a lonely year."

My heart fell out of my chest and hit the floor like a piece of glass on a winter day. Brittle, hard, and completely shattered—left to feel the full breadth of the cold. "Immi, I'm so sorry. I can visit more often. I can try to—"

"That's not the point. Just, thank you."

Thank you. Those two words carried so much weight that I could find no words in answer. So I merely accepted Immi's gratitude in silence.

"I'll wait for you here. And I promise, it won't happen again." She released her hold from my leg and returned to staring at the wall.

"I know, Immi. And I'll be back, after I speak to Rishi Ibrahm to make sure we get more visitors as well."

She didn't turn around to address me. "It's not his fault. The other masters forbid it. The Crow's Nest was their doing. Well, older ones. No Master Binder has ever wanted to have this place around." With that, she fell into silence, and I left.

When I passed by Krisham, he waved me a goodbye. "If you're coming back, see if you can bring me a piece of new fire, hm? The last one I grabbed burned my sword to cinders. Can you believe it?"

I waved back but didn't have the heart to reply. The doors of the Crow's Nest shut behind me and I walked across the Ashram grounds.

Darkness came earlier in the day now and, though we were only past fourth candle, the sky had taken on the deeper blue of late evening.

Pillars, which held brass bowls above them, had been erected throughout the main courtyard. Fires had been lit and kept burning by passing monks, creating a row of dancing bulbs dotting the Ashram sky.

Braziers, lower to the ground, continued the theme.

Fireflies joined in on the light show, adding their own minuscule motes of pale yellow glows to the flaming oranges.

Wherever you looked, you found something brilliant-bright to look at. The scene hypnotized me and left me staring. But a heavy hand smacked into my back, jarring me out of my dream of firelight.

Aram stepped in front of me, jostling me harder. "Hey, are you there, or have you finally gone as cracked as Rishi Ibrahm?" She whistled twice and waved a hand before my eyes.

I shook my head clear. "I'm fine, just a little tired. Long season. Classes, you know?"

She gave me a long look as if she didn't believe my reason. But being the friend she was, she didn't push it. "Fair enough. Have you eaten yet? I'm starving. There's a vendor who brought goat *kithas* here with yogurt sauce and buttered bread. I could eat half a dozen skewers right now."

I snorted. "Hardly. The last time you ate two you were so full we thought you'd burst . . . from both ends."

She glowered at me. "That's not true. It was just a queasy stomach from exams pressure and you know it."

I returned her earlier dubious look. "Uh-huh. Sure." My arm throbbed and Aram pulled her fist back, readying for another quick jab. "*Ow.*"

"Better me than Radi. He's in a foul mood." Aram held her hands in front of a brazier we passed, warming her fingers before stuffing them into her robe's pockets.

"What's got him twisted and turned today?" A part of me had an idea, but I wanted to hear it from Aram's mouth.

"Oh, he asked four different women to dance with him tonight, and you can imagine how that went."

I couldn't help a lopsided grin. "Well, knowing him, half a dozen of one, six of the other. Any say yes but then find out he'd asked others? Or did they all say no? Wait, did one of them slap him? How did he ask? Oh, Brahm's blood. *Who* did he ask?"

Aram's lips pressed tight and her eyes glittered. "They all said no. But *two* of them slapped him for the audacity." When she saw the look on my face, she explained. "Radi's already, erhm . . ." Aram broke off and gesticulated with wild hand motions, wiggling her fingers. "Gotten to know some of these wonderful women after a fashion. And, having a head with space only for music, he's forgotten them just as fast."

I winced and let out a low whistle. "That *has* to sting."

Aram raised both brows. "Not as much as both sides of his face. Though, can't say he doesn't deserve it."

I grunted in mild agreement. "Will he still show up for the fireworks?"

Aram nodded. "He wouldn't miss it. Radhvahni is one of the best nights of the year for him to play. He'll make more tonight than a season's work for many, and not to mention, I'm sure he'll find a way to charm some lady with his heartbreaking story of how his love was spurned." Aram rolled her eyes and I laughed.

"Nothing ever really dampens his spirits, does it?" I motioned for my friend to follow me as I set out looking for what Immi had asked for. As we searched, the sky darkened further, and a pale slip of soft moonlight bathed the part of the courtyard we walked across.

"Cloudless night. Stars above." Aram idly motioned to the sky.

"Mhm." I didn't feel like talking about the subject, still eyeing the various vendors in hopes of figuring out which sold Immi's glass tokens.

One merchant worked out of a wooden box, fitted with brass in places and as large as the man's torso. It must have been a pain to carry it up the stairs unless he'd enlisted help from Rishi Ibrahm. I'd heard you could pay him to open small doorways leading from the mountain base up to the top. Only, it was no small fee.

But from the number of students and town visitors leaving with his wares, it looked like his business would easily handle the cost.

I walked over to him. "May I see some of your tokens?"

The man beamed, revealing teeth as white as the moon. If only they were all there. The man's clothes hung off him even though he turned in enough coin to eat well. "Of course—of course. One for ten, two for eleven, and three for fifteen. An armful for a copper, and the whole of it for a piece of silver." He'd rattled off the prices so fast I nearly lost track of them all.

I did a mental tally and found myself grinning. "How many fall for it?"

That brought him up short. "Hm?"

"You're selling them higher and higher, making it seem like you're getting a bargain the more you buy because each piece is worth less and less as the number adds up. What do they cost a piece, *really*?"

His eyes turned to slits and he turned his head halfway away from me, giving me a sidelong look. "Clever."

"I've been told that."

"Now, I can't go around telling my secrets, you know?"

I agreed. "Can't have that."

"Let's say it then, for being a clever boy and all, and just as much for your discretion—hm—that we'll do one for seven, two for ten, and three for fifteen? They're really worth it." He held one up, angling it near a brazier. The moss green of the glass shimmered from within like it held crushed diamonds—no, stars. They glittered as they caught the firelight and burned like little embers.

"They do look to be that." I worked to keep my voice neutral and any of the excitement out of it. "But how about one for five. I don't really want one for myself. It's more a request for a friend." I shrugged, taking a half step away.

"Now-now, don't be like that. Wait a tick, boy." He raced around the box and cut me off, holding up the token. "I know it looks to be just a piece o' glass, true. But can't say it's not pretty. The sort of thing a boy like you ought to give a lady." He gave me another wide grin and elbowed me.

"It is for a lady, but a friend more importantly." I reached into my purse and pulled free five tin chips. "How about one for five?"

The man frowned, then looked around. Our conversation had led some of the students and visiting townsfolk to stop and listen in. He snatched the coins from my hand faster than I could blink and pushed the token into it. "Fine." He kept his voice low before bringing it to a basso boom. "Another satisfied customer! One for twelve, two for twenty, three for thirty! Best bargain—"

I walked away, smiling at the minor victory and shaking my head just as much at his performance. He'd been quick to capitalize on the show of coins and take in the crowd, though. I had to give him credit for it.

Aram continued following me, bemoaning her own lack of romantic companionship for the night. I consoled her the best I could, which is to say with a light pat on the back whenever she brought up the topic. She didn't really want a solution, just sympathy for the moment, and I could offer that.

We continued searching for the second thing Immi had asked for, when I crossed paths with Rishi Vruk. I set my staff and sack down, taking care to not disturb Shola as Aram addressed my mentor and friend.

"Master Philosopher." Aram inclined her head, keeping her voice low and respectful.

Rishi Vruk bowed back. "Aram." He then turned to me. "Ari. How are you?"

I shrugged, thumbing the token in my hand. Its texture was smooth as river stone despite being carved. Some glass lost that and grew rough and porous. Not this piece. "I'm fine; mildly upset at myself, though."

He frowned, turning to face me. When he did, bands of firelight washed over his face to tint his skin and cast a light yellow-gold glow across his eyes. It faded as soon as he finished moving. "Why's that? Something wrong?"

I shook my head, then nodded as I realized I'd been lying to myself. "I'm frustrated at my lack of progress with my bindings." Aware Aram stood at my side, I chose my words carefully. "I've been trying to get a better grip on them, performing another pair, as it were, and I've had nothing but struggle." It was true after a fashion.

His frown deepened, but it was the look of someone heavy with understanding. "I can understand that. It took me a long time to wrap my head around them. Still, you've displayed a talent in them before, like with the Nagh-lokh story. So I'm sure you'll manage just fine. Besides, Radhvahni is a magical night. Who knows, you might even manage one tonight." He smiled, and for a moment, the yellow returned to his eyes.

Before I could speak, he turned away to regard the sky. I followed the look to see a hint of smoke-colored clouds obscuring the barest sliver of moon.

He sighed. "Think she'll appear tonight? She always does." He hadn't addressed the question to me.

"I'm sorry, Rishi Vruk?" Aram leaned closer, cupping a hand to her ear, not fully registering what the master had asked.

"Nothing. Nothing. Talking to myself. Old man's mutterings, is all." An easy smile slipped over his face and he placed a hand on my shoulder, jostling me much like a father would a son. "Take it easy tonight, *ji-ah*? Give your mind a break from bindings. You might find they come quicker without thinking so much. Sometimes it's better to feel than think. Remember that."

"Thank you, Vathin." Aram stiffened at my side when I'd said that, but the master merely nodded and walked off.

"I should have figured that's why he always comes to pull your sorry Sullied ass out of the fire," said a voice I'd hoped not to hear for a long time.

I whirled around to find Nitham and his two friends, Thalib and Qalbi. But my eyes didn't go to his face for long, rather the things in their hands. My bag lay at their feet. One of them held my staff, another held Shola by the scruff, passing my kitten to Nitham.

Shola protested and flailed against the rough handling, swiping at Nitham's hand. He drew a few drops of blood as the boy yelped and drew back. "Bastard scratched me." He reached out and took hold of my cat.

Coals filled the pit of my stomach, quickly kindling to something hot. And yet, a hollowness, cold and vast, spread through my chest—taking my heart. "Don't. Please."

"What was that?" Nitham held the cat at arm's length, looking around to his friends in disbelief. "Did you hear him?"

Thalib and Qalbi laughed.

Aram raised both her hands hoping to calm the situation. "Nitham, just let the cat go. Come on, this isn't funny, and this trouble isn't worth it. You two have been at each other most of the year. The masters are tired, and this isn't going—"

"When I want your opinion, little merchant's spawn, I'll ask you. Better yet, I'll pay when I think it's time for you to think and speak. Otherwise. Shut. Up!" Nitham faced one of his friends. "What's the punishment for having animals on the Ashram grounds without permission?"

Thalib grinned. "The pet's removed from the grounds. The student is fined. And if the animal proves to be a danger, it's killed. Hey, Nitham, didn't it just scratch you?"

The pit grew wider—deeper. Cold leached into my bones. All the while, the fire in my stomach burned until I tasted acid in my throat, threatening to eat away the lining until it reached my heart and seared that too. "Don't." The word left me as a harsh, hard, and dry croak.

I looked around for help. For anything. Anyone.

Most of the students passed us by, not paying attention to the scene, all caught up in the fires, merchants, and their own business. The few that noticed decided to quickly lose that attention to and turn elsewhere, knowing how problematic Nitham's and my rivalry had become.

I couldn't blame them.

Thunder boomed. Pillars of metal spewed brilliant sparks into the air. Streams of fire, as varied in color as a child's dream could conjure. People cheered and let loose echoing gasps that drowned out everything else save my conversation with Nitham.

I searched for anything and found one pair of eyes watching us.

Vathin. He stood there, half paying attention to us, half glancing up to the sky.

The clouds cleared. The moon, in all her fullness, hung above. Pale and silver-white as a pearl. Vathin turned away from me to regard it and I lost what hope I'd found in that moment.

No.

"Well, there you have it, Sullied. Guess I should do it for you. I mean, it's a favor, after all. Can't have a *binder* with your promise distracted by this troublesome thing. And, it is a danger at that. It's already hurt me. Who knows what it will get up to when fully grown?" He turned his arm, holding Shola over one of the burning braziers.

Something flared inside me and my mind grew distant. The candle and flame came to me. The folds. But they stayed as dark and empty as most of the night sky.

Something snapped, hard wood failing with a bitter crack.

I looked to see Qalbi had taken my binder's cane—my staff, the dream of what I sought to be—and broken it underfoot into two.

The coals burned brighter inside me and the hollowness spread as well. Both fighting to take me.

I looked to Vathin, urging a silent prayer and plea. *Help me.*

He met my eyes, and they were as yellow-gold as that most precious metal. As the night a demon took my family. When I saw him then, he no longer wore

Vathin's face. My mentor, teacher, sponsor, Master Philosopher, and most of all, friend, was gone. They glittered with a cruelty and hunger I'd seen once in my life. His features reminded me of a wolf. This time, he did not look away.

Koli.

All this time.

Had I sent him up to Ampur with my theory? Had he done it to lure me?

My heart lurched. I froze. Coldness took me.

"How many lives do you think this thing has?" Nitham let Shola go, dropping him over the fire.

"No!" Something broke. The token slipped from my hand and struck the ground, shattering. Then I followed suit.

All around me, fire burned, and just as much inside me. The candle and the flame ebbed, then flared to fan a flame so large it filled the whole of my mind. Every fold.

I reached out toward the brazier and screamed, "Start with whent, then go to ern. I bind you flame. To spread. And. Burn!"

And the fire obeyed.

I saw it then, nothing but orange brilliance and the red of blood.

I felt it.

A wordless cry left me and the brazier's fire leapt to my command.

Shola vanished under a wave of flame as it surged toward Nitham, engulfing the sleeve of his arm.

He screamed.

The fire spilled to the ground, bringing the oil that fueled it along. It spread. It raced, growing all the closer. It passed to a nearby tree, catching it aflame as well. Branches burned and broke, bringing the fire down onto a section of the Ashram wall where it should have died. But it did not.

The wall burned. A brazier below it sent up its own tendrils to meet the new flame, feeding it another pool of oil as well. But that was what the onlookers would think.

In truth, something else fed that fire.

Me.

And it was taking me.

I screamed, willing, wanting for it to spread wider. To reach out and take Koli, who stood just dozens of feet from me. The space around me bent and bowed to make it happen. I tracked the flame in mind and heart and watched it flicker and fan across the grounds toward the Ashura.

I am burning now. Hotter. Quicker. Enflamed and engulfed by something I cannot hold. It is searing me, blood and bone, skin and sinew. It's taking me.

I see a world for the taking and a hunger that will not be sated until it burns me as its final price—its kindling.

I'm burning. And it hurts.

Hotter now. Hungrier still.

The fire wants more than I can give it. More than what the Ashram has to offer. That's its nature. It wants to live and grow and spread. It doesn't seek to destroy, only feed and fuel itself, for that's all it knows.

It's taking me. Mind and heart. Then my soul. Let it. Let it all burn. Let them all. I want to turn them to ash and bone and charcoal.

It hurts.

There is a piece of me feeding itself to the fire. It hurts. I'm breaking apart and burning deeper now with no end in sight. It's going to consume me like fire is wont to do. It needs more. Wants more.

And I don't have it in me to give it. To hold it.

I'm the kindling, and I'm willing to burn to end him too.

I stared at Koli as the fires roared into a wall that washed over him.

All the while, he looked away, smiling, catching one last sight of the moon.

I see the folds and they are fire. Violent oranges with a yellow that holds none of the softness of sunflowers. It's the promise of sparks with which to fan a flame that will take the school and those I hold dear.

I am burning.

Help me.

Please.

I was ready to die if it meant ending Koli.

But the clouds came, obscuring the moon, and then the storm broke out.

Rain fell from the sky, meeting my flames with the hateful hiss of oil to a hot pan. It did nothing to dull the pain and fire inside me. Nothing to give back control.

Koli spoke a word through the flames. I cannot say how I knew it, I just did. The flames lurched from his side as if blown away and the force of a bull struck me, throwing me to the ground.

I lay there, half-battered, writhing from the fire inside me that promised one thing: It would burn me from the inside out.

Rishi Ibrahm came to stand over me, placing a hand on my head and muttering something.

The world darkened.

My heart soothed. The heat inside me died, and the last thing I saw before the blackness were two golden eyes watching me. His smile. And Koli turned, opened a way, and vanished.

NINETY-THREE

The First Binding

When I woke, I rested in one of the Mendery's beds. The world swam before my eyes, and a haziness peppered my vision that left me sensitive to light. I winced against the morning sun and turned. "What?" The lone word took all my strength and left me hoarse.

"Don't talk." Aram's voice.

I groaned. Then realized something. "Nitham. My staff. Shola!" I rose, the whole of my body screaming and set to a new fire. Hands clamped to my shoulders and tried to ease me back down, but I resisted. "Aram, what happened?" My throat ached worse now.

Hotter. I grew hotter. Something surged inside me. "Aram!"

My cheek burned as my head snapped to one side. The blow cleared my vision and I turned to see Rishi Ibrahm standing above me.

His hand was raised above his head, ready to administer another full-arm slap. "Look at me."

I did. In that moment, he'd lost all of the cunning, the childish mischief, and the maddened gleam in his eyes.

"What do you see if you try to bring up the folds of your mind?"

I didn't bother asking what he meant by the absurd question, instead doing as he asked. The candle and the flame returned. Fire. Every piece I'd seen. An unspoken feeling of familiarity with it. A hunger. A need. A silent scream I couldn't give voice to, but which quickly took me and begged to be let out. My chest heaved and sweat broke out across my forehead.

I told him.

"Good. Breathe. Close your eyes. I'm going to teach you how to slip out of the folds without slipping too hard and fast. Come down with me now."

I obeyed.

"They're dying. Burning low. Do not try to snuff them out. Don't try to close that part of your mind to them. Acknowledge them. Listen to the fires. Hear them. Then, let them burn softer. Lower now. Dimmer then. Watch them ebb, like little candles struggling to stay alight. When you've done that. Wink one fold out of existence. Then the next. Softer still, Ari. I can feel you. You're pushing back."

He was right. A weight fell against me, telling me to resist. The pressure of Rishi Ibrahm's folds, gently testing mine—pushing.

I gave in and listened. Slowly, the folds fell and the fires burned out.

"Better?"

I took one heavy breath and sagged. "Yes."

"Good. Aram, leave us for a moment. I'd like to speak to Ari alone. If Master Mender tries to come back, tell him I asked for a moment of privacy, *ji-ah*?"

"*Ji*, Rishi Ibrahm." Aram gave me one last look before leaving.

I watched my friend go and felt all the winter chillness from the night before return. "I don't know what happened, I'm sorry, I—"

Master Binder raised a hand, staying me. "First, I thought you'd like to see this." He reached down and retrieved a sack that had been sitting at the foot of my bed. A familiar one at that. Mine.

He uncinched the top and tipped it onto the bed, nudging a small lump.

A kitten, orange as flame, scampered out of it, shooting the Master Binder a withering look. Once he saw me, Shola let out a rolling purr before bumping his head against my knee.

I wept, taking the cat in my arms.

Rishi Ibrahm watched us, saying nothing for a moment. "You called him Shola?"

"You can't tell the other masters about him." I'd spoken it as a command. Harsh. Hard. Demanding. In truth, it had been a plea.

He raised an eyebrow. "*Can't?*" Rishi Ibrahm's mouth quirked into an uneven smile. "Can't, hm? Been a long time since someone has told me that. I never did like that word. It's stupid, especially for a binder."

"*Please,* Rishi. I mean it. He has nowhere to go. He's not a nuisance. And—"

"Oh, stop. It's fine. I won't tell. Besides, I've a feeling the cat's more good for you than you might realize. The other masters don't need to know, but you will answer my questions now, hm?"

I nodded.

"Shola. Why did you call him that?"

I thought about it. "It means shy. He's skittish at times. I found him orphaned down in Ghal. Nitham and his friends were bullying him."

"Ah. That doesn't explain the name, though. Shola is Zibrathi."

"Yes, Rishi."

"It doesn't mean shy, though."

"It doesn't?"

He shook his head. "Shola means fire. Burning. The flame."

I hadn't known that. Had I misheard or misunderstood when I'd first listened in on the word being used?

"I didn't think you'd bind fire . . . and like that. And for that to be your first?" He sighed, some of the strength leaving him as he took to a chair.

The way he'd said that led me to wonder on something. "My first?"

He gave me a knowing look. "Come now, I know what really happened at Ampur, even if I went along with your little story before. I'm not a fool, Ari."

I shrunk a little at that.

"This presents a problem, though, Ari. What you did was dangerous. And had you not grown so weak in losing control of your binding, I wouldn't have been able to put you to rest. You would have ended up like those in the Crow's Nest—worse, by the looks of things."

Something else came to mind about the night before. "Rishi Ibrahm, there's something I need to tell you. It's about Vathin—Rishi Vruk."

"I saw." He didn't elaborate, but his voice had gone hard as iron and just as cold. The words carried a weight I felt in my heart and which banded my chest with lead.

"You won't believe me if I tell you more."

"Ari, I'm a binder. I've seen more than you could dream of. We will talk, then we can decide what I can and cannot believe. For now, keep your thoughts on the Master Philosopher to yourself and from the other masters. Can you walk?"

I thought about it, and in truth, I could. Though, it would be a pain. "Yes."

"Good. There's no time for you to rest. Master Mender will see to you quickly, then you're to go to the Admittance Chamber."

"Why?"

"Ari, you could have burned down the Ashram. You're up on the worst of grievances. They're discussing your punishment."

"Walking the fire?" I shook my head. No, too small compared to what I'd done. Expulsion? Wrong again. After what had happened, word would have spread through Ghal below. I'd be seen as a threat. A student who could bind fire and lose control like that? Only one option made sense.

"They're going to lock me up in the Crow's Nest?"

All of the color fled Rishi Ibrahm's face. "Or worse. Actually, I'm not sure which option is better."

Worse than the Crow's Nest?

He didn't answer. Instead, the Master Binder rose and left.

Master Mender arrived shortly after I'd hidden Shola back in my pack.

Once I'd been seen to and given something to dull the pain, I left as instructed to face my judgment.

The punishment for the first binding I'd ever truly done.

The headmaster called the grievance meeting to order. All of the masters were there in attendance save for one.

Vathin. The only one I could have once counted on for support and friendship.

Koli.

My fists tightened. But I took comfort in the fact I'd chosen to catch up with Aram and leave Shola in her care. No matter what happened to me, my kitten would be taken care of.

"Ari, you stand on grievances for employing a paired binding. Setting parts of the Ashram on fire. Binding an element you had no control over and even less of a right to attempt. Harming a student, leaving Kaethar Nitham with burns along his arms. Though he will heal, attacking a student is forbidden. Doing so with the ten bindings is immediate grounds for removal from the Ashram." He didn't say how that removal happened, however.

I shifted from side to side, looking at the masters, particularly, Rishi Ibrahm.

"I'm left with no choice but to bring up the only two methods we have for dealing with such a thing." The headmaster let out a long breath and hunched over, resting his elbows on the table. "To deal with a student improperly using the ten bindings and putting others at harm, we vote on whether Accepted Ari will be confined to the Crow's Nest . . . or executed under the Jadum laws for binders."

My heart fell into my stomach. "What?"

All of the masters ignored me except Rishi Ibrahm. He gave me a long-suffering look that said more of an apology than any words could have.

The masters conferred. Then they argued. Some of their voices rose. Finally, Rishi Ibrahm touched a hand to his throat and boomed over all of them. "Enough! There's a third option we're not considering."

Everyone fell silent.

My heartbeat followed, growing too quiet for me to even hear after its long thundering.

"Apprenticeship." The single word brought all of the masters to a similar and confused stop. "One year. Accepted Ari has demonstrated something few students do in all the seasons they study here. He's performed a major pair of bindings before us. More to the point, he's bound an element. Give me one year to privately mentor him along with his enrollment in the higher classes for binding. One year for me to turn him from a danger into something more.

"After all, it takes a village to raise a child, but only takes a child to raze a village. I'd rather help the boy than have him set to burning more things down. Especially if he decides to protest our little ruling."

I didn't know what to say. It was a preposterous request, no matter how much I wanted it. Would the masters even go for it? I'd caused so much trouble that I couldn't see it happening in truth. And Master Binder's closing argument wasn't exactly worded to encourage the others to see me as less of a threat.

They conferred again. Then the headmaster cleared his throat and addressed me. "All in favor of Accepted Ari being put under probation for one year under Rishi Ibrahm's tutelage? Should he prove himself to Master Binder . . . and should his testimony at a future time move the rest of the masters, Ari's punishment will be rescinded. Should he fail, we will vote on the original two choices."

One hand rose in favor. Rishi Bharia, Master Artisan.

My mouth dried.

A second, but many of the masters looked unmoved.

Master Conditioner crossed his arms over his chest, raising neither.

Master Mender's stayed stuck to the table.

Rishi Ibrahm finally raised his. Three. And there were eight masters total since Vathin's departure.

The headmaster looked around. "Three to five."

Master Lorist raised her hand, but something about it felt forced. Like she took pity on me more than anything else.

"Four to four," said the headmaster.

My legs were close to crumbling beneath me.

"It's been a long time, Accepted Ari, since a student has called fire. It reminds me of when I had dreams like that. I think the Ashram can stand a year to see what kind of man you might grow to be." The headmaster raised his hand. "And it's a very good thing my vote counts twice. Six to four.

"Accepted Ari is to be placed under Rishi Ibrahm's care and studies. He will be promoted as well to Kaethar for his display of binding prowess. And, he will be fined three silver doles for the damages to the Ashram. If he cannot pay, he will work off the debt. Is this acceptable to you?" The headmaster stared at me.

I grinned. "It is."

NINETY-FOUR

Revelry

News quickly spread of all that had happened and I enjoyed a new sort of fame in the aftermath. Some students gave me a wider berth. More stories sprung up about me and what I could do. The reasoning for why I'd gone unburned when I'd walked the fire.

I *really* was a scion of Brahm. Maybe him come again to test and watch humanity. I'd made a deal with the Shaen. My soul and blood for a mastery of the bindings. You know the kinds of stories people tell.

The night of drinking during the festival, and the one the day after my friends had treated me to, only served to worsen the spread and nature of these tales.

We'd met at The Fireside after I'd paid off my debt to the Ashram. Radi, Aram, even Estra and Eira joined us. Though, the latter looked to have come more for Radi's sake than mine. Other students gathered there as well, but kept far enough away from our table to be both polite, and leave me to wonder if they were afraid.

Shola was treated to as much as he could handle in food.

And I'd spent a full copper to get all of us properly and well-deservedly drunk.

I had a better time doing it than what I'd suffered in Volthi.

We talked of Nitham's suffering and toasted to his eventual departure from the Ashram. More a hope than fact, but why not hold to it? We'd seen stranger things happen.

They celebrated my rise in rank and my stay of execution as well as avoiding the Crow's Nest.

I'd called the first binding I'd dreamed of. Shola had survived safe and sound. My friends were around me. And I'd earned the Master Binder's attention and teachings. I'd learn even more of what I set out to.

Once the first part of our revelry had been enjoyed, Radi and Aram decided to take me out for a second swing at it. It turned out they were rather good at delinquency and, much to my old sparrow's heart, doing it on a budget.

We stumbled through the streets of Ghal, haggling for what we could with a handful of tin chips, more out of drunken curiosity and idiocy than anything else. We could have bought anything, but we were determined to see how far we could properly thrash ourselves for so little.

In the end, we left with half a pint of Vedh, a white spirit distilled from potatoes far west of the Mutri Empire. Sharp, strong, and enough to fell most kids our age. We procured an unopened bottle of a transparent spirit simply known as "Clear" for its appearance. Cheap, and mostly all grain alcohol that left it better suited to strip paint than consume. Some oranges and peaches fell into our possession as well.

I may have stolen those in a return to old ways.

I won't apologize for it, but will simply say that a drunken young man is prone to much foolishness.

We mixed our findings together and drank until we forgot the world's problems, and then the world.

Mistakes were made that night.

The morning after and the hangover came closer to killing me than my loss of control with the bindings.

NINETY-FIVE

Intermission—Masquerade

I stopped reciting my tale and raised a hand to help draw Eloine's attention. "I think that's as good a place as any to stop my story for the moment. A touch of happiness after times of trauma. Koli had bested my attempt to kill him, slipped my grasp, pretended to be my friend and betrayed me, and the Ashura were still out there as a whole. But I knew I'd find them again, all of them. And when I did, I'd be ready."

"I always did wonder about what happened in Ampur. The way people tell it now is quite something else altogether." She smirked.

I mirrored the expression. "I'm not surprised. So, has that sated some of your curiosity? Do I live up to the things you've heard?"

"Mhm. In some ways, surely. In other ways, a disappointment. Though, that's not a bad thing. I'm rather glad to hear the truths from your mouth. It tells me a great deal more about you."

I cocked a brow. "And what did you learn? Something interesting, I hope?"

She leaned forward. "Oh, very." Her eyes smoldered and she smelled of all the things a young man imagines a woman to smell like. Of firesides and sandalwood. Lemongrass and lavender. The slight sweetness of honey-gold drops, and the breathy scent of woodsmoke. And then she leaned closer, touching a hand to my cheek.

I felt her breath across my face and closed my eyes. Her fingers slid along the line of my jaw before tracing their way up into my hair. Her breath came harder now on me, but her hand pulled away. When I opened my eyes, she stood a foot from me.

I sighed internally. Partly cursing the side of me that had been foolish to hope, and just as much for wanting a thing I knew I couldn't have.

She smoothed her clothing, turning away from me. "There's to be a masquerade tonight. I hope to see you there."

"I thought the point wasn't to see who was there. Not really, anyway."

Eloine turned back to me and narrowed her eyes just enough to let me know she wasn't truly angry. Just a touch irritated. "I'm a lady telling you that I'd like to see you at a dance, don't get clever. Take it for what it is."

I blinked and got to my feet. "I'm not so sure I know what it is."

Eloine shut her eyes and blew out a heavy breath. "Promise me you'll be there."

"I will."

"Mhm. Good." She looked me over, starting at my feet, then stopping when she reached my face. "Do you have a change of clothes?"

I frowned and looked at myself. "What's wrong with how I'm dressed?"

She gave me a pointed look. "It's a masquerade. You have to dress up. Wear a mask. It's in the name, Ari."

"Is there something so wrong with my face I ought to cover it up?" A rhetorical question, of course, but she saw fit to answer it anyway.

Eloine turned her face, just slightly, and shot me a long sideways look before grinning.

I placed a hand to my heart and staggered. "I'm fine as I am. Besides, I can be stubborn."

Eloine let out a low moan. "Find me a man who isn't."

"Some women find it charming." I gave her the best smile I could manage.

"Oh, most women find it charming *some* of the time. Most of us find it tiring most of the time, however."

My smile faded. "Well, I'd hate to be tiring. Especially if you have a dance to prepare for. Will Prince What's-his-name be your escort?"

She bristled. "I don't need an escort. I'll be going by myself, thank you. And dancing with whomever I see fit." She turned and left before I could find the space to realize what my fool tongue had led me to do.

The word died in my throat as she stepped through the door. *Wait.*

But she wouldn't hear it, of course. The door shut behind her.

I went to my bed, stewing over what had just happened for as long as the desire took me.

It may have been a few hours.

I took another meal in my room, finding it more enjoyable than the last. More cheese than I cared for, but all of it came fresh and creamy as I could wish for. The bread had a hard crust, charred in places, but I found that favorable as well. I washed it down with a purple juice so thick it may as well have been syrup.

Satisfied with that, I went to my door and addressed the porter waiting outside.

He eyed me without turning his head. "Yes?"

"I've been invited to the masquerade tonight, and it seems I'm lacking the main requirement."

"A mask, you mean."

It took all my restraint to not drop my voice to something scathing. "Yes. I mean a mask."

"And do you have a particular taste, a style?" The porter rattled off all the possible variations.

A thought came to me and I smiled, something wide and feral—leonine. "I do." I told the porter the exact details of what I'd like and he assured me he'd find a fitting piece and bring it to me before evening. Failing that, one would be commissioned for me as a guest's gift. I didn't argue and retreated into my room.

Evening would come soon enough, and I felt it a better use of my time to prepare for the party. A few bindings would come in handy to that effect, and maybe a trick I'd learned outside the laws and lands of men.

The hours passed and brought with them an early dark. Stars sequined the velvet black of night like threaded gems of silver-white. My clothing had been once again pressed smooth and clean by a binding. I turned the mask I'd requested over in my hands to look at its face.

It had been fashioned in the perfect image of a lion. Mouth open, bearing at least four curved fangs that would obscure parts of my mouth. The full mask went on to boast a dark mane of fur along its fringes unlike the appropriate rust color.

I ran a hand over it, taking in its smooth features and murmuring the first binding I'd ever performed. "Whent." The folds spread through my mind and I reenvisioned the mask to be what I saw inside me. The smooth pale color of the sun had been replaced by something else—something deeper, richer, and infinitely more complex.

I brought out a mix of tones I knew would bring another life to the decorative piece. It was burnished bright like copper-gilded gold, within which it held a shade of red beneath—a red most better bold. An enrosened and emberant thing, the better red of blood-rose bright.

My hand moved over it again and I worked to impress my will on the object, bringing forth all the brilliance of sunlight, the warmth and hues of fire, and the colors of a man's heart. "Ern."

The binding took and the mask accepted. When I looked at it now, it could have been pulled from a Shaen story. It was no ordinary color to be found in our world. It looked to be fashioned out of stained glass and painted metals and just as much gemstone.

I smiled. It was a piece fitting a storyteller—a performer. And I intended to put on a show, though, for once, it would be for one person.

I made my way to the ballroom, mask donned. Stone tiles made up the floor, all polished so deeply they glowed as bright as the stars tonight. Tables lined the sides of the room, laden with silver trays and cutlery, heaped with all the food and drink any noble could want for.

Where one would expect to find candles on high to illuminate the room, there were black iron posts, hanging like a man with his head bowed. Lanterns framed in gold and paned with the cleanest glass contained the barest flicker of flames to cast a muted orange glow. What light we had came through a ceiling just as clean and transparent as lanterns' lenses. A glass dome to give us full view of the sky.

The moon hung above tonight, round and full—most brilliant white. She shone down on us and I took that as a quiet sign of luck.

Many of the guests and residents of Del Soliel had already arrived, mingling with one another. They kept to their guises, using them to move with a certain anonymity I realized moments later fell in line with their great game. Hands blurred and locked. Glints of gold and gems flashed, and I knew it to be the passing of rose pins and brooches.

Currying favor without names, all within eyeshot of one another, because what else could the masquerade be for if not that?

I held back a biting grin. A part of me wanted to applaud the fact that they held to their scheming even now, and my other half hated the idea of having to be on guard during this ball. I had my own desires. Well, just the one. And it meant a damn sight more to me than their foolery.

More people filtered into the room, instantly seeking others out. Most of them gave me space I silently gave thanks for. I didn't want to be embroiled in any more of their nonsense, at least not for now. Their attention, however, I would snare another way.

Once the remaining guests came onto the floor, the masquerade began in earnest. Musicians sat on a raised circular platform of the same material as the floor. Several violists, a lutist, and one harpist all worked in perfect concert to bring us lightheartedness—to set our feet and the strings of our hearts moving toward one another.

All as natural as breathing.

People at the ends of the room came closer, gravitating at random to partners that caught their eyes.

I joined in, searching for her.

But I didn't find Eloine at first. The first woman across my path had a familiarity to her. Something in how she carried herself. The tilt of her head as she regarded me. The half-moon smile, quick, cunning, and sharp as glass, from under her mask of polished black and silver studs. She wore a dress of saffron in milk, a pale yellow that was pleasant to the eye.

"My Man in Red." The smile grew.

Ah. The Lady Selyena come back again. I gave her a quarter bow before extending an arm.

"Do you know this dance?" She placed a hand in mine and pulled me just enough to know I should step closer.

I did. "No, so I'm afraid you'll have to take me into your lead then. But, I'm a quick learner and will fall into step fast."

"Will you? Fall into step fast, I mean. Shame." Her mouth formed an O of pouting before the smile returned. "I do like it when they're a bit stubborn at first."

She wouldn't be able to make out my whole expression behind my full mask. A good thing, that, as I buried a sigh deep in my chest.

Lady Selyena led me through a series of quick and short steps, moving smooth and fluid as water down the curve of a bowl. We circled, then again—half circle now. Fingers entwined. A motion of gentle tugging and letting go. Teasing. A cloying thing if you were to sum up a dance.

"How have you fared so far in your stay?" She'd asked the question in all sincerity.

"You mean after your husband threatened me?" One of my hands twitched, wanting to unconsciously fall to the pocket where I kept his black rose pin along with the others I'd gathered.

She huffed and almost pushed away from me, but decided instead to pull me along with her. "Don't mind Emeris. He's as much a hypocrite as me."

I arched a brow. Half circle, pull, ease—arm extended and let her drift away. Pursue, pull close. "Not a thing many would admit, Lady Selyena."

She rolled her eyes. "Many people are the worst sorts of liars. The kind that lie to themselves. He and I have no delusions of who we are and what we do. But we're honest in that, and for that, there's a certain . . ." She trailed off, biting one corner of her lip. "It doesn't matter. He lets his anger and jealousy get the better of him. Don't think too much on his threat."

"Hard not to. It's only my life, after all, and I do think a great much on that. Or, at least, of it." I gave her a lazy leonine grin.

She didn't return it, looking instead like a shark ready to sink its teeth into a fresh meal. Lady Selyena came closer in a move that had nothing to do with our dance. Her mouth neared my throat and I felt the heat of her breath where my pulse beat. Hot, heavy, and it set my blood quicker. "Let's leave. Stop this dancing and the dance we're doing with our words."

I had a strong idea of what she wanted to leave to do. "I don't believe that would be appropriate."

"Forget propriety and tell me of wants and needs. What are those? What are yours?" She leaned closer and I felt her teeth against my neck. No playful thing between young lovers. This was to mark, bruise, and take.

I didn't wince, instead tilting my head so my hair would hide her actions, and then pulled her close as if part of our dance. Once she'd pulled away from the hard-sharp embrace, I addressed her. "Truth, then? Yes, I find you attractive. Yes. My body has things it craves. To callously give in to that I often think would be better for my mind and heart. I'd be able to forget a great many things that way. But it wouldn't be true to myself. So, no. My heart's set somewhere else."

She broke from me then, cold and distant as a winking star on a winter's night. Her body stiffened and her voice followed. "I believe it's time to change partners."

I inclined my head, soon in the company of a woman wearing a red almost a match for my cloak. Dark ringlets fell to her shoulders, loose and flowing. She had eyes of cinnamon set under a film of warm honey. Her mask had all the green of emerald in it, trimmed with gold and set with sequins of silver. Part of it covered the left side of her face, only revealing a half smile.

She curtsied and I bowed. We took hands and repeated the steps Lady Selyena had shown me. "They talk about you, you know?"

I looked around to the guests and grinned. "I should hope so. It's a poor storyteller who doesn't have as many tales spreading about him as he can tell about others. So, what do they say?"

She showed me a new sequence then, leading me into a back step, hands still locked. We parted, pulled back together before passing one another along the sides. Turn, pull, and circle in place. "Some of them—the women at least—think you're like Araiyo. He was a crusader knight who went out east to the deserts along the Golden Road. A man in a red cloak of tatters, they say, made from the bloodstained patches of clothes from the barbarians he slew out that way. The desert nomads had designs on our lands long ago, and he went out with brave men and women to stop them.

"He stopped a flight of arrows with but his hand—staying them like God himself. An old story, one many forgot, truth be told. My family didn't, we knew of it long before traders came back speaking of his second coming and spread the tales again."

I gave her a paper-thin grin. "Stopped arrows midair, hm? Just like that? Sounds like an impressive man."

She nodded. "Oh, yes. You remind some of us of him, if only in dress."

I wish I didn't. And I wish the stories counted the arrows that flew by, and the places they landed. I cleared my throat from an imaginary blockage. "I think it's time we changed partners."

She frowned but didn't resist.

I flitted, dance to dance, searching still.

"Looking for someone?" said a voice I'd been hoping for.

I turned to find her, dressed in a white so pure and bright it could have been sewn from the dream of moonlight and snow. Her mask was mirrorglass and pearls. And she wore slippers that could have been fashioned from clearest ice. "I was, but now I think I found her."

Eloine smiled. "You only think? Shame, I'd hoped you'd know."

"I do." I extended a hand. She took it and we fell into the dance. For a moment, we moved silent and smooth like light pooling over a lake's surface. Then I found the words I'd been holding inside me since we'd last seen each other. "I'm sorry."

She said nothing, only eyeing me.

"What I said earlier. I didn't mean to snap. I just . . . it burns me when—"

Eloine raised a finger, pressing it through the opening of my mask to push my lips shut. "I know. And I didn't ask you to apologize. But I know." Her voice dropped to a whisper. "It happens around me—to me, more than you can know."

"Then I'm all the more sorry for it." I pulled her close but she pushed away. "Don't be. Just dance with me."

So I did. That much I still could do. "I don't suppose tonight's a night for that song about the moon." I looked up toward the heavenly body. A hand touched the underside of my chin and pinched the skin just enough to bring me back from my far stare.

"Eyes here tonight, please." She held no reproach in her voice. Just a sincere request.

"Of course."

"One last performance then?" Her mouth didn't quite break into a smile, pressing tight and pulling visibly to one side.

"A duet, of sorts." I pulled her close, and she let me.

She broke into a proper grin. "I'd like that. But first, let's build anticipation." And then she pulled away, dancing into the arms of another man.

Everything below my neck sank far below the floor for a moment. But I had no time to linger in the feeling as another woman swept by and took my hand. I fell into the now-learned steps of the dance, feeling like a puppet guided by someone else's touch. We traded partners until a man came to me.

He was dressed as dark as shadow over night sky. His mask was charcoal-dusted obsidian, and I remembered the hard stare from earlier in Del Soliel. Lord Umbrasio.

I inclined my head. "My lord. I didn't expect you to want to dance with me." I gave him a light bow, flourishing with one hand at my side.

"You're funny."

"I have been called that, among many things, Lord Umbrasio."

He gave me a smile too practiced to be honest. Cold, calculating, and forced for appearances. "I think I'm beginning to find you more than irritating."

"I've been called that as well. Did you want to dance?" I extended my hand.

He raised one of his own, almost as if to bat mine away, but resisted the impulse. "I came to ask for the return of something."

I froze, tilting my head.

"The black rose I gave you. While you are a maddening man, I may have acted rashly. I'll take it back, if you will."

I saw no harm in that. Though, I wondered why he had changed his mind. But sometimes the wheels of luck turn to favor a sparrow. One of my hands went into a pocket and I retrieved the pin, passing it to him quickly.

He made more of a show of taking it than I would have liked, examining it between a thumb and forefinger before stowing it. "Thank you. I'll be seeing you." He bowed his head and left.

I may have thanked many gods for our interaction being as short as it was. My mind turned from partners flitting by, only having the eyes now for Eloine's form as she traded men. But soon, we reunited.

"Done savoring the local flavors?"

She didn't frown, but shot me a look to tell me I treaded dangerous waters. "Please. I came back, didn't I?"

"You did. So, what does a singer need to give a storyteller a song? A little light? Lots? Only one ray to shine down and make you the focus for all sight? Tell me." I opened my mouth to speak more but she cut me off.

"That sounds lovely. All eyes on us, just for tonight."

I didn't give it a second thought and moved to execute bindings suited for two performers. The folds in my mind showed a darkened room, all bulbs of fire winked out to leave nothing but moonlight and stars above. But a lingering question remained: Could I do it?

I'd reached out to spaces beyond my own of late, remembering what I'd learned through my formative trials. Pieces of how to view the bindings returned to me—things I'd forgotten and could only apply when playing the role of storyteller. But now, to do this thing for someone else?

I would try it. I would believe.

The folds of my mind formed and spread. Four to six. Then doubled to twelve. Twenty now. An old number. One I had a hint of pride in. And it would be enough.

I broke from Eloine, leaving space between us. "Tak." I saw every flame snap from where it hovered into the open air between myself and her. "Roh." I fixed their point to coalesce and called them. Every thread of brilliant fire bound to that spot and formed a larger ball I quickly wrapped with another binding. "Whent. Ern." Keeping it active, fueled with air.

The scene drew gasps from everyone, stopping them in their tracks.

Then, once we had their attention, I let the fire die. I eased out of the folds and took away the last light save for that above. *Another shaping then.* A weak pale glow diffused through the room around us, but it wasn't enough. I reached out to the air around me, the space I shared with the world larger than myself, and I bid the light to intensify. To pull on itself. "Whent. Ern." And the shaping proved true.

A beam of moonlight shone on just the pair of us. "Will that do?" I raised a brow and smiled, knowing her answer before she gave it.

"It'll have to." She smiled back.

Then, she sang, bright and clear as starlight:

"Across darker skies and brighter snows,
here I am, I'm chasing you,
every night I howl my love, hoping you hear,
wishing you knew,
that my heart grows cold and with fear,
bleeding so dry,
and I hope that you hear me,
I hope you hear my cry.

"But I come to you then,
not as a friend,
hoping for just,
one more kiss,
one last memory, one last promise,
just like before, that promise of bliss.

"Then she turns from me now,
and leaves me wondering how,
how could she do this to me?
Doesn't she see,
what she's done to me?

"So I follow you now, and chase you still,
not giving up, not resting still,
until I have your heart,
and have gotten my fill,
I'll slake my thirst on the hunt, live for the thrill.

"And if you won't be mine,
then I'll go for the kill,
I'll chase you forever,
I'll chase you forever.

"Face in my hands,
I'll take what I want."

And the song broke. Eloine stopped, looking away through the crowd.

I tried to follow her stare, searching for what could have taken her out of the spell she'd woven on everyone. I spotted Lord Umbrasio in the distance talking to someone else dressed in flowing robes of white, clear and lengthy, and what I knew to be the mark of the pontifex. The man, however, paid little attention to the lord at his side. He kept his gaze fixed above to the ceiling—the sky.

Eloine stepped in front of me, pulling me close and brushing aside my mask.

"What are you—"

She leaned close, hands on my face.

Then she took what she wanted.

She pushed away my mask and stared at me before I could know what was to come. Her lips pressed against mine. Deep, full, warm, and sweet. To say it was blissful would do a disservice to the kiss. To say it was what I wanted would fall painfully short of describing how powerful a want a heart could have and the feeling to have it realized. To say it lasted as long as I wished for . . .

. . . would be a lie.

Thunder sounded above, drumming so hard I felt it rattle into me. The moonbeam faded as clouds passed overhead. Then the storm broke out.

In the dark, I looked for Eloine as she ended our kiss, but she slipped through the crowd. Leaving me alone. In the blackness.

I waited.

But she didn't return.

NINETY-SIX

The Black Rose Gambit

I ended the previous night in a foul mood that soon turned hollow. I'd left the masquerade, opting for the better company of a good bed. Then, I slept until the next morning when a heavy knock sounded at my door. It pounded again, and again, promising to shake the room nearly as hard as the thunder before.

I groaned, cursing anything and everything I could think of before answering it.

Marcos stood there, pillow in hand. He didn't meet my gaze.

I pulled the note from it. A summons, from Prince Arturo. I frowned as I reread the letter. "Should I fetch my brooch and pin?"

Marcos nodded.

"And may I ask why you, the runner for Lady Selyena and Lord Emeris, are delivering this and not someone else?"

"The Lord Umbrasio is breaking fast with Prince Arturo." It wasn't an answer, but from the boy's tone, it was the only one I'd get.

I fetched the brooch appropriate for visiting a prince and fixed the white rose summons pin he'd given me. A meeting, it symbolized. We'd see what sort soon enough. I thanked Marcos, but he looked reticent to accept my gratitude.

Someone had gotten to the boy again. I made a mental note to deal with that immediately after my meeting with the prince.

I left my room, asking the porter for directions. He offered to lead me. We arrived before a pair of wooden double doors bearing similar art to that of the palace entry. The porter left and I knocked, soon greeted by Lord Umbrasio.

He smiled, once again a thing plastered tight, wide, and utterly lacking in sincerity. "Ah, our performer. Quite a show you started last night. And the trick with the fires and light." He gasped, a bit too breathy to be real. Hand on chest, he made his eyes wide. "What magic. Though, I'm surprised you risked that. That sort of thing is ill-looked-upon in Etaynia. It's close to devilry."

I looked past him to the prince. "Well, I've been considered a devil by some before. I'm hoping the prince thinks otherwise and doesn't fear a little magic, especially if it's showmanship at best."

Prince Arturo gave me a tired man's grin. Lazy, half there, and completely uncaring about the dickering between Umbrasio and myself. He beckoned me with a hand. "Do you take tea in the morning?"

"I do." I shouldered my way past Lord Umbrasio, moving to take a seat by the prince. Emeris joined us, much to my displeasure, and I stifled a groan.

The prince poured me a cup of tea the color of water after passing through dark earth, a brown nearing black. The cup was fashioned from a material that had all the color of polished white bone and the look and fragility of glass.

"Porcelain?"

He nodded. "Far trade and gifts—both—from Laxina. We do little business, in truth, that far along the Golden Road. Other end of the world, practically, but I personally have a fondness for the look and feel of the material. Though, I think it odd they cut currency with it."

I gave him a small smile. "The world spends in gold as much as it wears it and fashions fixtures of it."

The prince tipped a spoon in my direction as way of acknowledging my point. "Sugar? Honey? Milk?"

"Honey, milk," I said.

He added those and passed me my drink. Then joined me in taking a sip.

It tasted as it looked, dark, cut softer by the milk, malty like a light beer, but made sweeter by the honey. I appreciated it.

"So, to business?" The prince set his cup down and I mimicked him. "I heard you're looking for stories." Before I could ask how he'd learned that, he waved a hand to move past the point. "We talk. My family, even if we're not on the best of terms. Other nobles and the gentry too, of course. I'm a collector of a sort, even if my brother is the one who visits the library more often."

I took another sip as I followed along.

"Do you know what fascinates me?"

I didn't ask, hoping the silence would do the job.

"It's a bit of a perverse thing, truthfully. A theory of mine, one that doesn't go over well with the church, so I try to keep my tongue from getting too loose from between my teeth."

Now he had my curiosity. Or maybe it was the simple act of rebellion against an authority. I knew that taste all too well. "What, Prince Arturo?"

"In all the stories I've read, the ones I've collected, I've long wondered about threads of commonality between them. Similar themes, sometimes a name, so very much like another a world away, yet different at the same time. Yet, the characters mirror each other here and there. Often, their quests and stories do as well. Little hints, little lies. It's like they all share some truths."

I sipped more and he joined me. For a moment, all we did was drink while I mused on his theory and he waited for a response.

Once he finished his cup, he set it down and steepled his fingers. "You think me mad? It's all right. I've heard it before, even if you won't give voice to the thought."

I shook my head. "Not at all. Just amused. I've often thought the same thing. That is in fact why I'm searching for the story I am."

Prince Arturo leaned forward with a curiosity saved for children wanting in on a deeply held secret. He reached out for the pot to fill himself another cup, but it ran dry. Rather than frown and lament the state of things, he merely addressed Lord Umbrasio. "Emeris, would you have someone bring me another pot?"

The lord moved to take the pot himself. "Of course." He headed to the door with it before returning to join us.

The prince motioned for me to go on.

"I'm looking for a story about the beginning of things. The first, the oldest I can find. The root of all things told today. I'm looking for the origin of The *Nuevellos*—your Nine. The truth behind the ten shadows and Antoine." Though I knew the truth of the story, I didn't know all of it. Nor how it began. "And I very much think that story exists. If not in one piece and whole, then in pieces scattered. That's why I came here. I wished to perform in exchange for access to your libraries."

The prince slapped a hand on his thigh and laughed. "Finally. Someone who understands . . . and has the courage to ask for what he wants. But, The *Nuevellos*? Children's tales. They're meant to scare folk, nothing more. There are too many of those to ever find a shred of truth in them. But stories of heroes? Antoine and Araiyo? There's something there."

Oh, I know it.

"I'll see your wish granted if you do me but one favor."

I shifted in the chair and my fingers flexed, unsure of what the prince would ask. I'd already been pushed and pulled around by the Etaynian upper class and their damnable game.

"I want you to share everything you find with me. Any theory, no matter how crazed. Any idea, any new thing. All of it comes by me, *sieta*?"

I agreed.

"Excellent." He then steered the conversation to the names of a dozen heroes. Some I knew, some I didn't. Then a dozen more.

Then . . . a dozen more.

By the time he'd finished rattling off stories and deeds, another pot arrived and he helped himself to a cup, offering Lord Umbrasio one. The lord declined, and my cup hadn't been finished at all.

A silence fell between us before Lord Umbrasio decided to end it. "There are other stories, Prince Arturo, that I think you would be very interested in as well."

The prince said nothing but looked up in curiosity as he took a sip.

"There are families that bear important names. Old. Old as the stories and carry those tales with them just as much. Names and things that go back before the shaping of the world today and how things came to be as they are. Names, that while they may have changed here and there, have remained untainted in their truth. Or, tainted altogether depending on your view of things." Lord Umbrasio stared at the prince, but his words didn't seem to reach the man. No. In fact, they sounded like they had been meant for someone else.

The prince took another sip, then frowned.

Lord Emeris Umbrasio then sang in a low voice:

"When his eyes go bright as gold.
Nuevellos. Nuevellos.
And comes the storm that is foretold.
Nuevellos. Nuevellos.
Time to pray. Do not stay."

Prince Arturo's color paled, then took on a hue of purple-blue. His eyes watered, only the tears came red.

"When their eyes begin to bleed,
Run all quick. Fetch your steed.
Race full hard. Flee full far."

Prince Arturo didn't protest as the life left him. No frothing or panic. He died, silent as a man can be.

I turned slowly to look at Lord Umbrasio.

The man pointed down at the table and I followed the gesture to find a black rose pin sitting on the tea platter. The same one I'd passed back to him last night. "Help!"

The doors burst open and I whirled about.

"He's murdered Prince Arturo. Poison!"

I opened my mouth to speak, all the while readying a binding to unleash. Something struck my head and the world cut from my vision. I remember the crack and shatter of porcelain. I stumbled, all thoughts of what I could do leaving my head.

"Look, a black rose pin," said Lord Umbrasio.

"I saw 'im give it to the lord last night, so I did," said one of the guards who'd come through.

I struggled to my feet but my attempt was cut short.

The butt of a spear came down on my head followed by several others, clubbing me to the floor.

"Arrest him and bring him to the dungeon. Alert the pontifex another prince has passed. Tell the families, the game is suspended, and the other princes must be looked to."

I lost consciousness.

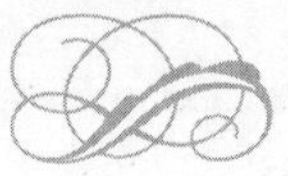

NINETY-SEVEN

A Prison of Stillness

I woke to a stillness. An emptiness. A silence.

Feet dragging across dark stone so heavy nothing could sound against it. A shade so deep it swallowed all noise as much as it did color. The quiet here was that of iron-hard bars that held back the protests of men as much as their hopes. This was the noiselessness of men too tired to despair. The grim gallows quiet of the hangman's judgment to come. It was the soundlessness of men too thin to do anything but think of talking, then decide even that took too much out of them. The hunger-deep stillness of a dozen men too hurt to hope for food for it would make them remember the pains of eating when so starved.

This was the quiet of a place so far forgotten beneath the earth that to make any sound was to upset the nature of the place. It was the place of half-swallowed hopes and dreams—where they were better left to die.

The silence hung in old stone so tightly mortared nothing could get through. Not sound, nor air, nor even light.

An open cell waited for me and they threw me into it.

I fell, hands bound behind my back and unable to break my fall. I lay against the cold and porous stone, taking in the damp from a puddle that formed in the curve of the floor. Even the droplets of water sliding along the wall moved with a respect for the silence here. They fell without sound, sinking into another part of the puddle.

I struggled to my feet, leaning against the bars of the prison cell for support.

Then I saw the prisoners around me stare. Long hollow-gaunt and forgotten men. They'd swallowed their own tongues and probably thoughts by this point. All they could do was look. They had no voices left to give.

So I would give them mine and answer the questions on their minds. The ones I knew them to have.

The silence belonged to me now. Mine to keep or end. And I decided to break it, like I'd done once long ago like a fool.

"Ask. Ask the thing you want to know. Who am I? Who is the stranger in the red cloak and cowl? What have I done? Why am I here?"

And the men asked.

The silence once again broken.

And I answered. "My name is Ari, and I killed a prince of Etaynia."

Only, the wrong one died, and not by my hand. But they wouldn't know it. And they wouldn't care.

Beyond the sides of good and evil, there is a field of curiosity and dreams. I will meet you there. At the end itself. Bring me your stories; live, love, and learn. I want to hear it all. I am waiting. Find me.

~ Brahm the Wanderer

Acknowledgments

To my editors, Christopher Morgan and Brendan Durkin. For their excitement over this book and series, their help, and making a dream come true. My agents, Joshua Bilmes and Stevie Finegan. For too many things to list. Christopher Yuastella. My oldest friend. The one who's been there through everything, for everything, and encouraged me without fail through all of it. To Brandon Sanderson, for listening to me talk about this project, and bouncing things back and forth with me.

Jim Hurd. For believing in me from the moment we met. Pushing me. Being there no matter what. And unfailingly seeing my potential and doing whatever he could to mentor me in life and navigating through the wacky parts of life. Chris Reed for all his support and friendship.

My alpha and beta readers, Katie Norris, Erika Marler, and Becky Tripp. To Nancy Green for the use of her cabin while I was trying to cram as many words as possible in on book one during a short summer vacation. Stone Sanchez. He knows why. LJ Hachmeister for being the older sister I never had. Kate Pickford for checking up on me, caring, and being a pillar of support. A. Lynn for the same, and being a rare caliber of friend who's been there through everything; the hardest, the heaviest, and some of the most vulnerable. Laura Etzkorn and Rachel Taylor for all their help, answering questions, and the serious patience they must have in putting up with me.

And my brother from another mother, Yudhanjaya Wijeratne. Years of brotherhood, friendship, brilliant talks at all times of the day and night, and being there in my corner no matter what.

About the Author

R.R. Virdi is a two-time Dragon Award finalist and a Nebula Award finalist. He is the author of the urban fantasy series the Grave Report and the Books of Winter. His love of classic cars drove him to work in the automotive industry for many years before he realised he'd do a better job of maintaining his passion if he stayed away from customers.

He was born and raised in Northern Virginia and is a first-generation Indian American with all the baggage that comes with. He's offended a long list of incalculable ancestors by choosing to drop out of college and not pursue one of three predestined careers: lawyer, doctor, engineer. Instead, he decided to chase his dream of being an author. His family is still coping with this decision a decade later.

He expects them to come around in another fifteen to twenty years. Should the writing gig not work out, he aims to follow his backup plan and become a dancing shark for a Katy Perry music video. You can get more news and updates on his website rrvirdi.com or by following him on social media.

f: rrvirdi
X: @rrvirdi
Instagram: @rrvirdi

Credits

R.R. Virdi and Gollancz would like to thank everyone at Orion who worked on the publication of *The First Binding* in the UK.

Editorial
Brendan Durkin
Áine Feeney

Audio
Paul Stark
Jake Alderson

Contracts
Anne Goddard
Ellie Bowker

Design
Rachael Lancaster
Tomás Almeida
Joanna Ridley

Editorial Management
Charlie Panayiotou
Jane Hughes

Marketing
Yadira Da Trindade

Publicity
Jenna Petts

Finance
Jasdip Nandra
Sue Baker

Production
Paul Hussey

Sales
Jennifer Wilson
Esther Waters
Victoria Laws
Rachael Hum
Ellie Kyrke-Smith
Frances Doyle
Georgina Cutler

Operations
Jo Jacobs
Sharon Willis